The Nightingale Trilogy

Submits / Rises / Triumphs

Cynthia Dane

BARACHOU PRESS

The Nightingale Trilogy

Published: 26th February 2016
Publisher: Barachou Press

Part 1

The Nightingale Submits

Entry #1

I'm not good with words. I'd rather program a machine to speak on my behalf than write down my own thoughts and feelings.

So, expect these entries to be sparse. The only reason I'm writing anything is because I need some sort of testimony in case something happens to me.

Because it's very likely I will die sooner rather than later.

Tomorrow I attempt my first infiltration of Xavier Crow's private club. I currently do not have a partner, which will prove most annoying when I have to hire someone to pose as my girlfriend. But I will do whatever it takes. I only hope the woman is discreet.

His end begins tomorrow.

Chapter 1

The first thing Nala noticed about the lounge wasn't the body odor vs. over-spiced perfume menagerie, but that women were actually capable of pairing flannel with lacy lingerie.

"Welcome to The Crow's Nest," a woman dressed in black and white plaid with matching fishnet stockings said. "Would you like something to drink?"

Nala, spying on a bearded man trying his luck with a woman bursting from a tight bustier, whipped her head around. "I'm sorry?" Her voice cracked in her throat.

The hostess's practiced smile faltered. "I asked if you would like a drink, Miss."

"Uh, sure. Rum and Coke."

"Right away. Please find a seat to enjoy. I'll be right over with your drink."

Plaid cotton sauntered away. Nala was left standing in the middle of the dimly lit and quiet lounge, a brand new staple of Portland's illustrious Pearl District. The Crow's Nest was a marriage of Pacific Northwest sensibilities and hoity-toity expectations. Craft beer, wrought iron umbrella stands, flannel and hoodies for days… and enough expensive perfume to choke a beaver,

That related to a question Nala was asked the moment she sat at the bar. "Ducks or Beavers?"

"Excuse me?" She looked up, meeting a bearded bartender's eyes. His skinny jeans slipped effortlessly beneath his red and blue plaid shirt.

His smiled broadened. "You like the Ducks or the Beavers? Football."

"Oh!" Nala nearly dropped her clutch. "Timbers?"

"Ha! I like that one. Prefer the *futbol* over the football?"

"Sure."

The bartender disappeared to the other end of the bar to tend to a patron's request. Nala was left, alone, wondering what the fuck she had gotten herself into. *Ducks, Beavers, Timbers, Blazers…* Fifteen years ago, when she was a child living in Portland with her mother and sister, nobody asked her such inane sports questions. Portland was a haven for people who didn't give a shit about *sports.* That was for the Texans and North Carolinians. Although so many of them had moved to Oregon in Nala's fifteen-year-absence that maybe they changed the game – literally.

Tasha would have said she liked the Ducks because her favorite color was yellow. It was those little details Nala remembered even now. Details that made her bite her lip and wave away the hostess as she brought by that rum and Coke. *Focus, idiot. You're not here to have a drink.* Nevertheless, she had to part with her precious money so she could access one of the richest men in the Pacific Northwest… no, *America.*

Maybe the world.

She pulled out her notepad and double-checked her research. *Xavier Crow, founder and CEO of Black Raven Pharmaceuticals, is also an avid real estate developer who owns many high-rises and businesses throughout Oregon and Washington. His latest addition to his empire is The Crow's Nest lounge, located on a block he owns in its entirety.* The picture in one of the articles she pasted into her notepad showed the fifty-five year old Xavier Crow sitting on the stool next to where Nala sat now. He was surrounded by his flannel-clad servers and bartenders, all smiling above a caption that read, "*Mr. Crow intends to make the lounge his second home in Portland.*"

He had to be around here somewhere. It was a slow night, but Nala had no choice but to come on Tuesday when the line wasn't halfway around the block. Without any great connections, there was no hope getting a glimpse of her sister's killer.

***

"*Nala,*

I hope this letter gets to you in time. I don't dare email or call you. I don't know who might be tracking me. Isn't it strange I have to go back to pen and paper in order to be undetected? Except it's the only safe way that I know of.

There may not be much time left. I know I'm not crazy. Men are following me. There was blood left on my apartment door yesterday. I don't say these things to scare you. I say them to warn you. If they come for me, they may come for you next. Don't tell Mother."

Nala could still remember the day she received that letter. She stood outside the dusty mailbox in Carson City, Nevada, wondering what she should do. For weeks, her older sister told her that she was becoming paranoid. Cars. Men in ski masks lurking in the shadows. Threatening notes. She went to the police, but all they said was that Tasha needed to be less "hysterical." Two days after Nala received that final letter, Tasha was found dead in her Seattle apartment.

Heart attack, the coroner said. Ridiculous. Tasha was still in her twenties. She exercised and was a vegetarian. Out of the three of them, Tasha had the best health while Nala ate like a dumbass and their mother smoked fifty packs a day.

So to say Tasha had a *heart attack* at her age was like saying Nala would choose a salad over a hamburger.

It had to be murder. It wasn't farfetched. Not in Tasha's line of work. She was a lead researcher for Black Raven Pharmaceuticals. Cancer cures. Medications. The type of shit every pharmaceutical company said they poured millions of money into researching, but always came up short. Not Tasha. She was brilliant. Determined. If anyone in the country was going to find some cancer breakthrough, it would be her, one of the greatest medical researchers anyone knew.

Xavier Crow may not have given Tasha her heart attack, but *he* surely made sure *somebody* did. Nala would bet her life on it. Since moving to Portland, Crow's newest home, she sort of had to bet her life on that fact.

She didn't know what she would do.

She didn't know what she *could* do.

But she would find the bastard.

And she would make him pay for his crimes.

***

"You look lonely."

Nala jerked up. There was that bartender again, this time with a beanie on his head. Did he think that made him cool? Did he like being a hipster stereotype? Nala furrowed her brows. Whenever she started thinking about her sister's death, she got angry. Easily. This man was one more condescending comment away from getting a fist through his man-bun.

"I'm relaxing," she said. *Please go away. For your own good.*

"What's your name? I like to learn everyone's name."

Nala had to bite back a testy reply. "Na… Natasha." That was a convenient go-to name. It's what her mother bellowed whenever she wanted both her daughters to come into the room.

"Natasha, huh?" What a chill-inducing smirk. "I thought you looked Russian."

What the fuck did that mean? "Interesting. I thought I left my *ushanka* at home." Damnit. She should have mispronounced it on purpose. Or said something maybe not, oh, Russian.

The bartender's smile disappeared, but he remained in front of her. "Uh… what's that?"

"Imagine a very cold Russian woman. She's wearing one on her head."

"Oh. Those fluffy hats?"

"Yes. Those fluffy hats."

He raised his hands in mock defeat. "Hey, this is a chill place. No need to be uptight. Enjoy your drink." He walked away. A bit too late to escape Nala's *chilling* glare.

No matter where she went in the country, men were the same, especially when they found out she was Russian. The idea of the feisty Eastern European sexpot was alive and well. Joke was on them. Nala was no sexpot. And her idea of *feisty* was slamming dudes in the balls, not teasing them with a thong on her way out the door. *They all need to leave me alone.* Nala considered herself "reluctantly heterosexual." She didn't like women – not that way – but here she was, attracted to men in theory, but unable to stand them in real life.

"I've never even been to Russia…" she muttered. Her parents immigrated right before the Cold War ended. Heard that there was a sizable Russian population in Portland and decided it was for them. Tasha was born in the Motherland, but Nala was born at the same hospital as her kindergarten classmates. The only Russian she remembered was whatever her mother muttered the most. *Tasha was the one with an interest.* Nala spent her life ignoring her heritage while Tasha taught herself Cyrillic… for *fun.*

So, great. Here she was, stalking a man she had no idea what to do with, and being propositioned by dudes with man-buns because they thought Kseniya Onatopp was hot in that one Bond film. Nala stretched her arms across the bar and tapped her forehead against the counter. *I'm so stupid.* Once again, her anger got the best of her. Yeah, she moved to Portland to "get justice," or at least discover the truth behind her sister's death, but that was as far as her mind ever let her get. Stupid Nala. Shot first, asked questions later.

Now she was paying for it. Literally. At least in Carson City her part time job helped her pay her share of the rent. Rent that went toward a whole bedroom in a sizable apartment she shared with a quiet girl her age. In Portland? Ha! Nala rented a closet. An actual closet. She could squeeze a twin mattress in there, but she had to hang her clothes above her and put her meager belongings on the top shelf. She could spring for a bedroom somewhere farther out if she could get a damned full time job.

Maybe it was a good thing she had this drink. First thinking about her sister, and now her living situation? Nala needed to get drunk, quick. Get drunk, go home to her closet, and lick her wounds. Who was she kidding? Of course Xavier Crow didn't hang out here on his nights off. That was publicity. This lounge was small. Maybe it seated thirty people comfortably. It was meant to feel intimate, not like a sprawling mess of stools and drunk people. Nala hated the bastard, but at least he had some taste.

She was woefully overdressed anyway. Her little black dress, the only nice outfit she owned, was too much for this plaid paradise. *I forgot that's considered formalwear here.*

"…Tell Chester that we still have the ten o'clock meeting." Two men in suits sauntered in. Nala barely noticed them… would've been happy to ignore their existence if they didn't sit one stool away from her and order a couple of Old Fashioneds. "All right. Thanks." The man on the phone shut it off and tucked it into his front pocket. "Finally, we can relax."

He had salt and pepper hair, muted cologne, and one of the finest business suits Nala had ever seen. The kind of guy Tasha would have said belonged at the altar with her. *She always had lofty ambitions.* Nala's sister was married to her work while in her 20s, but she said she wanted to establish her career and then go find a husband. *"I don't mind Mistress Medicine, if she'll have me."*

"This place ain't bad. One of the better lounges in this area."

The other man rubbed his clean-shaven face. He looked aloof, but that was par for the course in Portland. Hell, the Pacific Northwest. *Must be a native. No, a transplant.* Nala was starting to learn to tell the difference.

"I suppose. I don't get out much."

"Ah, if you stay in this business much longer, young Padawan, you'll have to learn how to get out and be social. It's mandatory."

"I suppose."

"You say that a lot."

The older man said that good-naturedly. Nevertheless, Nala heard a hint of frustration in his voice. *Is that his son? Nephew? Why do I care?* Anything to take her mind off her troubles.

"Crow hasn't done bad for himself in this town. Did you know he owns this whole block?"

The younger man tugged on his tie and adjusted his cufflinks. Aloof, indeed. "I had heard that. I don't get it, myself. Then again, I'm not interested in real estate. Or mergers and acquisitions. I just want to do my trade."

"Boy, you really are young and new to this."

"Let's talk about something else." The younger man, with his soft face and clean haircut, picked up his drink and clinked the ice inside. "Anything but Crow."

"We're in his place of business and giving him our money for alcohol. We can't avoid talking about him. Why don't you want to?"

"Suppose you could say he leaves a bad taste in my mouth." The younger man put his glass down and swished his drink around his mouth as if it really *did* leave a bad taste. His wince intrigued Nala, who watched this through the corner of her eye. "I also suppose the man can't be avoided around here. I mean, as you said, look where we are."

"Damn straight. It's amazing to see how things have changed around here in the past ten years alone. I remember when the Pearl was… well, not as nice as it is now."

They dropped that part of the conversation after that. Nala was content to finish her drink and leave, but then…

"All right. Let's talk about him. Xavier Crow, the man who owns half of Portland and developed half the medicine in your bathroom cabinet." The younger man sounded sarcastic enough to annoy even Nala, who usually loved a healthy dose of sarcasm. "He loves to take over half. Why is that? Is he only half good at what he does?"

The older man smiled again. "You really don't like him, huh?"

"What's to like about him? He's a narcissistic megalomaniac with a God complex. *What* is there to like about him?"

"Yet you're here."

"Well, it's like you said. I need to be mindful of my business pursuits." The younger man snorted into his glass. "Don't think we'll see Crow around here for me to butter up, huh?"

"I hear he comes here a lot, but nobody ever actually sees him. Sounds like shit to me. If I were him, I'd build an *exclusive* club to hang out in. Or stay home. He's got a beautiful place up in the West Hills. Was there for a soiree a few months ago. The man knows how to throw a party to please the people."

"I bet." The younger man turned his head away. "Thanks for having a drink with me, by the way. I know you didn't have to."

"And give up a chance to relax with my favorite young entrepreneur? Please, Vince, I'll pick you over my wife at home any day."

"Around this town someone might take that statement the wrong way…"

"Oh, I know."

They switched to talk about the older man's wife and kids, thereby losing Nala's interest. She slammed down her drink, feeling the liquor warm her body and help her relax. Not that she wanted to relax. What else was there to do? These strangers all but confirmed that she would not see Xavier Crow around there anytime soon. Her best bet was to do her reconnaissance elsewhere. Build up some evidence that the man had something to do with her sister's death…

Who was she fucking kidding? *No one.* The more the weeks went by and nothing happened, Nala considered moving elsewhere. Maybe not back to Carson City, but somewhere it didn't rain nine months out of the year and the sun could shine on her pale skin.

"Was everything to your… liking?"

It was the hostess in flannel and fishnets. At first Nala thought she was being spoken to, but when she craned her head around she saw a couple emerging from a back room. The man, also dressed in a pristine suit, had a lovely young woman on his arm. A woman wearing nothing more than a slinky red dress and a black mask on her face.

The way she curled her hand around the man's arm and batted her eyelashes at him said she worshipped the ground he walked on. *Gag.* Yet Nala couldn't look away. There was contentment to the woman's demeanor that Nala envied. She wished she could look so happy about her life. So… in love.

Ha. Love. Nala had a boyfriend once. Before Tasha died and took over her sister's psyche. That man? Nala thought she loved him. Then she realized that what she thought was love was merely a forced emotion that didn't mean anything at all. *I'm not suited for those sorts of emotions.* She both envied women in love and feared for their souls. Maybe they knew something she didn't.

"Everything was wonderful," the man said with a silky voice. "Starling and I will be returning soon, for sure."

"I'm glad to hear that, sir. If there's anything I can do for you in the future, please do not hesitate to ask."

"Oh, if you could go down and tell Mr. Crow that I'll be calling him about business tomorrow, that would be helpful. We were so… distracted… that I completely forgot."

The hostess chuckled. "I will do so. He will want his ten o'clock Chardonnay anyway."

The couple left. Although the men beside Nala continued to speak of mundane matters, she ignored them, her mind focused on only one thing.

Crow is here. He's behind that door over there. I could go find him right now.

Find him and do what? Ha! That didn't matter. Nala was young – and dumb. She may have more life experience and be more jaded than the average twenty-one-year-old, but that didn't mean she didn't feel that rush of sheer invincibility that told her to take over the world with her mind and body alone. If she owned a car, she would be exposed to bouts of reckless driving for the sake of it. If she were a partier, she would be in and out of hospitals with alcohol poisoning. If she had casual sex… well, that was neither here nor there. Point was, Nala had her stupidity vices like anyone else her age. Vices pinpointed on *vengeance.*

In her mind, she entertained images of stabbing Xavier Crow right in the heart. Bashing his head in with a club. Lighting his shoelaces on fire and watching him *burn.* When she had these fantasies, her blood rushed, adrenaline pumping in her veins like gas pumped into semis. Propane tanks. Exploding. Fire and brimstone raining upon the man who killed her sister and knew how many other people because… well, she still didn't know the details. All Nala had was her gut, and her gut told her to find Crow. The rest would fall into place after that.

Maybe I'll play the plucky young and driven gal who wants a job. Infiltrate his company. Lure him out of his shell. I'll… She stood up, stumbling from the whole glass of rum and Coke. She wasn't drunk, but she was definitely tipsy. *I'll fall down.*

There was one problem. The door said "Private," and it was not a large room full of shadows to lurk in. If Nala got up and tried to go in, someone would certainly spot her. This wasn't a dive bar where the worst that happened was getting a stern talking to. If Xavier Crow, resident billionaire who owned half of a major city, lurked behind that door, then… well, Nala could probably kiss her life in Portland goodbye.

I won't know if I don't try.

Maybe it was the alcohol that made her so brazen. If she were 100% sober, she may go home and regroup with her new information, but she wanted to find out *now.* So she went to a table by the door, stocked with water in a dispenser and many small glasses. She picked one up and slowly filled it with water, biding her time until nobody looked at her. The place wasn't busy. That meant she didn't have to wait long, but it also meant she was so conspicuous that a blind man could spot her.

The bartender was washing glasses at the far end of the bar. The hostess played coy with a single man in another corner. The two men in suits at the bar were getting up and shaking hands, paying her no mind. Now was the time to go for it. She could regret it later.

There were many things she could *regret* later.

Nala slipped her hand over the handle and found it deceptively unlocked. It opened, slowly, shadows filtering into the lounge. Good. It was a hallway. An unlit hallway she could fumble around in. *Good thing I wore a black dress and have dark hair.* While everyone in the lounge was still distracted, Nala ducked behind the door and shut it behind her.

Regret.

She waited. Assessed her environment. Listened for someone coming after her. Nothing happened. The hall was boring. More shadows. A long, long tunnel with a staircase at the bottom. Nala felt a lock on the handle behind her and wondered if that man and his little Starling were supposed to turn it on their way out.

She stepped forward, slowly. Each step was heavier, as if every one of those steps attached five more pounds of weight to her flats. *This is wrong.* She was trespassing now. One thing to go to Crow's lounge and order a drink. This? This wasn't legal.

Nala didn't care.

Although she didn't care, that didn't mean she wasn't aware of her heart fluttering in her chest and her forehead sweating. Crow was somewhere around here. Probably at the bottom of those stairs. Sure enough, as she advanced down the hallway as if she trudged through molasses, she began to hear the sounds of a party. Laughter. Shouts of glee. Applause. Any private party Xavier Crow threw was probably full of the Pacific elite. She didn't want to know them.

"Thatta girl!" she vaguely heard. Whispers in the constricted air. "Enjoy that!"

Smack.

Smack.

Nala didn't know what she heard, but people were having a good time. A better time than her, anyway. Something about that genuinely irked her. *Why do they get to have a good time while I…*

She didn't see the first step. Not in those shadows. So when her foot took an unceremonious step over the edge without her permission, Nala suddenly felt her beating heart surge into her throat and threaten to jump out of her mouth, bounce on the steps, and land dead at the bottom.

Or maybe that was her.

"Ah!" She was falling. Fell. *Fallen.* Her body lurched forward, arms shooting out to catch her fall, for all the good it would do her. *I'm going to die. Or break my arms.* Amazing what people thought when they were in the middle of falling down some stairs. It almost felt commonplace. Like it was naturally something one did every day. *Brush teeth. Check mail. Fall down stairs. Okay, ready for bed!* Nala wanted to berate herself, but she was sort of busy falling down some forbidden stairs.

Before her hands could catch on a narrow step and take the rest of her body with her, however, something miraculous happened. Or at least it felt miraculous when it happened. When one was in the midst of falling down some stairs, having a strong hand snatch out and grab said faller was definitely miraculous at the time.

"Oh my God!" Nala stared into the dark maw of the staircase, frozen in time and space. A man's hand was around her wrist, slowly pulling her back up to the top of the stairs as her feet tripped again and her heart gradually slowed down. "Oh my God, thank y…"

She whipped her head around and looked straight into the soft countenance of the younger man from the bar.

For some reason, she wanted to vomit.

Chapter 2

"You should be careful," the man said, voice steady. "It's dark here."

Nala stepped onto the top landing, her wrist still in the man's grip. "I'm sorry…" What was she apologizing for? For trespassing? For needing saving? Both? She wanted to cry. Her bones were saved, but she was also in a shitton of trouble! "I don't know what else to say."

Finally, the man released her, holding his hand up so he could yet again readjust his cufflinks as if it were a nervous tic. Perhaps beneath that cool exterior was a man as neurotic as everyone else.

The man stepped back. "You could thank me."

Nala looked back up with a start. *What in the…* "Uh, thanks?"

His reaction was… well, there was no reaction. Just a stoic look that said absolutely nothing at all. Oh, he was a good looking man. Even in those shadows Nala saw all the markings of a handsome specimen waiting for women to devour him. In another life, where she was both interested in such things *and* not busy sneaking around in the name of vengeance, she would be attracted to him. His demure, musky cologne did relax her, however. Not that she wanted it to.

"You're welcome." Just as Nala thought the man would turn around and leave, he said, "You're not supposed to be back here."

Caught! Twice! "Er… I got lost?"

By some divine intervention, the man's face softened and he smiled, wanly. It would've been reassuring if he wasn't so… standoffish. "I saw you in there," he said, gesturing to the door Nala snuck through. "You were making sure the coast was clear before coming in. You're not supposed to be here."

No matter how many times he reiterated that, it didn't sink into Nala's brain. She could be stubborn that way. "Please don't tell on me," she hissed, her fight or flight senses taking over. She couldn't be caught and thrown out. Not like this. Not before she saw a glimpse of Xavier Crow resting on his laurels stained in *blood.* "I had to see him for myself."

The man cocked his head in curiosity, his hands disappearing into his trouser pockets. "See who? You've got me intrigued now."

Nala looked down the stairs. "Xavier Crow. I heard he's in there."

They were silent. Music from both doors filtered into the hall. One was classical. The other was jazzy. Together they were noise. "What business do you have with Crow?" the man asked.

Nala looked back to him and the impeccable hair on his head. "My business is none of your business."

Her voice, unlike his, was laced in anger. She didn't mean to do it. She didn't mean to betray her own cool exterior. How could it be avoided when images of her sister lying still and dead in her casket flooded her mind? *I can remember that day.* Standing there. Staring at Tasha's lifeless face, surrounded by fresh daisies, her favorite flower. Tasha was dead. The flowers were dying. They died to be buried with her, long before their time was due to be over. The world – and nature – was cruel that way.

Any sense of feeling, especially negative, was the wrong thing to use in this situation. Nala needed to be as lifeless as her dead sister. *If* she were going to be emotional, then fuck it, she needed to be giddy and stupid. "*Oh, haha, I'm so stupid, L O L.*" Yet she couldn't fake that if she tried. Nala couldn't act. She was a creature who only knew how to act on instinct, and right now her instincts weren't giving her good advice at all.

"Hm." The man pulled his hands out of his pockets. "Perhaps it is my business. I'm going down to see Mr. Crow myself. Except I have an appointment. I doubt you do."

Nala was taken aback. She expected this type of attitude from this man, but nevertheless, she didn't like being on the brunt end of it. "Well…"

The man looked her up and down. *Checked* her out. Nala crossed her arms over her modest chest and summoned the best death glare she had. If the man noticed, he didn't let on, or at least wasn't fazed.

"I could get you in to see him."

Those words danced in Nala's brain, but barely registered. It was like she heard them, but they were so preposterous, so improbable that she wouldn't allow herself to hear them. *See… him?* "How so? You his friend or something?"

"Like I said, I have an appointment." The man looked at the door they came through. "Or I could go tell that nice, flirty bartender that I caught you back here where you don't belong. I doubt you'd be able to see Mr. Crow at all after that."

"Blackmail, huh?"

"Hardly. I'm giving you a fair choice."

"What do you want in return, Mister…"

The man snorted. "Lane. Vincent Lane. Doubt you've heard of me."

"Should I have?"

"Not at all."

"Good. Because I haven't heard of you before."

"You're caustic."

"And you're creeping me out." Nala shrugged. "I appreciate you saving my neck, quite literally, but I'm not sure if I'm interested."

"How badly do you want to see Xavier Crow? I don't care what your business is. I'll get you in. You only have to pretend you know me."

Pretend? This was sounding less than ideal. "I'm not a good actress."

"Then don't tell him we met because you were sneaking down to see him. Don't think of it as acting. Think of it as *lying*. Anyone can lie."

What a strange thing to say.

"Hey, this might be your only chance to see Xavier Crow up close. All I ask is that you don't go in there as my guest and embarrass me."

Nala looked around the hall, as if a trap were about to be sprung and catch her in its grip. "I see," she muttered. What was more important to her? Walking out of there unscathed, or accomplishing part of what she set out to do – namely, see the man who killed her sister?

She didn't know who this Vincent was, other than he wore expensive suits and cologne, but right now he was her only chance to not make the last few months in Portland a total wash.

"All right," she tried to say with conviction. "I'll go with you. As your *guest.* In exchange for you doing this and not telling on me – and I guess for saving my bones – I'll try not to *humiliate* you since that's what you're most worried about."

The corner of Vincent's mouth twitched. "Should I be worried about something else?"

Nala faced the staircase that tried to kill her. "Let's do this before I lose my gumption."

She didn't wait for Vincent to ask what she meant by that. Having to answer such a question wouldn't put her in the best corner – and Nala was already in a shitty corner.

"Well," Vincent said after her, when she was already halfway down the stairs. "I should still probably lead. I'm the one he's expecting, after all."

Nala stopped on a narrow step, but did not look over her shoulder as she listened to and felt him descend the stairs.

Vincent passed her. When he was one step beneath her, he extended his arm and looked up at her. He did not look any friendlier.

Nala raised her eyebrows.

"Take my arm. Try to look sociable."

Hesitantly, Nala wrapped her hand beneath his elbow and wrapped her arm around his. Sheesh, he was strong beneath this suit. It almost threw Nala off her game, and she was not a woman who fell for a man's charms – particularly when he wasn't exuding charm to begin with!

As they stepped down the staircase, side by side with Nala's head held high, she wondered what the fuck she was doing. *I met this man a minute ago when he was catching me on these stairs.* She didn't know him. Maybe he was lying. Maybe the moment they stepped through that bottom door he would do something sinister.

But Nala couldn't think that way. She relied on her instincts and gut feelings. Although her gut was currently occupied by a bevy of butterflies, she would listen to their vibrations. *Go with him,* they said. *Your sister sends her regards.*

Could butterflies talk to the dead? In her stomach?

If this was what Nala was thinking as she went to an uncertain future, then what was Vincent thinking? *That my ass is hot.* She expected no less.

They reached the bottom of the stairs. Vincent reached out and pushed a small button, eliciting a terse buzzing sound. Heavy footsteps approached from the other side. A peep slot opened, revealing two icy blue eyes.

"I am here to see Mr. Crow. I have an appointment."

"Password." That voice sounded like it had killed a couple of fools and dumped them in the Willamette River a time or two.

Vincent remained cool, his shoulders squared as if he had every right to be there. "Woodpecker," he said.

The peep slot slid shut with finality. Soon enough, the door opened, revealing another dark room. The sounds of music and happy voices intensified, and Nala inhaled the strong scent of perfumed air.

"Right this way sir, ma'am." A tall, wiry man in a butler's tails stood aside and bowed graciously to the couple. His white-gloved hand passed before him, gesturing to the small gathering inside. "Mr. Crow should be able to see you right away."

Vincent stepped forward with his thanks. He had to pull Nala beside him, because her knees locked up and her throat returned to her stomach. *Mr. Crow. Here. Right away.* Oh God. It was happening. It was finally happening.

She was going to look her sister's killer in the eye and know the true face of evil.

***

They entered a small circle of people sitting on low, comfortable benches. Pairs of men and women, each wearing masks as delicate as they were formidable, turned their heads in curiosity. Vincent nodded politely, but did not act as if he knew any of them. Nala kept her mouth shut and looked around for Xavier Crow.

He was *not* hard to find.

The man she had seen in a million publicity photos sat on a raised dais, as if perched on a throne made from the bones of his business enemies. There was nothing particularly special about his appearance. Older. Silver hair. Slight fuzz on his face. He wore a gray suit and black shined shoes that reflected the harsh spotlight shining above him. As if he were a *god.* By looking at the lingerie-clad vixens standing on either side of him? He did think himself a god.

Which was utterly delightful, because no man looked like he had a bigger god complex than Xavier Crow, patron saint and maybe deity of the Pacific Northwest's capitalistic hive mind. Nala's grip tightened on Vincent's arm, channeling her apprehension, anger, and hatred into a strange man's biceps.

"Mr. Crow," Vincent said in his quiet yet formal voice. "I hope you were expecting me."

That was a sinister smile if Nala ever saw one. It sent chills down her spine. Chills laced in arsenic.

"We most certainly were expecting you, Mr. Lane." Xavier's voice sounded gentle, but beneath that grandfatherly façade was a cold-hearted *killer.* The more Nala heard it, the more she believed it. *That's him. That man is the reason Tasha is dead.* She shook. Not in her skin, but in her heart. No, her body would remain firm and unwavering. Inside? Fair game to the wind. "I was just telling my friends here that we would have fresh blood starting tonight."

Vincent glimpsed at the masked faces around him. Most of them smiled, some of them in genuine friendliness. Who were these people? Cronies? Lackies? Hapless bystanders? Guilty by association, anyway.

"Pleasure to make everyone's acquaintance."

Nala didn't know what to do or so. She was frozen, hoping to blend into the shadows and take in what she could. If she were asked anything, she didn't know what she would do or say when bravado took over.

"Who is this gorgeous treasure?" Xavier Crow looked right at Nala. *Leered* at her. At least he didn't look at her as if she were a person. Then he may have seen the hatred she harbored in her heart. Instead, he merely saw a young female body prime for plucking. "I thought you would be coming alone for your first few meetings."

"Change of plans," Vincent said with masculine flair. Curiosity piqued all around them. More men leered at her. Women, too. They all struggled to catch a glimpse of Nala, some of them even straining in their seats as if she were some great celebrity come to grace their presence. She felt like meat, and suddenly wished she hadn't worn a barely-there black dress. *Somehow I don't think jeans and flannel would make me feel much better.* She was exposed no matter how she dressed. "I decided to bring someone I hope can get to know you all as well."

"Oh?" Xavier accepted a glass of Chardonnay from one of the women in lingerie. She smiled pleasantly, but from the look in her eyes, Nala could tell that this was a job to her. A prestigious one, probably, but a paycheck nonetheless. "Go on."

With every eye still on Nala, Vincent turned to her with a look of… adoration?... on his visage. It unnerved Nala to her unprepared core.

"This is my lovely sub, the Nightingale."

Chapter 3

His lovely… what?

The nightin… *what?*

Nala fought to retain her composure. *Don't react. Look as if nothing he said surprises you.* Was that lying? Or acting? Was she good at it after all? Could she really fool these people, including Xavier Crow?

"It's lovely to meet you, Miss Nightingale." Xavier sat up in his seat, both eyes firmly on Nala. *Don't react. Don't react.* Oh, did she want to. She wanted to… to…

She didn't know what she wanted to do. Probably something illegal. Nala never thought ahead, only *reacted.* Her mother would call her stupid. Her sister would call her "refreshingly brash."

"It's a pleasure to finally meet the great Mr. Crow," she said through gritted teeth. Vincent squeezed her arm in warning. Nala pursed her lips together with a grimace. *Be cool.* "I've heard so much about you."

"I'm sure you have!" Xavier laughed wholeheartedly, his self-indulgence spreading to his guests and making them chuckle alongside him. "I assure you, young miss, I would like to hear much about you as well. Anyone who enters my Aviary is worth speaking to."

Nala bowed her head. She hoped it looked honorary. Really, she did it in order to contain the sheer look of exasperation on her face.

"Please, have a seat and enjoy the festivities. Don't feel shy to ask the girls for any refreshments. We have even better stuff back here than up front. Oh, and you're in time. I have it on excellent authority that Sebastian and Quail are about to put on a delightful show for us. Don't worry," he continued, faking a haughty gloat. "We don't ask the newbies to perform the first few nights. Settle in and get to know the feel of The Aviary for a while. We only want members who will be absolutely comfortable here."

His smile disappeared into a firm, foreboding countenance. What did it mean? What was he talking about? As Vincent turned and pulled on Nala's arm, she found it impossible to look away from the man of the hour. The king of the castle. The god of the mountain.

The killer of sisters.

They sat on an empty bench at the back of the pack, behind a man in a gold shirt and black trousers and his partner, a woman in a barely there white… negligee. Nala tried not to stare. This woman was in her damned sleepwear. Sex wear. *Something* wear that was not appropriate for public consumption. The longer she stared, the more she realized she could see every luscious curve of this young woman's body. Her sides. Her hips. Her *ass.* Nothing was left to the imagination, except perhaps her pussy. If she stood, though…

The woman turned in her seat and flashed the newcomers a gracious grin. "Hi," she whispered. "I'm Robin." When her partner turned as well, she said, "This is my Master, Lucian."

Nala furrowed her brows. *These women all have bird names.* Quail. Robin. Starling, who appeared upstairs in her mask and red dress. And Vincent had introduced her as Nightingale…

"Pleased," Lucian said in a silky voice. "You really are just in time. Sebastian and Quail put on the best shows. Little Quail used to be a professional, if you know what I mean." He winked. Nala had no idea what the fuck he meant.

Vincent, however, seemed to understand. Yet before he could respond to the greetings, another nondescript woman in lingerie approached and asked if they wanted any refreshments. He ordered the two of them cocktails without asking Nala for her preference. Just as well. She had no idea what she would say. She was still the tiniest bit tipsy from the rum and Coke.

"What did you call me up there?" Nala asked after the lady left. "Your… sub? What does that mean?"

Vincent gestured to the front of the room. "Wait. You will see."

"No. Tell me now. Please."

Nala didn't mean to sound so pleading. Certainly not in front of a man she had just met and went with to see the man who… Nala looked into her lap. Demure. This was not like her. She was not a woman who stood to the side quietly. She did not stare into her lap and bite her lip while men did things around her, ignoring her. But she had to be "good" for now. She couldn't upset the balance she and Vincent already established. Nala didn't know what "sub" meant, but she would keep lying.

Vincent put a gentle hand on hers, in her lap. It made Nala look up, regarding him with unease. "I'll explain everything later," he said softly. "Please, let's get through tonight first." As two people got up in the front of the room and exchanged words with Xavier Crow, Vincent whispered, "We'll get coffee after this. It's the least I can do."

Coffee. They would get coffee. Okay. Nala could do coffee.

She focused on that as Xavier rose from his throne and sat on one of the front benches, gesturing to his seat. The women in lingerie dispersed, sitting next to their boss, petting his arms and whispering into his ears. Nala wanted to hurl. She did not come here to see *this*.

No, what she apparently came to see was something else entirely.

The couple, whom she surmised to be Sebastian and Quail, stepped onto the dais and bowed their heads to the several people in the audience. Nala remained frozen in her seat, not because she was shy, but because even if she knew the protocol for this situation, she would not have been able to react.

Vincent squeezed her hand before taking his away.

"Please enjoy our demonstration," Quail said. She was a petite woman, perhaps no bigger than Nala, although the woman with a feather in her pearl headband carried herself with greater gravity. She looked to her partner, a man twice as big as her and commanding. Nala did not ignore the way this man looked at her: as if Quail were the little prize he won sport shooting.

Quail, a woman with a sparkly gold dress that dazzled and jingled above the knees. With her curled, bobbed hair and bright makeup, she looked like a gorgeous silent movie come to life. Nala would be impressed, but women who dressed historically were a dime a dozen in Portland.

Besides, she didn't have the mental fortitude to be *impressed* right now.

"Position B, my sweet," Sebastian said, running his fingers down the bare back of his partner. His girlfriend? Fiancée? Now Nala was getting too technical for the situation.

"Yes, sir."

Gag.

Quail approached the throne, unfazed by the fact that the *great* Xavier Crow had perched upon it. Perhaps that was the point. Guessing from the way Mr. Crow looked up at the scene with the smuggest look in the universe, he was getting off on it. Nala had to focus on the stage before she flew into an impulsive rage that saw her hands wrapped around that turkey neck.

The golden woman knelt one knee on the seat of the throne, her fingers daintily curling around a sturdy, diamond encrusted arm. Her glittery stiletto pierced the air behind her as she drew up her other leg and knelt both knees, her arms supporting her torso in the seat of the throne. She looked like she was posing for a pin-up photo.

Quail gave her partner a coy look. "Am I presentable, sir?"

"You are presentable. I daresay you make quite the display for all of our friends here, including Mr. Crow."

Quail shot another coy look in Xavier's direction. "Am I presentable, Master Crow?"

The man held up an iced drink. "You're beautiful."

Nala couldn't tell if the smile on Quail's face was genuine or not. She was a poker queen.

"Now, my feathery little quail, go on and tell us your indiscretions from the past week." Sebastian stood to the side, giving the audience a full view of his partner. "Mr. Crow especially needs to know."

Something curdled in Nala's stomach. *Is this going where…*

Quail pouted, her fingers curling tight around the arm of the throne. Her ass wiggled in the air, enticingly, the light reflecting off the gold sparkles of her dress. "I didn't obey you two days ago. When you told me to wait for you at the coffee shop. I saw a jewelry store across the street and wanted to window shop. When you came back, you were cross."

"Yes, Quail, because I thought something terrible had happened to you. You know how downtown can get sometimes. All sorts of nasty people this time of year. A beautiful toy like you could easily be picked up by somebody else. I wouldn't be able to bear the thought. You gave me such a fright…"

"I'm sorry, sir!"

Nala's mouth twisted when Sebastian pulled up the bottom of Quail's dress, exposing two cheeks with a black thong running between them. "I don't believe you. Even if I did, I would have to punish you anyway. You must learn to obey me, especially when your safety is on the line."

A gasp tore through Nala's chest. In shock, in anger, and in a little awe, she watched as Sebastian's large hand came down on the nearest side of Quail's ass.

It was a smack that could sound across the world. Or at least through the bowels of Portland. Or definitely in that tiny, intimate room where strangers sat and watched a woman get spanked by a big businessman in a suit.

Nala looked around the room. Everyone was fixated on the stage, even Vincent, who sat coolly with his legs together and his spine straight. If Quail were the queen of poker, then Vincent was the undisputed champion. *No way I can read that face right now!* To be fair, she was highly distracted by the rough, pinking spanking going on in front of her.

Quail cried out in pain. Or at least it sure sounded like pain. Nala knew that sound when she heard it. It almost evoked a maternal instinct in her – or maybe a super feminist one. Her rage returned, imploring her to run up and stop that monster from hitting this poor, defenseless woman who… who willingly got up on that throne and… exposed herself… for…

What the fuck is going on?

"I'm sorry!" Quail cried out, her ass turning a hot, burning pink with every spank her partner bestowed upon her. "I swear I'll never wander off again without permission, sir! I swear it! Please forgive me!"

The words sounded frightened. *Everything* sounded off warning bells that should have made Nala call the police and cite a domestic disturbance. And yet, through the red veneer of anger clouding her vision, Nala saw something that she never expected.

Quail's body language did not say that she was scared, let alone in need of assistance. In fact, she looked damn comfortable up there on that throne, her mouth hanging open, her eyes squinting, and her body shuddering in…

In…

Pleasure.

This was insane. This world Nala had stumbled into was not what she expected. Oh, she anticipated some bullshit like the women in lingerie serving alcohol and pleasantries alike… but she did *not* expect to see a display of whatever the fuck this was. Wait. *Wait.*

Is this some fucking BDSM shit?

Holy shit.

Holy shit.

Holy *shit.*

Nala wanted to scramble over her bench and run for her life!

"Please, sir…" Quail moaned, her body finally relaxing as her ass turned a solid red. "I'm really sorry."

Sebastian stood up straight, pushing sweaty hair off his forehead. When he turned around, nobody was shocked to find a firm bulge in his trousers. *Oh my God. Get me out of here!* Nala couldn't. She couldn't do this. Not this kind of environment. Not…

Crack!

Nala leaped in her seat as a final spank hit Quail's ass. She shrieked, shaking, eyes rolling in the back of her head as she… came? Dear Lord, was this woman *orgasming* from a spank?

These people were insane!

It was only when the atmosphere in the room changed that people sighed and Nala realized she was halfway in Vincent's lap, clinging to his shoulder like a kid watching a scary movie. People clapped. Vincent eased Nala off and clapped as well, glaring at her to do the same.

Sebastian was gingerly helping his partner off the throne while Nala forced herself to put her hands together. *Am I really supposed to applaud this shit?* Quail was smiling, the mirth on her blushing cheeks nothing compared to the way she wobbled off the stage with a sore ass. One of the women in lingerie approached with a silk pillow to put on their bench. Quail thanked her, sat down, and let out a small puff of pain. Robin reached forward and patted the other woman's shoulder, congratulating her on a "stimulating show."

These people were certifiably insane. *Insane.* Nobody volunteered to be spanked and then got off on it!

Worst of all, Xavier Crow was still there, and he was very much enjoying the show.

It was the *worst* of all worlds for poor Nala, who could only sit and contort her face into a neutral demeanor so she could keep lying.

"Are you all right?" Vincent whispered, startling her. "I thought you had an idea of what kind of place this is. Don't you know anything about Xavier Crow?"

Oh, Nala knew a lot about the man. Like how he was a murderer. The whole BDSM thing? Went right over her head. If it came anywhere near her at all.

"No… I really did not have any idea."

"Oh. *Well.*"

Oh, well, he said! Nala was about to start wringing *his* neck next.

She froze in her seat. The bench had no chance of releasing the woman stuck upon it, for even if Nala wanted to get up, or even if an earthquake shook the ground beneath her feet, there was no way in hell she would move at all. Too much information swarmed her brain. How could she possibly process it all? Xavier Crow. A strange man already pretending to be her boyfriend. BDSM! Nala felt like a stranger on the other side of a horror show window. She didn't even pay admission. She stumbled down the wrong corridor, where nightmares lurked and she was trapped in a constant cycle of despair and all its trappings. *I want my sister to get justice… I want to know the truth.*

When Nala finally did move, it was to gaze upon Vincent's profile. That look… determined. Agile. Capable. The man was young, perhaps not much older than Tasha was, but there was a maturity to him that made Nala wonder what *he* had seen in his few days on Earth.

Then she remembered. Vincent was coming here with purpose. He had decided on the spur of the moment to use her as his partner to get in. To get into a BDSM club ran by the man who killed Nala's sister. No matter where Nala turned, she faced danger. Deceit. Intrigue, but not the kind that entertained her. This wasn't what she wanted at all. She wanted to use her rage and brash, impulsive decision making to end the monster that was Xavier Crow. Instead, she was in his den of depraved sexuality with a man she had known for ten minutes.

What had she gotten herself into?

Chapter 4

"Here you go, hon."

A cup of coffee landed in front of Nala. She blinked, taking in the sights of a family restaurant. Surly women in pink aprons. Kids coloring on placemats. Students trying to get studying done. It was a common sight, no matter where Nala traveled in the country. Yet after what she had seen back at The Crow's Nest? Everything was extraordinary.

When Vincent said he would take her out for coffee, however, this wasn't what she had in mind. Portland was teeming with coffee shops. You couldn't throw a rock without landing on a barista's head. *Fuck me.* She realized how late it was. None of the cozy coffee shops would be open now. A 24-hour family restaurant on the inner skirts of suburbia would have to do.

Nala vaguely remembered the hour leading up to this moment. After that sordid display of spanking revelry, they had to watch Lucian and Robin play with feather dusters and… a crop. A crop right against Robin's ass. Apparently it was a spank-a-thon at The Crow's Nest.

All while Xavier Crow happily looked on.

What a blur that hour was. Nala could barely think about it without wanting to bang her head against the table and cry. Except she couldn't.

Not only was she in public, but Vincent sat across from her, his suit jacket off and a skinny spoon stirring cream into his coffee.

"So…" he began. "I never really got your name."

"Thank you for coming tonight, Vincent. Nightingale." That's what Xavier said when sending them off at the end of the shows. *"I hope you'll join us again next week. Get to know us while we get to know you. Soon enough we'll know if you're a good fit for our group."* That was it. The only further communication they had before Vincent ushered Nala out of the lounge and into a taxi that he paid for.

"My name is Nala," she finally said, hands wrapped around her hot cup of coffee. A typical drizzle lashed against the window beside them. Although the heat was on in the restaurant, Nala still took solace in the way the coffee made her palms *burn.* "Nala Nazarov."

"Nazarov? That's very… Russian."

"You don't have to tell me twice."

"Sorry." Vincent leaned back. "I shouldn't have shared that thought."

"Everyone thinks that, though. I'm a stone cold Russian bitch."

Vincent didn't say anything. Apparently he was not a man to banter. Nala had no idea *what* kind of man she currently hung out with.

"So, Nala…" He sipped his coffee and waited for a waitress to walk by with plates of pie. "About what happened back there…"

The coffee cup shook in her hands. Eventually, Nala realized that it was her hands shaking. *I don't know what's going on. What do I even say?* Was she safe around this man? "What do you want from me?" she finally asked. "I mean… why me…"

"I'll be honest with you, Nala." The way he said her name was so smooth and gentle that it almost placated her – and Nala was *not* the type of girl placated by a man's voice. If anything, she didn't notice it at all. Yet there was a lot to notice about Vincent. He didn't broadcast much, but he couldn't hide his looks or the sounds he made. No man was that good, no matter how much he wanted to keep locked away from the world. "I wanted into that club. I wanted to get to *him* as much as you seemed to. I don't know why you do. You don't know why I do. But I knew that going in on my own wouldn't get me far. I had an invitation, but as you could see, it was more of a couple's thing. If I wanted to hang around for several weeks, even months, I would need to find a partner to bring with me. Someone to pose as my girlfriend."

Nala perked up. "Pose as your girlfriend?"

"You said you can't act, but you might be a fine liar. If you can lie and pretend to be my girlfriend, then you'll have access to Crow at least once a week, when that group meets. Not always on the same day, but almost weekly."

"That club was depraved." She said it so off-handedly that it almost sounded like she talked about shoes or skirts. "I should have guessed that a man like him is into that sort of stuff." She had no comment on the other people there.

"Yes, and I suppose you could say that this city is full of rich, depraved people. Just like any other city in the world."

Nala finished her sip and slumped in her seat. "And you? Are *you* rich?" He definitely had money, based on his suit and his connections to Xavier Crow. Honestly, that should have been enough to turn Nala away. Far, far away. She didn't mess with rich people. Well, more like they didn't mess with her… they didn't even know she existed in her tiny closet and at her shitty job working for a corporate donation center for the poor.

Vincent wasn't fazed, yet again. Did anything faze him? "I'm a tech entrepreneur. I develop and market apps. You might even use one or two on your phone."

"I don't have a phone."

Oh, finally. He was fazed. "Excuse me?" That was the most shock to ever grace that man's face in a month, surely. "You don't own a phone at all? In 2015?"

Nala frowned hard enough to feel the shockwave through her body. "Fuck you," she muttered, pulling out her dumb phone and plopping it on the diner table. "It's old. I might as well not have one. It doesn't do Wi-Fi and definitely doesn't do data."

Vincent glanced at the flip phone, possibly from 2005, 6, 7…. "You're not into tech?"

"Not like you, apparently." In another life, Nala would pack up and go live off the grid. TV was boring. Computers were too expensive. If she needed one, she would go to the library and do her research and job applications. The NSA was watching her regardless. "Look, I know what an app is. I probably have never used whatever one you created and made you rich. Sorry."

"Don't be sorry. It takes all types in this world." Vincent shrugged. "I came into the money this past year, honestly. Crow contracted my company to develop an app for him to personally use in order to manage his properties. The age of internal servers and websites is over. Everyone does everything on their phones. Including run multi-billion dollar properties."

"He's a medical guy, though."

"First and foremost. Don't know if you noticed, though, he owns half of Portland and is making his way through Seattle. I hear he wants east coast properties next."

Seattle. Where his pharmaceutical labs were located. Where Tasha worked and lived.

And died.

The cup shook so much that it sloshed hot coffee on her hands. She didn't notice.

"You okay?"

Nala focused on the man in front of her. "Yeah, sure." Lying. She couldn't act, but she could lie her face off. "I'm fine. Sorry. It's been a long night."

They were silent. Just as well, for a horde of rowdy kids ran by carrying balloons and screaming for chocolate cream pie. *I hate places like these.* Nala worked at one when she first moved to Portland. A local eatery chain, which tested her patience to extremes she never knew she had. *Turns out I'm not a people person.* She was fired when a customer complained about her demeanor. *All I did was pour ice water in his lap for telling me to smile for the umpteenth time.* Now she didn't deal with customers at all. Praise the Lord.

"So why do you need a fake girlfriend?" Nala was going to regret asking that, but something needed to change the pace.

Vincent sucked in his breath, elbows straining against the table as he rubbed his face. Fingers brushed through his combed dark brown hair. Now it wasn't so combed. It stuck straight up in places, making him look like a disheveled cubicle crony on the verge of having a nervous breakdown. Nala contained a smile. *That's more like the kind of man I like. You know, if I bring myself to care at all.* Men. Expectations. All that.

"Like I said. That club was for couples. I don't have a girlfriend, though. I'm also not looking for one. So if I'm going to be in Xavier Crow's intimate circle, I need a girlfriend willing to play along." He snorted. "When I saw you sneaking around trying to get a gander at him, I took what was given to me. Sorry if it shocked you. Didn't mean for that to happen. How was I to know what you did or didn't know?"

Nala almost cackled. "So let me get this straight. You want to kiss this asshole's puckered anus, so you need a fake girlfriend to get into his perverted circle. That's rich. I also don't know how that's going to work, considering what *kind* of club it is. I didn't see any cocktails and chats about the horse races or even the precious Ducks."

Vincent studied her. "Asshole, huh? For someone trying to sneak in to see him, you really don't like Crow."

"I'd rather eat it."

"I see. Go back, do you?"

Yes. We go back to my sister's death. Nala wasn't going to tell him about that, though. Not now. Not here. Not like this. "Let's say he fucked my sister over and I'm a bit sore about it."

She expected him to roll his eyes. To wave her concerns off and treat her like everyone else did when Nala expressed her disdain for one of the nation's wealthiest men. "*What have you got against the guy? I hear he has a lot of charities and pours millions of dollars into cancer research! His personal money!*" That was if people had even heard of him. For owning half of a city, most of its residents couldn't tell Nala who he was. Then again, most of those people were high most of the day.

Instead, Vincent Lane regarded her with newfound interest. "Fucked her over how?"

Nala looked away. "Enough to make me hate him forever."

She drank her coffee and stared at the tacky carpeting. Dirt. Grime. Food particles and lint. The same Nala's old restaurant always looked on a busy night of free pie and birthday parties. Now she was really going to puke.

"You must think I'm petty."

Vincent slowly shook his head. "Whatever you're guessing about me… I'm not trying to get to him because I want to kiss his puckered anus. I don't like the man either. It's personal."

That got Nala's attention. "How so? Business?" She snorted. "He fuck you over with money? Didn't pay for his app?"

The man sitting across from her did not smile. No. He frowned, so sour in countenance that Nala had to recall what she even said. He looked at her as if she had been purposely flippant.

"Let's say he has a lot to answer for."

This wasn't a man sour about money. Or business in general. This was personal, indeed. Yet like Nala wasn't going to get in her conspiracies about Tasha's death, Vincent wasn't going to share his thoughts. Probably a good idea. They barely knew each other. The most intimate thing they had shared thus far was watching two women get cropped and spanked.

Nala shuddered.

"It sounds like we have a lot to gain from one another, Ms. Nazarov." Interesting. He pronounced it correctly, and not with a stupid flair like most men thought it funny to use… as if she really were some Bond girl ready to rip off her clothes and soak in the ocean. Or whatever they did. "We both want access to him, for our own reasons, but we need each other to do that. It's probably our only way. That man is heavily guarded otherwise. Even when doing business with him, I only met with him once or twice. This was over months."

Nala shifted uncomfortably in her seat. The booth screeched, the faux leather rubbing against her thighs. "I don't know. That club was…"

"We probably shouldn't discuss those details here." Vincent gestured to the kids' party going on a few yards away. He reached into his pocket and pulled out a business card and a pen. His handwriting appeared on the back of the card. "Here." He slid it across the table. "The address to my office is on that card. I'm available Thursday evening at six. Come up to my office and we'll talk it over. Unless you have to work or have class?"

Nala shook her head. "I'm off work at three."

"Then I hope to see you."

Without a formal farewell, Vincent slipped out of his booth and slapped some bills on the table. For their coffees and the tip, he said. It was well over the kosher amount. The waitress was looking at a $13 tip.

Nala stared at the wad of cash long after her new friend left. She was far from home, with almost no money in her pocket and her bus ticket long expired. She needed a new one. Now.

Her fingers plucked three dollar bills from the pile of cash. When no one was looking, she pocketed them, feeling both guilty and shameless at the same time.

After the night she had, though? She wasn't going to feel bad about doing what she needed to do. She had accessed Xavier Crow. She had seen what kind of life he lived. She wanted to throw up in the process, but now she knew.

As for Vincent? He was convenient. Not only had he saved her back and neck, but he had gotten her into that club to begin with. Nala saw the value in that. Besides… he wasn't too bad to look at. If she was going to pretend to be a man's girlfriend to meet her vengeful end, he could at least be decent looking and rich. Especially if he offered to pay for everything. Like a taxi. And coffee. And Nala's bus ticket, even if he didn't know he was doing that.

She briefly wondered if this was a trap. Maybe Vincent was actually one of Xavier's cronies. Perhaps. Perhaps it was worth the danger to find out his true intentions.

"Let's say he has a lot to answer for."

What did that mean? Had Xavier Crow also ruined someone's life in Vincent's world?

The real question was…

Did she care?

As long as her formless plan continued along its path, oh yeah, she cared. The rage simmering in her stomach would have to dance with grief a little while longer.

For Tasha. She would find out what Vincent had to say. *For Tasha.*

Not those shining eyes of intrigue burning in Vincent's stoic face.

Not his strong arms holding tight onto her.

Certainly not for the look Nala recognized in him. The look of vengeance.

She didn't need to know the details. She just had to show up and lie.

Entry #2

Infiltration was a success. I've gained access to Crow's most private realm and met some of his closest business associates.

On top of this, something most unexpected happen. I met a woman who I think will make a good partner in this endeavor. She too wants something bad to happen to Crow. I can't help but wonder if he too has touched her in such a heinous way as he has touched me.

This woman is much younger than me, however, and I worry about her stability.

I have called her Nightingale and will call her this in my journal as to protect her identity should anyone else read this.

I'm not sure Nightingale knows what she's gotten into. I don't think she cares, and that's good for me.

Chapter 5

More boxes rolled down the shaft and in Nala's direction. With deft hands she grabbed them before they could pile on top of each other. She plucked a pen out of her mouth and marked the arrival down on her clipboard.

Great. More baby clothes. Granted, the donation center always needed more baby clothes to ferry out to the stores, but they were so *gross* to sift through, especially for minimum wage! Most days Nala didn't have the patience to pick up used bibs and onesies, inspecting them for poop and spittle. Half of them were like that. For some reason, frazzled parents thought it a great idea to donate their child's soiled clothing.

"Soiled. Soiled. Clean." She had to mutter beneath her breath, otherwise she would go insane. She often worked all alone in the receiving room. Two coworkers ran the donation counter and went through the bins in the neighborhood, but it was Nala who processed it all. Some days that meant standing around and twiddling her thumbs. Other days that meant working so fast that she wanted to pass out dead in her closet later on.

Yet it was Thursday. The day she was going downtown after work, to see Mr. Vincent Lane in his techy office. They were going to discuss the business of faking a relationship in order to access Xavier Crow's sexual den of sin and spanking. Lots of spanking.

Nala didn't dwell on that fact. They would discuss it that evening. First she had to make it through another round of "is this dirt or feces?"

Working at the donation center was better than the restaurant, if only because she didn't have to deal with people. Nala had never been a social girl. In grade school she often got in trouble for not playing with other children. In high school she fucked off from group projects. She didn't even bother with college. Just got a job doing clerical work for an auto parts store in the middle of Carson City. That worked fine until she got the notice that her sister was dead.

Now she was in Portland, the land of a million baristas with Masters Degrees. Nala had to hustle her ass off to get twenty hours a week at minimum wage. No wonder she lived in an overpriced closet and lived off crackers and coffee. At least she didn't have any debt!

Maybe that guy will buy me dinner. He wasn't haughty, but he stank of money. Tech money. Those days that's where all the money was. Nala didn't care that he was mega-rich, but she did care that he may pay for things here and there. Even at her angriest, there was a lot to be said for a full stomach and a free ride home.

"Hey, Nala." One of her coworkers appeared in the doorway. "We've got a big truck coming in. Hope you wore your wrist braces."

She glared at him. "Do I even want to fucking know…"

"Looks like practice jerseys and cleats and shit. One of the community outreach programs got new ones and is donating these. Have fun."

Nala dropped her clipboard on the rolling rack with a sigh. First baby shit, now the stank of athletes who forgot their deodorant. She really, *really* hoped Mr. App Man bought her some food tonight.

***

Still dressed in her jeans and blue work shirt, Nala ambled up a downtown sidewalk long after the sun began to set. She looked at the address on the business card for Lane Technological Solutions and crosschecked it with a transit map standing firm in the commercial district. The names of dead presidents went by with every block, until she came to the guy whose wife saved some portrait of George Washington or something. *That's literally all I know about him.*

The greeter behind the front counter looked at her with a stern face. No wonder. Everyone else milling about the lobby was dressed in their Sunday best and chatting about stocks and Ducks and Timbers and mergers. *All the same around here.* Nala slapped her handwritten appointment on the counter and hoped that her hair wasn't too greasy. She had washed it that morning, but sweaty athlete jerseys…

"Can I help you?" the elderly gentleman asked.

Yeah, kill Xavier Crow for me. "I'm here to see Vincent Lane of the tech… thing." Oops. "What floor is that on?"

The grizzly glare she received would unnerve the average woman. She, however, was anything but average in that regard. *I once had a neighbor who could've been this guy's brother.* Glared at everyone as if they had personally affronted him. Nala's mother said it had to do with families and KGB and some asshole named Gorbachev. *Come on, guy, tear down this wall between us and tell me what floor to go to!*

Nala was about to turn to the video monitor displaying floor information when the man said, "Sixteenth floor." He kept a careful eye on her as she walked toward the elevator. *Dare you to call security.* Yup. He was reaching for a phone.

No surprise when the elevator doors opened on the sixteenth floor and Nala was greeted by a young intern-y looking guy in a department store suit. Although behind his own desk, he looked as if he were expecting the young Miss Nazarov to announce she was there for a baby daddy check.

"Hi. I have an appointment with your boss." Nala slapped the business card down again, Vincent's handwriting up. "See? That's his handwriting." She looked up at the Lane Technological Solutions logo hanging on a wood wall. Bold. White. Red asterisk behind the L. Nala sniffed and checked for her wallet out of habit. Yup. Still in the back pocket.

Aggressive pan handlers hadn't whisked away with it yet. *It's the chain.* She liked chains.

The man forced a smile as he picked up the card. "Well…"

"It's okay, Andrew."

Nala looked to her left. There, standing in a nondescript doorway, was Vincent. A very different looking Vincent from Tuesday night.

That Vincent wore a suit meant for forty-year-old stock brokers showing off their wares. *This* Vincent wore pleated trousers, comfortable black shoes, and a burgundy button down tucked into a slim black belt with a simple gold buckle. No tie. No perfect posture. He was the epitome of laid back tech professional. Would be straight out of the Bay Area, but instead he had those PNW sensibilities that made him dress dark and probably carry a huge black umbrella.

Nala's eyes went straight to the big, bold silver watch on his wrist. Mostly because Vincent absentmindedly fussed with the clasp, like he had adjusted his cufflinks a dozen times the other night. *Every man has his tic.* If that was the worst of them with Vincent, then Nala should consider herself lucky.

"Come on in, Nala. Andrew, hold any calls. I don't want to be disturbed."

Andrew looked between his finely dressed boss and the girl who looked like she stepped out of a big box store staff room. Nala grinned at him before following Vincent into his office.

For a man of many apparent means, Vincent did not have grand tastes. In fact, they were quite subtle. His desk had no drawers. Just a black, sturdy table boasting a powerful graphics machine, printer, and telephone. The grandest piece of furniture was the office chair that looked like it hardly got any use. Two leather chairs sat before the desk, one of which Nala sat in while taking in the stark cream-colored walls and the few photographs around. There was one frame on the windowsill behind Vincent. Four pictures sectioned off. One was a middle-aged woman who looked enough like Vincent to be his mother. A college graduation photo. An old, worn photo that looked like it came from Ellis Island.

A recent picture of a woman with big, frizzy hair and a smile that could light up the night sky. *Sister?* Vincent said he didn't have a girlfriend, but, well, men lied.

"Sorry about the trouble." Vincent slumped into his chair and pushed paperwork aside. "I hate this building. Lots of old style types. Even the interns who canvas here are… well, never mind. It's convenient to the other offices we deal with, though, and the restaurant downstairs is pretty great. Do you want some coffee? I could get Andrew to bring us some."

Nala shook her head. Her stomach growled, and she hoped to God Vincent didn't hear. She hadn't eaten since her half of a turkey sandwich at lunch. *I've lost ten pounds since moving here.* Food was expensive.

"Anyway, I appreciate you taking the time to meet me. I honestly wasn't sure if you would after Tuesday night."

Nala suppressed an amused snort. "Why?" Like she had anything better to do?

Vincent's expression remained firm. *God, you're kinda scary.* Like a robot. Or was that an android? Cyborg. "You seemed very put off by what happened at the club. I know what you said in the restaurant, but I thought maybe you would have second thoughts. About everything."

Nala crossed her legs, dangling one foot in the air as she sucked in her cheeks and stared at her dirty fingernails. *Dirt or feces?* "I told you, Mr. Lane…"

"Call me Vincent."

She stopped mid-thought. "Fine. Vincent."

"Anyway…"

She fought to keep her eyebrows up. "*Anyway,* I recall telling you that I like that bastard about as much as I like passing a kidney stone. He and I have some serious unfinished business. Not that he knows me. I doubt he would even recognize my name. Look, I don't want to get you in trouble, but I'm telling you right now… you take me with you as your pretend girlfriend, and I may do something that reflects poorly on you."

Palms turned inward into fists. Vincent took a deep breath, his composure remaining, but the wheels turning so hard in his head that Nala could practically hear the gears screaming. "Funny you should say that. I was going to warn the same thing about me."

They fell silent yet again. *Secrets, secrets.* They were both keeping them from each other. Nala preferred it that way. She didn't want to share her conspiracies with a man she barely trusted, and she sure as hell didn't want to know his opinion on things. As far as she was concerned, she was entering a type of non-romantic partnership, regardless of what they had to do to play up a fake romance.

"Seems like we both want to do something brash around that man."

"Seems that way."

Vincent held her gaze for a few seconds before resolutely turning to a drawer. He opened it, fished out a piece of paper, and slid it across the table to Nala. She pricked it between her fingers and recognized Xavier Cross's personal letterhead. *I saw this in my mother's things after my sister died.* Offering his condolences, of course. The scum.

"That's the letter he sent me inviting me to check out his club. While he contracted this company, I found out about his predilections for… what we saw that night. I'm warning you, that was tame. The guy is an extreme voyeur. He surrounds himself with kinky couples to feed off their sexual energies. They put on shows for him, and in return he treats them to extravagant getaways and gives them important business connections. They're almost closer to him than his public friends." Vincent grimaced. "I hope you see where I'm going with this."

Nala ran her tongue across her front teeth. "We're going to lie about being a kinky couple." Lying and acting were starting to sound like the same thing.

"Nala…" Vincent leaned forward, his cologne growing stronger. Something about it relaxed Nala. "We *are* going to be a kinky couple. At least in front of Crow."

"Come again?"

"They won't make us do anything but watch in the beginning. Soon enough we'll have to perform like those other people. Not just on that stage. He'll scrutinize us, from the way we look at each other, hold hands, and even speak. He not only has to think we're in love, but into kink. Otherwise he might kick us out."

Nala shook her head. "You're kidding. You're going to…" She remembered Quail, her ass beet red and that look of surrender on her round face. "You're going to hit me?"

Fear laced her voice. Not enough fear to startle herself, but Nala was not happy with the amount that appeared. She didn't need this man thinking she was fearful of him.

Vincent didn't flinch. "Technically? Yes, and a lot more."

Nala turned away, chin resting on hand as she considered this. *He's going to spank me in front of those people. He's going to do God knows what else. Not just in front of strangers. In front of Xavier Crow.*

That sounded like heresy.

"Do we have to have sex in front of these people?"

She tried to keep her voice as even as possible. Matter of fact. Logical. Too bad her heart was thumping wildly in her chest as she imagined Vincent lifting up her skirt and parting her legs so he could get inside her… in front of people… in front of…

Her cheeks must've been on *fire.*

"Would that bother you?" No man seemed more asexual than Vincent Lane right now. Or perhaps that was solely Nala's perspective at the time. *No way. This guy is what most women would consider a total catch. Good looking and successful.* In another life, one in which she wasn't so jaded and angry, Nala would go on a date and maybe more with him. As it was, she hadn't been on a date since her sister died.

"N…" she tried saying no. To put up the façade that she would do anything for her sister, even if Vincent didn't know this was why she did this. She tried. Then she saw Xavier's face, twisting in sadistic glee as he watched the sister of Tasha Nazarov be smacked on the ass and fucked like a doll. "For fuck's sake!" She leaped up, towering as well as she could over Vincent. "Are you crazy?"

"No." He said it simply. "I don't want to go forward unless you know what's on the line."

"You need me that badly?" Who was she? Some girl he found snooping around a man they mutually disliked. She had no name. No clout. She was average looking and had the manners of a raccoon.

"I *need* you in that I have no one else to ask. My other option was hiring a woman to do this for me…"

"You mean an escort?"

"Something like that."

Nala sat back down, gob smacked. This man was willing to go as far as hiring a professional woman to pose as his kinky girlfriend. "At least a pro would be more familiar with that sort of thing."

"Yes, and pros can talk. I'd rather have a woman who also has something to emotionally gain from this arrangement. It doesn't matter to me what your issue with this man is. We both want to see certain things unfold. You can't get to him unless you're with me. I can't stay near him unless I have you."

"Unless I have you."

Tenderness abounded. They had yet to flirt one iota, and even so that warmth returned all over Nala's skin. She hadn't felt like that since she was seventeen, crying in her sister's arms because she suddenly missed their deceased father. She had almost forgotten what it was like to be coddled.

Not that Vincent was *coddling* her. This man seemed as affectionate as a wet fish.

"I'm not having sex with you."

Still Vincent did not flinch. "You will definitely have to play the sub in front of him."

"You used that word the other night." Nala pushed her fists between her legs, willing this excess energy to go away before she started rocking back and forth. "You called me your sub."

"Yes. It's short for submissive."

I was afraid of that. "And that other word… Nightingale. What was all that about?"

The sigh exuding from Vincent's body implied that was a long answer. "I'm sure you've noticed that the other women there had bird names.

Obviously, those aren't their real names. They're code. He calls his club The Aviary. A place where birds are kept. Men bring their submissive little birds there for his amusement. I knew this ahead of time and, well, when put on the spot I thought of the nightingale. You could probably change it if you want. It's not set in stone until we sign his NDA."

The nightingale… A bird that sang beautifully. A song of lament. A song of grief.

It was fitting.

"I wouldn't be able to stand going by my real name there anyway. I'll take it."

"So you'll do it?" Vincent almost sounded hopeful.

"Now hold on. So I have this straight, I have to pretend to be your girlfriend. You're not exactly expecting anything from me, are you?"

"No. This isn't a real relationship. If you have a boyfriend, I don't care. Hold up your end of the bargain by being a good liar."

"I don't have a boyfriend." Nala played with the end of her short ponytail. "If I do this, I still won't."

"Certainly." Vincent released a pent-up sigh. He sighed a lot for someone his age. "I'll also be willing to pay for any expenses related to this. It's the least I can do. Do you need a stipend? You may have to take time off work if he wants to go to the coast or something. Or Bali. I hear that happens a lot."

"Stipend? So now I am a pro?"

"Hardly. It's an inconvenience fee. How does a thousand a week sound? I can give you the first grand before the next club meeting Sunday night."

"A… thousand…" Nala hadn't had a thousand dollars to her name in years. Not since Carson City. A thousand a week? Dear Lord. "I mean, I think that's insane, but I won't say no." She wouldn't tell him that she needed the money. To eat. To get around town. To save for emergencies, because there would be some in the future. She didn't dare to think about moving, though. The closet sucked, but she didn't think she and Vincent would have this arrangement for too long. She didn't know why, but…

"All right. All right! Let's try this bullshit out for size. You said the next meeting is on Sunday? What do we have to do?"

"Watch and mingle. He's throwing a party in a hotel suite here in downtown. It would be a good chance for you to study the other women. They are all naturally submissive, and you need to pretend to be one too. We'll go over the details that night. Oh, do you need money for a dress? The one you wore the other night was okay, but I'm sure you saw how everyone else's popped."

"That's the only dress I own."

"I see." Vincent pulled out his wallet and a crisp $100 bill within. Air shot through Nala's nostrils. He wasn't kidding, was he? Apparently not, because he pulled out another hundred with it! "Here. Get something sexy that you're comfortable in. I'll bring the mask. I'll pick you up at six and we'll head to the party. Sound good?"

Nala nodded, although her head felt completely detached from her body. "Are you made of money, by the way?"

Vincent cracked a hint of a smile. "Something like that. I've had a very successful past couple of years."

"And you're single."

He frowned again. "I told you before. I'm not looking."

"But I'm sure women throw themselves at you all the time." Nala fanned herself with the money. It smelled like dusty old paper, ink, and traces of the cocaine she heard was on money everywhere. "I'll be the envy of every woman in Oregon. That may be the most annoying part of all."

"Don't worry. I'm rich, but I'm not high society. I doubt people will be watching out for who I date. This is Portland, not New England."

"I'll take your word for it. By the way, when do I get that first check?" Hey, she might as well milk this opportunity! A path of vengeance *and* thousands of dollars? Sweet.

"I'll give it to you after our adventure on Sunday."

"Awesome." Nala stood, stretching her arms above her head. "Well, Mr. Lane… I mean Vincent… I look forward to lying about being your submissive fuckdoll in front of a guy I would love to wring the neck of."

Vincent stood, holding his hand out for her to shake. "The feeling is mutual, Nala."

They shook hands. He was firm. So was she. There was no denying that they had something to benefit from in this situation. Who would fall first? Nala had to wait to find that out.

First, she had to go shopping. For a slutty dress that screamed sexual submissive. Whatever that meant. Surely, there was something at a consignment shop. Surely.

After that? She was already thinking about what she would do with the money. What she would do with her access to Crow and the evidence she could amass.

What would happen during her time with Vincent.

Him spanking her.

Kissing her in front of others.

Also, spanking her.

Why was she dwelling on that? Nala shrugged on her way into the elevator. Apparently she was fixated on the weird shit people could be into. At least it took her mind off all the terrible shit she was exposed to on a constant basis.

Entry #3

I had a meeting with Nightingale today. She is rougher than I initially took her to be. Younger, too. I already knew she was both of these things, but seeing how much so reminded me that I must be cautious. She could be a liability.

Business continues as usual. My personal life, outside of seeking vengeance… it becomes harder each day to separate my past from my present. Every day she is not with me is like two hands squeezing my throat. Some days are easier to bear than others, especially if I focus on my work. But recent events have forced me to think of her every day. Sleep does not come easy. It's been three years, and yet I feel like I've been suffering much longer. Such is Crow's reach.

I hope Nightingale is my means to an end. What will happen after? I cannot conceive.

Chapter 6

Vincent Matthew Lane, b. May 31st, 1985, the Wikipedia page said, in Fresno, California. Founder and CEO of Lane Technological Solutions based out of Portland, Oregon. Money Builder Magazine's #5 most eligible bachelor of 2015 with a net worth of over $1 billion.

Nala sat back in her seat, the cheap plastic of the chair squeaking loud enough to rouse her neighbor, an elderly man in serious need of assistance. "Does anyone know my password?" he kept asking, pointing to the email login screen. "I need to check my credit!"

The sounds of the local library continued to buzz around Nala, but she only had eyes for the grainy screen in front of her. "A billion dollars, huh?" Nala wasn't stupid. She knew that wasn't how much untaxed money he had sitting in his credit union account. Vincent Lane maybe had a few million at his disposal, tops. He was practically broke, like her.

"Thank you for visiting your local Multnomah County Library branch," a sweet voice said over a speaker. "We will be closing shortly. Thank you."

While the man beside her groaned, Nala fumbled for a few dimes and printed off Vincent's Wikipedia page. Would be good reading later.

A billion dollars… She slipped into her rain jacket and pulled her backpack onto her shoulders. *I can't even imagine.* How did a man make that much money? She knew that Vincent was in "tech" and developed "apps," but that was as far as her knowledge in that field went. Tasha would have known all about that. Truly, Nala and her sister were the opposite sides of the same coin. While Tasha was inside reading science books and taking apart computers, Nala was outside climbing trees – and falling out of them. In the beginning, it was their mother who came out to kiss the boo-boos and admonish the foolish youngest daughter for climbing yet another weak tree. Then their father died and their mother became a useless shell. *Tasha started coming outside after that.* She was the only one there to kiss her sister's boo-boos.

Well, she couldn't do that anymore. Not unless the zombie horde had finally come to take over the world.

Nala shuffled through a thick mist down the sidewalk. Her "house" was only a few minutes away from the library, but she wasn't in a hurry to get back. For one, her roommate Patrick was home. And for two, she had to get ready for her big "date" with Vincent the stoic billionaire, which sounded about as exciting as pulling out her toenails.

No, wait, she took that back the moment she walked through the front door. The thing as exciting as pulling out toenails was bumping into Patrick in the living room.

"Heeeeyyy Simba!" he called, already high off his rocker. The living room reeked of pot, but then again so did every house on that street. "Have fun learning books at the library?"

Nala shut the door behind her, scraped her feet on a mat, and went straight to the hallway closet where she slept. "Shut up. Don't call me Simba." He thought it was hilarious because her name was Nala. So when she displayed any aggression against that name, it made it worse.

Difficult for Nala to *not* show aggression when she wasn't supposed to. Should make tonight's date super fun.

"Whoa, that's quite the dress." Patrick hung over the back of the ratty living room couch, his chin scruff covered in cheese dust. "Where you going in that thing? Prom?"

God, he was in the clouds. Pot clouds, as thick as his head. "Uh huh. Prom. Cause I'm in high school."

"Haaaaa."

Rolling her eyes, Nala shut her "bedroom" door and dragged her new dress to the bathroom, also known as her walk-in wardrobe with water features.

The dress wasn't anything special. It was the best she could find on short notice and with "only" two hundred dollars to spend. Didn't Vincent the billionaire know that consignment shops in Portland were expensive? They appealed to the trust fund babies who thought making a lark with riding bicycles, dressing in dumpster dive wear, and working at cafés for "real world experience" was the epitome of one's 20s.

My ass is too flat for this shit. Nevertheless, Nala stood in front of the smudged mirror, pulling the skirt down until she was presentable. Oh, sure, she was going to some tycoon's sex club, but *she* wasn't one to put herself on display and lure in the leers. Quite the opposite. Nala wanted to blend in. Be unseen. So when she bought this body-hugging strapless cream-colored sequin monster… perhaps she wasn't thinking ahead.

I should have budgeted for shoes. Her same black heels from the other night would have to do. Hopefully there would be no stairs to fall down this time.

Nala wasn't a woman for makeup. Yet she knew that these assholes would want some semblance of propriety from a woman of her supposed standing. *What is my standing, anyway?* Vincent was paying her to be his fake girlfriend and submissive for however long it took them to get what they wanted from Xavier Crow. That could last weeks. Months, if Nala could stomach it. *I probably can't.* For all her bravado, deep down Nala was still a scared little girl who needed her big sister to come kiss her boo-boos after falling out of a tree.

"How does this even…" She had stopped at a pharmacy after buying her dress to pick up some cheap makeup. Now she stood in front of that mirror, wondering how eye shadow, eyeliner, and even blush worked. Nala could fake the lipstick… maybe. "I'm a fucking clown!" That was what she declared before promptly washing off the makeup and starting over. A dab of light pink lipstick. Some smoky eye shadow. That was it. They could deal with her tiny pimples.

Nala stumbled out of the bathroom and grabbed a small satchel. As she approached the front door, a black four-door sedan pulled up in front of the walkway. A masculine figure lurked behind the wheel.

"You were right, Patrick," Nala announced to her stoned roommate as she opened the door. "It really is prom night. Wish me luck in getting laid." Not really.

She wobbled down the path to the sidewalk, leaving the shambled craftsman home behind her. Vincent popped out of the driver's side and made to open the passenger side door before Nala made it that far.

"Hi," she said, her breath appearing before her eyes. Even though she threw on a heavy black sweater before leaving, it wasn't enough. The cold nipped right through the fabric. "Look at what two-hundred bucks buys you around here."

She said that flippantly, and yet Vincent leaned over the door and watched her get into his car. *Nice ride*. Leather interior. And clean! "It's lovely. You look… lovely."

With a huff, Nala situated herself in the comfortable seat and reached to close the door… except Vincent was still holding it open, his eyes boring upon her in that barely-there dress. *Okay, buddy…* Where did asexual Vincent go? Where was that stoic man from the sparse office? Where was the button-down and comfortable trousers? Tonight, Vincent wore a three-piece suit again, this time without the tie. His hair was styled in place, and a new cologne wafted through the frigid air. Very, *very* musky.

Nala may have been stuck in an endless cycle of tortuous grief and anger, but she was still a human. A human full of hormones and biological responses she couldn't control, no matter what her brain was doing.

So while her brain said, "What the fuck, girl? You've got a mission to accomplish!" her body said, "Hey, look at this hottie. He's pretty clean-cut and sexy. Sexsexsexsex *girl* hey how about that cock in his pants?"

"You should shut the door. It's cold."

Vincent's demeanor remained unchanged as he stepped upon the sidewalk and closed the door against Nala's arm. He sauntered around the front of the car before getting back into the driver's seat. The light of the day had faded, so all Nala could see in that dark car was the outline of her fake boyfriend. Who smelled really good.

And was putting his arm around her, coming in with his mouth…

His mouth…

"Wha…" Nala's skull met the headrest as Vincent lightly kissed her lips. His scent overpowered her, infused her with more of those hormones that demanded she unzip his pants and get a feel of him. *What? No way!* Where was that feeling coming from… and why was he kissing her?

The kiss did not last long. Surely, it was only a few seconds, but in Nala's world it lasted more than ten lifetimes. The universe slowed. Her eyes fluttered open and shut, one part of her wanting to lean in and savor those soft, tender lips and another part willing her to push him far away. Wasn't this assault or something?

Vincent sat back, his body looming over Nala's, in a non-threatening way. "We were going to have to do that eventually," he explained, returning to his seat. "At some point we would have to kiss in front of those people. They do it all the time." He started the car, the soft purr of the engine sending tingles through Nala's awakening body. "I thought it would be best to do it now and get the awkwardness out of the way."

His words settled in her brain, but they did not mean anything as he pulled away from the sidewalk and drove toward the nearest boulevard. Nala stared at her lap, at her hands clenched in it, wondering, *wondering* what this all truly meant. *I shouldn't feel like this for him.* This was a job. A mission. She didn't even know who Vincent really was, and she sure as fuck was not a girl who did things casually. She had never even been in love before. The last boyfriend? She thought that was love at first, but realized now she hardly missed him at all.

"Don't do that," she finally whispered. "If you're going to kiss me, warn me."

They were stuck at a stop sign. Vincent glanced at her. "I'm sorry."

Nala let out an exasperated breath. "You should be. You do that to every woman you take to sex clubs?"

The car turned, lurching poor Nala toward the window. "Apparently," Vincent said.

Things were quiet on the first boulevard. Nala gazed out the window, watching lights come and go as they headed downtown. Bridges loomed in the distance. Runners going for their nightlies jogged in place at lights and signaled to cyclists who didn't have a care in the world. *The man kissed me.* She touched her fingers to her lips. *He kissed me.* Out of the corner of her eyes she saw Vincent sitting silently behind the wheel, taking them to an uncertain future. He wasn't her friend. He wasn't even really a business associate. He was a means to an end. Nala thought that he felt the same way about her… until now.

No, he was right. We have to kiss in front of those people eventually. They'll want to see us do the bare minimum, at least. Kissing and touching and hugging… it's better than the spanking and the whipping. That's what she thought as they approached a notoriously long light.

"Vincent…"

"Hm."

Nala forced her spine straight and her face forward. "We should have a signal… some gesture for when the one needs to kiss the other. To keep appearances, of course."

He cleared his throat. "That is a good idea."

"Maybe a tap on the shoulder. A warning that a kiss is coming. I don't like surprises."

"I don't like them either."

"So no more surprises?"

"Certainly not."

Nala squirmed in her seat. "So a tap on the shoulder. Then I'll be ready for your lips."

She tried to sound jovial. Why not, in this situation? *Best make the most of it.* But when she glimpsed in Vincent's direction, she found him staring at the road and putting his foot on the gas so they could cross the bridge into downtown.

"I did some reading on you."

"Did you?" Vincent fiddled with the fan like he would with his watch or cufflinks. "Good. We should get to know more about each other before people start questioning us. Might not be a bad idea. What did you learn?"

"Well… you're a Gemini, for one."

Whenever Nala mentioned the Zodiac, she had no idea if she should anticipate laughter or scorn. Vincent seemed like the type of man who would go for the latter. "Is that a bad thing?"

"No. I'm an Aries. We're supposed to get along well."

"You don't strike me as a woman into horoscopes and all that."

"I'm not. My mother used to make a big deal out of it growing up."

"Your mother?"

"Duh. I have a mother."

Vincent scoffed. "So do I."

"Is that the woman whose picture is in your office?"

He glanced at her, forebodingly. "I do have a picture of her, yes."

"And the other woman? Is that your sister?"

"The other woman…" Vincent shook his head. "I don't have any siblings."

"Oh." Nala didn't pry any further. It was none of her business if Vincent didn't want to share. As long as he wasn't lying about not having a girlfriend, well, what did it matter to her?

"For the record, it's difficult to find out much information about you, Nala Nazarov." Vincent eased the car down another road, careful to avoid traffic congestion. "Even though that's a fairly rare name."

"There isn't much to know about me. I was born here. I moved to Nevada as a kid. I moved back here a few months ago. Didn't go to college and work some odd jobs. I'm nothing like you." Somehow, she managed to sound confident when she said that. "For one, I don't go around kissing people by surprise."

A chuckle filled the car. "Of course not. Do you have any family?"

"My mom back in Nevada. My dad died when I was a kid."

"I'm sorry. Siblings?"

Dread overcame her. "My sister died a little over a year ago."

While gremlins battled in her gut, Nala drummed her fingers against the arm rest and wished, for the first time since getting in the car, that they were at their destination already. Anything was starting to become better than sitting around being questioned by a billionaire who thought it was A-OK to plant his lips on any woman he chose. *He chose me, though.* No, no it wasn't like that. He *chose* her because she was convenient. Standing right there in front of him, ready to take on… something… stupid…

"I'm sorry to hear about that as well."

Nala closed her eyes and willed back the tears. Bad enough that Xavier Crow's presence was going to make her think of Tasha every single second. Did that pity party have to start now?

"She worked for Black Raven," Nala braved, her voice a mere whisper above the car heater. "Medical researcher. One of the top ones in the nation, and she was only twenty-seven."

They were at another light. Vincent stared at her, calculating, digesting the snippets of her life she had shared. "So we have even more in common than we thought." Deep. Menacing. Nala involuntarily moved away from Vincent's tone.

"How's that?"

He put too much pressure on the gas, lurching them across a busy intersection and garnering them a round of unhappy horns from other commuters. Nala gripped the nearest handle and sucked in her breath.

"Someone who is no longer with me used to work for him too."

There wasn't much time to consider that revelation. Vincent made an abrupt turn onto a side street and parallel parked in a part of town known for its vehicular break-ins. Before Nala could say anything, the engine turned off.

"We're here." Vincent tossed a simple black mask into Nala's lap as a valet emerged from a nondescript building. "Time to start lying."

Chapter 7

Crow's current party was held in a luxury hotel suite boasting four bedrooms and a large Jacuzzi. Nala stood in the middle of the brightly lit gallery in absolute awe, ignoring the comings and goings of more guests behind her. Xavier Crow had not yet arrived.

"You can see all of downtown Portland from here." An arm looped through Nala's, startling her as she was pulled up onto a platform near the sliding door. Beyond the window were a million twinkling city lights on display, with trees – so many beautiful, evergreen trees – dotting hillsides and lining streets. "See? There's the Willamette. The new bridge is gorgeous."

Nala sipped the champagne she picked up on her way in. It was only then that she recognized Robin standing beside her, scaring her more than Vincent had yet to accomplish. "It is a lovely view."

"What was your name again?" Robin finally released Nala's arm and looked her straight in the eye, as if she could see beyond the lacy black mask. *I sure can't see past her silk red one.* "Sorry if you have to tell me a few times. I'm terrible at remembering names."

Nala ran her tongue over her bottom lip before letting a single word pass it. "Nightingale."

"That's lovely! Who picked it out? You or your Master?"

My what? Nala caught a glimpse of Vincent talking to another man in a three-piece suit, their glasses of brandy nearly empty. *My Master? She's nuts, right?* "He picked it out for me." Like hell Nala was going to say the word *Master!*

"Oh, he must know you so well. It totally suits you! Is it okay if I call you Gale, though? It will be easier to remember."

"Sure." Whatever this fool wanted.

"Do you know the other girls yet?" Robin pointed an excited finger across the room, where the three other women of The Aviary gathered to talk submissive shop, or whatever it was Nala was expected to participate in. "They're dying to meet you. Especially Starling. She was the new girl these past few months before you arrived!"

"I'm afraid that I have not yet met them."

"Well, come on!"

Nala was hauled to the bevy of beauties in masks, each of whom looked up with a smile as they waved down their new friends. Robin stuck Nala behind the nearest couch, stroking her bare arms and cooing at what a beautiful code name she had.

"This is Quail," she said, pointing to the girl with bold red lipstick and a pair of shoes ready to dance the Charleston. "You probably remember her from Tuesday."

Nala couldn't help but blush as the young woman shook hands with her. "Pleasure to meet you, Nightingale." She had an even, airy voice that spoke of a submissive fun Nala never considered before. Confident, but deferring. "I hope you like this group. We do have a lot of fun." She winked. "Sometimes with the other boys."

"Oh, hush. Don't scare her off." Robin flicked her friend's pearl headband while Nala took another step back.

"She'll have to get used to it," said the buxom blonde, Starling. "That Master of hers is quite the punch of man. Hi." She extended her delicate hand to Nala. "Starling. That stud in the bold blue suit is mine, but you can have him if you give me yours for a night." She winked. Nala shuddered. *I don't even want to sleep with "my" man. Let alone yours!*

The third woman, who until now had been quiet, took her chance to lean forward and introduce herself. Nala was instantly captivated by her strong jaw, prominent lips, and shaved head with only a bit of black fuzz coming back in. Yet she was extremely feminine, wearing a dark, gold dress over her smooth black skin and a figure to die for. Her breasts alone caught Nala's wayward eye more than once.

"Maggie," she said. Then, smiling wider, "Short for Magpie. Charmed."

She had the strongest grip of all the women. While Nala was used to women having firm handshakes, for some reason she did not expect it in this submissive bunch. Then again, not much about Maggie seemed demure. Maybe her "Master" was only in this for the business connections, and, like Nala, Maggie was lying about being a submissive little flower.

"We hope you aren't too nervous about being here," Quail said, catching Nala's attention again. "The new couple aren't expected to do anything for a little while. Starling didn't put on her first show for us until a month in."

"Oh, and what a show," Robin said, sitting on the arm of someone's chair. "I got so wet watching her Master play with her that I begged for mine to fuck me done in the other room. Door open, of course." She giggled. Nala paled.

"The open door policy at these things is a little weird at first, but we're all a bunch of exhibitionists and voyeurs at the heart of it." Starling shrugged. "I don't mind if my friends peek in at me having sex with my soul mate. It's a beautiful thing, isn't it?"

"Uh…" Nala caught herself looking at Vincent, who happened to look over her way at the same time. They instantly looked away again, Nala's cheeks bursting in flames.

"It's okay if you and your Master don't have sex tonight. It can be weird at first."

"Weird? It's hot!"

"Of course you think so. You always make sure your ass is pointed toward the door so everyone gets an eyeful of your Master's cock."

"All right, ladies." Maggie stood, her long legs bringing her to Nala in one step. The gold mask on her face glittered in the light, like jewels. *There's something different about this woman.* Beyond her commanding abilities. "We're overwhelming the newbie. She'll get the hang of things soon enough."

She pressed her fingers upon Nala's shoulder before sauntering to her partner on the other side of the room. He welcomed her with an open arm, kissing her forehead before introducing her to Vincent.

Nala went off to get another drink and deposit the old glass on a counter. More of those women in lingerie came in and out of the main gallery, taking away drinks, bringing out food, and whispering to someone here or there to make sure they were "comfortable." When one went up to Vincent and whispered something into his ear, Nala felt a tinge of something that felt like… jealousy.

No way.

Vincent stepped away from Maggie and her partner before heading straight for Nala. She regained her composure, intent on staying focused before making a fool of herself in front of these new "friends."

"You should come over and meet the other men, too," he said, voice low. "Get all the facts before Crow makes his great appearance."

Right. That man was still nowhere to be seen, and this was his own party. *He probably likes making grand, late entrances.* Nala was sure to pick up a fresh glass of champagne before wrapping her arm around Vincent's and letting him lead her to Maggie and a man named Jay – quite the birdlike accident, he promised.

A flurry of names flew by her that night. When she wasn't learning names like "Starling" and "Quail," Nala had to remember the names of all the men who were not Vincent. She wasn't as bad as Robin claimed to be, at least. She could remember them, in time, but she couldn't say she was looking forward to it. These people would never be her friends. Their bright, fake smiles and constant flirting with one another unnerved her.

How many of them were there solely for the business aspect and had to fake the BDSM lifestyle? How many of them were super into the lifestyle and could barely contain themselves at these gatherings? What would be expected of Nala? Would she confide the lie she was already brewing? That Vincent wanted to further his business prospects with Crow, and Nala, his "girlfriend," was going to play along with it for the sake of her lovely man?

It was better to share than the truth, anyway.

God, the truth would get her killed, just like her sister!

"*Someone in my life is gone because of that man.*"

Nala gazed at Vincent while the group talked South Waterfront properties and the latest show at the opera. *Was someone in his family killed too?* Nala wanted to ask. She was getting to the point where she wanted to confide in someone again, but the last time she shared her suspicions, her mother threw a can of beer and told her to never bring it up again. "*Xavier Crow is a good man!*" she had bawled. "*He paid for your sister's funeral!*"

Because he was guilty. Nala was sure of it.

Sure enough, when the man and host of the hour arrived not five minutes later, Nala felt even more confident that she was not losing her mind and looking for someone to blame. There was something sinister lurking behind those old, playful eyes. The other women, most of all Robin, were utterly smitten with the way Xavier kissed their hands and asked them to "twirl around and let me get a look at you." They danced like music box figurines, blushing, giggling, and assuring the man who controlled their Masters' business destinies that he was the most interesting man in the room.

What's most interesting is that he hasn't had a date yet. Xavier either walked around alone, speaking to people here and there, or flirted with one of the servers on duty. Those women did the bare minimum to be polite and somewhat flirtatious back. Anything to keep their jobs.

"Everyone!" he cried, holding a glass of champagne in the air. Vincent nudged Nala, forcing her to lift a glass in toast as well. "Here's to another night of fun and relaxation. No shows tonight, unless you want to." People laughed, least of all Nala. "Eat, drink, converse and be merry. Oh, and, do make good use of the rooms in this suite. I'm paying a pretty price for us to *make merry,* if you know what I mean."

Even Nala knew what that meant. She forced a smile. Not acting. Lying.

Music came on a stereo. Lively orchestral tunes that would play in a fancy elevator or restaurant. Music to soothe the soul, loins, and heart… and easy to ignore, Nala noted. One moment she heard a song, and one shout from a man later, it was gone again. Always in the background, but never too distracting from the party around the room.

"How are you holding up?" Vincent's voice was suddenly in her ear as she went to get a third glass of champagne. "Don't get too tipsy. I know how you were the other night from that one rum and Coke."

Nala drank it in front of him. "I don't see any stairs to fall down around here."

"I don't need you losing your cool. I don't know what you're like when intoxicated."

Nala motioned to the glass of liquor in *his* hand. "And I don't know what you're like either. For all I know you get handsy and do more than kiss by surprise. So you watch it too."

This quiet conversation did not go unnoticed by Maggie and Jay, who came over with plastic smiles spreading across their faces. Maggie especially looked too curious for her own good. She reminded Nala of her high school guidance counselor, who made a habit of asking fifty times a day whether Nala had turned in her college applications. *No.* If she had joined a club to put on her resume. *No.* If she was doing okay on the anniversary of her father's death. *No.* They were off to a great start already.

"Mags and I were saying that you're a cute couple," Jay said with his broad smile. The way the both of them looked at Vincent and Nala made the latter take a small step back, as if she could use her new pal as a meat shield. "Got that fresh couple smell about you. How long you been together?"

Oh, shit. They hadn't even gone over such details yet!

Nala was going to open her mouth and lie, but then remembered she was supposed to be the submissive one and defer to the man of the relationship. *Gag.* Perhaps it was best for Vincent to spin the tales, anyway. Knowing Nala, she would twist her tongue until none of the lies made sense anymore.

"Six months," Vincent said evenly. "You?"

The seasoned couple exchanged loving glances. "Eight years."

"Wow," Nala let out. "That's a long time."

"Perhaps you two will be so lucky someday." Maggie winked, revealing shining red eye shadow that blended flawlessly into her surrounding skin. "See you around. Jay and I are going to, ah, relax."

Their chuckles were more than telling. The moment they walked away, heading for the hall of bedrooms, Nala turned to Vincent with gossip on her lips.

"They're not like the other couples here," she muttered, curling her arms around his so it looked like she whispered words of adoration into her "Master's" ear.

"What do you mean?" he asked. "Because I'm thinking the same."

Nala nodded. "She called him by his name, for one. All the other women say Master."

"And he didn't act possessive. Suppose I should work on that."

"You know, I'm not going to pretend I know everything there is to know about this BDSM thing, but I'm pretty sure you *don't* have to act possessive."

"Yes, but…" Vincent's grip tightened on Nala's waist as their shared enemy approached, his eyes reserved *just* for them. "When in Rome…"

Xavier Crow stopped two feet in front of them, his height conveniently between Vincent's tall gait and Nala's petite frame. It unnerved Nala how he looked at them like he looked at the other masked couples making their way down the hall to play for this man's amusement. *Open-door policy, huh?* Nala already knew that Crow liked to watch more than participate. That much was as obvious as the small wine stain on the man's white pant leg.

Will one of the lingerie-clad women clean that up for him? Nala had to stop before she started to gag.

"Ah, my new favorite couple." His voice was like listening to a benevolent dictator appear on the radio for the seven o'clock lies. When Vincent's fingers pressed deeply into Nala's flesh, treading dangerously close to her thighs, she did not feel the urge to push him away. If anything, he was the only thing keeping her from having a total meltdown in the presence of her sister's killer. "I trust that you two are enjoying the party?"

Nala kept her lips tight. Teeth dug into them, but she would rather bleed than say something she would regret later. Instead, Vincent spoke on both of their behalves, as he should have done anyway.

"It's a fantastic party," he said softly. That hand on Nala's hip slowly moved upward, wrapping tightly around her toned but small bicep. "Forgive us for not being too active. We're still taking in the sights and getting a feel for things." He gently shook his partner. "Especially this one here. She's not used to so much activity."

What a disgusting smile one man could have. Nala didn't know if she was so disgusted because of who he was, or because she knew it was directed at the supposed love life between her and Vincent. "No worries at all," Xavier said. "I'd rather new members be completely comfortable before getting too involved. We've had some… issues before."

"I'm sure you have," Vincent was quick to say. "We're a cautious couple, I suppose you could say." A fun loving smile broke his otherwise stoic demeanor. It took Nala back, who had yet to see such a thing on Vincent's face. "Although we're trying to learn how to loosen up."

His fingers tapped Nala on the shoulder. She barely had time to brace herself before her head tipped back and Vincent's mouth came for hers.

They must have looked the model couple. Nala, shrinking in her lover's embrace, holding her head back so she could accept the soft lips. No tongue, thank God. Yet the illusion was there, she was sure, especially as Vincent covered her cheek with his free hand and backed his mouth away without making it look like they no longer kissed. Now *that* was acting.

Nala almost let the moment go. She didn't care that Vincent kissed her, as long as he didn't get too handsy and he gave her warning – which he did. No, what threw her off balance was realizing that Xavier Crow stood and watched them, a wretched, no, *lecherous* smile on his slimy face as he probably started growing a hard-on.

I'm going to be sick.

"You really are a good looking couple," Xavier said wistfully. "Take all the time you need. Have a look around. Nobody here is shy… although right now it looks like I'm the only man to talk to."

He was right. The other couples had gone to separate rooms to do whatever it was they did. Deep down, Nala knew. Right now she wasn't going to think about it. Knowing she was surrounded by couples having sex was bad enough. She didn't need to actually *imagine* it.

"Excuse me," she muttered, gently pushing away from Vincent's embrace. "All that champagne is catching up to me." She wasn't lying. Her bladder was starting to do that knowing dance and threatened to embarrass her in this lofty suite.

"Of course." Xavier pointed down the hall. "Bathroom is all the way down there. Good time to let us boys have a chat anyway, eh, Vince?"

This was the second time Nala heard Vincent be called that, and both times the man flinched as if he would rather be called Dog. Nala put it in the back of her mind as she hurried down the hall, intent on making it to the bathroom before total discomfort settled in.

Since everyone else was busy making merry the old-fashioned way, Nala had the restroom to herself, although she could see makeup smears and discarded tissues on the sink. She was less impressed with the condom wrapper in the trashcan, but didn't think much about it as she did her business and attempted to rearrange her dress. The more she walked around, the more it rode up her ass and outdid a damn thong. Maybe she had actually gained weight since moving to Portland.

The hall was dark when she reemerged. Nala stood at the far end, opening her satchel to make sure her belongings were where they belonged. If Vincent had a habit of checking his cufflinks five times an hour, then Nala was allowed to be paranoid about her wallet.

"Yes, yes!"

Nala nearly dropped her satchel as that cry pierced her ear. Without thinking, she looked to her right and saw through a generous crack in the nearest door.

The sound came from Robin, who perched upon a large bed, her fingers wrapped around the edge while her knees dug into the plush bedspread. The skirt of her dress was hiked over her hips, exposing her round, rose-colored ass which accepted yet another spank from Lucian.

A man whose clothes were halfway off and whose cock was rammed deep into his lover's cunt. *Oh my God.*

All right, yes, this is exactly what was meant by *open-door policy*. Couples having sex in supposed private, but with the doors open to varying degrees so anyone – especially Xavier – couch watch with glee. *Hell no!* That's what Nala thought, and yet here she was, standing completely still while her gaze remained transfixed on the couple going at it.

"That's right," Lucian growled, his hand coming back down with a heavy *smack!* "You love having your cunt ravaged by thick cock, don't you? *Don't you?*"

Robin's usually sweet face twisted into a hedonistic gape as she accepted a hard and rough fuck. "Yes, Master!" she cried again, knees slipping farther apart on the bed. Her arms moved forward to gather more purchase, revealing both of her breasts bouncing from the top of her dress. Nala remained absolutely transfixed… and she didn't know why…

Okay, so she had never seen people having sex like this. Okay, not in *real life.* The woman had seen porn before, after all. But this was her unsolicited initiation into the life of a voyeur, and dear God, was she actually getting…

What the fuck…

Am I getting turned on?

No way. Nala wasn't a super sexual creature to begin with. Plus, she was in the presence of Xavier Crow, a man who could shut down her entire sex drive for ten years with one stinkin' glance. Yet here she was, standing in a dark hallway, peering through an ajar door and watching a beautiful woman get fucked by a man in a pristine – all right, now wrinkled – suit. The kind of man who probably spent his days put together for board meetings, video chats across the world, and the myriad of business associates who came in and out of his office. For meals in classy restaurants Nala could never afford. For limousines and Town Cars…

Holy shit, it was hot.

Her hand clasped across her mouth as she realized this, and shamefully – although she had no idea why she felt ashamed – she scurried to a darker corner of the hall and stared like a teenage boy finding his first Playboy.

For one blessed minute Nala was able to forget why she came to this party… why she was the consort of Vincent Lane, brand-new billionaire who was also on a mission to get back at Xavier Crow. She forgot the hatred, the anguish, and most of all the *grief* that had overwhelmed her for so long. For that one blessed minute, all that existed was Robin and Lucian, their bodies crashing together in insatiable lust as the one talked dirty and the other accepted it as if it were her God-granted right. Nala wasn't the type to clutch her pearls and run home. Nor was she the type to run in and ask, "Can I join?" However, she apparently *was* the type to stand there, watch, and happily realize that her nipples were hardening and her bottom lingerie became wetter with each passing second.

She didn't necessarily want Lucian to do that to her – although the quick glimpse she got of his cock told her that he wasn't bad at all. But Nala *did* want to be Robin for the briefest second. She wanted to feel that detached from reality, where all that mattered was the escape of sex. *It wasn't like that with my ex.* The man was as vanilla as they came. Make out. Take off clothes. Little fingering. Little head. Main event. Done. Sleep.

This was a different plane of existence. This was *sex*.

"Come in me, sir!" Robin pleaded, her whole body riding back and forth as her Master claimed her from behind. "Take me for yours!"

Lucian grabbed her shoulders and forced her down, Robin's long curls disappearing over the edge of the bed. Her cries intensified, but with the bed muffling her, they sounded like the ecstatic tears of a woman being granted the keys to the universe. Nala crossed her arms in front of her, afraid that her breasts would betray her propriety to the shadows enveloping her.

Before her, Lucian dug his fingers into the pink flesh of Robin's ass, throwing his head back and growling like a beast. Robin lifted her head, visage claimed with ecstasy even though no sounds fell from her open mouth. In those precious few seconds, Nala gradually understood what was happening and felt her nether lips tingle in want.

"Shit…" The couple came to a halt, Robin collapsing against the bed while Lucian slowly pulled out of her. His bare chest glistened in sweat, and the hair swirling out of his pants did nothing to cover the skin of his cock – which also glistened, but not in sweat. Nala had never seen anything like it. She didn't even think she was possible of being wet enough to make a man look like that as he softened and sank next to his lover, kisses caressing her shoulder and face.

Nala finally walked away, stumbling down the hall, hearing more sounds of revelry and seeing glimpses of sights before unseen. Quail was strung up in chains, being fed Sebastian's cock. Starling straddled her Master in a chair, slowly disrobing her dress in an elaborate striptease as he stroked himself with one hand and drank with another. The only room Nala couldn't see directly into was Maggie and Jay's.

By the time she made it to the main gallery, Vincent was sitting alone on a couch while Xavier entertained his lingerie-clad ladies with parlor tricks at the wet bar. For a man who claimed to love watching, he wasn't doing much of it tonight.

"You all right?" Vincent asked. "You look like you've seen something no less than shocking."

That caught Xavier's attention, who turned from his female friends and grinned like an old fool. "Someone was looking, Vince. I know that kind of face anywhere."

Disgust overcame Nala. She turned away, hiding her arousal. Even Vincent, who uncrossed his legs and stood from the couch, wasn't allowed to come near her and see what had happened to her body. What if he could see her nipples through her dress? What if he could sense her wetness? Nala wasn't afraid of her fake lover, but she *was* embarrassed and didn't need his judgment. She didn't need *anyone's* judgment.

"I'm fine," she said, struggling to get the words past her swollen throat. "Really. I'm fine."

No, she wasn't fine. She was far from this strange concept of *fine*. If anything, she was quickly descending into an infinite loop of arousal and disgust – two things that she did not want to associate together. Every time she allowed herself to feel a tinge of lust, she thought of Crow looking at her, *leering* at her, waiting for her to drop her panties and serve as expected. *I'm going through this for you, Tasha.* She held on to that thought as Vincent came to her, pressed his fingers on her shoulder, and kissed her tenderly. All an act, of course, and yet Nala was able to forget again. Forget the pain. Forget the disgust. Forget everything that made her come apart and quickly lose the pieces of herself.

If Vincent recognized this in her, then that was why he pulled her into a loose embrace and pretended to whisper sweet nothings into her ear. Nothings full of promise, of love, and of course – of sex.

Instead, he said, "You keep walking around like that, and we'll both be in danger. Lie, Nala. Don't start showing truths."

Frigidity claimed her limbs. "*We'll both be in danger.*" Danger from Xavier Crow… or danger from each other?

Nala glanced at Vincent's face and noted the slight color to his cheeks. He felt the heat in Nala's skin, surely. He saw the look of lust in her eyes, and smelled the pheromones that she couldn't control pouring out of her aroused frame.

Danger from him. Nala faced the nearest wall, unresponsive to Vincent's touch, even though she was pushing away images of him in Lucian's place, and herself in Robin's. *Vincent Lane is a dangerous man after all.*

She could not lose sight of her mission. Neither could Vincent, she was sure. *Maybe I'm the dangerous one.*

No matter where she turned, danger lurked.

Entry #4

Tonight was our first return to The Aviary. There were a few missteps we did not account for. I will have to have a preliminary meeting with Nightingale next time.

Speaking of her, I may have crossed a line tonight. I kissed her, to get it out of the way. I could have broached the subject better than I had, and now I must pay with guilt.

She is not the first woman I've kissed these past three years, but she is the first to make me feel a little… that old feeling I used to have. The moment I experienced it, I felt *guilty. I could not help it.*

I tell myself that Nightingale is more passionate, more intense than those few other women I've kissed since… there is nothing passive about Nightingale. She is posing as my sub, but I can tell that she is more buck than doe. The more animalistic side of me says that she would be a challenge to tame and break. I haven't come across a woman like that in a very long time.

Even as I write this, I'm swamped with deplorable fantasies. Tonight I saw her as more than my partner in this endeavor. She was more than a young woman who is more brash than brain. The dress she wore was almost too enticing.

I must steel myself. I cannot fall into temptation. Not now. It would be wrong.

Chapter 8

"I haven't gotten any notice, no," Nala said into her phone as she waited in line at the bank. "Also, it's not my fault if you're behind on your rent, Mom."

On the other end of the line, Yulia Nazarova let out the type of sigh that used to make child-Nala's spine shudder. *Used* to be that her mother was a formidable woman who could get her way with a snap of her fingers. Funny what double the grief did to a person. "You think it's my fault?" she said, her accent slipping as she grew angrier. Yulia spent most of Nala's childhood practicing her dialect so she would have a better chance at a career and help her children be made less fun of. For many years, it worked. Then she stopped caring as her life crumbled, and one family member after another was taken from her. *I'm still here, Mom.* Sometimes it felt like Yulia forgot that.

The line advanced one more person, but it being late Monday afternoon, that still meant ten people stood between Nala and some financial freedom. "Of course I think it's partially your fault. *I* pay my rent more frequently than you do. And no, I don't have any money for you to borrow."

"I wasn't going to ask!" Good. Nala had the desired effect on her mother. She didn't want to insult the woman, but she was definitely going to curb any thoughts that may have danced in her head. "For God's sake, can't a woman call her daughter to chat?"

That was absurd. Yulia never called "to chat" anymore. She was more likely to call to bemoan her financial fate – as if Nala's was any better – or to drunkenly cry on Tasha's birthday or other memorable day. It was like Yulia's existence centered around bringing more despair to her sole remaining family member. Oh, she could hold down a job. Barely. But her depression was so foul that she was a mere shell of the strong woman Nala once admired growing up.

"Fine. I'll leave you alone then." Sniffing, Yulia heaved another one of those now meaningless sighs. "Do me a favor, though. Step up and replenish this poor family. Marry a nice man and give me some grandbabies to live for."

"Mam," Nala said sternly, "I don't think that's going to happen anytime soon."

"Why not! Surely there's some surly man in that armpit stank of the world who can put up with your attitude. Just make sure he actually has money and doesn't pretend at it."

I could never tell her about Vincent. Not that Nala would go there, regardless of her relationship with her mother. "I'll make sure, Mam. Now I've gotta go. I'm at the… store." She didn't dare say bank. That would continue this talk of money and who had it and who didn't.

They hung up, and in time. Another teller window opened, meaning the line forked and put Nala second behind a man who merely wanted to update his address.

Ten minutes later, she walked out of the bank staring at a balance sheet. *$1055.76.* She could barely believe that number. Nala knew that wasn't a lot of money, but the check Vincent wrote her Sunday night before dropping her off at home would do so much. She could buy an actual bag of groceries. She could invest in some winter clothes. Maybe a fleece blanket for her prison of a closet. Coffee! Oh, sweet coffee before work!

Oh, and she should probably head to Ross and pick up shoes and another dress for The Aviary. Thinking about that, though… more shivers, and it had nothing to do with the frosty air that cold Oregon day. *For a summer that was sweltering hot…* Nala spotted the nearest discount clothing store and decided today was the day she got a real rain jacket. These other Oregonians could prance around in their wet hoodies all they wanted. Nala preferred to not look like a drowned rat when she showed up for work.

She was perusing a rack of clearance coats much too big for her when she felt her phone buzz in her front pocket. *What the…* She reached in, pulling out the ancient flip phone and seeing an unknown number in her texts. The only reason she answered it at all was because it opened with "Next club meeting this Friday night. Can you go?"

Right. She and Vincent exchanged numbers on Sunday, although she hadn't bothered to enter his into her phone because… why would she ever text him? Call him? Whatever. Besides, the last thing Nala wanted right now was to see Vincent's name every time she opened her phone. After Sunday? All she could think about when she saw that man's name was the way Lucian fucked the brains out of his girlfriend.

Nala turned her phone so she could painstakingly reply. "*I work during the day. I get off at five. Tell Crow he'll have to wait for my lovely face if we need to be there before seven. 'Cause that ain't happening.*"

She was in the checkout line with her new purchases when Vincent replied. "*Pick you up at six. I want to take you to dinner first. We need to talk.*"

Of course they did. At least she was getting free food. "*Sure.*"

She was back on the sidewalk, wearing her new coat sans tags when she received an unexpected text. "*Wear something sexier, if you can. We're going to a sex club and will be expected to dress the part.*"

Nala stopped, nearly slipping on a patch of ice. "*Excuse me?*"

"*You read that right. You're going to be ogled by every person there. To be fair, so will I.*"

"*I am so excited by this prospect. Unfortunately, I don't have any hooker clothes and I left the cheap clothing store.*"

"Hooker clothes won't do you any good anyway. I will send you something. What size dress do you wear?"

Nala had yet to continue her journey home. *"I'm suspicious of this, but, I wear a size eight, petite. That last part is important. I'm serious. Don't buy me a tent. There will be room for us both in there, and* not *in the fun way."*

"I will make sure it's suitable for your body."

Nala finally crossed the street and turned onto hers. *"Black and purple are my best colors. Also, I need shoes. Size seven, wide. Go all out."*

That last part was sarcastic, although she knew that didn't translate well in texts. Nevertheless, the final text she received from Vincent that day said, *"Got it. Dress, shoes, and anything else I think will work well. See you then."*

Nala put her phone back in her pocket and helped herself into the craftsman house that was supposed to be part hers. Thankfully, Patrick wasn't there, supposedly at his job, whatever it was this week. They had another roommate, but Paula had spent the past month visiting family back east. This meant Nala had the run of the house to herself, which didn't mean much when none of it was hers aside from what was in that closet and what she kept in the kitchen and bathroom. As cold as she was? A hot shower sounded delightful.

With nobody else home, she could take as long of one as she wanted. She let the steam fill the room while she undressed in front of the mirror and wove her long, dark hair into a tight bun. Her Cleopatra bangs continued to sweep across her forehead, but she would have to ignore those for now.

The hot water caressed her body the moment she stepped in. For as gross as Patrick was in the living room, at least he kept the bathroom clean – probably because he never fucking showered. Nala didn't care right now. Here, in the porcelain world of bath products and running hot water, she could pretend that she lived in a real home of her own. A fantasy that didn't exist very often.

That wasn't the only fantasy she had in that shower.

She looked down, groaning as she noticed her nipples hardening beneath water droplets. *Really, now is not the time, body.* Or perhaps it was.

She was alone in the house. Nobody would disturb her for as long as it took to get the job done. The hot water should last enough for a quickie…

None of that was the problem, anyway. The roadblocks standing in Nala's way were completely, 100% *mental.*

It felt wrong to be aroused to the point of touching herself. It felt *disrespectful.* To what? Her sister's memory? Surely, just because Tasha's life was stolen from the earth didn't mean Nala ceased to live and function. Of course not, but Nala was so used to being focused on the endgame – namely, getting justice – that spending even ten minutes getting herself off felt like the most selfish thing in the world. She should be plotting. She should be thinking about what she had learned so far from The Aviary. Nala had lasted weeks, even months without an orgasm. What was different now?

Vincent.

She didn't want to think about it. About *him.* That man with his dangerously stoic demeanor, with his body-pleasing outfits, and that fucking *cologne* that made him smell like the billion dollars he was worth. Fuck her life. Nala was *not* a woman who fell for men like that. Not even sexually. She had made it over twenty years without blubbering about or drooling over hot, rich men, so why would she start now?

This all started when he kissed me.

There was no passion in that kiss. Yet it woke something in her. Something tangible. Something dormant. Something so out of her fucking mind that here she was, standing against the shower wall as her hand traveled over her breast and to her stomach, stopping short of her mound.

This is wrong. Who was she? Was she a woman in control of her body, her emotions? Or was she a horny, dumb girl in need of being punished?

Wait, what?

Being *punished?*

There it was. A toxic image. A *deliciously* toxic image of Vincent Lane unbuttoning the front of his burgundy shirt and easing Nala to bend over. "*You're not supposed to be thinking about this, Nightingale,*" he would say. "*You're supposed to stay focused. Don't succumb to such base desires.*" The Vincent of her imagination caressed her naked body, touching her thighs and parting her nether lips with one expert finger. When Nala realized she was the one touching herself, she thought… well, fuck it. That's what she thought.

"I'm a gross pervert," she mumbled, snatching the detachable showerhead and directing the harsh spray of water first on her breasts, and then down to her mound.

She may be a gross pervert, but by all that was indecent in this world, she would be a sexually satisfied one.

"Oh, fuck," she muttered, instantly awash in rising pleasure as the water pounded against her clit. Nala's head tapped against the wall, eyes glazing over with steam before she finally closed them and gave herself over to the inevitable.

Not just sexual fantasies.

Sexual fantasies about *Vincent.*

Who else was there to imagine? Nala had no crushes on anyone, man or woman. It felt wrong to think of Lucian. Besides, she wasn't interested in him – just the act he performed on a happy little Robin. Nope. Nala's thoughts belonged to Vincent, the only man to have kissed her since one of the worst moments of her life.

Even though his kisses were cold, she knew there was life somewhere in there. He exuded a confident energy whenever they were together. He had pride. Desire. Blood, like any other healthy man his age. So much potential lurked in one man. Even though he came off as focused and determined as Nala in their mission, she wasn't going to write off his own sexual prowess. Surely, it was in there. Waiting for a reason to come out.

Waiting for *her.*

Nala was not a seductress. She barely knew how to flirt, mostly because she never cared to know. The men – boys, really – she dated approached her first. Sort of like Vincent, who suggested they join hands before Nala even knew what he was about.

So now here she was, water spraying her clit while her other hand pinched her nipples and clawed at her face. A healthy dose of need swelled within her. Nala's body was so starved for attention, for release, that for the first time in many, many months she allowed herself to think of nothing but a man and the way he could make love to her.

Ha! *Fuck lovemaking.* Yes, yes, that was it. She didn't want lovemaking. She wanted *fucking.* No strings attached sex that was all about the release, the thrill, the unknown she had yet to explore. A strong, confident man sucking her nipples, letting his teeth graze against them in a constant warning that he could *bite* if she stepped out of line.

Nala thought it was shower water at first. Then she realized all the water was currently between her legs, and the wetness she felt beneath her eyes were tears. Why was she crying? Was it the satisfaction of finally letting go of some of the misery bundled inside her? Was it reuniting with what it meant to be a sexual creature? Was it the reminder that there was a world of experiences outside of what she suffered in her short life? Sometimes it was hard to imagine other people going about their lives while their fellow men and women cried for affection. Nala didn't want to be swept off her feet and saved. She wanted…

I want to feel human again. I want to feel good.

It came now. Those foreign feelings of relief flooding her body as she began to orgasm. Nala's hand slammed against the wall as her knees buckled and her back threatened to slide down the wall behind her. Her mind was nothing but pleasure. Blinding pleasure that she hadn't experienced in such a long time, that she had almost forgotten it existed.

The thing that helped the most was imagining Vincent. He was a convenient stand-in for a partner. That and, well… Nala wouldn't go there for now.

What was he doing? Tasting her? Her nipples? Her clit? No, that wasn't enough. As orgasm spread through her, Nala's fantasy became brazen to the point she imagined herself impaled against that wall, Vincent's cock deep inside her and making her the kind of woman who did this sort of thing.

"*Slut,*" a voice in her head said. Was it his? Was it hers? Haha, who fucking cared?

"That's right, I'm a fucking slut," Nala muttered, dropping the showerhead and feeling it vibrate against the shower floor. The crash it created coincided with the end of her orgasm, when reason returned and she realized what the fuck she was doing.

Abashed, she stood there, kicking the showerhead so it no longer sprayed against the plastic liner. That wasn't a mess she wanted to clean up later. Bad enough she had a mess going on in her head and loins.

As long as it stayed far away from her heart, she could deal with it. Not that Nala foresaw that being an issue. Her loins may be a lost cause, and her head may waver between logic and *la-la-la-I'm-an-idiot,* but her heart was most decidedly too cold to care about anything but Tasha.

To be fair, she surmised as she finished her shower and got the hell out, her heart probably needed the release too. Couldn't be good for it to be so sad all the damn time.

Entry #5

We've been invited back to The Aviary. I'm almost afraid to go, because of the old feelings and images swarming my mind as of late. I had forgotten what it's like to feel this… stirring, let alone for a woman in my presence.

I must tread carefully. I cannot lose sight of our goals.

Chapter 9

The package from Vincent awaited Nala Friday evening when she returned home from work. *Finally, some nice clothes.* She knew she was a helpless cause when it came to picking out her own outfits. Especially outfits that were meant to impress the elite. Or at least keep them from gossiping about her terrible taste in, well, everything.

Nala took it into the dining room where Patrick wouldn't bother her. He was busy in the living room, watching cartoons and pontificating about the merits of non-gendered aliens in the media to no one in particular. Nala wasn't sure if he was on the phone or recording into a mic on his laptop. She honestly did not want to know. *I meet enough people who are talking to absolutely no one on the street.* She was pretty sure she worked with one too.

A pocketknife was all it took to open the box from a downtown boutique that Nala had never heard of. *I wonder who picked this out.* Did Vincent have an assistant? Did he use a personal shopper? He didn't seem like the type. He also didn't seem like the type to go shopping on his lunch break. Not for a dress anyway.

Nala pulled back the box flaps and hooked her fingers around soft black fabric. What she lifted from the box, however, was anything *but* what she expected.

Oh, it was sexy. Too sexy! Halter straps wrapped around the neck before blooming into two strips of wavy fabric meant to not-so-demurely cover the breasts. That wouldn't be terrible if it weren't for the giant, gaping hole over the stomach area. Nala could not figure out how the *fuck* these two straps connected to a miniskirt, but here she was, standing in a dining room with a high-class escort's dress in her hands.

"You've gotta be kidding," she said. Nala was so distracted by the dress that she almost missed the strappy stiletto shoes tucked at the bottom of the box.

So this was the outfit Vincent picked out. Even if he hadn't picked it out – and even if he hadn't *seen* it – he still signed off on it, like the total man he was.

On one hand, the fantasy enabler inside Nala liked the idea of that man picking out a hot outfit like this. On the other, it did color him in her eyes. Before now, he came across as relatively safe, surprise first kiss aside. Nala never felt threatened around him. She never felt anything but… protected. Granted, it was from a distance, but nevertheless, Vincent was the type of man to shadow her and make sure nothing befell her when she suffered bouts of stupidity. Or at least that's what she liked to pretend.

Until now.

She escaped into the bathroom to try the outfit on. The dress said eight petite, but she was suspicious that it was big enough to fit her at all. And yet, as she stripped down to nothing but her black panties, she quickly discovered that this barely-there dress *did* slip nicely over her frame and cover what it was supposed to… even if that was just her breasts, crotch, and ass. Because that skirt sure as fuck didn't go anywhere near her knees. She would be pulling this down more than any other dress she owned.

The shoes made it worse. They were taller and skinnier than any Nala wore before, making her wobble on the bathroom floor like an inexperienced teen girl. *I feel so exposed.* Not even her sweater would help her this time. The only way she could feel covered in any way was to wear her hair down that night. It fell, straight as a lonely board, over her shoulders and toward her bare stomach. A prepared woman would have a navel piercing to decorate the getup. As it was, she didn't even have nice jewelry to go with this. Her straight cut hair would have to do.

Her cell phone buzzed. "*Out front.*" Oh, sure, he was going to show up now, ten minutes early? Man probably left early so he could beat the rush hour traffic that Portland was notorious for. Yet here he was, acting like this was the exact time he was supposed to be there. Now Nala had to gather her bearings and walk out to the car – possibly with ice covering the walkway – and not fall on her fucking ass. Or freeze to death.

Somehow she did a passable job. She shuffled in those spiky heels to the front door, probably scruffing the hardwoods, and eased her way down the three porch steps and onto the concrete. Insufferable cold hit her legs and stomach, the two places her sweater couldn't protect her. The moment he saw her carefully walking down the front path, Vincent got out of his car and opened her door for her like a perfect gentleman. *Everyone in this neighborhood thinks I'm a fucking call-girl.* Well, she was being dressed and paid for like one.

"When I said I needed new shoes, these weren't what I had in mind." That was her greeting to Vincent as she lowered herself into the car without breaking an ankle. Miraculous.

The door closed behind her, leaving her to stew in the warmth of the car. The windows began to fog as Vincent got in on the other side and drove away without a word.

This was Nala's first time being in his presence since her Monday foray in the shower. *Hey, buddy, it's almost like we fucked. Trust me, entering a fantasy of mine is a pretty big honor. It doesn't happen with anyone.* Nala stared at him in the dark of the car, his profile firm and chiseled. He was wearing the tie-less three-piece again, only this time instead of a white shirt it was a silky black, decorated with glass buttons. *I wonder what he looks like under there.* Did the man work out? Was he a runner? Lift weights? All Nala knew about his physique was that he didn't look overweight and that he had hard biceps. Didn't exactly say too much.

"I hope the dress isn't too terrible," he mumbled, eyes on the road.

Nala scoffed. "I feel like I'm barely wearing anything. Who picked this out? You?"

He glanced in her direction. "Yes."

"Really?"

"Who else would have done it? I'm the only one who knows about this arrangement."

"That's…" *Weird.* "I thought maybe you had an assistant. Don't most men of your standing use assistants?" She thought of that Andrew guy, who was ready to escort her right out of the building before his boss stepped in to save her neck and maybe break his.

"I try to avoid using assistants whenever possible. They get in the way and rarely understand directions. I'm a big fan of if you want something done right, you must do it yourself."

Nala nodded. "I feel the same way. Although…"

Vincent eased on the brakes as they approached a light. *This is the smoothest car ride in the world.* The car didn't look like much on the outside, but from in here? Nala had to wonder how much a ride like this cost. *More than I'll ever see in my life.*

"What is it?"

Nala gripped the seat belt touching her exposed stomach. "What made you choose *this* dress? Is this the kind of stuff you're into?"

She expected him to give her that same expressionless demeanor he always had. Thus she was shaken to the core of that naked navel when he laughed. Not hard, and certainly nothing more than an ill-timed guffaw. It was enough to unnerve Nala, however, who stayed on her side of the car with a twist of the mouth.

"Hey, could be worse," he said. "I'm sure someone will show up in bondage gear."

The thought of this man buying her *bondage* wear sent a wave of nausea straight to Nala's empty stomach – which then promptly growled loud enough to compete with the quiet motor of the car.

Vincent stopped chuckling. "Hungry, huh?"

Nala kept her face turned toward the window so he couldn't see the embarrassment pinking her cheeks. "A little. I didn't eat after getting home." She did, however, eat a substantial lunch. Something she could get used to if Vincent kept paying her like a high-priced hooker. *That reminds me… do I get another payment this Sunday?* Check in the mail? Direct bank transfer? How was this going to work, exactly? Something to ask him over dinner.

"Don't worry, we're almost to the restaurant."

They had already crossed the bridge into downtown. *It's weird how there's so little traffic for this time of day.* Maybe the waves parted to admit a man of Vincent Lane's standing. As if the collective commuting consciousness knew to bow to him like a king coming through his court. *No, that's more like a Xavier Crow thing.* The man who owned half the town. What did Vincent own? *Besides me, apparently.* Nala nuked that thought from her brain.

"Hope you like seafood," Vincent said, pulling up to a valet and motioning for Nala to get out on her side.

"Do I have a choice?" The driver side door shut in her face before she had the chance to mumble some more in Vincent's direction. So much for chivalry.

"I've made reservations." Vincent extended his arm, waiting for Nala to take it as she stepped onto the quiet sidewalk. "Otherwise we would be waiting a while."

Nala looked around. The façade was yet another abandoned warehouse, a common sight along the Willamette River. Once upon a time – even back in Nala's childhood – this was a busy industrial village keeping the economy churning one day at a time. Now those time-honored businesses were long gone, replaced with empty, decaying buildings that were slowly being converted into lofts and cafes and whatever this was.

They stepped into a bright, warm foyer full of floral scents and the sounds of live piano. *Fancy.* Some said this was why they came to Portland – to enjoy the culture hiding within abandoned this and that. Nala never paid them much mind. Now, as she and Vincent were led through winding hallways to a private dining alcove overlooking the river, she wondered what other fancy gems hid within buildings like these.

You never knew because you never looked. Nala scoffed at herself. *You never looked because you know this world isn't for you.* Sometimes one had to tell themselves the hardest truths in order to get by unscathed.

"Let me get your sweater." Vincent had his hands on her sleeves before she could ask him what he said. *Well, then.* Soft fabric passed her arms as she was exposed to the warm air. Her hair kept out the chill, but it wasn't enough to stop her nipples from suddenly hardening within her dress. Nala felt silly turning around to sit in the nearest chair. "Here." Then Vincent was there, pulling out her chair like a perfect gentleman. *Who is this guy?* Was he being nice because he read her thoughts earlier?

She caught his glance as she smoothed down her skirt to sit down, a healthy helping of cleavage appearing before his widening eyes.

"You look…" Vincent stopped himself, hurrying to drape her sweater on the back of her chair before sitting down across from her. A small mauve flower arrangement and a burning candle separated them. *This is supposed to be romantic, I guess.* "You're beautiful."

Nala looked up from the menu she pretended to peruse. "Thanks."

Pages of fish names passed. *Where's the salads?* She wasn't used to big meals anymore.

"I'm serious." Vincent cleared his throat. "Not trying to imply you don't look great usually. It's… I did a good job picking out that dress."

Nala shuffled in her seat. "Thanks, I guess." It would be great if he dropped it there. She didn't take compliments well – made her feel like she owed the man something in return, and there was almost no feeling worse than *that.*

"Anyway." Vincent picked up his menu and promptly dropped it back down. For the first time since they first met, Nala saw the man more flustered than composed. He blushed in frustration as he fought to get the thing back between his fingers. "This place has a lot of good reviews. I ate here once." A waiter arrived, pouring them glasses of ice water and asking them if they wanted anything else to drink. Vincent was quick to order a small bottle of wine. Nala would have laughed if this behavior wasn't because of her body.

I get it. You realize I'm hot. She didn't take it as a huge compliment. Most men thought she was hot to some extent – after all, she was female and breathing. Nothing to take personally.

Vincent deciding she was hot enough to gush over didn't mean anything.

It really didn't.

"You should try the salmon. It's wild here. Not farmed."

Nala vaguely knew what that meant and why she should care. "It's okay to look, you know," she said, focusing on the words in front of her. "I've got tits. They're here. You bought me a dress that shows off the underboob. Go ahead. See what you bought."

Vincent peered at her from above his menu. "I do have some self-control."

"For that I commend you." Nala put her menu down, giving him full view of her bare stomach and the breasts barely contained in the dress. One wrong move and they would pop out below the sash, free-range nipples and all. "You've learned since kissing me that first time."

The waiter brought the wine. He poured it into two glasses, halfway, before leaving the bottle in the middle of the table next to the floral arrangement. During this time, Nala and Vincent played a coy staring game that would probably end with one of them turning away in a huff. The theme of the night was being twelve-year-olds. Or at least Nala had the patience of one, and Vincent was probably being reminded of the first pair of tits he saw in middle school.

"Anyway," he muttered yet again, breaking eye contact. "I'm going to have…" he rattled off some convoluted seafood title, a list of sauces, and a request for his rice to be of a certain variety not listed on the menu. *Rich people.* Nala wondered how long it took to get acclimated to being so demanding. Or was Vincent naturally like that, and she had yet to see the full extent?

"For you, madam?" The waiter stood expectantly next to her.

"That," she said, pointing to a random salmon entrée. "That's good."

The waiter took away their menus and left them alone in their silent alcove. Vincent sighed, folding his hands on the table and looking anywhere but in Nala's direction. *Typical.* She said the man could look, and he did everything in his power to do anything but.

"Is there a reason you brought me to dinner first?" Nala asked. She ran her fingers along the stem of the wineglass, admiring the deep, flushing red before attempting a sip. "You think I'm too skinny and need some feeding?"

Vincent remained frozen in his seat, although Nala could tell a battle of wills fought in his addled brain. "I don't think you're too skinny. As long as you're taking care of yourself, well… it's your business. I shouldn't have even gone that far."

Scoffing, Nala dared a sip of her wine. It was sweet, bitter, a healthy mix of the two as it caressed her tongue. *I haven't had wine in forever.* Certainly none as good as this… yet she wouldn't make a show of it. Didn't want Vincent thinking she was some uncultured rube this far into their "relationship." "You act like you don't have an opinion on the way I look, talk, and act. Of course you do. Don't be ashamed of it. I've been judging you since the moment we met."

"Oh? What did you surmise?"

Nala put her glass down, crossing her ankles beneath her chair. The long stiletto heels pierced the floor and put so much pressure on the soles of her feet that she winced in discomfort. "You're a man of means who doesn't say much and has some agenda with Xavier Crow. You won't tell me anything about it, though. Not that it's a problem. I'm not exactly in a hurry to share my own tale with you."

"That's actually why I invited you to dinner first." Vincent downed half his glass already, his head tipping back and Adam's apple pulsing. "We need to go over the details of this relationship. We got caught on the spot last time when we were asked how long we were dating. We need to figure out how we met and where we're going. Also…" He cleared his throat, still refusing to look Nala in the eye.

"What?"

Finally, his frosty blues bore into hers. "I would like some transparency. I need to know exactly what you want from all of this. I know you want something negative from Crow, but what, exactly? What do you want from me besides an excuse to get close to him? Money?"

Nala slumped in her seat, breasts sagging against the table. "The money sure is nice. I'm not going to pretend otherwise.' She shrugged. "You're paying me more than any job I've ever had before. By the way, am I getting another check soon? You said a grand a week."

Something twisted on Vincent's face. "Of course. I'll make sure you get a check Sunday."

"Nice." More winter clothes! Rain boots! Nice ones!

"That doesn't answer my other questions, though. Why do you want access to Crow?"

"Why do *you* want access to him? More business opportunities?"

Another grimace. Everything Nala said seemed to be a harpoon to the man's gut. "You're deflecting, but I'll humor you." He tossed his wallet onto the table, letting it flip open to a picture of the woman from his office. This one was candid, with her long, curly tresses bigger than her smiling face as she perched on a picnic blanket and wrapped herself in a baggy striped sweater. *She's pretty.* Prettier than Nala, anyway. Not that it was difficult to be plainer than a girl who wore no makeup and kept her hair straight out of convenience.

"Who is that? You had a picture of her in your office."

"Yes. I keep her picture there to remind myself every day that she's gone."

"I see." Dread twisted in her stomach. She wasn't sure she liked where this was going.

"Her name was Desirée. She was my classmate at Stanford. And..." Vincent looked Nala head-on, daring her to defy what he was about to say. "I believe that Xavier Crow is involved with her death."

Shudders rippled from his side of the table to hers. Nothing sexual about it. This was pure, conniving hatred that they shared on a mutual base level. *So he killed this woman too.* No, that was the wrong way to look at it. *Had* her killed. Nala wasn't dumb in all of this. She knew Xavier Crow would never kill a woman himself. He would hire someone to do it. He had the money and the means. Why dirty his own hands when plenty of people were willing to do it? How much had the deaths of Desirée and Tasha cost, anyway? A million dollars? Hundreds of thousands? Mere thousands? *Nah, he would hire a real pro. He has too much to lose.* That's why their deaths were better than whatever they were going to do to him and his business.

"Why would he do that?" Nala asked carefully. "He would have to have a good reason."

Vincent studied her reaction. "You don't ask me how I know. So you believe me?"

"I certainly believe your suspicions are not unfounded. However, I would like to know why you thought this. Did she work for him?"

"Yes. An intern at one of his real estate firms. Desirée was at Stanford doing the same coursework as me. Namely, computer engineering and app development. She was working on a project to help real estate agents manage their properties… the app I did for Crow may or may not have been the finished product of what she started."

"I see. Why would he kill her?"

"Had her killed. Don't be stupid."

"I'm not."

Vincent narrowed his eyes. "I don't have a lot of details. In her last few months, she was working closely with him, and was becoming more and more paranoid. She said that she thought she was being followed. When I asked her what she was working on, she remained hushed and said it was confidential. I didn't see how. Everyone knew about her project, most of all me. So why was she holding back? It didn't make any sense."

Nala leaned against the table. "Then she ended up dead?"

Shadows cast themselves across the room, summoned by Vincent's wary countenance. "It was a late, rainy night. She told our friends that she would meet us for drinks after she got off work with Crow. Next thing I know, I'm getting a phone call saying that she had ran off the road and fallen fifty feet. Broke her neck. Instant death." He snapped his fingers for emphasis.

"Well, it was a rainy night." Nala didn't like playing devil's advocate, but she wasn't about to jump into telling her own tale until she got more details from Vincent. Sometimes she still had the sinking feeling that this was all a scam to get her to admit nefarious details about herself. As if Vincent were really the one working for Crow and sousing out whether or not Nala should be the next target.

"Desirée was one of the most cautious drivers I knew. She would have never fallen asleep or not paid attention, *especially* if it was raining. An investigator said there was evidence of her breaks failing on the curb. Nothing came of it. Crow was generous and paid for everything, including any investigation fees." Vincent shook his head, disgust riddling his features. "He paid for her funeral."

He paid for her funeral. Images of Yulia barking that her daughter should be grateful that her sister's funeral had been paid for entered her head. Admission of guilt? Perhaps so.

"So you see, I need to find out the truth. I don't know how I'm going to do it, but I'll find out whether or not Desirée was killed by Crow's order… but most of all, I want to know why she was disposed of."

Something didn't add up. "Why are you so invested in her? Was she your girlfriend?"

Vincent remained still, face ever unchanging. "I told you, she was a classmate of mine. We were good friends."

"Uh huh." *They were totally boning.* Nala didn't believe in the goodness of men that well. Vincent wouldn't still be so invested if it weren't for Desirée being *that* close to him. "Anyway, that's quite the deal. I don't envy you in the least feeling that way."

Vincent sat back, almost as if he were offended. "And you? What do you want him for?"

"Even after hearing that, I still don't think you'd believe me if I told you."

"Try me."

That commanding grate in his voice caught Nala off guard. One moment she was thinking about this Desirée woman, and the next she was back in her shower, blasting herself between the legs to images of this man thrusting himself into her. *The first fantasy I've had since before…* Nala still didn't know how much she could trust Vincent.

"My sister. I told you that she died."

Those set lips barely parted when he spoke. "Yes. You didn't mention anything else."

Nala considered the red wine swirling in her glass. Anything to avoid looking at the man sitting across from her. "She was a medical researcher for Black Raven."

"Go on."

"You ever hear of Tasha Nazarov?"

"Not off the top of my head, no."

"I'm not surprised. You probably wouldn't have unless you read research papers and magazines. She was becoming fairly famous in the world of cancer research." Yulia still kept every clipping, from both print and online, mentioning her daughter's progress in the world of medicine. *She doesn't keep anything about me.* Nala had nothing to show for her life thus far. "She was hired at Black Raven right out of college. Worked her way up until she was researching cancer cures in the main lab up in Seattle." Nala stopped, bile in her throat. "She would come home for holidays and say that she was close to a breakthrough. There were promising trials. The science made sense, she said. The more the months went on, the more excited she became. Until…"

"Until she became paranoid."

Nala sat up with a start. "Yes," she said, trying to contain the first bit of excitement she felt in so long. "Men following her, like Desirée."

"What happened?"

"Heart attack. In her late 20s."

"Let me guess… the trials magically stopped, the notes disappeared, and nobody spoke of what your sister was up to again."

"That's right." Nala wished she had her sweater back on. Everything was frigid in that room now. "I didn't understand. I still don't. It wasn't until I was surfing the internet one night when I came upon a conspiracy theory that pharmaceutical companies don't actually want cures for things like cancer and HIV. They'd rather make more money keeping those poor people alive than cure them and lose them as customers."

"Yes. I've often wondered about that as well." Vincent shook out his sleeves, those cufflinks needing more love. "I've done a lot of research into his companies…"

"So have I."

"…And the thing about Black Raven Pharmaceuticals is that they talk a lot. They pump a lot of money into many things, but they never, ever have anything to show for it. It's a multi-billion dollar setup thanks to, as you said, the medicines they provide to keep millions around the world alive, but never cured. Xavier Crow would lose most of his foundation if a cancer cure came around. Your sister must have come too close to becoming the woman who would cure cancer."

The woman who would cure cancer? That didn't sound like something that would happen in the Nazarov family. *Isn't that why my parents came to America? For those opportunities for their daughter?* Nala hadn't existed yet. Tasha was already a promising science student even back in the USSR. Some people were like that, Nala guessed.

"Why would he hire her if he doesn't actually want to find cures? You'd think he'd hire researchers who are middle-of-the-road in achievement. Less likely to have to dirty his hands that way."

"Because PR. It's always PR. I guarantee his stocks went on huge upswings whenever there was great news of some kind. Not merely hiring your sister, who must have shown great promise out of college, but every step she took toward finding a cure, short of actually finding it, would have meant more money in his pocket. It looks great to investors."

"You'd think he'd take the credit for the cure, take the money, and use it to expand his real estate hobby."

"Real estate is too risky, which is where he gets the thrill, but he's not stupid. People may go homeless, but they will still get sick."

"That's terrible."

"Unfortunately, that's capitalism."

Nala's throat betrayed her when she said what she was wondering, but didn't want to dare to actually ask. "You're not like that, are you?"

Vincent smiled, slightly, enough to assuage Nala's nerves. "Money is nice. Money means I've paid off my debts and can live comfortably for the rest of my life. But even if apps stopped being a thing tomorrow and I never moved on to the next big tech thing, I would be content with how much I have. It takes a certain type of personality to make it as far as I have… but it takes a completely different one to make it to Xavier Crow's level. I am only one of those personality types."

"The successful kind. Not the sociopath."

"I hope so."

Their first course arrived. French onion soup, with a side of freshly baked bread. The scent took Nala on a journey far, far away from her fears and dread over her sister. She hoped Vincent felt the same way, if only for a little bit. *I don't know who this Desirée woman was to him, but he clearly cared enough about her to want vengeance like I do.* It almost seemed too coincidental. Two women taken down by Crow's cronies. How many other people were there? How many had fallen because they got too close to something or someone? What had Desirée done to "deserve" such a gruesome death?

When the waiter departed, Nala lined her lap with a napkin and broke off a piece of bread to dip into her soup. "So, here we are," she said, watching the bread turn dark from the soup. "Two people trying to take down Xavier Crow."

"Is that what we're doing?"

"Well, I suppose. What else do we want besides justice? Have you thought through what we're going to do?"

"The first step was the easiest. We got into his club. The whole point of getting in, for me, was to try to gather evidence to take to the authorities."

"Me too!"

An uncharacteristic smirk appeared on Vincent's face. "What a formidable pair we make. Now, let's start with the basics. Where did we meet?"

Over dinner, Nala and Vincent concocted a story surrounding their supposed romance. Apparently, they had met at a convention, at which Nala temped. Well, one thing led to another, and wouldn't one know it, they were taking vacations to Vancouver (the Canadian one, not the one across the river) and exploring the finer points of a heated BDSM relationship.

Before their previous conversation, this would have been awkward at best, but after knowing Vincent's real motives and their shared pain and frustrations, Nala felt free to be more open with the man she called her fake boyfriend. Not that they were sudden bosom buddies or anything. More like business associates who were about to go down a very dangerous path, now that they knew what the other was about. *I can't believe we're doing this.* They had played at being a couple before, but now they felt more like a unified force hell-bent on revenge and all its trappings. Or maybe that was Nala feeling the surge inside her veins. Who knew what Vincent was thinking? The man was as easy to read as an ancient Sumerian text.

It almost felt… fun. Until she remembered the rules of The Aviary's game. That eventually she and Vincent would have to take their lying to a new, uncomfortable level.

"What is it?" he asked over their main course. "Is the food making you sick? You really don't look well."

"It's only…" Nala stared at the fish left on her plate. "It's one thing to pretend to be a couple. We can fake that easy enough. Some kisses here, some jokes there… but what about the other stuff? We can't just talk about our fake kinky sex life." Water. Spray. Showerheads. Nala hid a cough in her napkin. "Eventually people will want more from us."

"Indeed. I thought we would take things one step at a time. I know how uncomfortable it must make you feel."

"No, no... the only thing that really bothers me is the people watching. I've never done something like that before, so I'm not sure I could..."

"Wait... the *voyeurs* is what bothers you the most?" Vincent dropped his fork, letting it ping against his plate. "I would think it's the act itself bothering you."

"The act itself?" The spanking? The groping? The tying up and putting on a display for the other kinksters? Oh, right. That was pretty bothersome.

Sort of...

I'm embarrassing myself. Vincent had barely kissed her a couple of times. What gave her the right to not only fantasize about him while bringing herself to orgasm, but flippantly shrug off the idea of him bending her over his knee and swatting her ass while calling her a naughty tramp? *Oh my God, what is wrong with me?* These conflicting emotions had to end before she suffered whiplash. Anger one minute, sexual arousal the next. Not exactly a winning combination for anyone's life.

"Well, I can distance myself from that," she asserted. "Dealing with everyone else's reactions is something else. I have no control over that. What if I don't give a convincing performance?"

"Again," Vincent said, holding his palm up to her, "let's take things one night at a time. I doubt we'll be asked to do anything like that soon. How's dinner?"

Dinner was fine. Fantastic, even. Nala hadn't devoured a meal like that in a long damn time. Could Vincent take her out on more dinners in the near future? *I'll take his money and the food right off his plate.* Now that she hid no secrets from him – well, besides the fact she found him attractive enough to orgasm to – she was free to imagine all sorts of crazy scenarios. Driving his car. Harassing his assistant. Using his credit card to order takeout. Maybe she should ask about an expense account.

After dinner, Vincent helped her put her sweater back on, his hands lingering on her shoulders after the fact. "Excuse my hair," she said, pulling it forward and over her chest. She tried to not think of his touch sending ripples through her barely-there dress and centering its strength in her core. *Maybe I should sleep with him.* How would she even bring that up? *"So, hey, I know we're playing at being a couple, so maybe we should fuck to make it more believable. I know I'll be able to lie better if I know how big your cock is."* She cleared her throat and stepped away from him before she made a fool of herself.

"Your hair is fine," he said. Nala turned, wondering why he wasn't following her out of the alcove. "Your hair is quite lovely."

He walked past her, informing the host that he would need a valet.

No one comments on my hair. Most people told her she needed a better style than the plain Cleopatra look. Bangs were out. Fringe was in. Apparently there was a difference.

They got in the car the moment they stepped out into the chilly air. Vincent was quick to put his foot on the pedal and wheel them out of the old industrial district and toward the downtown center.

"You're kidding," Nala said. "There's a sex club downtown?" She thought it would be more on the outskirts, maybe even around where they were. A place where people wouldn't question what was going on. People who went to sex clubs liked a semblance of privacy, *right?*

"There sure is." Vincent pulled into a large parking structure. No valets here. However, he had access to a private floor that had extra levels of security. The benefits of being rich, especially in a town known for its numerous break-ins. *People need money for their drugs.* Heroin was the new marijuana.

The engine shut off. Nala undid her seatbelt, but Vincent remained resolute behind the wheel.

"What is it?"

He slowly turned his head toward her. "You ever been to one of these places before?"

"No. Have you?"

He didn't answer that. "I know you can probably guess that there will be a lot of… play going on in there. I wanted to make sure you were prepared for that. Even seasoned men and women can get overwhelmed."

"I've seen people have sex before." Nala didn't mention that it was Lucian and Robin going at it at the last party she attended. "I have a good idea of what BDSM means, and I know everyone in the group now. You don't have to look out for me that badly."

"All right." Vincent opened the door. "Don't say I didn't warn you."

He came around and helped her out of the car, hand going to her hip and lips appearing in her ear. *Oh my…* No woman should feel so coddled in a freezing parking garage.

"From now on tonight, you're my sub, Nala. Or should I say Nightingale?"

Nala forced a smile through her budding arousal. *Go away. I don't need you mucking up my head.* "Indeed you should. Nala Nazarov doesn't play in The Aviary." She curled herself around Vincent, inhaling his deep cologne and telling herself that this man was hers to adore tonight, whether she lied or not. "Only the Nightingale does. Chirp chirp, mother fucker. Let's take that son of a bitch down."

Vincent squeezed her hip before directing her toward the parking garage entrance.

Really, how *bad* could this be?

Chapter 10

What. The. Fuck.

Nala hadn't been in the sex club for fifteen minutes before she saw her fourth penis and smelled her second whiff of a woman so aroused she could no longer contain herself. The entrance lounge, full of clothed people flirting and drinking at a bar, was nothing compared to the downstairs depravity. So. Many. People.

Doing God knew what!

Nala kept a straight face as her sweater was taken in a coat check. She managed to not let her voice waver when Vincent asked her if she wanted a drink. And by some sweet, Godly miracle she kept her shit together when they entered a large VIP area and came face to face with four other couples wearing glittery masks.

"Gale!" Robin called, jumping up from her couch and rushing in their direction. "Come here and check this out! Oh, if your Master will let you."

Fuck calling this guy my Master. Nala covered her sneer and morphed it into a sweet smile. "I'm sure he will. Won't you, *sir?*"

Vincent gently pushed against the small of her back. "Go on, then. I've got business to talk anyway."

Giggling, Robin led Nala away to a terrace overlooking the sexual revelry going on below. Although they were in a subterranean level, there were still multiple floors, with the VIP area high above in a private corner, full of leather couches and complimentary drinks. Xavier Crow never spared any expenses, regardless of where he hosted his voyeuristic parties.

Holy shit, this town is full of perverts. Surely, every town in the world was full of pervs, but Nala couldn't comment on the level of depravity occurring in Carson City or in her mother's hometown of Korolyov. She only knew about Portland right now, and Portland was looking to be one of the biggest hotbeds of sex freaks Nala had ever heard of.

So many naked people. *So many.* People who weren't in their birthday suits tottered about with tits hanging out or dicks slapping against thighs. *There is more cock in this room than in a gym locker room.* Nala knocked back some of her highball in order to erase the image from her head, if only for a few seconds. God knew it would pop back in soon enough. Oh, like now, when she glanced down and had the misfortune of seeing a woman in a sparkly yellow halter top drop to her knees and taste a random man's cock.

"You ever seen anything like it before?" Robin asked. The mirth on her fair face made Nala want to shake her head. "I'm glad I'm not down there. It's bad enough all those people will flirt with me and make my Master jealous. He can get pretty possessive." She giggled again, informing Nala that this aspect of her boyfriend's personality did not bother her. *Weirdo.* Even if Nala were in a real relationship with Vincent, there was no way in hell she'd let him be *possessive* like that. Gross.

My mother would've said that I'm a woman of the '90s. Fine and fancy free. And wearing a lot of flannel. That was Portland in a nutshell.

"Come on!" Robin pulled on Nala's arm, urging her to join the group of girls meeting by the terrace. "Just because we can't join them down there doesn't mean we can't be admired."

Sure enough, Robin perched on the arm of a sofa and wiggled her fingers at a group of guys passing by downstairs. They whistled up at her, and she blew them a kiss.

"You hussy," Starling admonished with a grin. "If Master Crow finds out you're being a bad girl, you might get Master Lucian in trouble."

"Sir can fend for himself," Robin said with a huff. "He doesn't need me protecting him. It's his job to protect me."

Nala knew this was her opportune moment to get some information. "What do you mean he could be in trouble? Why does Mr. Crow care?"

"*Master* Crow," three girls corrected her. Maggie was the only one silent, although she appeared amused by the situation.

"Sorry. Master Crow." Gag. "So, why does he care? It's your business what you do."

"Maybe out there, but in The Aviary, we have to play by Master Crow's rules," Quail said, curled up in a corner of the couch. "He puts all our Masters to shame when it comes to controlling what we do. After you perform the first time, you'll have to sign a contract saying that you'll remain loyal to only your Master – and any other man in the club who wants you."

"What?"

"Didn't anyone tell you?" Maggie asked. "We're all pretty birds in a cage. Meant to be admired, to sing for the men passing by, and, most of all, to go to any Master who calls them. You may go home with your *Master*, but while you're here, you have to do whatever Master Crow says. If Master Lucian approaches him to sleep with you, well… if Master Crow decides he likes the idea, he'll tell you to do it."

Nala's jaw dropped into her lap. She looked at Robin, who remained nonplussed by the idea of her "Master" dallying with another woman in the group.

"Relax. It's what you sign up for joining this private club. It's great fun, really. Last month Master decided to get a taste of Quail, if you know what I mean. Hmph. Doesn't matter to me. We made a proper swap out of it."

"Beyond that, we don't kiss and tell," Quail said.

"Master Lucian has told me that he thinks you're lovely," Robin continued, grinning like an idiot. "Maybe we'll swap."

That was weird. This was *weird.* Seemed to Nala that one of the cornerstones of BDSM was staying true. Maybe the occasional dalliance with the other's approval, but to make a lifestyle out of it? Well, she wouldn't declare herself an expert by any means. She was playing all of this by ear.

"If you don't like the idea of your Master sleeping with one of us…" Quail said, interrupting Nala's thoughts, "then you need to discuss that privately with him. You should consider it, though. If he lets you sleep with one of the Masters, he'll get a nice kickback for his business from Master Crow."

"Oh, yes." Maggie forced back a chuckle. "Master Crow really gets off on using us like his play dolls."

"We don't have to… with him… do we?" Nala hadn't considered that. Until tonight, she thought The Aviary was a sexual club for dedicated couples. She knew Maggie and Jay were married. Robin and Lucian were together forever. Starling and her Master, Joseph, were as good as engaged, or at least the young woman couldn't stop talking about wedding plans. Aside from Nala, Quail was in the newest relationship.

"Oh, no, Gale. He doesn't touch us. Just watches."

"And watches and watches." Maggie pulled out a cigarette, holding it away from the gaggle of girl talk.

"This is a lot to take in."

"Would've thought you knew already. Can't imagine Master Crow letting a couple in without at least the Master knowing the details ahead of time. Didn't Master Vincent tell you?"

"I feel like there's a lot he hasn't told me yet."

The other women exchanged glances. "Young relationships," Maggie said carefully. "I've almost forgotten what it's like to not have a psychic connection with Ja… my Master."

Nala held the older woman's gaze for longer than was kosher. During that time, Maggie winked, a delicate pink fingernail pressing against her lips – out of sight from the other women around them. *What is up with her?* Nala wasn't unnerved by Maggie, but she was definitely suspicious of her. Her instincts were rarely wrong.

The party continued around them, the general rabble of Portland's sex fiends having fun down below while The Aviary fluttered about in their VIP loft. Xavier Crow's arrival was marked by a gorgeous woman stepping in with bondage gear clad all over her nubile body. The men whistled, the women expressed their jealousy, and Xavier Crow put his arm protectively around the woman he dubbed Hawk and said she would be joining them for the evening.

"Reconvene by the bar," Vincent muttered in Nala's ear as they passed each other. "I suppose you could say that's an order."

It should've been a joke, but coming from Vincent Lane, it was more like a dry attempt at poor humor.

"This club is fucked as fucking fucked up," Nala whispered the moment they had a semblance of privacy. Vincent stood between her and the rest of the party, including Hawk, who offered to demonstrate on Robin's ass how one properly used a paddle. To the sounds of that girl squealing in delight with every smack of her skin, Nala continued, "You didn't tell me that if one of the other guys wants to fuck me I have to say yes or get us kicked out."

"Thought that would come up later."

"Fuck off. You knew and didn't tell me."

"You said you would do whatever it takes to avenge your sister. Well?"

"Well what? Would I fuck one of the other guys here if it means staying in this club?" Nala snorted. "Fuck. Off. You don't get to ask me that."

"All right. While you were finding that out, I discovered that Miss Hawk here is the first date Crow has brought pretty much since he founded The Aviary a year ago."

"A year?" That was the only piece of information Nala cared about. "It's been going on that long? Surely he didn't have a couple members for so long."

"No. There have been other couples who are no longer members. Some of whom… disappeared."

"Who?"

"Nobody knows, because their real names weren't known. Especially the women."

"You think he had them killed too?"

"I don't know." Vincent poured himself a hasty drink, knocking back liquor like it was candy. "We both need to tread lightly. *Don't* piss him off. He likes us, for now. He'll like us even better if we fall in line and don't bend the rules too much."

"You mean…"

"Vincent! Nightingale!" Xavier appeared behind them, his stocky gait making him waddle as he propped himself up with a silver-tipped cane. Nala heard something about a trip in his office. *And I'm the mayor of Portland.* "Isn't this place absolutely divine? Do take the time to enjoy Hawk's displays. We'll also have a demonstration by Joseph and little Starling in a few minutes. They say they've been practicing all week."

Nala nodded politely, choosing to stay close to her "Master." Thus far she had built up an image of a girl who was quiet around the other men in the group. *Hopefully that doesn't make me attractive.* She didn't think she could take any propositions. She wasn't even sleeping with Vincent. What made anyone think she would fuck Lucian or Sebastian or Jay or Joseph? *Fuuuuck that.* Nala entertained the idea of being loose enough with her morals to take on Vincent for a night or two, but those fantasies belonged trapped in her head – and loins.

No fantasy was happening in the presence of Xavier Crow. *One step at a time, Nala.* There were many bridges to cross, but they had come upon few of them so far. Nala couldn't get ahead of herself. Otherwise she would go mad.

"We'll be delighted to enjoy the show," Vincent said on both of their behalves. "Thank you again for inviting us."

"Ah, think nothing of it. Say, this time next week, you two may become full-fledged members. Think about it, would you?"

Nala bit back her lip. Vincent remained as smooth as ever. "I don't suppose that means sharing a bit of ourselves with the group, would it?"

Naturally, Nala assumed that Xavier would speak directly with Vincent. He was the Master, after all.

Instead, he turned to Nala, sharing with her a despicable smile stained in the coffee of the day. If bile had any other flavor, it would be that. Right there. *Smite me now.*

"Only if the lady is up for it. What do you say, Nightingale? Would you sing us a pretty song next week?"

Her heart thumped so hard in her chest that she thought she would die. *This man is asking me to perform… sexually…* She had to grin and bear it, however. For the sake of Tasha. For the sake of Desirée, and any of the other people this man had murdered. *Too many.* In the realm of the world, people went through worse things to see justice served. *I can do it. Maybe. I'll detach myself like a total badass.* Nala had been practicing something similar ever since her sister died.

"I'll have to practice my scales, of course," she said timidly. How much of that was real and how much of it was show… she couldn't say. "I'm sure I could come up with a tune. With the help of my Master, of course." Nala looked to Vincent, smiling, willing him to finish this farce on her behalf.

"Nala is very talented. We both look forward to sharing."

Not what I had in mind, buddy.

The look of expectation passing between them sent a tangible shudder through Vincent's frame. "I look forward to it as well. Anyway, I must be off. Do enjoy the show." Xavier waved over his head as he returned to the mischief going on between Hawk and Robin. *Does that woman even know I've seen her have sex?* Of course she did. She probably assumed everyone had seen whatever there was to see and then some.

"Well," Vincent began, letting out a heavy breath. "I didn't expect that to happen quite yet. Looks like I'll be smacking your ass sometime next week."

"Hell no," Nala mumbled. "Keep your hands to yourself."

"If you insist." Nevertheless, here came Vincent's arm, snaking comfortably around Nala's waist. "Let's go get this over with."

Joseph was already setting up a small stage next to the balcony. Below, the sounds of partying and general merrymaking wafted up into the VIP area, full of music, shouts of joy – and orgasm – and smacks to asses and thighs. Glasses clinked as Quail served a round of shots. Nala was obliged to take one, and thank God, because Starling was already topless when she made it to the stage where her Master awaited her.

"There's my lovely bumblebee," he said, his neatly groomed goatee spreading with his smile. Joseph was a tall man with tanned skin and a dark ponytail that hovered above the back of his neck. Starling, in all her model-tastic blond glory, was exactly the type of woman Nala expected to see with a man who also looked like a model. *Nobody could say they're not beautiful.* Even Starling's breasts, which were an ample size for her petite figure, were still perky and tipped with pink nipples that hardened with a whisper in her ear. *Oh, God, here we go.* Nala sat in the back with Vincent, where they wouldn't be scrutinized because they were only politely watching, and not actively playing voyeurs as expected of them.

Well, maybe. That was Nala's intent, anyway. Yet the moment she caught a glimpse of the way Starling's breasts moved with every slight undulation, she was fighting back the urge to see what happened next. Not like she didn't know how things ended between Robin and Lucian. *A happy ending for the both of them.* Nala got up long enough to grab another drink. As an afterthought, she grabbed one for Vincent too, since it would be expected of her. When she returned to the couch in the corner, there was Starling on the stage, one hand bound above her head with the lights of the club below splayed behind her.

"Sweet pet of mine," Joseph said, picking up a small crop and lightly touching one of his sub's nipples. Nala felt her own peak in her dress, and she forced her eyes into her lap, where both her hands wadded up fabric. Her throat swallowed a large lump. "How much do you enjoy showing off for our friends?"

"Very much so, Master," Starling was already breathless, her legs shaking. Below, a man on a speaker announced a gangbang about to commence in the center stage. Nala couldn't see anything way back where she sat, but she heard the cheers, and she saw Robin curl her arm around her Master's shoulders and bite the tip of his ear. Her hand disappeared between his thighs, stroking his bulge.

"Oh, boy," Nala muttered. She hoped Vincent was containing himself.

His arm drew her into his embrace. "We shouldn't look so cold and unfamiliar."

He was right, but this was the *last* place Nala needed to be. The last time she watched something sexual like this unfurl, she went home to fantasize about this man fucking her raw in the shower. *Come on, hormones, get a fucking grip.* She couldn't let that happen right now. She couldn't inhale this cologne, mingled with this man's natural musky scent, and let her imagination get away from her.

Yet her heart fluttered. Her hand absentmindedly went to Vincent's thigh, feeling the thick muscle there. She didn't dare draw her hand up farther.

Sweat traveled from his palm to her bare shoulder. In front of them, Starling gasped in surprise as the crop smacked her right breast. Nala nearly jumped as well.

The show was everything she expected – and everything she did not need. Namely, she watched Starling be stripped of the rest of her clothes, each one fluttering to the ground as her breaths increased, heaving her breasts up and down. Down in the gallery, a woman groaned with a microphone broadcasting how good her damned gangbang felt. How many men was she taking on? Why in the *world* was Nala wondering that? *It's not like I'm into it.* Yet that woman continued to groan in sync with Starling's breaths, her legs slowly spreading open as her dark and handsome Master loosened his collar and planted a heavy kiss on her lips.

Something terrible happened while this went on.

Nala forgot why she was there. She forgot that Xavier Crow sat in some shadows somewhere, watching this unfold with the most perverse sense of glee any man had ever felt. Blood dripped from his hands, and yet these people were able to enjoy themselves – including Nala, who slowly realized her biggest obstacle had nothing to do with Crow's presence, but the sick sense of shame she felt watching this spectacle… and getting aroused from it.

Shame? What shame? There was nothing shameful about listening to a gangbang, including a woman's orgasm followed by a tender laugh and a demand for a fresh cock. Shame had nothing to do with the naked woman in front of Nala, the woman who felt hands all over her and let a tongue snake into her ear while a pair of strong fingers aimed for her cunt. She shrieked in joy, nether lips spreading to admit Joseph as he pumped his fingers into her in front of the entire Aviary.

She looked so happy.

That was the thing that struck Nala the most. Starling looked *happy*. She was loved, she was caressed, and above all she was pleasured by this man Nala could only assume she loved in return. It didn't matter that they did this in front of an audience. Whether they got off on it or not, it didn't matter. *All* that mattered was the connection between them. The charisma. The chemistry. Not only were they a good looking couple, but they clicked in such a way that the one could anticipate the other's next move. Even with her old boyfriend, Nala couldn't say she ever experienced that before.

She was reminded of Vincent's arm around her when his fingers pinched her flesh. Nala jerked in his embrace, nearly falling over to her side until Vincent caught her, like he had back at The Crow's Nest over a week ago.

Had it only been a week?

"Beg for it," Joseph commanded, his fingers all but disappearing into his sub's body. "Tell me how much you want my cock."

Eyes rolling back in her head, Starling nodded, her hips going back and her ass pushing into the air, as if to give her Master greater access to her inner chambers. "Please, sir," she muttered, body shuddering. "Fuck me."

"With what?"

Nala's mouth watered in anticipation of what Starling would say. "Your cock."

A familiar giggle echoed in front of Nala. Before she knew what she was watching, Robin bent down and unzipped Lucian's pants. *Oh my God.* This party was officially underway.

To the sounds of one unknown woman taking on her third man in fifteen minutes, Nala watched as Robin licked a long trail down her Master's cock. *So that's what it looks like up close, I guess.* Only a few more feet away, Starling's leg was lifted up, *her* Master making short work of any humility she had left. *And that's what his looks like.* Soon, the only cock Nala *hadn't* seen would be Vincent's!

"Well, this is happening," she said, hoping her partner-in-crime would say something witty in return. Instead, she got silence from his direction. Unbearable, unnerving silence.

Nala slightly turned her head, making sure she still saw the debauchery unfolding in the corner of her eye. Vincent sat, arm around her, his legs crossed and eyes neither focused on the scene nor on the floor in front of him. *Will of steel.* Or so Nala thought, until she happened to glance down and saw the tent struck in Vincent's trousers.

Oh no. This is turning him on. Well, to be fair, he was a man. Just because Nala joked to herself that he was asexual didn't mean he *was.* As a healthy thirty-year-old man, he probably got hard-ons every day from existing. Being in a sex club? It was amazing he lasted this long. *Men can only have so much self-control.* After all, here Nala was, fighting off her own arousal so she could stay focused on… on…

What was she trying to focus on, anyway? Because as far as she could tell, the whole point of her being here tonight was to get horny as fucking *hell.*

Forget the darkness.

Forget the anger.

Forget *everything.*

Sit back, the world seemed to say. Sit back, relax, and remember that you're human and only young once. She was twenty-one. She was *supposed* to be enjoying her youth, whether that meant traveling, partying, or, well, exploring every facet of her sexuality that she could.

It was almost liberating, being able to forget all the crap.

Of course, all she had to do was crane her head to the right and see Xavier Crow muttering something in Hawk's ear. The dominatrix laughed more than once, stroking the man's cane and playing with the paddle still in her hand. As long as she didn't look over there, Nala belonged to a group of people who celebrated life by getting aroused and having endless sex.

Without thinking – because who could think while Robin's head bobbed up and down in Lucian's lap and Starling begged for her Master to come inside her – Nala kneaded her palm against the inside of Vincent's thigh, thinking back to that night she imagined him doing the same exact thing she saw before her.

She came dangerously close to his cock, but it was at that moment she snatched her hand away and Vincent turned his body in the other direction. *I'm sorry.* She didn't know why she thought that. *I shouldn't be focusing on this.* Wasn't it okay, if only for a few minutes? Surely, a few minutes out of her long, grueling day could be dedicated to life's simple pleasures.

Really, she was a bit put out that Vincent was acting like this. Maybe he had award-winning self-control after all. *Jealous.*

His hand moved from her arm to her shoulder. Fingers tapped her there. Fluttering commenced in Nala's heart, and on cue, her head hit the back of the couch and Vincent's mouth was on hers.

"Yes!" Starling cried, her whines competing with the woman's below. "I'm coming, sir!" Grunts filled the air. The scent of heady sex met Nala's nose as Vincent's cologne mingled with it. *Oh my God, ohmygod.* Her hand untangled from his and shot into his hair, her mouth parting to accept his tongue the moment it plummeted down her throat.

Joseph climaxed with an intense roar that nearly knocked Nala over the back of the couch. Except Vincent was there, caressing her bare arms, her stomach, and treading so close to her thighs as he kissed with that burning, crippling passion that Nala was so scared to experience.

Her hand went to his cheek, fearing he would leave her otherwise. *I've never been kissed like this before…* Certainly not her ex-boyfriend. She had seen these kinds of kisses between other people over the years, mostly on TV, but never felt it for herself. And for everything she ever thought about Vincent, she had to admit that this… well, this was like ripping open one of her old scars and seeing what had transpired beneath.

Rush. Rushes of desire. Rushes of heat. Rushes of waves upon waves of *give me more of this.* Nala clung to Vincent in a vain attempt to make him awaken even more. *Would it be so bad if you took me home with you?* No, no this wasn't the Nala she trained herself to be. She was supposed to be bitter. Fed up with the world and what it had thrown at her. Not… not hopeful.

Not desperate for affection.

Certainly not head over heels in exploding lust for this *man.*

"Vincent…" she managed to utter in between heavy kisses. "I want…"

He knew what she wanted. Vincent took her hand and brought it to his erection, letting her feel the size of him as he grew harder with every passing heartbeat. Every drop of blood in his body must have been rushing there.

"Oh, fuck me." That self-admonishment escaped from Nala's ear and disappeared into her throat, where Vincent's lips went, sucking her skin and releasing one groan after another as she rubbed his cock. "I'm a fucking mess."

"Me too," she whispered, relieved to feel him come as undone as her. At least they were equal in that regard.

"Ha! I told you they were as horny as the rest of us."

Vincent leaped off Nala, sending her upside down as she nearly tumbled off the couch. In front of them, Lucian grinned, languid from a climax as Robin continued to giggle into his chest. On the stage, Starling was released from her binds, her skin so flushed that she needed some pats to the cheek to come back to reality.

If anything killed Nala's libido then and there, it was Xavier Crow gazing at her from his spot on the other side of the VIP area. There was something… strange, about him. More than usual. Hawk was nowhere to be seen, but Xavier remained transfixed on Nala, pleased.

Hell no.

"I've gotta go to the bathroom," she announced, getting up and scurrying away as quickly as possible. The nearest bathroom was down a dark hall. This time there were no bedrooms full of people fucking to distract her.

She didn't have to go, but she did have to stand in front of the mirror and splash water on her face. It helped, a little. Not enough to completely calm her down from her sexual high, but enough to placate the heat turning her inside out. *Calm down, slut.* Nala was damn close to saying that to her reflection, but she decided to go with fixing her hair and making sure her dress was as decent as could be.

Every time she tugged on the fabric, however, she remembered Vincent pawing at her, exploring her figure with a single hand. He had been determined to pinch her nipple, feel her heat before they were interrupted. God, Nala was sure of it.

The bathroom door opened. Starling stumbled in, barely with the fucking program as she fought with her clothes to get them back on. "Oh, hi," she said, tripping over her feet to get to the single toilet stall in there. "You ever get dick drunk? I am so dick drunk right now."

"Er…"

"You fuck your Master tonight?"

Nala shivered, quite involuntarily. "No, not yet."

"Mm, you better get on it. People are going crazy out there. If he's like any of the other guys, he'll be needing you pronto."

Starling opened and shut the stall door behind her. Shoes scuffed against the floor, toilet paper turned in its wheel, and one woman bemoaned how much cum she had to clean up.

"I need a priest," Nala mumbled, splashing more water on her face. "A priest, an exorcism, and maybe a margarita."

"You can get at least half of those out in the club!" Starling called.

Nala had to get the fuck out of there.

She wasn't sure where she was going to go. Oh, at least her impulses were back. She may forget the anger and bitterness for a little while, but she could never fully get rid of the brash decision making that led her to trying to flee from the club before she had to face some unsavory emotions. Not just lust. Definitely not love. But something spoiled inside her stomach, and it wasn't the seafood dinner.

All she knew was that she had to get far away from Xavier Crow. And Vincent. Definitely get far, so very far from that man who had nearly shown her what was what.

That was the mad plan as she dried off her face with paper towels and left the bathroom. That was her plan as she scurried down the darkened hallway, wondering where in downtown Portland they were and how she could get home to her dingy closet. Fuck the money. Fuck the mission for now. Vincent could make up a story about her having food poisoning. Surely that would get out of her Crow's line of sight for…

"Nala."

Vincent was there, like an arch-angel – no, a glowing demon – gripping her shoulders and halting her. *Oh, no, please… let me go.* Nala kept her eyes downcast as she struggled to think of what to say to him.

"We need to talk."

Well, he wasn't wrong about that.

"Okay…"

"This way."

Vincent hooked his hand around the bend of her arm, hauling her farther down the empty hallway and into the darker shadows encroaching there. An abandoned leather chair sat in the corner where they finally came to a stop, Vincent forcibly turning Nala around with such strength, such determination that she felt like she was on a carnival ride.

"What do we have to talk a…"

Oh.

That.

Chapter 11

Now that they were alone, Vincent was not gentle. Not in the least. He practically slammed Nala against the corner, pulling her legs into the air until the only thing keeping her from sliding down the walls and onto her ass was his sheer strength alone.

"Vince…"

"Shut up, Nala." Who was this? This wasn't the stoic and collected Vincent Nala met a week ago. This wasn't the quiet man she met in that sparse office. This definitely wasn't the bereaved individual she had dinner with. Whoever this was… well…

She rather liked him.

"I don't want to hear a word out of you." Stern. Commanding. More effective than Lucian, Sebastian, Joseph… any man out there doing a mediocre job at whatever it was they did. "Make all the noise you want, but don't distract me. Got it?"

Nala nodded, the flow of her blood reversing in an instance.

"All I want to hear," Vincent growled, yanking her short skirt up and ripping aside her lingerie, "is that you want it. Tell me you want me, Nala. Tell me!"

Vincent's deep voice usually sounded so soothing. Like a man people instantly trusted, because they knew he would do them no harm. *This isn't that man.* He could hurt her. He could hurt her heart, her body, make her walk funny and burn her ass until it was too sore to touch. *He's gonna do it…* Those fantasies she had were nothing like this. Vincent was never forceful in her mind. He did her hard, a little rough, but not like *this.*

No. This was better.

This was the kind of wild escape a woman like Nala needed.

"Do you, *Nala?*" Fuck her! The way he said her name, spitting it out like a fucking beast was doing things to those torn panties. Namely covering them in her slick wetness that demanded to be used. "Go on…" she whimpered, hands splaying across his shoulders before feeling his chest through his silk shirt. Fingers played with glass buttons. "Do it."

"Say you want it, and then shut the fuck up."

Well!

"I want it." Three words that hadn't meant so much before. She clawed his shirt, tearing apart the buttons and feeling the warm flesh beneath. "I want it!"

Then she needed to shut the fuck up.

Not that she could get any words out thereafter. Vincent slammed her again, harder, pushing her body up the wall as he undressed her in one tear of the hand. The sashes covering her breasts gave way. The zipper in the back of the skirt fell down. Gasping, Nala felt every bit of her skin be exposed in front of this man, whether he could see a patch or not. In those shadows? He probably couldn't see anything but the dark of her thick, straight hair and her darker nipples protruding in the air. *Ohmyholyshit.* His mouth was on her, sucking her throat; his tongue tasted her, flicking against her nipple. Nala moaned, as if this were her lot in life, and let herself be carried away by the current Vincent Lane brought to sweep her up into his arms.

"Don't say a word," he reiterated, one hand fumbling with his zipper while the other held her up by the ass. "If you say anything, even my name, I'll stop and leave you here to suffer with this wet cunt."

Like fuck she was going to say anything in response!

"That's it." The more he spoke, the raspier his words became. Was there smoke in the corner? Nala couldn't smell it. All she smelled was that insane cologne making her lustier. *Oh, fuck me.* Her spread legs wrapped tight around Vincent's waist. The position made her open up, wetness dribbling from her body, down the underside of her thigh, and touching the crease of her ass. *I'm so fucking wet.* Wetter than she was in the shower with her comparably *tame* fantasy. "Take me, Nala."

When she thought there was nothing to take yet, she felt it – the head of his cock, attempting to push into her wetness.

She bit back a cry as she braced herself, fingers digging into his back as she fought to both open her legs wider and to enclose them around his waist. Either he was big, or she was tighter than she gave herself credit for – maybe both. *He's definitely bigger than my ex.* Was that guy average? Who cared? Oh, shit, he was in, in, *in,* his tip entering her before he pulled out and went for it again.

This time she could not stay quiet. Nala could forbid coherent words, but she couldn't be completely silent. Vincent's cock ruptured her, forcing its way in, down deep, far back, out again, in, out, in outinoutinoutin…

"*Ohhh,*" she moaned, the pain nearly unbearable at times. So long since a man had last been in her. Was she prepared at all? Not like this. Not for a man Vincent's size and determination. Nala felt so tiny compared to him, a giant, a monster, an incubus making her forget all her pain with a new pain of his own.

"You're so God damned tight," he growled, stilling his cock inside her as his fingers wrapped beneath her thighs and attempted to pull her cunt wider. Nala slammed her eyes shut, feeling him inch in a little more, past a part of her that had lost its wetness. *Too rough!* She didn't say anything that would make him stop. For all the discomfort, for all the pain, the thrill was still too real. Nala did not want to let it go.

Finally, a bright light flashed before her eyes – he was in. Deep, hard, most definitely in.

However, she could not relax her hold on him, nor could he release his strength binding her to the corner of two unsuspecting walls. Because now he had to fuck her.

There was nothing loving or tender about the way he thrust into her, using her body as a means to his own generous end. Nala went through spells of being absolutely enthralled with the pinching pain and blinding pleasure both… and spells of wanting to push him away, to slap him across the face and tell him to fuck off.

Which would win out?

Her ass slammed against the wall. At first she couldn't feel why, and then she felt it happen again: Vincent tried to pull out too fast, his cock still hooked within her and attempting to bring her with him as he moved. This resulted in a mere inch slipping out of her, but her whole pelvis following him three more until he slammed forward again. A shoe slipped off Nala's foot and clattered to the ground. Her throat released a cry of shock and pleasure both. *This is so fucking unreal.* It happened again. Again. *Again.* Each time Vincent impaled her against the wall and rammed his cock deep within her core.

Nala had never felt this split open before. Because *split open* was the only way to describe what Vincent was doing to her.

Eventually he caught on to what was happening and held her hips still, thrusting faster and faster until she was undeniably wet enough to take him like this. *I didn't know I could do this.* It was rough, it was sudden, and it was absolutely wonderful.

"You fucking seductress," he managed to murmur against her chest, lips diverting to her breasts as her hands pushed strands of dark hair between fingers. "I'll teach you a real lesson."

Nala didn't know what that meant, but he was about to force an orgasm out of her if he kept this up. *Do it. I want to know what that feels like!*

"Fuck you!"

Nala nearly fell to the ground as Vincent suddenly pulled out of her, letting her legs collapse into their rightful position. She moaned, betrayed, her body begging him to fill her again and to give her back that beautiful pleasure she had never experienced before.

She opened her mouth, lips about to sputter disbelief. Vincent slapped his hand over her gaping maw and slapped his other hand right on her wet nether lips, pressing against her engorging clit.

"Fuck you, Nala Nazarov," he said again. "Fuck you for what you've made me feel." Vincent forced her around, bending her over the arm of the nearby leather chair and lining his cock up with her opening. "Fuck you and your tight cunt." Nala's knee appeared beside her shoulder as Vincent pulled her leg up by the thigh. The only thing helping her with their height difference was the stiletto heel piercing the ground beneath her. "Fuck you and your Siren song, Nightingale."

He entered her, hard, spearing her over the arm of the chair and sending her and a loud, echoing moan into the seat. Vincent's hand covered her mouth again, muffling any further sound as his cock furiously penetrated her depths over and over again. *He's going to come. He hates it, but he'll fuck me until he comes.* Would he let her come? Was she even allowed to? A part of her didn't care. The wild ride she took on his cock was enough to sate her for now. But another part of her demanded it. Because she was the Nightingale, a creature he had named himself.

If I am yours, then I demand to be treated as your treasured possession. All well and good in her heart and head. Then she felt the way he broke into her, taking whatever he needed without any regard for her pleasure.

Or maybe it was with every regard.

"*Mmf!*" She couldn't contain that. Nala moaned into his hand, her own braced against the couch as she became more and more determined to stand up to his fucking. Fingers gripped leather. Knees turned red from whatever burns they endured. Sweat dripped down her forehead and cum stole down her legs. There was no escape for Nala now. Not that she would run. She was a willing prisoner. A prisoner who defied her Master. His cock may swell within her, but she would endure it, welcome it even.

After all, in the end it felt like the greatest moment of her life.

"*Ugh!*" A surge of heat, wet with fury, expanded inside Nala's loins. She braced herself for the next shot of his seed, gripping all that she could as she willed her cunt to open more to his length. *You're not all the way in. I know it.* Not even at that angle, with him driving right into her. *You have me stretched every which way to Sunday. It hurts like fuck. I know I'll pay for this later. I want more. I want your big fucking cock in every nook of my body. Give me more of* your *seed, dirtbag. I can take it. I can take anything.*

She stared triumphantly at the black leather in the shadows. Nala would have cackled in glee if she wasn't concentrating on the third hit of seed expanding within her. She hadn't felt it quite like that before. It felt... amazing? Welcoming? *Right?* It was so wrong. She wasn't supposed to have unprotected sex with a man she barely knew... but she couldn't help herself. This was what she was meant to experience.

"Holy *shit.*" With that, Vincent spent himself at last, holding himself within her as he lost the last of his strength.

Nala released the tension in her tendons, but she did not release his cock. She locked herself around it, tears of victory falling down her cheeks as her tongue snaked between his sweaty fingers. When Vincent finally won the battle of their wills and pulled out, Nala welcomed the hot stream flowing out of her and covering the leather chair. She felt it with her own fingers, guffawing against her arm.

"What the fuck is it..." Vincent leaned against the wall, watching her.

Nala eased her sore legs together, holding him inside her. "You underestimated me. You didn't think I could take that."

"The fact that you did means nothing."

The taste of salt hit Nala's tongue as she sampled what happened when they came together. "It means everything. Your macho male bullshit thinks it's claimed me, but really, we both know that it's me who owns your ass now."

"Whatever."

Nala stood, inhaling the sweet, musky air of victory. Maybe it was all in her head. It didn't matter. Right now she felt much more like her old self that it was endearing. Not to Vincent, no… but to the person she preferred to be.

"Now I've gotta go clean up," she announced, clasping her hand on Vincent's arm. Nala took in the sight of his disheveled shirt, of his flaccid cock sticking out of his pants. Vincent hurried to zip himself back up, but it was too late. "When I get back, you're finding an excuse to take me home. Because I am so done here. You made sure of that."

She made it sound like she was admonishing him. Perhaps she was, a little. *I've gotta stay ahead one step of this guy now.* Otherwise he would walk all over her, and Nala Nazarov was not a woman a man could walk all over.

Her mask threatened to slip down her nose as she strolled back to the bathroom. *Neither is Nightingale.* Her persona would have to be even stronger than her real self in order to survive this bullshit.

***

The car pulled up to the same spot it always made use of. Nala waited for the engine to shut off, but it never did.

Vincent remained silent behind the wheel, eyes planted on the quiet residential road. He hadn't said a damned thing since they left the club, telling Xavier Crow that poor Nala was feeling under the weather and needed to head home for the evening. The man had waved them off before going back to a heated conversation with Hawk.

Now Nala was trapped in a car with a man who wanted nothing to do with her. Was it because she "seduced" him, making him shed that resolve that was usually so resolute around her? Or was it fatigue? Vincent was not going to offer her cuddles. Not that Nala wanted any.

"Goodnight, I guess." Nala opened the door, feeling the cold air back on her skin. "Thanks for the slutty dress. I see why you picked it out now."

Vincent bristled, but did not otherwise react. *What an ass.* Nala should have guessed he would be like this when pushed. Men didn't stay docile for long. *Telling me to shut up so he can fuck me.* Didn't she like it? *Beside the point.*

"By the way."

She waited until he looked at her, brows furrowed and nose flaring in disgust. With her? With himself? For the way they acted like common animals in a stupid sex club? What, was Vincent a candles and body oil kind of guy? *Fat chance.*

"Now what?" he snapped.

"Next time we do it, make sure you let a girl come."

Nala stepped out of the car, slamming the door behind her. As she stepped onto the sidewalk, the window rolled down and Vincent reached across the passenger side seat to catch Nala on her way.

"You mean you didn't?"

She stopped. "You mean you couldn't tell?" Nala could barely hear herself over the car. Plus, the cold. The *cold.* "Or were you so caught up in your dick that you weren't even paying attention to me?" No way was she sticking around for his answer. Nala walked away, finally mastering stepping in those huge heels in time to reach the front door. She heard the car take off behind her, but did not turn around to watch Vincent go.

For all her righteous bravado, Nala became crestfallen as she searched for her house key in her satchel. *Fuck, that was hot.* Girl needed a shower, but…

The door opened. The lights were off. Patrick was apparently out for the night, giving Nala free reign to do as she pleased. Like take a shower and make love to the showerhead, finishing the job Vincent started over an hour ago. The man in her fantasies always made sure she came, no matter how rough he gave it to her.

Entry #6

As it turns out, Nightingale's motives are exactly like mine. Crow had her sister killed. This woman was a medical researcher beneath him, and it seems she came too close to harming his bottom line.

But that's not what I'm focusing on tonight. At The Aviary, I crossed a line that I can never transgress again. I took her. I took Nightingale in that primal way I've been fantasizing about. In that way I haven't felt in such a fucking long time.

It was not love. It was barely respect. I lost complete control of myself. But hearing her say that she wanted me… that she wanted me to do those things… do you know how long it's been since I succumbed to my most base desires.

I feel him awakening in me. The dormant Vincent of these past three years is rising to the challenge set before him. Nightingale is trainable. She is willing. I could feel it in her body as I took her. Perhaps it's her youthful folly and she'll come to realize I'm more dangerous than she thought. But I don't take her for that great of a fool. Tonight's dinner conversation proved she's been through almost as much as I have. Perhaps she is more mature than I give her credit for.

Nevertheless, she continues to haunt my mind. I can't stop thinking about her. The guilt invading my heart is unlike anything I've felt before. I want her. I want to make her all mine. I want to repel her, to tell her to get the fuck away from me.

I'm afraid if I'm put in that position again I'll cross yet another line. I'm even more afraid that she'll want it and I'll have no reason other than my shame to turn her down. I had hoped I was past those passions. Turns out they're alive and well.

Chapter 12

The surprising thing wasn't that Vincent still sent her a check via courier mail on Sunday afternoon – because of course a rich guy could make that happen. No, what shocked Nala was the phone call she received late in the morning.

He has never called me before. She stared at his number lighting up the tiny screen on her cell phone. *What does he want?* Ever since she woke up with a clear head Saturday morning, Nala dreaded talking to the man who fucked her raw.

"Nala," he said the moment she answered. "I'm glad I got a hold of you. We need to talk."

Spare me. She sat in the living room, which reeked of Patrick's leftover pot fest the night before. Or maybe it was that morning. "Not sure I have anything to say to you, sir."

"Are you mad at me?" Was that a tinge of worry in his voice? Did Master know he messed up by not even letting a girl come on his dick? "Tell me the truth. We need to clear the air right now."

Nala snorted into the phone. "Mad? Nah, but I feel like you owe me an explanation about what happened."

"I don't know what to say other than, I, well…"

"Never mind. What do you want?"

Vincent held back a breath. "I was calling to apologize about what happened. I feel like I owe you a few explanations."

"Uh huh." Nala stretched out across the pot-infested couch and stared at the popcorn ceiling. "Go on then. Give me your explanations."

"I'd rather not discuss it on the phone. I was wondering if you had free time today?"

Nala turned over, burying her face into the back of the couch. "I don't work today, if that's what you mean."

"Great. Got any plans?"

Calm down. A man of his means had some friends, surely. Even the most antisocial billionaire in the world had to have *friends.* Whether or not they were any good friends was another matter. "No plans, unless you count sleeping on this couch and trying to enjoy my day off for what it is."
"But you don't have any concrete plans."

"Vincent Lane, are you asking me out on a date?"

She said it flippantly, imagining him sitting in his bare office with an unchallenged look on his face. "Is that what you want?" he asked. "For me to take you out on a date?"

Did she *want* that? Ha, no. She couldn't imagine her and Vincent on a real date if their lives depended on the charade. Bad enough they were faking the whole thing for an audience to begin with. "I don't know if the word 'date' is what I want, but I would like something more than a rendezvous in your car and dinner in some squared away hole in the wall. I mean, don't get me wrong, the food was great there, but it takes more than that to impress me. You wanna impress me, right?" Maybe it didn't matter anymore. Lots of men lost interest, let alone interest in impressing women after they had done the deed. *Guy's marked me. All of Portland can smell him on me.* Or maybe that was Patrick's pot. "Let's go for an outing. Look, the sky has cleared! We could actually do something in this rainy-ass city."

Vincent made some strange noise on the other end of the line. "Fine. As long as we have a frank discussion somewhere in there."

"Yeah, whatever. When are you picking me up?"

Something tapped on the window behind her.

Nala pushed herself up on the couch, craning her head around to see a shadowy figure dancing behind the lace curtains. *No way.* What a fucking creeper. Nala dragged herself off the cushion and went to the window, pulling aside the curtain and staring Vincent right in the Portland-pale face.

"You stalking me?" she said into the phone.

"You could say I was in the area."

Nala didn't have much more time to think. She grabbed her wallet out of her bedroom-closet, made sure she had her keys, and locked the front door behind her. It wasn't as cold today, but she huddled within her hoodie, afraid she would feel as exposed around this man as she had two nights ago.

His car was parked in its usual spot in front of the walkway. Nala beat Vincent to it, waiting for him to unlock the door before flinging it open and hopping in. *Still smells like the weirdo.* Speaking of weirdos, here he came now, rounding the front of his car and getting in on the driver's side door.

"You're… casual, today," Nala said. She stared at his dark wash jeans and the black, plain hoodie covering his muscles. The only reason she was able to recognize him was because of the strong, musky scent coming her way. *Do other women smell that stuff? What about men?* Nala couldn't be the only woman around who was aroused by that scent. *Why do I care? Not like he's my real boyfriend.*

"It's Sunday." Vincent strapped himself in and started the low purr of the motor. "Not many opportunities to wear a suit on Sunday."

"Only if we're going to someone's sex club."

"Uh huh." Vincent placed his hands on the wheel but did not step on the gas. "Where are we going, anyway?"

"Hm? Thought you would have a place in mind."

"Not really."

Nala slumped in her seat. Her finger wrapped around the end of her hair and twirled it until she felt the pressure on her scalp. *I wonder what it feels like to have my hair pulled…* Where did that come from? One moment she was thinking about food and fun, and the next she was back in that sex club, feeling Vincent's cock swell within her while she imagined her hair tight against her head. "*Pull my hair, asshole!*" she would cry, and by the cosmos he would.

The man sitting next to her did not look like a man who would go around pulling hair and fucking women from behind. He looked like Average Joe trying to get from the supermarket to the bank before heading home. *Not so sexy*. Now, if Vincent were in his work clothes, or, better yet, his Aviary attire? Ohoho. Nala was becoming a little too comfortable around that Vincent. This guy looked like he could be her cousin come to pick her up from the mall.

"Take me to your favorite place in Portland."

"Huh?"

Nala patted his arm and gestured to the steering wheel. "Take me to your favorite place opened on a Sunday. I'm sure a guy like you has his haunts he likes to go to. Pick a place we can chill and talk."

"My favorite place in Portland…" his mouth twisted, as if to say, "*You think such a place exists?*" Nala would like to see him try to say that. Even she had her favorite place. It was a park at the end of the street, but it had a great view of downtown. "I've never had someone ask me about that before."

"Well, let's go."

"Sure. Let's."

It was Nala's first time seeing the car pull away in broad daylight. From this vantage she could see the undersides of all the trees lining the street. A camera crew wandered up and down the sidewalk, perhaps looking for another scene in Grimm, or one of those other TV shows they filmed in the city. *Been late to work more than once because they shut down a street to film.* Nala looked away, catching Vincent's profile as his head emerged from his hoodie. Shorn dark hair glistened in, what, sweat? Rain? The man was so tragically casual that it was hard to tell. *You'd never guess he was a billionaire looking at him.* Nala had to be careful. Hanging around men dressed like this made her drop her guard. At least when Vincent was in a suit she felt no need to open up or order him around.

They crossed the nearest bridge into downtown – and then kept going. Soon they were entering the hills that would either take them to nearby Beaverton or some of the swankier homes in the area. *Is he taking me to his place? Is that where a man hangs out on his days off?* Nala had to wonder how a man like Vincent lived. He didn't seem like the type to keep a mansion in the high hills. Nah, more like a penthouse apartment. A smaller one. Something easy to keep clean, even with the help of a maid.

"Oh, I see." Nala chuckled as the car veered toward the rose gardens. Seemed like a poor time of year to view them, but who knew what a billionaire kept up his sleeve? "You like roses?"

They drove past. "Not really. Why? Do you? Should we go back?"

"No." Nala remained focused on the road before them. "Where are we going?"

"Here." The car made an abrupt left into a small parking lot at the bottom of a hill. A shuttle waited to take a new crop of tourists up to the top of the hill, where the world famous Japanese gardens lurked in a small corner of Portland. "Hope you don't mind I picked something outdoorsy."

"Mind? My people were made to be hardy in the out of doors."

They exited the car, Nala's arms stretching above her head. "Your people?" Vincent asked. The car doors locked with a soft click.

She lowered her arms. "Them stocky Russians. Haven't you figured that out yet?"

"I may have thought it, but with a name like Nazarov, there isn't much room to guess. You're either from that part of the world or in denial."

They walked a couple feet away from one another as they forewent the shuttle and started the trek up the hill. Little streams of water coursed down pavement, circling potholes, and emptying into natural ditches full of dead leaves and dirt. "Do you know where your family is from?" Nala had met tons of people who had no idea where their ancestors came from. It was such a strange concept to her. Being "Russian" was such a huge part of her identity growing up, even if her parents did their best to quash it so they could assimilate into American culture easier. *Especially back then.* The Berlin Wall had fallen before she was born, but even Nala still saw traces of the Iron Curtain drawn between her old communities and their all-around American neighbors. TV shows did not help.

"I think they're from Germany and Britain. Boring stuff."

"You think?"

"I really don't know. Maybe Dutch. My family has been here for hundreds of years. My mother joked that her grandfather came over on the Mayflower."

"My parents came from around Moscow in the '80s. My mom still has a bit of an accent."

Vincent asked the same thing every person ever asked her. "Do you speak Russian?"

"Speak it? Nah. I understand some of it, though, if it's my mom's dialect. She spoke it at home a lot, especially after my father died and she didn't care anymore."

"I'm sorry to hear that."

"Why? Wouldn't it be better for me to be exposed to it? You know what a lot of those first generation parents say. They regret holding their culture back from their kids because they were afraid they would be bullied or have troubles getting work. My parents were that way. I think they would have regretted it." Nala snorted. "My sister taught herself a lot of Russian anyway. Minored in it in undergrad."

"That's cool. I tried learning Mandarin. Didn't take."

"I know nothing but English and some dirty, casual Russian. My Spanish classes in high school have not stuck."

"It's the true American way. Everyone is monolingual, unless they secretly aren't."

"Monolingual, immigrants, or overachievers who speak several languages a piece, none of them very well." Nala had met a ton of those since moving to Portland. They always knew Spanish, German, and Japanese. *Always* Japanese, as she was reminded when they started up a winding walkway surrounded by bilingual signs. "Anyway, you like this place? Your favorite in the whole city?"

"That's open right now, yeah." Lo' and behold, Vincent pulled out a year pass as they approached the front gate. Tourists mingled in the gravelly entrance. Schoolchildren complained about wanting to go home. An artist carted in an easel and set of paints, and a plethora of photographers took turns coming in and out with their heavy equipment. It was the sort of sight Nala expected to see at one of these places. She had heard the Japanese gardens of Portland were world class, but had never gotten around to going. It cost money to go there and get in, after all.

Vincent flashed his pass and announced that Nala was his complimentary +1. "I've never been here before," Nala said. "Took a stroll through the Chinese gardens in Chinatown once. Doubt they're alike?"

"Not really. Come on." Vincent waved his hand for her to follow. "Check this place out."

"Yes, *sir.*"

Nala followed with a lackadaisical smile, but it was Vincent who stopped and glimpsed at her with a tired expression. *Don't like me even joking about that, huh?* Fine. Nala could mind herself, especially if another paycheck was on the line.

The gardens had no particular route to follow. Some people went right, some went left, and all wandered around aimlessly. The occasional sign pointed the way to a landmark, like the Zen garden or teahouse. For every corner that was devoid of life and as tranquil as one's own blank mind, there was another packed with people taking pictures and pointing out different plants to one another. Nala didn't know anything about that. She knew nothing about gardening, art, or even much about East Asian culture. *He says he took Mandarin. Is that similar to Japanese?* She would never ask that out loud, out of fear of embarrassing herself. For all she knew, it was like asking if there was a difference between Russian and Ukrainian. In her experience, most monolingual Americans assumed a flat *no.*

The two of them walked along a single path, stopping here and there to observe something in silence. Sometimes Vincent would catch her attention regarding a leaf or the way plants were laid out. Other times Nala would hold up their progression so she could squint and read a sign. It was interesting, to say the least. Interesting, but not something she would choose to do on her own.

So what does this guy like about this place? Vincent looked neither bored nor enthralled. He walked and spoke as he always did, mouth taut and eyes narrowed. He always looked as if he were about two seconds away from either popping a man's head off or lying down for a long nap. Before, Nala assumed he was a stoic, antisocial mess who worked too much and didn't care about "fun." Now, knowing what she did about his past, she realized that a lot of the fog swarming his frame was that familiar face of grief.

This man was in as much pain as she was. Because of Xavier Crow? Nala continued to steal glances at him as they stood in front of a pond, watching carp swim in their brilliant orange glory. Vincent's eyes followed every trail they weaved, his face finally relaxing. Nala half expected him to say, "I used to come here with Desirée all the time."

They were in love. Nala didn't need him to tell her that. Vincent wouldn't be vengeful if Desirée were "just" a classmate whose project he completed in her memory. He may keep an interest in finding out what really happened to her, but he wouldn't go as far as he had. He wouldn't have infiltrated The Aviary, let alone with a woman he just met. *They were really in love.* Crow had crossed the wrong man. Somehow, Nala had been lucky enough to meet him.

Vincent sat on an empty bench overlooking a wide, man-made lake en route to the teahouse. It was quieter here, although some people continued to pass before him. Nala lingered by the railing, watching water ripple and trees sway in the breeze, before quietly sitting next to him and trying to see what he saw.

Peace. Reverie. A slice of the world that was built for meditation and reflection. Even Nala, who shivered a little beneath her hoodie and had to stuff her hands in her front pockets, had to admit that the world was a better place when she sat here.

"It's a nice spot." Her voice acted as if it broke the fragile glass surrounding Vincent's space. He turned his head toward her, elbows resting on his bent knees. "I can see why you like it. No one bothers you here."

"It's easy to sort out of my thoughts. Business, personal…" Vincent shrugged. "I might have come here today anyway, even if you didn't suggest it."

"But I didn't…"

"You asked me to take you to my favorite place, right? Well, now you know. Even my assistant doesn't know he can find me here."

Nala gripped the edge of the bench, her fingers burning in a cold breeze that blew by at that moment. "Thanks for bringing me here. What did you want to talk about? Friday?"

It seemed so far away now. This man was different. This feeling was different. What happened on Friday? Eh. It didn't matter. So what if Vincent had a lapse in lust and reason? Wasn't like Nala didn't want it. She was still a bit tiffed he didn't bother to make sure she came too, but he knew now…

"No, not here," Vincent said, interrupting her thoughts. "We should be in private for that discussion. But it's good to clear my mind, I guess."

"You didn't have to do it with me, so, I'm thankful, I suppose."

"No problem."

They remained a respectful distance. People passing by, like the young family trying to get opportune photos with their toddlers, and the German couple gruffly discussing the map, would have never guessed they were a couple. *Because we're not, I guess.* It didn't bother Nala. She wasn't looking for love, especially with a man she was in an undercover mission with.

Still, boundaries had fallen the other night. The man had touched her. *Intimately.* He had taken her in such an animalistic way that she couldn't help but feel connected to him even now.

"I'm not mad about Friday," she muttered. "It was kinda weird, thinking about it, but I won't pretend I didn't like it."

Vincent remained silent. Wind rustled in the dormant cherry trees above them.

Nala scooted closer, perhaps searching for some warmth, but with a man as closed off as Vincent, the best she could hope for was some of his hot breath as he talked in her direction. "I've been trying to stay distant because I don't want to lose sight of my sister. I was in a relationship before she died, you know."

A curt voice entered her ear. "No, I didn't."

Although he didn't ask, Nala continued. "Nothing serious, although it lasted a couple years. We didn't even live together. Just hung out on weekends, talked on the phone sometimes, and, well… did couple stuff." Vincent was right. Best not to directly talk about sex in public like this. "He was more like a best friend than a real lover. When my sister died… I couldn't do it anymore. I didn't want anything to do with anyone. Some people rally others around them when they're grieving. Me? I pushed them all away. My mother was the same. We pushed each other away. She had lost her husband and a child. How could I compare that to losing a sister? It didn't matter that I was still around. One daughter was alive, but the other was dead. Let alone the golden child who was probably going to cure cancer."

"I see."

At least Vincent was able to pretend he cared about what she had to say. "So I dumped my boyfriend. Is it weird I've never missed him? I mean, sometimes I wish he was around to play video games and forget about life with, but I don't like… miss his *touch* or weird stuff like that. He was super average."

Vincent leaned against the bench, hands disappearing into his hoodie pockets.

"I don't know why I'm telling you this. It's not like we're actually friends. I guess I've gone so long without talking about myself to someone that… well, after Friday, we don't have much left sacred between us."

"Only emotionally."

"Only emotionally," Nala agreed. "You seem like a possibly nice guy, Vincent. A hurt guy. A really guarded guy, but potentially nice. I don't blame you for any of that. God knows I can't let go either."

The world continued to go by at a snail's pace as they sat there, taking in the scenery. *I bet in the spring this place is gorgeous.* Cherry blossoms. Plum blossoms. Greens and sunlight as far as the eye could see. Did crickets chirp in unison during hot summer evenings? Could you see the stars twinkling above the ponds? Would Nala come here in a few months and be completely blown away, her heart ripped to shreds because it couldn't contain such natural and man-cultivated beauties? Was this where Vincent came to think through making a billion dollars? The man had since picked up a small twig and began writing equations in the dirt. After he had smeared and rewritten them half a dozen times, he pulled out a pad and pencil and wrote down a hard copy. *Oh my God, he's officially a geek.*

"You'll be able to let go one day," he said, long after Nala's last reply. She had almost forgotten what he referred to. "As soon as we make Crow pay for his crimes."

"How will we even do that?"

"I have no idea. One step at a time."

"I would hope a genius billionaire like you knows what to do next."

He shrugged. "Fucking beats me today." His last equation disappeared in the dust as he stood and stepped all over it. "Let's go. Sun's going down fast."

At that time of year, such a thing was a given. But he was right. The longer they sat there, the faster the sun disappeared behind the surrounding trees. Fewer people walked by. A nip entered the air that was not there before.

Nala got up and walked by Vincent's side. They were slow going, not because of foot traffic blocking the paths, but because the tall man's strides did not wish to outpace Nala's smaller ones. Their hands remained in their pockets, hoods covering their hair and ears, and breath as frosty as snow every time they exhaled. At least it wasn't raining. For once.

When they stopped at a pedestrian turnout in a grove of growing cherry trees, Nala caught a look on Vincent's visage that said the man hid more than a few words of pain. Whatever he thought about, it was making him think of things – and people – lost so long ago.

Nala drew her hand out of her pocket and tugged on his arm. When his hand fell from his hoodie pocket, she wrapped her fingers around him, willing what warmth she had into his body.

They stood there, awkwardly, Nala's affection not going unnoticed, but unremarked. Vincent did not shrug her off, but he continued to stare ahead, fixated on a contraption that made noise every few seconds when it filled with water. Once the top was full, it *banged!* downward and spilled the water into a receptacle. A sign said it was a classic contraption used to frighten raccoons and other small critters. If anything, Nala found the rhythmic sound soothing.

Her hand squeezed Vincent's. A heavy breath racked his body, sending shivers through Nala, who cleared her throat and hoped they would soon move on. They weren't too far from the path that would take them back to the entrance.

When they continued, it was hand-in-hand, their fingers tentatively entwined in what was perhaps the barest minimum in regards to affection. Yet for two torn up people like Nala and Vincent, hell, it was more than efficient at reminding them that nobody had to be alone, no matter who they were or what they had been through.

Nala needed reminding of that.

Chapter 13

She didn't ask where they were going when Vincent pulled out of the parking lot and drove with purpose back into downtown. They got stuck in some late afternoon traffic, but it wasn't enough to trap them on the infamous Burnside Street. They drove past historical hotels, the biggest indie bookstore in the world, and parts of Chinatown that even Nala hadn't explored before. Vincent whipped to the left before they hit the bridge, taking them up a road weaving through barren industrial parks.

If I thought he were a serial killer, this would be it! By now it was all but black outside, with the occasional light twinkling either from a building or from a plane coming in for landing. Nala didn't think much of anything when Vincent pulled down a dark street lined with big, brick buildings that looked like they hadn't been used in years.

Even so, he pulled into a small carport blocked off by a secure fence, cell phone in hand as he called for a pizza delivery.

"You hate anything?"

"No anchovies."

Nala stood outside the car, taking in the smell of the Willamette River half a mile away. A freeway passed by, high enough in the air for cars to wink in and out of existence as they went on their way. A drizzle began to fall. A part of her was glad to be led up a flight of metal stairs, while another part of her wanted to continue to stand and take in the past of Portland.

She shouldn't have been surprised by how Vincent lived. A young, affluent bachelor like him was either the penthouse lover or someone drawn to converted lofts. Of course he was all about the latter.

Exposed brick, exposed beams. Open living that would make most middle-class yuppies salivate. The wide, open living area went straight into a dining area and then a spacious kitchen with all the trimmings. A guest bathroom sat to the side, sporting one of the only doors in the loft aside from closets and a back door permanently shut. Up a twirling, wrought-iron staircase was the loft itself. Even from down by the entrance, Nala could see a king-sized bed draped in cream-colored comforters, pillows, and who knew what else.

It didn't *look* like much, but between the location and how trendy such a place was, Nala was sure it cost at least a cool mil. It looked well lived in, so Vincent probably purchased it before he became an uber rich asshole.

If there were any great lights in the place, Nala never got to see them. Vincent seemed content to live in the dark, with only a few, soft glowing lamps illuminating the kitchen, dining area, and the bed upstairs. Nala didn't ask for permission as she flopped onto a leather couch facing a large flatscreen TV. Video game consoles were neatly stacked beneath the coffee table. An advance copy of the latest *Fallout* game lay on top of the glass. *Of course he likes playing games about total desolation. Of course.* This man was so damn angsty inside that it almost made *Nala* laugh.

"Pizza will be here in about five," Vincent said. "Guy knows me well. Always gives me first dibs on his route."

"How often do you order pizza?"

"I dunno. Once, twice a week? I also tip well."

"Oh, I'm sure." The man had no qualms slipping her a grand a week for pretending to be his girlfriend, so the pizza guy probably got a Benny for putting Vincent first on his delivery route.

Nala had to hand it to Vincent. He had a great view of the river from here, including of the boats gliding effortlessly back and forth like tiny white dots. Inner east Portland lit up as the evening wore on. There, in the comforting warmth of Vincent Lane's loft, Nala almost felt at home. It was better than Patrick's place, anyway.

"It's not as cozy as a craftsman like yours, but…"

"Hm? You think I own that house?"

"Well, no, but…"

She cut him off again as he offered her a glass of water. "I barely even live there. I pay three-hundred bucks a month, plus my part of the utilities, to say I live there. Really, I live there on paper. It's not a home." Nala wouldn't mention the sleeping arrangement.

"Forget I said anything."

The pizza arrived in three minutes. The man was more than happy to take Vincent's generous tip before going on his way, and the smell of veggie pizza smacked Nala right in the hungry stomach.

"You play?" Vincent asked, pointing to his video games as he sat down with pizza on plates. Nala helped herself to the two slices he gave her, mindlessly taking note that the box was on the kitchen counter with more slices inside. "I don't have as much time anymore. Too busy coding this shit to play it."

"You make video games, huh?"

"Not anymore. I dallied in college. Then…"

"Then your girlfriend died and you decided to go the app route like she was going to."

Vincent put down his pizza and glared at her. "I never said she was my girlfriend."

"I deduced." The pizza was the perfect balance of greasy and tasty. "And I don't really play. Not anymore. That was more my ex's thing and I played with him." Fallout, though. Anything by Bethesda was good shit. *I had the most kickass Nord mage on Skyrim.* Oh, the things she lost when she dumped her boyfriend because of grief.

Apparently Vincent was not going to talk about video games anymore. "Desirée wasn't my girlfriend," he said, his voice low. "She was my fiancée."

"Ouch." Nala hadn't figured they were that serious, but that was only because Vincent seemed as personable as a fruit fly. When he wasn't fucking her, anyway. "I'm sorry." That explained a lot, though. Fiancée probably conjured up a different kind of grief from girlfriend.

"Thanks. We were two months away from getting married when she died. That was three years ago, though. Feels like yesterday."

"It feels like yesterday when my sister last called me to make plans for Christmas." Grief had a funny way of bending time like that.

Was there anything more to say? Nala wiped her fingers on a napkin and sank deep into the comfortable couch. Vincent remained silent, as he always did, jaw working on pizza while countenance whirled in thought. The man spent a lot of his time thinking… Nala supposed that was necessary for someone who made a living off being on the cutting edge of technology.

"So, there was something you wanted to talk about," Nala said after a long, unperturbed silence. Plates were empty on the coffee table. Drinks were half consumed. She and Vincent lay sprawled on their respective couches, staring at the dark, lofted ceiling while thinking of God knew what. Even Nala wasn't sure what went through her mind right now.

"Yeah. A couple of things."

Neither of them moved. Neither of them said a word.

"Well?" Nala sat up, hoping that some movement would get him talking. "You've dragged me around half of Portland and brought me home, where you plied me with pizza and a few words about video games and your dead fiancée. I think it's time you started talking."

"If I may confess…" Vincent joined her in sitting up. "I had a lot more resolve earlier."

"What happened?"

His stare was unwavering. "You did, Nala."

"Oh, come on." She laughed. "Be serious like you usually are."

"I am serious. When you were a woman helping me with something… before you had a real identity to me… it was much easier to tell you things bluntly. Now I feel like I have to cushion everything."

"Why?"

"Because I don't want to scare or hurt you."

Nala shuffled in her seat, thighs going up and down as she stuffed her hands farther beneath them. Her own natural heat was the only comforting thing in that big, cold loft right now. "I can take it. Whatever you need to say, I can take it. Even if it scares me a little, it's worth it, if it means getting vengeance for my sister. And your fiancée, I guess. And anyone else he's hurt. What is my pain and discomfort if it means having a chance to take down that son of a bitch?"

Vincent had an uncanny way of studying her. Uncanny because it vaguely reminded Nala of her sister, who used to stare at her much in the same way, as if she were dithering between giving her the cold, hard truth of a situation or continuing to coddle her because she cared too much. *This man is definitely not my sister.* The implications were too grim.

"Go on. Tell me what you want to tell me so badly."

"It's actually two things." Vincent reached into his back jeans pocket and pulled out a small envelope embossed in gold. Had he been carrying that thing all day? "Guess I'll tell you this one first." He handed Nala the envelope. "It's an invitation to the next Aviary meeting on Wednesday. It's at The Crow's Nest, where he holds most of the weeknight meetings."

Before Nala could pull out the letter and read it, Vincent gave her the bomb.

"He wants us to become official members, which means we need to perform."

She didn't bother to read it. She didn't need Crow's words telling her to bend over and get spanked in front of him.

"I didn't think you'd be excited." Vincent picked up his glass and wetted the back of his throat. "It's good, though. It means he trusts us and wants us in his inner circle. We'll soon be invited to his house. I have plans for that, if you're interested."

"What kind of plans?" Nala tried to focus on that and not the conflicting images entering her mind. *BDSM play with Vincent… but in front of those weirdos. And Crow.* Fucking Crow.

"I dunno, are you a sneaky woman?"

"You mean can I sneak around?" She grinned. "With the best of them. When I was a real shit I used to sneak money out of my mom's purse to get gum and stuff. Let me tell you, she is *not* easy to get past. I still don't know if she knows I did it."

"Good. If I can get you near his office or something, I'll need you to infiltrate."

"Like a spy? Awesome." It was a scary thought, and yet Nala's adrenaline was already pumping in anticipation. *I'll find the evidence, Vincent. You play your smooth businessman game, and I'll get the evidence to take him down.* Damn, they could make a good team.

"We'll still need to perform. Be convincing."

Nala came down from her productive high. "I see. So you gonna swing me over your lap and spank me?"

Perhaps she said it too candidly, for Vincent's eyes widened in disbelief. "We don't have to do that, but we should plan something out. Something you're comfortable with."

Butterflies twisted in her gut. "I'm not going to be *comfortable* with anything, but not wanting to die would be great."

"No spanking."

"You'll have to buy me a few more dinners first."

Vincent ignored her. He rubbed his chin, lost in thought as if he were figuring out a complicated algorithm instead of guessing what to do about Nala and her nubile body. "We could do a bondage show. No actual touching, but you'll have to make sure you look like you're getting off on it. Can you do that?"

Nala nodded. "Tie me up. Whatever. Better than you spanking me."

"All right. I'll have to brush up on my bondage knots. I'm a bit rusty."

Nala almost missed that. "Excuse me? A bit rusty? What, do you tie bondage knots for *fun* in your spare time?"

She couldn't imagine it. This cool and collected man getting a hard dick from tying knots of all things. Sure, spanking was erotic with the right person. God knew the man was hard as shit fucking her the other night, acting like some badass who owned and controlled her person. *Calm down, Nala. That was us getting the sexual tension out of our systems.* Explosive chemistry. Yup. Bottled it up too long and then *bam!* Body fluids everywhere.

Yet Vincent did not falter. He held her gaze, challenging her to defy him – if she dared.

"That's the other thing I wanted to talk about." His voice… how low and gruff it was, devolving into that beastly growl he acquired the other night when he thrust Nala against a dark wall. *Oh, shit.* She knew what was coming now. Something she had long suspected ever since that first night when Vincent's strong, commanding grip saved her from herself.

Oh, shit!

Vincent stood, hands slapping against either side of Nala's head, his fingers gripping the back of the couch so tightly that she cowered beneath him. Not out of fear. Out of a natural respect that made her think he was a man worthy of shrinking before.

This wasn't a game to him.

The next few words out of his mouth? She expected the first part, but the latter hit her right in the chest. In the heart.

"I'm a Dom, Nala. That's what makes this infiltration so easy for me to play at. Because I'm not playing. I'm really like those other 'weirdos' at those meetings. And let me tell you, *Nala…*" His hot breath hit her face, threatening to kiss her lips if she turned her head back too far. *Oh my God, no!* She couldn't fall for him like this right now. The other night? That was all hormones. Nala was supposed to be in control of them now. In control!

His nose traced a line from her cheek to her throat, catching her words there, her complete and utterly forgotten sanity.

"Let me tell you. From that first night I met you, I've wanted to do nothing but take out all my latent frustrations on you. Because you're making me come undone, Nala Nazarov. I haven't felt like this in so fucking long. I didn't even think I was capable of wanting a woman like that again. It scares me. It makes me feel like I'm losing my vision. You want to stay focused on your mission of vengeance? Well, so do I, but with you unknowingly seducing me at every turn, I am finding it very, *very* difficult to stay focused. One minute I'm planning my takedown of Xavier Crow, and the next I'm fantasizing about your body beneath mine, writhing as you struggle to take my cock."

Fingers lightly touched her arms. Even through her thick hoodie, Nala tingled. *Oh. My. God.* Her nipples hardened in her bra. Her thighs heated up in her jeans. *No, stop… no, don't stop…* Her lips lifted toward his. Any other man, and Nala would have made the first move. This was Vincent, though. She wanted *him* making the move. Like Friday night, when he gave her the best sex of her life, even without an actual orgasm.

"So if we're going to keep doing this, Nala…" God, she loved the way his tongue slipped off the roof of his mouth when he said her name. Like it was honey he flicked off his precious organ. *I wonder what it would feel like on me.* She knew what it felt like in her mouth, down her throat, and even on her neck. Elsewhere? This man could do some serious damage. "I need you to know where I stand. I want you. I want your body. I want to tame this wild, contrary streak of yours. I need to know that I can trust you, and the only woman I can trust in this venture is one who knows how to follow my directions."

"I…"

"No." He pushed himself away. No longer a danger of kissing her, but still imposing above her body. His arms had her trapped – not that Nala wanted to go. "I'm serious. I'm not looking for love. It's best if love isn't even on the table. Let me tell you, though, I've gone to bed more than one night since meeting you and thought of nothing but making you my sub."

Nala's lips parted, her mouth dry.

"Let's put it this way. We have to be a Dom/sub couple to be a part of The Aviary. I'm fine with that. I'll Top you until the end of time – or until that man is either dead or in jail. I'll fuck you. I'll tie you up, spank you, consume your whole body both in private and as a performance. On my end, it will be real. I'm not acting, Nala. I'm showing both you and Crow who I am. To that end, I will gain everyone's trust. What will you do?"

Her hands clasped upon her chest, as if her meager barrier was enough to keep this new side of Vincent at bay. *No, it's not new. He's been this way the whole time.* Kissing her. Leading her around. Telling her what they were going to do. Sending her money. *Fucking* her like that. The man was a Dom through and through. Nala had been too much in denial, too consumed with her own mission to have seen it.

Until now – no, until Friday – she never thought such a thing would turn her on.

"I don't know anything about that," she said, meeker than she ever intended. "I've never done that. I don't know how to sub."

"I'll teach you. I'll make it so you're not lying. Because…" One hand lifted, caressing Nala's cheek. She looked away, her breaths ragged and her arousal threatening to betray her. "You won't be lying. You'll know exactly what to do. And you'll want it."

"No… no I'm not like that."

"You're not? You seemed to like it the other night."

"Vincent, you're scaring me."

"I'm sorry." He put a little more distance between them, but it wasn't enough. "It's not about scaring you. It's about owning you, even for only a few hours a week."

Owning me? No man owned her. No man controlled her. She wasn't like that. She wasn't into that. No… no she wasn't…

Them, in bed, naked, his hips thrusting between hers as her fingers clawed at his chest…

Them, on this couch, clothes barely off as he treated her to round 2 of Friday night, this time with her climax matching his…

Them, sharing tender moments, because that's what one did in a relationship.

"Don't be scared, Nala. I'll take care of you in ways you've never experienced. You won't want for anything. In return, I'll trust you, wholeheartedly. Without trust, we cannot succeed in our mission."

He spoke a language of flowers. No, not poetry. Flowers, as in he promised her a sunshine-laden meadow as opposed to the muddy valley she trekked through now. Except Nala didn't rely on anyone but herself. She couldn't. She didn't know how.

So, perhaps he would trust her, but would she trust him?

"Do you want me, Nala? Do you want to make love to me in the way I want to make love to you?"

Against her instincts, Nala nodded, frightened of herself. Of her body. Of her heart.

"Like I told you, I will teach you how to submit to me in a convincing manner. No one will suspect we're not a real Dom/sub couple. Because we *will* be. Do you understand?"

Nala wanted to say no. Then she thought of Tasha, of Desirée, of all the men and women who died because they knew too much or almost did too much good for the world. *Their sacrifice is nothing compared to mine.* Perhaps it was a dangerous way to think. Nala didn't care. She would do whatever it took, no matter how much it went against her perceived nature.

"I'll do it," she muttered. "Teach me, Vincent." New resolve surged within her, rising to the challenge she now set for herself. "I will submit."

"Good. We don't have much time, so we better start tonight."

His kiss almost destroyed her.

Chapter 14

Never before had Nala forgotten her woes so easily. One minute she was focusing on what she had to do for the good of her mission, and the next she entirely forgot what that mission was. Deep inside her subconscious, she chastised herself for this, but the greater parts of her knew it was futile to feel bad about it. Because sometimes a girl needed to feel *good.*

Vincent made her feel fucking good.

"Like that," he muttered on her lips, still overtaking her on the couch. She had barely moved, but here she was, sinking so deep into the leather couch that she thought it might swallow her whole. Assuming it could beat Vincent to the punch, of course. His lips were devouring her, sucking on her mouth, plundering it, and exploring some of her innermost parts before diverting to her ears, her throat, and sweet, reddening cheeks. "Don't be a wilting flower. It doesn't suit you."

That's right I'm not a wilting flower! She felt a bit wilting beneath Vincent, but she knew what he meant. *You're not the kind of sub who is passive. Be active in our experiences. Defer to my orders, and my wants, but don't pretend to be a doll.* The fact she understood that so easily made her shiver beyond control.

Vincent sensed it. "Fuck me, Nala. I'm glad you want this."

She gasped as he sucked her throat, his hand pulling apart her ponytail and threading fingers through her thick, straight hair. "Would you do this if I didn't?"

"No. I would die of lust, though."

Her arms wrapped around his shoulders, trying to bring him down upon her. "Me too. Fuck me, Vincent."

"Fuck me, *sir.*"

"Fuck me, *Master.*"

He bit her earlobe. A squeal of delight echoed against his shoulder. "Good catch." Vincent pulled back, still threading her hair, letting it fall in a wispy veil to her body. "I don't mind you calling me either one. Although Master gets me harder, and hopefully you wetter."

"Everything is getting me wet right now."

"Good." He kissed her again, his grip on the back of her head unrelenting. "I'm going to hold back, unlike the other night. For fuck's sake, if only you knew what you were doing to me in that dress."

"That you picked out."

Vincent lifted her hoodie, pulling it above her head and casting it onto the other couch. His hands went to her breasts, hiding beneath a T-shirt and bra. As he massaged her, aroused her, he said, "I didn't think that far ahead with it. I thought I could handle you. Thought I could *behave* around you." Her T-shirt went up. Thick, masculine fingers yanked her bra cups down and immediately pinched her nipples. *Fuck!* Nala writhed on the couch, as he wanted. "You're too irresistible for me, though. You're a succubus, Nala. Maybe you don't intend to be, but from the night we met you've been both the best and the worst thing to happen to me in so long. Fuck me every which way, I *want* you."

He pinched her so hard that she cried out in pain. Sweet, delectable pain. *This wouldn't have felt good with my ex…* Because that guy wasn't a Dom. He wasn't a man who made that sort of thing feel good. Nala was lucky if he got her off. *I was used to doing it myself.*

"Do you want me? Like this?"

There was almost a hint of desperation in his voice. Careful desperation. Like hell Vincent Lane would be *desperate* around her. "Yeah…"

"That's not good enough. I want to hear you *say* it." Vincent pinched her again. Nala sucked in a shriek before her hand slapped over her mouth. *I doubt anyone can hear me.* That was both fantastic and dreadful.

"I want you…"

"What do you want me to do?"

His fingers rubbed her breasts, as if that could soothe the delightful pain she experienced. "I want you to teach me how to submit to you."

"And?"

Man wants an end game. "Fuck me. Please."

Vincent stepped back. At first Nala was afraid he would trip backward over the coffee table, but he remained firm, neither swaying nor flinching. "It's not enough to submit. You'll have to serve me, too."

You like that sort of thing, huh? Nala wasn't surprised. Why would she be surprised at this point? Men who made it to his level of success and fortune – let alone so early in life – had to have this streak in them. *I wonder what he's like during board meetings.* Nah, that was boring. Nala wanted to know what he was like in his *bed.*

"I'll serve you, Master."

She couldn't hide the sarcasm in her voice. Nevertheless, she didn't lie. *You want me to bring you a drink, sir? I'll do it if it means getting that dick right now.* Girl had to keep herself from drooling.

If Vincent was displeased with her tone, he didn't say anything. He was more interested in taking her hand, pulling her off the couch… and swinging his arm behind her legs.

"Whoa!" Nala was in the air, legs kicking in his grasp as she flung both arms around his neck. Safe to say she had never felt this… possessed… before. *I'm his thing. I belong to him, right now.* The baby feminist in her was about to have a shit fit. Good thing she knew how to shut that asshole up. "Dude, you're strong."

He said nothing as he carried her across his loft and began their ascent up the stairs. Nala closed her eyes, hands squeezing his hoodie as her nose inhaled the heady musk of his cologne. *I want this scent all around me. I want to smell like him in the morning. I want to smell like… his.* The more she submitted to this idea – and to him – the more heat swelled between her legs, and the more her nipples begged for that rough attention. *Pinch me, bite me, pull my hair.* She was so horny she was almost game to put on a saddle and be ridden around like a pony. *Tame me, fucker.*

Each step was like entering another layer of hell. No, not Dante's hell. The hell of anticipation and eternal sexual frustration. Not like Nala forgot how she was left Friday night. *He better make me come. Multiple times.* She was submitting to him, and that meant she wanted a real reward.

She knew she would have to earn it.

"Don't worry," he muttered, stepping onto the landing of the lofted bedroom. "I'll make it up to you. Friday, that is."

Nala landed with a hard *wumpf* on his bed. His soft, pliable bed that shuddered beneath her petite body. She braced herself, breasts still hanging out of her bra and shoes dirtying the end of the comforter.

"I was so wrapped up in my need for you and your body," Vincent continued, standing beside her and grabbing the hem of his sweatshirt, "that I couldn't think of anything but my drive to have you. I wasn't going to stop until I saw myself spilling from your cunt." The sweatshirt came up, taking his T-shirt with it. *Oh my sweet, merciful deities upon high.* The man was *toned.* Those abs! Nala could have licked her breakfast off them! And those arms… this was her first time seeing them. No wonder he was so strong.

Getinmegetinmegetinme! She was rubbing her own breasts and barely realized it.

"You're going to come so much," he snarled, pulling Nala's legs apart so he could kneel between them. "You'll be begging to make it stop so you can breathe again."

That was a winning endorsement if Nala ever heard one!

"Come here." Vincent hooked his fingers around the waist of her jeans, tugging hard enough to make her slide down the bed. "I want to look at you. Don't be shy."

Shy? Me? She thought that, and yet Nala had her arms crossed in front of her breasts as if she had any chance of modesty. When Vincent gripped her wrists and held her hands above her head, letting her fingers play with the bottom edge of a pillow, she felt so exposed that she couldn't help but defer before him. The way he devoured her breasts with his eyes reminded Nala of a hungry wolf about to consume its prey. *If you fuck me like a wolf, I might be yours forever.* She kept thinking about his cock surging into her Friday night. It had barely made its way in there. Would she be better prepared tonight?

"Stay still." Vincent's hands traveled down her arms, to her shoulders, to her breasts, where they grabbed and kneaded her until she was whimpering in near-worship. "You're mine to explore right now."

Nala had never been put beneath this kind of spotlight before. So when Vincent dragged his nails down her stomach and then quickly unbuttoned her jeans, she sucked in a desperate cry, if only because she didn't want to appear meek before him. *Relax, girl, this guy thinks you're so hot he can't control his dick around you.* There was nothing she hid beneath her clothes that could possibly turn him off. Not her stretch marks around her hips, not her coarse tufts of pubic hair covering her mound, and certainly not the slick folds of her pussy as he pulled down her underwear and spread her legs before his famished gaze. There was enough light shining from downstairs for him to see the pink of her insides.

"If you're not confident in yourself," Vincent said, teasing the inside of her thigh with his fingertips. "You damn well should be. Because you are gorgeous."

No one had sincerely called her gorgeous before. Pretty, yes, plenty of times. Beautiful? Occasionally. *Gorgeous?* Next he would call her stunning!

"You've almost stunned me into silence."

Close enough.

"Nala," he muttered, leaning down and covering her chest in kisses. "I love saying your name. Nala. Nala. *Nala.*"

She loved hearing her name. Especially as he continued to whisper it against her skin, lowering his head more and more until his breath touched her nether lips. *Oh my fuck.* Nala closed her eyes, sighing against the bed beneath her. It had been so long since anyone paid her this kind of attention that she had almost forgotten how wonderful it could be. Her guards continued to lower. Pretty soon Vincent would enclose himself around her heart and send her for a tailspin she could never recover from.

Two weeks ago, even one week ago, Nala would have never guessed that she would be happily spread on Vincent's bed, feeling his tongue push into her folds and lick languidly, heavily along her slit. The tip of his tongue flicked against her clit, sending ripples – no, *waves* – of endless pleasure through her body. *Holy shit, he's good.* The man feasted on her like the caught prey she was. No pathetic little licks. No bare minimum attention so he could say, "Hey, I went down on her, okay?" Nope. This was what the sex in oral sex meant. The man was making love to her pussy with his tongue, and Nala could barely contain herself as her clit became more sensitive with every passing lap.

I'm gonna come on his face. It was a plan by that point. Her skin shivered, nipples tingling in arousal as her center released an endless stream of little resistance. Really, drowning him was the least she could do after Friday night. Man was gonna pump her full of liquid? Oh, two could play at that game! *He better prepare himself.* Fuck that. Nala better prepare *herself!*

"Oh!" His tongue was heavier now, Vincent's hands bracing themselves against her thighs as he went as far in as he dared. In *her.* That world-shaking tongue slipped from her slit to her insides so effortlessly that it felt like it glided between heaven and nirvana. Nala's hips began to buck at his face, willing his tongue deeper into her. *Fuck me with your tongue, stud.* The ripple of his muscles as his head moved up and down was one of the most erotic things she had ever seen – never mind what was happening between her legs.

Nala went from pleasured to orgasmic within another second.

"*Fuck!*" She threw her head back, hips thrusting wildly against Vincent's face as one torment of ecstasy after another overcame her. She thought she was going to drown him? She was the one drowning now, cast away in a sea of conflicting thoughts and feelings that would destroy a lesser woman. Yet every time she began to worry, Vincent would caress her with his tongue, and she was gone again.

It felt good, it felt guilty to give herself completely over to sex and all its delicious trappings.

She opened her eyes and found his staring intently back at her. "Oh my God," she whimpered, coming down from her orgasm just to have another one. This man needed to mind his abilities before he killed her.

Well, he did say she was going to come so much that she would have to beg for it to stop…

"Shit," he muttered, pulling away from her as Nala whined in defeat. *Okay, you win, I'm all yours.* "Shit, shit." Vincent's chin was wet. His thumb slipped against her thigh easily, drawing small streams of wetness across her skin. "*Shit.*"

"Uh huh," Nala responded. "Shit."

Vincent sat up, wiping the lower part of his face with his right hand. When he hooked it beneath Nala's left knee again, she gasped at how wet it was. *Wet with me, of all things.* "You smell so damn good."

His head went down again, nose nuzzling against her wet folds, dipping into her, taking her for who she was. Nala bit her lip and refused to say anything that would ruin the moment, whatever the moment was supposed to be.

"Kiss me," Nala whimpered. "I want to taste myself on you."

She didn't think he was going to do it. After all, it hadn't been his idea, and Nala figured that *everything* was supposed to be his idea from now on. Then his lips came, bruising hers as they had bruised her elsewhere. Nala dared to lower her arms and feel him within her embrace, wrapping between her legs and pushing the bulge in his pants against her thigh.

"You're mine." One growl after another passed from his lips to hers. "When I'm done with you, you'll understand that well."

Nala hoped that all this heavy kissing and petting would lead to him drawing himself out of his pants and into her. Heaven knew she was ready. Legs spread, slit wet, and body eager to be invaded and claimed. Yet Vincent held back, content to press his lips against her, to touch her breasts and throat and nothing else.

"I've made up the other night to you, don't you agree?"

There was only one correct response. Nala nodded, wordless. Vincent squeezed her breast so hard that she gasped into his ear instead.

"Good. Now that you know what I can provide you, it's time for me to know what you can provide *me*."

He sat up, his back straight and tall as his knees dug into his bed.

"Serve me, Nala."

Those were her only orders. Nothing specific, nothing that could tell her what it was he wanted, if anything. *Serve him, huh?* Did he want a massage? A bath drawn? Something to drink? Is that what he meant? Or did he want some sexual service? Nala eased herself onto her elbows, legs slowly closing as she turned her hips toward him. Her face was dangerously close to that toned abdomen laced in sweat. Even after what had happened a few minutes ago, Nala had never felt so *carnal* in her life.

"Yes, Master," she whispered, a light flickering in the back of her mind when she called him that.

Goodness, she was turning into one of *them*.

"Sort of sad how quickly I've got you calling me that. I was hoping you'd put up more of a fight so taming you would be that much sweeter."

Oh, Nala was not going down *that* easily. "Tonight I'm suggestible," she explained, lightly running her nails down his chest. "Tomorrow is another day and another chance for you to see the wild side of me."

"You seem pretty wild right now."

"You said…"

"I said I wanted to tame you, not strip you of what makes you *you*." He snatched her hand, taking it from his chest down to his zipper. "I don't dare think you would obey any other man but me. The day I see that spark leave your eyes is the day I give up being a Dom for good. I want you to enjoy every minute we spend together like this."

"Enjoy it, but obey you."

"You think those are mutually exclusive?"

His tender touch to her head and back placated her for now. "Not at all," she said, lowering his zipper. "Why don't you lie back, sir? I hear somebody wants to be served, and I only know one way to do it."

Vincent raised his eyebrows, one of the only ways *he* knew how to express anything. *We'll figure that out later.* If he wanted Nala to make some changes, then she expected the same in return. Like learning how to be a feeling human being again.

Nala watched in minor triumph as Vincent lowered himself to the bed, slumping slightly against a pillow with one arm propped up and the other resting lazily against his side. He watched her, expectantly, eyes burning in curiosity as she knelt on the bed and took off the last of her clothes.

"You're very beautiful with your hair down like that," he said softly, finger rubbing his upper lip. "You're pretty with it back, too, but this is better."

"I wear it back because it's easier that way, *sir.*"

"Just don't ever cut it. I'll be gutted."

He looked as if he wanted to reach out and touch her hair, but refrained. Yet Nala took his comments to heart and brought her hair forward, over her shoulders and framing her heart-shaped face. Locks of black landed on his jeans, tickling Nala's arms and scraping across the bed as she leaned forward on her hands.

She didn't know why she wanted to please this man so much. Well, it wasn't really about pleasing *him.* Right now it was about having fun, letting loose and exploring a facet of her sexuality she never considered before. So what if it led to more trust between them? That wasn't bad at all. *Just because I can put it out of my mind for a few hours and learn to breathe for fun instead of the sake of it… doesn't mean I forget who I am or what I'm about.* She wasn't afraid to tell Vincent to step off if he stepped out of line. He could strut around saying he was a Dom all he wanted. If he *wanted* Nala to happily obey his whims, then he would have to earn it.

She had a feeling that a good Dom knew that.

We're having fun, girl. Nothing more. This wasn't a commitment. Nala still held all the cards she wanted.

Besides, she thought as she smirked at him and finished unbuttoning his pants, she owed him nothing.

A pleased growl rumbled from Vincent's throat as Nala rubbed his erection beneath his black briefs. *Finally, I get to experience this thing under my own terms.* Funny! The man thought *she* was serving *him?* Nala was doing whatever the fuck she wanted!

And Nala wanted to check out what a man like Vincent Lane had going on in his pants.

Hello, there. She pulled his briefs down over his erection and ran her finger along his growing length. *This here is a cock, all right.* The man shuddered beneath her touch. Now that was power.

"Fucking hell, Nala," he muttered, hand stroking her head and hair as she wrapped her fingers around the head of his cock and pressed her lips against the rigid length. "You're a tease. I knew, but try not to kill me."

Would that be so bad, though? Nala would almost take it as a point of pride if he came right now. *How much can you hold back?* She blew against his skin, flicking her tongue against a vein and feeling a bit of precum with her fingertip. When she tasted it, making sure to look up at him with her finger firmly in her mouth, she noted that it had a lovelier taste than what she experienced the other night. *Why men gotta be this way?* Whatever.

She wrapped her hand around him beneath, on top, and any other direction she could conjure. No matter how she approached him, he remained firm, and her tiny, petite hands remained unable to completely circle his girth. This was the thing that struggled to get in her wetness the other night. She thought it might have been the position back then, but maybe he really was that big in comparison to her.

Only one way to find out.

His fingers tangled in her hair as she wrapped her lips around his tip, hand working its way down his shaft and feeling his sack beneath. Vincent relaxed more into his bed, content to let Nala do the work. She was content with that too. *Just let me have my fun. Let me explore you like you explored me.* Part of this exploration included tasting more of that sweet liquid coming from the tip of his cock. Nala wasn't shy around this stuff. She wouldn't tell Vincent that her only experience was with her ex, but it hadn't been a problem back then either.

Mostly because she was eager. With the right man, this was fun.

In fact, she wanted to prove that she was so *not* a demure little flower that she made a point to not break eye contact with him. With him lying back against his headboard, that was easy. All she had to do was keep her mischievous eyes on his, even when he closed them and retreated into his own world. *You looked at me, so it's only right I look at you.* He slipped farther into her mouth, resting on the back of her tongue as she attempted to take as much as possible. *Maybe I really do have a big mouth.* What was difficult to get in her body on Friday night was now almost simple.

She let him fall out of her mouth so she could reorient her breathing. Spit broke between her lips and his tip. *So, I'm doing that.* Nala slightly tilted his cock so she could move her face in closer, teeth grazing his hidden sack and the salty taste there. His musk was almost overwhelming. This whole time she thought it was his cologne! Apparently it was part cologne, part natural scent.

"Fuck, Nala," he groaned, fist tightening in her hair. Nala's grip meandered along his shaft, feeling it swell in preparation. "You are so damn hot."

Vincent's hand landed gently on her ass. She shook, surprised but not shocked. As his hand kneaded her ass, she continued her oral onslaught, realizing that this man was about to come with or without her.

Like hell she would let him come without her.

Although he was big, Nala felt so relaxed around him that she didn't think twice swallowing half his length, feeling his tip rub against the back of her throat and dance around her gag. Her hand tightened around his base as her tongue went wherever it wanted, swirling along his length and attempting to futilely wrap around his girth. Her eyes flickered between his and the abdomen before her. Sweat trickled down his stomach and toward his navel. As her breaths increased, so did his – and so did the force pulling at her scalp.

Vincent hissed, his cock swelling to an unusual size in her mouth. Nala knew it was coming, and yet she was almost unprepared for the sudden taste of seed hitting the back of her throat. She swallowed quickly, mouth and hand bobbing on his cock, taking every last drop from him like she did Friday night.

An orgasm for an orgasm. Sure, hers was apparently in return for going without two days ago, but Nala wasn't naïve. She didn't believe for two seconds that more would happen now that Vincent got his. He was totally a one and done dude. Unlike Nala, who was pretty sure she could go on and on and on…

"Ah!" She toppled on the bed, Vincent's strength too much for her to resist as he flipped her. She was in mid swallow, and some of his seed broke past the corner of her mouth right in front of his gaze.

"You've had your fun." He smirked, wiping the mess from her mouth. That taste of salt continued to go down her throat, even after he kissed her and sampled what he had given her. *Oh my God, that's hot.* Nala was getting wet again. "Now we get serious. You still don't know what submitting means… just because you gave me head. Please."

He stepped off the bed and opened a drawer in the far away nightstand. From it he pulled three silk ropes, his eyes lighting up in a glee he probably hadn't experienced in a long, long time.

"I told you I had some practicing to do." The ropes landed next to Nala. "And you still have some learning to do."

She could only gape in astonishment as he rolled her back over and slapped her hand against the headboard.

Chapter 15

Until now, everything was familiar to Nala. She knew what it was like to get head. She knew what it was like to give head. She even knew the ins and outs of this man's cock by now. What she *did not* know, however, was what it was like being tied up in a man's bed for his own twisted pleasure.

Although Vincent occasionally muttered and cursed other things beneath his breath because he was more than a bit rusty in the world of erotic knot-tying, Nala still felt like she was in the hands of a professional. Maybe that was because she didn't know any better. At any rate, she obeyed whenever he told her to move this way or that, to hold her hand in such a way, or to stay in one position above another. Whenever he got a knot right, he smiled to himself.

Occasionally he walked around the bed, admiring his handy work and wondering what he should do next. It was difficult for Nala to see, but she saw an intricate web of long ropes woven above her, creating a design that reminded her of a dream catcher. Her arms were nothing more than spread, and her legs were free, but nevertheless, she stared in awe as art was created above her head. *Here I hadn't even noticed the headboard.* It was perfect for tying unsuspecting women to. Especially if Vincent liked fucking those women where he tied them – because the man was starting to get hard again, and all he did was play bondage prisoner with Nala.

She didn't say anything. She was almost afraid to fuck up his flow and lose the momentum. The greater the art became, the tighter her wrists were held to the headboard. No way was she going anywhere now… not that she wanted to.

"This is almost passable," Vincent said, standing near her head. His cock was half-erect. "Not as good as I used to be, but I can get back into form soon enough. Fuck, I'll need to practice every day… not on you, of course."

Oh, well thank heaven!

He loomed over her. "Unless you want me to."

"One thing at a time."

"Obviously." The bed jilted beneath his weight as he climbed on and pulled on one of her legs. A small scarf was in his hand. *I have a feeling I know what that's for.* Nala bit her lip in anticipation. Vincent situated himself between her legs and proceeded to pull the scarf taut between his hands, biceps flexing in the minimal light. The longer he sat there playing with the scarf, the harder his cock became again. With her legs spread, all Nala could think about was getting a proper taste of his lovemaking abilities again. *I'd say I'm embarrassing myself down there, but… nah.* She did hope, however, that Vincent had the means to wash his bedspread tomorrow. Nala had made short work of it.

"Are you going to fuck me now, sir?"

She didn't smile. Nor did she squirm as he tickled her knees with the silk scarf. "Is that what you want? Because I have some orders for you."

Of course he did. "I want it." It felt like Friday again, when Vincent pinned her against the wall and demanded she tell him *right then* that she gave her consent to him taking her roughly in that corner. *Is he going to be rough again?* Nala wouldn't mind if it went in that direction, but she wasn't in the mood to start off that way. *Ease yourself in first this time.* Assuming this went well, there would be plenty of opportunities for him to jump and take her like that again. *Oops, there I go.* Didn't take much, apparently.

Vincent circled her nipples with the scarf. "First, close your eyes."

She wasn't surprised when the scarf touched her face. Vincent knotted it tight behind her head, blocking out the last of the light. Even when she opened her eyes again, all she saw was shadows. *I've never been blindfolded before.* Let alone with a rock-hard man kneeling between her spread legs. Let *alone* when her arms were spread and tied to his headboard.

"Well, here you are, Nala Nazarov. Blindfolded and bound naked in my bed. How does that make you feel? Make your words count."

She didn't have to think twice about what she wanted to say. "It makes me feel good, sir."

"I'm glad to hear it. Now do me a favor and don't say another word until we're done. Remember the other night when I told you to make all the sounds you wanted, just don't say anything?"

Nala nodded.

"Let's do that again. If you can take me and still obey, I'll make it worth your while."

She sucked in her lips, afraid to speak.

"If you speak, we're done. So, I guess if you want me to stop, say so."

Nala remained silent and unmoving as Vincent pulled her thighs apart and fingered her slit. She heard him lick his hand before it smacked against her clit. *Holy shit.* If he wanted her wet, then that's what he got.

"Did you like it when I talked dirty to you the other night?"

I suppose it's okay to gesture. Nala nodded again, remembering those erotically callous words. *Call me them again. Put me in my place, asshole.*

"Good. Because I doubt I'll be able to help myself."

Breath swept through Nala's nostrils when his rounded tip touched her opening. It moved up and down her slit, stimulating her clit and reminding her of how much she wanted him to fuck her. *Guess he's hard again.*

Oh, he definitely was. Her body parted to let him in, Nala's mind escaping to another plane of existence as she was slowly filled by Vincent's stiff cock.

She whined. She had to make *some* sound, and that was the best she allowed herself since she couldn't tell him how good it felt. *I need to come up with other ways to tell him.* As Vincent slid out, waited for her to get wetter, and then began to enter her again, Nala curled her toes and arched her back in reverie.

"You look good on me." He grunted, pushing himself to the hilt. Nala spread her legs wider, cursing herself for being so petite. *He must look like a monster compared to me.* The demon was back, and she was expected to swallow him whole. "This time I'll make sure you come on my cock."

The bed creaked and groaned as he began to move. At first, it was in slow, gentle strokes that gradually opened Nala up and made it easier for her to take him. *This is what I'm talking about.* She didn't want to make slow and easy love, but she *did* appreciate not feeling like a train wreck after the deed. Nala kept her teeth on her bottom lip so she wouldn't utter a word. This was too good to let slip through her fingers

"Fucking damn it all, Nala." His grip on her hips tightened, directing her ass up as he rose on his knees and slipped deeper into her. "I have you exactly as I want you, and all I can think about is tearing you apart."

She showed him her teeth, a smile as dreadful as any of his. "*Then tear me apart, Master,*" it said, and she was ready.

Or so she thought. The scream of surprise as he rammed into her, hard, scared even her.

One thing for Vincent Lane to slide his big cock in and out of her like a gentle soul. *Quite* another to feel like the sky itself came crashing into her every single second. Nala let out a long, pathetic wail as her body was used like a toy, Vincent's grunts becoming louder and more sadistic the longer he fucked her from above.

"You don't know what kind of man I am," he growled, bruising her hip with one hand and snatching her breast with the other. Nala was manhandled – groped during lovemaking, and marked during a round of day-to-day fucking. "You don't know what I can do to you."

A flicker of fright shook her heart as she struggled to meet his intense thrusts. *It's too much!* Yet it felt so damn good, the way this otherwise composed man split her in two and acted like it was the most life changing thing in his world. She made sure that every sound passing her lips made it seem like she enjoyed it, even though it hurt a little. *Pain is fine… this is fine…* True to her thoughts, an orgasm built within her battered groin.

"Or maybe you do know." Vincent stilled, but it was not to come within her. He lifted his hips, taking her with him. But being tied so well to his bed meant it lifted her back and made her head sink deep into the bed. *Oh my God!* No man had found his way this far into her before. She didn't know anyone *could* go that deep! *Is that my…* Even by herself Nala had never found her most precious place within her. Vincent had found it their second round having sex. "You're mine, Nala."

What happened in her mind as he came inside her was something she could have never anticipated. She alit in a flurry of hormones, riddled with a type of lust that seemed to come from the core of her being and strained to touch Vincent wherever it could. The only way she could touch him right now was with what wrapped around his cock, so she squeezed, tight, refusing to let him go as undulating waves filled her. The crazed sound coming from Vincent's throat made her feel so small, so needed, and so at the whims of a frenzy no man could control. She was left to a fate that had no certain end.

Except for his own climax as well.

She unleashed a cry that almost drowned out his. The warmth consuming her was soothing, of course, as if this mighty hunter had finally caught his vixen and wanted to tame her right there in the wild. *So hot, so fucking hot!* Nala wanted to be a vixen. She wanted Vincent to be her hunter come to mark her before releasing her back from whence she came. Anyone to catch her afterward would find that she already belonged to another man. Normally this type of scenario would disgust her, but Nala was so swept up in her orgasmic paradise that this was the only way their relationship could end. *Fuck me, fill me, and tell the world I'm yours.*

Nala was almost too wet to contain Vincent by the time his thrusts finally slowed. He groaned in fatigue, letting Nala's ass and hips hit the bed with him on top of her. She too came down from her high and remembered where she was and that they were two simple people in this big, fucked up world.

She wasn't prey, and he wasn't a hunter. They were just man and woman.

"You get really fucking tight when you're coming," Vincent muttered, his cock easily slipping out of her now. *My God, that is a hole.* Seed spilled from her, dribbling down her ass and coating the bedspread beneath her. *That's a hole, and it's hot as hell.* If she weren't so spent right now, she'd beg him to find something to fuck her with again. "I'll keep that in mind in the future. I wanted to learn your responses since last time… guess I did."

Just when Nala thought it was over, he pushed back into her, his groan that of a man who was very satisfied with his current lot in life. *Money and pussy. Typical.* Nala wasn't complaining. She'd save that for later.

When all was said and done, it could've been worse. *Who am I trying to kid? It was awesome.* During the moment. Once the binds and blindfold came off, Nala was able to roll over and use her body as she wished again. The first thing she did? Put her hand on Vincent's face and push him away to the other side of the bed as she got up and shuffled to the master bath a few feet away.

She tried to play it cool. So he tied her up. So they had sex. So he said some weird shit that would've been threatening if she didn't kinda-sorta know him by now. *He keeps saying he owns me.* Nala cleaned up, even going so far as to briefly run the spacious shower so she could rinse out – and in. *Does he?* Of course he didn't. Not legally.

Except he was her in when it came to getting to Xavier Crow. He was her only means of revenge, if Nala did go the vigilante justice route – and she had thought about it several times. *In the end, I don't have the guts to go to* jail. . Plus, he was giving her money. A thousand dollars a week to pretend to be his girlfriend, and now they were having kinky sex.

All of that was fine. Except Nala liked it.

"Dumbass," she muttered, toweling off in front of a huge mirror above Jack and Jill sinks. "What do you think you're doing, getting involved with this guy?" Vincent wasn't any good for her. He wasn't even a real relationship. It was sexual tension blowing over. He didn't think of her as Nala. Not Nala the person. He didn't even *know* Nala the person!

That was it. Nala had to do something right now to prevent a potential disaster.

She walked back into the loft with a towel wrapped around her body. Vincent was on the bed, still naked, his hands beneath his head as he dozed. For a moment, Nala was foolishly taken in with his lean, muscular physique. *I mean, he fucks like a champion.* Who knew? She had expected him to be a lazy lay because he was rich and good looking. *I may have known a man or two like that in my short years.* Never boned any of them, but certainly heard stories…

"You can stay the night," he mumbled, as Nala bent down to pick up her clothes strewn across bed and floor. "I have work in the morning, but can drop you off somewhere."

"No thanks." Nala dropped her towel, pulled her hair back into a *boring* ponytail, and started putting her underwear on. "I'm gonna go home now."

Brows furrowed, Vincent sat up, one foot landing on the floor by the bed. "Do you want a ride home?"

"No." She found his pants and his wallet within. Right in front of him, she opened his wallet and pulled out a Grant. *Perfect.*

"What are you doing?"

"*You're* paying for a taxi. I'm not taking transit through here this time of night."

"I said I would take you home."

He was halfway out of bed, grabbing his briefs and jeans as if he could get them on in time. Maybe he'd pull a real PNW move and put on the hoodie and go commando down below. *I'd almost pay to see that. Walk down Burnside with your wang hanging out, buddy.* Nala nearly hooted at the thought.

"Nah, I'd rather go by myself. Let's not complicate this any more than it has been."

Vincent was cute, what with being too confused to function. Nala bet that didn't happen often. "Did I do something? Say something? You came, right?"

Rolling her eyes, Nala finished dressing and pocketed the money in her jeans. "Yeah, I came. Thanks."

"Then what's the problem?"

Oh dear Lord, he was *such* a man! "You're confused, Vincent, and I'm not in the mood to deal with your confusion."

"I guess I am pretty confused right now, but only because you're not being clear with me."

"Look." Nala put her hand on his bare chest, ignoring the warm sweat and other sources of heat emanating from his hard frame. *I am this close to climbing in his lap and kissing him.* The stupid part of her brain wanted her to cuddle next to him and feel protected by the man who made such short work of her. The smart part told the stupidity to fuck the hell off. "We can't lose sight of what's important. Getting justice for my sister and for your *dead fiancée.*"

Now may not have been the time to get weird about that detail, but…

"Thanks for bringing her up. Feels really great."

"I bet." Nala ruffled his hair, sending him back on his ass. "I'm sure you're a decent guy, *sir,* but I can't afford to find out any more than I have. Don't worry. I'll learn how to play the good sub for The Aviary. I will follow your plans, because God knows I'm too fucked up to come up with any of my own. You saw what happened the last time I had a non-plan." She pivoted, making for the stairs. "But I won't be *yours.* We'll have sex, if it seems like the thing to do. I ain't saying you're bad at it." She raised her voice as she began her descent, Vincent scrambling to grab his clothes and chase after her.

"Nala!"

"That's the thing, Vince." Nala stopped at the bottom of the spiral staircase and looked up at him. "You need to separate the two of us. I'm not Nala when you're acting like a territorial alpha male. Because nobody owns or controls Nala Nazarov. Understand that right now."

He braced himself against the railing, eyes boring into hers even from that great of a distance. "Then who the hell are you!"

"Don't you know? You named me." Nala fetched her sweatshirt from the living area and tugged it tight around her frame. When Vincent still hadn't responded by the time she reached the front door, she turned around, finding him wanting. "I'm the Nightingale. Every time you see me like this, I will be the Nightingale."

The door was heavy behind her. Vincent did not come after her, which was fine. She didn't want him to make a scene as she entered the frosty night air and walked toward the nearest boulevard where she could hail a cab to take her home. *You pay for what you named, Vincent.* The Nightingale would call him Master. The Nightingale would bow to his command and *be* the perfect submissive to his domination. The Nightingale would become a queen of espionage and stand in the face of danger, whose name was Xavier Crow.

It was best for Nala Nazarov to step out of the light and let Nightingale shine. Nala was brash, foolish, and a liability to stone-cold justice. The Nightingale, on the other hand, was the perfect identity for Nala to give her new focus, and to act as a burner should she need it.

The Nightingale would submit. Nala would stay where it was safe, where she could keep her identity – and heart – in a treasure box.

It was all she had. It wasn't much, but she wouldn't let someone like Vincent Lane or Xavier Crow take that away from her too. *I can be both Nala and Nightingale.* She had to be. For her sister's sake.

Even for Desirée's sake.

Entry #7

If you're out there, Desirée, then I apologize until my soul has been forgiven.

I am more man than brain. Having Nightingale to myself all day was both reassuring and the worst decision I've made in the past three years.

I took her again. In my home. In my bed. I made love to her. I made her feel the strength I've kept inside this long. I filled her with everything I had, in the vain hope that it would heal me.

It didn't.

If anything, I am even more confused and frustrated. After all that, she left, taking my money right in front of me so she could make her escape.

There is no denying that she has enjoyed everything I've thrown her way. Tonight, I tapped into my old friend bondage. I had forgotten how calming the ropes make me feel. It's good to get back into it, because I will need a skill to barter with The Aviary, and it will keep us from having to have sex in front of the others.

Right now, I only want to keep that to ourselves. I will share my art with the world, but my sexual needs and releases are for Nightingale only. There is still so much more I can show her. So much more to the deepest sides of me to reveal.

I'm afraid. I need, but I am afraid. The more of myself I give to her, the more I feel my vision coming apart.

Chapter 16

Two weeks after making her grand debut in The Crow's Nest, Nala was back, arm hooked around Vincent's and descending the secret stairs with nary a trip of her stiletto heels.

"You sure you're set to go?" Vincent asked, stopping their steps at the bottom of the stairs. He waited for Nala to catch her balance before continuing. "This place is too small for us to meet for a private conversation. Ask me something now before we go in."

Nala stood up straight, tugging at her body-hugging lavender dress delivered fresh that morning. *Just gonna let the man pick out my outfits.* Obviously, he was male and capable of a healthy erection or two around her, but Nala wanted to make sure the others knew how much he wanted her around the clock. *If I can't get a spring in his pants from one glance, then I'm obviously not his real girlfriend.* No one had told her this. She had deduced it on her own.

"I'm ready," she said lightly. "Nightingale, reporting for duty."

His hand squeezed her shoulder. "You can be yourself."

"No I can't." Vincent knocked on the door, making that creepy butler appear. "They wouldn't like Nala. They *like* Nightingale. And after tonight they will think she's the shit."

The door opened. They were welcomed with a proper announcement, forcing three pairs of heads around to greet them. Quail and Sebastian appeared to be running late.

"Gale!" Nala could always count on Robin being the first to welcome her to these things. *I sort of like her.* Robin was crazy obsessive with the lifestyle and a bit too chipper for Nala, but she may be the ticket to best friend stardom for Nightingale. *Rope her in. Make her your solid ally in this place.* Quail was a bit too reserved to read, and Starling self-absorbed. Maggie? Well, Nala was still trying to figure that woman out.

In the times since seeing her new best friend, Nala had deduced that Robin was a true lifestyle submissive. She enjoyed serving, as evident when she hauled Nala to the wet bar and insisted on pouring her a cocktail.

"This is for your Master." Her chipper attitude was almost infectious. "I know you probably want to make your own drink for him eventually, but everyone *swears* by this. Get him started with a sip or five of this, and he'll be the sweetest guy in the room."

Yeah, I bet. Nala took both drinks and forced a pleasant smile. "Thank you so much, Robin. I really appreciate how you've taken me under your wing, so to speak."

Nightingale had the softest voice Nala ever heard come from her own throat. *Submissive, but not a pushover.* That was the persona she was building for Nightingale. *Nightingale* loved to make her Master happy and shower him with adoration, but she did it because it brought her genuine joy. That was the part Nala had to remember. *I'm becoming an actress after all.* Either that or she was becoming more comfortable around the other members of The Aviary. The female members, anyway. She remained suspicious that some man would try to arrange a rendezvous with her.

Robin took a step back, flustered. Her pink cheeks turned cherry red as she hid a grin behind the palm of her hand and giggled out that sweet mirth. *No wonder she landed a man easily.* Nala didn't swing that way and *she* was starting to have a crush on this woman. *Or maybe Nightingale swings that way.* Her next smile was slightly flirtatious, as if to say, "*You know, if your Master demands a threesome, I might go for it.*" She didn't dare send that grin to Vincent. Might give him the wrong idea.

Nala returned to her Master with two drinks in hand. "Here you go, sir," she said sweetly, her newly free hand rubbing the top of his suit jacket. "Robin kindly made us drinks. I made sure to bring it to you myself, though."

A flash of surprise flittered in his eyes, but Vincent quickly blinked it away, sampling the cocktail with a swish of the tongue. "Thank you, darling," he said, his words burrowing deep into Nala's psyche. *I sometimes forget he's a better actor than me.*

"Anything for you, Master." Nala leaned her head against his shoulder, using it as a chance to survey the room. The other couples milled about, Starling breaking off to greet Quail and Sebastian as they finally entered. As of yet, Xavier Crow was nowhere to be seen. "I look forward to tonight's show," Nala continued. "You're going to wow them, sir."

Every time he looked at her, it was with a hint of intrigue. *I told you this was going to happen.* They had several phone conversations since Sunday night. Vincent convinced that he had somehow wronged her; Nala telling him again and again that this was what was best for her. The more she separated herself, the easier it was to play the part necessary to get the justice the universe demanded.

Joseph approached them, shaking Vincent's hand and asking him about business. Nala made sure to nuzzle her Master's arm, acting as if anything Joseph said was nowhere near as important as making sure Vincent was happy right now. *There's that cologne.* Nala glanced at his crotch and was almost disappointed to not see a bulge there. Maybe later. *Nightingale loves sex.* Okay, so did Nala, but Nightingale loved *Vincent's* sex. *Starting to freak myself out now…*

It didn't take long for Crow to make his arrival. He came through the secret door all smiles, his usual bevy of lingerie-clad beauties in tow and heading straight to the wet bar to get everyone drinks.

"Good evening!" Unnerving how easily he smiled. *Man is a true psychopath.* Or maybe it was because he wasn't directly involved with killing people. He gave the kill order, like a capitalistic dictator. "Pleasure to see everyone here already! Unfortunately I was caught up in traffic. Almost had my driver hop out and cobble a pedestrian or two."

Vincent and Nala exchanged glances. He was probably thinking what she was thinking… driver? Assassin? Same difference.

"You know these blasted Oregonians," Crow continued. "Law gives them too much pedestrian right of way. Idiots think they can jaywalk whenever they damn well please…"

Nala hated to break it to him, but that happened in Nevada too.

Once Xavier was over the terrors of driving down Burnside, he welcomed everyone to have their seats while the intimate party began. The benches were arranged in a semi circle this time, allowing each group to eye each other as they drank, cuddled, and whispered nothing into one another's ears. Vincent led Nala to one on the far end, letting her take the seat right next to the stage – and where she could hide the best.

"Who here is from Oregon?" Xavier asked, sitting upon his throne. "I admit, I hardly even visited here until about ten years ago. Now it's practically home, with all its… trappings." A woman brought him a glass of brandy and draped her body across the back of his chair. *Women: victims and decorations.* Nala had to keep her eyebrows in check. Nightingale was expected to be a vision of decorum and class.

Only one person in the room admitted to being from Oregon, and that was Lucian. "Grew up in Tualatin," he said briskly. "Doubt many of you have heard of it."

Nala suppressed an eye roll by half-burying her face in Vincent's shoulder. *There's a bus that goes out there! It's in the fucking metro area!* Good Lord, rich people. Didn't even bother to know the names of towns and neighborhoods in their area that didn't concern them. If only Nala could be so privileged.

This conversation led to people going around the room and talking about where they were from. Most were from California. A couple, like

Quail and Starling, were from the east coast. Vincent told the truth and said Fresno. Nala, on the other hand… well, she would let Lucian be the only "real" Oregonian in the room.

"I'm from Nevada," she said sweetly, although her lie didn't stop there. "Henderson."

Vincent glanced at her, but said nothing. *You know why I'm lying.* So far nobody knew who Nala was. Just as well. She had her secrets that must be kept from Crow. If he knew that Vincent *and* a Nazarov were in his inner circle…

Now Nala had to store this lie in the back of her mind, cataloguing it with any other lie she had concocted. A woman had to keep her story straight, after all.

She had to briefly wonder if anyone else in the room was lying.

"We're both from Texas," Jay said, motioning to Maggie beside him. "Met there, married there…"

"You're married?" someone asked.

"Yeah, we've mentioned it… how many times?"

Maggie pursed her lips. "At least once a meeting."

"Of course they're married," Xavier said. "A handsome couple like them? Dare I say… it was our dear Magpie who made sure Jay committed?"

Laughter spread through the room. Those pursed lips turned into a taut smile that could have eviscerated lesser people. *I still can't get a reading on this woman.* If anyone was more guarded in The Aviary than Nala, then it was definitely Maggie. *Ten bucks says she's not even a sub.* The theory that she was here purely for her husband's business advancement was looking more plausible. Poor woman… not that she couldn't hold her own with this group of people.

"Maggie is a woman who knows what she wants." Jay patted her knee, fingers flecking something off her skin. "When she said she wanted me, well, how could I resist?"

Vincent brushed his hand against Nala's arm. His other hand disappeared into his pocket, tapping something away on his phone. Within another minute, Nala's cell phone buzzed with a message.

She stole a look when all focus was off her. "*That man is not a Dom.*"

Nala hoped he would elaborate later. Not that she wasn't getting the same vibe as well. *If there is kink in that relationship, then Maggie is holding the reins.* What were they playing at? Why would Xavier Crow invite a couple who didn't totally fall in line with his image? Then again, neither was Nala… but Xavier didn't know that.

"Tonight we have a special itinerary planned," the host said, standing from his throne and putting the spotlight back on Vincent and Nala. She made sure to sit with her posture facing Vincent, one hand clasped adoringly on his shoulder. *Nice muscles. Have I said that recently?* Nala fought back the images of him looming over her, talking about taking her to new and exciting places with her body. *Down, I say!* There would be time for sex later, if she still wanted it – and if Vincent wanted it.

She glanced at his tightening muscles. Oh, yeah, he wanted it. He was being a gentleman.

"I've invited Vincent and his sweet Nightingale to join us in The Aviary as full-time members. They've graciously accepted, which means tonight they shall be inaugurated into our Hall of Fame, so to speak."

Polite applause rippled around the semi-circle, with Robin clapping the most enthusiastically. Nala tried to relax her shoulders and exude a warmth that she was not used to producing. Vincent, on the other hand, remained his stoic yet gracious self.

"Vincent has shared with me that he's quite the bondage aficionado. I thought we would start the evening with their initiation. A simple – or not so simple, if you're our Vincent – bondage demonstration with Nightingale as the lovely model is on the menu tonight.

More applause. *We're doing it now?* Xavier and his beauties stepped off the stage and took seats on a bench behind Maggie and Jay. Maggie shifted in her seat, eyes glancing behind her with a frown threatening to consume her countenance. *Interesting.* Nala focused on that as she followed Vincent onto the stage. Better than focusing on the fact she was about to be erotically tied up in front of these people.

"Please get into position," Vincent said, loud enough for the people nearest them to hear. Nala stood in front of the throne, keeping her chin up and the clean bun on her head back. Vincent wanted her to have her hair down, but for the demonstration it was best if it were out of the way. *"I'll eventually get to the point where I can braid your hair with the ropes. Perhaps."* That's what he said on the phone the day before. Nala thought it silly at the time, but now wondered if it would feel good…

Vincent was a silent demonstrator. He wasn't the type to talk to the audience while he worked, preferring to let his artwork speak for itself. *My quiet gentleman.* That's what Nightingale would say, if she were allowed to speak right now, but they both decided it best that she speak as little as possible, in case her temper got the best of her. So Nala lowered herself to her knees, taking care that her stilettos didn't accidentally pierce her ass when she leaned back.

One silk rope after another landed in front of her, coloring the stage in deep crimson. Nala had no idea what design Vincent was going to do. The only planning they did together was deciding what position Nala would start off in. Vincent told her to follow his lead after that.

"Good." He tickled the back of her neck, his caress sending unexpected shivers down her back. Someone swooned in the audience. Probably Robin. "You're doing great, darling."

So that was the pet name he settled on. *I wonder if it's natural.* What did he even feel about her after Sunday night? Did she care? *Right now I can't afford to care. Not like I love the man.* And yet…

"Above head."

Nala raised her arms and cupped her hands above her head, barely missing her bun. She thought Vincent would tie them together, but instead the first rope went beneath her arm and looped across her shoulder.

The key was to not look at the audience. Easy, since Nightingale was a submissive mare, tamed and ridden. It didn't mean anything if Nala stared at the stage before her knees, waiting for a command to shift in this direction, to turn her head this way, or lift her chin just so. Always, however, her eyes remained pointed at the floor. She did not need to meet Xavier Crow's lecherous gaze as she became more vulnerable before him.

Still, it was not a quick demonstration. Xavier Crow would not be content with that for their debut as a sexually available kinky couple in his circle. He wanted a *show.* Nala was a passive doll tonight, who barely had a finger placed on her, but she still had to perform. She had to sit perfectly still while Vincent tied knots, moved her limbs, and gave her the occasional soft touch that made her tremble – quite involuntarily.

Murmurs echoed in the audience. Women leaned in toward their Masters; Masters became more animated. *What is he doing?* Every so often her arms were tugged upward, until finally she had to get up on her cramped heels. Pulleys squeaked behind her. Her shoulders ached, and her back threatened to become sore for the next few days.

It wasn't a lot of weight. Even with the ropes intricately tied above and behind her, it wasn't *that* much weight, thanks to the pulleys. Yet as Nala became more wrapped up in the world of bondage, she began to feel that dull curiosity that begged her to look up and see what was happening.

Except she couldn't look up. A rope was knotted tight beneath her bun, keeping her head pointed straight, chin parallel with the stage. *I'm not sure what's going on.* Some of the audience stood, pointing high above her as the squeak of the pulleys recommenced.

Her arms held out straight above her head. Nala wobbled onto her stilettos as she was forced to stand. By the time Vincent came to stand beside her, a slim look of satisfaction on his face – the same kind of look he had the other night – even Xavier Crow was standing and taking out his glasses to see better.

"I say…" He pulled his phone out of his front pocket and held it in front of him. A flash blinded Nala. *He did not just…* He had. He had taken a fucking picture of her up here on this stage, tied up like an asshole.

So had Vincent, who hopped off the stage and documented his handiwork.

Nobody else took a picture, however. That would've been uncouth. Instead, they marveled, talking excitedly to one another before erupting in vigorous applause. Sebastian came up and clapped his hand on Vincent's shoulder, welcoming him to The Aviary and asking if he was keen on doing a bondage workshop for the group – with Xavier's blessing, of course.

Nala was the only person who wasn't allowed to see what had happened. Nobody was sharing a picture, nobody could find the words to describe it, and, well, she couldn't exactly step outside of her body and have a gander for a few seconds. *Besides, I'm fucking tired.* Her arms were turning to jelly, her shoulders were threatening to pop out of their sockets, and her knees were wobbling as she tried to keep her balance in her shoes.

"That is amazing, Lane," Lucian said from his seat. "But you should probably get your birdie down from there. She's shaking like a seizure."

"What a sport, though," Xavier said, as the first rope came undone and alleviated some of the pressure on Nala's left shoulder. *I never thought such a thing could feel so relieving!* "There's nothing like a girl who can take whatever her Master is serving, sexually or otherwise."

Oh, vomit.

Slowly, with the care of a man who knew what he was doing, Vincent untied Nala and helped her lower to the throne. *Hey, here I am, sitting in his massive throne.* She slumped over, stretching out her shoulders and arms. Giving her feet a rest was a top priority as well. Vincent fielded questions and comments about his artistic abilities, someone even going as far as to ask if he considered doing a public show. "This is Portland," a male voice said. "They would love you two at one of the alternative galleries."

Vincent said he would consider it. Nala almost nodded off to sleep before Robin sideswiped her on the throne and gave her a friendly hug.

"I'm so jealous of your Master's abilities." Her giggles were almost infectious. At the very least, they rejuvenated Nala until she was able to sit up straight again. "I've been trying to get mine to take bondage courses so we could give it a whirl. There's something so intensely erotic about… well, I don't have to tell you! I bet your panties are so wet right now."

Nala stared at her. *No, girl, you're Nightingale.* She smiled. "Maybe a little." Nightingale loved getting tied up and fucked. *Okay, maybe I do a little too.* Not the actual tying up part. The fucking part.

There were other demonstrations that night, of course. Robin was spanked for what felt like hours. Quail took a crop right to the pussy and came with her legs shaking in the air. Starling demonstrated a mewling submissive who was a queen of dirty talk. Maggie and Jay also did bondage, but their piece was more about restraint than artistic expression.

Two weeks ago, this would've been scandalous. Now Nala could hardly care. She was still disgusted with Xavier's presence, but that would never go away. Not with him being in control, and all. *I hope nobody else tries to sleep with me.* She scooted closer to Vincent on their bench, attempting to look 100% his possession. Her hand slipped between his legs and lightly stroked his cock when Quail started screaming in ecstasy from the crop.

She caught his glance. *Why, yes, I am doing this, sir. I am the Nightingale, after all. I am here to serve your every sexual whim.* Why, did Vincent not care for playtime in this situation? He was probably as grossed out being around Crow, but last week proved he didn't mind a rough quickie as far away as possible. Neither did Nala. *It might be good for someone to catch us fucking. Word will spread. We'll be more legit.*

After the demonstrations, two couples left. Robin and Lucian departed, saying they had to leave for a trip early in the morning. Starling and Joseph thanked everyone for a wonderful evening and expressed how tired they were. After seeing them off, Xavier took the opportunity to approach Vincent and bring up the NDAs.

As full members of The Aviary, they were expected to sign some suspiciously illegal documents that passed as NDAs. Except Nala was supposed to use her code name. Worked for her, but it only served to remind that she and Nightingale were different entities.

"Come up to my office. I have one on the second floor upstairs."

They couldn't say no even if they wanted to. One of the fishnet-clad women led the way, weaving upstairs through The Crow's Nest, and up another set of stairs pointing out a regional office. One side of the room belonged to the on-site lounge manager, who had stepped out for this private meeting, and the other was the neat and tidy property of Xavier Crow.

"Are you all right?" Vincent asked, as they sat in the chairs in front of Crow's desk. "We haven't had much time to talk tonight."

Nala looked around, noting a camera in the corner – and mics only God knew where. "I'm fine, sir," she said. "Why? Are you not pleased with me?"

Vincent sat back, frowning. "You're more than pleasant. I'm… worried about you."

Nala cocked her head with a reassuring smile. "We can discuss your worries later, yes?"

"Sure."

They were their usual silent until Xavier arrived ten more minutes later, swinging his jacket onto a coat rack and letting out a hearty sigh as he sat behind his desk. "Vincent. Nightingale." His smile would've been friendly if they both didn't know the truth behind it. "That was a wonderful demonstration you put on earlier. I had no idea you were so handy with a set of ropes, Lane."

Vincent nodded. "I've dabbled in it over the years. Was practically an Eagle Scout with my knowledge of knots growing up."

"I'm sure." That leering smile turned to Nala, who managed to retain her poise even under this much scrutiny. *I'm getting good at this.* "You remained so docile during that trying experience. You two must have a lot of history to know one another so well."

Nala pulled her cheeks into a smile. "You could say that. My Master and I are very in tune with one another." She turned her smile in Vincent's direction. "Wouldn't you say so, sir?"

Vincent didn't say anything. He didn't have to.

"At any rate, there are a few boring formalities we have to go through before you can fully enjoy the privileges of The Aviary." Xavier opened a drawer and pulled out a single sheet of paper. Nala was too far away to see the words on it, but she knew it was the sketchy NDA. *Where do I sign, fucker? Then give me the keys to your house so I can go through your shit.* Finally, a real smile. Except she had to hide this one. "Vincent, I will need your statement when you can get it to me over the next week. Both of you need to sign the non-disclosure agreement saying that you will not talk about The Aviary or its members to others, *especially* anyone who could compromise these people's careers. I take that very seriously."

Nala nearly swallowed her tongue. *I bet you fucking do.* That's why Tasha was dead. That's probably why Desirée was dead.

Vincent picked up a pen, perused the paper before them, and signed his name at the bottom. When it was Nala's turn, she saw the name "Nightingale" in small print beneath the solid line.

I really am a different person now. The name rolled from her fingers without contest. The longer she stayed in the headspace of Nightingale, the more she felt at home.

Xavier took the paper and pen back with a happy sigh. His eyes lingered on Nala, staring uncomfortably at her face. "You know, dear Nightingale, you look strangely familiar. I can't quite place it. Do we know each other from elsewhere?"

Nala politely shook her head. "Until two weeks ago, sir, I had never met you before." A new thought sparked in her mind. "I have a distant cousin who is a model. Perhaps it's her I look like. Everyone in that part of the family looks the same."

"I don't cavort much with models."

Nala didn't think so, but now she had thrown a red herring at the man, and that was all she needed to keep him from thinking of Tasha, one of his top researchers he always kept a close eye on. *To make sure she didn't get too close to something that would stop his money from trickling in.*

"Thank you for this." Xavier tucked the paper into a locked drawer. "Now, as full members, you'll be delighted to know that we'll be taking a sojourn to Cancun in the coming weeks. Just a weekend jaunt. I've rented us a scattering of cottages right on the beach. Have you ever been?"

They both shook their heads. *Shit, I need a passport.* Nala tucked that into the back of her mind so she wouldn't forget to tell Vincent. If it was in the coming weeks, she would need him to help her get an expedited one.

"On top of such treats, I have regular parties at a ranch I own down south, toward Salem. You of course will be invited to come. Oh! And…" Xavier stood, prompting both Vincent and Nala to stand as well. "Drinks are on the house here at The Crow's Nest. Also, you can come and go as you please from the downstairs club room." He shook Vincent's hand, winking at him. "Lots of fun tools of the trade down there. Have fun."

Vincent twisted his mouth in such a way that Nala took a step back. *They look like they're in on some joke.* She reminded herself that it had everything to do with the game they played. Still…

"We might take a jaunt down there now," Vincent said, buttoning up his suit jacket. He gauged Xavier's reaction, but the man barely breathed. "I know that my little bird is, ah…"

Nala looked away before she met another disgusting leer. "Happens all the time with such women, and especially after the demonstrations earlier! I can't blame you. You two have fun. I must be getting on home before I turn into a pumpkin."

His endearing grandpa shtick could stop anytime. Thankfully, Crow seemed serious about grabbing his coat, hat, and scarf and heading downstairs. Vincent and Nala followed him out, watching him lock the office before leading the way down.

"Let my man behind the counter know when you two are done having your fun." Xavier put his hat on his head and nodded to the customers gathering at the bar. "He'll lock up."

They waited until he was out the door before heading for the stairs. *He must have the same idea I do.* Time to snoop.

Granted, Nala didn't expect to find anything substantial in the club room. No way would Crow leave incriminating evidence lying around a place a dozen people came in and out of on a weekly basis. *I still have to look.*

Before she could start upturning benches and sniffing through chests of tools and toys, however, Vincent took her by the arm and drew her into his embrace. His kiss startled her.

"Lay low," he muttered into her ear after diverting his lips. "There are cameras all over this room. You bet your ass he'll review them tomorrow."

Nala didn't know what to do – so she encircled her arms around him, hoping it was a convincing enough pose should someone see them later. "He takes video of the club meetings?"

"Of course he does. It's a liability otherwise." Vincent's warmth enveloped Nala, but she tried to not be taken in by it. *Focus.* Her hands slipped to his collar and tugged on it. Her body trembled as his hot breath moved from ear to throat. "It's no secret either. It was written on the NDA that everything that happens on 'his' premises is recorded for security reasons."

"I'm sure he likes to review his security quite often."

"He's a world-class voyeur. He gets off on that harder than he gets off on those women who hang all over him."

"He likes the idea better than the actual thing."

Vincent's hold grew tighter. "You know what we have to do, right?"

Yes, great, thanks Vincent. Thanks for bringing me down here knowing that. "I am trying to avoid that man seeing me naked or having sex. I would rather fucking die."

His lips pressed against her throat. "I know where the cameras are."

"Not helping."

Nala tripped on her shoes when Vincent pulled away and steadied her shoulders. "Let's look around first. Just… try not to look like you're looking for *evidence.*"

She wasn't looking for much of anything as they took a tour around the room, poking their heads into toy chests and looking behind curtains. To anyone watching the security feed, they looked like a frisky couple getting hard and wet over the possibilities. After all, most of what they saw was in the vein of erotic art or equipment. No doubt Xavier crow encouraged his couples to have sex in here whenever they pleased – so he could watch.

That man is never seeing my body, so help me God. If Vincent wanted to whip out his cock and twirl it around in front of the camera, boy howdy, he sure could do that. Nala would show herself out first.

"We're not going to find anything here," she finally lamented. "We had to look, but…"

"Don't sound so hopeless. The real chance will come when we have access to his home. A man like that has to keep evidence around. He's a big enough sociopath to keep *some* sort of recognizable trophy."

Nala was ready to head out, to go home and take a long shower, but Vincent put a firm hand around the back of her neck and guided her to the rear of the stage. "What the…" A thick, black curtain hung there, concealing a small space in the back where a padded pommel horse was stored – and a few other weird items that probably belonged in the realm of "too kinky for me."

"The cameras can't see us back here." Vincent tugged on the curtain, shrouding them in darkness. "He can't see you."

"Vincent," Nala said, bracing herself against the pommel horse. His hand cupped her chin, pointing her head up and making her look back into his face. "What are you doing?"

"What the hell do you think I'm doing?" Vincent yanked down the zipper of Nala's dress, giving him plenty of skin to caress with his soft fingertips. She really, really wished it didn't thrill her – a little. "Taking what's mine."

Chapter 17

"*Now?*" Nala swatted his hand away and attempted to stand up. Yet one hand remained clutching the leather of the pommel horse, and there Vincent was, taking her other hand and kissing it as if he really were her regal lover.

"You said so yourself the other night." Lips pressed against the inside of her arm. "Every time I see you like this, you're Nightingale. And Nightingale belongs to me."

Oh, fuck, I did say that. At the time it sounded good. Sexy, even. "You seriously want to fuck me right now?"

"Nightingale," he said, and a part of her missed the way he could say her real name. Yet when Vincent inched his hand into the inside of her dress, touching her breast and rubbing against her hardening nipple, she had to admit there was a dark undertone that turned her on. *I don't want to be turned on right now!* "You said you would submit. Did you forget that I am your Master? Then I need to teach you even more than I thought I did."

Trapped between two identities, Nala had to make a quick decision. She could tell Vincent to fuck off, but he was right… she *had* said that shit the other night. No wonder he was under the impression they could go to The Aviary and then bang afterward. *Sometimes I forget that under this guise is a horny Dom.* Shivers claimed Nala. Oh, yes, she *did* want to go another round with Mr. Rough and Ready. But here?

"Why don't we go back to your place?" She tried to sound sweet. Docile. *Compliant.* "We'll have actual privacy there." *I won't feel this veil of shame all over me.* Nala may be able to slip into Nightingale's shoes without too much effort now, but some things could not be avoided.

"You are seriously suffering from a lack of understanding, *darling.*" Vincent grabbed her chest, hoisting her back up and into his embrace. She stared into the darkness behind the curtain, wanting to cry out in, what? Anticipation? Fear? Neither was happening now that Vincent had his hand on her mouth. "I said I wanted it now. Not later. Not at home. *Now.*"

The longer she knew him, the more Nala came to realize that the façade he projected around him was that – a façade. Vincent wasn't the silent, brooding type he broadcasted to keep people at bay. He was mired in grief – and desire. *I'm probably the first woman he's really gone for ever since…* Vincent's hand squeezed her breast, his knee pushing her legs open.

"I've been hard for you all damn night. All *week*. Just one thought of you and this happens." He snatched her hand and brought it back, letting her fingers feel the hardness bulging in his pants. *Oh, dear.* The worst part? If it weren't for where they were, Nala would be totally, 100% turned on. "I've been looking forward to tonight because of what you said Sunday. If you're Nightingale right now, then you're *mine.* She – you – belongs to me. I can do whatever the hell I want to you." Nala's hem worked its way up her thighs, revealing her simple black lingerie that was embarrassingly wet. "Do I need to prove this to you?

Nala was allowed to stand on her own, her head craning around so she could look the madman in the eye. "No, sir," she said, conjuring the soft voice she had been using as Nightingale all night. "You should have said something earlier."

Vincent glared, hand plucking the tie from her bun and letting her hair cascade down her shoulders. "Will you submit to me and obey? I'm not playing around, *Nightingale.*" His teeth came dangerously close to her lips, forcing Nala to grab the pommel horse behind her. "I need to fuck you like

I need to breathe. God knows why. I'm starting to suspect you really are a succubus. You get me hard and then suck me dry of my vitality. The only thing I have going for me…" Vincent grabbed her ass, pinching it until she began to whine from the surprising pain. "Is that I can take you however way I want. I can punish you."

Even though he said these intoxicating words, his touch to her cheek, to her hairline was gentle. Nala closed her eyes, lips slightly parted as she swayed beneath his promises of sex. *Who the fuck am I right now?* Whether Nala or Nightingale, she was enthralled. *Because at the end of the day, it's this stupid body rushing in hormones and demanding to get fucked.* So maybe Nala was the one involved right now… he didn't have to know that.

"Do you know why you need to be punished, Nightingale?"

She melted in his backward embrace, feeling her thighs inflame and his cock continue to harden against her ass. "No, sir," she whispered.

"Two reasons. The first is because of your insubordination. You need more proper training. You need to learn how to be a better, more obedient sub for me when you, Nightingale, are around. Because…"

Nala swallowed, hard. "Because?"

"Because no matter who you are at the moment, I hate the fact that I want you so much. Don't you get it?" His harsh whispers spat into her ear, both arousing and scaring her, a little. Enough to make the arousal worse. "I'm supposed to be able to control this. Yet here I am, aching to feel your cunt all around me. Do you know what that does to a man like me?"

Nala knew she wasn't supposed to actually answer, but she couldn't help herself. "It makes you resent me. Because you wish I were your fiancée instead of some dumb co-ed your dick gets hard around."

It was a low blow. One she would have to pay dearly for.

Vincent shoved her back down, tearing at her dress and promising to get her back for that. *It's okay. Really.* Riling him up was becoming like a game. How hard could she get him, *and* how passionate? Didn't matter what kind of passionate. Nala was quickly learning that these rough quickies were some of the best fun of her life.

They weren't in love. They were barely partners of any kind. If anything, life was easier pretending to be his on-call sex worker. *Got body, got services. I'm here for you, sir!* She wasn't like Robin, who salivated to call her man Master and get on her knees to blow him. She also wasn't like Maggie, who looked like she should be anywhere but at The Aviary. *Fuck me.* She almost wished Vincent would. It didn't matter what he did to her, as long as he meant it, and it felt good.

"You make it incredibly hard for me to go easy on you." A zipper came undone. Nala's breasts fell from her uniform, a dress Vincent had bought for her so he could show her off and then fuck her senseless. When she felt cool air hit her pussy, she knew it would be quick, and hardly easy. Sure enough, Vincent's fingers helped themselves to her wetness, making Nala grip the pommel horse beneath her. *Finger me, fucker.* He did, not for her pleasure, but to make sure she was wet enough to take him right now. Well, it pleasured her anyway, and that made Nala – and Nightingale – grin against the taut leather.

"Don't go easy on me," she hissed, rubbing her ass against the rough material of his trousers. Nala searched for his cock, now free from its confines. "Punish me, sir. Teach me a fucking lesson."

Her hair wrapped around his hand, tugging at her scalp, pulling her up, letting her breasts graze in joy against the pommel horse. "You are something else," Vincent muttered, almost bewildered. "You'd almost be fun if you also weren't such a confusing pain in my *ass.*"

"Don't hold back how you really feel." Nala grimaced as he pulled her hair again. *That's why you like it loose and long, sir.*

"Don't you dare either."

Was that a challenge? Well, he hadn't told her to shut up this time…

"*Ho,* shit!" Nala's fingers pierced the pommel horse as Vincent drove into her, his cock already swelling to his near-climax size. *Fuck me is right!* It was like last Friday again, when her body struggled to open wide enough to take him. It ached again now, stretching, testing itself as Vincent all but forced himself into her.

"Why do you have to be so fucking tight, Nightingale…"

His growls did things to Nala that no man had been capable of doing before. Namely, they made her so hedonistic and wet that she felt like she could take two of him. That was silly, of course. One Vincent Lane was almost too much for a petite body like hers to handle by itself.

"Damnit, open up for me!"

"I'm trying!" Nala lay her cheek on the leather, smelling the age of it as she stepped on her tip-toes and tried to pull her legs wide. "Fucking take me! I don't care if it hurts! Punish me!"

She got her first punishment when her ass stung from a sharp spank.

Another one. Nala cried out, knees buckling as Vincent held her cheeks apart and barged into her. Dear cosmos in the sky, it *hurt!* Regardless of how wet she was, it wasn't enough to accommodate a man when he was like this. *Yet it somehow feels so good.* This rough way of lovemaking – if it could be called that – was a just punishment for being so insolent a while ago. *I'm sorry, not really, but I'm sorry.*

"Yes!" The best part? Being able to mouth off for the first time since they started having sex almost a week ago. "Fuck me, sir!"

Every time he pulled slightly out, she became wetter – and every time she became wetter, he informed her how easy she was. One of his hands held her down while the other pinched her ass, reminding her that he was there, owning her, making the shortest work of her libido.

"Do you like it, Nightingale?" It helped that he kept calling her that. It fueled the fantasy building, the one where she was a lawless, loose woman who was into the sorts of things Nala Nazarov would never in good conscience do. "Do you like it when my cock devours you?"

"Yes!" Her forehead tapped against the pommel horse with every hard thrust he gave her. "God, yes!"

Vincent stilled within her, squeezing her hips as he pulled up one leg and slipped deeper into her. "Do you like getting fucked as if you're nothing?"

"Yes!"

"What do you want, Nightingale? Do you want to come for your Dom?"

My Dom. There's a phrase she never thought she'd hear. "Yes… oh my God, please!"

Her body shook with the need to orgasm. Vincent was her ticket to heaven, and most of all, he still carried a loaded gun. *I want to feel him inside me like that again.* Filling her, spilling from her, marking her skin and letting her feel the tangible proof that he had been there and felt good as well.

"Let me come, Master! Come inside me, please!"

Vincent showed her body so little mercy in the next minute that Nala thought she would fall onto the floor and *die.* His cock owned every inch of her cunt, his hands clawed at her skin, pulled her hair, and poked at the edge of her mouth. When he slipped between her legs and began to stroke her clit, she whimpered to the point of tears.

"Oh my God!" she cried, riding the sudden orgasmic wave crashing over her. Nala's body tightened around him, holding him there with such determination that it was any wonder he was able to keep fucking her at a steady rhythm. "I'm coming!"

He increased his speed, pushing her through her orgasm. "Do you want this?" he heaved into her ear, each breath more harried than the last. "Is that all you want now?"

Still high on her climax, Nala sobbed into the leather beneath her with such relief. "Yes, holy shit, *yes!*" It would be the most delectable cherry on this sexual sundae. Nala loved cherries.

"Fuck, Nala!" Vincent grunted in satisfaction, his cock so stiff that Nala had nothing to do but prepare for the first burst. *I'm ready. You don't know how ready I am right now.*

So when he pulled out and climaxed on her bare back instead of inside her, Nala stared in disbelief at the back of her eyelids.

"Too bad. You don't get it."

She lay still, his seed spilling down her back while her own wetness claimed her thighs. While she was sated with her own heavy orgasm, Nala's disappointment at not being able to feel so *one* with him was indeed a punishment she never anticipated. *Oh my God, is this what it feels like to disappoint your Dom? Is this what he means by punishment? To deny me what I want?* Nightingale was mortified. Nala was pissed.

"What a mess," Vincent mumbled, zipping himself back up and tucking in his shirt again. "Suits you, though. You're a mess in and of yourself."

Pride shaken, but not shattered. Nala stood up, feeling the physical manifestation of her messy self streaming across her skin. *Don't care.* Wouldn't be the first time she bathed in body fluids. "And you're an asshole."

He watched her zip up and fix her hair. "An asshole who makes you come hard."

"That's not necessarily something to design your life around." Nala faced him. *I wonder where the bathroom is.* She wasn't leaving The Crow's Nest without visiting. *Or I guess I could smear his little swimmers all over that nice interior of his car.* Nah, he'd like that. The more Nala got to know alpha male Vincent, the more she realized his world revolved around what his cock could do. "You're also an asshole who doesn't kiss much."

"I'll kiss you if I feel like it."

"Obviously."

Nala pulled back the curtain, ready to find that bathroom and demand to be taken home.

"Well."

Both Nala and Vincent paled at the sight of Jay and Maggie near the door. Jay clucked in his throat and shook his head while Maggie grinned like a naughty aunt catching her family in a scandal. "Looks like someone owes me money. Here I thought you two weren't a real thing."

Vincent put a firm hand on Nala's shoulder. She wavered back and forth in her stilettos. *They were watching... or at least listening to me…* Better than being on camera for Xavier Crow to jack off to, but not exactly Nala's idea of a cool fetish. "Did you enjoy the show?"

"Oh, we enjoyed both today." Maggie pulled a cigarette from her purse and lit it without any regard for Jay, who kept a respectful distance behind her. "Looking forward to more."

Vincent stepped forward, taking Nala by the hand and pulling her behind him. "We'll let you have the room to yourself, then. We need to be going."

"I'm sure." Maggie winked at them as they went by, a plume of smoke obscuring her perfectly white teeth. "See you at the next meeting."

The first thing out of Nala's mouth was asking where the bathroom was. Vincent pointed it out once they were back in the lounge, the sounds of people chattering and ice clinking against glasses almost welcomed. The second thing out of her mouth was expressing a "bad feeling." Vincent did not hesitate to agree as he stood outside the ladies' room and waited for Nala.

Entty #8

We are official members of The Aviary. And I am officially a fucking idiot who can't keep his dick in his pants. The Dom in me has awakened, and I cannot keep him contained around that damned woman. Every time I take her I wake up more and more. All that careful planning is coming undone because I am more beast than man.

I want to punish her for making me feel this way. But I'm afraid that will only make it worse.

I can't win. At this rate, she will be the only winner. My majestic Nightingale.

Chapter 18

"Got another batch coming through, Nala!"

Before she could cry uncle, a large box appeared on the rolling tray running through Nala's station. She still hadn't finished sorting through the current batch of T-shirts and jeans donated earlier that day. Now she had…

She took a cursory glance of the contents. *Lingerie?*

Hell no! How did this make its way to her? The company had a very strict no lingerie policy, no ifs, ands, or buts. Apparently, a boutique had gone out of business, and these were the items they couldn't sell during their liquidation. *So, brand new and never worn, but I still can't process these.*

Just another day at Nala's job. She was getting *beyond* fed up with it, but what was a girl to do when her current thousands of dollars was coming from the equivalent of a sugar daddy?

She laughed into the box of new-used lingerie. Vincent! A sugar daddy! Would he even *know* what to do with a sugar baby? *"Oh, baby, let me buy you some pizza and come on your back."* If Nala didn't stop hollering in laughter, someone was going to come back and see what looked like her huffing a box of lacy panties.

Nala set the box off to the side so she could finish processing the T-shirts and jeans. For once, the donator didn't completely fuck up the rules and managed to deposit a sizable amount of usable clothes. No crazy stains, no terrible tears, and the fading was what one expected from seriously used. That was great for the company, but annoying as hell for Nala's remaining time.

There was only fifteen minutes left on her shift by the time she returned to the box of lingerie. *What do I even do with these?* Normally donated panties and the like had to go to the incinerator. These weren't technically used. Banged around a bit in boxes and sitting on shelves for who knew how long, but a simple wash would make them usable.

Nala held up a pair of black lacy panties, amazed that a simple string was supposed to keep them on a woman's hips. *Oh, but they're adjustable that way.* A woman could tie them as tightly or loosely as she wanted. *That would be great for my hips.* Depending on the hormones of the month, Nala could have her version of thick, curvy hips, or stick-like bones protruding. Finding granny panties that stayed on or didn't strangle her once in a while was a trial.

Now she supposed she had to dress her undies up too. If not for The Aviary performances, then for Vincent, her stupid sugar daddy.

Good job, thinking about him yet again. It had been three days since they last had sex, and Nala was already turning into a cock-starved nut. She imagined herself splayed out across a fainting couch, fanning her face as she claimed to have "a bit of the hysterics," her hand constantly moving toward her thighs and demanding a man come take care of her. *"Oh, Mr. Lane! You're what the doctor ordered to cure my hysterics!"* Whoops. Time to laugh in the underwear again.

In the end, Nala stuffed about six pairs of underwear, a bra that she *could* have processed but decided not to, and a couple of sheer negligees into her tote bag before leaving work. The rest of the goods were left in the box with a note for her supervisor – minus any mention of things Nala may or may not have lifted.

"Have used undies, will sell," she muttered, sneaking out of work one minute after she was off the clock. She wondered if Vincent was the panty sniffing kind. *God, no.* The only panty sniffing that man did was what a woman was already wearing as he prepared to disrobe her. *One of those guys in that club has to be a panty sniffer, though.* Her money was on Lucian. Well, a girl needed something to think about as she walked home in forty-degree weather.

She got home in time for the mailman to stop by. Trailing right behind him was a private courier, who detoured around the mailbox and even the path leading up to the craftsman house. He walked right up to Nala, who carried a new collection of undies in her tote bag.

"Nala Nazarov?"

She stopped in the middle of the sidewalk, clutching her bag to her shoulder. "Yeah. Need me to sign for something?"

"No need. Here." The man handed her a letter before jogging down the sidewalk as if someone were after him.

Nala glanced at the letter. It was addressed to her, but there was no return notice. *Is that legal?* No sense reading it out there in front of God and everyone. She took her things inside the house, passed by Patrick smoking a bowl in the living room, and sequestered herself in the bathroom.

The bright lights came on. The door locked. Nala leaned against the counter and tore open the envelope, fully expecting to see some suspicious white powder come pouring out. Instead, she got a thin piece of paper with tiny typeface scattered upon it. There was no signature, no name to go with the strange words.

We know who you are.

We know why you are after the man.

We will keep your identity secret from him.

Because we are on your side.

You have friends.

Nala folded up the paper and stuffed it in her front uniform pocket. Although slightly shaken, she forced herself to remain straight faced and collected as she picked up her tote bag and went back outside. No need to settle into her closet right now.

She walked to the end of the street and took a bus into downtown. As she sat in one of the hard bus seats, she thought about what she would say. *"I told you I had a bad feeling." "Is this a joke?" "So, uh, sex?"*

The bus dropped her off by Pioneer Square in the heart of downtown, making her trek a few blocks to Vincent's office building. He told her to come by there if she had an emergency. Well, this *seemed* like an emergency. Not that Nala felt like she was in immediate danger… but this was definitely something Vincent needed to know about before anything else happened.

Unfortunately, it was Andrew who greeted her at the front desk of Lane Technological Solutions. *Unfortunately,* because his mouth turned at the sight of her, as if hordes of lice were about to start jumping out of her hair and all over his department store suit.

"Hello," he said, trying so damned hard to not sneer. *I know, I'm here in my uniform again.* Nala picked something off her dull blue shirt and straightened her back. "If you're looking for Mr. Lane, he's currently in a meeting."

Nala checked her watch. *No way he's having a meeting a half hour before he's supposed to go home.* "You might tell him I'm here. Tell him I have something he really needs to see."

Andrew cocked a disbelieving eyebrow.

"No, really, he likes me. Go watch. He'll drop everything he's doing for little ol' me."

This was kinda fun.

Andrew cleared his throat, standing stiffly from his desk as he smoothed down the front of his suit. His sandy blond hair was practically plastered to his scalp from too much product. "I will check in with him. You might want to have a seat, though."

"Not necessary. He'll see me within five minutes."

What a cute scowl!

That's right. Go along, little puppy. Your boss is my sugar daddy and is taking down one of the biggest billionaires in the area with me! He'll see me even if he's sitting on his private toilet! God, she hoped not, honestly.

Andrew disappeared into Vincent's annex, coming back less than a minute later with red on his face. "He said he'll see you now," he mumbled. "Just so you know, he was working on a very important proposal."

"Oh, I'm sure he was." Nala twiddled her fingers as she made a grand show of sauntering into Vincent's office as if she had the run of the place. Briefly – *very* briefly – she imagined being Mrs. Lane and pissing all over Andrew's dreams of showing her up. *I'd ask Vincent if he could be transferred to my services. I'd make sure he got paid more to ensure he followed through!* Sometimes she could have quite the mean streak.

Vincent got up from his desk the moment Nala stepped in and shut the door behind her. *Oh, hi.* The three sides of Vincent Lane – the scruffy PNW hoodie guy, the decked out Aviary man in a suit, and this plain business gentleman – all had different effects on poor Nala. She went from wanting to be his friend, to wanting to be *dominated* by him, to… well, whatever she felt right now, it was greatly influenced by that dark blue button down and those loose black trousers. *I know what's in there.* She averted her eyes.

"What is it?" Vincent asked, tidying up papers and tablets on his desk. "I'm guessing you wouldn't come all the way here if it wasn't serious."

Nala pulled the note from her pocket and handed it to him when she had the chance. "I got home from work, and this was delivered to me with impeccable timing. Like the deliveryman knew when I would be home."

Vincent read it over as Nala sat on a couch along the edge of the wall. Her heavy tote bag sighed into the seat beside her. She watched for Vincent's reaction, but all he did was fold the note back up and deposit it into one of his desk drawers. *I should've made a copy.* Wasn't like things belonged to her anymore once she handed them over to Vincent.

"So? What do you think it means?"

He turned toward her, but remained firm against his desk. "I think it means exactly what it says. Someone knows who we are and what we're about."

"They say they're our friend."

"We'll see about that soon enough." Vincent's poignant visage did not instill any confidence in Nala."

"*Well?*"

"Well what?"

"Who do you think it is? What do you think they want? They came to *me,* Vincent. Did you get the same note?"

"Not that I know of."

"Geez! Okay, so go ahead and stand there, acting like it's not a big deal. Some weirdo delivered me a message from someone who claims to know who I am. Not a big deal. Right."

"Nala," Vincent said, too calm for the situation. He pushed himself away from his desk and joined her on the couch, his body language in no way inviting. Nala's tote bag remained between them. "Don't think I don't care or won't look into it, but I'm not sure what to tell you. This person says they're an ally, but they said it in such a threatening way. They want us to remain cautious. They didn't tell us anything about themselves, so they have an identity to hide. They went to you because… well, I don't know that off the top of my head right now."

"Because I'm cute, duh."

She said it flippantly, but Vincent snorted nonetheless. "Maybe." His face contoured into a serious look again. *He's good looking when he smiles… but there's something about Mr. Emo Lane that does me in.* Nala truly was a product of her generation, heaven help her.

"Well, it freaks me out. If they could find out who I am that easily, then so can Crow. It's only a matter of time before he finds out I'm Tasha's sister. He must already know your history."

Frowns abounded on that couch. "He mentioned it a few times when we were working together. Offered me a ton of condolences and expressed his happiness that I was continuing Desirée's work. It extremely unnerved me, but I had already decided to get under his good graces so I could pursue answers regarding her death. Then I found out about his club, and… let slip that I was into it. It worked. I was invited to join his club when he had an opening because the last couple moved to another country."

"Yes, but he finds out who *I* am in conjunction with you… he may start to suspect something. Then bam! We're dead too."

"Please don't act like I don't know that myself." Vincent lifted his hand, brushing against the tote bag and accidentally opening the top. He happened to glance at the contents. "Is… is that…"

Nala sat up with a start, snatching the bag and shoving the disrupted lingerie to the bottom, beneath her wallet, scarf, and extra tampons. "You didn't see anything. Don't snoop in a woman's bag!"

Vincent's ability to suppress laughter was nowhere near as good as his marketing skills. *Had* to be, because he ran a billion-dollar business while being completely unable to control his emotions right now. *How often does this guy laugh, anyway?* Probably not as much as Nala, and that said something.

"Those are some serious panties you're carting around."

Caught, Nala opened her bag and pulled out the nearest pair of lacy undies she could find. "You want a pair, Mr. Lane? They would look fantastic on your nicely kempt hair. Oh! Even better! Give a pair to your uptight assistant. At least he'll have an excuse for having something shoved up his ass."

Vincent plucked the panties from her fingers and noted the tag still hanging off them. "Didn't this place close a week ago?"

"How would you know? Go shopping for lingerie a lot, do you?"

He rolled his eyes. "The place used to be on my commute home. Stuck out in my mind."

Nala shrugged. "I work at a donation center. Someone brought them because they couldn't be sold… but we can't resell them because they're lingerie, so…"

"So you… took them…"

"What do you want from me! Girl's gotta need fancy panties, right?"

"Holy shit. You're gonna wear donated panties for me."

"Excuse you! *For you?*"

Vincent wasn't listening. He was swinging the black lace back and forth in front of his nose, guffawing with every muscle in his abdomen. *I've never seen him laugh like this before.* Almost like he was human. Almost like he wasn't a Portland robot who functioned on passive-aggression and quoting Edgar Allan Poe. *Next you'll tell me he doesn't smoke pot.* Or wear plaid. Or grow a beard. Or dye his armpit hair blue.

"That's amazing." He dropped the underwear back into her tote bag. "You came here with a note… and with a bag full of donated panties to wear to The Aviary…"

"Yeah, well, never let it be known that my life isn't super serious all the time."

When he finally stopped laughing, Vincent had a flushed face the color of Mars. "After the work day I've had today, I really needed that."

Nala didn't ask. She figured she wouldn't understand anyway.

She caught Vincent staring at her shirt. At first she thought he was checking out her tits, as they were *totally* glamorous under a thick blue shirt, but then she realized he was reading the stitching above the side pocket. "I didn't know you worked for that company."

"You don't know much about me, really." *I don't know that much about you either.* Nala preferred it that way. Fewer emotions.

"No, I suppose I don't. I know what matters."

"Yes, you do."

Why did they have to get so serious so soon? Nala was almost enjoying a side of Vincent she rarely saw. As opposed to the one reaching across the bag to cup her face and turn it toward him.

"I don't want you to worry about anything," he said, on the verge of using the growl that emerged during sex. *Ah, fuck.* "Don't worry about this note. Don't worry about having to get second-hand-but-not-really clothes. I'll take care of you, Nala. Say the word, and I'll make sure you get it as soon as I can."

Her eyelashes fluttered, but it wasn't in arousal – for once. "I'm PMSing, so you're going to have to talk slowly… do you mean you're gonna throw more money at me?"

Vincent's grip tightened on her chin. "Is that how you see it?"

"How else should I see it? You're not really my boyfriend. I pretend to be your girlfriend for The Aviary. The sex is casual. You pay me so I can be available for The Aviary. Oh, and be presentable. You don't have to do more than that."

Something faltered in his eyes. *He didn't really think I was his girlfriend, did he?* "What if I want to do more than that?"

"Don't." Nala sank into the couch, crossing her arms and holding her tote bag close. Whatever walls she could build. "Don't complicate this, Vincent. I'm not your Nightingale right now. I'm Nala. The best you can get with Nala is a tenuous friendship."

The look on his face said it all, even though his voice didn't. *"You keep people at a distance, like I do. You're afraid to open up to anyone out of fear of losing them, like I am."* Great. Like Nala needed a list of reasons they were the same. *Don't make me start falling for you.* She was already sexually attracted and available most of the time. The last thing Nala wanted was lovey-dovey emotions on top of that… if she was even capable of such a thing.

"All right," he said, although his lips came dangerously close to her throat. "I bought you pizza that one time, but all right."

"Oh, nice. Buying me pizza means you get access to my pussy whenever you want, huh? That's the kind of sugar baby I am, huh?"

She did not protest when he lightly kissed her skin, his hand snaking beneath her tote bag and rubbing the outside of her thigh. *Men.* Vincent was getting too comfortable around her. They were having too much sex. Pretty soon he would not only delude himself into thinking they were a couple, but that they had a healthy sex life that went along with his whims. *It's not like that.* Nala needed to start drawing some lines, now.

But it was difficult when her body warmed to his touch and wanted nothing but affection. So few people gave it to her. Vincent may not be her real boyfriend, but he was *real,* and he was evidently attracted to her enough to want to fuck her every time they saw each other now. *Even though he never once asked me about birth control. He assumed.* Sometimes Nala thought about sending him a text that said, "I'm on HBC, btw. Thanks for checking before getting cum all over my vag multiple times." Not that she ever protested – or wanted to, for that matter. "

"Is it wrong of me?" Vincent finally said, his breath hot against Nala's ear. "I told you, Nala, you do things to me that I haven't felt in a long, long time. I'm not putting any labels on it. Excuse me if I want to pursue something that makes me feel like a fucking human being, though."

Good for him, really. Grief had obviously been hard on Vincent. Nala didn't have to ask to figure that she was one of the first healthy hookups he'd had in the time since Desirée's death. But that wasn't her job. It wasn't even what she wanted. Vincent needed to find that sort of emotional relief elsewhere. All Nala was good for was the physical kind. *That* they could share. When it was pertinent.

It was not pertinent right now.

"Stop," she whispered, before her body could come alive in lust and desire. Vincent backed off, hand still hovering over her leg. "It's not a good idea."

Her body protested. *Um, of course it's a good idea! This dude is gonna fuck you if you give him the signal!* Hot sex. *Eager* sex. If Nala wanted, she could turn off her brain, turn off the negative thoughts constantly plaguing her and go to a place where all that mattered was feeling good and getting off.

If she wasn't careful, however, she could become addicted. Like some people going through the grieving process became addicted to drink, drugs, and other destructive behavior, Nala could find herself on the path of relying too much on Vincent's worldly pleasures to help her escape reality. *And vice versa.* She wasn't deaf to his comments about how she was the first woman to make him feel sexually alive in a few years. *Don't become addicted to me, and I won't become addicted to you.* She was not Desirée, and that was who Vincent was chasing.

What was Nala chasing? *Don't go there.*

"I'm sorry." Vincent backed away, taking his touch with him. Nala hated to admit that she missed him already. *This is what I mean, though.*

Vincent got up, returning to his desk, which he leaned against and used to keep himself upright. Someone needed to tell him to stop looking so good, so approachable. Granted, he didn't look any different. He had a northwest goatee starting, but Nala knew that this man's facial hair grew at the speed of light – he had probably shaved it that morning. Imagining him standing in front of his sink, shirtless, shaving his overnight stubble was almost too hot to bear.

I wonder what his stubble would feel like down… Nala shook out her hair and stood as well, hoisting her tote bag onto her shoulder.

"Do you want to fuck me, Vincent?"

She stood right before him. He sucked in his breath. "Only if you want me to."

"That's not a real answer." Nala opened her free hand, drawing lines around his thighs before cupping his half-erect cock. Vincent gripped the desk, startled, but saying nothing. He hardened in her grip. "I'm asking if you want to *fuck me*. Every time you see me? Every time you think of me? Do you imagine ripping off my clothes and driving yourself into me until you come?"

Vincent chewed on the inside of his bottom lip. All that renewed energy had to go somewhere.

"Do you wanna fuck me in your office? You wanna show your sugar baby what's what?"

His lips parted enough to speak. "No comment."

"Hmph." Nala tightened her grip, feeling his cock come to life as all the blood in his body rushed there. "You said you were gonna take care of me, though. I know that doesn't come for free." She toyed with his zipper, gauging his non-reactions. "Face it. You want to see me get down on my knees and suck your cock."

Vincent narrowed his eyes. "Of course I fucking do."

Nala glanced at the bulge appearing in his dark pants. *I did that. I'm kind of awesome.* "Well, you don't get to. Because I'm not Nightingale right now, so you don't get to boss me around until I give in to my own temptations. Nala Nazarov doesn't play that game."

She could practically hear the next eye roll happening in the back of Vincent's head. *Whatever.* When she removed her hand from his crotch, she diverted to his back pocket, plucking his wallet and flipping it open to his small wad of cash. A five was sufficient to help her get home, since her ticket was already expired.

"I've gotta go. Call me when you hear something. I'll try not to make too many shady friends out there."

Nala left, bidding no further adieus as she tossed the wallet on the desk and bypassed Andrew glaring at her. She rode the elevator down to the ground floor, now full of businessmen and women starting their commutes home. The transit mall along the street outside was fuller than usual, comprised of eco-friendly businesspeople and the service staff that helped operate the surrounding buildings. Nala tucked herself beneath a glass enclosure as a drizzle began to fall on the already darkening streets.

Her phone buzzed in her pocket. She almost didn't read Vincent's text, because she wasn't in the mood for him to change her mind about things. *I must remain resolute.* Usually that was easy for her… and then she thought about the way the man controlled and fucked her. *Remain resolute!*

Since the bus was still another ten minutes away, however, Nala pulled out the phone and saw that it was a mere image attachment. A single line accompanied it.

"No matter what name you go by, you will always be her."

It was the picture he took the other night, at the end of their bondage demonstration. Nala stared, at first in confusion, and then in wonder.

The ropes twirled together, blending in, blending out, criss-crossing in an intricate design that represented an angel's wings.

No, not an angel's. A bird's.

Nala knelt on the stage, head bowed and long, dark hair cascading like a veil on either side of her face. Her arms held out above her head, attached to the wings preparing to take off in flight. To attack. To run.

Anyone else modeling, and she would say it was very beautiful, and that was it. Being her? The Nightingale? There was a sinister air in the way the wings began to flap. Her bowed head made her look injured, but determined. Grief and a thirst for revenge comingling in the most dangerous way possible.

It was her. It was Nala. It was the Nightingale.

Tears attacked the edges of her eyes. Nala turned against the wall, hiding her emotions from the people standing around her. *He really is an artist.* Was he? Had Vincent captured her essence? Had he tamed an angry woman with a thirst for blood? Or was she a willing canvas, waiting to be exploited by the first man to show a genuine interest?

"I'm going to do it," she muttered into the back of her hand. "I'm going to take that son of a bitch down." Xavier Crow had been in awe of this image. Awe? Fright? "I'm going to need him, though." Vincent was her means. Her means to revenge, her means to justice… her means to freedom.

Her eyes were dry by the time the bus pulled up and a dozen people got off and on. Nala clutched her phone in her hand, purchasing a new ticket before sitting next to a woman with sleepy eyes and perfume as strong as the wind kicking up outside.

"You'll help me, right?" Her thumb lingered above the send button before smashing it.

"I'll give you whatever you need."

"For Desirée?"

A minute passed. The bus stopped farther down the transit mall, letting more commuters on as the place quickly became standing room only. When Nala's cell phone buzzed again, it was with a man with two shopping bags standing right beside her, threatening to smack her if he even so much as turned around.

"For you, Nala."

The phone tapped against her lips as she bowed her head. Nala undid the clasp in her hair, letting it fall as it had in that photograph. She needed to shield herself the rest of the way home. None of these people could know why silent tears fell down her cheeks. They couldn't begin to understand the horror inflicted upon her. The upheaval Xavier Crow brought to her family… and the heart-crushing emotion Vincent Lane bestowed from behind a stoic façade.

"Thank you."

It was the first time she truly realized she could not do this alone. The enlightening thing? She didn't want to do it alone anyway.

Vincent would help her. Vincent would be by her side. Whatever happened along the way – and whatever happened afterward – Nala could count on at least one person to protect and guide her on the road to bringing down her sister's killer.

She had to not fall in love with him. That would lead her astray. That would lead to her heart shattering into a million more pieces she could not afford to lose – not without also losing the last shred of her soul.

"You have friends," the note said. Nala didn't know who it meant, but she knew who it should mean. *Vincent.* Friend first, lover second. She hoped it would stay that way. She didn't trust that it would.

Part 2

THE NIGHTINGALE RISES

Entry #9

Things continue to escalate. Nightingale has received a note detailing her identity and with references to The Aviary. I assume they know who I am as well.

Is it bad that my first concern was for her safety?

And that my second concern was that… as soon as she came to see me about it, the first thing I did was try to seduce her?

I fear becoming too comfortable around her. It's bad for her. And me. I can't afford losing another person I care about. Let alone in that way.

If there's a God, I will need all the divine intervention possible. On one hand I want to believe, because I need to believe that Desirée is still somewhere out there, being happy and well taken care of. But on the other hand, I am merely a shell of a bitter man, and I can't believe in such a thing. I have no faith.

Second chances don't exist like that, even for a man of my new means. I think Nightingale feels the same way. She is my muse, both in my recurring art and in helping me stay on track. If she ever succumbs to me… we'll be doomed.

Perhaps she really is the stronger one.

Chapter 19

"How the hell do you use this thing?"

Nala turned the smartphone upside down, wondering if that was the key to getting it to turn on. For being twenty-one, she was woefully a Luddite. Her flip phone had lasted her a good few years, and she still saw no reason to upgrade. Yet here she was, sitting at the dining room table trying to get a phone to boot up for the first time.

"*It's about time a 21yo join the 21st Century,*" said the note on top of the box, hand delivered by one of Lane Technological Solutions's best and brightest couriers. At least it wasn't Andrew, the young assistant who always regarded Nala with disdain whenever she stopped by her sugar daddy's office.

"Wish he would butt out of my life." Nala continued to mutter as she smashed buttons and futilely searched the instruction manual for a simple answer. She felt like a senior citizen at a computer class at the local library. If she were an old man, she would go outside and yell at some clouds – and in Portland, there were plenty of clouds to yell at.

She finally turned on the phone by accidentally pushing a certain button on the side. *The fuck?* What was it doing there? Holy crap! Why didn't phones have real buttons anymore? Her old phone had a lovely dial pad begging to be touched and played with, like a frisky wife after a lot of wine. Also, the startup sound the new phone played when it finally got going was liable to make her jump out the window.

Vincent told her that everything was set up, and all she had to do was customize it and make sure it was in her name. "*Don't worry about the bill. I'll take care of it.*" Oh, joy, and probably keep track of her. Nala may have been a Luddite, but she saw the stories about parents tracking their teens through parental switches and doohickeys and whatever. Vincent was a good ten years older than her. Did he think he was going to snoop whenever he felt like it? Read her texts? (To him?) Check out her pictures… if she ever figured out how to take them?

Nala wasn't stupid. She would keep the old phone to talk to everyone but Vincent. Better safe than sorry. Especially now that he gave her enough money every week to pay off her dumb-phone bill.

Still, playing with a new phone and getting acquainted with functioning technology gave her something to do on a rainy Thursday evening. It would be even better if her roommate Patrick weren't hosting a "party" for all his pothead friends.

At least they weren't smoking. No, all their cannabis was consumed via a healthy batch of brownies that had baked all day. At first Nala thought they smelled delicious. Herby, but delicious. Then she made the mistake of sampling some of the batter and gagging, flushing her system with heaps of water in the hopes of not becoming high. *I think I avoided it. Maybe.* The default background on the phone was sort of trippy.

"I feel like… man, life is so much more than whom you're boning, you know?" That was Steven. Or was it Stephen? Patrick's best friend, at any rate. He often came over to get high, but today he had his girlfriend – or was it fiancée? – in tow. And another girlfriend. And the other boyfriend his two girlfriends shared. *This shit doesn't happen in Carson City.* Nala could barely handle her fake boyfriend right now. Who expected her to deal with more than one? Let alone a girlfriend on top of that…

"Totally," one of Stephen's girlfriends piped up. "I'm so glad to be poly, man. We can chill without any drama. So many cuddle dates…"

Nala's new phone buzzed with life. And buzzed. And fucking buzzed.

Everyone in the living room turned around to look at her before going back to their super cool conversation.

"Am I queer if I'm into kink?"

"Oh my God, man, don't say queer. The lesbians don't like it."

"But I am, like, totally a lesbian. Or at least I was born one. I love women! Loooooove."

"Ahahah Steve, oh my God, you are not queer for being into kink. You are totally a lesbian, though."

"Aw, my boyfriend is genderqueer enough to be a lesbian!"

"We should have, like, more kink in this world, yo. Wouldn't it be great if we could come together for some BDSM?"

"There are so many clubs around here for kinksters. I've thought about joining them, but I'm shy! Someone go with me!"

"What do you like, Kathy? I'm sure we got some whips."

"Oh, I'm not so much into that. I want a man or woman to tell me what to do and then have their way with me."

More phone buzzing. Nala was vainly attempting to text Vincent, but all that was happening was randomly opening apps she had never heard of. Instagram? Snapchat? What the fucking fuck were those?

"Hey, Nala, come hang out with us!"

She perked up, seeing Patrick wave his hand over the back of the couch. "Oh, no thanks."

"Come *on,* hon, we wanna know about your hot boyfriend!"

Nala bristled, but not because she hated people assuming Vincent was her boyfriend. Why wouldn't they? She dressed up super fancy for him. He picked her up in the evenings and sometimes didn't bring her home until much later – eventually, he would probably drop her off the next day. Whenever Nala was seen returning, it was always with that "Back off, I've just been fucked" face. There was no doubt that Vincent was *someone* to her. No, she didn't want to talk about it.

"There's not much to say about him," she mumbled, trying to look focused on her phone.

"What's his name?"

"Not telling."

"Ah, come on! I see that guy out there all the time in his nice car! You've gotta spill."

"Yeah, spill!"

"Her? With a hot boyfriend?"

"Patrick's bi. He totally knows what a hot boyfriend is."

"Damn straight."

"You mean damn queer."

"See, this is why the lesbians don't like it."

"Fuck the lesbians."

"I'm sure you'd love to."

Nala had enough. She stood, happy to take her new toy into her closet of a bedroom. *Don't give these people all that satisfaction.* She turned toward them, boxes in hand.

"You wanna know about my boyfriend? All I have to tell you is that he's a Dom." Nala waited until their eyes lit up in curiosity, especially that Kathy girl who was talking about wanting to be bossed around, or whatever. "Yeah, he doesn't take shit from anyone, least of all me. You wanna know what it's like to be tied up? To be punished because you stepped out of line? You should wish to know a Master like him. Pshaw. You wouldn't be able to handle him. Now, excuse me, sugar daddy bought me a phone so we can phone sex in the closet. Bye."

As if on cue, the phone in her hand rang. Kathy jumped up, startled. "Oh my God, is that him? Is he omnisexual?"

"Dumbass, you mean omnipotent."

"Yes. And yes." Nala opened the closet door and popped in, turning on a fan she had clipped to the rod. She hoped it would be loud enough to drown out the stoners while not being too loud to talk to Vincent.

"I see you got the phone working." Amazing! His voice was so much clearer on the new phone. *It almost sounds like he's right here.* Boy, that would be cozy. "Congratulations. I thought I would already be leaving you a voice mail, and then hoping you figured out how to access it."

"Haha. Very funny. What's up?"

Vincent cleared his throat. "I have an unusual favor to ask of you. Are you available tomorrow night?"

"Yeah. Why? Last minute Aviary meeting?" As far as Nala knew, there wouldn't be another one until Sunday.

"No. Something more personal. I'm having a business dinner with clients and another couple. It would be rather awkward for me to be the only one there without a partner, so…"

"Vincent," Nala growled, taking a hint from his manner of speaking when they were alone. "I know you're not asking me to play your girlfriend for your business deals."

"Well… not quite."

She could have reached through her shiny new phone and throttled the man. "What if that starts some gossip? What if Xavier Crow finds out who I really am? I don't think I'm even on his radar right now, other than him probably wondering what my tits look like."

"Nala… I will make it worth your while."

Great. More money. Make her feel even more like a sugar baby. *Why not? It's what I'm good for.* Her mother would be so proud.

"To put up with that shit? You better."

"How does five-hundred sound?"

"Five-hundred what? Thousand dollars?"

"I see your point. I'll give you an extra thousand, and treat you to some shopping."

"What kind of girl do you think I am? You think I can be bought for dates like that? You really are my sugar daddy."

"Wow."

"Wow, what? You suddenly got a conscience?"

"Not at all. I never thought of myself as being old enough to be someone's sugar daddy."

"You're thirty, Vince. So old."

"Anyway, call me whatever you want. I would be grateful if you came as my date tomorrow night. Nothing serious, of course, but the others there don't have to know that. Besides… the man I've proposed to – now hold on, not *like that* – is also in town doing business with Crow. You might want to come and use your wiles to get what he knows out of him."

"Use my what?"

"Never mind."

Nala flopped back on her thin mattress and stared at her clothes hanging above her, at her tote bag swinging back and forth above her feet. "All right. I'll go, but only because I don't have anything else to do and because I like money." She had over three-thousand sitting in her account right now. That wasn't including the several hundred she made from her shitty job every month. "This doesn't mean I'll do this regularly, though. Like you asked, I'm mostly doing this as a favor to you, got it?"

"Got it."

"By the way…" This was Nala's chance to ask, since she hadn't talked to Vincent in a few days. "Did you find out the source of that note I got?"

"Not yet. I mean, there wasn't much to go on, but I've been doing some clue hunting in what spare time I have."

"Before or after you fall asleep playing *Fallout*?"

Vincent didn't miss a beat. "Before, of course. I'm a responsible man."

Says the dude who stuck it in unprotected. Nala wasn't going to go there right now, though. "What should I wear? The lavender dress?"

"No. Nothing from The Aviary. Sends completely the wrong message."

Oh, I bet. Vincent probably didn't want to be constantly reminded of sex while they ate dinner with business associates, anyway. "I don't have anything to wear."

"I figured. That's why I've gone ahead and sent someone over with my credit card to take you out shopping and to get your hair done."

"What?"

"You heard me. It's my treat. There's a spending limit, of course, but it should be sufficient to get you a few nice things and some pampering." Vincent chuckled. Nala did not care for his chuckles. "Unless you don't *want* pampering. You could suffer for the sake of it."

"Shut up. Okay, I'll go, but not because I particularly want to."

"Of course not."

"It's not Andrew coming, is it?"

"It's not Andrew. It's someone you'd much rather go with, if you had to choose."

"Oh, well, if I *had* to choose."

"What time is it? They should be there any minute."

"Wait, what? You went ahead and sent someone over to take me shopping, even before I said I would do it?"

She could practically hear him shrugging on the other line. "I didn't think you would end up saying no. Anyway, the worst that could've happened was that I had to call and tell them to not bother. Then pay for their time. It's not a big deal."

It's a big deal to us little people.

"Don't worry about anything today, or tomorrow night. Pick out something nice but safe, and I'll come pick you up around six. Come hungry. It's a five-course meal."

"Of course it is."

"I hope you have some fun, Nala. Even if you're not too into shopping, it will be a different experience downtown."

"Yeah, sure. Thanks."

She hung up before he could say anything else. At that lucky moment, the doorbell rang.

Nala burst from her closet before any of the stoners could get to the door. *Oh hell no!* She had no idea who was coming. She didn't *want* to know, but here she was, huffing it to the door before Patrick could stumble off the couch and answer with a cheese dust-infested grin.

The door opened with nary a squeal of the hinges. When Nala looked up from the heels greeting her, she almost lost the ability to speak.

"Gale!" Robin took up the entire doorway, sunhat flapping with raindrops on the rim. "Look at you! Let's go shopping!"

Nala began to close the door again before realizing that was a very rude thing to do.

Chapter 20

Nala stepped onto the porch, closing the door behind her instead of in Robin's face. *What the fuck!* She had yet to see any of the people from the club outside of its confines. Yet here Robin was, dressed like she was ready to attend an expensive luncheon after Sunday mass.

"You ready to go? Oh, didn't you know I was coming? You're dressed like…" She looked up and down Nala's ensemble, a simple hoodie and jeans combo. "Never mind. Do you want to change before we go? I can wait in the car.' Robin gestured to the Rolls-Royce idling on the street. *Oh my God.* What was going on?

"I… had no idea you were coming. Nor that you knew Vincent."

"He and Lucian have recently started doing business together. Vincent called and asked if I would be able to take you out shopping for a day. Said you were… not so into it, but needed a new wardrobe… and thought maybe you'd like a friend to help?"

Nala couldn't help but crack a smile. *She's ditzy, but she seems genuine.* If Nala had learned anything since moving back to Portland, it was that people could be faker than money sharks in Vegas. But when you found a good soul who clicked with you – or as much as one could with Nala – it was best to hold on to them.

"It was very nice of you to come all the way out here from…"

Robin perked up. "Oh! We live down on the South Waterfront. It wasn't *that* far to come out. The bridges ain't nothing this time of day."

"I'm sure." Nala pulled her hands out of her hoodie pocket and placed one on the door handle. "Give me a few minutes to put on some shopping clothes." Whatever those were.

Robin went to wait in the heated car while Nala perused her slim selection of cute clothes. Cute clothes that wouldn't leave her to freeze and drown in the rainy weather, anyway. *Are jeans too uncouth?* Most of hers were second-hand. So, probably.

The best she could do was her nicer work trousers and a dark blue blouse that made her look more chic than homeless. *Please fit into the Portland aesthetic.* It was her best bet, because she could never hope to dress like Robin in her slinky red dress and bold makeup.

"Hey, girl, let's go!" The car door opened and enticed Nala to come inside. "I know all the best shops downtown. Mr. Lane gave me his credit card for safe keeping. You're so lucky! Ten thousand spending limit!"

"Ten… thousand?" Nala had barely shut the car door behind her and buckled her seatbelt when she heard the news. In the front seat sat a dapper man with white gloves and a black, flat-topped hat. The moment Robin told him to head downtown, the car pulled away from the pot-reeking craftsman house.

"What? Does he usually give you less?"

"Well…"

"Hm." Robin crossed her slender, waxed legs. *I need to shave mine.* She started shortly before going to The Crow's Nest the first time, and she still wasn't used to it yet. It was a miracle Vincent never mentioned her stubble. *Oh, right, guys don't actually notice that shit.* Yet here Nala was, staring at a woman's smooth legs. "No matter. We'll get you squared away. He said that you have a big business dinner tomorrow night and you needed a new outfit. He also mentioned getting other similar outfits and some… well, you already know."

Nala caught a hint of blush on Robin's face. "No. What? He hasn't told me anything other than something about a dinner."

"Oh?" Robin's lips were pretty when she formed that round letter. "He said you wanted to go to that lingerie boutique. You know, *the* one."

"No, I don't.'

"Um… okay."

What are you doing? Don't blow your cover, girl. "I don't go shopping much." Nala forced a smile intended to save her current relationship. "And I only moved here a few months ago. So I'm afraid I don't know much about what's available, shopping wise."

"That explains a lot," Robin muttered, studying Nala's clothes again. "You're always done-up so pretty – albeit simply – for the club. I figured it's what your Master liked best, but now I see you really are plain-styled. Not that it's a bad thing!" She held up her long, manicured nails in defense. "It really suits common styles around here. At least you're not lumberjack-chic, though. There's only so much I can do with that." Robin grinned. "I have a degree in fashion consultation and cosmetology, you know."

"I had no idea."

"Yup. That's how I met Lucian." Robin tossed her hair behind her shoulders as they approached a bridge into downtown. "His daughter is thinking about going into cosmetology and stopped by my school a long while ago. He came to pick her up while I was stepping out… the rest is history. Guess I'm really his type to make him stop and look."

"He has a daughter?"

"Yes. Eighteen, from his ex-girlfriend."

"He doesn't look old enough to be a father of a teen…"

"To be fair, the mother was close to the same age…"

"I see." Teenage Lucian knocking up his equally teen girlfriend of the time didn't seem too farfetched. "Do you get along well with her?"

Robin shrugged. "Well enough. She lives with her mother in Colorado, so I don't see her much. I don't really feel like a stepmother, which is fine with me. I'd rather be like a big sister."

All right, that's weird.

"Do you have kids? Or does Vincent have kids?"

Nala pursed her lips. "I don't have kids. *We* don't have kids," she corrected herself. *I don't think he has children.* Did he want them? Did Desirée want them, and were they planning to have kids by thirty-five? *They could afford it.* Not many, like Nala, could say that. *He's a loose cannon downstairs, though.* Coming and going in whatever pussy he pleased. Some men got off on that thrill, though.

"You two haven't been together that long, have you?"

"What gave that away?"

"You're both a bit reserved, even around each other. Plus the way you both talk about the other, as if you're talking about a distant roommate instead of someone you've been with for a long time. Not that it's bad. It's rather obvious that you're still getting used to each other."

"I suppose it hasn't been that long in the realm of the world."

It was about a month since they met, Nala falling down the stairs of The Crow's Nest and Vincent grabbing her in time. *Everything changed after that.* The Aviary. The bondage. The *sex*. Nala always knew she liked it a little rough, a little dangerous – and Vincent offered both. Underneath that cool exterior lurked a beast waiting to take her to new heights. Nala still didn't know how to process it.

"So! First, I'm going to take you to my friend who is a personal stylist. She has an office downtown and I've already called ahead. Since I don't know you *that* well, Gale, I thought it best to get a professional opinion instead of going by intuition alone. You game?"

"Couldn't be more game." It sounded like torture, but Nala couldn't be picky. If she had to choose, then going to a personal stylist and shopper was probably better than going by Robin's tastes alone. *I could not pull off her look.* Vincent would laugh before refusing to let Nala get in his car.

They pulled into a parking garage in the middle of downtown, the driver letting out both Robin and Nala before the former took the latter by the arm. Like a couple of perfect – albeit polar opposite – besties, they walked into a nearby building and took an elevator up a few floors. When they stepped into a stylish, pristine office covered in gilded mirrors and marble tiles, Nala instantly noticed Vincent's office building across the street. For some reason, nerves claimed her stomach.

"Georgina!" Robin exchanged kisses on the cheek with a woman emerging from a back office. Lacquered nails, tight stockings, stiletto heels, and a body full of Gucci took in Nala without a second look. "This is my friend Nigh… Gale. This is Gale." She sent an apologetic look. *We still don't know each other's real names.* That was more than fine, but it did create a few awkward situations. Like this woman looking at Nala and clearly thinking that she didn't look like a damn "Gale" at all.

"What can I do for you, Gale?" Georgina's voice was buttery, reminding Nala of the fresh biscuits her mother used to pull out on rainy Sundays.

"She needs a new formal wardrobe," Robin interrupted. "She's got a big business dinner with the likes of Vincent Lane tomorrow." She pulled out his credit card. "Mr. Lane will be taking care of all associated costs."

"Ah." Georgina snatched the card without a second thought. "This is good. Any instructions?" She still looked at Nala, but it was clear that her ear was open to Robin, the woman running this show – and running the cards coming in Georgina's direction.

Robin produced a small, handwritten list of items she probably jotted while on the phone with Vincent. *What were they saying about me? Did he really call this woman up to discuss my fashion sense?* Vincent's new business relationship with Lucian must have been really good for the girls to be going out for shopping and new hair.

"He has asked for darker colors, particularly for the formal wear. Black, blues, some deep purples and reds. He's also made a point to ask for her hair to be cut no shorter than two inches, to account for any split ends."

Nala picked up a clump of her hair and looked at the ends. Were they split? She had no damn idea. Most of these terms were like Greek to her.

"I can work with this." Georgina tentatively extended her hand and fingered Nala's hair before looking over her current clothes. *I bet she can tell how cheap they are…* Not ideal in the least, but hey, Nala was here to spend Vincent's money, apparently. "Yes. I know where to start. Meet me downstairs in fifteen minutes while I arrange things here with my assistant."

Nala had never been on a shopping spree of this caliber before, and she wasn't sure she could ever survive another one.

Boutiques, department stores, and even private collections from Portland designers sped by in the remainder of the afternoon. Nala's tired legs carried her from one location to the next, where Georgina and Robin discussed what colors and cuts were best for her skin and frame. They agreed that Vincent had good tastes in colors. The black, dark blues, and crimsons were the biggest hits, with a few white pieces a respectable distance behind.

They dressed her in body-hugging dresses, loose and tight bodices, and skirts that flared out above her knees. Many gowns and skirts had to be tailored to her height – a first in Nala's short life. *My mother used to hem some of my clothes, but nothing was tailored.* When she thought about it, all of Vincent's clothing must have been tailored to fit so well on his body. *Why am I thinking about him?* Oh, because she was spending his money? Every time that black credit card passed to a girl behind a register, Nala wondered if it was really okay.

Wondering that made *her* feel okay about being treated like a doll. They could dress her however they wanted. Every time they called her Gale, Nala was reminded that she was the Nightingale, who would be more than happy to accommodate her Master's wishes. Whatever he wanted. Whatever he desired. As long as it was comfortable enough to put up with for an evening at a time… well, what did Nala care? Her opinion was rarely asked. Even dithering between two colors of the same outfit mostly came down to Georgina and not Nala. The only time she expressed her mood was when she was asked her favorite color.

"Dark blue. Paired with silver."

"Very regal," Georgina said. "I can see it. With this hairstyle… you can look like a queen."

That made Nala smile in the mirror.

The last thing they did with Georgina that day was go to a salon. The hairstylist washed and conditioned Nala's hair, taking the time to carefully pick it before evening the ends and getting rid of the splits. When Georgina asked what was so important about keeping the style the same, Robin replied, "You know how I am with Lucian? That is how Gale is like with her fiancé."

Stop calling him my fiancé. Nala tried to not let it get to her. *That was Desirée.* She shouldn't care, and yet… *I'm the one who is alive, not her.*

The stylist created a new, simple makeup pallet that Nala could maintain on her own. Lots of smoky eyes. Dark lipstick colors. Red rouge. They went over this while she had the first manicure of her life.

In the end, nine bags from nine different locations were accumulated. Robin's driver carried a bulk of these from the shops to the car. *I've never owned so many nice clothes.* Where was she going to put them?

They thanked Georgina for her help, Robin giving her Vincent's contact information so they could go over her commission. Nala received a kiss on the cheek from this woman who was still a relative stranger. When she finally left, Nala assumed that it was time to go home – although she hoped Vincent's credit card could buy her dinner as well.

Nope. Robin had one more place she wanted to check out. That boutique Vincent claimed Nala really wanted to visit. For lingerie.

It was a small place off the main streets, but after being in so many other fancy places that day, Nala could tell that this boutique tailored to a certain clientele as well. *Rich people. Rich skinny people.* She wasn't skinny, but she could probably fit depending on the hormonal fluctuations.

"Georgina knows a lot of things about style and fashion, but I'm the best when it comes to figuring this stuff out." Robin touched a black bustier displayed on a headless mannequin. "I know what men like ours like on their ladies. Of course, we want to get you some things that make you feel confident as well!"

Nala stared in awe at the racks of panties, bras, garters… anything that could be used to underline her new dresses or draw Vincent into bed. *Do I really need help with that?* She was already fending off his advances…

advances she so dearly wanted to give in to. "I'm not used to this sort of thing. I'm not sure what you would even call most of these things."

Dresses and skirts were one affair. She was willing to be dressed up, paraded, and even admired in someone else's tastes. Lingerie? That was so intimate that she almost began to shake in her new boots. *Do I get what I like, or what he would like?* Normally Nala wouldn't wonder such a thing. It was her body, her style, right? Except Vincent was paying for this, and she would only wear them when she was playing Nightingale in their undercover play. And Nightingale… would pick things that made her feel sexy while her Master undressed her.

"If you're not used to wearing this sort of stuff, I could see how it's intimidating. Don't worry. We'll get you fitted for a bra and go from there. What size do you think you are? I'll find someone to help us."

Nala stared at a rack of pink, frilly bras in various sizes, from super tiny to super *big*. "I dunno. 32B?"

"Oh, honey, you're bigger than that!"

"I doubt it." She looked down at her breasts, hiding beneath her blouse. "I mean, it's okay that they're small. It doesn't bother me." She couldn't comment on Robin's, er, *tig-ass bitties.*

"It's not really about whether or not you feel good about the size of your breasts." Robin flagged down the nearest helper and motioned, quite evocatively, at Nala's chest. "It's about wearing a bra that feels damn good and gives you the support you need! Most women are wearing a bra that's too small for them."

"About that…"

When Nala, Robin, and the helper ended up in a changing area, Robin slapped her hand over her eyes to discover her dear new friend was completely commando beneath her blouse. The helper barely blinked as she pulled out her tape and instructed Nala to get into position.

"Girl, you ain't got a bra on!"

"Because these things are not that big." Nala shrugged. She was in the presence of women who didn't wish to leer at her breasts. No big deal… or so she thought. The helper tugged on the loose tape and wrote something down on a pad. Robin peeked through two fingers and shook her head in awe.

"I could never get away with that. Even when I try not wearing a bra, my boobs are too big to feel comfortable. I even sleep in one… how do you manage?"

"It doesn't bother me."

"Well," the helper interrupted. "Let's start you at a 34C. I think you'll find it's comfortable."

"That's cool."

Nala supposed her breasts could have grown since she was last measured at a lingerie shop years ago. After all, she had been seventeen then. Now she was twenty-one and with a more womanly body. When the helper brought a plain black sampler to try on, Nala shrugged into it, surprised to find it fit. The helper pulled on the snaps and announced they may want to try a 32 next after all.

"I don't really like wearing bras…" Nala said.

"Gale, honey…" Robin put a kind hand on her friend's shoulder before sidling close and whispering into her ear. "This isn't your run-of-the-mill lingerie shop. I mean, you could wear some of these things on the daily, but it's *more* about… you know…" She faked a cough. "Being sexy. For your confidence, *and* to put your Master's Mr. Happy in a fun place. You know. For your benefit. Ahem."

Did she say Master's Mr. Happy? Robin was a trip. Nala would have to be caught dead with psychedelics strewn around her corpse to be caught saying something dumb like that. "I see. Thanks for the perspective." Good to know Vincent sent her here to get sexy undies *for him.* Sure, he'd tell her they were for The Aviary, but she knew his real motive. *He wants to see me in lingerie like this.* Lace. Silk. Satin. Rioting colors and soft pastels. Panties with holes in them and bras that came apart in the front.

Nala was ready to leave. Nightingale, however, was deeply intrigued.

I wonder how hard I could get a man like that. It could be a game. Get Vincent aroused, make him endure a striptease with underwear like this as a treat… and then see if she could get him to come without touching him.

Nala hurried to get her blouse back on and rushed into the gallery, where racks upon racks of lingerie awaited. Robin hustled to keep up, and the helper followed as well, asking if she could get Nala started with anything.

Yes. I need five bras, ten pairs of panties, and whatever these corset things are. I need to be on fire. A man is paying me to dress up like the classiest hooker he's ever had the pleasure of purchasing the services of, and I intend to deliver for my sugar daddy!

Robin attempted to help Nala shop for lingerie, but *someone* was a tornado of grabbing, trying on, rejecting or accepting, and furiously asking a million questions about style, color, and materials. Would this make her itch? Would this shrink in the wash? *How* should she wash this stuff, anyway? If the panties were thirty a piece, did that mean she could ask for more on the sexy black market? Girl had to think long term past Vincent's weekly payments.

"*Hey, guess what,*" she texted Vincent while waiting for her purchases to be rang up.

"*What?*"

"*You bought me fifty pairs of underwear.*"

The fact it took him so long to reply – when they were in an elevator with Robin on the phone and asking her driver to meet them up front – made Nala wonder if he were this busy after five or having a moment to himself in the bathroom. *Latter one, please.* Robin talked about lingerie giving her confidence, but Nala was pretty sure mentioning underwear to a man and getting him to take it to the corner was better. Or at least for someone like her it was.

"*I couldn't have you tramping around in used panties, now could I?*"

Nala was surprised he remembered that. "*I don't have room for this stuff at my place. Can I dump most of it at yours?*"

"*I'll be home at six. Anytime after that is fine.*"

What was Nala supposed to do until then? It was barely after five.

As if Robin read her mind, she said in the elevator, "Let's get dinner. Lucian won't be home until late, anyway. We haven't had time for a real chat anyway."

"Sure. You pick." Nala plucked the black card out of Robin's hand. "I'll take this over for now. I'm sure my *Master* won't mind." Besides, she could give it back to him later.

They reached the bottom floor and stepped out onto the sidewalk. The rain had let up, but crowds continued to swell in the dark. With so many cars passing by, they would have to wait a few minutes for Robin's driver to make it around the block and reach them with the skin still on his back.

"Hey! You ladies got any money?"

Robin leaped out of her stilettos, instinctively hiding behind Nala even though the other woman was a good head and a half shorter. Nala, on the other hand, could hardly be bothered by the homeless man sauntering up to them and putting his hand out.

"Sorry. No cash," she said. *Even if I had any money, I'm probably going to be asked five more times tonight. What do I tell those guys?*

"Baaah!" The man, who smelled like alcohol and an allergy to baths, tossed his hand into the air and sent Robin a stink-eye. "Look how rich you are," he sneered, turning on his foot and marching away to harass someone else. "Can't spare even a dollar…"

Robin waited until he was at the end of the block before stepping out from behind Nala. "That was scary. I had heard the homeless problem was worse down here but… I don't normally go shopping without a man in present company."

I bet. "They're mostly harmless. Just tell them you don't carry cash and they'll be on their way. Be firm." She shrugged. "Then again, I look poorer than you. That probably has a lot to do with it."

"You're not poor, though," Robin said, as the car pulled up. "You've got Mr. Lane."

Nala didn't have the heart to tell her. Not that she would, anyway.

Robin took them toward Burnside, to a restaurant sitting atop a historical building and boasting some of the "best seafood" around. *What is it with rich people and seafood?* Was it a Portland transplant thing? Even when Nala moved back from the desert, she had no desire to try the local fresh caught salmon. Or the factory farmed, for that matter.

They had their own corner in the half-empty restaurant. Robin claimed a booth while Nala sat in a wooden chair across from her. The waitress hadn't come by with water and taken away their orders when Robin opened her big, gossiping mouth.

"So, Gale, tell me everything," she said, teeth bared. "How big is Mr. Lane's cock?"

The glass Nala held dumped on the table. Water spilled everywhere, including in Robin's lap.

And that was how Nala responded to the least invasive question that night.

Chapter 21

"Sorry, so sorry," Nala apologized, helping Robin and the waitress clean up the mess. "To be fair, though," she muttered, once the waitress was gone, "that was a banger of a question."

Robin inhaled deeply, composing her long limbs and making sure her red dress went back into place. "Never mind. Just thought we would have a bit of girl talk. I can see, though, that you're jitterier expected. Also, shy."

Shy? Was Nala shy? *I'm the girl who had no problem with Vincent tearing my dress apart the first time we had sex.* Nor did she have issues dropping his pants and putting her mouth all over him. She didn't have a problem with a *lot* of things. "I wasn't expecting a question like that, let alone so soon. Sorry."

Her mumbling did not go unheard. "Okay, so I was quick to jump into that, but come on! We know so little about you two. Lucian and I speculate about you and Mr. Lane all the time…"

"You do?" Why in the world? Because business was happening now?

"We are a couple of gossips. The man spends more time chatting on the phone than I do… but, that's not the point. Hey, Gale, I think you're a sweet girl. Bit quiet and understated, but a loudmouth like me needs that kind of foil in her life. I thought maybe you and I were pretty similar deep inside our brains."

The way she said *brains* made her sound like a hungry zombie. "*Braaiiinnnss.*" Nala hid her laughter with a new sip of water. "I'm not shy, but give a girl some warning next time."

"Will do! Should I start talking about Lucian's? It's pretty big, if I do say so myself…"

What was with this woman? She started yapping about her boyfriend's dick as if Nala would naturally want to know about it. *I already know. I saw it.* She would never admit she stopped and peered at the show Robin and Lucian put on back at the hotel. *The one that turned me so on that I…* started fantasizing about Vincent. That's what happened. Which then led to the couple fucking each other dead at the sex club. And then at Vincent's place. And then…

These people were all about sex. Nala knew it, and yet she remained shocked at nearly every turn. Even in everyday life, Robin spent most of her time thinking about her Master Lucian. How often did they have sex? Were they always kinky? Were they real lifestylers like they presented to The Aviary? Robin didn't act very submissive when she was out with another woman. Was that something she gave only to Lucian? Again, was it a lie? Or a falsehood at best?

"That's… congratulations." Nala didn't know what else to say. What did one say when a new friend started talking about her boyfriend's big dick?

"I suppose. You know, in this game, men of our boyfriends' standing come in only two flavors. Big dicks or little dicks." Robin giggled into her handkerchief. "Someone like you must have discerning tastes, Gale. I can guess what Mr. Lane is like."

"Er, well…" She had no idea how many inches Vincent sported. She wasn't counting. Nala could only go by the difficulty he sometimes had entering her, but that could've easily been her as well. "I'm not complaining."

"Good! We deserve men who make us happy in all areas of life. Oh, Lucian is so doting. Even when he's being strict with me and on the verge of punishing my ass, he feels so tender and loving when he does it. I could never ask for a better man. Let alone a richer one."

"That's great."

"What about Mr. Lane? Is he the affectionate type? He's hard for anyone to read. If you ask me," Nala hadn't, "he's not interested in anyone but you."

Nala looked up from her elaborate napkin folding. *I was once a champion at origami in second grade.* "You think that?"

"Why, yes. Would that be weird?"

Idiot. She thinks we're in love. Apparently, Vincent was doing a great job making people think that. When Nala thought about it, she realized he spent a lot of their club meetings lightly touching her, whispering whatever he had to say into her ear as if he said nothing but sweet affections. *He's a good actor.* "Not weird at all. It's just, well, Vincent is not very forthcoming with his feelings and emotions. He doesn't tell me that he loves me."

"What? Really?"

Robin looked as if Nala told her a cat was dead. "Well, no, but that's okay. I know he cares about me." He had to. *Wait, what am I thinking? He only wants me for sex and to get to Xavier Crow.* Nala snorted at her own absurdity.

"Oh, I'm sorry about that. I don't think I could live this lifestyle if my Master wasn't openly affectionate. It would be really hard otherwise, you know?"

Nala had to pretend she did. "I don't like a lot of affection, anyway. So, you really do live the lifestyle?"

Robin laughed in disbelief. "Of course I do? We all do. It's a requirement to being in The Aviary, silly."

"Of course. I'd forgotten."

If Nala got any more head turns and tilts from the people around her, she would start wondering if she had magnets hanging off her chin and the populace had metal implants in their scalps. "You're a funny gal, Gale. I like that about you, though. The other girls in the group… they're nice, but not really my type."

"Oh?"

"Uh huh." Robin almost looked as if she didn't want to gossip in that direction, but then explained, "Quail has been in the lifestyle for a long while, but Sebastian is a pretty new partner for her. Starling… well, she's too new for me to know well, but she doesn't seem interested in returning calls or getting to know us. Maggie, though… hells bells, nobody knows about her!"

"I'm flattered you think so highly of me, then."

"You're so blissfully normal, Gale. You're the kind of girl I want to spend fun days with, even if it means going to the movies or museums. Or shopping! I had a lot of fun today, and I wasn't shopping for myself…"

"I'm glad to hear you say that." Really, she was. Nala didn't want to waste anyone's time. "You seem nice, too. How did you and… your Master… get invited into The Aviary?"

"Oh." Robin looked away, blush touching her alabaster cheeks. "We're one of the oldest couples in that club. One of the first to be invited when Master Crow started it a while ago. He and Lucian go back a good ways. Lucian is in trading. Not just stocks, but physical products like cars and the like. He's helped Master Crow with marketing his medicinal stuff a lot. So, they've known each other a while."

"I see."

"I think it was knowing us that spurred him to start his club. It's been interesting. Lucian and I always look forward to the meetings, although we can't always make them."

"Naturally."

"Anyway…" Robin leaned across the table, lowering her voice. "I was asking those personal things earlier because Lucian is… well, he has a healthy appetite, I gotta tell you, Gale. I knew that getting involved with him, so it doesn't bother me, but he's one of the reasons the club has that swinging policy. The only woman Lucian hasn't touched so far is Maggie, and I'm pretty sure it's because Jay won't have it. Worked something out with Master Crow so they don't have to swing as often… anyway… I'm sure you can see where this is going." Robin bit her lip and looked down into her lap, sheepishly.

"Yes." Nala pulled her napkin into her lap and began pounding it like dough. *How about no?* No to Lucian feeling her up and getting to stuff his cock in any of her orifices. Heeellllll no! *One billionaire is all I can handle right now, and I've told him no as often as I've told him hell yes.* "I get the gist."

"I don't want to scare you or anything. He's a really great lover, and, well… it's only right for my Master to offer me in exchange… and…"

Nala almost snickered at the thought of Vincent and Robin in bed together. *I would actually pay to watch that.* Big tits swinging and Vincent wondering what the fuck he was involved with. *They're both hot… but no chemistry at all.* Robin would be a good one-night match for any of the other men in The Aviary, but not someone like Vincent. She doubted Robin was the type of woman Vincent would pick up at a bar and take home without knowing her name. *I guess I'm more his type.* That didn't say much.

"It's okay if you don't want to discuss this, but I thought I'd put it out there so it didn't come as a huge surprise later on. We okay?"

Nala nodded. "Absolutely fine." She wasn't bothered by the idea of Robin and Vincent in bed together, but she *was* bothered with being expected to sleep with Lucian. She would have to discuss this with Vincent. *Can we get out of the swinging? Please? These other guys don't understand what I'm doing here. I don't get off on being bartered with other men. I don't think I do anyway…*

Right now she only got off to Vincent's brand of… whatever it was he did.

Thankfully – *blissfully* – Robin changed topics. Choosing to talk at length about herself. This didn't bother Nala, as she was glad to get the focus off her and on someone else for a while. She didn't mind hearing about Robin's upbringing, her siblings, her last Christmas party with her family – with Lucian in tow – and all that other stuff people talk about when talking about themselves. Sometimes she would ask Nala a question about her life, but she was able to eschew it by either playing dumb or telling a white lie. For example, she mentioned she had a sister, but didn't mention that said sister was dead.

By the time dinner was over, Nala had learned everything there was to know about Robin's personal world – which wasn't much at all. *I wish I had learned something more about Crow.* Robin probably didn't know much to begin with. She was a pawn in The Aviary. A pawn who was happy to be overshadowed by Rooks and Kings.

Robin gave Nala a ride to Vincent's loft. She didn't feel strange about this, since anyone, especially of Lucian's standing, could look up Vincent's address. What was the harm in showing Robin how to get there?

Once Nala confirmed that Mr. Sugar Daddy was home, she grabbed her bags out of the trunk and waved goodbye to Robin and her driver, bags hanging from hands, shoulders, and elbows. The car pulled onto the nearest main road before something buzzed by the front door leading up to Vincent's loft.

"Get up here before the local wanderers figure out what you have in your bags," came his tired voice over the intercom.

The door unlocked. Nala finagled it open and began her ascent, hearing the door close and lock behind her.

Vincent sat in his kitchen, bathed in warm light and going over a stack of files next to him. *Wow, that is some boring work he brought home.* Nala dumped her bags by the dining table and leaned against it, letting her hand brush against Vincent's shoulder. The man wore a cotton T-shirt and jeans. Probably what he changed into the moment he arrived home.

His eyes grew wide when he ascertained the amount of bags at his feet. "Did you turn into Crow when I wasn't looking and buy out half of Portland?"

"Haha, very funny. What did you want after I was put into the hands of a stylist who had access to your credit card?" She produced said card from her pocket and dropped it in front of Vincent. "Nice touch sending Robin. Didn't know you two were friends."

"I'm not friends with her, but I called in a favor with Lucian."

Do I tell him now?

"Speaking of him, this shit's all for a project we've started working on together. He's hired my company to create an app to manage the cars he oversees before they leave port. Could lead to some very nice international deals, especially with the Koreans and Japanese."

"They have all the money right now." See? Nala read some news too.

"Basically. Did you buy anything nice?"

He opened the nearest bag – which was of course the lingerie bag.

"Uh oh." Vincent pulled out a lacey black thong and dangled it from his finger. Nala pretended to be unperturbed, but for some reason she couldn't look him in the eye while he fondled her purchase. "What were you planning to do with these?"

"Wear them, duh."

Vincent touched the bottom of her hair, letting his finger trail along the trimmed edge. "You look good."

"I'm not wearing new clothes. I already owned these."

"I know."

Nala stiffened. Did he have to get right to flirting? "Can I leave these here? I'll take what I'm wearing tomorrow home, but I can't bring these back to my house." She left out the part where she had completely run out of room to store things in her closet. Er, her bedroom.

"You can leave whatever you want here, but as for going home…" Vincent scooted his chair back. "You don't have to do that."

"Um…"

His hand grazed her hip. *Oh no.* She didn't come here to have sex with him. Hell, she was feeling quite unaroused when she arrived. Now? *Calm down, libido.* If she didn't rein in her sex drive, she would quickly find herself on her knees with her face buried in his lap. *Why is my imagination going straight there?* Shit, she was in trouble.

"You can stay here, if you want. I know you already had dinner, but…"

"Let me guess,' she brusquely said. "Sex for dessert?"

"Only if you want. We don't have to do that."

He kept complicating things. *I get it. You get hard for me.* Vincent had said more than once that she reawakened yearnings he hadn't had since

Desirée's death. Yearnings like famished fucking. *Yearnings* like BDSM bullshit. *He wants to tie me up and stick it in me, hard.* Nala crossed one leg in front of the other to keep them closed. *Maybe I want him fucking me on this table.* Okay, *that* she might have a really hard time saying no to.

"You're an okay guy, Vincent, but I'm not ready for sleepovers."

His hand curled around the front of her waist, touching her bare stomach beneath her blouse and tugging at her waistline. "Then don't stay the night. I'll give you a ride home later."

He stood. Even though Nala knew what was coming, she still was not prepared for Vincent to kick aside an expensive boutique bag and lower his lips to hers.

I'm a fool. She let him kiss her, and in truth, she kissed him back. Maybe not as much as he was kissing her, but she was definitely into it, even if for a few seconds. Seconds that were long enough to let his tongue dip into her mouth and explore the near back of her throat.

Nala's hand went around his neck. She held him upon her lips long enough for Vincent's hand to make its way up beneath her blouse and discover she wasn't wearing a bra.

"Naughty girl," he purred into her ear. His whole body shuddered, threatening to take Nala down to the floor with him. When he pinched her nipple, Nala finally snapped out of her stupor and yanked his hand out of her blouse. "What is it?"

She looked at him, taking in his muscular physique beneath that cotton T-shirt – taking in the bulge growing in his jeans. *A quickie. We could have a quickie and then I would be on my way.* No, no… that was a bad idea. "I spent the whole day with a member of The Aviary, talking about the other members and Crow himself… and your first inclination is to get into my pants?" She should have anticipated this. "I may have been playing for Robin, but I assure you that I'm not in the mood for your games right now."

"Fine." Vincent sat back down. "What did you find out?"

Nala didn't expect that spotlight to be shone upon her so quickly. "Er… nothing, really. She told me a lot of junk, but it didn't relate."

"You mean you spent the *whole* day with her, and didn't learn a thing?"

"And Lucian? You learning shit from him?"

Vincent leaned an elbow against the table. "Touché."

"So we both suck."

"I've got a business to run in the interim. This is a big week for us, with the proposals going out and having to hire new staff… I spent all day yesterday conducting interviews for more programmers. There isn't a short supply of them around here."

How utterly fascinating. Nala patted his shoulder and pushed off the table. "I'll be going then. I'll take the bus home before it gets too late. I've got work tomorrow before our big date with your business associates. You owe me, you know. This shopping spree doesn't count, because I bought clothes to wear around you… and because I don't care that much for shopping."

She should have figured his hand would reappear on the front of her body – right next to her crotch, to be exact. *Oh, brother.* "Tell me what you want, and I'll give it to you."

Ha! Just like that? This man was showing off his god complex if Nala ever saw it. *I guess some women find that sexy.* She found it sort of creepy. Definitely off-putting. *Where's the guy who wanted to play video games and eat pizza?* Maybe she should ask for that. "I don't want anything but to go home."

Vincent's hand lingered on her stomach. "What's wrong, Nala? If you're not in the mood, say so."

"I'm not in the mood."

He took his hand off her. "Sorry I assumed."

All Nala could do was conjure a glare. "Have you ever considered getting a *real* girlfriend? I'm sure it's great to have your dick get hard again, but I'm not really available for that every time you see me. Maybe you should get an honest woman who wants your cock as badly as you want it sucked every day."

Vincent sat up in his seat. "What's gotten into you? You've implied numerous times that you're not put off by us having occasional sex."

"Yes, Vincent, and *occasional* means just that. Not every time we see each other."

"Fair enough. Can you blame a man for inquiring, though?"

"So, getting that real girlfriend?"

He frowned. "I don't think that's a good idea right now. Maybe after all is said and done I'll be able to start looking again."

Somehow, Nala was amazed that he was able to say that so casually. Was it something he had been thinking about? "Well," she began, "that's true. Best not to get another woman wrapped up in this bullshit. Besides…" she picked up the bag containing her outfit for the next day. "I *did* imply numerous times that I'm okay with playing cock and pussy with you when I'm up for it. How about tomorrow night, after the dinner?"

Vincent looked as if he couldn't believe what the hell she was saying. "Are you making a sex date with me?"

"Yes. As Nala."

"As Nala…"

"That means you don't get to hold me down and do that dirty girl stuff. Trust me, Vincent, I want you too. Carnally, at least. By that, I mean I want to have my way with you like you keep having your way with me. What do you say? When your dinner is over, we'll come back here and hide your salami in my taco."

"That's… not the sexiest talk I've ever heard."

"You mean I'm not good at this dirty talk stuff? Darn."

"We'll see where the wind takes us tomorrow. But it's a date. After dinner, we'll come back here, and do something."

Date. He said date. Nala had not thought of it as a date. This was a business transaction at best. *Oh my God, I'm officially a sugar baby.* If she hadn't thought it before, she thought it whole heartedly now.

Either way, *something* was going to happen the next day.

Entry #10

Tomorrow night has nothing to do with The Aviary and everything to do with it at the same time. It's so important that I have paid for Nightingale to have a shopping spree. Knowing her, however, she'll do everything in her power to not spend any money. Thus I arranged for a fellow Aviary member to take her out and make sure she gets the clothes and accessories necessary. It's imperative that we look like a real couple, and that means only the best clothes for her body – that I paid for, as her boyfriend, of course.

She will be surprised to see who is at the dinner. I've done a lot of digging since she received her note, and I have some pretty good hunches. It will be interesting to see what transpires.

Meanwhile, I must be on my best behavior. I cannot afford to lose myself around a woman who would barely be in college if she went. When I was in grad school, women her age seemed so young. That was only a few years ago. Now she doesn't seem so young. I think it's the age of her mind making her seem much older than she actually is.

Even more dangerous for a man like me. Women wise beyond their years are my #1 weakness.

Chapter 22

"I have no idea what to do or say," Nala said Friday night, standing at the front of the restaurant. Vincent was beside her, dressed in a silk white button down that left the top two buttons undone. Oh, and that suit jacket and pants… *I'm trash.* Nala kept her eyes off Vincent when he picked her up, drove her to the restaurant, and then escorted her in. He, on the other hand, had a difficult time keeping his eyes off *her.*

To be fair, even Nala admitted she was a knockout in her designer black sweater dress that clutched her frame and tapered off before her knee. A thick, gold chain illuminated her neck and rested above her breasts. Rings sparkled on her fingers. Shoes that were easy to walk in but were still sexy clacked on the hardwood floors of the restaurant. The only thing he probably wasn't crazy about was her hair, tied back into a high, shining ponytail sporting a big, gold clasp around it. *Wish I had more than studs to wear in my ears.* Diamond studs, but studs nonetheless.

"You don't have to say anything," Vincent reassured her, putting his hand on the small of her back as they followed the maître d' to their table. "As for do? Don't be rude. Simple as that."

Maybe for you. Nala didn't think that because Vincent was better bred than her. For someone like her, it was difficult to maintain certain levels of propriety. Especially when nothing lay on the line for her. *I'm his hired girlfriend tonight. That's it. That's all. No espionage.*

Or at least that's what she thought until they reached their table.

Four people already sat there, with two chairs pulled out for Nala and Vincent. Two of the guests were men Nala had never seen before. An older gentleman, relaxing with a cigar while the younger man next to him carried on the conversation at the table. They looked related. Perhaps father and son.

The other two people? Made Nala stop in her tracks and Vincent stop to fiddle with his cufflinks.

"Why, hello." Maggie turned to them, her smile both curious and delighted at once. Jay looked up from behind her, flashing them his usual silent grin. *What the…* Nala looked to Vincent, who was not looking back at her. "How lovely to see you two."

She held her hand out. Vincent, the consummate gentleman, kissed the back of it. Nala nodded her head in acknowledgement, but did not hurry to look like she knew either Jay or Maggie. At least in this amount of light she could see the wedding rings glistening on their fingers. *I guess they really are married.* Not that she didn't believe it before…

"We ordered wine," Jay announced, gesturing to the other guests. A round of introductions occurred, with Nala being the least interesting person. Regardless, she was introduced to Dominic and Ian Mathers, the father and son team in town to get funding for a hotel they were renovating on the east coast. Nala quickly gathered, as dinner commenced and she was forced to listen to idle business talk, that they were also in talks with Vincent, who had submitted a proposal to write them a hotel managing app.

Everything really is run by apps these days. Nala had barely begun playing with her phone and finding out what her apps could do. One of the first she downloaded was developed by Lane Technological Solutions, an earlier app that helped manage music files on a person's phone, without having to download other music programs. *He likes managing things.* All his programs had this theme to them. It apparently brought him a ton of money, so…

As for Maggie and Jay, whose real names were not revealed throughout the course of the meal? *Damnit. Does Vincent know who they are?* They were investing in the Mathers' hotel, but Nala couldn't figure out why they were at the dinner. Vincent was supposed to be schmoozing the father and son to commission a program from him. So far, not much of that was happening.

She had her chance to find out when the other trio of men all had to go to the bathroom at once, and Maggie decided to check on her husband's car. *Or is it her car?* Nala had yet to be convinced that Maggie and Jay were a real Dom/sub couple, regardless of what Robin claimed.

"This is crazy," she said to Vincent, the moment they were left alone with wine and salads. "Did you know they were going to be here?"

"I had a hunch. That's why I really wanted you to come tonight."

"You had a *hunch?* Then what are their real names?"

"Don't know. All I was told was that the other couple joining us tonight were black, and there aren't a lot of black power couples in this city."

"Not in the rest of the state either," Nala mumbled. She gave Vincent credit for noticing, though. "What do you want me to do?"

"Listen for any subtleties they say. Out of all the couples in The Aviary, they're the most perplexing."

"You don't say."

"I have my suspicions about things."

"You're really helping to clear things up."

Vincent shot her a harsh look. "I can't do my business and pay attention to them too. The Mathers invited them along. Look, I don't need you to do much tonight. Be pretty, be charming, and above all, *pay attention* to…"

"Got it! Sheesh, and here I thought you really wanted me to be by your side tonight." She was almost put out. Almost. Nala wouldn't lie and say she didn't find it invigorating that Vincent wanted her to be his pretend girlfriend in other areas of his life too. *He thinks I'm beautiful. He keeps spoiling me. He can barely keep his hands off me. The man might be falling for me.* It definitely wouldn't be good for their undercover gig, no matter how it may have seemed so on the surface. If they got too close to one another… well, things could be compromised. Opportunities could slip through their fingers.

Vincent put a hand on her bare knee. *Stop it.* "I do want you here. If not as my girlfriend, then as my partner in… well, something."

If not as my girlfriend… Was it something he thought about? Considered? Nala stared at her half-eaten salad, wondering if Vincent really *did* want her to be his girlfriend. *That would change everything.* Not for the better.

"I'm stronger for having you around, Nala. Perhaps I'm not good at expressing it, but there it is."

She squared her shoulders and attempted to look not only presentable, but functioning as well. Nala needed all the divine interference she could get. "You're terrible at expressing it," she finally said. You either want me to be your real girlfriend or not. It's one thing to pay me to fake it for others, especially if they're from The Aviary, but don't put me on weird spots where I have to wonder what you really feel about me."

Vincent's lips remained taut. "I'm not good at expressing myself in words. In all honesty, I'm not sure I could express to you how I feel even in binary code."

"Sexy."

Nala tried to not let it get to her as the others returned. First the men, laughing as they sat down with the arrival of the soup course, and then Maggie, slipping into her seat between Vincent and Jay as if it were completely natural for her to be flanked by these two men. She exchanged a coy smile with Vincent before digging into her soup.

These people. Rich people. She didn't understand them. She didn't really want to understand them. It was that stink of money that made men like Vincent feel free to say, "I don't know how to express myself in words, har har," and get away with it. *Fuck that.* The more Nala sat in her seat, the more she wondered if she was a plaything, a doll, or a girlfriend.

She looked up and happened to catch a glance from the man sitting next to her. Ian Mathers flashed her a friendly smile before perusing the drink menu once more, his soup untouched in front of him. *How old is this guy? Vincent's age?* Thereabouts. Yet while Vincent was grim and moody, Ian had an energy to him that made him seem younger than he was. Every time he was caught looking at Nala? She saw an opportunity to find out how Vincent *really* felt.

"So, Mr. Mathers," she said, sweetly, as if sugar poured from her mouth. The other people at the table were deep in marketing conversation, something she couldn't care less about. Ian looked about as interested as a boy in school, too. "Are you enjoying Portland so far?"

"Please. Ian." He jerked his thumb in his father's direction. "That's Mr. Mathers." When all Nala did was graze her teeth along her lip, he dropped his smile and said, "Portland is very nice, rain aside. It has a nice atmosphere."

"We're very relaxed here."

"I've seen that."

Nala thought back to the conversation happening at her house a few days ago. "*Very* relaxed, if you catch my drift." Her hand "happened" to slip beneath the table and over Ian's unsuspecting knee. He tensed, but did not change his expression. *It's the same kind of expression Vincent has when he's thinking about something… regarding me.* She had seen that careful façade before getting rammed for the first time.

"I catch your drift, Miss…"

"Gale," she said, switching to how the Nightingale would respond. *She'd seduce this man, for whatever gain she had in mind.* "You can call me Gale, Ian."

"Well, Miss Gale." Nala's hand was plucked off Ian's knee and left to dangle between them. "I'm afraid I will have to decline any invitations tonight. You're a beautiful woman, to be sure, but I sort of have… someone."

"Oh, dear. Never mind little old me, then."

The soup dishes were taken away and replaced with tiny plates of the main course. *What the fuck is this?* Nala kept on her fake smile and decided to not take her chances with suspicious looking food.

She took her chances with Vincent instead, who was also not eating. He was glaring at her, at Ian, and the hand still dangling between them. *Oh, did you see that?* Nala suppressed a cackle of glee.

"Nala," Vincent said so low that she could barely hear him. His hand snatched her bare knee, squeezing it until she shifted uncomfortably and the skin surrounding his grip turned white, then pink. "Behave yourself."

Who did he think he was talking to? His plaything that he didn't want to share? Or… his girlfriend? *Which one do I want to hear?* None. She would assess his reaction and go from there. *Oh, but he's so jealous.* So jealous.

That alone was kind of fun. Jealous Vincent… he could be a *lot* of fun. And since Nala had already promised to go home with him after this…

"I am the epitome of good behavior, sir," she said, batting her eyelashes. "You should eat your dinner, by the way. Wouldn't want you to go hungry later. You might have to eat something low in nutritional value." Her. She meant her.

"Uh huh." Although Vincent returned to the conversation at hand, it was with furrowed brows – and a hand still protectively clutching Nala's knee, as if she were going to leap up and run off somewhere. With Ian Mathers, probably. Nala picked at her meal with a smirk threatening to split her face.

Five minutes later, when the waiter returned to take away their dirty dishes and promise them the next round, Nala heard a familiar voice on the other side of her jealous date. "Gale, dear?" Maggie sounded suspiciously sweet. "Would you mind running to the ladies' room with me? Just for a few minutes. I seem to be having a… well, never mind that."

With this situation forced upon her, Nala had only one possible thing to say. "Oh, of course. Just a second." She straightened her dress, fingered her hair, and stood with nary a facial reaction. *Learning from Vincent too well here.* "We'll be only a few minutes." She lightly touched Vincent's shoulder. "Don't forget about me."

She got the exact response she wanted – a hand brushing against her thigh, almost possessive.

Nala followed Maggie to the back of the restaurant, where a cordoned off women's restroom awaited, empty. Although two stalls were available, Maggie turned and locked the main door behind her. Nala spun on her heels, eyes widening and wondering if she should *run. Oh, fuck, she's Crow's assassin!*

But Maggie did not lunge for Nala. Nor did she pull a gun out of her golden, glittering pouch. Instead, she sauntered to the nearest sink, pulling lipstick from her purse and touching up her hostile smile. Her eyes never left Nala's reflection in the mirror.

I could leave right now. Nala was by the door. Not like she couldn't unlock it and make a break for it. *Jay wouldn't try something funny out there, would he?* Like kill Vincent? Shit, Nala needed to check her paranoia!

"So, *Gale,*" Maggie said, that sweetness more like salt in a wound. "How are things with your *Master?*" Why was she talking like that? As if she didn't believe a single word coming out of her mouth?

Nala shifted on her feet, pretending to be unfazed by Maggie's glare in the mirror. "Things are great. Wonderful, even. Yup. Everything's good."

"Now, hon." Maggie stood up straight, plunking her tube of lipstick back in her purse. "You don't have to lie to me. I saw that display out there. Making him jealous so he would pay attention to you? That's no way to keep a relationship going. Especially with a man like Vinc… Mr. Lane."

The more she lurked around Maggie, the more suspicious she became. She didn't act like a submissive woman, either in The Aviary or out of it. She had too many tells. Plus, she couldn't keep her names straight. Most of the girls from the club were reverent to the other men, even if they didn't date. That meant no first names. So far, Maggie was doing a bangup job calling Vincent by his first name all the time. Not to mention the sheer disdain and venom dripping from her canine teeth every time she said a word like Master.

"He likes feeling jealous." Nala had to be quick with her words. *Don't let her think we're not a real couple… or at least haven't been together for a few months instead of weeks.* "So sometimes we play a game like that. It doesn't mean anything serious, really." Was her smile real enough? Or was she no better than Maggie right now?

"You can drop the act. I know you and Mr. Lane haven't been together long enough for him to even see you on your period."

That's not true. Nala had resisted the urge to get pregnant recently. She was blessed with short periods – not that they didn't do their damndest to make her as miserable as possible. "I don't know what you mean. Vincent and I have been together for six months." That was their story, right? Shit! Nala needed to write this stuff down!

Maggie faced her, leaning against the sink with her arms crossed. She looked too formidable to be anyone's submissive, let alone belong to a sweet man like Jay.

"Keep lying if you want, but I can guarantee that if you keep lying in the club, it will come back to bite you in the ass. Trust me. Crow is very, very good at sniffing out a weasel, and he's not afraid to take drastic measures to maintain harmony in his group of pervs."

She is definitely not a sub. Nala didn't know what to do. Not here, not later when she would be alone with Vincent again and could relay everything that happened. *What do I tell him?* So far, Nala probably didn't know anything that Vincent didn't already know.

"I certainly don't want to get us kicked out, because it's done so much for Vince… my Master's business."

Maggie took two slow steps – steps big enough to bring her only a foot away from Nala. "I'm not talking about getting kicked out of the group, Gale. There is a lot more going on behind closed doors than couples getting it on. A lot of people have gotten hurt for going against Crow. You know it, don't you?"

Nala checked to see if she were shaking. Not yet. "I may have heard a few things, but what does that have to do with me? Vincent?"

"I'm only going to tell you this once. You may be totally innocent. I dunno, but I *do* know that it doesn't take much anymore for Crow to decide you're an enemy that must be dealt with. Tread carefully, Gale. I don't say this to anybody. If there's a reason for you joining the club outside of Vincent's prospects… well, keep them to yourself. Keep your head low and don't say anything stupid. Follow the rules. Do things you may not want to do, because otherwise… I probably don't have to tell you." She unlocked the door, but did not yet open it. "I would hate to see someone else get hurt."

Someone else? Who else did she mean? Let alone lately?

"Should I… tell Vincent?"

Maggie let her hand linger on the door handle, her visage softening into light concern. "Do whatever you want. I just wouldn't be able to live with myself if something happened to you and a simple warning from me could have stopped it. That's all." The handle jostled under the weight of her hand. "I don't dislike you, if that's what you've been wondering. You have a good head on your shoulders for someone your age, but I also remember what it's like to be twenty. You're brash and decisive, aren't you?"

Nala didn't say anything. *I mean…*

"Before you jump head first into *anything,* think long and hard about it. I've seen so many girls your age take a tumble that could have been prevented with some foresight. You are not invincible. Vincent is not invincible, even if he seems like a superhero to you at times. I don't know how you really feel about each other, but if you care at all… yeah, perhaps you should tell him. Say the warning came from a friend you can trust."

Maggie left the bathroom, letting the door latch behind her. Nala remained near the sinks, digesting the words.

"Say the warning came from a friend…"

Isn't that what that note said? The one Vincent claimed to be looking into? *"You have friends."*

Nala decided to wait it out a few more minutes in the bathroom. Who knew what awaited her when she returned to the table? Who knew how Vincent would react… to her? To the information she had to share?

It was at that moment Nala realized how much danger she might really be in.

Chapter 23

As she and Vincent drove down Burnside that night after dinner, Nala swore she saw malicious shadows in every corner. All right, so some of those were drug deals going down and people picking fights with other pedestrians because… well, she never knew why those things happened around Portland, but they weren't the everyday occurrences she expected whenever she went out at night. These were directed right at her, even if she were nowhere near them.

"What has got you acting so bizarre tonight?" They sat at a notoriously long light, Vincent tapping the steering wheel while he waited to hit the gas again. "First you embarrassed yourself like that at dinner, and now you're acting like every homeless person we pass is going to run up and try to open your door."

To be fair, that happened to my roommate once. Or Patrick could have been hallucinating.

"I'm not acting bizarre, thanks." Nala pulled herself away from the window and stared straight ahead. Rain began to patter, anyway, forcing Vincent to turn on his windshield wipers. "I'm paranoid. You would be too if Maggie cornered you in the bathroom and gave you a *warning.* And what the fuck do you mean by embarrassing myself? Excuse you."

"Wait, cornered and warned you? About what?"

The light turned green, but Vincent was slow hitting the pedal. The face he kept on Nala while he drove did not inspire confidence in her. "She said that it was really easy to make an enemy out of Crow."

"Not like we didn't know that already."

"You do *not* get it. She was really concerned that we were somehow going to mess up in the club and not only get kicked out… well, I don't remember exactly what she said, but it was really sketchy. I honestly do not think she and Jay are a real couple. Not any more than we are."

"I'd be shocked if they weren't actually married." When Nala looked at him incredulously, Vincent explained, "They act like a married couple, just not the kind that shows up to The Aviary."

"Exactly. Maggie is totally not a submissive. She's acting. Or lying, if I want to relate."

"That means they have a very good reason for risking it in the club," Vincent continued for Nala. "Crow does not like women he can't control. That's why he likes looking at submissive women being ordered around and possessed by their supposed Masters so much. He not only gets off on it. It comforts him."

"For a guy who says he really is a Dom, you don't sound impressed."

"Why would I be? Being a Dom isn't about possessing and controlling. Not to that degree. Even the other men at the club are playing it up. I don't believe for a second that Lucian is that way with Robin when they're in private."

Wouldn't be too sure about that. Robin was, uh, really into it.

"Okay, but what do you mean by *embarrassing myself?* Can we go back to that?"

Vincent turned onto his street. "Do I really have to explain?"

"Uh, yeah."

He didn't answer until he was in his enclosed parking space, setting the car alarm and listening to the rain fall a few feet away. Nala wondered if she should get out. Then she saw Vincent still gripping the steering wheel and leaving his seatbelt on. His countenance was cold.

"What were you doing, flirting with that man?"

Nala stifled a gasp. *The way he says it…!* As if she had been serious in any way! "I wasn't doing anything. Having some fun. Why do you care? You're not my boyfriend."

She went to unbuckle her seatbelt, but Vincent's hand slapped upon hers, sending fright down her spine. "You weren't having some fun, Nala. You were trying to get a rise out of me."

"It worked, didn't it?"

Vincent's hand nearly squeezed hers off her arm. "Why? Why were you doing that to me? Like you said, I'm not your boyfriend, so…"

"So it doesn't matter, right?"

"If it really didn't matter, Nala, you wouldn't have done that. Now tell me why you did it."

What insolence! Nala bit her lip before she could say something so testy, so hurtful that Vincent would have no choice but to drive her back home and kick her to the curb. If he would bother driving her back home at all.

"Nala."

"Why are you talking to me like I'm six?" Nala did everything in her power to *not* look like she was a six-year-old about to throw a giant temper tantrum. "I'm not going to tell you anything unless you start treating me like an adult."

She knew that he was almost a full decade older than her, but Nala also knew that it didn't mean much in the realm of the world. Some people her age were really mature and had a ton of life experience. Some people Vincent's age still acted like they were ten and barely knew what life was. *I'm not saying I'm super mature. I'm saying he's not giving me enough credit right now.* So what if Nala never went to college? So what if she had never held more than a minimum wage job and had yet to change the world in any way?

"Fine." Vincent leaned back in his seat, inhaling a deep breath. "Please tell me why you did that."

That wasn't much better, but Nala wouldn't argue anymore. "I wanted an idea of how you really feel about me."

"What?"

She looked at him for the first time since they arrived. The rain continued to pound behind them, but there in the warm car all Nala could think about was curling up next to him and resting her eyes. *I can do that inside.*

"You said so yourself that you're not any good with words. Well, it doesn't take a genius to gather that anyway. All this back and forth you and I have been playing ever since we met… fuck, you think I can't tell that you like me? Maybe you don't know you're exuding more than lusty thoughts my way, but sometimes I get the feeling that you want more from this relationship than we currently have. But not only am I not super interested in that, I'm also not into the idea of giving you more of myself and feeling nothing in return. I flirted with that man tonight to see how you would respond. I wanted to see if you got jealous or not."

"That is so archaic."

"And you're so dumb."

They stared each other down in the car. Although dark, Nala could see the lights of his eyes and the heave of his chest. *Stop being so attractive.* She had to remain firm. Not melt into this man's embrace as if it were the most natural thing in the world to do.

"Are you happy now?" Vincent's voice practically pierced Nala in the chest. She gasped, feeling like an admonished child even though she had asked to be treated like the adult she thought she was. "You got a rise out of me. You know how I really feel."

"No I don't," Nala barely whispered. "I don't know anything. For all I know that jealousy was you being possessive of some woman you're sleeping with. It doesn't mean you feel anything good for me. Not beyond your dick, anyway."

"*Nala,*" Vincent growled, his fingers tightening around her wrist again. "I would *not* have acted like that if I didn't feel something for you. Don't you get it?" His hiss burrowed deep into her ear, tickling her mind and stimulating the rest of her body in the process. "The whole reason I have been distant from you is because you make me…" Vincent's voice may have cut off, but it did not stop his grip from traveling up her arm and making short work of her bruising limb. "I don't like how you make me feel. It's not something I'm meant to experience for a very long time. Maybe not ever. Don't you see? I'm fighting back feeling *anything* for you beyond common decency and concern for your safety."

Nala sat back, shocked by his words, shocked by the grip still threatening to break her arm. "Why are you fighting anything?"

"The same reason you're fighting your feelings for me."

"I'm not…"

"You wouldn't have played such a trick on me if you also weren't feeling things. Don't be daft."

Nala could only gape in his direction.

"You wanted me to feel jealous to feed into your ego. To make you feel better about *feeling* anything for me. Don't think I'm that dumb. I know we're both fighting back more than physical attraction right now, but neither of us wants to lose sight of the most important thing. There's no time, no energy to get involved more than we already have, and most of all…"

Nala waited for it.

"We don't want to become disconnected from the people we're trying to avenge."

In a way, he was right. Yet at the same time, the man couldn't be further away from the truth if he started this car up again and began driving in the other direction. "That's not fair. I lost my sister, but it wasn't romantic or sexual love, obviously. I lost someone precious to me that I will never get back, but I don't feel *guilty* being with you, Vincent! *You're* the one projecting shame and guilt onto what's going on between us!" She didn't wait for him to counter with a different argument. "You're still not over Desirée. You feel guilty every time you stick your dick in me. You think that if you start having feelings of any kind for me, you'll be shitting on her memory. What if I told you that it's been three fucking years? I'm not saying 'get over it.' I'm the last person who should be telling you such a thing but, holy *shit,* Vincent, no woman wants to be the rebound who gets shafted because you're busy feeling like the biggest asshole in the universe because of a *dead woman.*"

Silence befell the car. Vincent's grip lightened on Nala's wrist, until he completely backed away, considering the steering wheel in front of him. In time, he undid his seatbelt and opened the car door, stepping out and slamming the door behind him.

Nala didn't know what to do. Go after him? Head down to the bus stop? That latter thing was probably what Vincent wanted her to do. Except there was no way in fucking *hell* Nala was going to let him get away with skulking off like that!

She fought with the seatbelt and the car door, convinced that both were out to prevent her from getting her way, from getting to Vincent the moody, grieving billionaire. *Grieve all you want, asshole. Just don't treat me like this!* Nala finally won the battle of wills with the two-ton car, emerging in the cold night air with nary a sweater to keep her warm. She tore up the stairs after Vincent and caught him as he was about to close his loft door in her face.

He relented, stepping away from the door and letting Nala in. She closed and locked the front door, but did not remove her shoes. They instead clamored over the hard wood floors, helping her chase down Vincent into the kitchen, where he pulled down a bottle of whiskey and poured himself a shot.

"I want one too," Nala demanded.

Vincent glared at her.

"I'm twenty-one! What, suddenly you worry about stuffing me with alcohol?"

They both knew that wasn't why he glared at her. Nevertheless, Vincent took down another shot glass and poured Nala a drink.

No cheers. No clinks. Vincent downed his shot, and Nala followed, letting the whiskey burn her esophagus like she damn well deserved. *Teach me to ever open my big mouth again.* She probably needed punishing, too.

Except Vincent was about as interested in her as she was in him right now. The man wandered into his living room, tearing off his jacket and tossing it on a couch as he sat with a new drink. He leaned back, sinking as far as he dared, with his head resting on top of the couch and his arm outstretched. If Nala didn't know any better, she would think he was relaxing after a stressful day at work – not trying to process what she said to him in the car.

Nala approached from behind, staring at the top of Vincent's dark head and wondering if she should go. But as she lurked next to the couch, her fingers treading dangerously close to his hair, he said, "You're a real spitfire, Miss Nazarov."

She said nothing.

"You'll probably be the reason we ultimately get killed."

Her eyes widened, but yet again she said nothing.

"You're not wrong, though. You're right. That's the problem." Vincent took a drink, ice clamoring against the side of his glass. "I hate that you're right."

Nala took two more steps, bringing her to the couch. She looked down into Vincent's face, his eyes closed, his posture unforgiving. "I know I'm not Desirée," she said softly. "I don't want to be her. I'm only me. You can take me or leave me, but if you take me, I expect no mind games. I don't need or want your love, Vincent, but I do need to be treated like a human being. Not saying you've been *that* bad…" She plucked his glass from his hand and finished his drink for him. *Gotta cut myself off after this.* Wine at dinner, and now following it with two drinks of whiskey? "But I have a short temper for that kind of behavior. You need to decide. Will you move on? Or will you continue to hold onto her as if she's going to come through that door at any moment?"

"I'm not stupid, Nala. I know she's not coming through any door. She's dead. Forgive me if it's been difficult to deal with."

"Of course I understand." She traced one of his crowning worry lines on his forehead. Vincent sighed, but did not shrug her off. "My sister died only a short while ago. It feels like yesterday, honestly. I know it wasn't. I know it was a long time ago in the realm of the human lifespan. In olden times, we would have been forced to move on. It's only recently we're allowed to take time to grieve."

"Don't have to remind me."

"Nor me. My dad died when I was a girl. I've seen what too much grief does to a person. My mother… she's not the same anymore. She wasn't the same even before Tasha died. All that did was solidify my mother's inability to ever move on. Her life from now on will be dependent on grief. I don't want to live that way. I want vengeance, but once I get it, I want to move on. It doesn't mean I've forgotten Tasha, or what she meant to me. I'll never forget her. She was a huge part of my life, and someone I thought I would have until the end of it, or at least until near the end."

Vincent relaxed beneath her tender touch, but did not invite her to continue. Even so, Nala let three of her fingers graze against his skin, lulling him into a welcomed sense of security. His hand loosened its grip on his now empty glass, letting it tumble against the leather. Nala fought the urge to wrap her arms around his shoulders and offer him whatever comfort she could spare. *Underneath it all, he's still a human too.* When it came to alpha-type men like Vincent, it was easy to forget that fact.

"She was my soul mate." The forlorn tone to his voice gutted Nala. "No, you don't understand. It was deeper than average love. I had thought I was in love before, but then I realized those women didn't mean half of what Desirée meant to me. When you lose your soul mate, what the fuck do you do? How do you move on from that? You know what they say. You only get one soul mate. That's the whole point. Whatever. She always told me I was too romantic for my own good."

Romantic? Almost seemed impossible to see this man as *romantic.* Vincent was about as romantic as a fish flopping out of water.

"Would you believe me if I told you that… between her death and meeting you, I could count the amount of women I've had sex with on one hand?"

"Yeah, I believe you." Nala would be shocked if it were more than two. Vincent was so sold on the idea that Desirée was his soul mate that it probably felt like cheating on her. Nala had met a few men with that mindset over the years. Lots of the elderly men in her neighborhood growing up had a difficult time moving on as widowers. Even the ones who barely knew how to take care of themselves because their wives had done everything for them. When pressed to find new wives to spend the rest of their days with, they often said it felt too wrong. Too soon.

"The women I met and slept with between then and now were barely human to me. I'm not saying I treated them like animals. I did my best to be gracious and to treat them well, but I could sense that *they* sensed I wasn't into it. It felt good. It was relieving to get the sexual tension out of my body. Just because the heart grieves doesn't mean the loins stop working… as I unfortunately found out."

Nala sighed, fingernail lightly scratching the skin above his right eyebrow.

"It was all wrong, though. I didn't feel better after those encounters. I felt worse. Like I was a weak man who couldn't keep my dick in my pants. It made me wonder terrible things, like if I would have cheated on Desirée during our marriage. I had planned to spend the rest of my life with her. Then she died."

"Come on. You can't expect to stay celibate for the rest of your life. Do you think she would have wanted that?" Nala had no idea what Desirée was like, other than good enough to win the eternal love of a man like Vincent. "If you had died, wouldn't you have wanted her to move on and find love again?"

"Of course. But…"

"And would you really be that upset if you found out she moved on a year after you died? Two years? *Three* years? Especially so young?"

"Of course not. It would be normal… I would be happy that she was happy still."

"Then don't you think she would say the same thing about you?"

"That's different."

"How so?"

Vincent opened his eyes, full of more life than Nala had seen as of late. "That was her. This is me we're talking about."

Are you fucking kidding me? Was this a male thing? Or a stupid Vincent Lane ego thing?

Nala stepped away, rounding the couch, heels catching her off balance more than once. *These fucking things.* But if she were going to exude the confidence she felt inside her bones, she needed to stay on her feet. "I know this is you we're talking about." She faced him, still slouching in his seat, but eyes entirely on her. "The only Vincent I know is the man I met a month ago. That man? Has a ton of potential to move the fuck on."

To prove it, Nala stood before him, steeling herself for any negative reaction as she pulled down her dress zipper and shimmied out of the body-hugging ensemble. It pooled at her feet, revealing a lacy black bra and panty set she purchased the day before. The very same underwear Vincent pulled out of her bag with a laugh. *The man wanted me. He wanted to have sex with me right there. He was going to flirt and make us both feel good. Again.* Nala would be damned if this man was so up the ass of "soul mates" that he found it impossible to find some sort of happiness three years after the death of his beloved fiancée. It was sweet that he had loved her so much. It was endearing that she would always be in his heart, like Tasha would always be in her sister's heart, but the man needed to *move on.*

"Just because you get hard for and enjoy fucking another woman doesn't mean you're dishonoring her memory. You're human, damnit. You've got needs, don't you? You can't spend the rest of your life jacking off while bitterly thinking of what happened to her."

He didn't wince, but he did frown at that image.

Nala kicked her dress away from her, content to stand with her body exposed in lacy lingerie. *Oh, look at that.* Lo' and behold, Vincent was starting to stiffen in those nice pants. Point being proven.

"I know you're mad that you're attracted to me. I know you want to take it out on me. All that frustration ready to burst in you." She tugged on his collar, feeling the sweet silk and the way it touched her skin. "You think I mind? I'm not looking for a relationship either, but if there's a man who makes me feel alive and able to forget my problems for a while… I'm hesitant to say no. Because I would be a total fool to pass that up."

Nala straddled his lap, not touching him, but so close that she may as well open his zipper and take him right there.

"Do you want me, Vincent? Don't lie."

He breathed deeply through his nose, every breath careful and controlled. *Too careful.* This guy was about two seconds away from throwing Nala on the couch and fucking her until they both ran out of sweet energy. *I wouldn't say no.* It was taking Nala every ounce of reserve stored within her to *not* suggest that right now.

"Yeah," Vincent grunted, hands hovering over her waist. "I fucking want you."

Before she could kiss him, his finger appeared before her lips. She kissed his fingerprints before touching anything else.

"But I want Nala. I'll give in to her tonight."

Nala braced herself against the back of the couch, her breasts a mere two inches away from his mouth. *Are you kidding me?* This might come as a shock to you," she muttered, undulating her hips against his chest, "but Nala has always been here. This whole time. Like, I'm kinda her."

Finally, his hands gripped her hips, fingers digging into her ass while his mouth slightly parted and eyes fluttered shut. "I'll give you whatever you want, Nala."

The kiss did not disappoint. Nala fell right into it, hips rolling in his lap, feeling him awaken between the legs with every gentle thrust. *You silly man.* Vincent could deny her all he wanted. He could fight his attraction to her, only to be miserable… and for what? A woman who hadn't been alive in three years? *That's noble and all, but if this man were my fiancée, my first wish after my death would be for him to get some.* Perhaps Nala didn't have the same association with sex that Vincent had. When she heard that her ex was already dating an old mutual friend of theirs, Nala didn't care. Good for him. Their mutual friend was a nice girl.

Maybe Vincent really was a romantic at heart. A romantic who didn't know how to let go after life punched him in the heart and loins.

"You deserve to find happiness," she mumbled on his lips, letting him kiss her harder, harder, tongue penetrating her mouth and hands running up her sides and to her breasts. His hips raised, hardness brushing against her slit. *Fuck me, damnit.* "I don't say people deserve anything very often."

"Shut up." Vincent's fingers dug beneath her ass, spreading her thighs apart until a single fingertip touched her beneath her lingerie. *Oh my hell.* "You talk too much."

How dare he! Nala took that as a challenge, wrapping her hand around the back of his head and pushing her touch against his skull. She bit his bottom lip, dragging it far away from his face until it snapped out of her mouth. The moan falling from both of their throats practically made her wet enough to take whatever he offered. *All of it. Offer me everything, Vincent.*

"You can't make me shut up tonight." She threw her head back as his lowered and immersed itself in her cleavage, tongue snaking against both breasts and searching for a nipple. "If my name is Nala, then you can't tell me what to do. Not tonight."

"Fair enough. I'm going to ignore you, though."

Her fingers felt the slickness of his hair between them as she laughed into the crook of his neck. "Fair enough, indeed."

He wanted her to be quiet, but he was anything but. Every other breath out of Vincent's body was some form of her name, whether a whisper, a cry, or something so beyond human that Nala barely recognized it. The farther they went, the more her knees dug into the couch, her thighs lowering to his as his fingers pulled aside her lacy underwear and plunged deep within her.

"Shit!" It felt good. It felt wonderful. It felt like the end of the world come to take her away from the mortal realm. *Why does he feel so good?* Vincent was the man who showed her it was possible to feel as good as the movies portrayed. Before? Nala thought it was only a lucky few who got to have such powerful lovemaking. The kind that ripped out hearts and brought on knee-shaking orgasms – all from a simple touch of the hand.

Vincent may have been deep within her, wetting his fingers in her essence, but it wasn't enough to sate a woman as needy as her right now.

"More," she whimpered in his ear, arms wrapping tight around his shoulders. "Please, Vincent."

Her hips met the thrusts of his fingers, Vincent's other hand fumbling with his zipper and struggling to get himself out. Nala was barely coherent enough from the climax wracking her body to see his cock emerge, hard and ready to take her.

She shuddered on his fingers, easing herself off as he wiped his knuckles against her ass. Vincent kissed the mounds of her breasts, still encased in her bra. "I like it when you beg," he said matter-of-factly. "Be careful, Nala. You think I don't get to tell you what to do, but if you keep doing this to me, I'll have no choice but to show you who I really am."

Dry though her throat was, Nala still found the ability to speak. "Don't give me any ideas."

Vincent chuckled, pulling aside her underwear again as his other hand lined his cock up with her opening. "Are you ready for me, darling?"

Darling? That was what he called Nightingale when they were undercover. He claimed to want Nala, not the identity she sank into when trying to make the lies easier to pass. *He's calling me darling…* It shouldn't make her heart flutter, and yet here she was, clinging to his shoulders and continuing to whimper into his throat as he slowly guided the head of his cock into her.

"I'm trying," she groaned, feeling him struggle to open her enough to take him. *Damnit, why is it sometimes so easy, and sometimes so difficult to get this man inside me?* It didn't matter how wet she was. How aroused. What position. Whether he was slow or forceful. Sometimes Vincent slipped right in, and other times were like now, with the head of his cock clearing the way for the rest of him. It hurt, a little. Discomforting. Yet it was also so damn relieving to have him fully inside her, triumph overcoming the both of them. They weren't quite there yet.

"Relax, Nala," he whispered into her ear before tasting the outline of it. "Don't clench up. Not yet. Relax and meet me halfway."

"I'm…" she was going to reiterate her intention to *try,* but Vincent had lifted her hips and pulled himself out, too easily. He licked his fingers and ran them along her clit, forcing her body to ready for him again. Her arousal slipped from her nether lips, charging a course down her inner thigh and dripping on the head of his cock. Vincent's growl of satisfaction as he felt her drip on his skin made Nala even wetter.

"You've already ruined your brand new designer panties," he chastised her. "You'll probably have to leave them here. Can't have you wandering home with these things on."

Nala laughed as she remembered her thoughts about panty sniffing. *What a world.* "I've ruined them because of you." She didn't tell him that a simple wash would fix everything. For next time.

"So you have. I better take advantage of this glorious situation."

"I really don't know what's stopping you."

His satisfied smile turned slightly down. "You, Nala. I need you to relax. I don't want to hurt you."

"Don't see how you could."

"Don't tempt me."

She shivered. *That might be nice.* Really, really rough. That wasn't about the physical aspect, really. It was about feeling his sheer power claiming her, taming her. *I keep thinking those sorts of things.* Was she really a woman in need of taming? Maybe only in the bedroom. It was nice to give up control and know that there was at least one man out there who knew exactly what she needed… but not tonight.

"I bet you like it, though," she teased him, trying her damndest to relax when she knew she was about to have a great lay. "Feeling like the biggest man in the world because little ol' me is who she is."

"I don't take that much credit. You're tiny."

"Uh… huh…" Her fingers dug into his shoulders, his cock making an easier way into her now. *Holy shit.* It never got old. No matter how many times he filled her. No matter how often he took her and became intimately familiar with every curve of her body. *This should be illegal.* The illicit nature of it would make it even hotter. Forbidden. Held back. Nearly forgotten, until now. That's what Nala thought about as she pulled herself off him and then eased back down. Amazing how it got easier every time.

"God," Vincent said, his head resting against the couch and his eyes half closed. "You're amazing. You know that?"

She gently kissed him, distracted by what happened between her legs. "It takes two. I'll only take a fraction of the credit."

"A big fraction, I'm sure."

"Hey, you're the math guy." Nala kissed him all over, from his lips to his cheeks, to his throat, back to his forehead and then all over again. "Fuck me."

Thank God, he did just that.

Nala wasn't an easy woman to impress, but not only had Vincent done that more than once, but he did it yet again, lifting himself into her, over and over, unrelenting. Nala held herself as steady as possible against the couch as he had his way with her, using everything he had to take her right where it mattered most.

"Yes!" she cried into his throat, feeling the exquisite way his cock continuously slid in and out of her. Her body accommodated him by stretching around him, inviting him to keep his hold on her while he did whatever he damn well pleased. "Vincent!"

His hands kneaded both sides of her ass as she lifted up and down in his lap, taking his lovemaking as if she had no other choice in the world. *I've got all the choice. I choose to be here, doing this.* That thought made her cling harder to the couch before grabbing his shoulders and holding herself steady over his lap. *Just let him do it, girl.* The sheer power behind his thrusts was enough to make her whine so loudly that, if Vincent had neighbors and his loft wasn't so well insulated already, they definitely would have heard.

Her mouth finally meandered to his, tongue penetrating her up top as she was below. *Just kill me already!* Although she wasn't bound, gagged, or in any situation that gave her any less power than usual, she found herself unable to do what she wanted – whatever that was. Nala was naturally deferring to Vincent's whims, letting him control every movement, every moment they shared on his leather couch.

"I'm gonna come," she murmured between his lips. Nala could feel every spark of an orgasm get ready to fire in her body. "You gonna come with me?"

Nala's hand landed lightly around his throat, indulging in the silk of his shirt and the softness of his skin. She didn't get a response. Not right away. She was too busy giving herself over to the throes of orgasm, letting it expand like a blast through her. The epicenter was her thighs as they fought to stay as spread as possible.

"Vincent!" Her voice pealed through the loft, fingers scrambling for purchase either on his shoulders or the back of the couch. He continued to pound into her, letting gravity bring his hips down before defying it again with his strength. It prolonged her climax, taking her down, up, down again until she thought she might pass out from exhaustion.

When she finally came down for the last time, it was to the side of his erection, one knee slipping off the couch while the rest of her followed until she lay across his lap, avoiding his cock. Her pants disappeared into the couch beneath her face as Vincent continued to massage her ass and the thighs beneath.

"No," he growled, hand passing from Nala's curves and to the erection still springing from his lap. Nala thought he would finish himself off before she had the chance to sit up and use her mouth to bring him to the final moments of his pleasure. As she was about to plead for him to hold off, Vincent reached beneath her and brought her up into his arms. He stood, Nala hoisted over his shoulder as he made for the spiral staircase.

Chapter 24

Although recently sated from their frenzied lovemaking, Nala now looked at the loft below her as they ascended the rounded stairs… and shivered in anticipation. *He's going to throw me down on his bed and consume me.* What was once sore and begging to be left alone now woke up again, begging the man who controlled half her destiny to completely have his way with her. As Nala.

Sure enough, the moment they entered his bedroom, Vincent brought Nala back down into his arms and let her land with a hard hit to his bed. It seemed to swallow her, Nala's body at the mercy of her own energy levels, her desire to feel more of Vincent's overpowering lovemaking, and…

Oh my sweet merciful justice, he is hot. Her thighs trembled as she wiped sweat from her forehead. Vincent stood beside the bed, ripping off his shirt and discarding his trousers. His cock, wet and glistening from Nala's climax, faced her and prompted her to open her legs, each toe curling around the edge of the bed as she propped herself up on her elbows.

"Now say that you want me." His voice as he completely disrobed before her made Nala tremble. "I want to hear you say it. I *need* to know what you want from me."

Both of her hands pressed against her forehead in a futile attempt to recharge. "I want you to completely take me over. I…" She wasn't going to say it, and then she saw him standing before her, his lascivious eyes drinking her in as the rest of him became firmer, harder, more determined to devour her in this bed. "I want you to own me."

Those were not words Nala Nazarov would say out loud, even if she fleetingly thought them. She was supposed to be independent, a woman who didn't bend to the will of a single man – not like she was wanting to now, as she gazed up on Vincent's muscular form and felt herself completely melt into his bed.

Those were words Nightingale would say… but that identity was pushed away for now. Realizing that every thought she had belonged solely to Nala, her true self, was almost scarier than anything Vincent could physically do to her.

"That's funny," Vincent said, crawling between her legs and spreading them wide with a touch of his hand. "I was hoping you would say that."

"Are you going to do it?" Her meek voice belonged to someone else. As much as she wanted this, she was afraid. Afraid of what? Losing her independence? Any respect Vincent still had for her? *Why should I be ashamed? I told him to stop being ashamed! Now I'm getting what I want!* She should be happy that Vincent was willing to give her his all after feeling so bitter and guilty a while ago. "What are you going to do?"

"Do you want to hear?"

She bit her lip. "Yes."

He was between her legs, hovering above her, head lowering until his arms bent on either side of her head and his breath, hot and commanding, touched her ear. "I'm going to own you, Nala. I'm going to take you until you know, well and good, that you belong to me and no other man – or woman. Nobody else can have you like I do. You've awakened the beast in me. Now you must face him."

Vincent held her arms above her head, his hands clasping hers. She knew to leave them there when he lowered his hands and cupped her breasts, freeing them from her bra and pinching nipples already hard from arousal. Nala nearly cried from the renewed pleasure it gave her.

"I'm ready," she whimpered, legs wrapping tight around his waist. Although her thighs were sore, and her slit almost too wet to bear, she was ready. "Do whatever you want to me. Make me feel like there's no other man in the world but you."

The look he flashed her said that he could make that sound easy… but deep inside, he would be doing his damndest to make it a reality. Even men like Vincent couldn't make the world bend at the knee. They had to earn it.

"Tell me you want this," Vincent said for the hundredth time that night. He guided his cock to her opening, pressing it into her folds. *I feel so easy right now.* Nala was not a woman of any upstanding quality. She had already been used by Vincent once tonight. Just a matter of time before he used her again, this time for his own ends. "I need to hear you say it."

"Fuck yes, I want your damned cock." Nala felt her whole body jiggle as Vincent sat up and moved the bed from his weight alone. "And this time I want you to finish."

"That won't be hard." He made her close her eyes, every inch of him slowly taking her again. *There's no resistance now.* Nala's body was prepared. It knew what to expect. It *wanted* him, tonight, tomorrow, probably a year from now.

"And I…" Nala bit back her words as she was temporarily shaken with new pleasure. "I want you to talk dirty. For fuck's sake, give me the full treatment like you almost did the first time we did it."

"I was angry then." Vincent loomed over her, his cock back where it belonged. "I'm not angry right now. I don't want to be angry at you."

"I didn't say to be angry. I said talk dirty, *sir.*"

"Oh, it's like that?" His cock thrust into her, once, eliciting a gasp of surprise from Nala's throat. "You want to hear what kind of girl you are?"

The smile on Nala's face could break bones if anyone gazed up on it. "Only if you're as harsh on yourself too."

"I always am, darling."

His body crashed into hers. From how quickly he pulled out again, Nala knew this conversation was over for now.

Fine.

Her nails, cut nearly down to the cuticle because she could never be assed with them, attempted to dig into his shoulder blades as he thrust into her again and again. She wailed, she cried out, she whimpered in surrender as Vincent Lane, a man she happened to meet completely by chance and shared a similar history with, showed her all the reasons she belonged to him, even if only for tonight.

"You're so tight on my cock even now," he growled into her ear, taking her to a new level of pleasure – the level she briefly experienced the first time he fucked her. "Even after all that, Nala, you're still exactly what my cock needs. You fucking succubus."

Yes, yes, that was it. Nala wanted to know she was a demon, like Vincent was. They were both broken, shoddy angels no longer good enough for Heaven. They lurked in the shadows, sipped from the cup of bitterness, and spent their days searching the earth for their next victims. So happened that succubus Nala set her sights on an incubus like Vincent. What a formidable pair.

"More," Nala pleaded, wondering how much longer she had before Vincent finished inside her. "Please!"

"How dare you, Nala. How dare you do this to me? I've made it this long without faltering. Then you…" He stilled within her, reorienting himself. "Then you come along and transform me back into this insatiable beast. All I want is your damned cunt. The wetter and warmer you get, the more I want to feast upon this body of yours."

Oh, *Heaven!* A glimpse of the Heaven she had been cast from!

"Take it!" Vincent clasped her arms, holding her shoulders down on the bed as her hands flailed above her head. Her legs shook in the air, the bed straining beneath the force of Vincent impaling her. "Take it, you fucking she-demon. You…"

Say it! Nala wanted to hear how easy she was. How much she loved this sort of thing. How disposable she could be, if her Master no longer found her amusing. *He'll never. He'll want me forever.*

The word fell off his tongue and burrowed in her ear, filling her body with the new spark needed to set off her biggest orgasm of the night.

Soon nothing in the world existed outside of Vincent. *Vincent. This man.* He had achieved what he set out to do, which was to make Nala think he was the only thing in the world that mattered. Not hard to accomplish when she was solely at the whims of the fate they conjured together. So great was this moment that Nala could feel her heart split in two: the side that rejected any and all emotions, dismissing them as futile. And the side that went straight to Vincent, begging him to take her in and keep her safe forever.

"Nala!" The roar echoing in her ear only brought her back to reality for a moment. That moment was long enough for her to see the look of exquisite pleasure on his countenance as he held himself within her, directing her hips up so she could catch every drop of his passion.

The warmth flooded her with promise. The swelling of his cock, rippling through her loins, made her feel more vulnerable than she ever had before. It was beyond her comprehension, this experience. What made her think that such a thing could happen to someone like her? How had she seduced this man again and again? Who was she, other than some stupid girl too brash for her own good? The only thing bringing them together was their thirst for knowledge and justice. What kept them together?

It wasn't…

No, it couldn't possibly be…

Nala wanted to laugh, but she was too involved with the feelings surging through her body in the form of a man named Vincent Lane.

He collapsed on top of her, breathless, his cock lodged deep within her. He moaned her name a few more times, languid kisses falling on her throat and sauntering up to her lips. She lay like a lifeless doll, too exhausted to function.

"That was amazing," Vincent muttered into the crook of her neck. "You're amazing."

Nala pushed her hair out of her face and took a deep breath, forcing herself back into the real world. Not an easy feat after what had transpired.

She was in a fog, a haze as Vincent dislodged from her and attempted to bring her into his hold. She didn't want to fight it. Everything in her heart told her to turn over and give in to the temptation, like she gave in to all the others so far.

It was intimate. It was *romantic.* Her, in his arms, feeling him breathe steadily against her body as his seed emerged and reminded her to whom she belonged. Yet as the haze gradually dispersed from Nala's brain, her fight or flight response kicked in, yelling at her to *leave.*

"Oh, no you don't." Vincent pulled her back down as she fought to get up. "I know you want to leave like you always do. I'm not saying you can't go home tonight, but give me at least a few minutes of feeling your body next to mine."

Good Lord, she would find the one man in the world who wanted to *cuddle* after sex. Nala gave into it, letting him rest against her as his fingers slowly caressed the curve of her back. She leaned her cheek against his chest and stared into the darkness before her.

Don't fall in love.

Her heart leaped in her throat at the prospect.

Don't fall in love.

She squeezed her eyes shut, inhaling the natural scent of the man she so wanted to flee from. Soon. She could go home soon. Until then, she was his prisoner, fighting to escape.

Entry #11

Nightingale's words continue to echo. What I did to her replays even more.

Other things happened tonight, but what I remember most are her harsh admonishments about how I behave toward her. And what I do to her.

I told myself I would not feel anything more than physical desire for her. It's just sex, I tell myself. We're hopped up on desire because of the nature of our infiltration. Surrounded by sex all night. It's only natural for me to get a hard-on around a beautiful young woman. Let alone one who apparently finds me attractive as well.

But isn't it fucking hilarious that I'm *acting like the needy one. ME! I had to beg that woman to stay a few extra minutes tonight so I could, what, "bathe in the afterglow?" I don't know how else to say it. I gave her everything I had. I told her that she had awakened the beast roaring inside of me, and she had to face it. She did. She did so well that I think she may actually get off on how rough and coarse she makes me.*

We are a sick pair.

It's insane. Even now, spent from sex and with the usual droopy eyelids, I can only think of everything I want to do to her. Tie her up until she can't move and at my whims. I want to mount her like a monster and leave my mark all over her tiny body. I'm not a really big guy, by all accounts, but she's so petite that I feel like a giant compared to her. It's so easy to wrap my whole body around her and consume her soul.

No woman has made me feel like this. No woman, ever. Not even Desirée stirred such monstrously possessive feelings inside of me. I'm sure the potential was there, but I was a normal guy back then. I didn't know what it meant to be so angry and bitter. I didn't have those black emotions to channel through sex. The first woman I was with after Desirée… well, after she died… the first woman was five months later. I felt so guilty, so ashamed that I purposely got fuck-plastered drunk with a woman and probably spent a whole two seconds inside of her before we both passed out only to wake up with regretful hangovers.

I've prided myself on staying true to her memory, even though I know it's not realistic. Most men have moved on by now. They still care, they still love the woman they've lost, but they move on. Nala reminded me of that tonight. The idea that I could love again… that there is room in this fucked up heart for more than one person is so beyond me. Desirée was it. I knew she was the love of my life two months into dating her. The way our hearts sang together was like the art we created in bed.

Now I hear a bird chirping at my window this late at night. It's hours after dusk and even more hours until dawn. Yet it sings. A nightingale. It's all in my head, but it's there, nonetheless.

Nightingale may have ran from me, but her spirit is here, singing to me. The most beautiful voice I've heard in three years.

Is it wrong? Was she right? I wish Desirée were here to give me an answer.

Would you be mad, Desirée? Can I still see you in Heaven if my heart moves on?

The only thing I fear in this world is losing someone I love. If I love Nightingale, I will have to fight to keep her alive. And fight to keep her by my side, never running away again. I feel that the first will be easier than the latter.

Chapter 25

"*New info came in,*" said the text from Vincent. "*Next Aviary meeting is at Crow's house in the West Hills. This is going to be our big chance to find evidence. Hope you're ready to put that sneaky body to good use.*"

Nala looked up from her phone and stared into her half-eaten bowl of oatmeal. *I wish I had work today.* As much as she liked a good day off to rest and recharge, she hated sitting around that crappy house. She couldn't afford to go out and sit in a café for a while. The weather was too shitty to go to the park – besides, last she checked, a new homeless camp had set up there. Nala often wasn't *that* bothered by them, but her last few strolls down a busy avenue led to her being harassed more often than not. A girl could only take so many dick flashes and requests to smile.

Finally, she replied, oatmeal spoon in her other hand. "*Sounds good. Tell me when.*"

"*Tomorrow.*"

Oh, joy. Work and then tearing up Crow's fancy mansion. Where *would* Nala find the time?

"*How are you doing? It's been a couple of days.*"

Ah, shit. Vincent wasn't getting clingy, was he? Ever since Nala finally snuck out Friday night, she had been avoiding texting him, even if she had a question he could quickly answer. *I think I inspired him too much.* When Nala told him to get over his shame for being human, she hadn't anticipated him focusing his romantic efforts on her. *What is a girl to do?* A handsome, athletic billionaire wanted her pussy 24/7. In a perfect world, Nala would be counting her good fortune and calling her mom up to brag. However, this wasn't a perfect world. There were many barriers left up between them, and besides…

There was no way they could ever pursue a real relationship until this Aviary thing was *over.*

Men. They were so high maintenance.

Because she wasn't being tortured enough, Kathy and Steven stopped by to shoot the Mary-Jane breeze with Patrick in the living room. Nala pulled out headphones to block out their asinine conversations, but she couldn't escape that sweet, heinous smell of marijuana as it sparked up and seeped deep into the living room walls. *The worth of this place is totally shot.* It being Portland, however, probably meant the shoddy house was only worth 500k instead of 600k.

Once she finished up her meal, she escaped into her closet, since that was better than being subjected to the pothead triplets. Nala curled beneath a blanket and played on her new phone. *This thing is cooler than I took for granted.* Vincent had bought her an unlimited data plan, meaning she could look up anything on the internet that she wanted. Watch videos. Listen to music. Play on social media. Finally, after who knew how long, Nala was finally starting to feel like a real young adult. Too bad she couldn't print from her phone and still had to go to the library to do that.

While she perused an article about the dying bee plight, her phone buzzed with another message from Vincent.

"I have something for you. It was supposed to be delivered to your house, but there was a miscommunication and it was delivered to my office instead. I'm leaving early. You home?"

"You don't have to do that. You can give it to me the next time you see me."

"I'd like to give it to you before tomorrow."

"Maybe later."

She thought that would mean later that evening. Maybe that night. Not five minutes later when she heard someone knock on the door and one of her stoned housemates stumble to answer.

By the time Nala realized that it might be Vincent, it was too late. She was up in her closet, but her closet door was also opening without her permission.

"There she is!" Patrick said, his finger pointing right down at a mortified Nala. "This is her room! Have fun!"

Oh. My. God.

Nala's mouth dropped open so Vincent's wouldn't have to. His eyes bulged, however, taking in the sight of Nala's bullshit of a "room." Did not help her ego that he was dressed in his work outfit, slacks crisp and burgundy shirt hiding beneath a plain black suit jacket. She could smell his aftershave all the way down there. *This is it. This is the pinnacle of my shame.* Nala had to look away before she cried.

"I, uh…" Vincent pulled a hand from his pocket. Whatever he had intended to give her remained in his pants. *For once it's not his dick.* Oh, God, why did she look there?

"This has happened." Nala forced herself up, nearly knocking her head into the closet rod holding all her clothes, including some of the nice dresses Vincent had given her. "Get a good look right now. I live in a closet."

"*What?*"

Nala had never been forthcoming about that. It was not any of Vincent's business, although surely he had assumed she rented a whole bedroom like a decent human being. Now he faced the brutal truth. Nala, his fuck buddy and sugar baby, was living in a dilapidated house for potheads and barely had a closet space to call her own.

"Okay, get the closet jokes out of your system now. I've heard them all. Just do it."

"Nala. Get out of there."

"Nala, come out of the closet? I didn't know you were a lesbian fetishist, Vincent."

"*Nala.*"

She pushed him out of the way and stepped into the hall, refusing to let her wounded pride show.

"Were you ever going to tell me about this?"

"Why the hell would I? You're not my boyfriend."

He stepped back, as if her words stung. *You're not. Just because I fuck you doesn't mean we're serious.* Nala was having a devil of a time keeping eye contact with him. "Nala," he said again, this time more evenly. "This isn't okay. This isn't healthy. Honestly, I'm shocked. These people…" He glanced at the pot party going on in the living room, as if Nala's "boyfriend" wouldn't give a shit – hell, they probably hoped he would join in. "These people shouldn't be doing this to you," he hissed.

"Would you step off?" Nala had half a mind to stick her finger in his chest. His hard, muscular chest that spent most of last night rubbing against her breasts. *Fuuuuck.*

Surely he noticed how embarrassed she was becoming, right? Apparently not. "Come on, Nala. Pack up your most important things. We can get the rest later. You're paid through the rest of the month, right?"

"What?"

Vincent reached in and started grabbing hangers full of clothes. "Do you have a suitcase we can put these in?"

"*What?*"

He swung toward her, that composed face now turning into something more… bereaved. "You're coming to live with me, Nala. I can't let this situation continue."

"Who the fuck are you!" Yet she stood there, in shock, watching this big ol' businessman pull down a small rolling suitcase from the top shelf. Vincent emptied the contents and started stuffing it with the clothes he held in his hands. "What are you doing? I can't go live with you!"

"Nala." He snatched her wrist and brought her close to him, his minty breath consuming her face. *That's not all I want him to consume… wait, what am*

I thinking… "Stop this. Stop being so stubborn. You don't have to stay with me long-term. Come stay with me until we can find you a place more suitable."

She didn't want to argue. God knew she wanted a new place to live… but with Vincent? Even if it was only temporary, that sounded like a recipe for a plague to end the ages. *Besides, I don't need him acting like a knight in shining armor.* That only complicated what relationship they had. Nala would feel like shit, and, well, maybe Vincent would think she somehow owed him.

"You ever think that maybe there's no such thing as gender?" Patrick, high as a fucking kite, asked the air before him. "Oh! Or maybe each of us are *all* genders. Yeah, I'd like to believe that I'm all genders… and you too Nala…" he reached out for her, but she was too quick for his touch. "You're a budding goddess of gender equality."

"What the fuck?"

"Nala, *please.* My car is out front."

"And this guy here! I don't know who you are, man, but you're super pretty. Would you be my girlfriend?"

"Nala!"

"All right!" She kicked open the suitcase and started dumping her underwear and T-shirts in as quickly as possible. "Get me the fuck out of here!"

She may not have owned a lot, but it felt like an eternity getting her shit out of the closet and into Vincent's car.

***

By nightfall, Nala's suitcase and assorted bags of clothes and items were shoved into a corner of Vincent's loft. He promised to clean space out of a closet for her, no pun intended, but until then, she was left with living out of a suitcase… which was slightly better than her last situation.

In the meantime, she told him the story of how she had come to Portland months ago, searched high and low for a place she could even dream of affording… and how every one of those places dried up because she wasn't best friend material enough for them. Eventually she took what nobody else would even touch: Patrick's coat closet. It wasn't home, but it was warm and dry.

Vincent glared at her the whole time she told this tale, as if he couldn't imagine being so poor that he had to stoop so low as to live in a pothead's closet. *Of course he doesn't have to think about those things. He's a billionaire.* Had been a millionaire at least for a while. Probably grew up upper middle class and always had the biggest bedroom in the house. Sigh.

"I'll buy out the rest of your lease," he promised. "We'll get you set up somewhere much better, if you don't want to stay here. Would a one bedroom apartment downtown be good enough?"

Nala sat on the couch, curled up into a tiny ball of rage as she thought about what Vincent was trying to do for her. *Don't make me owe you, asshole.* "Even the rent alone is outrageous. Last time I looked, downtown apartments cost like a thousand bucks a month."

"I'm not talking about renting. I'm talking about buying you a place. I'll invest in the taxes so you don't have to worry about that. Pay for your food and the electric bill."

"Are you crazy?" Nala sat up, almost blinded by all the lights turned on in there. She had never seen Vincent's loft so bright. "That's a couple hundred grand, at least!"

"It's nothing, if it means you're happy."

"I won't be happy with that kind of arrangement," she mumbled.

"Fine. Two bedrooms. That's my final offer."

Nala couldn't be more exasperated if she tried. "That's not my problem, and you know it."

"Then what in the world is your problem?"

He sat at his dining table, sorting through his mail, still dressed in his business best – although the jacket was hung up in the closet he promised to clean out for her. "Nothing." Nala wasn't going to argue with him right now. *Emotions are still too high.* If Nala pushed this issue, she might make a bigger ass out of herself than she usually did. That would be a feat.

"Look, don't worry about putting me out. I'm not here during the day anyway. You can have the run of the place. Bathrooms are yours to use. Feel free to stock whatever you want in the kitchen. Cook whenever you want, although don't worry about tonight. I'll order us something."

Nala rolled her eyes, pulling a pillow down to her edge of the couch and looking around for a blanket. She was ready for a nap after all that crap.

"What are you doing?"

"This is my bed, ain't it? Last I checked you don't have a guest room. Please point me in the direction if you do, though. Otherwise I'm claiming this couch in the name of the great state of Nala Nazarov, one of the final frontiers real estate Xavier Crow has yet to touch."

Vincent tossed his mail onto the table. "Don't be stupid. Of course you can sleep with me."

"Oh, I have every assumption that says I would be allowed, even welcomed to do that." Vincent would probably like it. *He's been aching for a proper sleepover ever since he decided his boner for me was more than okay.* Yet there was a reason Nala kept leaving before the cuddle party could totally start. She was not going to push herself now. "But I'm not interested. Probably a bad idea."

"Why?"

"Come off it, Vincent. You know we should keep things separate. Especially if this is only temporary. When you buying me that apartment, again?"

Although she didn't turn around to find out for herself, she could feel his glare burrowing into the back of her skull.

"I'll look into it when I can. Possibly starting tomorrow."

"Thanks."

Vincent grumbled into the back of his hand before scooting his chair and getting up. "You can be a pain in the ass, you know. Not because I *want* to find you a new place to live, or because you're staying here for now, but because you're such a stubborn ass about it."

Nala crossed her arms over the blanket enshrouding her. *Where's the TV remote? Time I took this big bad boy for a spin.* For once, she didn't mean Vincent. "I have my boundaries. Don't press me."

"Boundaries are one thing, Nala. You're pushing me away."

"As we established earlier, you ain't my boyfriend, now are you?"

"No. No, I'm not." He stood behind her, finger tracing a gentle line down her side. *What the?* "But I should at least be your friend by this point. After all that crap you said to me last night? What makes you think you can keep getting away with closing off your heart and pushing everyone away?"

Nala tightened her hold on herself. "Don't wanna talk about it."

Vincent rounded the couch and sat down by her feet, reaching into his pants pocket and withdrawing a small, rectangular black box. *Is that…* "This is what I had come by to give you."

Nala was afraid to sit up. Whatever lurked in that box was nothing good.

"Don't give me that look. Stop stewing in your perceived misfortunes and learn how to take a gift."

Scoffing, Nala tossed back the blanket and sat up in a flash. Her legs swung around, her hands disappearing beneath her thighs as she regarded Vincent with a half-interested look. "All right, lay the diamonds on me."

"They're not earrings." Vincent opened the box in front of her face. "Nor diamonds. Those things wouldn't suit you."

Nala tried to not look at the contents. Something glistened, catching her eye and then her full attention as she realized a long, silver chain illuminated in the loft lights.

"What is…"

Vincent pulled it out of the box with one hand and pulled back her hair with the other. Her neck was barely exposed because of her hoodie, but somehow, Vincent managed to get the silver choker around her throat. Thank God it was adjustable, because initially it was much too tight before he loosened it enough to let her breathe comfortably.

She touched the pendant hanging from the center, feeling the outline of a bird taking off in flight. She didn't have to ask what it was.

"It's a Nightingale," Vincent confirmed. "This is your new collar for The Aviary."

"My collar…"

"Surely you've noticed the other women wearing theirs. I should have bought one for you sooner, otherwise people will start asking questions, but…" Vincent sat back. "I wanted to pick out the perfect one for you. It's customary for the Dom to choose it, you know."

Who says? Nevertheless, Nala felt it with her fingertips, swallowing hard, making sure she still could. *The bastard has collared me?* No, it was only for The Aviary, where Nightingale would be expected to prance around showing off how "owned" she was. *Oh my God, I asked him to totally own me last night.* Nala looked away, in half disgust and half shame. *This isn't me.* This showed how imperative it was to have separate sleeping arrangements… if not living ones.

"I'm sorry if it's not to your tastes. I tried to keep what I knew in mind when I went and picked it out. It's custom made. The man who made it comes from a long line of jewelers in the area. It's one of the best qualities a woman could have."

"What about you? What do you wear to show everyone that *you* belong to me?"

"Well… it doesn't really work like that."

"Maybe it should," Nala mumbled. "It's not that I don't appreciate it," she said, louder. "But it's out of left field, and after what happened last night…"

Vincent stiffened beside her. Suddenly her body called to his, for comfort, at least. Neither of them succumbed. "I hope you don't regret that. I know it was a night… I don't expect anything out of it. This is for The Aviary. I don't actually think you're my…"

How sad that neither of them could say the word. "I know. I *know* we're on the same page, theoretically, but then things go to some other level and I'm not sure what's going on anymore. It confuses me. I don't really want to be your *sub*, Vincent. I don't mind the sex, but I want to make it clear that I'm not your girlfriend, and you're not my boyfriend. Even though it might be best if we remain exclusive until we're done here."

"Yes," he readily agreed. "That's a good idea. Things are already complicated enough as they are, and we don't know what's going to happen."

"Not that I was dating anyway."

"Neither was I."

Nala leaned back in the couch, the collar still lingering around her throat. "You could really have any woman you want, you know. You should tell me who your ultimate type is. Maybe I can help you get a real girlfriend after all this is over."

Vincent looked askance at her. "You're something else, Nala."

"What? I'm serious. I'll take good care of you. Find you a nice girl who would really appreciate your *charms* and what you do for a living. Oh, and the money, duh."

"I'm not sure about that."

"In return, maybe you could introduce me to some of your rich business buddies. After I've lived with you long enough I'll be used to a certain standard of living. Don't wanna let it go too soon. Especially if it means I get more gifts like this." She touched the nightingale charm again.

"What makes you think I would let you anywhere near those men? None of them are your type."

"Neither are you, really."

"How so?"

"Really? You're way too uptight for me. I need a man who can relax and enjoy himself, and not just with sex."

"Then you're not going to like *any* of my buddies. If you think I'm uptight? You've never met another million or billionaire. I am the chillest guy at the country club."

"You actually go to a country club?"

"It's a figure of speech. I hate golf. Only do it when I have to for work."

"What a hard life you live."

Vincent propped his elbow on the back of the couch and regarded her with mild amusement. "Yes, and now your life is going to be so hard by association. All the healthy food you can eat. If you have a license, you can use my other car…

"You have another car?"

"…There's a lady that comes by once a week to deep clean the whole loft. We're first on every takeout list in the area, and you can put whatever you want on my tabs there. My accountant pays them off for me once a month."

"You're right. It sounds like a hard life. How will I know what restaurant to order out from?"

"I go with the darts method. Or follow your stomach."

Nala sighed, her whole body moving with her breaths. The choker constrained her throat, but she could still fill her lungs, and that was all that mattered. "Could you please take this thing off me and put it away? I don't want to wear it until tomorrow."

Vincent unclasped the collar and took it away, upstairs, into a drawer Nala didn't have to know about. *This is almost too much for me.* Living with Vincent. Possibly sleeping with Vincent. Letting Vincent pay for her food and services. Using Vincent's cleaning lady to help her do laundry…

"I'm going to keep my job," Nala said the moment Vincent came back downstairs. "I'm not going to entirely rely on you, and I still want my thousand a week stipend." She had to build her own savings before this all came crashing down like an old, demolished building. Nala had no reason to believe it wouldn't end like that. *I'll lose my temper. He'll decide I'm too high maintenance to deal with. Rinse and repeat until I'm out on my ass, maybe in that tax-free condo for however long he decides to keep paying the taxes on it.* That still seemed too good to be true. Nala didn't believe in good fortune like that. Her life was built around losing, not gaining.

"Of course you'll keep your job. I wouldn't have suggested otherwise." Vincent went into the kitchen and picked up his phone. "So, what should we have for dinner? Should we get out the dart board?"

Nala curled into the couch again. "I want something healthy and filling. I've only had oatmeal today."

"There's a bistro down the way that will deliver turkey dinners. How does that sound?"

Absolutely ridiculous. How could she say no to a free Thanksgiving dinner long before it was Thanksgiving?

Vincent ate at the dining table, typing on a laptop and occasionally talking business on the phone. Nala ate with a tray at the couch, watching TV with the volume low enough for Vincent to hear his phone calls. *Good. Don't eat dinner with him.* Would be one thing if she were visiting. Living with him? No. That blurred the lines of their relationship way too much.

As gracious of a host as Vincent tried to be, there were many things he continuously overlooked and nearly drove Nala to her death with. Didn't he know that she needed her own towel? One that she would probably use every day? What did *he mean* that was gross? What kind of upbringing did he have where there was more than one towel per person? Oh. Right. Upper middle class kid from Fresno.

Nala forgot her toothbrush. Did he have any spares? Ew! She was *not* using his – she didn't care how often they had kissed!

How did one turn off the TV? Okay, so what if she wanted to play all his pre-release games? The man had a fucking copy of *Fallout* before anyone else!

No, she would not wait for the cleaning lady to do the dishes. No, she would not wait for the cleaning lady to fold her clothes and put them away somewhere. *No,* she would not wait for the cleaning lady for anything! Damnit, Nala was an adult and would damn well clean up her own messes after making them. This didn't mean, however, that she was suddenly Vincent's maid. He could keep paying the cleaning lady for that.

"I'll change in the bathroom," Nala mumbled, after Vincent refused to understand why she might want some privacy, even though he had seen her naked enough times by now.

Nala made herself a bed on the couch downstairs, content with watching TV until her eyelids were too heavy to keep open. Vincent, however, insisted on bringing down the other pillow from his bed for her to curl up with. He also brought down a spare blanket and tossed it over her body when she least expected it.

"The offer still stands to come upstairs," he said more than once. "The bed is way more comfortable. Trust me. I've fallen asleep on this couch countless times."

And fucked on it, I'm sure. Nala tried not to think about that. "Thanks. I'll be fine here."

At least he didn't try to kiss her goodnight.

He did, however, go take a shower while Nala watched TV. Oh, sure, that was perfectly normal. Men took showers, after all, but did all men then come downstairs and scrounge around… wearing nothing but cotton pajama bottoms?

Spare me. The moment Nala caught a glimpse of Vincent's bare torso standing before the fridge was the moment she pulled the blanket over her head and attempted a journey into sleep.

During that time of cautious tossing and turning on a leather couch, Vincent turned off the lights downstairs and went up, leaving one soft lamp on while he coughed and creaked on his own bed.

The loft grew cold.

Nala tried to ignore the strange feeling of sleeping on Vincent's couch. She watched TV until it drove her insane. She played on the phone he bought her until she couldn't think of a single Wikipedia article to check out next. *You need to sleep. Crow's party is tomorrow. Also, work.* At least she had her priorities sorted out.

Even so, Nala could not convince herself to sleep. The air around her was too stiff, too… devoid of life. At least in her closet, Nala could pretend she was in her safe home, snuggled deep into a cozy corner and unaware of the world around her. She was not claustrophobic in the slightest. If anything, people might say she was agoraphobic in the traditional sense. *I don't mind crowds, but this whole big open space thing is unsettling.* She often felt that way living in Nevada. Big, sunny desert with no end in sight. What if something got her?

Nala turned to the back of the couch and tried to snuggle there. All she could think about, however, was how this leather felt against her hands and feet as she straddled Vincent's lap a few days ago… the way his body surged into hers, taking her, *owning* her.

No matter how deeply she sank beneath the blanket, she kept thinking about him, about this huge loft with its exposed beams and the cold nature of the brick walls. Lots of people found this intellectually stimulating, but Nala wanted to run back to the craftsman house with its potheads and sink piled with dirty dishes. At least it felt human.

There's another human here, you know. Nala certainly knew that, but it was hard to reconcile her need to put barriers between her and Vincent and her need for companionship.

"I'm ridiculous." Nala sat up, tossing the blanket aside so she could swing her legs over the side of the couch. The pillow held fast between her fingers as she dragged it across the hardwood floors, her feet taking her to the spiral staircase and to a fate she never signed up for.

"Hey there." Vincent was sitting up in bed, lamp on and tablet displaying some important missive, Nala was sure. When she glanced at it as she climbed onto the other side of the bed and put the pillow back in its rightful place, she realized it was a novel. *Even billionaires read before bed.*

"Hey." Nala was glad he didn't ask about her sudden appearance. Either that was his personality, or he knew her well enough by now to know to not say a damn thing. *Thank God.* Nala sighed as she lay in the comfortable bed and instantly felt cozier. It helped having a warm human by her side. Plus, the lofted bedroom brought her closer to the ceiling and some nearby walls. She already felt better.

Within a few minutes, Vincent put his tablet on the nightstand and turned off the lamp. He got properly into bed, shaking it enough to wake Nala back up again. She stared into darkness. She felt and smelled the man she had given herself to enough times by now.

Don't do it. Don't do it.

She did it.

"We're not having sex," she insisted, curling her arm around Vincent's abdomen and resting her head against his chest. "I'm going to sleep, okay?"

"Me too. I'm not in the mood for sex either."

Nala snorted against his skin. "Like you would say no if I went for your cock right now?"

"I said I'm not in the mood. I said nothing about him."

"I'm pretty sure one influences the other."

His fingers brushed against her hairline, lulling her deeper into slumber. *Fuck me. I'm falling for this.* Maybe not for him… but definitely *this.* "You might be surprised."

"Good night, Vincent."

"Good night, Nala."

She pulled the blankets up until they nearly touched her nose. Between the heat of their bodies and the scent of his skin, Nala convinced herself that this might actually be a slice of heaven. After that, sleeping was easy.

Entry #12

Nala moved in with me yesterday. I had to force my hand, since the moment I saw her deplorable living conditions… what other choice did I have? I could not – would not – let someone live like that if I had the chance to change it.

So now her things are in my house, and for the first time ever we shared a bed for a night. At first she insisted on sleeping on the couch, but within five minutes she was in my bed, in my arms, and feeling like she belonged there.

It was also the night I gave her the collar I had made. At first, I had it made solely for *The Aviary… but now that she's living with me, I can't help but wonder if there will be other chances to see it around her throat.*

I am more beast than man now. There will come some night soon where I will have to claim her once and for all. I'll show her what it means to submit to me, the new Vincent. It scares me as much as it liberates me. I don't know what I'm capable of.

Chapter 25

Nala had never been up in the West Hills before. It was a lofty, natural place that she could never dare to afford, so why would she go there?

Xavier Crow lived here when spending time in Portland. As far as Nala knew, it was his primary residence ever since he decided the area was where his newest ventures would take place. *Get him a quick drive to the airport, and it's weekly meetings in Seattle for this guy.* Even though the sun had long set by the time they ascended the hills, Nala was still in awe over the lights illuminating large houses and even tiny, albeit adorable cottages.

"He lives way up here, huh?" They drove for several minutes, with the houses becoming sparser and the trees denser. It was hard to believe they were still in Portland.

"He's one of the richest men on the coast. Of course he lives all the way out here, if he's not living in a penthouse condo."

"Oh, well, excuse me."

"You're excused."

Nala almost smacked his shoulder until she realized that this was Vincent's dry humor striking again. The more she knew this man, the more she realized that his sense of humor was a bit… off. Oftentimes, Nala was more offended than amused. She supposed that happened when she was involved with one of the most aloof men around. Even for Portland, Vincent Lane was…

"We're almost there." He pulled down a marked lane, slowing down as he looked around for any guards or other people hired to keep out the riff-raff. *Do the crazies make their way up here?* It would be quite the hike. Nala didn't put it past them, though. "You ready?"

Nala subconsciously touched the choker around her neck. Her *collar. The moment I step in Crow's mansion, I am Nightingale. I belong to Vincent and have to do whatever he says.* Nightingale was also a master spy, and tonight would be the first real night of espionage.

"Good. Did you review the layout earlier today?"

"Of course." Vincent had sent her the public domain plans to Xavier's mansion. He had it on Lucian's authority that most of Crow's home parties were hosted on the second floor, east wing, which also happened to be where his main office was located. It was their hope that, as soon as the couples broke up for "playtime," Nala would be able to sneak into the office. How would she get in? They still had yet to figure that out.

"*Good.*" Vincent pulled into a roundabout and then switched gears as they went up a dirt road lined with Christmas lit trees. At the end of the road was a baroque mansion with all the trimmings. Gaudy as hell. Like Crow. *His business buildings and residences are all super modern, and then there's his personal home.* No wonder he liked to watch spanking so much. "We're here. Time to put Nala away, darling."

She was already changing her outlook. Nala pulled her long hair around her face, framing it and her breasts as they pushed out of a black bustier. She wore one of Vincent's smaller dinner jackets to keep out the chill until they got inside. Otherwise, it was corsets and miniskirts… and big black boots. *I'm feeling more and more like a Nightingale as time goes on.* Excellent. She could get shit done that way.

"Welcome sir, madam." The butler from The Crow's Nest came out to greet them the moment Vincent pulled up. "Parking is around the corner.

Please meet us inside the foyer. Master Crow has asked everyone to gather there before heading upstairs."

After Vincent found a suitable parking spot, he helped Nala out of the car, leading her by the hand to the front marble steps. The butler waited at the double doors, already ushering in Joseph and Starling. When Vincent approached, the butler bowed again, showing them to the far side of the grand foyer.

Nala felt like she was walking into a five-star hotel as opposed to someone's home. Here came those open spaces again. *How can people stand to live like this?* She liked intimacy. She liked knowing where the walls were and that she could touch the ceiling if she had a ladder. Then again, Xavier Crow was all about showing off what he had.

Four out of five couples were there, minus Crow. A conservatively dressed maid offered Vincent and Nala some champagne, which they accepted graciously. The others were already halfway to tipsy-town.

"Just think, Lane, you could live like this sometime soon!" Lucian clapped his hand on Vincent's shoulder, almost knocking the champagne glass out of his hand.

"I'm fine with my loft for now. It's more my style."

"I know what you mean! But, well, I've got a little woman who likes the finer things. You're lucky. Yours seems like she'll do whatever you desire. I know Robin loves her."

I'm right here, you know. Robin also wasn't that far away, although she was deep in a flippant conversation with Quail about shoe sales.

"If I may say," Lucian continued, addressing Nala. "You are very beautiful tonight, Gale. A woman who can pull off a corset like that is one in a million." He winked with the eye out of Vincent's view. Nala took a small step back, clutching tight to Vincent's arm. *Okay then.* Robin had mentioned something about Lucian thinking she was good looking enough to swing with. *Not tonight, buddy.*

"Thank you," she said, nodding her head in appreciation. Nightingale was a thankful woman. She loved receiving compliments, especially if it would elevate her Master's status.

Lucian wandered away after that, leaving Nala with Vincent. "This is already a crazy party," she muttered into his bent head. "Try to keep that guy's hands off me, if you would."

"Don't have to tell me twice. Remember, you belong to me tonight." His hand went to the small of her back. Nala sucked in her breath. This was a far cry from the guy who tenderly held and caressed her last night. Nala had woken up to Vincent curled protectively around her, cloudy sunlight streaming through the nearby window and lighting up his sleeping face. He had looked so peaceful, so easygoing that Nala had to fight the urge to kiss him awake.

Now he was clutching her ass, reminding her that deep down this guy was a stone-cold Dom who liked to tie her up and call her dirty things. Good thing Nightingale was into it.

The butler returned to the front doors to welcome Jay and Maggie. Nala steeled herself. This was her first time seeing Maggie since their encounter in the women's restroom in a fancy restaurant. The one where she all but threatened poor, confused Nala. *Did she threaten me?* With a woman as tight-lipped as Maggie, it was difficult to tell.

"How lovely to see you two so soon," Maggie greeted, standing in front of Nala and sipping her champagne. Jay came up behind and put a light hand on her shoulder. *It's not the same as the other men.* These two played at being a Dom/sub couple, but the more she got to know them, the more Nala realized something was incredibly amiss. *They make me nervous.* She wondered if she made them nervous too, and they were better at not showing it.

"Lovely to see you too," Vincent said, managing to sound amicable. "You look particularly lovely this evening, Maggie."

She batted her long eyelashes as her lips wrapped around the edge of her glass. "You're such a gentleman, Master Lane. Almost as much of one as my Jay here."

Were all of these conversations going to be so boring and yet strange? Nala was almost grateful that Xavier Crow finally made his appearance at the top of the stairs to invite everyone up. Almost! Because he had a familiar guest with him.

Hawk. Wearing a feathery mask and carrying a cat o' nine tails at her hip. She too wore a corset, a leopard print one, paired with fishnet stockings that didn't do much to cover her tanned legs. The way she looked at the gathering felt like a tiger overlooking a herd of gazelle.

Everywhere Nala turned, there was someone setting out to make her feel uncomfortable. First it was Lucian's subtle sexual advances, then it was Maggie's veiled threats, and now Hawk was about to make her the most uncomfortable of all. Crow might be too busy to keep track of what his guests were doing or thinking… especially as he got drunker and his pants started filling out. Hawk? She had gained her name for a reason. She was watching them all like a bird of prey.

Nala and Vincent brought up the rear going upstairs. Nala made sure to cling to Vincent's arm, knowing he was the only man she could trust in this place. This place wasn't anywhere close to being neutral. Every door was guarded by Crow's men. Every window watched. Every woman? Leered at like meat.

Nala was used to that last part. Even as they entered a spacious salon stocked with plenty of liquor and a small stage for "demonstrations." *I hope we're not expected to perform tonight.* Nala couldn't handle being bound or spanked in Crow's place of residence. It was bad enough that she and Vincent would have to go into a bedroom and pretend to have sex. *Or really have sex.* She was Nightingale. If Vincent decided the time had come…

In the end, she wasn't surprised when they were expected to sit and watch one of two demonstrations that night. The first was Quail and Sebastian, her subservience unparallel even for that group. Anything he told her to do, she did, including disrobing half his clothes – and then her own. Nala was getting used to this environment, but it still unnerved her to see such displays acted out right in front of her and other people. *How can she do that comfortably in front of Crow?* Nala could never. It was bad enough when Vincent tied her up for artistic purposes. To be degraded, verbally and physically? No way. *Doesn't help she looks like the happiest woman in the world.* Nala appreciated the rougher forms of loving Vincent provided, but this was on a different plane of existence.

The second show was not much easier to handle. Hawk was formally introduced as Crow's "old friend," a dominatrix who stopped by town every few weeks for business. *What kind of business?* Wait, Nala didn't actually want to know.

She was the guest demonstration that week, calling upon Starling to be her volunteer. Nala wondered if this was arranged beforehand, or if she had barely not been called up. *I would have to find a way to avoid that.* She would *have* to!

Nala thought that over and over once the demonstration was under away. Why wasn't she surprised that it was *spanking?* Not any type of spanking, either. This was purely about erotic pleasure, since Hawk and Starling did not know each other and thus had no other kind of relationship. It wasn't like watching a Dom spank his long-time sub. No tenderness. No blooming love for one another. Even naïve Nala was learning the difference now.

"Ow!" The sound echoed in the room in tandem with the smack on Starling's bare ass. Her face was more pain than pleasure. Even Joseph uncrossed his legs and leaned forward, his easygoing smile disappearing in favor of concern. "I mean… thank you!"

A large red splotch appeared on her skin. Nala shuddered, instinctively taking Vincent's hand and thanking any god out there that this wasn't her. *I'd kill her.* Hawk wouldn't live long enough to bring down another spank on Nala's ass. Worth going to jail over.

"You have good resilience," Hawk said with her grating voice. She patted Starling's ass, eliciting a hiss through the teeth. "Your Master has done a fine job training you, sweetie, but there is always room for improvement. My subs are used to taking much harder spanks from me. Maybe one day you can join their ranks, hm?"

Starling did an admirable job controlling her reaction. Although Nala could tell the young woman wanted to cry out, maybe say something testy to someone considered a Domme, she didn't. Instead she expressed more gratitude, thanking Hawk for her kind words and kinder hand. The only "tell" she had was a quick nod to Joseph, keeping him in place on his couch even though he looked ripe to jump up and pluck his girlfriend off the stage.

Yet as everyone assumed that part of the party was over, Hawk raised her paddle and brought it down – *hard* – on Starling's other cheek. The girl screamed so loudly that Nala's seat shook. She grabbed Vincent's hand with both of hers and tried to hide her face in his shoulder. Even he wasn't looking directly at the stage.

"This isn't eroticism," Nala hissed in his ear. "This is abuse."

He squeezed her hand back. "I'm glad that isn't you." He then stood, excusing himself so he could use the restroom down the hall.

Joseph heaved an audible sigh of relief when Starling was finally released from the stage, walking like a bow-legged fool to her boyfriend's arms and lying askance on the couch so she wouldn't have to sit on her bruised ass. She somehow managed to not let any tears fall. Nala had half a mind to go up to the stage and ask Hawk what her fucking problem was, but was afraid of the repercussions.

The only person not frowning – for Maggie looked like she was about to light the place on fire – was Xavier Crow, standing up to applaud both Hawk and Starling as if nothing was amiss. Nala had to remain stiff in her seat so she wouldn't smack him next.

"I don't know about the rest of you," he said, much too jovially, "but I'm starting to feel the mood of the evening. Why don't we retire?"

Usually the "mood" was a lot less sinister than this. Nala could tell that most of the other couples – especially Joseph and Starling – were interested in doing anything but retiring to a bedroom and leaving the door open.

"Yes, indeed," Hawk reiterated. She raised a glass of champagne. "Here's to everyone having a fine time tonight."

Everyone, including Nala, raised their glasses and chimed that they hoped to have fun too. *Where is Vincent?* Granted, it hadn't been long since he went to the bathroom, but Nala wasn't comfortable being in the middle of this foray without her "Master" to protect her. Lucian winked at her again as he led a giggly Robin out of the salon. Maggie flashed her a stern look as she and Jay left the room as well. The only person Nala willingly made eye contact with was Starling, who put on a brave face and tried to walk as if her ass wasn't in serious pain. Joseph led her carefully, their low voices discussing what they should do that night. "Don't touch me down there, please," was all Nala heard on Starling's end.

Soon she was left alone with Crow and Hawk, two of her least favorite people. When Xavier saw her sitting alone, he came over, sending nauseous chills down Nala's spine.

"Why, Nightingale, it appears that your Master is not back from his sojourn. You can stay here and wait for him, if you want, but my butler will also show you to your assigned room."

When she saw the way both he and Hawk leered at her, Nala was fast to get on her feet. "I'll wait for him in our room," she said, channeling her inner Nightingale so she would think of nothing but Vincent and his hands all over her. *Don't actually get horny though.* "I have to, um, get ready."

Wrong thing to say. Both Hawk and Crow looked at her as if she were suddenly a piece of food on a sampler plate. *Run, girl!* The last thing she wanted was for Hawk to make her the next anal victim while Crow watched. Where the fuck was Vincent?

The butler saved her by offering to escort her down the hall. Nala went immediately, following the spry old man and downing the last of her champagne. She hoped there was more alcohol in the room. She needed it.

Nala went in and instantly tried to close the door as the butler walked away. However, she found out that the door did *not* close all the way, let alone latch. *Making sure the open door policy remains in effect.* Nala looked around the room, searching for cameras. She didn't doubt there were some in there, but did they have sound?

I guess this means Vincent and I really have to do something. Maybe she could get him to bind her to the bed with more artistic, elaborate designs. No actual sex, but by now people might start thinking they both got off on it. *They don't have to know the truth.* The truth that Nala kinda did get off on it…

She sat on the edge of the bed, out of sight from the door. Nala opened her satchel and checked the contents. Makeup. Wallet. Notebook and cell phones. The spare key Vincent gave her to his loft. Everything was still there. She wasn't sure why she was so worried. Who would have had the chance to steal from her so far?

"You here?"

Vincent's voice wafted into the room. Nala stood, alert, her satchel plopping to the bed behind her. "I'm in here. Hurry up before that crazy lady comes and breaks my ass too."

He did enter, also trying to get the door to close behind him. Once he realized it didn't, he turned around with a huff. "You okay?"

"Barely. Wasn't that awful?'

Vincent sat next to her on the bed, readjusting the buttons on his jacket. "It wasn't pleasant. Definitely not arousing."

"Blech." Nala squished her legs together for emphasis. "Did you have fun in the bathroom? Thanks for getting up and leaving me there with that mess. I was almost afraid they would pick me next for mandatory volunteerism."

"I didn't go to the bathroom. That's what I told them."

"Then…?"

He leaned in, champagne-laden breath touching Nala's ear. "I went looking for Crow's office. I found it. Only a few doors down from here. Looks like a standard lock, which is low-key for a man of his standing. Here." Vincent plucked a pin from Nala's hair. It happened to be the pin holding some of her hair back, so now it fell, obscuring her face and making it difficult to see Vincent right next to her. "I'm sure there are cameras in there, but if it's like any other watched room, they probably focus on the center. Stick to the sides."

"If I'm caught?" Nala held her pin between her fingers.

"Tell them you got lost and thought that was the salon."

"Wow. Nobody is going to believe that."

"I don't know what else to tell you, Nala. This is one of our only chances. You want to go find evidence or not?"

When Nala fantasized about this moment, she always imagined her busting down the door and seeing a file folder on Crow's desk labeled, "People I Had Killed." This was different. It was real, and it wasn't anything like her fantasy. Not the fantasy where Nala Nazarov was like those hot Russian spies every man her age thought she should be. Not even the fantasy where the Nightingale in her head could get her way with a bat of the eyelashes. *What would happen if Hawk caught me?* Crow would surely start making the rounds later, looking for couples to spy on as they did their thing.

"I want to go. I'll be quick. I even brought these." She pulled out the final items of her satchel – two leather gloves she picked up on her earlier shopping spree. "When I get back, Nightingale wants a kiss."

"Don't get caught, and she might get more than a kiss."

Nala sat back. "What are you saying?"

"You know what I mean." Vincent affectionately pulled her hair back from her face, letting his hand cup one of her cheeks. "I don't want you to get caught… not just because it would incriminate me too, but because I don't want you in too much danger. I don't want you in any danger, to tell you the truth, but it can't be avoided. Do a good job and get out of there. Use the camera on your phone to take pictures of evidence, if you find any, and if you don't… well, we tried."

Nala was a fool if she thought she could revel in this moment. Vincent, concerned for her safety but still willing to let her go out and do what she set out to do. Vincent, touching her as if she were the most precious thing in his life. *What if I am?* Nala couldn't dwell on that. She needed to leave.

She kissed Vincent, her head turning so she could taste the whole of his lips. He froze beneath her touch before gradually lifting his hand and stroking the side of her head. *He really does care about me.* This man with his guarded heart, his inability to let go and move on… he was graciously accepting her tender kiss and not expecting anything more in the moment.

Nala didn't want to break away from him. She wished they were back in his loft, where she could take her time exploring this moment between them. *Don't fall in love.* That was the most dangerous thing that Nala could not afford to do. Falling in love with Vincent was more dangerous than attempting to break into Xavier Crow's office.

As Nala was about to end their kiss, however, the bedroom door flung open and admitted two of the least – okay, most – likely people.

No, it wasn't Crow and Hawk, thank God, but it wasn't much better. Because how did one react to two supposed friends stumbling in, tipsy off their asses, and declaring it was "group fun time?"

Both Nala and Vincent stared before them, still wrapped in each other's arms. Good thing, too, because Robin was halfway to falling over already. Lucian wasn't faring much better himself.

Oh my God.

Chapter 26

A whole bottle of champagne landed on the bed. Thankfully, it was unopened, but Nala felt compelled to jump off the bed anyway.

"It's a good thing we… good thing we didn't drink anymore…" Robin sat in Nala's place, holding out her arms as if she couldn't protect her balance any other way. Lucian wasn't far behind her, flopping down near the pillows and jostling the whole damn thing. "Because I want this to be *awesome.*"

Nala stood near the wall, keeping her satchel close to her chest. "What are you guys doing here?" That was all Nala, not Nightingale – because Nightingale knew damn well what "group fun" meant. *They want to have group sex. I can't believe this. No wait, yes I can believe it.* That sort of kinky shit was right up Lucian and Robin's perverted alley.

"This bed is way more comfortable than the one we got," Lucian revealed. "That one is all squeaky. This one is nice and sturdy." He patted it to reiterate his point. "You're a lucky guy, Lane." Lucian's attempt to put his hand on Vincent's shoulder ended with him landing on his stomach in the middle of the bed. *I can smell the alcohol over here. How plastered are they?*

Robin she could see being a lightweight. Lucian, on the other hand, either set a record for a guy his size or had nearly drank Crow out of his home.

"*Hi.*" Robin attempted to climb in Vincent's lap, but was met with a firm hand against the shoulders. "Wow, you smell good, Master Vincent. Doesn't... doesn't he smell good, Lucian?"

"Like *roses.*"

Nala briefly met Vincent's eyes from across the room. "*Don't you dare,*" Vincent's said. "*Don't you dare leave me with these crazy people.*"

"Um, I gotta go to the bathroom first," Nala announced, shuffling toward the door. "Little girl business. You three go ahead and get started!"

She ducked out of the room before Vincent could forbid her.

Uh oh. Nala stood in the hallway, alone, looking back and forth for anyone who might be watching her in turn. Yet not even the butler was there, although she did hear the occasional voice of a reveler somewhere in the hall. Luckily, none of them were Hawk or Crow.

Vincent had told her that the office was a few doors down. Well, she still had her satchel and the pin in her possession. There was no reason for her to not make a go of it, assuming she could find the office.

Look for a room closed all the way and with a normal looking lock. If pressed, she could say she was looking for the bathroom around there. Nala started to shuffle, trying to be quiet, but also convinced that the echo of her heartbeat could be heard from Timbuktu.

She looked all around, stopping whenever she heard a loud voice pounding through the hall. With so many doors ajar, it wasn't hard to hear someone get spanked or someone else cry out in pleasure. She was pretty sure, as she passed one such bedroom, that she witnessed Quail being stripped of her clothes – again – and pulled upside down onto the nearest bed. Someone was about to get very lucky.

Nala shot her eyes away and continued her search. She was reaching the end of the hall. Had she gone the wrong way and Vincent meant the other direction?

As she thought that, she came upon the final door before another one marked *RESTROOM* on a gold plaque. No wonder Vincent had been able to find the office so easily. As Nala searched, she realized that it was the only unmarked door closed all the way. It also had a key-lock that was prime for picking.

Nala forced herself against the hall wall. She looked behind her again, making sure the coast was clear before jamming her hair pin into the lock and jostling it about.

What the fuck was she doing? She had no idea how to break a lock! All she knew came from the movies. Spies were able to put in hairpins, fingernails, pretty much anything and break into a room with nary a sweat broken in turn. Except this was Nala. This was real life. She couldn't jam a hairpin into a key lock, let alone the lock to a billionaire's primary office, and…

Something clicked. Nala turned the handle and watched the door miraculously open, admitting her without a second thought. *Oh, shit!*

She looked around again, convinced that at any moment the police would come storming down the hall and arrest her for breaking and entering. That was the kind of kinky shit she really wasn't into. She also doubted that Vincent liked the gruff handcuffs as opposed to his silky ropes.

When she was sure that nobody had seen her, Nala stepped in, keeping to the wall. The lights were off, which was good for cloaking her – although any security cameras were probably night vision. Regardless, Nala stayed close to the wall, pulling out her cell phone and using it as a light to see her way around the office.

It wasn't that big. In fact, it was almost sparser than Vincent's downtown office. *This doesn't look right…* Had Vincent gotten it wrong and this wasn't Crow's main office at all? Nala thought it was suspicious that such a place was so close to the happenings of a party. Wouldn't he keep that far out of the way from where anyone may be snooping around? Like her, for one.

What am I doing? Her cell phone and the light coming through the window picked up few things, mostly furniture and decorations on the wall. Still life paintings. Race dog photos. Old pictures from Crow's childhood and before even that.

Nala was about to turn and rummage through the desk when she came upon a series of recent photographs that piqued her interest. Mostly because the first photo was of Robin and Lucian, embracing as they smiled for a more candid than not photo. Since Robin was wearing a glittery red mask, Nala had to assume that it was taken at an Aviary party. Perhaps one hosted here in Crow's house.

There were others. Every couple, including one of Maggie and Jay looking more stoic than usual, hung on the wall wearing sexy outfits and the masks of The Aviary. Little printouts beneath each photo held their names. Not the women's real names, of course, but their code names as plain as day.

What intrigued Nala the most, however, were the older photos of couples no longer in the club. There were only three of them. One, called "Lewis and Bluejay," featured a man with tan skin and an Asian woman vying for Maggie's stoic title. Another, of two red-heads, was called "Othello and Sparrow." The last photo was missing, but the tag remained, too ominous to bear.

"Xavier and Raven."

Whoever Raven was, it certainly wasn't Hawk, and she must have once been Crow's partner in the Aviary, perhaps when he founded it over a year ago. Nala hurried to punch these names into her notes before moving on. There was one last space on the wall for a new couple. No doubt Crow would soon be asking for Vincent and Nala's photo to hang on his wall of deviants.

Nala moved away from the wall, focusing on the desk behind her. It was all but empty, with only a leather office chair and a comfortable pad for writing longhand on. An ink well was filled, and plenty of pens stuffed together into a simple box. There wasn't even a computer to snoop on. Nala put on her gloves, however, and started opening any drawer that didn't have a pesky combination lock on it.

Most of them were empty, aside from some candies and extra legal pads that had hardly any scribbles on them. Nala grumbled, dropping her satchel and hurrying to pick it back up again.

She was about to give up and get out of there when she found a few printout papers in the bottom drawer. At first they weren't anything out of the ordinary – a few business receipts from a week ago that Crow probably had yet to file with his other receipts. Nala wished there was something incriminatory, but the best she found toward the top was one receipt for chauffer services around downtown Portland.

Dinner receipts. Tech receipts. Even his phone receipt. Nothing was out of the ordinary. Not until Nala unearthed one piece of paper that had two familiar names on it.

RE: Othello and Sparrow.

Funds transfer status is confirmed. $5,000,000 has been cleared from primary account ending in x679 and deposited into account ending in x4535. Awaiting further orders. Please advise. New target location: Hamburg, Germany.

RE: RE: Othello and Sparrow.

Hold off for now. Hopefully they will keep quiet. We don't need an unnecessary mess. Keep an eye on their private activities for the next two years and report anything that may be defamatory to BRP.

Nala didn't understand any of this, but it sounded shady as fuck, so she snapped a picture with her phone and hurried to close the door.

Now she had to get out and hope nobody could see her coming out of the office. She pressed her ear to the door, listening for footsteps or voices in the hall. When she was fairly confident that everything was clear, Nala slowly opened the door and stared into the bright lights of the hallway.

When she didn't see anyone, she opened the door wide enough to let her slip through and was sure to close it behind her. She kept close to the wall until she was near Quail and Sebastian's room again.

"Fuck me, sweetheart, you have the best pussy in Portland."

Nala hurried past their door and veered into the middle of the hall…

…And right into Xavier Crow as he emerged from her and Vincent's room.

"Nightingale!" he greeted, almost relieved. "I was asking Vincent where you were, since I noticed he was all alone in there."

Nala's heart beat so furiously that she worried it would pop out of her chest. "I, uh, was in the bathroom." She pointed behind her.

"That's what Vincent said. Hope everything is fine."

"Yeah. Things are fine."

He continued to stare at her, as if attempting to peer into her soul and read the lies painted upon it. *I haven't done anything, I swear!* That was the message she broadcasted from her brain, hoping someone as business shrewd as Xavier could pick up on it.

"Do take care, dear Nightingale. Please excuse me. I must tend to something."

She let him pass, bowing her head so she wouldn't have to look at him. *Don't go in your office. Don't go in…* Sure enough, Crow pulled a key out of his pants and opened the office door before going inside.

Nala hurried ass into her assigned bedroom, relieved to find Vincent alone. Bedraggled, but alone.

"Well?" he snapped. "Did you get anything? Because things have been peachy in here."

Nala slowly sat down on the edge of the bed, her eyes never leaving his tested countenance. *I probably should not find that hot.* Nala shouldn't find a lot of things hot, and yet here she was, already thinking about what she heard Sebastian tell Quail two minutes ago. *Would Vincent ever say something like that to me?* Nala didn't know if she wanted to hear it or not.

"You go first. What happened with Robin and Lucian?"

"Oh, *that.* After they both – yes, both – tried to rope me into a threesome for you to return to, I managed to fend them off and said that you and I hadn't really discussed such things yet. They told me to have the chat with you right now so they would know if we would be game next time. Then I think they went back to their room to screw around."

"Oh."

"Yes, Nala, *oh.* Because *then* none other than Xavier Crow peeked in to try and watch us in the act. Did not end well for him because I was all alone, trying to regather my bearings after what had happened. I told him that you were in the bathroom. So?"

"Yeah, I ran into him out there. I told him the same thing."

"Good. And?"

"And…" Nala sighed. "I didn't really find anything. That can't be his real office. It was super empty, aside from some pictures and receipts. Before you can ask, no, I'm not sure I found anything, but I wrote some things down and took pictures anyway. I'll show them to you later."

"Fuck."

"Right?"

They leaned against one another, Vincent still stewing in whatever bothered him. Nala didn't feel much better. She wanted to take her toys and go home. Between being in Crow's house, watching that horrendous display of "spanking," being harassed by people she considered friends, and rummaging through Crow's office… Nala was over it. Over everything.

Vincent put a reassuring arm around her, allowing Nala to embrace him. She buried her nose in his chest, feeling "safe" for the first time all night. *How crazy is it that this guy I still barely know is my only real friend? The only guy I can trust?* He stroked her skin, pulling back more of her hair so he could touch the spot behind her ear. Sighing again, Nala sat up and intercepted his lips for that kiss they were denied what seemed forever ago.

She thought it would be an almost loving kiss. That was all she could bear in the moment, anyway. *Let me feel safe again.* And again. And again.

Instead, she felt his tongue punch into her mouth, devouring her throat as his hands grabbed the back of her head and drew her in closer.

"Mmf!" Nala could have choked on him! When she finally pushed him away, it was with a gasp, her hands splayed in front of her as she stared at him in disbelief. That was the first time he was *that* aggressive! "Let a girl breathe, huh?"

She thought he would apologize. He usually did, unless… oh, no, he was in irate Dom mode, or whatever the fuck this was.

"Don't be insolent," he hissed at her. "You think this is a lovey-dovey game? I could have gotten us in serious trouble with Crow a few minutes ago. You're lucky you timed it right coming back. I know he would have gone into his office."

Nala didn't mention a certain tidbit.

"This is a different world. *We* live in a different world when we're here. Just like you separate yourself to deal with this, so do I. From the moment I walked through those doors downstairs, I became the Dom I usually keep locked up inside me. So, let me say… from the moment we walked through those doors, my mind has been in overdrive with you, Nightingale."

Her eyes widened. "Vin… I mean, *sir.*"

"Good." He tucked more of her hair back, fingers playing with the edges of her mask. "We're being tracked. Maybe not in terms of our snooping around yet, but we are definitely still on probation. They want us to get over our shyness. Do you know what I mean?"

She swallowed. "Yeah."

He tipped her chin up, forcing her to look him in the cold blue eyes. *Oh my shit. He is so fucking hot.* Dom Vincent was a different kind of hot from everyday Vincent, but *damn* if he wasn't as hot! *No, this is wrong. This is the wrong time for this!* They were in Crow's mansion… liable to be *seen* by him at any time. Nala may be willing to try out exhibitionism under different circumstances, but this was definitely *not* the right circumstance!

"Good. I'm not going to make you expose yourself…" he glanced at her chest. "Or so I thought when we were getting ready to come here.

Then you walked down my stairs wearing this corset, taunting me. Do you know what that does to a man?"

Nala didn't have to guess. *I can tell you what it does to me…*

"Take them out."

"I…"

"Now, Nightingale."

He spoke directly to the obedient woman inside of her. The one who would drop everything to do whatever her Master commanded. That was Nightingale's identity. That was who Nala tried to be ever since coming here.

It would make… things… easier.

She loosened her corset, eyes flitting to the opening in the door. Someone was screaming in ecstasy from down the hall. Maggie? Quail? Robin was probably passed out drunk, but hey, maybe she sobered up enough to play a game with her equally toasted Master.

"Don't dawdle. If you do, I'll have to punish you."

Nala stopped, looking him in the eye. *Is he serious?* Of course he was. He was a Dom. She was a sub. Her disobedience would lead to sexually frustrating places… *here* of all places!

She released her breasts from their casement, careful to keep her back turned toward the door. Vincent's gaze hovered on her breasts, his hand coming to pinch her nearest nipple.

"Vincent…" Nala tried to deny the pleasure erupting in tiny spurts within her. "Please don't make me have intercourse here."

His fingers caressed the underside of her breast, lips descending to kiss her bare chest and then whisper in her ear. "I won't 'make' you do anything. I'll do my best to protect you, but you must obey to the best of your abilities. You never know who is watching and waiting for us to prove ourselves unworthy."

Strokes of gentle compliance eased down her back. Nala wanted to sink into his embrace but refrained. He hadn't told her to do that, after all. *I hope you're enjoying this, Nightingale.*

"We have to hurry. Everyone else is already having the times of their lives." Vincent eased Nala down onto the floor – in particular, onto her knees. Her back remained toward the door. *Yet I feel like everyone can see me.* "You don't have to have finesse. Just do it."

"Do what?"

"Come on, don't play dumb. It's not cute on you."

Nala furrowed her brows. "I'm serious. What are you talking about?"

He yanked on her hair, pulling her head back. Nala braced herself against his spreading legs, her boots digging into the carpet and her ass threatening to land behind them. "Suck my cock, Nightingale."

She had a feeling he was going to say that.

Perhaps if they were home – and it was still strange calling it that – she would be into this. Him, dominating her, making her half undress and get on her knees to pleasure him. But they *weren't* home. Nala was constantly aware of where they were, and who might be watching.

Don't think about that. Think about him. Think about what you might get out of this. A brief escape in a world out to get her.

Nala really didn't have any time to lose. She had to hold on to the feeling flooding her as she unzipped his pants and rubbed her hand against his half-erect cock. Vincent propped himself up with one hand while the other combed through her hair. "Is it wrong of me to say this is kind of hot?" he murmured.

Why are we going there? Nala didn't want to say that hearing him hiss through his teeth as she pulled him free from his pants made her hot between the legs, but yet here she was, already imagining him throwing her down on the bed and fucking her.

He was right, wasn't he? At some point someone would peek in and expect something to be happening. Even if no one caught Nala giving Vincent quick head, they would definitely hear the way this man came. Better him than Nala, who wouldn't be able to perform given the conditions. In a way, he was taking one for the team, or at least sparing Nala as much embarrassment as possible.

As for loosening her corset? Vincent had already made it known a time or two he found her breasts hot, and looking at them – let alone pinching her nipples – was a surefire way to get hard, fast.

"This is hot, sir," she said, not intending to sound like a damned robot. Her hand wrapped firm around his base, breath coming dangerously close to his tip. She could smell his musky scent even before lowering her head and tasting the precum already emerging.

Nala was glad she had volunteered to give this guy oral a while ago, because this was only her second time, and she didn't trust that a first time would be any shade of good. *I barely know what he's like giving it to me missionary style.* She wanted to learn more, though.

Vincent was fully erect by the time she wrapped her mouth around his girth and began massaging the heavy sack beneath. For all his composure, Vincent struggled to not force himself into her throat. Thank goodness. Nala already had troubles taking as much as she did into her mouth. The last thing she needed was him fucking her face.

That could happen some other time. When they were home and she could be seen exerting *some* control over situations.

"Fuck," Vincent murmured, one hand pulling her hair while the other ran down her bare back and tickled her filling throat. "*Fuck.*"

He said that she could use little finesse and be quick. Under usual circumstances, she would draw this out, make him beg – in the only way Doms can – for release and then take it from her. But they needed to get this over with. There were things to discuss, like… like…uh. *I don't remember. Whatever.*

She had fully escaped into the world Nightingale occupied. As far as she was concerned, this was a game to see how quickly she could get her Master off.

His cock was already swelling in her mouth by the time he started talking dirty. Loudly. In case anyone was listening in the hall, Nala supposed.

"Look at you," he growled, both hands pushed into the thick of her hair. Nala braved glancing up, catching a visage full of dominance. "Taking out your tits for me and sucking my cock. Do you like it, Nightingale?"

Hearing him say her code name gave her as many shivers as her real name. She relaxed her gaze so he knew she liked it.

He called her a few choice words. *Loudly.* Nala wore those words as a badge of honor, taking the challenge head-on as she felt him grow larger within her and prepare to come.

Sure enough, as if she couldn't have timed it better herself, Nala brought her mouth down along his shaft as the first wave of his climax occurred. It brought with it the taste of a man who had been forced to come long before he intended. Of course, this was all Vincent's plan – but Nala didn't doubt that he would like to take his time and hold back as much as possible. What man didn't want to enjoy this aspect of a woman's attentions?

Nala continued to lick whatever her tongue could find as he finished on the back of her throat. She relaxed her gag as best as she could, breathing through her nose so she could swallow everything he gave her before pulling off his cock. When she finally did, she met the languid eyes of a man who damn well wanted to enjoy the afterglow of this kind of lovemaking.

"Shit, that was good."

"You think anyone noticed?" Nala wiped him from the corner of her mouth. Vincent reached over, grabbed a tissue, and handed it to her.

"If you didn't notice me making all that noise, then I don't know what to tell you. I'm practically famous in the club now, I'm sure."

She hadn't heard anything, but that was neither here nor there. *I must have been really into it…* His scent overwhelmed more than his voice did. *That* was the epitome of erotic. That and taste. Nala could indulge in that all day if given the chance. *Maybe I will be one day.* It wasn't coming anytime soon. When they weren't having quickies in the club, they were passed out dead in his loft. Or Nala was running away from everything…

Vincent helped her up onto the bed. At first she thought he would push her down and give her pleasure, but – thankfully – he merely brought her into his embrace and stroked the back of her head.

"I'm sorry for making you do these things."

She patted his back. "You don't *make* me do anything. I know what our situation is as much as you do."

"I don't delude myself into thinking that this is ideal for you, though."

"I'm sure it is for you, though. Mr. Dom who likes controlling women during sex."

He laughed, almost tragically. "I won't lie. It gets me off pretty damn good, but even so, it's not really under my conditions. If I had to redo these past five minutes…"

Vincent didn't have to tell her. *It would've been a lot more fun for me too.*

She put on a brave face. After all, Nala couldn't let her world turn into a pity party because she couldn't have a whole night's worth of great sex with Vincent. *Yes, that's the problem.* That's what she told herself as she broke out of his hold and fixed herself up in the nearest mirror. Vincent fixed his clothes and kept his eyes on her back. Even though she no longer pointed her breasts at him, he still found something to stare longingly at.

Nala cracked a smile. *When do I tell him about what I found?*

First, she needed to go to the bathroom. For real, this time.

Eventually Nala would learn to stop going to the bathroom at these club meetings. Nothing ever, *ever* good came out of them.

This time Nala's punishment came in the form of Hawk, leaning against the wall outside the bedroom door. The smirk on her pointed face as she uncrossed her arms and faced Nala nearly struck her dead right there and then.

"Good job, Nightingale," she purred, voice laced in arsenic. "I was starting to suspect that you and Master Lane didn't have much going on."

Nala's spine bristled. "We have plenty going on, let me assure you." Her tongue would be the death of her. "Want me to describe how his cock feels in my ass?" Whoa, sometimes the lies got away from her!

"That's quite all right." Hawk's smirk did not waver, and that disturbed Nala more than anything else. "Oh, don't worry that pretty head of yours, Nightingale. You and Master Lane are his favorites right now, and that's not a terrible thing to be. Just… keep in mind that his whims change. A lot. You don't know what he's capable of."

Nala had a pretty good idea, but did her best to not react.

"I'll leave you to your cleanup then. Wouldn't want to keep your Master waiting for you."

That was her cue to leave, so Nala did, stealing into the bathroom at the end of the hall as Xavier Crow's office door creaked open to let him back out.

Nala locked the bathroom door behind her and held herself there, chest heaving in exasperation as her knees buckled beneath her. The potpourri scent filling the room made her want to gag. The black walls and stark, white plumbing frightened her in ways no décor should. *What is happening to me?* Was it the thrill of the espionage? Was it the arousal Vincent brought out of her when he forced her to her knees and opened his trousers for her awaiting mouth? No. No, it was Hawk, who had been standing outside their door listening for the sounds of sex.

Although Nala knew that people would be watching, it wasn't until now that she realized *people would be watching.* Not just the occasional giggly Robin and her ravenous boyfriend Lucian. Xavier Crow. And Hawk.

They would be watching, waiting for them to mess up.

They would be watching, waiting to see Nala and Vincent in their most intimate moments. Waiting to see what they thought was Vincent humiliating his girlfriend.

Nala.

No, Nightingale.

Maybe Nightingale didn't care, but it was times like these that Nala found it impossible to separate the two identities. How was she supposed to, when the heart she and Nightingale shared were the same? Their spirits? She could say that their minds were one, but separate, but that was hogwash. At the end of the day, they were the same women, both struggling to fight back their anger, their feelings for…

Their feelings for Vincent.

Nala sucked up her pride and whatever else she felt as she went back to their room and made a grand show of placating and servicing whatever Vincent wanted. This followed them out to the salon, where two other sexually sated couples waited with drinks and canoodles. Nala whispered in Vincent's ear that he should insinuate what they had done, all while stroking his arm and inner thigh, pointing her chest to him and employing every bit of body language she had to make it look like she craved her Master's machinations.

The more she detached and let Nightingale's mind takeover, the easier it was. Nala had to retreat, deep into her mind, her body, forgetting the shock and pain she felt the moment she realized how far into this world they were. Somehow she managed to stick out the rest of the night. Vincent didn't suggest they leave until three other couples had. By then, Crow and Hawk had been engaging him in tech talk while Nala gradually loosened the ties on her corset again. Never enough to let her breasts pop out, but enough to imply she wanted her Master to do her good when they got back home.

I feel so dirty.

Vincent led her downstairs when it was time to leave. He was parked deep in the shadows, and it wasn't until the headlights of his car turned on that Nala realized they were still on Crow's property.

She stayed strong as they pulled down the dirt road toward the main road. She stayed strong as they descended the hills, weaving in and out until they hit Burnside again, the road that would take them home.

Home.

Vincent's loft was now home.

Nala could never escape the world she found herself in. There was no retreating to her closet, where the worst she dealt with was cramped legs and the smell of marijuana in the living room. Where her roommates and their friends said stupid shit but were otherwise harmless. Where she came home to eat oatmeal for dinner before lounging in the bath for an hour.

Instead, she lived with Vincent, the man who started this whole endeavor. The man who made love like a beast unleashed from its cage. The man so broken inside that he would be as likely to admit his feelings for Nala as she would be to confess whatever she felt to him.

There was no escape there. Everywhere she could possibly turn was infested with proof that her life was now totally, utterly consumed by Xavier Crow.

Nala held it together until Vincent pulled into his personal parking garage. She held it together until he unsnapped his seatbelt and sat there, waiting for her to say something.

Not a single word came out of her mouth. Just a long, mournful wail as everything she tried to contain burst forth in a slew of salty tears.

Nala crumpled into her lap, burying her tear-stained face and attempting – vainly – to stifle the howls and wails she so often kept bottled up inside. Vincent remained sitting in his seat. He wasn't being disrespectful. Not in Nala's cloudy eyes. No, he was letting her cry it out while still remaining in her presence. His hands gripped the steering wheel as he looked away. Whenever Nala wiped away her most recent slew of tears, she saw him sitting upright, arms shaking as he too fought back his emotions.

"What's wrong?" he finally asked. That deep voice wasn't the most comforting thing in the world. This wasn't a man who was about to grab her and tell her everything would be all right. This was a man who was ready to whip the car around and run some poor mother fucker over if it meant Nala would feel better. *That's sort of sweet.*

Nala sniffed up more tears, only moving when Vincent presented her with a handkerchief from his pocket. She snatched it from him and blew her nose, although her biggest problem was the tears staining her face as opposed to any snot accumulating in her nostrils.

"I don't wanna talk about it."

Vincent shifted in his seat. "You should. I want to know what upset you so badly."

"You wouldn't understand."

"Try me."

Nala looked at him through bloodshot eyes. Although his visage was stern, everything else about him was relaxed, almost kindly. *Men don't like seeing a woman cry, I guess.* Nala held back her urge to touch him. That way led to too much danger.

"She was watching us, Vincent. She was *watching* me blow your dick."

"They do that, yeah. I knew she was out there spying on people. Why do you think I was in such a hurry?"

"I know, but… I feel… I felt… right now I am so disgusted I can't handle it!"

Although she tried to hold them back, Nala couldn't contain the new tears falling from the corners of her eyes. *I'm so pathetic.* Of course she knew people might watch them fool around. That was the point of the club!

"That man had my sister killed, Vincent. It's because of him I have to do all of this to begin with. It's the only way I can possibly get justice, and I don't know how to do even that!" She slapped her hands against her face, shaking, *convulsing* as she remembered the way her sister's killer looked at her as if she were a piece of meat to devour. "What am I doing? What am I doing with you? Do I really think I can do something to get that man taken care of? What chance do we really have? I'm doing things I never thought I would. I left Nevada for this expensive purgatory, and… and…"

Finally, Vincent reached over and put a hand on her shoulder. "You're doing what you think you have to do, like I am."

"Don't." Nala wanted to shrug him off, but his touch was too reassuring. *Damn him.* "We're in no way equal. This is your *thing* anyway. What are you sacrificing? What's keeping *you* up at night through this?"

His grip fastened tighter. "I'm seeing you in pain right now. I'm seeing the man who killed the woman I loved more than any other… I'm seeing him hurt someone else now. If you don't think that makes me burn with rage in my gut, then I don't know what to tell you, Nala. I don't express myself well, that's true. I keep things bottled up and channel that energy into other things. It's not healthy. I know that, but it's how I am… and don't think for two seconds that I don't care what you're going through as well. I'm not naïve. I know you're taking the brunt of it."

Nala shook her head. "I hate this. I want it to stop. I want… I wanna go home, wherever that is."

"Home is where that man can't haunt you anymore."

Her lips vibrated in the need to cry even more.

"Come here." Every time he said that, Nala felt more secure. That was becoming code for "let me hold you" or "let me take you to a place that will blow your fucking mind." Right now it was the former, his arms encircling her as his chest came for her cheek. Nala melted right into his embrace, clutching him, crying into his silk shirt and wishing there was a way to have Vincent and none of the crap hanging over their heads, lurking in the shadows, or breathing down their necks.

Nala clung harder, the stick shift of the car separating them, but not enough to keep her out of his hold.

"I'm sorry, Nala," Vincent said softly. "I'm sorry I dragged you into this. I'm sorry if I've ever made you feel uncomfortable. I'm sorry for what he's done to your life."

He took away the one person I loved the most. Vincent was right when he said that earlier – Nala felt the same. They thought of two very different people, but just because they were different didn't mean they were any less deserving of their love and admiration. Vincent lost the love of his young life. A brilliant tech mind who could have created the next great wave of personal aids. Nala? She lost her big sister, her caretaker, the one person she could count on to make her smile and understand what she went through growing up without a father and a mother who slipped further and further away from reality.

"You don't have to be sorry," she said. "I made the choice to pursue this. You've never made me do anything I didn't want to do or understand why we had to do it. Anything we've done in private… I wanted to do it, Vincent. Don't ask me why. I just did."

His fingers pulled hair back from her sticky face, and… were those his lips brushing against her forehead? "I'm not the best man in the world when it comes to helping other people feel better. I admit I don't really know what to do, but I want you to know that I'm sorry you're in so much pain right now, Nala."

"You dumbass," she muttered against his chest. "That's all you have to say. You've got it down pat."

He kissed the space between her ear and cheek, easing himself back and pulling his seatbelt on again. When the car started once more, Nala got the hint and sat up in her seat, seatbelt still strapped against her chest. "Maybe it's all I have to say, but there are a few things I can do. Hold on. Let's escape for a while."

Chapter 27

"Eat the damned curry already."

Nala stared at the plate of rice and brownish sauce stuffed with carrots and onions. An unknown scent claimed her, and she wasn't sure she liked the foreign spice or not. "Except what if it's too hot? What if I cry again because my mouth is on fire?"

"That's why I got the mildest one available. I'm pretty sure they're laughing about us in the kitchen."

"Oh, excuse me, my PNW sensibilities…"

"You mean your inability to eat anything slightly spicy?"

"Okay, Mr. Fresno."

"Being able to withstand the hottest spices is a time-honored Californian tradition. Don't let the yuppies tell you otherwise."

"I can't believe I'm sleeping with a Californian. I'm losing *all* of my street-cred."

Vincent reached across the table and latched onto her wrist. "I may have upped the property taxes when I bought my loft, but at least I live there and am contributing financially and socially to my immediate community."

"Holy shit. You know how to spear an Oregonian right in the heart."

"Baby, we are the Romeo and Juliet of House Bear and House Beaver. Together we can accomplish anything between our rivaling families."

"Must I remind you that they died in the end?"

"*Eat the damned curry already.*"

Nala shook his hand off her and leaned back in her booth, picking up a large spoon and dipping it into the curry. *I hope I don't regret this.* Under Vincent's watchful gaze, Nala put a small amount in her mouth, swallowing it as quickly as possible.

"See? It's not that spi…"

"Fuck!" Nala nearly knocked over Vincent's water glass as she grabbed her own, downing it in record time. When she polished that off, her tongue continued to burn, forcing her to grab his water and make short work of it too. "*Fuuuck.*"

"Amazing." Vincent scooped some curry in her spoon and ate the whole thing in one bite. He didn't even wince, let alone take more than one sip of water remaining in his glass. "It's barely spicy, and yet here you are."

"*Shut uuuuup.*" Nala yanked her spoon back and scooped up plain rice, hoping the bland taste of it would take over any spice left in her mouth. "I do not want to hear it."

"You know, I had some Russian food once. It was fairly spicy, even by my standards."

"Shut up. Shut up!" Nala collapsed across her leather bench, rousing the attention of a group of friends dining out late nearby. One of them began to laugh. Probably because Nala's breasts were about to spill from the top of her corset. Vincent's baggy jacket could only cover so much from this angle. "My mother cooked the blandest Russian food in the universe. My father was always dumping stuff in it at the dinner table."

"I'm sure."

Nala sat back up. When Vincent pulled up to this late-night eatery on Burnside, she did not expect to be dying on the bench – from food that was too spicy, no less. Yet when Vincent insisted that she try some traditional Indian cuisine offered at the restaurant, she didn't want to say no. After all, she was Nala Nazarov, a woman who never said no to a challenge. Not usually. Vincent's food challenges may be too much for her.

"Dare I ask you to take me to a Mexican restaurant one day?"

"Only if you can handle *real* Mexican food."

"I might surprise you."

"Doubtful."

He said it with a shit-eating grin that Nala didn't often see on his face. She picked up her napkin and tossed it at him. Naturally, it only made it halfway across the table before dying an honorable death on top of the curry.

"Aw," Vincent said, plucking it off so he could eat more food. "Should I get you something else? I'm sure they have crackers for a palate as delicate as yours."

She didn't take his bait this time. "I want another beer." She pointed to her empty glass. "The only calories I need right now."

Vincent tracked down a waiter and got Nala her refill. This interruption to their good time meant she had a few seconds to regroup and think back on the past hour. Vincent brought them here, a hole in the wall by billionaire standards, but he was familiar enough with the menu that he was probably coming here to eat by himself long before he became an official billionaire. There was something endearing about his continued patronage.

Once her refill came, Nala put on her serious face and pulled out her cell phone. Vincent took an immediate interest, returning his countenance to his usual grim features. *Is it bad that I think both sides of him are hot?* "Here," she said. "These are the pics I took in his office. I'm gonna show you now before I forget later and you're at work or something."

Vincent glanced around the sparse restaurant before taking her phone and swiping through her gallery. His brows furrowed as he stared at the paper Nala uncovered and the various pictures hanging on the wall. "Not surprising, but weird. That guy is *weird*."

"At least now we'll know what he's doing if he wants a picture of us next time."

"Indeed." Vincent forwarded the pics to himself before handing the phone back. His own phone buzzed with a message in his pocket, which made Nala stifle a tipsy giggle to rival one of Robin's. "Speaking of next time, I have it on a few of the guys' authority that we're going to Mexico for a weekend. You better clear your schedule."

"Mexico? Holy fuck, dude, I ain't got a passport!"

"I know. You need to apply for one tomorrow."

"Don't those things take like… six months to process?"

"Turns out that Sebastian is wrapped up in that sort of thing. I talked to him about it, and he said if I use his name when I call up the department to talk about your application, they can put you at the top of the list."

Nala frowned. "Is it wrong that I kinda wish I couldn't get a passport in time so we wouldn't have to go?" Nothing sounded worse than dealing with The Aviary in the air… and in a foreign country, even if it would be a billionaire's cocoon. Nala would officially feel trapped, and there was almost no worse feeling than that. *I would really be a bird in a cage.* She ran her fingers along the collar around her neck, searching for the security the nightingale pendant provided.

"It's not wrong, but it won't help us any. If we have to bow out because of something like that… it would look suspicious."

"Why?"

"Because Crow might wonder why I've never taken you abroad, especially if we've been dating over six months now. We have to keep our lies in order."

"I guess."

"Besides…" Vincent took out his phone and looked at the photos he sent himself. "This must be the couple who moved abroad and had to quit The Aviary because of that. The ones mentioned in that paper you grabbed."

"Yeah. Looks like they moved to Germany."

"That's not weird in itself. What's weird is Crow and whoever he's corresponding with talking like this."

"What does it mean?"

Vincent squinted, as if that would help him decipher the words better. "I don't know, but if I read between the lines, it sounds like Crow instigated the move himself. The funds could refer to the couple's payoff to give Crow a wide berth, but it seems awfully low for people as rich as them. I am more inclined to believe the money is for the person he's talking to in this letter. Who is probably a…"

He didn't say it. He didn't have to. Nala was frozen in her seat, beer hovering against her lips. *An assassin.* The same person he paid to kill Desirée? Tasha? Any other number of people? Or did he have a network of assassins? How did that even work?

"Let's not talk about this right now." Vincent took her hand and rubbed his thumb on top of hers. "I brought you out here to help you cheer up. Is it working at all?"

Nala shrugged. "Well enough. Thanks. Beer always helps."

She said that, and yet the thing helping her most was Vincent's casual presence. Spoiling her. Cracking jokes that were so unlike him. Doing everything he could to take her mind off things – and probably his too. *I guess we do need each other like that.* The more they came to depend on each other, the more Nala worried things were growing deeper between them.

"So I have a question," Vincent said, folding his napkin ala origami. "Your last name is Nazarov. Shouldn't it be Nazarova?"

"Ugh." Not the first time Nala had been asked that. She pushed her hair behind her ears and pretended that she wasn't annoyed. "Yes, *but* when my parents immigrated they decided to standardize their last names to keep the US government happy. When my mother left the Motherland, her last name was Volkova. When she signed documents in America, however, she suddenly had the same last name as her husband. Well, almost. She still goes by Nazarova because Nazarov was too weird for her. She would rather see herself as her father-in-law's daughter than a man. Or something. Whenever she ranted about it, it was in Russian and I didn't really understand it."

"And you and your sister?"

"We didn't have those preconceived gender and naming notions when we were born, right? So I was a Nazarov from birth and my sister's A was dropped from her last name when she was brought over. She only remembered Nazarov."

"Fascinating."

"I guess." Nala shrugged. "I guess I should be impressed from a feminist perspective, but it's still your father's name and patriarchal. Plus, I'm glad my mother almost had the same last name as me. She had a hard enough time communicating with school admins when I was a kid. My father was fluent in English when they came over, but she had to learn almost from scratch."

"My parents are the most Anglo-Saxon you can get. Although I hear Koreans use similar naming conventions in their culture."

"I honestly have no idea." Nala had heard that before. Because people always mentioned that as a way to sound smart. She wanted them to drop this nonsense right now – she was tired, and now too tipsy to deal with it.

"Never mind then." Vincent put his hand on her again, this time stroking the top of her knuckles. Was that supposed to calm her? Maybe… "I'm taking a day off two days from now. I'll be between projects and I like to take even a small break to reset my brain. I was thinking… why don't we do something together?"

"You mean like a date?"

"Sure. Nothing fancy… well, nothing fancier than going to the Japanese gardens the other day."

"I, well…" Nala stared at the crane Vincent created from a paper napkin. "Why do you want to go on a date with me? I thought we weren't serious like that."

"Who said a date is serious? Okay, don't think of it as a date. Think of it as hanging out for a day."

"While you pay for everything, I'm sure."

"Why wouldn't I?"

Because you're still paying me a grand a week to be with you. Nala wasn't super into blurring their lines. It made her feel less like a partner in crime, and more like an escort. A prostitute, if she wasn't mincing words. "Sure. I guess. Nothing fancy, though. Hanging out. I have that day off."

She grabbed her phone off the table and opened her satchel to put it away. Time for another neurotic check. Wallet. Tampons. Change. Old cell phone. Key…

Wait.

Key?

Nala started pulling things out of her satchel, piling them on the table while Vincent continued to eat their curry. He watched her with mild interest, but once Nala emptied the whole contents of her satchel and still couldn't find the spare key to Vincent's loft, her stomach somersaulted into her throat.

"What is it?" Vincent sounded way too lackadaisical.

"Your key… the key you gave me to your loft isn't in here…" Nala turned her satchel upside down and hoped the key would come falling out. "What the fuck!"

"Don't worry about it. It was tiny and you didn't have a key ring on it yet." Why was he shrugging? Didn't he understand what a big deal this was? "I'll get another one made for you."

"You better change your locks too!"

"I will. Do you know what the odds are of someone even knowing where it goes, let alone trying to break into my house?"

"Doesn't matter. You're rich. You should get your locks changed."

"I *will.* Sheesh."

They left shortly after, Nala still uptight enough to question whether or not Vincent should be driving, let alone down Burnside at night. He reminded her that he had two sips of her beer and usually drove more intoxicated than that thanks to all the contact highs one got wandering through downtown Portland on a regular basis. "Most of my clients come in high as shit now," he explained, starting his car. "It's like going to the Netherlands for a ton of people here."

This time they actually entered his loft after pulling into his parking space. Nala clung to Vincent's arm to keep her body steady. She wasn't drunk, but she was tipsy enough that walking up in those boots made life more uncomfortable.

Like brother and sister they took turns showering, the hot water refreshing Nala so she no longer thought of the night or tottered about on tipsy legs. She suddenly had the munchies and came out to find Vincent heating up leftovers in the kitchen to snack on.

It was too late to watch TV or see what it was like playing video games with this guy. Instead, Nala announced she was going to bed, not sticking around to see what Vincent had to say about that as she went upstairs and curled up in his bed.

She faced away from his side, but she still smelled remnants of that cologne and the way he naturally smelled. *Is it so bad?* Not according to her addled brain.

Within the half hour, Vincent climbed in next to her, turning off every light before lying down with a heavy sigh. They were both quiet the first five minutes. Perhaps Vincent thought that Nala was already asleep, but in truth, she stared at the dark windows, trying her damndest to not think of what happened earlier that night.

She didn't protest when Vincent's arm looped around her midsection and drew her into his embrace. Why didn't she protest? *Because this is the safest I've felt all day.* How dangerous was it that the only way she could feel safe now was in some man's arms?

Not just any man's. Vincent Lane's.

"I'm sorry about today," he muttered into her ear. Rumbles of desire took her over, and it was all she could do to keep from turning farther into his arms. "I wish I could make things easier."

You already do. Nala ran her fingers along his arm, feeling the hairs growing from his skin. She touched his wrist, where he was always fiddling with something. *I couldn't do this without you.* She clamped her mouth shut before she accidentally said it out loud.

"If there's anything I can do…"

Nala thought of how she felt that night… *before* discovering Hawk outside their assigned room. Aroused. Powerful. Like she was in control of her destiny and half the world by extension. *If only it really worked that way.*

She turned over, feeling Vincent's body move slightly away from her to accommodate *her* movements. "You're already doing it."

He held her tighter, letting her retreat deep against him, feeling his strength, his heat, the aura emanating from his heart as it beat against her cheek.

Vincent began with a kiss to her head, fingers massaging the back of her neck until she was lulled into serenity. Then he kissed her nose, pushing her away far enough to bury his hand beneath her shirt and feel the bottom of her breasts. Nala whimpered, but did not protest once more. She looped one leg over his and felt him press forward, lips on hers and fingers pinching her nipple.

It was the gentlest thing he had ever done to her. Nala wrapped her hand around his neck, holding him to her, waiting for the real Vincent to erupt and take her as he always did.

Except he never did. Because this was *also* the real Vincent, a man who could be as tender as he was rough with a woman he cared for.

I'm the first woman he's probably been this way toward since… Nala couldn't think about it. Thinking about Desirée dragged up too many bad memories. Memories as old as her childhood. Memories as old as when she first met Vincent only a month ago.

"Don't worry, Nala. I'll make sure you don't think about anything else tonight."

She laughed against his lips. "Idiot. I'm going to be thinking about you."

"Is that bad?"

Nala tightened her legs around him. "Not at all. Just make sure I'm only thinking good things about you, Mr. Lane."

"Ms. Nazarov, you flatter me."

"Mmhmm." She muffled any further sounds against his mouth, inviting him to taste the inside of hers – and perhaps the back of her throat, where he had been only a few hours ago.

But this wasn't quick. This wasn't powerful. This wasn't even the slightest bit rough. This was everything on the opposite end of the spectrum. This was *real* lovemaking.

The thought should have scared Nala. Yet as Vincent slowly undressed not only her but himself as well, she came to realize that, yes, this was exactly what she needed right now. She needed to feel his strong, protective body overtake hers, gently, but so assuredly that she would never have to worry about a thing again. Or at least for that night.

I am doing the most dangerous thing possible. Snooping around Crow's office, going up against possible assassination attempts and having her identity discovered was nothing compared to making love to Vincent, a man who had the power to completely uproot everything she ever thought about herself and what she wanted to achieve in her life.

A blip of her heart realized that she was falling in love with him, and no matter how much she tried to quash it, she knew it was impossible. Nobody could stop love. Nobody could have stopped her from loving her parents, from adoring her big sister who always watched out for her… and now not even the force of the world could stop her cold heart from thawing under the heat of Vincent Lane's body.

"You're…" It was the only thing Vincent said. By that point he was halfway inside her, taking his time, *biding* his time until she was completely ready to accept him. Once she was, however, she felt the sky split open and reveal a chasm of stars she had never seen before. *Because I never bothered to look up before now.* Tasha the romantic scientist would have told her that was because she had a different outlook on life. *Not anymore.*

Nala held him close, feeling him roll gently into her over and over again. She was falling in love. She loved how rough he could be with her. She loved this tender side too. Vincent was learning exactly what she needed, and when. If that didn't say something about the way he felt for her… but they were both the most unlikely people to ever admit it. That session in the car earlier was the first time Nala had cried in weeks. When was the last time Vincent cried?

Crying out in ecstasy didn't count. Yet that's exactly what they both did when their climaxes came together, Nala reaching up to touch those blissful stars out of her reach.

She wouldn't be allowed to wrap her hand around one of those until what she set out to accomplish was over. She knew that, and yet she wanted to race ahead of herself anyway.

I love this man. It was one of the only times she would allow herself to think it without a drop of guilt or shame. She wondered if he thought the same way about her.

Entry #13

Last night, Nightingale cried in my arms. I saw the full extent of the fear she keeps buried within her, like I bury it within myself. Regardless of what happened at The Aviary, all I can feel is this immense need to protect Nightingale and make sure she never feels that fear again.

Is this love? I don't know. If it is, then it's a very different kind of love than I have experienced before.

I used to think that was a bad thing. Slowly, however, Nightingale is showing me that it doesn't have to be. Maybe every love is different, and this is the kind of love we offer one another.

Soon. I hope tomorrow. I'll show her.

Chapter 28

"Get up, darling." A knee nudged Nala. "Rise and shine. It's a sunny and bleak Portland day, and you told me we could go on a date. Get *up*."

She rolled over, warily opening her eyes to see half naked Vincent standing between her and the morning sunshine. *Oh, go away.* Not Vincent. The sun. Nala liked her days cloudy and drizzly with a side of wind. *Life in Nevada was hard.*

"Don't make me yank you out of this bed." Vincent threatened to do that, hooking one hand beneath Nala's arm and yanking her gently across the bed until she looked at the hardwood floors over the edge. "I am serious. I have breakfast cooking downstairs, damnit. Are you going to waste your life sleeping when you could be eating food *I* cooked?"

Who is this annoying fucker and why is he bothering me? Nala shook him off and sat up, the long hair she tried to keep in a neat bun for sleep falling out all over the place. Half her hair fell down her side while the other twisted in snarls on top of her head. *I must look the sight.* If Vincent was frightened, he was clouded by his need to shove food down Nala's throat.

"Do we have to start so *early?*" Nala was up, barely. She dragged herself out of bed while Vincent jogged to the window and opened the sheer curtains all the way. *Holy fucking hell!* Nala nearly fell over again from the blinding rays of, well, hell. What right did the weather have being so damn *nice* today? Disgusting.

"We've got a lot of nothing to do," Vincent said. "Besides, it's ten. It's not early."

Nala woke up when he sauntered past the bed wearing nothing but those loose-fitting sweatpants. *Hello, sexy.* She scratched the back of her head and remembered the way he made love to her two nights ago. Last night he had gone to bed long before her, and was snoozing by the time Nala got out of the shower and joined him, curling up in his arms.

"Speak for yourself, handsome." Nala let out a morning burp and scratched her side. If she had any chance in hell surviving today, she would need a quick wash up in the shower.

She came out, only a little refreshed, and descended the spiral staircase to find Vincent back in the kitchen, humming a nonsense tune while turning sizzling bacon and slapping toast on plates. The moment he saw Nala, he patted the counter lined with barstools. "Sit down and enjoy the tastes of Café Lane, Ms. Nazarov."

"Who the fuck are you?" Nala slumped onto a stool and held her head up with one shaking hand. "I don't know this Vincent. Where's the guy who downs coffee and a bagel before driving to his office and getting catered there?" He had told her about it before.

"Sometimes it's entirely possible that a man gets a great night's sleep and is looking forward to what is supposed to be a fun and relaxing day." Half-naked Vincent – okay, so this aspect Nala was definitely into – deposited seasoned eggs onto a plate and served it to Nala. Every time he moved even *slightly,* his muscles flexed, and Nala woke up more. *Good to know that I'm alive in there.* She yawned, stabbing eggs with a fork and feeling dubious that they would be any good. She had never, ever seen Vincent cook anything outside of a toaster or microwave, and Nala trusted other people's cooking about as much as she trusted Xavier Crow.

"Shit, I guess you can cook. Somewhat." Eggs fell unceremoniously from her mouth and littered her plate. "Thanks for this, by the way. Sorry. I'm totally not awake yet."

"No problem." Vincent turned off the stove and rounded the counter, joining Nala on the other barstool. He reached over and landed a kiss on her cheek before digging into his breakfast. "I'm starving."

Nala touched her cheek, feeling the traces of his early morning kiss. *What is happening?* She barely saw him the day before since he was finishing up that project and getting ready to take time off. *Is this left over from two days ago?* Once Vincent got it in his head that Nala needed reassurances, he started going overboard. Not that Nala minded. She wasn't… *used* to it from a man like him. Where was stoic Vincent? Where was heartbroken and mad at a grieving world Vincent? Okay, so she didn't *want* him to always be that way… but this was such a 180 from how he usually was that Nala couldn't help but wonder if she fell asleep in one world but woke up in another. *Is my sister alive in this world?* She would stay, if so.

While they ate, Vincent attempted to make plans for the day. "Loose plans," of course, since they were supposed to be relaxing. All he would tell her was that they had somewhere to be by eleven – but not to worry too much, because he had parking already handled.

"Dress warm," he said, washing dishes in the sink while Nala went upstairs to freshen up and change. "We'll be outside a lot of the day."

Oh, boy.

All Nala could assume was another trip to some gardens. Bearing that in mind, she dressed in simple jeans and a T-shirt, layering with her thickest sweatshirt. Too bad for Vincent she pulled her hair back in a high ponytail.

"Perfect." He snuck up behind her, wrapping his arms around her midsection for a few seconds while kissing the side of her neck. "That's absolutely perfect."

Vincent wandered to his dresser and started pulling out similar clothes for himself. Nala could only watch in awe, wondering what strange planet this was – besides Portland.

By the time they were ready to go, they looked the similar pair. Except everything Vincent wore was of the highest quality, from his sturdy designer jeans to his super soft cotton T-shirt with pithy tech sayings Nala did not understand. *He's gone geek today.* This was further proven when he pulled on a thick "Stanford Computer Science" sweatshirt styled with binary in the background. The dark red looked striking on him, and Nala had to hold herself back from sneaking into his arms and wishing he would pick her up. *I'm awake, I guess.*

"Meet me in the car downstairs, darling," he said, disappearing into the bathroom a final time. "We don't want to be late."

"Late for what?" This was Nala's tenth attempt at finding out what was going on. Alas, Vincent's lips were sealed.

His car was transformed from a business man's no nonsense car to a young, hip thirty-year-old's wheels. Nala buckled herself up the moment Vincent appeared at the driver's side door and helped himself in. When the car started, Nala wondered if she should start making the signs of the cross or relax for once in her life.

Then again, she really, *really* did not like surprises. Knowing her luck, Vincent was taking her to a cock fight, or, even worse, a *nerd* fight. *What would that be anyway? A Magic the Gathering brawl?*

He braved morning traffic on Burnside, turning on the radio for the first time in Nala's presence. Adult contemporary blared from the speakers, and Nala wondered what kind of music a man like Vincent Lane listened to. She half expected to find a Maroon 5 CD in the glove compartment. *CDs? Pshaw. This man's got Sirius radio.*

Traffic became more congested the farther west they went on Burnside. They were held up momentarily outside the big bookstore. Nala looked out the window and saw people coming in and out with large paper bags stuffed with books, looking pleased with themselves for supporting one of the biggest indie enterprises in America.

Vincent caught her looking. "We can go there later, if you want. I've been thinking about stopping by to check for a few things."

Nala remained noncommittal. If Vincent wasn't going to tell her what they were doing, then she wouldn't be forthcoming about what she wanted to do. *That's against my best interests, come on.* Nevertheless, she could be ridiculously stubborn like that.

"Oh my God," she gasped, watching Vincent whip a sudden left near Providence Park. "Don't you dare tell me." People were cramming their cars into parking, jumping out wearing green and white scarves and carrying TIMBERS pennants like they were running toward the rapture and angels themselves were making an appearance. "You are way too nerdy for this shit."

"Nobody is too nerdy for soccer." Vincent put up his parking permit sticker and hopped out before Nala had the chance to further protest.

She thought back to that night they met, when she told that bartender she didn't care for Ducks or Beavers. Only Timbers. Was this irony's way of getting her in the ass? Not that Nala hated soccer or even sports by an extension… but her idea of a rip-roaring day did not have anything to do with soccer.

Thanks to Vincent's connections, they went straight to the front of the line, complete with drinks and some popcorn to get their day started. *I can't believe we are doing this.* He had good seats. Not great, but it was apparent that not even this billionaire was buying boxes at sporting events. He seemed a lot more at home surrounded by people wearing war paint and waving their pennants in pride. Nala had no idea who the opposing team was. She didn't recognize any of the chants. She barely knew the rules, but was determined to figure them out before resorting to asking Vincent, who booed the officials with the best of them. *Who the fuck* is *this guy?* Nala didn't know if she was endeared or frightened. Ever since the other night… Vincent had changed right in front of her.

Changed for the better? God, she hoped so.

"Okay, what the hell does offsides mean?" She asked him this three times, but over the rabble of the other people around them, Vincent never heard her. When she tugged on his sweatshirt sleeve, he brought her into a hug, as if that's what she wanted. Eventually, Nala remembered that she could look things up on her phone. She quickly became one of those terrible people who spent more time staring at her phone than staring at the game. Then again, in her defense, she was researching soccer stuff!

I only know "we're" winning because the score is in our favor. She knew that scoring goals got points. The other nuances of the game, however, were completely lost on her. It took her about an hour, but she finally realized that understanding the game didn't matter. It was more about spending time with Vincent, the man she was slowly starting to consider her boyfriend. Not a fake boyfriend, either. A *real* boyfriend.

She gazed at his profile as he cheered for his team. There was so much renewed energy in him that Nala was a little scared. Was this what he was like before Desirée's death? Was this the Vincent that woman knew? Nala had never met him before. When she curled her hand over his knee and he barely noticed, that somehow made her happy.

Nala looked around the audience, seeing the usual suspects. Groups of buddies going all out with their cheering. School kids making the most out of their youth. Older people, younger people. Men and women. Men and women *together.* Oh, hell, women and women, men and men. *This is a huge date spot.* Obviously, Vincent enjoyed the game for what it was – he also came here often, it seemed. But did he often bring dates here? Or was Nala that special?

He said he hadn't really been with a woman since Desirée. Sex, yes. Anything beyond that? Not likely.

Nala remained seated for the whole game, which let out while the sun was still out and people were going about their days. Even after the game ended, she stayed curled next to Vincent, wrapping her hand in his and watching the world go by. People on either side of them left. The field cleared. The sun came out again, illuminating this enclosed world in endless light. Nala let her hair loose across her shoulders, and Vincent raised his hood enough to cover the back of his neck from the blaring sunlight. *Someone burns easily.* Was he sure he was Californian?

"What do you want to do now?" Vincent asked, once it was clear enough for them to make their escape. "Bookstore?"

"Sure."

Still holding hands, they walked out of the stadium, heading toward their parking space and silently praying that nobody had broken into

Vincent's car. Thankfully, it remained untouched, and most of the cars around it had left. That didn't mean traffic was any better, however. They sat for a while, watching cars and trucks go by, departing from the game and going elsewhere. People who lived in the area could walk. Others who lived by the Streetcar or on the MAX or other nearby lines could take those and avoid too much congestion.

The sad thing was the bookstore wasn't even that far away. The *sadder* thing was that trying to find parking in the area was like looking for a tie on Vincent's person. While Vincent muttered under his breath, swinging laps around the same blocks over and over, Nala rolled down her window and soaked in the warm sunshine, watching people wander around enjoying their days.

There was something blessedly *normal* about this day. She hadn't felt this kind of reassurance since before Tasha's death. Back when she was in a relationship with her ex. Back when she could feel relatively safe stepping out of her house and then coming back home later. Such days seemed so far away now.

No. They're right here. Danger lurked everywhere now. Nala knew that the world wasn't as good as it used to be. People died. Others were born, but the odds of her getting to know them well enough for it to matter were slim, especially at this point in her life.

The only reason she felt this way was because of Vincent, who finally found a parking space near the park and signaled for Nala to get out. They walked side by side toward the bookstore, the man checking for his wallet and Nala following suit. *I wish every day could feel like today.* Perhaps when it became sunny in the summer again, however many months away that was. For now, Nala was content to be secure in her jeans and sweatshirt, walking twice as fast as Vincent to keep up with his strides and hardly breaking a sweat.

Powell's World of Books boasted to be the largest indie bookstore in the world. Nala didn't know how true that was, as she had barely been to any indie bookstores in her life, let alone around the world, but the building took up its own city block and had multiple stories. The one time

Nala had been in here before, she remembered rooms of various colors and carrying all sorts of fiction and nonfiction goodies. Right after a ball game – and on a sunny day no less – the place was packed with families, couples, and singles scoping out the wares as if they would never have the chance to again. For some of the tourists, that was probably true.

"Where the hell do we even begin?" Nala asked, standing in the opening foyer with her eyes scanning *maps* on the wall. Not maps of Portland. *Maps of the store!* "Do you know what you want to look for."

"Sure. Why don't we reconvene in an hour?"

"What?"

"It's awfully crowded to look together, and I'm sure you want to look at different things from me. So let's split up for now and meet up again later and compare notes. Or books, in this case." He smiled at her. "Pick up whatever you want. It's my treat."

Vincent went on ahead, going a hard right while Nala was left to be pushed by more people coming into the store behind her. *Where do I start?* As a woman who didn't read as much as she should, and didn't have anything in particular she wanted to find, all she could think to do was start from the beginning and make her way through.

She started in the cookbooks. Cookbooks from all around the world, from Japanese to Thai, from Brazilian to Latvian. Nala fingered the worn out spine of an old Russian cookbook. Eventually she pulled it out and flipped through, wondering if she could find some of the dishes her mother used to make. Sure enough, after wracking her brain to remember what her favorites were called in the mother tongue, she found some easy enough recipes she could possibly try. *I wonder if Vincent would like any of these.* He would probably find the dishes Yulia made too bland for his Californian tastes. Luckily for him, Russian food boasted a lot of spices and dishes too sour to handle as well.

I don't cook much, but… The man had cooked for her. Maybe Nala should give it a try too. *What am I doing? Thinking I'm Suzy Homemaker for that guy…* Would he appreciate a home cooked meal? The guy probably hadn't had one since he last visited his mother.

Nala continued to stare at a page in the cookbook, but she wasn't reading it. Instead, she realized that she knew nothing about Vincent's personal life. Nothing about his family, other than he had a mother. She never heard him mention a father. Did he have siblings? Nala couldn't remember if he said anything about that or not. Surely he had cousins. Old friends from school? New friends in Portland? He didn't live a completely solitary life, did he?

Nala held the book to her chest and went down the next aisle, eventually looping into the next room that was apparently a children's and YA section. Nala scanned the pretty book covers before braving a horde of kids as she veered into the literature section.

I haven't read anything substantial in so long. Once again, she didn't know where to begin. Aisles opened up before her. Letters passed by, signaling where one author ended and another began. She had her pick. Western literature. Translated literature. Books by men long dead and books by women having their voices heard for the first time. Books by white people talking about Asian life. Books by black people discussing daily life in 1400s Italy. Books by East Asians and South Asians about everything under the sun. There were authors Nala heard of a million times over but never read. Then there were authors she never heard of but was sure were great.

She didn't like to do it, but Nala went the "judge a book by its cover" route. She picked ones with bright colors and read their blurbs. Most she put back again. Every once in a while, however, she found one that piqued her interest and made her carry them around like precious possessions. Eventually a volunteer offered her a basket to carry everything in.

The hour wore on with Nala meandering upstairs and discovering books about philosophy, religion, travel, music, and anything she could ever dream of. She knew nothing about these subjects. All she *did* know was that her knowledge seriously lacked in so many areas. *Is this because I didn't go to college?* She knew she was still young, but it seemed like there were so many things to learn out there. Suddenly, Nala imagined herself making a career out of being a student. Traveling the world. Learning how to write code like Vincent. Learning to play an instrument. *I wanna learn how to play guitar!* She picked up a book showing beginners how to mind their frets and strums. *I wanna go to China someday!* She picked up a book about Shanghai and the fun things to do there. *Ooh, what's flower arranging?* This place was dangerous.

The farther back she went, the more adult certain things became. Nothing was held back behind glass – unless it was that old or valuable – so when Nala came face to face with "BDSM lifestyle" books, she nearly dropped her small basket and begged for a Dom's mercy.

They write books about this stuff? Apparently it was more mainstream than she ever thought. Nala looked to her left, then her right, making sure no stupid stranger judged her while she plucked two random books off the shelf and shoved them at the bottom of her basket. As if he were a mind reader, Vincent chose that moment to text her.

"I'm in the café. Come join me when you're done."

Nala tried to lift her basket and found it a good fifteen pounds. *Guess I'm done.* Now, where was the café? She wished she had grabbed one of those maps when she had the chance.

When she did find the café, she was greeted with the smell of coffee, tea, and so many sweets she could barely stand it. The place was also packed. Tables nestled between shelves of comic books and romance novels – because those were totally the same thing. *Hm. Maybe to me they are.* Nala looked around the room, assuming that Vincent would be easy to find. Except a tall guy in jeans and a sweatshirt blended in like smoke on a cloudy day. She couldn't throw a book from her basket and not give a guy like that a concussion.

Naturally, she did find him before the sun could go too far down to see in the spacious room. Vincent sat with his back to her, along the window, a stack of books in front of him as he flipped through one book with his right hand and fiddled with his phone with the left.

Nala almost ran up to him, but there was something… tugging at her. As if she were at the end of a string, and someone was at the other end yanking for dear life. Except she didn't move anywhere. She was trapped where she stood, left gawking at this gorgeous man who was at a soccer game one minute and now flipping through books the next. The same man who had seen her cry. The same man who had shown her a chasm of stars.

She put her basket down before resting a tender hand on his shoulder. Vincent glanced at her, smiled, and went back to his book. Strange formulas and what looked like programming code flashed before Nala's eyes. Of course he was.

"Anything good?" she asked, pulling out the chair next to him. "I'm dying to know what a guy like you looks at."

He backed away from his book and let her take a better gander. "You know Java?"

"Coffee?"

"Not quite."

Nala pretended to be fascinated by the lines of code demonstrated in the book. "You should teach me some of this. We've got some good scientists in my family. You never know. I might be one too, and I never realized my potential due to shoddy teachers and little drive."

"It's not that complicated. Of course, I can say that because I understand it. To someone who doesn't think like this, it's an encrypted language." Vincent barely had those words out of his mouth before he started snorting. Those snorts shortly turned into laughter. "Encrypted language… I crack myself up."

I don't get it. Nala figured she didn't have to. "Whatever. Look at this bible I got."

Vincent looked at her as if she were being literal. *Not quite.* She plopped down the cookbook and pointed to a picture of soup on the cover. "My mom used to make me that when I was sick. You'd hate it. Really bland."

"Are you going to cook for me?"

"Cook for *you?* You'll be lucky if you get the leftovers I make for myself."

"I made you bacon and eggs…"

Nala nudged his shoulder with her own. "What else did you get?" She squinted at the spines in front of them. More coding books. A biography about some tech giant. *He's probably met him.* Another book about Apple and Steve Jobs. *Probably met him too.* The only thing in that stack *not* tech related was a John Steinbeck novel. That seemed… hilariously ironic, given Vincent's status in life.

He caught her looking at it. "It's good to be reminded of what people went through and what they still go through today."

"So I see."

"What did you get besides a book of food you're going to make me?" Vincent started to dig through Nala's basket. "Traveling, are we? Say the word and I'll take you to Beijing. I have…"

"Connections there, I'm sure."

"Why, of course. I'm glad you're realizing what goes on around here."

Nala rolled her eyes. She smacked his hand away before he could dig too far into her basket. *I've got naughty stuff in there, Mr. Lane.* "Go back to your funny formula books and make me enough money so I can buy these ingredients. Did you know there's a recipe in here that calls for seventy eggs?"

"Holy chickens. Think of the cholesterol."

"I dare not."

Vincent pulled out his wallet and slipped her a ten. "Get yourself something from the counter and get me another one of these." He shook his empty coffee cup. "Would you, please?"

Nala made a grand show of getting up and taking his money. She folded up the precious Hamilton and stuffed it in her sweatshirt pocket, smacking her lips before pushing through the throng of people huddling around tables and dithering about what to order from the café menu.

Today isn't so bad. Nala was almost able to forget what lurked behind the shadows when she wasn't careful. It was nice to be among *normal* people for once. To be on a date with her… boyfriend.

Her heart warmed at the thought. She pulled out Vincent's money and smiled at how easily it slipped through her fingers before being caught again. *That looks good.* There was a blueberry scone in the case that had their names on it. When she reached the register, Nala ordered herself a latte, Vincent a coffee, and got the scone for the both of them.

While she waited for her order to be thrown together, she perused the nearby romance and erotica section, wondering if any of the women in those stories had lives as fantastic as hers. *If I'm doing better than a romance heroine, then the world has some explaining to do.* Then again… she snatched a BDSM romance off the shelf and barely had time to glance it over before they called her order up front.

"What's that you have there?" Vincent asked when she returned.

"Blueberry scone. I figured the marionberry one was too much for you Californians."

"Ha ha, I mean the other thing." Vincent took his coffee and gingerly placed it next to his book. "I didn't know you read romance."

"Neither did I. I'm discovering all sorts of things about myself today." Nala briefly showed him the salacious cover before taking it back into her possession. "You wouldn't understand this though. The hero of this book is probably a lot nicer than you."

"*Nicer?* Nala, you ever read one of these books before? The heroes are anything but nice. They're usually pretty rough with their heroines."

"Ooh. Rough. Don't you know that I like it rough?"

A hint of darkness crossed Vincent's face. "I have found that out a time or two."

Nala tried to keep smiling through this strange look of his, but eventually found herself shaking in her hoodie. *Okay, so that's how it is right now…* Vincent the Dom was alive and well in there. Nala put her romance book in the basket and pretended to be more fascinated with her latte and scone. The scone she kept trying to feed the man who owned Nightingale.

Wait, if Nightingale is his girlfriend, then who am I? She really needed to stop asking herself these things.

The hour they spent sitting together in front of that bright window, perusing their books and deciding which ones to keep and which ones to put back, was almost too simple in its comforting beauty. Nala only got up once to use the bathroom, a good two stories above her head and too busy to be done with quickly.

When she returned, sauntering into the café as if she owned the place, she found Vincent anything but alone.

Chapter 29

Oh, hell no.

In Nala's seat, which was still clearly marked with her basket of books and half-consumed latte, was a sweet looking brunette tossing her bob about as she batted her eyelashes at Vincent. The man in question leaned back in his chair, hands folded on his stomach as he took in the woman's words with a shit-eating grin. *This piece of…*

It was obvious that this strange woman was attempting to flirt with Vincent. Why? He was a good looking guy, but there were a lot of good looking guys in that room. Was he the only one who reeked of money? Nala couldn't tell that. She didn't know what money smelled like, outside of Vincent's expensive cologne. The only thing she knew was that *her* Vincent currently had some bobble-headed hussy flirting with him.

She knew it was flirting. That much she was sure of. The woman's fake smile basically screamed for Vincent to fuck her. The way she kept extending her hand to touch the top of his would've been hilarious if Nala weren't somehow involved. This was a mating ritual she often made fun of when witnessing it out in the wild. Except now she was the doe being tossed out of the back of the hunter's truck in favor of a bigger one. *OH HELL NO.*

Nala could only stare in disgust as this display went on. First the woman laughed at everything coming out of Vincent's mouth. Then she went on to ask him about the books he was reading. "Oh, I don't know anything about this. *Giggle.* It seems like it takes someone soooo smart to do it. *Giggle.* Oh, you own your own company? Wow, that's amazing! *Giggle.*" Damnit, why did Vincent have to mention he was a business owner? Now that girl was a shark circling the lone survivor of a shipwreck. She smelled that money on this hot guy.

That was it. Nala couldn't take it anymore.

"Hey, I'm back!" she said as peppy as possible, letting one hand snake down the front of Vincent's sweatshirt. *That's right, smile at me, playboy!* To be fair, Vincent hadn't been flirting back, but he also hadn't shaken this woman. One strike against him already.

"Excuse us," the woman said, so much snot dripping from her voice that Nala had half a mind to offer her a tissue. "We were talking."

"Oh, I saw plenty of talking back there, but I hate to tell you that you're in my seat."

She looked Nala up and down, attempting to decide whether or not she was a worthy adversary. *Try me.* Nala knew how to tango with the best of them.

"You're kidding, right?"

Nala glanced at Vincent, who had one hand covering his mouth as he watched on. *Hope you're enjoying this.* He probably was.

"I'm not kidding. You're trying my patience. Back off."

The woman scooted back in her chair with a loud screech, leaping to her feet and dwarfing Nala by a good few inches. "Who the hell do you think you are?"

Nala wasn't intimidated by women taller than her. That would be ridiculous, since almost every woman was taller than her. She waltzed up to the woman, coming up only to her mouth, and put hands on hips. *You think I'm gonna back down?* The woman was in for a sore surprise. Much like the sore surprise she would've gotten on her ass had she ever gone on a date with Vincent.

"I'm his girlfriend."

Two pairs of brows went up. The woman's in disbelief, and Vincent's in sheer curiosity. Nala's, however, stayed planted where they belonged.

"Besides, trust me, honey," Nala continued, curling her arm around Vincent's shoulders. "You wouldn't be able to handle what he dishes out."

"Excuse me but…"

Nala tipped her basket over, revealing one of two books about living up the BDSM lifestyle. The woman glanced once before taking a visible step back, shrinking away as if she saw something foul and dirty. *Oh, yeah, baby.*

"Don't assume so much about a person…" The woman left, mumbling about how rude Nala was. Rude? Her? That woman was the one trying to snatch another girl's man! *I make it sound like he belongs to me.* Didn't he?

"That was, uh, special." Vincent lowered his hand and plucked the book Nala dumped out of the basket. "I didn't know that I had a girlfriend."

Nala sat in her seat, stinking of cheap perfume. "I didn't know that I had a flirty boyfriend."

"Hey, now, she's the one who came over here and tried chatting me up. If you think for two seconds that I actually found her interesting, then you have another think coming. She was incredibly boring. I don't go for girls like that. Because they bore me."

Nala nudged the book in his hand. "Ahem."

"Yes, yes, she didn't seem the type into this either."

"That's right."

Vincent waggled his eyebrows as he handed the book back to his girlfriend. "But you totally do, Ms. Nazarov."

"Mr. Lane, I will have to ask you to refrain from flirting right now. You are on probation after that event. Besides, there are children present. We can't talk about those things until later."

"Yes, ma'am."

I'll never hear that very often. Nala had to admit it sounded pretty good. *He doesn't say ma'am a lot in his life, does he?* How many women did he pay respect to in his job? Surely there were female programmers… but none he would call *ma'am.* Clients? Did a lot of business-minded female clients come in and demand his respect? Now Nala was asking the hard questions.

Although they couldn't talk about those things, she could certainly read about them. Nala plopped her book open, taking care to avoid any pictures that may be too obscene for public consumption. Which was most of them. Including the ones displaying the implements and general tools of the BDSM trade.

I am in way over my head. She didn't know what most of this stuff was. Sex swings? Paddle benches? Latex body suits? Was Vincent into this stuff? She looked over at him, covertly, studying the profile of a man nose-deep in Java code, whatever that was. He looked so damn average like this, but Nala knew the truth. Deep, deep in that genius mind was a guy who got off on being rough and domineering in bed. *He's also really tender too.* Two sides to the same man. Whichever one Nala needed the most could come out nearly on command. Who was really bossing who around?

Vincent pulled a pad and pen from his pocket and started jotting down notes. No wait… they were lines of code. Formulas. If he had thought ahead, he probably would've brought a laptop to run his experiments on. Meanwhile, Nala sat beside him, in utter awe that he could do these things so quickly.

Nala shoved aside the BDSM book. She tucked it beneath the cookbook and then bundled those in the basket so prying eyes couldn't see. Instead, she snatched one of Vincent's coding books and flipped to the beginning, determined to make some sense of it.

Alas, she didn't have her sister's analytical and scientific brain. Also alas was the fact that this book was advanced enough to start with some heavy shit. *It assumes I'm level four of this. Whatever level four is.* Vincent was level four. At least.

Sighing, Nala returned the book to Vincent's basket and picked one of her novels to look at instead.

She wasn't two pages in when Vincent leaned on his elbow and looked at her with a knot tangled in his visage. "Are you really my girlfriend now?"

Nala dropped her book in exasperation. "If you have to ask, then I guess I'm not."

"You were jealous of that other woman, though."

"Jealous? Ha! I knew she couldn't handle you from the moment I saw how she was flirting. She wasn't going to get that though. So I had to play up the jealous girlfriend to get her to buzz off. Did *you* have time for her?"

"Honestly? I was hoping you would get back in time to see her and get a bit roused by it."

"Aroused?"

"I said *roused*. But aroused works too."

"I don't think so." Nala was about as interested in that woman as she was interested in kissing one of the bearded hipster wonders wandering around the café. "Don't flatter yourself."

"Wouldn't dream of it…" Vincent nudged her. "Darling."

Now it was Nala's turn to lean on her elbow. "You can be such a ham sometimes."

"Says the woman who is my girlfriend one moment and totally not the next."

"Why? Do you *want* me to be your girlfriend?"

Vincent continued to look at her, noncommittal. "Do you want to be my girlfriend?"

"Are you asking?"

"Pshaw."

"Thought so."

They went back to their separate worlds, Vincent engrossed in his notes and Nala reading about a man who was trapped in the Siberian wilderness. Yet her mind kept wandering. One moment she was staring at the spine of that BDSM book, and then the next she glanced at Vincent's profile, wondering how deep the kink could get with him.

She didn't think he was a *lifestyler* like Lucian and Robin. If anything, Vincent was into "normal" relationships until bed time. Even then, he had two speeds. Maybe three. The usual lovemaking, and then full-speed rough and binding. Nala shifted in her seat, feeling heat erupt between her and Vincent.

The spine appeared again. For some reason, her first thought wasn't "*I wonder if he's into sex swings,*" but "*I wonder if he did those things with Desirée.*"

She wanted to ask him, but knew that now was not the time or place. Vincent was trying to enjoy his day off. To ask him such a thing would surely ruin it. Nala didn't want to be responsible for that.

As the hour wound down, Vincent suggested they take their purchases up front and move on. Nala was happy to, deciding to keep the cookbook and put the BDSM books away. She also put the travel book away. Some of the novels followed her home, all thanks to Vincent's generous credit card.

He put his arm around her waist as they left, like he always touched her whenever they went to The Aviary. At first it made Nala uncomfortable… and then she realized she liked it. As if she were his bird riding high on his perch.

The car idled as they waited for traffic to let up enough to leave. Nala stared at her bag of books. *I don't have those BDSM books because I can look that stuff up online.* "I had fun today," she said. "I know there's still dinner, but…"

"But what? The day is hardly over. The sun is only starting to go down now."

"I know, but…"

"Buuuuut?"

Nala knew she had to look him in the eye when she said it. That was about as easy as admitting what she wanted to say in the first place.

"I think I wanna be your girlfriend. Your real girlfriend."

Vincent's gaze held hers, neither of them faltering. *What is he thinking?* No, she didn't want to know. It was probably salacious. As salacious as her thoughts? Who knew anymore.

"Nala…" He glanced at the steering wheel and then back at her, his tongue punching the inside of his cheek. "If you're my girlfriend, not every day is going to be like this. A lot of days, yeah, but most will be… different. You have to be able to handle that."

A big enough gap passed. Vincent decided to not pull out into traffic yet – he was still invested in how Nala would react.

She was prepared for that. So she put on the most serious face she could muster without looking too scary. *Not easy.* Not that she thought Vincent was easily frightened. Let alone of *her.*

"I know. Don't underestimate me, *sir.*" She let that word sizzle off her tongue like an exquisite hiss. It had the desired effect: Vincent sat up to attention in his seat, his breathing heavier than it had been all day. "I can take whatever you throw at me. In fact, I rather wish you would show me how wild you can get." She glanced out the window and saw a happy family pass by on the sidewalk. "Not here, obviously. At home."

"Obviously." Much to Nala's surprise, Vincent's voice adopted that decadent growl. *Whoa, slow down there underwear.* It wasn't time to get that wet yet.

"You would have to really try to freak me out." She slipped her hand between his thighs. Vincent watched her move toward his cock, but when she got too close, he took her hand and plopped it between them.

"Let's get dinner," he said, almost cheerfully. "I know the place."

Nala had to force the smile on her face. "All right."

Vincent pulled out of their parking space and said nothing more on the subject.

***

Dinner was sushi and ice cream for dessert. Although Nala knew how to use chopsticks, she wasn't super great at it, requesting her new boyfriend to help her get the hang of sticking two pieces of wood between her fingers and making a go of feeding herself. Luckily, Vincent minded her complete lack of taste buds and kept the spicy and sour stuff away from her. *I'll get him with this Russian cookbook.* It was big enough to be a weapon, anyway.

Vincent started driving them home once they were done with dinner. The traffic had finally dispersed, giving them a clear berth to his loft.

He parked in his space but did not move. This was becoming more and more common in Nala's life. *What's he gonna say now?* Did she even wanna know?

"Wait here for ten minutes after I go in," he said, voice deep. "When the time is up, I want you to go into the loft and kneel in the living room. Take off your sweatshirt and put your hands on your head. The moment you step into that room?" Vincent sent her a look that said he was not joking, whatever he was about to say. "You have to obey every single thing I say until the sun comes up again." He tossed his sunglasses onto his dash and opened his car door. "We'll see if you can handle being my girlfriend. We'll see if Nala and Nightingale really are different."

He got out of the car and unlocked the door to his stairwell. Nala was left in her seat, absolutely gob smacked.

Gob smacked, and bristling with anticipation.

You asked for it, shithead. No matter how hard Vincent was on her tonight, Nala was guaranteed to be even harder.

Chapter 30

The loft was dark when Nala turned the unlocked handle. She entered warily, as if the wrong step would get her kicked out of Vincent Lane's den of domination.

Naturally, he was the first thing she noticed. He stood in the bedroom, overlooking the living area from his high pedestal and surveying the entirety of his kingdom. Of which Nala was a part of. A trifle trinket to be toyed with.

His watchful gaze followed her into the living room, where she stopped, pulled her sweatshirt over her head and tossed it onto the couch. *I'm cold now.* If the heater was on, he only recently set the thermostat when he came in. Not enough time to make it warm enough to take off the sweatshirt. *Thanks, nipples.* Although she wore a shirt and a bra, she could still see tiny bumps emerging from the cotton enshrouding her breasts.

Nala kicked off her shoes and socks and sank to her knees. Her hands slowly came to her head, fingers locking together as she glanced back up at Vincent.

He also was not wearing his sweatshirt anymore. Or his shoes. The man watching her with a steady eye wore nothing but his shirt and jeans, both tight enough to outline every muscle beneath. The time of day meant stubble was quick to spread across his face. As he leaned down and crossed his arms across the guardrail, Nala swore she saw a gleam in his eye.

"That was the easy part," he called down. "I'm not going easy on you tonight."

Nala didn't say anything. He hadn't told her to speak, had he?

"Go ahead and tell me that you're excited about tonight."

She looked up again. "I can't wait, sir." That was almost impossible to say without sounding sarcastic. Nala could only hope she succeeded in portraying how much she wanted to please him tonight. If that meant pleasing him with her obedience and service? So be it.

"I know you can do better than that."

Nala cleared her throat, hands still on her head. "I'm excited about what you have planned, *Master.* I'm sure I'll not only enjoy it, but in ways I can't even comprehend right now."

"Do you like doing that?"

Nala shook on her knees. "Doing what, sir?"

Vincent grinned. "Calling me Master."

She hadn't thought about it until that point. *I guess so.* Every time she did it – when they were in private, anyway – it was like giving up one more care or tribulation in her life. Master would take care of her. Master would make all her problems go away. Master didn't need Nala to worry about anything ever again. She was his, which also meant her issues were his to solve while she went about her life.

And, boy, did she have a lot of shit she could call issues or tribulations.

"I like putting myself in your hands, sir."

"What will I do with you once I have you in my hands?"

Nala didn't miss a beat. "Whatever you please. I'm okay with that. More than okay."

Without a word Vincent backed away from the guardrail and went to the spiral staircase, treating each careful step downward as if it would be his last. Amazing how one man could be so graceful, so steady as his body moved languidly, almost as if he too had been waiting for this moment for a long time – but didn't want to make it look like that was the case. After all, he had an image to maintain, even around Nala.

"You stay still so well," he praised, sort of. Vincent stood in front of her, out of reach, but certainly present. "So far you're obeying as I told you to. Like I said a few minutes ago, though… this is nothing. This is the easy part. Any woman could come in here and kneel in my house. What is it to me? I'm not impressed."

What do you want from me? Nala had to suppress a sneer of defiance. That would get her nowhere. *I can't tell if he wants me to make it or not, though.* Perhaps he wanted to break and tame her some more. Or maybe he wanted her ready to go out of the box. Nala had a good idea, but… she wasn't about to attempt the risky guess.

"Do you know what would impress me, Nala?" Vincent didn't wait for an answer. "Unwavering loyalty. Even if you falter, I will still see your motives. Your intent. If you falter and I can tell you desperately wanted to behave but are still green behind the ears… that's fine. That's admirable. So don't worry about disappointing me. Only worry about that if your heart isn't into any of this."

Nala swallowed. "Yes, sir. I'll give you my all, sir."

"Good." Vincent approached, each step its own brand of torture. *He's coming for me, but will he do anything? Will he satisfy me yet? Will I have to satisfy him first?* Nala thought of her last night as Nightingale, when she got on her knees and serviced him to climax. She had sensed how much he wanted to savor the pleasure with her. Did he want a mulligan now that they were alone? "I know this doesn't come naturally to you, Nala. That's okay. I prefer my women – my girlfriends – to be feisty. I don't like the demure types of submissives, except for every great once in a while. For everyday life, I like a girl with a lot of punch and power. Do you know why?"

Nala shook her head. At least she really knew now that the woman in the bookstore wouldn't have been able to satisfy her Master.

Vincent touched her cheek with his knuckles, caressing her skin with a tender touch that brought with it a ton of warning – warning to not indulge in it too much. "Because you're so much more satisfying to tame."

She knew it.

Vincent reached around her head, gently pushing it to one side as he surveyed the white of her throat. Then he inspected the other side before grabbing her ponytail and yanking *up*.

"Ah!" That was the only sound escaping Nala as pain surged through her scalp. It was fleeting, as all Vincent did was rip out her hair tie and force her hair across her shoulders, but it was enough to give her a taste of what was in store that night. *He'll show me no mercy. He'll make me up to be exactly what he wants before breaking me in.* Nala didn't yet know what it meant to serve or to obey. That night of his bondage practice didn't count. As hot as it was… it didn't count.

"You are so…" Vincent shoved his fingers down her shirt, tugging on the front collar of the fabric. "Damn…" He pulled down harder and harder, nearly bringing Nala down to the floor as her balance floundered and she struggled to keep her hands on her head. "Gorgeous…" With a terrifying tear, her shirt came apart. So. Damn. Easily.

Nala stared, aghast, at her bra now on full display. The light gray of her plain cotton shirt was in two, as if the man's bite and claws was taking her apart. *My mother would call him a* volk, *like her maiden name.* A wolf. A terrifying, wonderful wolf making her its prey. Yulia had warned her daughters of such men. *Uh oh…*

The only reason she didn't panic about her clothing was because it meant nothing. A simple T-shirt could easily be repurchased, especially by a billionaire. *No, the real reason I don't care is because he can do whatever he wants to me.* Like pull her shirt free from her body, tossing the ruined cotton onto her sweatshirt.

"Look at you. If I always had my way, you would spend your whole life on display to me." Vincent rubbed the tops of her breasts, crouched down so his breath blew hot on her face. "I've spent this whole day thinking about what I want to do to you, Nala. I never thought you would give me the chance to express it. Not like this." He yanked her bra cups down, freeing her breasts and most of all her nipples – which he continued to pinch, as he always did. *Oh my God.* Here they went. Here *Nala* went. Pretty soon she would be so suggestible that she would walk on hot coals to get to this man.

"I want only to serve you, Master."

Her voice shook. For the briefest moment, as Vincent stroked her flowing hair and ripped down her bra straps until the whole thing started to come apart, Nala wondered if she were retreating into Nightingale's space. *But we're the same person. How can I want to be anyone else but who I am?* Nala didn't need to be any other identity. Not around… the man she loved.

He discarded her clothing until she was half naked, her hair the only thing keeping her modest. Nala shook in the cold, and from the anticipation. *I want him to do whatever he's going to do right now. I can't stand the wait.* She had no idea what to expect. She had no idea what kind of man lurked beneath this kindly shell. For all she knew, Vincent's true self was using BDSM as a guise for something terrible, like other members of The Aviary.

"Do you trust me, Nala?"

She looked up, catching a flash of concern on his countenance. *He's still the same Vincent. He still wants to protect me.* "I trust you," she said softly. "You won't hurt me. The only pain I feel will be pleasure."

Nala didn't have to read those books. She didn't need to talk to those girls at The Aviary. She knew these things like she knew her own heart. *This is a part of me. This has always been inside of me.* Her ex hadn't been a bad guy. He wasn't super bad in bed, either, but he never held Nala's interest, in part because he couldn't *really* give her what she wanted. For all her bite and desire to be seen as an independent young woman, she enjoyed this more than anyone had the right to. Every time Vincent took her deeper into his world, every time he made her more and more into his ideal sub, Nala realized that this was part of her true calling in life.

It was exhilarating. It was pleasurable. It was so fucking hot that she thought she would explode beneath his domineering touch.

"If you want me to stop at any time, the safe word is…"

"Tasha."

Vincent didn't say anything. He simply touched her chin with his fingers before reaching into his deep pockets.

"Please…" Nala begged, as she saw the nightingale collar emerge from Vincent's jeans. "Don't hold back. I can take it, I swear. I trust you, Vincent. Do whatever you want to me. Make use of my body and what I can do to you. Deny me whatever you want. Give me as much as you want. I want to know what it's like."

"What it's like… to be my sub?"

"To be your girlfriend."

Something glistened on the collar, and it wasn't the pendant. A silver chain fell from the nightingale's beak. A leash, one of the most debasing things Nala could have thought up. Even she balked for an instant.

"You're not a dog." Vincent slipped the collar around her throat, making sure it was snug but not too tight. "But you need training. You might get overeager otherwise. No matter how much you think you want it like that, I can't be sure until I've made you feel like this."

He tugged on the leash, bringing Nala down on all fours. *What?* She couldn't help it. No matter how she tried to position herself, she couldn't achieve anything but hands and knees, head pointed up toward Vincent. Her ass was still covered by her jeans, but it stuck out behind her, and her breasts swung dangerously close to the floor. *If something touches my nipples, I'm done.*

Vincent wrapped the leash around one hand while the other ran down the soft curve of her back and toward her ass. "What are you, Nala?" he asked with a biting tone. "What are you, my darling?"

She knew what she damn well looked like. "I'm a bitch, sir."

"Is that what you want to be? You can be anything you want. As long as it fits the situation. Now's your chance to change that statement."

"Well…" he had said she wasn't a dog. That was already established. Besides, *bitch* wasn't really sexy. Not to Nala, anyway. "I can be your whore, sir."

"You've asked me to call you that before."

"It's true, isn't it? You're paying me to pleasure you, sir."

"In a way, I suppose. I have never thought of you as a whore, though. I've never thought of any woman that way."

Noble, but not what Nala was fishing for. "Like you have your needs and desires, sir, I have mine as well. I like to think you can meet me halfway."

"Fine." Vincent climbed onto the sofa, but kept Nala steady on her hands and knees. "If that's what you want to think, you're free to do so. When I ask you again what you are, you can change your answer."

Nala nodded.

"First we have other matters to take care of." His hand was back, grabbing her ass through her jeans, fingers shoving between legs and teasing her slit. *Make me shiver, why don't you.* It was still cold in there. Did he turn the heater on at all? No? Well, then. *I'll sit here and suffer with my dying nipples.* "Do you know why subs get some of this, Nala?" He patted her ass, enough to let her know that he could go harder – and would.

"Uh…" Here it came. One of the few moments she dreaded since first walking into The Aviary. "Because it feels good?"

"See, my sweet? This is why you need to be trained. There's still a lot to learn." He patted her bottom again, almost good-naturedly. "Yes, it feels good. There are some who love it so much that spanking becomes a reward for them, but not purely for physical reasons. Spanking is often a form of punishment. If you've transgressed a line and need to be reminded of your place, then a spanking might be appropriate. Now, why might I want or have to spank you, Nala?"

What a cruel game. *Let's play it, already.* "Because I did something wrong today."

"What might that have been?"

Nala said the first thing to come to her mind. "I undermined your power at the bookstore. I told that woman off. I got too possessive. I made decisions on your behalf. I…"

"Yes, yes, that's enough."

Nala braced herself for a spank, but it didn't come. Not yet.

"It's not enough to understand *why.* In theory, you could give me a whole list of reasons I, as your Dom, would want to spank this firm ass of yours." His fingers flicked against her jeans. The more he drew this out, the more Nala… awaited it. *That's his plan. He wants me to enjoy it. Why wouldn't he?* Never had Nala gotten the inkling that Vincent received glee in exchange for anyone's pain. "But until you've felt the sting of a good punishment, you're not going to completely understand why it's done."

His pats grew harder, stronger. He was warming Nala up for the real thing, and her fingers curled deep into the rug beneath her. The more this went on, Vincent revving up his touch, the more Nala wanted to hang her head, to bury her face in the rug and retreat into herself. Not out of shame. Not out of fear, but because she assumed this was expected of her.

"No, no." Vincent tugged on the leash, forcing Nala's head back up. Her hair slapped against her breasts, parting enough to let her nipples poke through. "Keep your head up and your back straight. I may not be able to see your face from here, but I can feel your pride in your posture. You can close your eyes, if you want, but keep your arms and spine as straight as possible. Tip your chin up if it helps. If we ever perform like this in front of people, this is what we would show them."

Did he really have to bring that up? *I am not doing this in front of anyone but him!* Nala wasn't even sure if she could tolerate it yet! Just because she was adventurous tonight…

Smack!

Nala let out a yelp of shock, surprise, and, yes, pain. The sting of Vincent's not-so-gentle-hand warped her, bending her elbows and almost sending her torso to the ground. *Ow…* To think her jeans were protecting her!

"Stay *up.*" Vincent tugged on the leash again, keeping Nala in the position he wanted. *You bastard…* His voice may have been firm, but his demeanor was that of a Dom desperately trying to train a sub still wet behind her pretty ears. "Be good, Nala. If you can take three spanks from me without flinching in anything but pleasure, I'll reward you. Do you understand?"

She grimaced. "Yes, sir." Nala struggled to remain in position, but she knew what was coming.

A spank. As hard as the first, but this time keeping her in place.

It wasn't any less shocking or painful. The only thing his spanks did was numb her to the frenzy overtaking her body.

"Tell me why I'm doing this, Nala. Tell me why I have to spank you."

He continued to smack her ass in between his words, making her tremble, whimper, and wonder how much more her flesh could take. "Because I undermined your authority… sir…"

"Good. Why else?" He spanked her again. This time Nala did not flinch, but she did cry.

When she had control of her voice again, she replied, "Because I got jealous, sir."

"Why else?" His next spank wasn't as tough, but still, Nala trembled. "There's one more reason, not relating to the bookstore."

Nala searched her brain for any reason Vincent would use to hit her ass like this. He was alternating cheeks, sometimes going hard, sometimes easing up, but always using a firm hand. *Am I getting aroused by it?* Nala couldn't tell. "Because I need training and this is a part of it. Every sub can expect to be spanked at some point in her training." She was bullshitting, but nevertheless, she hoped she was right.

"Very good. You're catching on." Vincent massaged her worn flesh with one hand and then eased off the leash. Nala knew better than to think she was allowed to bend down. If anything, Vincent was testing her resolve. How well would she behave? How well did she understand what he had been saying this whole time? "Now can you take three spanks in a row without flinching? Do you want a reward for your upstanding behavior these past few minutes?"

She nodded. "I want to be rewarded, but only if I deserve it."

"What are you, Nala?"

Her lips turned inward, letting her tongue wet them. She said the same word from earlier. Vincent did not react.

Instead, he spanked her hard enough to make her flinch – but she remained sturdy where she knelt, refusing to buckle. She wanted this to be over after the three spanks she deserved the most. So far, she had made it through one.

The next one came, hitting her in the exact same spot. This should have made her buckle, but she forced herself up, flinching only in the slightest. *I hope he didn't notice that.* It would depend on how aroused this was making Vincent. *I hope it's getting him so hard he doesn't know what to do with himself. Besides fuck me.* She imagined him pulling down her jeans, kneeling behind her, and driving himself into her until she came uncontrollably. *That would be nice…*

Smack!

`Nala almost went down. *Almost.* As the pain washed across her body, shooting up her spine, tingling in her breasts, and centering in her mound, she felt her knees shake and her arms attempt to move. *I won't.* She thought it, over and over again, like a mantra. *I won't, I won't I won't.* She refused to disappoint him. While Nala could never be the perfect sub on her first real try, she would at least strive for as much perfection as possible. This seemed like the least she could do.

The pain subsided. Nala was left looking at the ceiling, wondering what Vincent thought of her performance. *Did I do a good job? Did I pass his test?* She had no way of knowing unless she looked over her shoulder. *I won't risk that in case that's the wrong thing to do.* Nala wouldn't put it past herself.

"That's good enough. You did very well." Vincent tugged on the leash, helping Nala lean back on her heels as gingerly as possible. "For your first time, I have no complaints."

Nala let out a sigh of relief. At least she could say she got through that.

"What now, sir?"

"You don't have to be so eager. When it's time to move on, I will let you know."

Nala sat expectantly, flicking dust off her pants and wondering how long it would take for the pain in her ass to subside. *And that was with my* jeans *on.* Did that make it worse? Easier? She had no idea. That's how inexperienced she was. "I'm sorry you have to put up with me, sir. I must be a lot of trouble for you."

"You'd only be trouble if you weren't willing to learn. Since you are, it's no trouble at all. In fact…" Vincent caressed her cheek and combed her hair with his fingers. "It can be a lot of fun training a new sub. I only wish our circumstances were better."

Nala didn't have to ask what he meant by that. She had to force herself to never think of The Aviary, otherwise she would panic and run.

"You're very obedient for your general personality. Are you enjoying yourself? I don't want you to force this."

Nala shrugged in an effort to stretch her arms. "I am enjoying it, sir. You said there would be a reward?"

"Ah, yes…" Vincent leaned back in the couch, looking like any guy sitting back to watch TV or play lazy video games. "Come up here and lie across my lap. I'll give you your reward."

Although her leash was still in his hand, Nala was able to maneuver onto her feet and shuffle to the couch, ass beginning to burn in her jeans. *Ow, ow, ow…* She kept reminding herself that it was better to experience this for the first time with Vincent and not someone like Hawk. *Why are you doing this to yourself? Stop thinking about those people for one moment.* This was about sharing something special with Vincent. This was about getting closer to *him,* not distancing themselves with more heartache and grief.

Nala climbed onto the couch and straddled Vincent's lap, lowering herself until she carefully lay across his wide lap and buried her nose into a throw pillow. Vincent pushed her long hair out of the way so he could stroke the curve of her back, his cock stiffening beneath Nala's bare stomach.

"You're beautiful." His soft voice entered one ear and escaped out the other. Nala sighed, turning her head to one side so she stared at the black TV only a few feet away. "Turn over. I want to see your breasts."

Did he now? Nala hid a chuckle as she turned over with his help, looking into his shadowy face as she rested her head against the pillow and let her sore ass nestle between his legs. His hand instantly went to her stomach and teased her with his touch.

"Am I only beautiful, sir?" She tried him, that was for sure. "A girl even in my position right now needs to know more than that from the man touching her like this."

"I'm sure." Vincent forked his fingers around one of her nipples, stimulating her to the point they peaked again. "I have to admit that right now I'm mostly caught up in your striking beauty. If you want to know more, I also think you're a very strong woman."

"Hmph."

"What is it?"

Nala cracked a smile. "Few people go so far as to call me a woman."

"Aren't you? Womanhood is more than your age. It's what you've been through, how you carry yourself, what your goals in life are, your maturity…"

"So I'm a woman then. That's relieving."

"I'm serious, Nala." His fingers came together, gently pinching her nipple as her hands clasped across her stomach. "Why would I be with anyone else other than a woman?"

She wasn't going to seriously answer that.

"Anyway, your reward. You still want it, right?"

"You mean this isn't it?"

"Only a taste." That clean-cut – okay, so his shadow was coming back in at this time of day – guy in a T-shirt and jeans was almost too much to bear as he pinched her with one hand and tugged down the zipper of her jeans with the other. "There's a lot more I can offer you right now. Don't be shy to take it."

"I never would be, sir. I have nothing about my body to hide from you." Not at this point. Besides, Nala was about as shy as a woman who had been around the block a few times and made a living walking naked down the street. She was sure such a profession existed somewhere in a city like Portland. "Please, feel generous with my reward."

"Now, don't get too cheeky…" Vincent pulled the front of her jeans apart and let his fingers touch the top of her mound. "Although I do like a certain level of cheek from you."

His fingers cut a trail along her skin, sliding between her breasts, dipping into her navel, and coming so close to giving her true pleasure that Nala couldn't do anything but shudder where she lay. A reward? This was a huge, drawn out tease meant to make her even hornier for him. *Okay, so it's working. Shut up.*

Finally, after what felt like an eternity, he stroked one of her nipples, eliciting a wave of pleasure through her torso and beyond. *Now this is what I'm talking about.* Nala's hips slightly undulated against Vincent's lap, especially when he shoved his other hand down her pants and rubbed her slit through her lingerie.

Nala closed her eyes and let herself slip away into another world, one where they were the only two people to ever exist. Thank God for that. Because Nala was tired of experiencing an existence where she had to rely on people, had to make her own way, had to deal with the unpleasantness that was life. *People say I'm so cynical for my age.* Growing up, the elders in her neighborhood simply said she had an old soul. An old, adventurous soul that shirked learning how to keep house and do other "womanly" things such as cooking and childrearing. Those were more Tasha's bag, although she was able to get away with not doing them too much either because she had her studies to tend to. Nala didn't have an excuse beyond "I don't want to." Yulia would drag her in from outside, force her into the kitchen, and try to teach her "practical" skills so her un-academic daughter would have something to fall back on one day. *Tasha was guaranteed a good career. The best my mother hoped for on my behalf was a good marriage.* That wasn't happening unless Nala could cook.

So when Vincent insisted that she was a woman earlier, she felt lost. Lied to. Even for a split second, it felt like the biggest farce in the universe. How could Nala be a woman? She was too young, too inexperienced in what really *mattered* that she still felt like such a girl inside. Sure, she worked for a living. Sure, she took care of herself. Sure, she relied on hardly anyone, because she had run out of people to rely on. Did that really help make one an adult?

Having sex didn't make a person an adult, like having a job didn't necessarily make one an adult. Young teens could do both of those things. *I'm not a teenager anymore.* Every passing day took Nala further and further away from that. Soon she would be forty, looking back on her life and wondering where the years had gone. How had time gone so quickly? How had life without Tasha continued to go on?

Where would she be in twenty years? Would she finally have her revenge? Would she be with Vincent?

Would she be happy, regardless?

Nala came back to Earth when Vincent cupped his fingers around her slit, forcing her lingerie inside her as he *threatened* to finger her like that. But the cloth of her underwear created an impenetrable barrier, even if it stretched more the wetter it became. *You're going to tease me to death!* Her eyes opened, meeting Vincent's in the darkness of his living room. Nala's breaths became more erratic. Her hands stretched out, curling around his muscular arm as he slid his fingers deeper into her jeans.

"Will you let me come?" she asked, pitifully. "I mean… please sir."

"I'm sure you would like that. How many orgasms should I let you have tonight? There are two schools of thought when it comes to training a sub and utilizing orgasms as rewards and tools. One says I should let you come as often as possible, as it helps you associate everything that happens with incredible pleasure." His fingers pulled her lingerie aside and dipped into her wetness. It took all of Nala's power to not gasp in absolute frustration. "The other school says I should reserve them for only the most pivotal moments. Orgasms have to be earned. The training is in the tease."

"What school of thought do you belong to, sir?" Her breath was leaving her. Soon she wouldn't be able to speak at all unless Vincent forced her to.

"I belong to whichever one I feel like indulging in."

His fingers drew a slow, languid line along her clit, turning Nala into a moaning, almost begging creature that subsisted solely off the pleasure a single man could give her. *Oh my God!* This coincided with a pinch to her nipple. A very, very delectable pinch to her nipple. *I'm turning into a sex fiend because of this man.* What a life that would be!

Before she could enjoy the full gamut of an orgasm, however, Vincent pulled his fingers out and patted her stomach. *So that's how it's going to be?* Apparently Vincent believed in the second school of thought.

"You're doing great, Nala. I couldn't be happier with your behavior tonight."

So did that mean she got a treat? Is that what her reward was? Some bones, some scraps thrown in this bitch's direction? *He's gonna make me homicidal at this rate.* Heat had swollen in her stomach, begging for release. So much energy, so much tension… did Vincent know what kind of fire he currently played with? He really shouldn't underestimate Nala Nazarov. She always got her way… eventually.

"Sit up."

She obeyed, with his help, sitting up in his lap. Vincent eased her off the couch and back onto the floor.

"Turn your back to me and put your hands behind you. Trust me."

She already did, but she wouldn't tell him that… again.

When she was in position, Vincent pulled one last thing from his deep pockets. A single silk scarf. Nala shouldn't have been surprised… and yet she was.

"Don't worry, darling, you haven't misbehaved," Vincent said, as he secured her wrists behind her back. "I want to see how well you take to being, ah, hands free."

She had no idea what he meant by that. She was sure she would find out soon enough.

"There. Is it too tight?"

Nala barely noticed the scarf tied around her wrists. "No, sir." Her fingers wiggled freely. She was secured, but it would take considerable effort to break free. Only if she really wanted to. *And I don't. Just don't give me a reason to try.*

"Good. Let me know if they're too tight and you're uncomfortable."

"I will, sir."

"Listen to you." Vincent pulled her hair back, ensuring he had the best view of her body – and her face, of course. Nala did not miss the hard bulge in his pants. *Let me guess where this is going.* She wouldn't complain. Yet. "I never thought you would be so compliant, let alone during a training phase. Do you enjoy submitting?"

Nala looked away, studying the creases in the leather couch as if they held some mystical answer for her to consult. *Do I?* She was pretty sure she did, but she was still new to this world. Yet it felt right. It was something definitely worth exploring. *If I'm going to explore it with anyone, it better be someone like Vincent.* The man who had the ability to make her smile with one of his own. And, well, he wasn't too bad in bed.

"I like what I've done so far."

"You say you like it rough?"

"I like both rough and gentle." Nala held back her smile, forcing her lips to curl inward and make her look even cheekier than usual. "With you, anyway. You do both very well, sir."

If Vincent were the type of man to blush, surely this would be his shining moment for it. "You flatter me, Nala. I know you can't be an easy woman to please. Normally I'd chastise a sub for trying to suck up to me, but I don't think you are. I think you're telling the truth."

"I am. I like both rough and gentle with you. The only scary thing is how easily you tell which one I need in any moment." Nala twisted her fingers in their binds. "Which one do you think I need right now, sir?"

She got the reaction she wanted. Vincent, pulling on her hair and bringing his face close to hers. "I think you need to be put in your place before you get out of hand."

He kissed her, hard, his tongue prying her mouth apart and diving deep. Both hands clasped her face, steadying her – a happy fact, since she didn't have her arms to keep her balanced. *I love the way he kisses.* Vincent never half-assed it. Every time he kissed, it was with true, unadulterated intent. Nala could wrap herself up in his arms if it were possible.

"You know how to rile me up, Nala," he muttered on her lips, one hand going to his hips and unzipping his jeans. Nala spared a look for the erection coming out of his clothes. The man hadn't even taken off his T-shirt, and here Nala was, knowing exactly what was expected of her. She only hoped it would be in the manner she wanted most right now. Not that she would tell him. Just as he trained her, she trained him to learn the movements of her body and what it was she wanted. She practically trained him to *read her mind.* Vincent would not be the type of man to wave away a woman's whims as "They're mysterious. Who knows what they're thinking?" He wanted to know what Nala was thinking. Even when he tied her up, gagged her, spanked her, *whatever,* he still wanted to know what thoughts ticked in her head. That's what made him so respectable on the outset.

"Is there something I can help you with?" she asked sweetly, knowing full well what was expected of her. She only had to glance in his lap again to get a glimpse of her imminent future.

He kissed her again, his hardness surging toward her stomach. "Put that wordy mouth of yours on my cock." His breath soared in her ear, diving deep, deep down into her heart and eliciting a gasp from her throat. "You talk too much for a sub, even one I'm being patient with. Perhaps I should punish your mouth."

He could have easily done that with his unforgiving kisses, but of course, that would be too easy – and not get him any sexual relief. When Nala's head was shoved into his lap, she inhaled deeply, taking in the scent of his strong musk and everything that entailed. At this point, nothing else could have excited her as much. Let alone excited her to dart out her tongue and lick his stiffening shaft as soon as possible. The first swear word of relief to fall from his lips nearly tickled Nala to death.

"That's it. Good. *Good.*" Now Vincent was the one controlling his breaths, gently guiding Nala's head over the tip of his cock. Salt and sweat touched her tongue, delightful, *delicious.* Nala wrapped her tongue around it as soon as possible, showing Vincent how eager she truly was to please him – and be pleased in return. *I definitely am pleased by doing this.* She couldn't explain it. She didn't know why she liked doing this so much. Maybe it was because it was for him. Was it possible to enjoy serving a man so much?

Nala barely had a hold on him with her mouth before he yanked her hair, sending a thousand thrills through her scalp and forcing her eyes up toward his. Until then, her eyes had been closed, savoring the moments as they went blissfully by. Now she was forced to look him in the soul, wondering how much of this came from Vincent the man or Vincent the Dom.

Does it matter?

"Keep it up," he growled, one hand holding tight to the back of her head while the other continued to pull her hair. "Inhale my cock, darling."

Used to be Nala could take or leave that name he called her. Now she came to love it, knowing that it wasn't a term of endearment he pulled out of his ass on the spur of the moment at The Aviary. He had probably thought about it. "*What do I want to call her? What name fits this woman the best?*" He had settled on darling, for one reason or another, and now he used that word whenever he wanted to make sure Nala felt special. *That isn't hard to do anymore.*

Vincent gave her enough reprieve to reorient herself, steadying her breaths through her nose as she worked her way up and down his ever-hardening cock. *Is he going to come soon?* Nala was sure that was part of the plan, although now that Vincent had time to enjoy the moment, he would probably hold off until he absolutely could not anymore.

Nala realized that this was a service to her Dom. Even so, there was no denying the pleasure it brought her, in unconventional ways. She enjoyed the challenge of pleasuring him like this without the use of her hands – although she longed to wrap one fist around his shaft and squeeze him, feeling the raw power residing within. It would also make taking him deeper into her mouth easier to bear. Yet without her hands to rely on, Nala had to be more patient, more resourceful. She used her tongue to draw him toward her throat, relaxing whatever stood in the way of her taking him down to places he had yet to explore. Not even his passionate tongue could reach this far into her mouth.

Don't you dare fucking choke, idiot. Not only would Nala be embarrassed, but it would ruin the mood. *He's expecting me to do this. So do it!* Nala rarely backed down from a challenge. A man asking her to practically – no, actually – deep throat him? Yeah, sure, no problem. Or so she told herself.

In reality, it was not an easy feat to do, let alone on her first try, and without the ability to use her hands to steady herself.

Vincent encouraged her, giving her the occasional tip when he had the mind to. Nala was sure that was becoming more difficult as time went on. After all, it could *not* have been easy to stop his fantasies in order to tell her what she needed to do to not choke or otherwise hurt herself and him by extension. While Nala appreciated it, she was also sure she could have figured it out on her own. Eventually.

When they fell into a rhythm that suited them both, Nala let herself go and rode the wave of power coursing through her. She had given up all control, but she was still a major part of this moment. It could not have existed without her, as it could not have existed without Vincent. *We're both equal in this. Just because he's calling all the shots… doesn't mean he doesn't need me here.* Could Vincent have achieved this pleasure on his own? Surely not!

Perhaps he couldn't even achieve it with another woman. Such a thought took Nala by surprise, but she let it go, choosing to instead focus on the moment before her.

Not that Vincent could let things go on course. He always had to up the ante, which he did the moment Nala let her guard down. Soon enough, her hair pulled at her scalp, her breath pounding through her nostrils and her fingers fighting for freedom as Vincent lifted his hips off the couch and fucked her damned throat.

She cried out, muffled by his body, by the sheer amount of need coursing through the both of them. Nala had to concentrate more than ever, but her heart thumped wildly, accepting what had happened with grace and as much dignity as she could muster. If anyone saw them in this moment, she would not be upset about it. In fact, she would be proud, because not only could she take this, but Vincent had *chosen* her. That in itself brought her pleasure.

The sounds coming from his throat increased, becoming more intense, threatening to burst from his chest before the rest of him was lost to pleasure. In the last moment of his sanity, he warned Nala. She knew what was coming.

Him.

She could not suppress the alarm going off in her head as Vincent came, one wave after another surging down Nala's throat and filling her mouth. His cock swelled to unusual size, her mouth working it, draining it of every last bit of his vitality. There was no time to savor his taste. No time to feel the ripples of his body as he shared this moment with her. There was only him, her, and what happened in her throat.

"Fucking shit, Nala." Vincent sank back into the couch, his cock falling from Nala's mouth. She gasped, gulping in the first deep breaths she had in minutes. "That was the best."

The best what? The best oral? The best sex? The best she ever gave him? Nala knew he wouldn't divulge that detail. Not yet, anyway. So she leaned her head against the couch, panting, some of his seed already dribbling from the corner of her mouth. She was too tired to do something about it.

His hand came for her, stroking the top of her head until she looked up at him with the softest expression she ever felt on her own face.

"You're adventurous," Vincent said. "I knew that already but… you surprise even me."

Nala braved a few words. "What do you mean? Didn't expect me to like that?"

"You're not the type of woman a man would take for being a submissive."

"Yeah, I give off that vibe." Nala grinned. "Does that make it more fun for you? Knowing that I will do these things and like it?"

"Maybe. Like I told you before, I'm a lot more into the feisty type than the demure. I like a girl who makes me feel like I'm accomplishing something as opposed to being serviced."

"Accomplishing? You mean like breaking a poor girl in?"

"Over and over."

"Mm, Mr. Lane, you like a girl with some resistance."

"Playful resistance."

"Of course."

Vincent bent down, tilting Nala's head back. "I like you, Nala. I haven't said that to someone in a very, very long time."

Not since Desirée, I'm sure. "You're not so bad yourself, Mr. Lane."

"You're a mess already." Vincent lightly kissed her lips. "Something tells me you enjoy being messy."

"I was quite the tomboy growing up. Always climbing trees and getting muddy."

"I like it."

He kissed her harder, delving between her lips and tasting himself on her tongue. *That is so hot.* There was no shame between them. No thoughts of disgust or ambivalence. If it weren't for her wrists becoming sore in their binds, she could have easily spent half her lifetime kneeling there in front of him, feeling him kiss her, explore her, and indulge in some of life's simple pleasures that they so rarely allowed themselves.

"I think it's time I took you upstairs."

Chapter 31

Vincent stood, gently bringing Nala to her feet before swooping her up in his arms. With her arms bound behind her, however, Nala was truly at his mercy. *I trust him.* Only an accident could bring her pain now, and she trusted Vincent enough to be careful so that never happened.

His steps were slow going up the spiral staircase to his lofted bedroom. It gave Nala time to relax in his arms, feeling her hair hang beneath her head and scrape against the shining metal around her. None of that compared to the heat radiating from beneath this man's T-shirt. His breaths were steady, his need to have her so quickly abated. Nala didn't worry about her own pleasure. She knew that Vincent would take care of her needs.

His strides across the bedroom were quicker, his arms lowering Nala to the neatly made bed. *Won't be neat pretty soon.* Vincent freed her arms, but squeezed them so she knew to not move them. He was merely changing their positions before binding them again.

There was no hurry. Vincent took his time disrobing his vixen, as he called Nala more than once. She had graduated from succubus, apparently. Never mind. Nala would continue to play up those fantasies in her head.

Me, a demon. Him, a demon. Together we dance in darkness in order to release our most carnal desires. Entire cultures sang songs about their unions.

"You must be more beautiful than the day you were born." Vincent knelt between her bent legs, pulling his T-shirt off in that strange way guys do. Nala never knew how they were able to grab their back collars and yank a fucking shirt off like no big deal, but damn, it was always hot. *It makes them look so strong.* And Vincent *was* strong. Over the past few days, she had seen him working out around the house. Pushups on the floor here. Stretches against the couch there. Early morning jogs. A punching bag hanging in a corner. Vincent didn't have a lot of time to dedicate to a gym, so he took breaks from work and life here and there to punch something or use his body as an exercise tool. Almost a shame he hid those muscles beneath clothes, *especially* sweatshirts in his down time.

Not now, though.

Nala drank him in as he loomed over her, teasing her with a smirk. *He looks so happy.* Was she doing that to him? Was she making him feel like this for the first time in forever? How often had Vincent felt like this with another woman since the death of his fiancée? Was this… the first time?

With her, of all people?

"You will have to take that up with my mother, sir." Nala could be cheeky again. "I think she has the final authority."

"Let's not bring your mother into this."

He knelt down, sampling her nipples between his teeth, his eyes never leaving hers. It was erotic and emotional all at once, leaving Nala in a nether space between desire and an emotion she had never felt so profoundly since the last time they made love.

I remember the chasm of stars. A million of them, twinkling in time to their lovemaking. *I fell in love with him that night.* Here she was again, turning into a foolish girl at the sight of a man who liked to tie her up and fuck her throat.

"Nala," he whispered, after his tongue drew a long, tantalizing trail down her cleavage. "I want to take you to places. Places you can't even imagine existing. Will you let me?"

She forced back a knowing smile. "Of course, sir. My body is yours to command. Tonight, anyway."

He caressed her face while turning her over on her stomach. "Every night we want. What are you?"

This game continued – he had not forgotten after all. She said the same word as the previous two times, and Vincent hopped off the bed to take what he wanted from the nearest nightstand.

"You still think so?" He drew out two long silk strips, weighing them in his hands, testing their durability while his muscles flexed. The color of the silk was such a deep purple that they looked as black as a midwinter's day. *No, the twinkling of the silk makes them look like the chasm of stars.* Nala braced herself, partly in infatuation, as the strips landed softly on the bed beside her. "You're free to think that, for sure, but know that I will continue to see you differently."

What does he mean?

He was his usual silent self as he tied a tight, intricate knot into the center of the headboard and drew the two ends of the silk strips taut toward Nala. *Naturally.* Her wrists were bound again, still together, but now hanging from the taut strips in front of her. So much resistance bundled in those strips, but if Nala pulled hard enough, they still gave. Just like her.

The rest of her was free, for now. Vincent laid her legs out straight on the bed beneath her, pushing them together and letting his hands roam up her ass and back as he straddled the space behind her knees.

Kisses heavier than the ones he gave her mouth landed on her supple flesh, almost ravenous in their pursuit. Vincent had nothing to be shy about as he ravaged the dimples between her cheeks and thighs, his tongue lashing against hidden spaces and his hands squeezing her so hard that it was almost more unbearable – in the best way – than the spanks from earlier. *This man wants me to moan myself to death.* She wasn't opposed.

"I have one more test for you tonight, Nala," Vincent said against her skin. "If you can make it through the next few minutes without uttering a single sound, I will give you whatever you want."

She swallowed. "You ask a lot of me."

"I know. That's why I ask it."

"I'll do it, sir."

"We'll see."

She knew that with a challenge like that something pleasurable was coming. First, she had been asked to endure pain without flinching. Now she was asked to endure pleasure without sound. Her obedience was being stretched to new destinations, and in turn, she learned what Vincent wanted not from a sub, but from *her.*

Here it came.

Not a spank. Not dirty talk. Just his tongue, his pinching, both making their way all over her nether regions, dipping into folds, drawing lines up slits, and plunging into areas they had no business being in. Nala channeled the pleasure into her slight movements, attempting to avoid a single sound falling from her lips – if she could help it. Not easy. Vincent had such a way with his tongue that Nala writhed back and forth, biting back screams of ecstasy, words of adoration, and even the whimpers demanding to be freed. *This is impossible!*

Yet she fought to control herself. In time, Nala grew to realize that submission wasn't always about being controlled by another person. It was also about controlling oneself. Submitting *to oneself.* There was a lot to learn from these situations that Nala could apply to other aspects of her life. She needed to mature. To learn to be less brash and hotheaded. To control her temper. She may be an adult, but oftentimes she found herself in situations that could have been prevented if she simply sat back and *looked* at what she was doing. Submitting to Vincent forced her to face these parts of herself. She would always be a rebel and contrary. That was who she was, from the day she was born. Vincent didn't want to change that. He wanted to teach her how to *control* it. *That* was the role of her Dom. Not to exert force over her, but to bring out the best inside of *her.*

The man she called Master wouldn't be her king. He would be her teacher.

In the meantime, she would love him.

So even though she wanted to scream, to cry, to heave the loudest breaths in history against the bed, she didn't. She wanted to make Vincent proud. Not just to get her reward, but to prove to him that she was worthy of being his obedient student.

And worthy of his love.

When the test was over, with nary a peep from Nala's clenched lips and stifled throat, Vincent sat back, letting his fingers round her ass with a ticklish sensation. Nala finally let out a breath laced in a moan.

"What do you want, darling?" Vincent asked. "I'll give you anything."

Can you give me your heart? Nala had to shake that thought from her head. There was no sense asking for the impossible.

"I want you," she said, knees pushing her hips up. "I want you to take me. Please, sir."

Was it working? Was her ticket to success bumping her ass into the air and enticing the man? *I'm really fucking wet.* She could feel it on her thighs, running down her leg, and from the air hitting her between the folds. Nala didn't know how much time had passed since Vincent's first climax, but she hoped it had been enough time for him to get hard again.

"What else, Nala? I know you want something else."

Oh, there it was. Vincent drew her hips up and knelt right behind her, his stiff cock touching, taunting her. A fury of desires wound themselves up inside Nala. *Now! I want it now!* She had been denied all sorts of things tonight. First she couldn't flinch. Then she didn't get her orgasm. Then she had to be quiet while she was pleasurably tormented some more. Was this it? Was this finally her reward for a job well done that night?

She knew what she wanted.

"I want you to talk dirty to me, sir." She breathed deeply, filling her lungs with much needed air. "That first night you took me as yours… part of what made it so exhilarating was how you talked to me."

"You're strange," Vincent immediately replied. "I've never met a woman who likes that level of filth."

"Of course, it means nothing if you don't really mean it, sir."

"I was coming from a dark place that night. I resented how guilty I felt wanting you. If I did it now, it wouldn't be the same."

"I think it would."

"Why is that?"

Nala looked over her shoulder. "Because deep down, I really am a seductive demon who has been spending these past few weeks seducing you into feelings you haven't allowed yourself for a long, long time. It doesn't hurt to be reminded of what I *really* am."

She grinned, assuring him that this was a joke, of course. Vincent smiled back at her, removing his jeans and the briefs beneath until he was as naked as her.

He reached to touch her as he had all night, but Nala knowingly disobeyed, moving her legs to one side and fighting against his need for her.

"What are you…"

"You're going to have to do better than that, *sir*." Nala's hiss stung the air, and she watched as Vincent went from the gentleman to the demanding Dom in about two seconds.

This was the wildest game they had played yet, but it exhilarated Nala's heart in ways she could not express even to herself. If she was going to see Vincent as her teacher, then he would have to continue to earn her respect. He would have to prove himself, over and over, matching wits with the flighty bird who would never be content to be kept in a cage all day. She would always be trying to break free, because that was her nature.

She *wanted* to feel him forcefully hold her hips down, spread her legs and mutter into her ear that she was a terrible demon who needed to learn her place. She *wanted* to feel him sit on top of her as he reached into his drawer of bondage gear and pulled out more silk scarves and strips. And, oh, *she wanted* to feel her knees wrap in those beautiful silks, the other ends tied tight to the headboard so she was nearly immobile. The bird couldn't fly away. The demon was caught, the succubus finally getting her way with the man she had chosen as her target.

Vincent didn't tell her why he didn't gag her. Nala knew why. He not only wanted to hear her make a shitton of noise and talk back to him, but he intended on being rough, and wanted to give her the ability to use her safe word if necessary.

He did blindfold her, though. The darkness overcame her, and all she had to go by were the sounds of their bodies and the feel of the bed as it sank beneath Vincent's weight. Nala's torso was lifted, her nipples barely grazing a pillow to a tortuous effect. Her knees were also connected to the head board, forced apart with her ass high in the air. The trapped demon was not only unable to flee… but she was presented on a platter to the man who would fuck the mischief out of her.

The way he spoke to her would never be like that first night again. His heart was dark that night, and it would not be tonight. This was pure role-play, but Vincent could certainly deliver on other fronts. He played along with Nala's fantasy, fulfilling the idea that she was a bad, bad succubus who needed to be tamed and taught a serious lesson. With his body, of course.

"You can't take me," Nala growled. "I'll never be docile or demure. I'll never be a pretty princess who serves a king."

He spanked her raw flesh, sending shivers through her body and a hiss through her teeth. "What a pity if you did turn out that way. I'd much rather fuck the filthy street girl than some cleaned up, soulless princess. You're lower than a filthy street girl, though, aren't you? You're lower than the dirt on my hands. You're the kind of menace who preys on the people who want nothing to do with your kind. The only way you'll learn is if a man like me forces you to learn."

Oh, what a delightful word. *Force.*

Although her legs were "forced" open already, Vincent clapped both hands on her hips and pried her thighs farther apart, opening her folds and making her arousal slip effortlessly from her body. *Do it in one stroke. I dare you.* Nala wanted to feel him inside her what felt like hours ago.

One stroke? Who was she kidding? Maybe if they were different kinds of people built in different ways. Yet no matter how aroused she was, Nala would never be able to take that man in one swift thrust. The universe would never allow it.

"*Shit!*" one of them cried… or was it both? Either way, Nala was pierced, like an arrow to the bird's breast. Yet the arrow did not go deep. It pierced her flesh, but it would not lodge, and the hunter was forced to shoot another arrow at her. Again. Again. Each time deeper, but every time making her cry in pain and delight both. If this were gentle lovemaking, then Vincent would take his time entering her, making sure she felt nothing but good things as his body became one with hers.

Not tonight.

"*Why* are you always so difficult?" he demanded, spanking her for her insubordination. He fell right out of her again, his tip barely inside to begin with. "Why do you fight me? Why do you fight your destiny, succubus?"

Nala bit back a cry of relief to feel her arousal reemerge from her body. Every time Vincent attempted to shove himself in, she dried up a little, making the friction that much more intense. "I don't fight anything, *sir,*" she spat. "Perhaps it's you who isn't worthy of *me!*"

Before they moved from Portland and sold most of their belongings to pay for the costs of moving and a funeral, Nala had gone through some of her parents' books. One of them was a book of Russian folklore and fairy tales written in the original Russian and English translation both – Yulia had used this to practice her English. Although Nala was never as smart as her sister, she was able to read at a fairly young age, and from this book she learned of spirits, nymphs, and other mischievous types whose purpose was to lure handsome young men and become their demise. Sometimes they were called *rusalki,* who sang siren songs from lakes and rivers. In some of these stories, specially trained hunters would track these nymphs down, pretend to be lured in by the songs to which they were actually unaffected, and then either slay the nymph or "take her in." Some of these spirits became mistresses, and as she grew, Nala wondered if there were erotic undertones to these stories. Now she didn't wonder. She was living such a story.

Maybe I really am *a demon.* A demon of vengeance who also felt the extremes of sexual desire and anger. Vincent was the hunter, lured in by her siren song, but remembering at the last minute what his duty was. To take her down. To punish her. To tame her so she could behave in society and no longer exact her anger on the innocent.

So to insult not only his manhood, but to imply he was a terrible hunter… Nala knew exactly what she was doing. She was the siren, the succubus, and she would only be taken down by a hunter who proved himself absolutely worthy of her body and essence. To submit to a lesser man would bring imbalance to the universe and never fill that chasm of stars ever again.

"You think *really* highly of yourself for someone who was dumb enough to be trapped."

"And *you* think really highly of yourself for someone who can't even fuck a cunt!"

Nala knew she would pay for that. She would be really, really disappointed if she didn't.

Vincent delivered. He slapped his large hand over her mouth while the other hand pulled her spread thighs toward him, his cock ramming between her legs and piercing the bird right in the heart.

She squealed against his palm, feeling him finally fill her, and not gently. She was the siren claimed, her fate now bound and set. The hunter had her. The hunter *took her.* It wasn't a mere matter of fucking her. This was raw. This was passion at its core, taking them both to another plane of reality as Vincent reached deep into her and made sure she knew what it felt like to have her Master teach her the real lesson.

Nala held up her end of the role-play by struggling against him, although every inch of her body begged for her to sit still and take it. Except that wouldn't have been as thrilling, as satisfying as playing it out *this* way.

"*Fuck!*" she screamed, still muffled by his hand, Vincent's fingers slipping against her lips as he pulled out and slammed back into her again. Nala tried to flail her arms in pleasure, but the binds were too tight. She was immobile. She truly was trapped and at the hunter's whims. His words of filth and defamation, of pride and alpha tendencies filled her ears as his body filled hers. Nala wouldn't even remember most of them later. Her mind was so lost to the ether, soaring high above the room, watching the scene play out below her… that it would have been impossible to retain everything he said to her that night. Whatever it was, it came from a real place. Not real as in that's what he really thought of Nala, but real as in those dark emotions still lurked deep within him – Nala had a helluva ability of bringing them out during sex.

Vincent rocked into her with increasing force and speed. Nala's small body could barely take it, but she had to – what choice did she have? Using her safe word was not an option. It wasn't that she didn't want this or couldn't take it. It was that her heart raced so quickly that she almost feared the hunter really *would* take her down.

Any pain, any discomfort disappeared as Vincent made it all the way inside with one favorable stroke. They were one. They said terrible things to one another, but they were *one.* No matter how awful they felt, no matter what crazy fantasies they played out, this was it, this was the real reason they did it all. Who else could Nala take these feelings out on? Who else could *Vincent* finally express himself with? They had come together as total strangers, and now Nala was in love. Every hard thrust, every deep touch of her body as she remained tied for his easier access made her feel like she was free.

With a mighty growl, Vincent pulled her hips onto him while his other hand clutched her shoulder. He rode her, his movements steady enough to lull Nala into a sweet rhythm. She continued to float in her mind, her words leaving her for the first time in minutes as she gave herself over to the endless expanse of space.

They were both wordless now, the only sounds leaving their lips being exclamations and formless groans. Nala released the tension in her body; Vincent began to swell within her. With any luck, they would climax together, ending this scene and bringing them back to reality.

Nala would welcome that, but Vincent had other plans.

"What are you Nala?" he shouted, driving into her so quickly that she cried in surprise. "What the fuck *are* you?"

So overwhelmed by her rising orgasm, his barrages, and the sheer amount of power flowing from him to her… how could Nala find any way to respond? She was ready to spit her usual response, but that dirty word was not what came from her heart, the sudden understanding of what Vincent *really* thought of her this whole time.

"I'm your girlfriend!" she cried, his hands all over her as both Vincent and their bed made love to her. "Holy shit, I'm your girlfriend!"

Siren, succubus, foolish 21-year-old girl. None of those identities mattered when Vincent surged inside her, his mouth coming for the back of her neck and teeth clamping hard against her skin. Nala screamed, her climax exploding within and turning her into a trembling, tightening mess beneath Vincent's beastly body.

He was everywhere. On her. Beside her. Beneath her. *Within* her. Nala couldn't escape into the chasm of the stars even if she wanted to. Vincent held her back, leaving every mark, every claim to her that he knew of.

He bit her. He scratched her. And by fucking hell he unleashed himself within her, his liquid heat emptying in her with the most hypnotic pulses of his cock. Nala gasped, unable to move, but also not wanting to.

Vincent clenched her stomach and continued to suck the skin of her throat, his hips stilling his cock inside her. Nala couldn't have gotten away from it if she wanted to. *I don't!* Just when she thought the moment was over and Vincent was finished, he spared her two more releases of his cock, his seed spreading within her and making sure Nala knew that she was the only one who got to feel something as amazing as this.

She felt both like a creature and a woman. The creature accepted its fate, claimed by the hunter, but the woman moaned in relief, her body more than a vessel for this man's pleasure. He was sharing the most intimate part of himself with her. Not merely his climax, but the ensuing flood of emotions that came with it.

His joy, his heart was hers, even if only for this moment.

When the pressure finally lifted from her body, Nala whimpered. All things had to end, though, including their unconventional lovemaking.

"Please don't leave me," she whispered, afraid to feel him pull out. "You went through all that trouble to get in there and share yourself with me. Why leave now?"

"Who said I was leaving?" Although gruff, there was tenderness in his voice as he lightly kissed her throat and shoulders, hand brushing away her hair and cock softening within her. "Don't underestimate me, darling. I'm happy where I am."

"Am I too tight?"

He untied the strips holding her arms up. Relief flooded them as they, and her torso, were allowed to fall into the pillow. Vincent rubbed her sides and ass as he moved within her. "No. You get hung up on the strangest things."

She waited for him to untie her knees. That didn't happen for another minute, and it was such a slow undertaking that she wondered if he was prolonging it so it would be easier to stay so deep inside of her. For the moment her knees were free, they naturally sank toward one another, and Vincent had to quickly pull out before she fell off him instead.

Oh my God, I am dead. That was when the fatigue hit her, a breath of fresh air if she were telling the truth. Sleep would be easy after the perfect day.

She thought she would be left to lie and feel him spill from her body. Instead, Vincent rolled her over and stuck two thick fingers inside her as her legs spread wide, giving him access.

This wasn't sexual. This was him asserting the last bit of authority he had over her.

"What are you trying to do?" Nala asked, eyelids heavy. Vincent propped himself up on his elbow next to her, his face near hers as his fingers stayed inside her, keeping *him* inside her. "Impregnate me? Good luck. I'm on the pill."

"No. I'm not trying to do that." Vincent kissed her forehead, fingers slowly circling within her. What would usually be sexual pleasure was now a mere conduit for his affection. "I'm making you think about to whom you belong. Close your eyes."

That wasn't hard to obey. Nala let her eyelids droop as she sank deep within their bed. His intimate touch lulled her into a doze, and knowing he was right there watching her made Nala feel safer than ever. Yes, she could feel his essence within her, trapped, like she had been a few minutes before.

I'm trapping it. He trapped my body, he marked it with his essence, but I'm the one trapping that inside of me. It's mine. All mine.

"I belong to you," she muttered, indulging in his warmth. "But you belong to me too."

"Yes, darling." His words were the last thing she heard that night. "It goes both ways."

As she fell asleep that night, Nala knew that everything would be different when she opened her eyes again.

Entry #14

I don't need to write down what happened tonight between me and Nightingale. If I have no other memories of my life, I will have this, at least.

She is my girlfriend now. I have no choice but to protect her with every ounce of my being.

I am elated. But I am also more fearful than ever. For now, I will forget my fears and focus on rebuilding any shred of happiness I can reach out and grasp within my hand. At the moment, that means Nightingale.

Chapter 32

The day Nala received her super-expedited passport was the day she and Vincent received a very apologetic letter from Xavier Crow informing them that the trip to Cancun had to be canceled "for personal reasons." Instead, he invited his club members to join him on his ranch down south for the weekend.

This wasn't what surprised Nala the most. What did was the transportation Vincent arranged to take them down near Salem. Well, *he* didn't arrange it. He merely announced that they would be sharing a car with Lucian and Robin, their two designated buddies in the club.

While this suited Vincent fine since it meant he didn't have to drive, Nala was more anxious than usual. Usually her time in the car before a club meeting was when she put her game face on and got into the headspace of Nightingale. Being picked up in a stretch limo with Robin already shrieking and Lucian making one bawdy joke after another meant she had to be "on" from the moment she stepped out of Vincent's loft, wearing a brand new outfit from him: a knee-length A-line dress with a faux-fur coat that made her look like a puffy blackbird as opposed to a nightingale.

She and Vincent climbed into the modest limo – if there was such a thing – before hauling ass out of town to the tune of laughter and a champagne bottle popping.

It was almost too much energy for her to handle. Robin and Lucian were a *loud* couple when left to their own devices. Their voices naturally carried, especially in such a small space, and their movements clacked, clanged, and banged as if they were giants tearing through a village. Vincent looked completely unfazed as he leaned back in his seat. *He looks too casual for this.* Since they would be outside on a ranch, the men were asked to mind anything too formal or likely to get dirty. So Vincent wore one of his pairs of business trousers and a linen shirt beneath a typical PNW jacket. All very nice and formal enough for a play date outdoors, but a far cry from the formal suits he usually wore to Aviary meetings.

Nala had to look away from him multiple times that evening. *Things are both so awesome and so weird right now.* Ever since their incredibly passionate night, they had barely said more than was necessary to one another – although this did include the occasional words of affection and light, playful admonishments. Vincent made a move one night to feel up Nala's breasts while they watched TV, but she gently turned him down, citing terrible, crampy PMS. Sure enough, the red demon slashed her insides open the next day. Nothing more than light pats on the ass while passing one another in the kitchen or brushing teeth together after that.

Yet Nala understood that there was a fundamental change between them. They may have kept to themselves, but the air was different. Vincent was much more relaxed around her. He spoiled her with her favorite foods and let her decide what video games they played and what movies they watched, whether he felt like doing them or not. *Because I'm his girlfriend now.* They never discussed it after the fact. As Nala came to understand, they were the type of couple who didn't use words to communicate much. Between Nala's monthly maladies and Vincent diving head-first into a new project at work, they didn't see *that* much of each other anyway.

This was the first time, however, they were in a more public situation. Sure, Lucian and Robin already thought of them as an established couple, but Nala wasn't lying anymore. She really *was* Vincent's girlfriend, and she had no idea what to do.

At first she relied on what she knew Nightingale would do, such as offer to pour him champagne in a moving vehicle, but soon there was nothing else she could do. Nightingale wasn't overly affectionate. Neither was Nala, although by the time they were on the freeway heading south, she felt the extreme urge to reach across the seat between them and touch that fine lining beneath his jacket.

Nobody said anything – other than continuing Lucian and Vincent's conversation about the Timbers – as Nala lost her seatbelt and climbed into Vincent's embrace. *This is so weird!* She was genuinely happy to be there, against his body, and taking refuge in the safety he offered. But it was *weird* having Robin nudge her boyfriend with a new giggle on her lips.

Is this really so bad? Nala wasn't happy about where they were going or who they would see, but in the precious hour or so it took them to get to Crow's private ranch, she was able to relax and be in the company of her boyfriend and their friends. *These aren't bad people. They're a bit much, but they're playing a game like we are.* Lucian had a tendency to take his jokes too far, and Robin had the most annoying laugh in the universe, but they were genuine to a fault. Even when they grew serious enough to apologize for trying to drunkenly start an orgy the last time they all met, Nala could tell that they really were embarrassed. *I wonder if we would go for it now?* Sometimes a girl still remembered the way Lucian could fuck his woman. *I mean, if Crow is gonna make my boyfriend and I swap with someone…* Might as well be these sexy fools.

The more she loosened up, drank some champagne, and laughed at tasteless jokes, the more Nala felt like a normal girl. Someone who went out with her boyfriend. Someone who had friends and wasn't afraid to be herself around… and someone who was *happy.*

The way Vincent danced his fingers upon her throat as they went down the freeway made her shiver. The way he kissed her when he didn't think anyone was looking was exhilarating – and then embarrassing, because Robin shrieked and told her boyfriend to kiss *her* like that.

It was the greatest shame that the good feelings eventually had to come to an end, and not for natural reasons, but because they arrived at the ranch. The driver opened the doors to reveal a bright, clear night with few chills. Nala still hugged her coat to her body as Vincent put an arm around her and led her to the ranch house, where the surly butler pointed them to the party happening out back.

Whoever threw Crow's parties needed a raise. Beautiful white Christmas lights lined the large open space; cushy chairs and carefully laid out tables full of candles and snacks awaited them. Music played from small speakers while warm breezes flitted through. Best of all, Xavier Crow was nowhere to be seen. While more guests arrived, the butler informed them that their host would be late "due to personal reasons," and for them to enjoy the three courses of supper without him.

It was like any other dinner party without that man around. Some people Nala liked more than others, but for the most part she was able to relax and enjoy the roast brought out for them to savor. Without Crow around to inspect their every move, Nala noticed that some behaviors changed. The only women going out of their way to coddle their men were Quail and Robin, and one was a lot quieter about it than the other. Maggie and Jay barely interacted, as if they detested each other. Starling and Joseph were painfully normal, with Starling whining and Joseph giving in to one demand after another. Nala and Vincent? They were the most publically lovey-dovey they had ever been before. Some people commented on it, but the only one who caught Nala's eye was Maggie, who studied the way they acted as if she had to write a dissertation about it.

During dessert, Nala caught a glimpse of a shadow in one of the ranch house windows.

At first she ignored it, and then she looked again, realizing that the figure was none other than Xavier Crow surveying his dolls through a pair of opera glasses.

"Vincent," she hissed, lightly jabbing her elbow against his arm. "It's him. It's Crow. He's watching us."

Vincent looked away from his conversation to snatch a quick look for himself. "He means business," was all he muttered before going back to his dessert and laughing at a joke.

Business, huh? What kind of business? This wasn't the perch of a voyeur getting off. This was a man spying on them, looking for a wrong move, a wrong glance. Nala had to keep her eyes on her plate instead of meeting Crow head-on, hair bristling on her neck and heart racing like a hummingbird's. The only things keeping her safe were Vincent beside her and the nightingale charm resting on her chest.

Nala and Vincent were the only ones not surprised when Crow showed up a few minutes later, giving his apologies and brushing away any concerns the others had. He sat at the head of the table and thanked everyone for coming. His eyes lingered for a long, *long* time on Nala.

What does he know? The amount of judgment shooting in her direction was unreal.

"I still think you look very familiar, Miss Nightingale," he said in a low voice as the dessert plates were taken away. "I know you insist that we have never met before you joining The Aviary, but my eyes know."

Nala tried to brush his comment off with a placating giggle, but neither she nor Crow believed it.

Luckily, he dropped it after that, but Nala felt his watchful eyes on her all night, even when she buried her face in Vincent's chest during a toast and acted like a kitten around Lucian. Her flirtations were subtle, but not unlike her – not too much. The more she stood in the wake of Xavier Crow, the more she realized he knew more than he let on.

Does he know who I am? Nala broke away from Vincent to talk to Robin about absolutely nothing. Their laughter and sweet talk did nothing to drive Crow away. *Is he going to do something to me?*

But Crow didn't do much of anything there on his private, isolated ranch. Hell, he could have had them all killed with the rain of hellfire, and nobody would ever know. So why wasn't he using this to his advantage? Did he cancel the trip to Cancun so he could bring them out here to the middle of nowhere and start things all over again?

The shows began after everyone had enough time to digest dinner. Tables were cleared away so Lucian and Robin could properly demonstrate what happens when a woman's aroused body was exposed to the outdoor elements – a lot of hardening, apparently. Starling and Joseph went as far as they usually did, and Vincent did not stop himself from rubbing the inside of Nala's thigh and whispering in her ear that he would very much like to do some of that to her. Nala could not return his flirtations because she was too weirded out.

Crow retired early, stating the usual "personal reasons." He encouraged his guests to stay as late as they wanted, but warned that there weren't many available rooms in the ranch house. That was code for "go back to whence you came." Nala looked forward to getting back into the limo and returning to Portland, but Lucian and Robin were… busy… very busy. So busy that Quail and Sebastian openly watched with haughty laughs threatening to burst from their lips over the absurdity of it all.

Nala wanted to sit and wait for her friends to be done fucking so they could leave, but Vincent pulled her into his arms and covertly slipped her hand over his thighs, letting her feel his hardness.

"Really?" she said. "Here? In front of these people? *Tonight?*" Nala was a lot more comfortable than she used to be, but she would hardly say she was *comfortable.* Especially after the way Crow was acting.

"No. Not here. Come with me."

When nobody was watching, Vincent led Nala away from the after party, deep into the black and empty fields that probably never saw a bovine or sheep in their lives. On any other night, Nala would find her boyfriend lowering her to the soft grass and overtaking her beneath a blanket of twinkling stars the craziest thing ever. Except it didn't feel crazy. The moment Vincent put his mouth on her and started moving clothing out of the way was the moment Nala realized he was doing this to take her mind off dark and terrible things.

Probably himself as well.

Nala never closed her eyes. She looked up into the real chasm of stars, feeling Vincent's strong and sturdy body take her in the cold. Her skirt hiked above her hips. Her lingerie tore away to take his cock. Busts were pulled down so her breasts could welcome Vincent's teeth and tongue. The only foreplay they needed was the rush this gave them. Nala didn't cry out when he entered her, but she did breathe hard into his ear and raise her hips to meet his every thrust.

Out there, in the wild, beneath the stars and with a cool breeze caressing her skin, Nala felt the freest a woman could possibly feel. Someone was always watching – that was the nature of this game, but she didn't care. Let them all watch from afar. Let Xavier Crow peer out of his window with his opera glasses and watch two wild beasts go at it the old fashioned way.

"Remember," Vincent whispered, "You belong to me. I'l protect you."

His climax was much stronger than Nala's, but that was fine. She enjoyed her low-key pleasure while enjoying his more. The way he growled into her shoulder and the ground. The way he thrust into her, unrelenting. The way he smothered her against the grass. Grass that would never hurt anybody.

Nala accepted his kiss the moment he released within her, and she accepted it readily, remembering what he did a few nights ago. He did it again, now, holding himself within her long after he was finished and letting her know that this went beyond their bodies.

"Fuck me," Nala muttered. "This is going to kill us."

"Maybe, but I'll die knowing it was worth it."

Whether he meant her or Crow, Nala didn't know. She also didn't care.

Entry #15

Something ominous hangs in the air. My vigilance is lacking, however. Where I should be spotting threats, I only see Nightingale, luring me to her. The taste of normalcy, of happiness I had tonight was beyond anything I could have ever hoped for again. Friends and a partner. It's too good to be true.

But as always, I am haunted. By Xavier Crow and his crimes.

Chapter 33

Nala emerged from the Russian grocery store with a bag laden with fresh goods and cans written in a language she never bothered to learn. When she entered half an hour earlier carrying a list of ingredients from her new cookbook, the one clerk on duty had been more than happy to load Nala's basket up. When he asked, in his thick but friendly accent, what Nala was cooking, she was almost sheepish to admit to near-peasant staples her mother cooked every week. Then Nala remembered that this wasn't Vincent's world of fancy eating and exorbitant delicacies. This was the *real* stuff.

Her time at the grocer's would've passed by otherwise non-eventfully, but then the clerk asked where Nala was from and who her parents were. Since the Nazarovs had lived in this exact area nearly twenty years ago, the clerk came to the edge of tears as he said, "Nala! It's you?" Apparently she had attended kindergarten with the man's daughter.

The sun was bright and full for the first time in days. Nala folded up her umbrella while carrying her bag with the other hand. She made it to the bus stop in time, meaning she should be home before the hour was up. Plenty of time to start cooking.

I'll show him how good the food I eat can be. Nala mentioned that morning that she would cook Vincent a traditional Russian dinner. He stood in front of his dresser, fixing his cuffs and pulling on a tie to wear to a big meeting with his new client. *My hardworking man.* Nala smiled to think it.

It should have scared her how much like her mother she was suddenly becoming. The Nala of six months ago would have never deigned to prepare a meal for a man *after a hard day at work*. Yet as her relationship with Vincent deepened, she realized that it wasn't about being a good *domokhozyayka,* but doing what she could to contribute to the household Vincent so graciously let her join. Nala wasn't going to make a *habit* out of cooking for them, but once in a while it wouldn't be so bad.

"*Just bought a ton of food ;)*" she texted Vincent. "*Someone's getting spoiled with Russian food tonight.*"

"*Should I be scared?*"

"*No, but I'm pretty sure you should be working.*"

"*I just got off work. I'm going to be home early. You there?*"

"*Not quite. I'm on the bus crossing the bridge right now. You?*"

"*Just pulling onto Burnside.*"

"*OMG, stop texting while you drive!*"

"*I'm at a very long light.*"

"*Dumbass!*"

"*You're cool too.*"

Nala didn't hear from him again until she stepped off the bus and began the few block trek to Vincent's loft. *I guess it's my home too…* It was still a strange thing to think. Now that they had established themselves as a couple, Vincent no longer brought up buying Nala an apartment. They went on their merry way, assuming that for now they would simply live together and hope for the best. *My mother would be so scandalized.* Good.

Her phone buzzed as she turned the corner onto their street. The weight of the shopping bag was starting to get to her, but Nala found the ability to pull out her phone.

"*Hello, gorgeous.*"

She looked up, seeing Vincent's black car on the other end of the street. Nala waved before putting her phone away and hurrying her steps. If she timed it right, she could make it as he parked. *Then he could help me haul these groceries upstairs!* His true job! Put those muscles to perfect use!

Alas, he made it before her, although he remained seated in his car, stuck on the phone. Nala waved, made a face unbecoming of a young lady, and started the onerous climb up the stairs. The bag was heavy enough to pull her down on one side, so she waddled more than walked.

She put the bag down on the landing, fishing for the key in her pocket. Vincent hadn't bothered to get the locks changed yet, but Nala did have a new key to make up for the one she lost somewhere along the way.

The door opened, light spilling into the stuffy loft. Nala kicked rather than pulled the heavy bag of groceries inside. Behind her, she heard Vincent's car door open. As Nala walked inside, she wondered if she should get started with the cooking right now, or cook something *else* with her sexy boyfriend. *If I could do both at the same time, I totally would!*

Yet Nala didn't have the chance to think about doing both at the same time, or the logistics therein. Her eyes blinked, adjusting to the shadows of the large, open space, although a huge stream of sunlight poured through the windows. The black leather couches were illuminated, heating up, and the glass coffee table…

And the glass coffee table…

Broken, the shards sprinkled across the throw rug beneath.

Nala stared in disbelief, her breath, her voice caught in her throat as her eyes traveled from the surprising mess to the body sprawled between both couches.

Blond. Fair. A pretty red sundress frayed at the hems and torn wherever glass shards had pierced it. Some parts of the dress were darker than others. It took daft Nala too many seconds to realize it was blood.

It took her even longer to realize who it was.

"*Robin!*" she screamed, running to her friend's body, shaking her, slapping her face, staring into half-dead eyes that once shone so brightly.

Nala's cries of alarm echoed through the loft, as if she were the one fending off an attacker in a strange home.

The front door flew open. Vincent, in his suit and tie, rushed in to the harrowing sounds of Nala's voice. He saw her, then Robin, his strength shoving Nala out of the way as he immediately knelt down and checked for a pulse.

"She's alive! Call 911!"

Nala stood there, aghast.

"*I said call 911!*"

The world slowed. Nala stumbled over the couch behind her, patting her sweatshirt and looking for her phone. What was happening? Why was Robin there? *Like this?*

Nala was about to call for an ambulance when she looked down at her feet, a piece of paper sticking out from beneath her shoe.

Against her better judgment, she picked it up before doing anything else, no matter how much Vincent yelled at her.

Your first warning.

Miss Nala Nazarov

Hopefully this birdie beauty gets along with Tasha

As well as she got along with you

I never got to hear either of them scream but

Desirée screamed. A lot.

I wonder.

Can you scream as beautifully as she did?

A bird of prey always lives for the thrill of the kill

Run away, little Nightingale

Run away so I can hunt you down

Nala fell against the couch, Vincent still shouting, the sun still shining, and Robin still dying.

Somewhere, in some corner of time, Desirée's screams echoed, and Tasha fell asleep, never to awaken again.

Part 3

THE NIGHTINGALE TRIUMPHS

Chapter 34

The hospital was chaos. A heavy frost in the morning meant a plethora of accidents, both on the roads and at home. People came in and out of the emergency room, crying, bleeding, and in shock. Those who didn't need medical attention were asked to sit with their waiting loved ones or to kindly sit far, far away from the counter and the emergency doors.

This was where Nala sat, staring at the scenes unfolding before her. One man had a broken wrist, iced and wrapped, but in further need of care. He sat in front of Nala, rocking back and forth, muttering nothing in an attempt to take his mind off the pain. His only companion was a ten-year-old boy Nala figured was his son.

Two rows in front of her was a woman swaying back and forth in her seat, complaining of incredible stomach pains. Her family did their best to make her comfortable.

I'm hiding here. Nala's eyes both darted around the room and kept to themselves. She was alone, friendless, loverless. She didn't know where Vincent was. After he drove them to the hospital behind Robin's ambulance, he pulled the fact that he had been a healthy benefactor to this very hospital the previous year and got both him and Nala in to follow Robin even though Nala would much, much rather run away.

She hated hospitals. Hated them almost as much as she hated living in fear of…

Nala pulled the crumpled note from her pocket and stared at the words. If she didn't need further proof that Hawk was an assassin, the bird tracks signing the message said everything she needed to know.

What do I do? Why was Robin selected? *Why* was Robin dumped in Vincent's place? *To send a message. To me.* Robin was Nala's only friend, let alone in The Aviary. Not only would she send a message to Vincent and Nala, but she would send one to every other member.

Fear crept into Nala's blood again. *What do I do?*

Her phone continued to blow up with messages from Vincent. He tried calling her multiple times, but they went straight to voicemail. "*Where are you??? Come back here now! Do you know what's happening? You can't be by yourself!*"

Nala wanted to curl up on the plastic seats of the emergency room and pretend she was ten again, with her sister coddling her as she always did. Then she would eat some of her mother's home cooking. *I was supposed to cook for Vincent tonight.* The groceries were left to rot in his living room.

Eventually she had to get up and wander away. She didn't dare go outside. Besides, she needed to know how Robin was doing. When she last saw her, she was coming out of surgery still in critical condition.

Nala only sent one text. "*What room?*"

"*C67. Get here now.*"

She was too shaken up to be annoyed with his tone. *He's worried about me.* Nala was worried about him too. If Vincent thought *she* was brash? He hadn't looked in a mirror.

C67 was a good hike away, and by the time she got there Nala had encountered an unfamiliar name. *Clara Montgomery.* She stared at it, the only name by the single occupancy room.

It had to be Robin's real name. To see her as a woman named Clara was both natural and completely strange.

Robin – or was it Clara? – lay in her bed, hooked up to a million wires and tubes. Some feeding her, some monitoring her. A mask covered her face. *She can't breathe on her own…* Bandages covered her arms and upper chest. How many times was she sliced by glass? Was that what that was about? Nala felt woozy as she stood in the doorway.

Then she felt absolutely awful, because curled up on the side of the bed was Lucian, hand gripping his girlfriend's as the blanket beneath his face was constantly bathed in fresh slews of tears.

"Nala!"

Vincent sat in a waiting area not too far away. He stood up, jacket and tie off and in a crumpled pile in a seat behind him. For being so put together that morning when he left for work, he now looked so disheveled that Nala barely recognized him.

Indeed, she barely knew the man grabbing her arms and shaking her where she stood.

"What are you doing?" Vincent was crazed, his voice growling, hissing, sending ripples of anything but pleasure through Nala. "You don't leave my side. You don't wander off. You don't disappear from my line of sight. Do you understand me?"

He sounded like a frazzled father who had let go of his daughter's hand in the middle of a fair. Now that she had returned, Nala felt like that ten-year-old again. Only this time her sister wasn't there.

Vincent didn't wait for her to respond. He pulled her into his embrace, holding her head close to his chest and wrapping his arms so tightly around her that she forgot how to breathe. "I can't lose you too, Nala. You've gotta understand. I can't lose you too."

Nala lifted her arms and let her hands rest on his elbows. "I'm sorry. Is Robin okay?"

Vincent broke away from her enough to look into her eyes. "She's alive. That's all that matters. Because they intended to kill her."

Do I tell him about the note? As far as Nala knew, Vincent hadn't seen it. He was much too busy giving Robin CPR and yelling at Nala to get her head screwed back on and call 911.

So much had happened in so little time. The police came, cordoning off Vincent's living room and asking them a thousand questions they couldn't answer. Why was Robin there? How did they know her? What was her name? What had happened to her? The only reason neither Vincent nor Nala were currently in holding was because of Vincent's standing.

Nala fell back into his embrace. She didn't want to talk. She wanted to be held.

"Vincent."

Lucian stood in the doorway. If Nala didn't know better, she would say the man was drunk. His eyes were swollen. His cheeks pink. His staggering so erratic that he could barely keep himself standing straight.

"She'll be okay, Lucian."

"What if she's not?" Instead of letting his tears fall in front of them, Lucian slapped the doorway, rousing the attention of a nurse down the hall. "You heard the doctor. She'll be lucky to get through the night."

"She will."

"How do you fucking know?" Now the nurse was jogging, summoned by the loud voice. "What was she doing in your house anyway? What were you doing with Clara?"

Nala knew that look on Vincent's face. "*We could ask you the same thing, but we won't.*" "We found her there, Lucian. We've got questions too, but now is not the time to be searching for answers." That was a big fat lie.

But it placated Lucian enough to send him back into Robin's room, where he slumped into his seat. The last thing Nala heard before disengaging from Vincent was, "Your parents are coming, honey. Hold tight. Your mama wants to see you and I know you want to see her."

Nala wiped something from her eye as she insisted she go to the bathroom. Since it was within Vincent's sight, he let her go, and Nala was so, so relieved to duck in there and claw at her own face in private.

Tasha died alone. She was all alone. Desirée died screaming…

She pulled the note out of her pocket, staring at those damning words again and again. Poor Tasha. Poor Desirée. Poor Robin.

Poor Nala.

"Vincent…" She couldn't let him see those words. Not now. Not ever. Nala had half a mind to throw the note away, but she carefully folded it back up and put it in her pocket. She washed off her face, straightened out her half-soiled sweatshirt, pulled back her hair into a neat ponytail, and stepped back into the hospital.

A crowd of people ambled by. Family members visiting Robin's neighbor. They carried balloons, flowers, teddy bears, and half a dozen children of varying ages. This surge of pedestrians trapped Nala against the wall, and blocked her off from Vincent, whom she could vaguely see still sitting in the waiting room a good pace away.

Nala turned her head and saw someone else.

She was almost hard to recognize without her bold, glittery makeup and sequin dresses. Yet the hair – or lack of it – was unmistakable, as well as her dark skin in a sea of Scandinavian descendants wandering this way and that. She may have worn dark wash jeans and a light denim jacket, but Maggie always had the same stern expression no matter where she went.

Nala sucked in her breath. Yes, the most concerning member of The Aviary was definitely standing a few feet away, looking right at her frequent object of apparent disdain.

"Gale," Maggie said softly, hoisting a cloth tote bag on her shoulder. "I'm sorry. Robin's a nice person and doesn't deserve this."

Nala wanted to say that nobody deserved anything Crow ordered, but that was neither here nor there. "Thanks."

Maggie pulled one strap of her tote bag off her shoulder and fished out a large manila envelope. "I wanted to give this to you. Don't open it here, and don't show it to Vincent unless you're sure about it."

"What is it?" Nala snatched it anyway. *It's not heavy.* Papers, surely.

"No, not here. You might wanna have a drink before taking a peek, though."

That did not inspire any confidence.

"Is it you?" Nala finally whispered, the people behind her still clogging up the hallway with their balloons and laughter. "Are you the one who sent me that mail?"

Maggie rearranged her bag and pulled a pair of sunglasses onto her face. "His reach is far and unyielding. Don't trust anyone, especially in The

Aviary. There's a stinking rat in there who answers directly to Crow. He's on to you. They're all on to you. They know who you are and will either want you to play along like a good little birdie or…"

She didn't have to finish her sentence.

"If you know all that, then surely you know who I am too."

Maggie was not good at smiling as a way to relieve people of their worries. Yet she tried, her forced grin not doing much to make Nala feel better. Especially when she said, "Yes, Nala. I know who you are and what that man has done to you. I know what he's done to Vincent as well."

"Who are you?"

"Someone who is well aware of the danger that permeates wherever Xavier Crow goes. He's a textbook sociopath. He plays with toys until they break or he has to throw them away. If they have too much information… well, there are ways."

"They were sending me a message through Robin."

"Yes."

Nala shook her head. "What does he want me to do, then? Run away, scared for my life?"

"Yes."

"And what about you? Has he done something to you?"

Now Maggie frowned, her body turning away from Nala. "Just know that you're not the only one searching for justice." She turned back around after hitting the elevator button. "This conversation never, *ever* happened."

"Of course not."

Maggie disappeared into the first elevator that popped up. She did not wave goodbye.

Nala stuffed the manila envelope beneath her sweatshirt before going back to Vincent. Not once between their stay at the hospital and heading out to his car did she bring up Maggie, the envelope, or the assassin's note. She was still trying to process it all.

Chapter 35

Not only was the loft still a crime scene, but both Vincent and Nala agreed that it was much too dangerous to stay in. Vincent found them a hotel downtown and checked them in under assumed names. Nala worried about toiletries, but Vincent returned from the lobby with enough shit from the gift shop to get them through a week's stay.

Suffice to say, Nala had never owned so many pieces of "Portland" and "Oregon" merchandise.

"I'm going to need two suits delivered to my office by tomorrow afternoon," he said into a phone while they ate their dinner of takeout. "I know it's short notice, Andrew. I don't give a shit. I can't go home and I need clean suits. Do *you* want to be the one responsible for running the dry cleaning? Didn't think so."

Nala said nothing through the course of the evening. When Vincent was in the bathroom, she took off her sweatshirt, making sure the manila envelope was secured within and everything folded neatly in a chair so Vincent wouldn't touch it. Since they were settling in for the night, she pulled her bra out from beneath her T-shirt and took off her jeans. The heater was on, meaning she could sit like this on the end of the bed without a care. Well, she had many cares, but that was beside the point.

The shower turned on. Vincent probably wanted his privacy to sort out his thoughts, so Nala tried to busy herself with the TV. *No good.* She turned it off, her eyes continuing to linger on her sweatshirt and the manila envelope she knew was in there. Should she look at it now? What was in there? Did she actually want to know?

Vincent's shower was short. Or maybe Nala spent that whole time staring at the floor, thinking about Maggie, Robin, and all the people Xavier Crow ever had hurt. Was Hawk his only hired help? Or did he have a crew of assassins around the world? Maybe Hawk was in charge of the PNW branch of killers.

When Vincent emerged from the bathroom, clad in nothing but a white terrycloth towel, all Nala could think was that she was glad to not be alone. How would have things went down if she still lived in Patrick's house? Shit, what had happened to Patrick? Anything? He was an annoying stoner, but didn't *deserve* that shit!

"Nala."

Although low, Vincent's voice was hardly soothing. Nala looked up from her folded legs and the breasts poking through her thin white T-shirt. *Don't tell me I'm inappropriate, boyfriend.* She didn't see lust in his eyes.

Perhaps it wasn't lust, but his next few actions were definitely fueled by something as powerful.

"Vin…" Nala's mouth was covered with his, his intentions clear when he snatched the back of her neck and let his towel fall to the floor. *Whoa!* Nala flung her arms behind her, bracing herself against the bed as her boyfriend inhaled her throat and sucked her nipples through the cotton of her shirt. She moaned, involuntarily, her mind trying to catch up with her body as it quickly turned to thoughts of sex.

He said little, preferring to rub his body against Nala, kiss her skin wherever he could find it, and gently tug on her ponytail whenever his hand wandered up that way. When he did speak, it was with embittered desperation. "Please, Nala," he said. "I need you."

She needed him too.

"Okay."

"Okay?"

This time it was her who started kissing first.

She didn't expect him to be gentle, but she also didn't expect the frenzy that erupted once she gave him consent to do whatever he wanted. As it turned out, it was what Nala wanted too. While she was sure Vincent acted on his own desires and nothing more, it was almost as if he read her energy and decided to throw them both into a sexual hysteria that would hopefully either knock them out or make them forget what happened that day. Or both, if the world suddenly turned into a perfect place.

I don't care what he does to me. Just make me forget. Surely, Vincent was on that same wavelength. He sucked her skin hard, leaving behind red bruises that would take more than a day to go away. His hands squeezed her, from her breasts to her ass, taking stock in her body and making sure it was still there, still warm, and still breathing. *I'm here, Vincent. They didn't get me.* Likewise, she pawed his muscles and ran her fingers along his fine hairs in an effort to imprint everything about him into her eternal memory.

Nothing was as sweet as when he ripped her lingerie off her hips, his hardness immediately coming for her with almost no warning.

She cried out in both awe and pain as he shoved himself in, grunting into the crook of her neck while the rest of his body completely overpowered her. *Yes, yes, make me forget. Take me over and let me know I have nothing to worry about but what we do together.* She was ready, she was willing. Nala wanted him fucking her even if it meant her body hurt and her thighs regretted it in the morning.

"More," she whimpered, her Vincent growling in frustration as he tried to do too much too quickly. "Don't worry about hurting me! *Oh!*"

Once he was in, nothing mattered anymore.

Sometimes he embraced her tightly, bringing their bodies harmoniously together as he thrust as hard as he could into her small body. And sometimes he sat up, slamming his hands on either side of her as he told her to open her eyes and look into his. Nala did. Every time she did she felt like she was disappearing to another planet, another galaxy. Vincent filled her in ways no other vice could. Thank the heavens, because it was all Nala needed.

He's here. I'm here. We're okay. That's what's most important.

Whether he tired of the intimacy or wasn't comfortable enough as is, Vincent eventually released Nala and rolled her over onto her stomach, his hands grabbing her hips and pulling her up toward him. Nala deferred immediately, letting her legs spread over his as he grabbed the base of his cock and directed it inside her again. She barely had time to bask in the relief of having him inside her again before he was pounding into her, his anger, his fear, and a thousand tons of frustration channeling into Nala's body as she grabbed the comforter beneath her fingers and moaned loudly into the hotel pillow.

She didn't need him to talk dirty tonight. Every stroke of his cock and pinch of her ass and shoulders told her that Vincent *needed* her. He was right in the moment, whether his brain was in reality or somewhere else too. *I'm helping him and he's helping me.* This wasn't lovemaking, per se. This was searching for evidence that someone else was alive – and then searching for peace.

"Fuck me," she groaned into the pillow, feeling his thrusts increase in speed as his skin smacked against hers. He probably couldn't hear her under these conditions. It didn't matter. "Fuck me!"

She knew he was close to orgasm when he grabbed her by the collar of her shirt and yanked hard, the cotton tearing against her skin while his cock impaled her and began to swell.

There was a layer of primal desire to his actions. Particularly when he shoved her down into the pillow and released into her, one wave of liquid warmth after another filling her and taking her to a level of comfort she rarely felt, with Vincent or not. *I'm his. I'm protected. No one will come near me if they know he's here.* Was that how her ancestors did things out in the wild? Have sex to keep predators away? *Think of all the noise it creates. All that rustling and moaning. And then the smell should be enough to keep the asshole tribe from infiltrating for another night.* Would that work in the 21st Century? Nala had to believe it to get through the next few minutes.

That and a hard, rolling orgasm on her end helped. If she didn't start coming before Vincent, she could always count on his jumpstarting hers, and vice versa. They were well synced that way.

Vincent squeezed her hips so hard that it hurt, but Nala did not protest. She needed to feel him buried within her, doing what he did best at the end of a rough round of sex – make her feel like this moment was the only thing in the world that mattered.

"Shit," he muttered, slipping out of her and collapsing nearby. Nala's hips dropped to the bed, his seed already attempting a great escape. Vincent did not stop it. Nor did Nala, who was too tired and too worn out from the day to do anything besides letting him get all over the comforter. "Shit, shit, shit."

Nala didn't know what that meant. Either Vincent was finally relieved, or he was more pent up than ever.

She didn't hang around to find out.

"Where are you going?" he asked, as if he had initiated snuggling and she rejected it. "Did I hurt you?"

"No." Nala stood beside the bed, losing the torn T-shirt and pulling her neatly folded sweatshirt into her arms. She was naked, so exposed and so vulnerable that she almost considered what ran down her thigh to be some barrier of protection, like the hair on her head. "I really need to go to the bathroom."

"Hurry back."

"Uh huh." Nala headed for the bathroom. "You sit there and suffer through your recovery period. Round 2 is coming up in twenty minutes. I want that same thing again." And again. And again. "You're young. You can do it." That was the last thing she said before disappearing into the bathroom and latching the door behind her.

Nala sat on the toilet and tossed her sweatshirt onto the side of the tub, pulling out the manila envelope and finally opening the damn thing.

It was a large, glossy photo. That much Nala could tell without pulling it out very far. She was in no hurry, either, because written on the back, near the top where her fingers smudged the material, was a handwritten note in Xavier Crow's careful hand: Xavier and Raven.

The missing photo from his office. Nala held it in her hands.

It could not be anything good.

It could not be anything good.

That was her mantra as she slowly slid the photo from the envelope, knowing full well what she would see, and yet denying it at the same time.

Her body shook. If Vincent thought he was angry earlier? Nala was so disgusted, so livid that every fiber of her being vibrated, threatening to give *her* an honest to God heart attack at the age of twenty-one. Or at least a *seizure.*

"You fucking pig bastard," she snarled, nails clawing at the face of Xavier Crow, haughty and amused with himself as he wrapped his arm around a woman slightly shorter than him. *Raven.* A woman with a svelte body, long, black hair and the kind of smile that inspired confidence and warmth, even when that smile looked tentative and… scared.

Nala threw the photo down on the bathroom floor, her shout of exasperation probably alerting Vincent on the other side of the wall.

"I'm going to get you," Nala muttered, hands covering her mouth as she leaned on her knees. "I'm going to get you, and when I'm done with you, they won't know who you are anymore because I fucking *destroyed* you!"

Her eyes kept going to the picture of Tasha. Her heart and mind were full of darkness.

Entry #16

A girl, whose name I shall omit, was tortured and dropped off in my home tonight. It's the work of Crow if I have ever seen it.

To say that Nala and I are in danger is an understatement. I must protect her at all costs. If I lose her, I have lost everything.

Chapter 36

Nala's existence was based in a dark, conspicuous cloud that loomed over her head for the next week. Her life was silence. Wake up. Work. Change hotels. Dinner. Sex. Sleep.

Nothing stood out. Everything refused to leave her alone. The haze Nala found herself in was unlike anything she ever experienced before – worse than the fog of grief she had swam in twice in her short life. Grief made sense. Everyone experienced grief. There were even stages to track one's progress through grief. Were there stages to figure out when Nala was done being *so fucking angry?*

She was used to the kind of anger that manifested itself in fits, tears, and finally, stone-cold acceptance as one fell asleep in the hopes of waking up refreshed. This wasn't normal anger. This was poison brewing in her body. She was in so much shock from the photo – which she kept hidden in a backpack Vincent bought her to keep her clothes in – that her mind both rejected it and chewed it over, tasting every bitter, rotten morsel as if it were the only sustenance she was allowed.

It was a dangerous way to live. One day she woke up and it was Thursday, and she had no idea how she had arrived there from Monday. The only thing that could have spared her from this ill fate was Vincent, but he was in his own toxic world, and they enabled one another until the only words they exchanged had to do with hotel locations and what to order for dinner.

I'm fucked up. He's fucked up. This manifested every night when Vincent emerged from his shower and took Nala wherever she waited – for by the second night, she recognized the pattern and appropriately prepared herself. Sometimes she sat on the couch, watching nothing on TV, and the next thing she knew she was beneath Vincent's body, succumbing to the frenzy of intense, sudden sex. Other times she flopped on the bed the moment she heard his shower turn off. Once, she sat at a table – until she was rather *plastered* against the table.

Like most sensations, these rough rounds of sex were a blur to Nala. Yet they were a single ounce of escape. Whenever Vincent wandered into the bathroom to take his shower, Nala became more alive than she had been in days. *Take me away from here. Make me forget.* Unfortunately, the only words they said to each other during the act were grunts, moans, and the occasional wail if something was exceptionally memorable.

By the third day Nala's body warned her that she couldn't keep doing this. Not the rough stuff. She was sore, but her brain in such a haze that she barely registered the discomfort. It wasn't until the fifth night, when Vincent finally noted the way she shuffled around the hotel room as if she had been sitting split-legged for a week. *I have, dumbass. Sitting on your cock.* That night he found other ways to take her and give her the escapist pleasure she deserved.

It was funny. Until that week, Nala was still counting the amount of times they had sex. *I only needed two hands to do it.* By the end of that week, however, she no longer had any idea how many times Vincent was inside her, let alone until completion. Sometimes she stood at work, trying to count when she should be counting tank tops and torn jeans instead. *Has it been ten times now? Or thirteen? Did the head I give him last night count? Of course it counts, duh. Okay, I'm still confused…* It was better than constantly wondering if an assassin was going to burst through the door and take her out, leaving her to die in a pile of donated jerseys.

In all her wondering, she didn't stop to think of something crucial until Friday night, when she and Vincent stayed in a mid-tier hotel on the outskirts of downtown.

He had emerged from his shower naked, as usual, dragging Nala across the bed and using his mouth to leave a mark on her neck. Within minutes he was between her legs, fucking her with the rawest power he could muster while she groaned in the ecstasy she was desperate to embrace.

She didn't think of this crucial thing until he came within her, as he usually did, with his hands holding her hips down and his animalistic growls echoing in her ears. Nala came down from her own orgasm feeling less like a sex-starved demon and more like a forest animal in heat.

Oh, no.

Vincent rolled off her and stared at the ceiling, chest gradually stilling from heavy breaths. His hand searched for Nala's until their fingers lightly clasped together. Nala turned her head away and stared at the dark window overlooking the river.

"We forgot my pills."

Vincent's eyes bored into the back of her head. "What?"

"My birth control pills. They're still at your apartment. I haven't taken one in almost a week now."

"I'll send someone to get them tomorrow." Not the first time Vincent had an assistant go into his loft and pick up a few things.

"Dumbass. All it takes is one missed pill, and we've been fucking like dirty rabbits all week."

"So then what?"

"So I could be pregnant."

Vincent sat up on his arms. "*Could* be pregnant?"

"I'm just saying. We're both young, healthy… and you come in me."

"You only thought to tell me about this now?"

"Excuse me for being in a shitty fog all week. I didn't think about it until now. Other things have been on my mind."

"Fuck."

"Don't worry about it. I only wanted you to know. I need my pills. Or something."

"Or something?"

"Look, man, you're shooting a loaded weapon at me and I no longer have my bullet-proof vest on."

"Mother fucker."

"I'm trying not to be a mother right now. Let alone a fuckin' one."

Vincent slapped one hand on his face and groaned. First time in a while Nala didn't hear a pleasurable one. "I will get you your pills, and I'll get some damned condoms."

"Honestly, after tonight, I want a break. I love fucking you and all, but after this past week I feel like a very used fleshlight down there. Your pounding game has been too strong and I'm starting to feel it."

She expected Vincent to be testy with her, but instead she heard the first lighthearted joke from him in a very, very long time. "I always knew I had it in me."

"You're a dick. I hope you know that."

His arm wrapped her, followed by his strong, not-so-clean-anymore body folding around hers in the most protective embrace he had shown her all week. "We've got enough to worry about right now, darling." Shivers went through Nala like water through a river. "Let's focus on what we can control right now. We need to figure out what to do next."

Yes, next. Nala looked in the direction of her backpack, wondering if she would ever have the courage to face – let alone talk about – that photo Maggie happened to hand to her.

***

When Vincent finally had some time off that weekend, they formed a plan. This came shortly after hearing word that Robin was not only up and walking, but slated to go home in another week. The police came to Vincent's office no fewer than three times, asking questions, subtly threatening to take him in, and finally leaving him alone as – even though

Robin was left to die in his home – every path toward Vincent being the primary suspect turned into a dead end.

They could not implicate Xavier Crow or even Hawk, whose real identity was as vague as Robin's had been before she was admitted to a hospital. Not only would he create his own dead ends, but it would put a bigger mark on Vincent and Nala's backs. There were no more threats or attacks as of yet, but Vincent didn't know that Robin was merely a warning. As long as they kept their heads down and stayed in line, Xavier would not try to touch them. Yet.

Their plan was terrible, but it was all they could come up with: Vincent was going to hire the best lawyer he could find, even better than the one he usually had on retainer. This lawyer would hear their side of the story, dole out his professional advice, and well… they would go from there.

Nala laughed to hear it.

"That lawyer is going to tell you what you already know," she said, draped across his body on a couch. His hand stiffened around her leg. "The only way to take Crow down is to either wipe him out with our bare hands or have so much irrefutable evidence that doesn't even make it into the hands of police. No way. We need to get evidence, make copies, and send it to the press… that preferably aren't owned by him. Does he own any media?"

"I think he has some stakes in a few newspapers. Not sure." Vincent rubbed his chin. "What kind of evidence would we even get? Come on, Nala. We've already tried robbing his office, and nobody will tell us a damn thing. All we've got is that letter about a previous couple. That's not enough. It's conjecture."

"I know. That's why we're going to get a confession out of him."

"Excuse me?"

"The only evidence that would ever be strong enough is if he's caught on camera committing a crime – which he would never be – or if we get him on tape confessing. I'll do it, Vincent. I'll get to him about Tasha."

"You're talking crazy. Don't."

"It's the only chance we have."

"If we do go that route out of total desperation…"

"We will."

"…Then it will have to be the most carefully planned thing in the universe."

"I'm not saying let's go bust down his door this weekend, but you know I'm right, Vincent."

He pulled her into his arms, lips nibbling her cheek and the bottom of her ear. "You're dangerous when you're right." When his hand went to his breast, she shrugged him off. "Sorry."

"I'm not ready for that again yet." Nala disengaged from him and sat up on her side of the couch.

"Have I hurt you?"

"No." The soreness was gone. *I needed a break. Not a trip to the ER while some camera crew bursts in and asks how sex sent me there.* "It's not only that. There are other things."

"Like what?"

Like sure I like it rough, sir, but not every damn time. "Maybe a girl wants some tenderness once in a while."

"To be fair, this past week has been a doozy for the both of us."

He didn't say.

They curled up in bed later that night, Vincent stroking her temple until she finally fell asleep against his chest. *Okay, good. Now give me some tenderness in the other kind of bed.* Nala remembered the way he *made love* to her the night she cried in his car.

The fog slowly lifted. The haze dispersed. Soon, all Nala was left with was a healthy dosing of fear, regret, and a huge pile of secrets she was keeping from Vincent. They would have to be released soon.

Entry #17

Nightingale and I are doing what she calls "hotel hopping." Since I currently do not trust my own home, I have had no choice but to move us from hotel to hotel in the vain hope of keeping an assassin off our tails. Although there has been no formal threat, fi*nding a half-dead woman in one's home will tick off the paranoia.*

Nevertheless, Nightingale and I are not living the healthiest of lives. There is something ticking like an old and worn clock beneath everything we do. We are time bombs. Every day we come closer and closer to losing who we really are.

All I want to do is sink into her body and forget all the pain, all the worries plaguing me at every turn. Used to be I escaped into my work to forget my troubles. Now I want to escape into Nightingale, both literally and figuratively.

I didn't think it was possible to find another woman to want like this. I hate myself for *being so distracted by her while people die all around us.*

Chapter 37

An invitation was stuffed in Vincent's mailbox the next time his assistant Andrew drove by to check on things. *And to set off any bombs there, let's be real.* Nala had suggested that Vincent hire a temporary bodyguard, but Mr. I Box For My Workouts shrugged her off. Yet when Vincent brought an invitation to their hotel room Monday evening, Nala turned milk white and excused herself to the bathroom to vomit. *Fuck, I'm pregnant.* She knew worrying about it this far away from her supposed period would only make things worse. But even though she was back on her pill and Vincent brought her two pregnancy tests – that she still had yet to take – Nala worried about everything.

She emerged from the bathroom to find him composing a polite response at the table. "*Due to previous work commitments and the sorrow we feel for our fellow indisposed club member, Nightingale and I must regretfully decline this week's invitation. We shall make sure to put on a grand show the next time we can make it.*"

When Nala asked what this work commitment was, Vincent announced he was taking two days off from work starting the next day and driving to the coast.

"Why the coast?" She asked this, and yet Nala was already packing for another hotel move. *He better get me clothes for the beach.* "You'd think we'd want to be as far away as possible."

"Because it's a good place to go on short notice. Be ready to go early in the morning. I want out of here. I can't breathe."

Nala made sure everything was delicately packed up before going to bed that night. Sure enough, at the crack of dawn, Vincent dragged her out of bed and into his car so they could start the long, *long* drive to their destination.

When he said the coast, Nala assumed somewhere around Astoria or Cannon Beach, a respectable hour or two away from Portland depending on weather and traffic. But *noooo.* The moment they were in the car, they were going south on the interstate, Nala's heavy eyes making her fall asleep again until she woke up three hours south in Eugene. It was only then that Vincent finally headed west, into the mountains.

Nala was used to sparse landscapes and utter solitary living. She had lived in Nevada for years, after all. Rural Oregon was different. The mountains and hillsides were covered in evergreen trees, trailing to wild rivers and weaving in and out of suspension bridges and tiny hamlets that looked like they never left the 1930s, 1950s if they were lucky. These blew by as the sun was shining upon them, a riot of oranges and golds spreading across water, asphalt, and the hood of Vincent's black car.

"Where are we going?" she asked, sleepy.

He kept his eyes on the road, sunglasses masking them from the harsh angles of the sunrise. "Somewhere far away from the bullshit. Go back to sleep. It'll be another couple of hours."

The radio came back on once they broke free of the mountains and turned onto Highway 101. Nala kept her eyes out for the ocean, but Vincent informed her – to the tune of John Mellencamp coming in and out of the speakers – that they wouldn't see it for a while. Still sleepy, Nala leaned her head back and willed herself into another nap. This was the most sleep she had in days.

She didn't know the name of the town they stopped in. Some port, some bay, some Native American word or some English word nobody knew the meaning to anymore. Mispronounced French words abounded. Even the Spanish titles were hilariously off. Down here, the citizens lived in their insular worlds where they welcomed tourists – as long as they had the money. Vincent had plenty of money to spare, as evident when he got them one of the nicest hotel rooms in town and immediately went out to buy some snacks and even more spare clothes for Nala. Andrew had brought some of her shirts and jeans, but he refused to go near even her clean underwear. Over the past week, Vincent gradually brought her the plainest cotton fare around. Today, in celebration of them getting out of Dodge, he dropped a pack of colorful underwear on her as she continued to snooze in the hotel bed.

By the time she was awake, Vincent sat on the patio overlooking the beach. *I didn't even notice where we were.* It was a cloudy, slightly drizzly day on the coast. Then again, what day wasn't that time of year? Nevertheless, Vincent looked content sitting at a small bistro table wearing his jeans and hoodie, snacking on a bag of potato chips as if that was what one did when they came to the Oregon coast.

Nala leaned in the doorway, shaking off the chilly breeze by wrapping her own sweatshirt closer to her body. "Can I join you? Or are you contemplating the Pacific Ocean by yourself?"

Vincent pulled out the other chair without another word. He also pushed the rest of his chips in Nala's direction after she sat down. She chewed on one, letting the salty, crunchy texture wash over her tongue in tandem to the salty ocean waves crashing on the beach.

"You ever been here before?" Vincent asked.

Nala shook her head. "I've never been to the beach before." She tried to not look too impressed.

"What? You lived in Oregon before."

"I lied a little. I've been to the beach when I was a kid, but it was such a long time ago that I barely remember it." Before her father died, they would sometimes take short family trips when they could afford it. A couple of those trips veered toward Cannon Beach or Newport during the height of summer, when it was sweltering in Portland. Nala's parents, who were not used to such a hot climate, would pack up and go somewhere cooler along with the rest of the Willamette Valley.

"If I had known that, I would've brought you here sooner."

Nala smiled in his direction. "Oh, would you? Taking me on romantic getaways, are we?"

"If that's what you want to call it."

"It is."

Vincent smiled back at her, but did not say anything.

Does this man love me? It wasn't the first time Nala wondered that, but it was the first time she seriously considered it. Vincent was not a man who shared his emotions. Not verbally, anyway. She had felt the gamut of them through sex. Anger, bitterness, grief, guilt, shame… no, not merely negative emotions. There had been a lot of joy and gratefulness in there too. Sometimes simple tranquility. Except he had never verbalized any of these emotions.

That was okay. Nala didn't need to hear "I love you" from anyone. Not from her sister, not from her mother, and certainly not from Vincent. She had learned the cues over the years. A kind gesture. A small, tender smile. Words of worry and praise. Her family had never been big into expressing positive emotions the traditional way. Tasha was the first one to start saying "I love you" to family members. She was also the last person to tell Nala that she was loved.

She slid her hand across the small table and brushed against Vincent's. He did not shrug her off. Instead, he looked at her and said, "Let's go for a walk."

With only chips in her stomach and the plain clothes on her back, Nala got up and followed Vincent to the beach.

The sand was hard and compact here. *The tide must have gone out.* Sure enough, kelp and seaweed were strung here and there, with pieces of fresh driftwood beached for the crabs to climb over. Far, far away was the stench of some poor dead creature coming down on the wind. In time, they either walked far enough away or Nala's nose chose to no longer recognize it. *I'm hoping for both.* After the week she had, the last thing she wanted to see was some poor dead sea lion decaying on the beach. Or whatever it was.

Nala pulled her hair back into a ponytail, tucked it into her sweatshirt, and pulled up her hood so her hair would stop whipping in her face. Sometimes the breeze died down enough that she could stop and admire the loud waves rolling upon another, tossing boats around and drawing in squawking seagulls. Other times the wind was so strong that she felt like she walked against a hurricane. The only creatures on the beach not affected by the wind were dogs, running up and down as if in the most blissful hysterics. Their owners stayed far away, sometimes throwing sticks, but otherwise sitting in peace with their camera phones or books.

It was far from tourist season, so they mostly had the beach to themselves. Even so, Nala still felt like she was in her own world, where Vincent strayed at the edges but never committed to fully crossing her borders. Sometimes he stopped to contemplate the water. Other times he stopped to dust off a shell or throw a stick for a dog that ran by. Most of the time, however, he ambled aimlessly, Nala along for the ride.

Yeah, that about summed up their whole relationship.

"Are you hungry?" he eventually asked, facing a steep staircase that went up to a restaurant. "Let's get lunch."

Seafood, of course. Seafood and coleslaw for him, while Nala loaded her plate with French fries. He stole some of hers occasionally, and she was in a good enough mood from the fresh sea air to not chastise him for it. Their seats, overlooking the beach down below, gave them privacy from other diners, but not from the waitress making the rounds in and out.

"We get a lot of cute couples around here," she finally said, bringing Vincent his bill. "You guys take the cake this week. If I didn't know any better, I would say you guys are brother and sister." She stopped, suddenly horrified. "Oh my God, if you are, I am so sorry."

Nala turned her lips downward, but Vincent laughed, taking out a wad of cash. "That's not my sister. That's my girlfriend."

The waitress sighed in relief before walking away with Vincent's payment. Whatever she did with his generous tip was on her.

"So I'm still your girlfriend?" Nala asked. Her hood slipped down her head, freeing some of her long hairs as they blew around in the breeze.

"Yes." Vincent took her hand on the table and gave it a single squeeze. "I'm sorry I've been a terrible boyfriend this past week."

"Don't apologize for any of that." Nala shrugged. "You've done the best that you can. We only decided who we really are to one another a moment before…"

"Yes. Before Robin."

Nala looked away before she could see the anger alight in his eyes again. "I know they picked her because she was my friend. I can't help but feel guilty." That was an understatement.

"I know, but trust me, they wouldn't have ruffled Lucian's feathers if he weren't on Crow's shitlist too. I don't know what he did to piss Crow off, but I'm sure it was a double-whammy. Freak us out, and scare Lucian shitless. I don't doubt that Robin was okay to die. If they only wanted to hurt her a little to send a message, they wouldn't have gone to such violent…"

"Stop it." Nala kept thinking about that note. "*Desirée screamed a lot.*" She didn't need more visuals.

"I'm sorry. It's stuff I've been thinking about."

"You think I haven't been too?" Vincent didn't know. He still didn't know what Nala did.

His hand returned to hers. Their fingers interlocked across the table, a stray French fry flying off the balcony thanks to the wind. "I don't want to think about it anymore today. I only want to think about you."

Nala lifted her chin, eyes meeting his. His steely blue visage had softened for the first time in a whole damn week. This wasn't the man who emerged from a shower and took her to crazy places. This was the man who held her in the car, who took her to a soccer game, and who first showed her that sea of stars flowing gently by the universe.

Technically, it was the man she fell in love with.

"There's nothing else we can do today about our situation," Vincent went on to say. "Besides make the most of it. I'm here. You're here. We can breathe a little. Let's pretend none of that other shit exists. For today."

Nala couldn't help but smile. "I'd like that. I've never had the chance to fully appreciate what it means to have a boyfriend. Not with you, anyway."

"Then what are we waiting for? A sign from God?"

"Maybe."

Vincent scooted back his chair and stood, hand still interlocked with Nala's. "We're at the damn beach already. What other sign do you need?"

Absolutely none.

It took a few minutes for Nala to force herself to relax, but once she was able to take her cue from Vincent, everything fell into place.

The wind never died down, and the occasional sprinkle of rain washed over them, but sometimes the sun came out and glistened in the water, in the sand, and against Nala's skin as she and Vincent wandered up and down the shoreline hand-in-hand. The poor man had never been shown how to skip rocks, so whenever the water was still enough, Nala tossed one at the ocean and watched it take two, three great skips before sinking. Vincent wasn't quite as talented.

They packed their pockets with shells and agates that would eventually be emptied out somewhere else. They picked up sticks and poked bubbles in the kelp, Nala making heinous faces as the slimy stuff slid around the sand. And they definitely entertained the constant stream of dogs running up and down the beach, happy to jump in the surf and roll around in the sand.

A break was called for eventually, and they sat on a large piece of driftwood lodged deep into the compacted sand. Vincent still had a stick from his walk and, to no surprise of Nala's, started writing foreign languages in the sand.

"What in the world is that?" Nala knew what it was, but not what it meant. She wrapped her arms around his and leaned her head against his shoulder. "I imagine you sitting in restaurants by yourself jotting down codes on napkins."

"I do. Especially on my lunch breaks. Never hurts to figure out the next thing I'm working on."

"Is that what that is? Homework?"

Vincent covered his current codes with sand, erasing them. "It's calming. Some kids wrote stories or drew pictures. I did math. Numbers are great. They always make sense and fall right into place. Only not everyone yet knows what places they can fall into. It always makes sense, though."

Speak for yourself. Nala was as good at math as she was at Cyrillic. Which was to say… not at all. *Why do I put myself down like that?* She stared at the numbers, the symbols, and the equations they formed. When Vincent had his base down, he moved on to writing codes.

"You should teach me what this means one day," she said, attempting to sound chipper. "I'd like to be able to admire your work on the back end. Not just the front end when I punch shit in my phone."

He glanced at her, but his attention remained fully on his numbers and codes. "If you'd like. I'm not a great teacher, though."

"Oh, you'll find ways to teach me." Nala squeezed his arm and rubbed her cheek against his sweatshirt. *Damn, it really smells like him.* "I'm really susceptible to certain forms of tutoring. You have no idea."

That made Vincent keep a careful hold on his stick. "Sounds like you would get constantly distracted. Or I would."

"Shut up!" Nala drew her legs up on log and practically climbed on Vincent's back, her arms wrapped over his shoulders. "Now take me home to my castle. Your princess demands it."

Vincent rocked back and forth beneath her weight, stick dropping to the sand as he hurried to fish out his phone and take a picture of his codes. "What do I do with a princess once I get her home? Do I get a ransom?"

"I ain't got any money. I'm a poor princess."

Vincent stood up, grabbing Nala's legs and pulling them forward around his waist. His knees bore the brunt of their combined weight until he was able to start walking across the beach. "Excellent. I'll take my ransom in other forms, then. I hear you're not a virginal princess."

"Haha, you're funny!"

"I aim to entertain you on our journey to the castle, your *highness.*"

He walked slowly back to the hotel, careful to not lose grip of Nala's legs while she in turn clutched carefully to his torso. On one hand it was so commonplace that Nala thought nothing of it, but on the other she realized that this was perhaps the most intimate thing they had ever done together. That wasn't sex, anyway.

It was easy to pretend that they had no problems outside of themselves as she leaned her head against the back of his and watched the ocean continue to fold upon itself. The ocean didn't care about the affairs of men and women. It didn't care that there were powerful, evil people who made others' lives hell. All it cared about was the moon's gravity and the creatures swimming within.

Vincent let her down when they reached the hotel. Once they were outside their door, however, he pulled her back up into his arms, mumbling something about claiming his ransom.

"I wanna make love," Nala muttered, her body floating through the air before Vincent lowered her to their bed. "You know what I mean."

He loomed over her, his countenance too kind to be real. "Funny. I was thinking the same thing."

"That you know what I mean?"

"Yes. That." His following kiss was exactly what Nala wanted. No, *needed.*

Foreplay had never been so slow, so gentle. Vincent's hands lightly touched Nala's body, teasing her here, taunting her there. Every time she sighed, he kissed her, sometimes pulling off an article of clothing and other times acting as if he would put them on again. When Nala tired of his teasing, she yanked off her clothes herself – and then his, happy to see his familiar body be anything but rough for once.

Now it was her turn to cover his body in kisses. Now it was his turn to lay back and learn what it was like to be doted on for a change. Even so, Vincent didn't let her get far, for he had every intention of smothering her with his affection. Even though Nala wanted to protest, she didn't, because this suited her fine. Particularly the part where Vincent disappeared between her legs and lovingly took her to the height of pleasure with nothing but his tongue.

"Shit," he said afterward, kneeling between her legs and unzipping his jeans. "I forgot a condom."

Nala rolled her eyes. "It's a bit late for that. I'm back on the pill again. If I'm already pregnant, then I am. You ain't knocking me up today, though. I ain't worrying about it until my body says otherwise." Nala was sure as hell not lingering on that today. *I'll cross that bridge if we ever get to it.*

"Did you take those tests?"

Nala shook her head. "I'll do it when we get back. My period's not due for another couple of weeks so I guess I should." She *tsked* in her throat. "What are you waiting for? Besides, I don't want to use a condom. If I'm making love to my boyfriend, I want to properly feel him, damnit."

"As it so happens," Vincent growled, delectably, as he slowly pushed her into the bed, "I prefer the same."

"Yes, that's right." Nala turned her head, letting him gently suck the side of her throat as he guided her legs around his waist and searched for her opening with the head of his erection. "I demand the highest form of lovemaking."

"Oh, so they're *your* demands?"

"Today I'm power bottoming."

"Is that what it's called?"

"Uh huh."

He silenced her with a kiss the moment he entered her.

Nala had almost forgotten what it was like to make love to this side of Vincent. Just because the sex was more methodical did not make it any less passionate, however. It was simply a different kind of passion: a kind that fueled her with every good feeling imaginable. Good feelings that reawakened her ability to open her heart and reach out to another human being. From the way Vincent lightly groaned into her ear with every slow, easy thrust, she had a feeling he felt the same way.

It all felt lighter, airier than the very air they breathed. When Vincent sat back, drawing Nala into his lap and letting her control their thrusts as she looked into his eyes, she felt like she was racing into the stratosphere, where she flew high, higher, highest with the stars twinkling in the daylight.

"Vincent," she whispered, arms wrapped tightly around him as she moved up and down in his lap. "Don't let me go."

His strength tightened around her as well, lips maneuvering to her ear. "I won't. I'm never letting you go, Nala."

Emotional – hormonal, really – tears appeared in her eyes as she prepared to ride him for all they were both worth. "Good. Now do it."

He did.

The way his body surged against hers, lifting her higher off the bed with every movement, allowed Nala to forget every ounce of trouble in her mind and body. The only things that existed were Vincent and this moment they created together. The more their passion inflamed, the more Nala opened her heart.

Good feelings. Only good feelings. This was a purge from the previous week. From all the tragic events and terrible news. Nala wouldn't allow herself to think of any of it. There were still wonderful things in the world, and even a pair as cynical as them could find some sliver of happiness.

"Vincent," she said again, her climax cresting. "I love you!"

He pushed back onto the bed, her voice a loud, silvery echo as his hips increased their power in preparation of claiming her for the day. *Remind me that I'm yours.* Nala confessed her love once again, bracing herself against his strong shoulders as her legs shook in the air and Vincent expressed himself without words.

They lay in content silence afterward, Nala's legs strewn over his and his fingers brushing against her forehead. Such peace had seemed unachievable. Yet now, to the sounds of waves, gulls, and wind, Nala felt so much at peace that she wondered if she even continued to exist.

"Can I ask you something?" she finally said, turning her head toward him. "It's something I've wondered for a long time now, but I never asked because I didn't want to upset you." Now seemed like the best chance.

"Go on."

His voice was soft, but trepidation lurked. Nala would have to be careful with her tone. "Did you and Desirée… do the BDSM stuff?"

The answer was obvious, but Vincent had never been clear about it before. He either talked about BDSM or Desirée. Never together.

Now, Nala was told what she already knew. "Yes. It was how we met. A group at Stanford." He chuckled, surprising Nala. "We already knew each other from our studies, but it was the first time we found out the other was into kink. I asked her out a week later. We built up to it, over time. Learning each other's limits, and the like. Our first time was… well, I will always remember it."

Nala snuggled closer to him. "She wasn't your first in the lifestyle."

"No, but she was the first serious one."

Nala wasn't sure how that worked, but left well enough alone. She nuzzled her nose against his arm. "I was serious, you know. What I said now. I really do love you."

The last thing Nala expected was a word. Indeed, Vincent turned over, pulling her into his arms and breathing softly against the top of her head. Kisses dotted her face, as well as the most tender hand she ever had the pleasure of feeling on her skin. Nala took this hand and kissed it, letting it drape across her face as the scent of sweat and the aches of the body overcame her, as if there were no other scent in the world to experience.

"It's okay," she muttered against his chest. "You don't have to say it."

His hold on her was firm, then firmer. Nala couldn't breathe for a small second, but it was the longest second in the world. When Vincent's fingers played with her hair… no, she didn't need to hear the words. The man loved her. There was no doubt in her mind or heart, but like he was not the most articulate man in the universe, neither was he likely to confess such a thing anytime soon. Not with his wounds from Desirée's death still so large in his heart.

The fact he came this far in his healing journey said enough already.

Nala submerged herself in their world a little longer, surfacing only when she had the courage to say what she had to convey to him in his afterglow.

"I've been hiding a couple of things from you," she said. "I didn't mean to… I couldn't face them myself, and you were upset with other things as well. So… give me a second."

She pulled herself out of bed, away from his strong arms and toward her backpack. She took the whole thing into the bathroom, where she washed up and went through what pitiful evidence she had. Showing Vincent the picture was the least of her concerns. Her biggest issue was the note left by Robin's would-be assassin. Mostly the line about Desirée screaming toward her death.

Nala pulled a marker from her backpack and scratched that out. *If* this were ever entered into some sort of evidence someday, the rest would be enough to implicate Hawk. Or so Nala hoped.

When she reemerged in the bedroom, Vincent was sitting up cross-legged, hands resting on either knee as he watched Nala cross in front of him and rejoin him on the bed. The first thing she handed him was the note, freshly purged of the most damning thing.

Vincent perused it, his eyes certainly lingering on the line Nala blacked out. However, she was glad he could no longer read it. *I don't want him relapsing into that anger.* If Nala never had to see him *that* angry again, she would be happy.

"This has to be Hawk," Vincent agreed. "I can't believe it's anyone else. The signature is everything… and she's being cheeky like she knows you well."

"The only thing I'm unsure about is who she's referring to in The Aviary. The person working directly for Crow."

"Do you think it's Maggie? Or Jay?"

Nala considered the dated patterns on the comforter. "No. I don't get the feeling that Maggie at least wants anything to do with Crow." She thought of the way that woman's brows furrowed whenever she spoke of The Aviary. She was doing her best to bite back disdain. "I don't know who it is. I mean, it's not Robin or Lucian, for sure. Hawk wouldn't implicate Lucian the same day she takes out Robin. That leaves two other couples." Sebastian and Quail. Joseph and Starling. Both were mostly enigmas to Nala. She thought they were couples trying to get by, but now…

"I wish you hadn't kept this from me," Vincent said softly. "I wish you had given it to me the moment you found it."

Do you know what you would have read? He must have, for he didn't ask about the crossed out line. There was sadness in his voice, though, as if he were forced to think of other unpleasant things. *Is he thinking about when he found out Desirée was dead?* Was he more upset that night than when Nala found out about Tasha's death? *As least she didn't scream.* All Nala knew about induced heart attacks was that they came in the form of poison. Tasha probably ingested something before leaving work, or maybe her water bottle was spiked… and then she fell asleep, never to awaken again. Poison completely undetected during autopsy. *It makes me sick.* At least she hadn't suffered…

Desirée, on the other hand…

"There's something else," Nala finally said, clearing her throat. She picked up the manila envelope and pulled the photo out, holding it to her chest so she wouldn't have to see her petrified sister in the arms of Xavier Crow. A sympathetic tear appeared in the corner of her eye, and she brushed it away before thrusting the photo in Vincent's chest.

He pulled it away and stared at it for a long time, occasionally turning the photo over to see the handwriting on the back.

"You remember those photos I took a picture of in his office? This was missing. It was labeled someone named Raven and everything." Nala covered her face with her hands. "I had no idea… I've tried so hard not to think about it."

"You said it was missing in there… how did you get it?"

Nala bit her lip. "Maggie gave it to me at the hospital."

"*Maggie?*"

Since having sex, that was the most emotion he had yet to show. Apparently his energy was coming back now.

"So, wait…" He put a hand on her shoulder. "When we were at the hospital last week, Maggie gave you this picture from Crow's office?"

"Yeah. She said… well, I can't remember what she said, but I didn't get the impression that it was a threat. She warned me about getting further involved, but not in a scary way. I think she was really looking out for me."

Vincent looked at the picture again. "Nala… this implicates something very, very disturbing."

"You think I don't know that?" Nala didn't want to think about it. She didn't want to think about her dear sister in the Aviary, let alone as Crow's *girlfriend.* Because it wasn't bad enough those facts existed. On top of everything else, there was this picture of Tasha looking so scared, so hesitant that Nala's mind kept going back to *she didn't want to.* Even now, Nala could not look directly at the picture. Every time she did, she felt another piece of herself swell up and die. "I don't know what to make of it. I have no other information. Tasha never talked about something like… this." Nala had replayed every phone conversation with her sister during the months leading up to her death. Yes, Tasha was becoming more paranoid toward the end… but did that have to do with her work, or with the unfortunate world she found herself in? Tasha *did* work directly under Crow. He would have had plenty of access to her.

Nala looked at Vincent. *Desirée worked directly beneath him too…*

It was one thing to see her sister that way. It was quite another for a man to see his *fiancée* that way. *The woman he talks about would have never done that.* Vincent never talked about Desirée straying… let alone with Crow! Then again, sometimes Vincent didn't mention anything at all.

"This is a lot to process." Vincent put the photo down with a shake of his head. "I'm sorry you ever had to see this. I will…" he looked away. "When we get back to Portland, I am going to ask around. I don't know *who* I will ask. Normally it would be Lucian, since we talk about kink a fair amount and he's been in The Aviary since the beginning, so he would know about any partners Crow had… but now would be a really bad time."

Nala sighed. "I know. I *know* how dangerous things are right now, but at the same time… Vincent, I don't care! This is going crazy. This man has got to be stopped. There must be *some* way we can take him down, even if it's finding the evidence to take to the cops!"

"Fuck the cops. He's got them all paid off, I'm sure of it." Vincent snorted. "We would have to go way higher up. This is FBI levels of insanity. Pretty sure he's been killing people all over the country. Washington and Oregon, at least." Vincent rubbed his chin while looking at a painting on the wall. "There might be something I can do. I'll have to take more time off work to do it… and it will be really fucking difficult… but if I can pull it off, *well.* Nothing will stop me from getting the information I need."

"What is it?"

He smirked. "Geek shit."

"Of course it is." Nala hurried to put the damning evidence away and bury herself back in Vincent's arms. "I totally would start dating and fall in love with a geek."

"A very rich geek."

"I bet you got made fun of in school and everything."

"It was the early 2000s, so not really. Computers were cool by then. My braces, though…"

"Oh my fuck. You in braces."

"I also weighed about thirty more pounds. *Not* muscle, by the way. If I watched my weight but didn't exercise and lost my muscles… I would weigh a lot less."

"Say it isn't so."

"Ah, Nala…" He pulled her down onto the bed, feeling her naked skin against his. "I'm glad that we at least have each other through all of this."

"We'll still be together when it's over, right?" Nala had to believe that the fight against Crow would be over someday. Hopefully soon, before either she or Vincent ended up hurt. Or dead. "I've read about people who get together because of high-adrenaline situations. It almost never works out."

"We will still be together." Vincent squeezed her, enough to tell her that he was serious. "I promise. Do me a favor, though. Don't leave me. Not like that."

Nala didn't have to ask what he meant. *Don't leave him like Desirée did.* Nala knew that by being with him, Vincent would always be in some state of grief. She didn't want that to change. Yes, she wanted him to move on, but not to forget. They were both forever changed by the people they lost… but they were also forever changed by being together."

Or at least that's what Nala believed. She curled up in Vincent's arms for the rest of the day, trying not to think about what awaited them back in Portland. She only wanted to think about Vincent, their relationship, and what could build from it. Nala was young. Her previous relationship wasn't the best, but it wasn't bad either. She thought that was normal. Vincent, however… he was wonderful most days. The other days? She could take those as well.

There was no use obsessing over things she could not currently control. Like Xavier Crow. Like her job. Like the possibility of something happening inside her body.

I need to take that test when we get back. She tried to pay attention to her body, wondering if it could tell her something like she sometimes heard about. She didn't hear anything. Nala wasn't stupid. Stupid wives tales anyway.

Nevertheless, she held herself closer to Vincent and hoped beyond hope that he could protect her from what was to come.

Entry #18

Is it possible to have a good day in the midst of hell? Because I had a good day today and don't want to let it go.

But I have to. When we get back to Portland, I will have to work harder than I have ever worked before. My plan is crazy. It's the only hope we have. I hope I am as good as I think I am.

Chapter 38

Upon returning to Portland, Vincent decided it was time to move back into his own damn house. After hiring a security team to sweep the room for bugs – of which they found two, one behind the TV and the other in a bedroom lamp – and traps, he hired a *different* security company to start a bodyguard detail for both himself and Nala. So whenever Nala went to work, some guy in a black suit followed her. The only saving grace was that her work cut back her hours and now left her more grateful than ever that she had Vincent to take care of her financially for now. *I don't have the mental ability to find a new job. I don't have the time, either.*

Vincent worked for two days before announcing to his team that he was taking at least another week off. While Nala was not there for the uprising that almost caused, she did hear Vincent on the phone haggling new benefits for his employees to make up for him not being there. "If it's a dire emergency," he told Andrew the first night off, "I will deal with it. Otherwise, don't bother me. I have a very personal project that demands my attention right now, and I will be using all my work energy on it."

Nala found out soon enough what that was.

It began with a single computer on the dining room table. Parts splayed across the surface, and when Nala asked, Vincent simply told her he was a building "a very powerful machine." As someone who had no idea about that sort of thing, Nala left him to it.

Then another computer appeared. Then a high-powered laptop was unearthed from Vincent's bedroom closet. *How many computers does this guy have?* Nala had seen his work laptop plenty of times. He was always working on some code, answering emails, or surfing the web before bed. The last casual website she saw him on was a *Fallout* message board where those who received advanced copies could report bugs and their other thoughts. "*Good game. I even got used to the dog. However, my game gets significantly lower FPS at…*"

There was no more time for games now. Vincent had three computers set up at the dining room table – banishing Nala to eat her meals on the couch – and a large, brightly lit box that he revealed was a security device. Naturally, Nala assumed this was *his* security. Soon enough, she found out that the box wasn't meant to protect a damn thing at all.

The screens were almost always black, with green, white, and yellow typescript appearing whenever Vincent touched his primary keyboard. Sometimes he had to get up and type on another computer. Other times he brought in the bodyguard hanging around outside and asked him to help with moving a large piece of equipment that was too big for Nala to help with. *What in the world is he doing?* He said this was his big plan for taking down Crow. So far, all she saw Vincent doing was working on a huge program to do… something. *I really wish I could read this shit.* It might as well have been Chinese.

Nala couldn't help. She spent those first two nights on the couch, either playing video games or pretending to be fascinated with TV shows. Yet whenever a commercial came on, she sat up, staring at the side of Vincent's head as he sat in a hoodie and jeans like he did every time he was home. Sometimes he became so wound up in frustration that he ripped off the sweatshirt and kicked it across the room.

Nala had seen nerds explode before. Most of those nerds didn't have a six-pack to eat dinner off of or a billion dollar company at their disposal. So when Vincent wanted to punch a hole in the wall because his project wasn't going the way he wanted, he got up, went to the corner, and gave his punching bag a good one-two. Then he would come back, sit down, and get back to work with grumbles on his lips.

Leave him alone. When Vincent was done for the night, he would go take a shower and then pull his small laptop into bed for some "light research." Nala would cuddle next to him, ask him how he was doing, say a little something about herself, and then go to sleep with a laptop glare in her face. Sometimes she tried to help him *relax*. Because, well, a girl had needs. So did Vincent, surely, but either he was getting off in his shower or he had mastered the ability of completely turning off his libido for the time being. *Jealous.* Nala wished she could do that.

The only time he completely relaxed with her was when he put his laptop down early, pushed himself down, and welcomed Nala's hand around his growing erection. She got a little something in return, but she had to mostly take care of herself when he wasn't around. One time she got so loud up in the bed while he was on his computers down below that he actually called up to her to *please be quiet.* She yelled back at him to put on some headphones. So he did. Heavy metal blared from them while Nala came to the thought of him taking her from behind.

Heavy fucking metal.

Three days of this passed. Nala was the only reason he ate. She brought him take out and some simple homemade things like soup and wraps. Vincent thanked her halfheartedly, his attentions so fully focused that Nala didn't have a snowman's chance in Miami of getting through to him.

Finally, one night he slumped on the couch, taking a breather and complaining about his wrists. Nala went into the bathroom and finally faced the one thing she was currently most afraid of.

Don't be blue. Don't be blue. Don't be blue. Had a few minutes in the bathroom ever been as nerve wracking as they were right now? Nala tried to distract herself with her phone, convinced that her fate was not as tied into a stick as it was right now. *Because Vincent would totally be the most fertile man in the world.* Nala had made it this long on HBC without a known pregnancy, so it wasn't *her*. Totally.

When she had her result, she went downstairs and dangled the stick in front of Vincent's droopy face.

"What is this?" he asked.

"Something I peed on. You're welcome."

"Thanks." He took the end she held and looked at it in the wan light. "I don't know what this means."

"It means I'm not pregnant." Nala sat down next to him with a relieved sigh. "I mean, I'll take the other one to be sure, but don't be shocked if I'm bleeding in another week."

Vincent glanced at her but didn't say anything as he gently set the test on the coffee table. He leaned back in his couch and closed his eyes.

"Well? Aren't you happy that I'm not pregnant?"

He opened one eye and looked at her, beyond tired. "Of course I am. Now would be a terrible time to have a kid."

He wasn't whistling a snappy Dixie tune. "You okay?"

Vincent put a hand against her outer thigh. "I'm fine. Tired."

Nala glanced at the test and then back at her boyfriend. "Did you *want* to have a baby?"

He snorted. "Not right now, that's for sure."

"But… like…"

"It's neither here nor there."

Nala tilted her head, as if she could read Vincent any more than she already could. "It's everywhere, isn't it? Should we talk about this?"

"Not right now we shouldn't."

Nala rolled her eyes. "Typical response. When I thought I might've been pregnant with my ex one time, he was the same way. Didn't want to talk about it! How does that help me any?"

Vincent held her gaze with two crisp eyes. "Fine. The whole kid thing is a bit of a sore spot with me."

Nala bit back her lip, but it didn't stop her speaking. "Why is that?"

It took Vincent a while to respond. When he did, his hands were to himself, and he stared at the ceiling as if looking in Nala's direction was suddenly the worse thing possible. *Oh, boy. Here we go.* "Desirée was pregnant about a year before she died. Came as a surprise, since we were always so careful."

"I see…"

"She had a miscarriage four months in."

"I'm sorry." What else could Nala say?

"I took it harder than she did, honestly. When she told me, I think she had already started moving on. We hadn't seen each other in a couple of weeks because she went home to tell her family while I had to stay behind and work on a project. It happened while she was there, before she even had the chance to tell her family."

"Damn."

"So by the time I found out… well, I had surprised her with a diamond ring. Fuck, that's when I proposed to her. Right after she told me."

Shit.

"I was still adjusting to the idea at the time. Here I was, still feeling like a kid even though I was older than men of my father's generation when they started having kids. I spent more time feeling nauseas with worry than I did focusing on my work. You know, as a guy, I always know that every time I have sex there's a chance I'll have a kid, and there's no say in it. It's the chance I take as a man. When I was finally faced it, I realized it didn't scare me as much as I thought it should. I knew it would be hard. I knew that I had no idea what I was doing, but I loved Desirée, and having a family with her seemed natural. I was in the mindset that I was going to be a father and I would have to provide for my wife and child… so I worked hard. Every day I thought about my future kid. I didn't know if it would be a boy or a girl, but I knew it didn't matter. It would be different either way, but I would love them no matter what… that's what I felt in my heart."

Nala leaned back next to him and pushed her body toward his. Her fingers played between his own. "I'm sorry."

"I guess I don't deal with grief well. I will never know how Desirée really felt about losing the baby, but she seemed to bounce back a lot easier, and *she* was the one carrying it. I had no physical stake in it. All I had was this image in my head and the words of my own father growing up.

When we talked about it later, I told Desirée I would like to try again when we were ready, and that if she ever found herself pregnant again, I would be happy."

"You're a good guy, Vincent."

He wrapped his arm around her, kissing the top of her head. "When you told me about what was going on with you, I had all those emotions come back. I tried to be rational, but I couldn't be. While I'm relieved that you're not pregnant right now because of everything going on… a part of me is also thinking back to those days."

I didn't think he would care so much. Yeah, if she *were* pregnant… but she assumed that not being pregnant was a non-issue. A relief.

"Don't mind me, Nala. I've been thinking way too much these past two weeks."

"What *are* you working on over there?" Finally, a natural topic change.

Vincent glanced at his setup on the table. "Do you want to see?"

"Sure."

They got up, Nala still thinking about Vincent's past. *I didn't know Desirée had been pregnant and miscarried.* No wonder the man was so attached to her and grieving so hard after so long. First he lost a child that never had the chance to be born, and then he lost the mother, the woman he loved and wanted to make his wife. Nala still thought of these things as she stood behind the dining room chair and looked at a screen covered in strange white numbers and words.

"Is this some sort of program you've been writing nonstop?"

"Sort of." Vincent pointed to a particular line. "This is what I'm having trouble with. It's a security bypasser, but the security I'm trying to bypass is too strong. Some of the hardest shit I've ever gone up against. My hacking is a bit rusty since college…"

"Wait a second. You're *hacking* something? Into what? Xavier Crow's servers?"

"Exactly that."

The look of determination on Vincent's face was almost unreal. Nala looked at the screen again, hoping that it would suddenly make sense if she stared long and hard enough. *Is this the insides of Crow's security? For what? His business? His personal computer?* Nala wasn't sure exactly what Vincent was hacking, but it had to be difficult!

"You used to hack?"

"Who didn't? In my world, anyway." Vincent shrugged. "Hacking was a point of pride as a kid. It was how we showed off to our peers. Who could hack into the school's website and put up something funny? Who could hack a social media profile? Who could hack the website of a hate group? Stuff like that. As we got older, the sites got harder to hack and it became more a point of proving shit to ourselves. I stopped hacking a few years ago to focus on my actual studies… you know, building stuff, not breaking into it."

"Noble."

"So like I said, I'm a bit rusty. It doesn't help that Crow has some of the hardest security to crack that I've ever seen. Not surprising, though. He's got a lot to hide."

"Seriously! What exactly are you trying to hack?"

Vincent waved his hand as if that would make what he wanted suddenly appear. "I'm going back and forth between two different things, hoping taking a break from one will make the other easier. Specifically, I'm trying to hack into his email accounts and his home computer."

"You can hack into his home computer?" This was starting to get beyond Nala's ability to comprehend.

"Of course I can. Anything can be hacked if it's on a network. Trust me, that man's home computer is on a network. It has to be."

"Okay. So how's it going?"

"I told you. I'm having trouble with the security. It might be another day or two before I'm able to break through. If it takes longer than that… well, I'm afraid it might be impossible *for me,* or I might be detected. I'm rerouting my IP address through half a dozen countries to throw them off my trail, but if someone worth their shit takes a look at who's breaking in, they'll figure it out soon enough."

"That sounds scary."

"It could be. We're already on his shitlist. If I fuck this up, we're as good as dead. No way they'll let either of us hang around for much longer. You know, Nala… I've been thinking…"

"Yeah?"

"If this keeps going deeper, you might have to run."

"What do you mean?"

Vincent sat back in his chair and glared at her. "I'm not going to be responsible for your death. I'd much rather shove a stack of money in your hands and send you off somewhere you'll be safe under an assumed name. Do you understand? I can't lose you like that too. I'd rather break up because it's the safe thing to do… than see you die like Desirée did."

Nala put her hand on his shoulder. "I'm not going to die, Vincent. Do you understand me? I have no intention of going down to that man or any of his cronies."

"That's all well and good, darling, but…"

"We're not even going to talk about this right now." Nala began to walk away. "You get back to your hacking, and I'll leave you alone so you can do it. You better hack into it, Vincent. I'm serious. I wanna see what that lunatic is hiding."

"If I can."

"Like I said, I'll stop distracting you." Nala chose that moment to go back to the living room and start flipping through channels. While Vincent continued to type on his computers, Nala thought more and more about what she had learned that night. What he was doing, where he had *been* in his life. *I should take that other test to make sure.* On one hand, it was nice to know that Vincent would be there for her if she decided to have a baby. Hell, he'd probably be ten times more excited about it than her. *I dunno, I've never been pregnant that I know of.* On the other hand, that was a lot to bear, both literally and figuratively. Nala wasn't ready yet, if she ever would be. Besides, there was too much on the line right now. What if Vincent sent her away for her own good and she was pregnant? What would happen then? Mysterious money in her accounts? Meeting up in secret in the middle of deserts? Would the kid even know that Vincent was its father?

Nala had to stop thinking about these things. She was living in a toxic soap opera, but in this show all the deaths were real and the threats looming in every shadow. A woman almost died in this room. Nala would have to go visit Robin soon.

The TV stopped on a 24-hour news network. Nala usually blocked out the "SHOCKING ANNOUNCEMENT: SOMEBODY DIED" headlines for her own sanity, but tonight, she was hooked from the moment she saw the picture appearing on the large screen.

"Vincent!" she called, hoping her voice was loud enough to break through whatever bubble he hid himself in. "Look!"

She felt him behind her within a few seconds. Just in time, too, for the news network broke from a sponsored product to the actual story at hand.

"This just in from Germany: multi-millionaire and shipping giant Othello Gainsborough died in a car accident outside his home in Hamburg. Also in the car with him was his long-time girlfriend Melanie Marcus. She is currently in critical condition at a local hospital. On-site investigators say the accident was caused by reckless driving, as photos from a local intersection show Mr. Gainsborough texting on his phone shortly before he crashed into a median and flipped his car three times. Doctors say he was killed instantly. We'll report more as soon as we can."

Vincent took the remote out of Nala's hand and turned off the TV. "Shit," he muttered. "Time to get back to work."

There was no need to discuss what had happened. Othello was the man mentioned in that letter Nala found in Crow's office. Melanie must have been Sparrow's real name. Now both were dead, or almost dead.

I wonder what they did to piss him off. Were they moved away on Crow's insistence, on pain of death? Or did they move on their own, to get away from Crow and people like Hawk? Did it matter? *Not really, because either way, it was Crow who had them killed.* No wonder Vincent wanted to get back to his project. The longer he sat around doing nothing, the higher Crow's kill count got.

Nala couldn't help but wonder when she would be targeted.

Entry #19

Operation hack into Crow's personal database is underway. It's more difficult than I thought it would be, and I was giving myself a high level of difficulty to achieve. The man has some of the toughest security I've ever seen. If I have any hope of cracking it, I will have to spend all my days, all my energy and know-how on doing this one thing.

How funny. My life has come down to doing something illegal after all. This comes after I swore to myself I would try to run my business with as much integrity as possible.

Well, I suppose this isn't business. It's much more personal than that.

Please hang on, Desirée. I'll find out the truth soon enough. I'll bring you the justice we deserve.

Then… perhaps I will finally be able to move on.

Chapter 39

"It was really nice of you to come, Gale," Robin said, sitting upright in her bed. Her skin was still covered in light bandages, and seeing her without any makeup and with the flattest hair in the universe was like seeing an unphotoshopped photo of a supermodel. Nala pretended she recognized her friend upon entering the room carrying a small bouquet of get well flowers and – most importantly – a chocolate bar.

"I would've come earlier, but I had to go out of town for a while." That was all Nala said as she sat on a stool next to the bed. Across from her, she saw the permanent indent Lucian had left from all his time sleeping by Robin's side. *That's sweet. He must really love her.* Nala didn't know why that surprised her. Apparently she assumed that all the relationships in The Aviary were as fake as her and Vincent's had been. *But if we fell in love, then they must be too.* The only couple she wasn't sure about was Maggie and Jay, but there was a lot she wasn't sure about there.

"It's okay. I'm glad you came at all." Until now, Robin had put on a brave face that said she wasn't hurt or scared. She had been in the hospital for a while. Wasn't she well enough to go home yet? Or was Lucian's money able to keep her here until she was emotionally ready as well? *She must feel safe here.* "Not many people have visited me, besides Lucian, of course." Robin looked away, biting her lip. "Nobody from The Aviary has come. Not until you, anyway."

Nala sighed. "Maybe they didn't want to find out your real name," she teased. "You know that's supposed to stay hush-hush."

"I like my name, though!" Robin's face lit back up, much to Nala's relief. "It's your name nobody knows, honestly. Well, yours and Maggie's. I could easily tell you Quail and Starling's real names."

"I thought you weren't supposed to…"

"No, but we're not at a meeting, now are we?"

Nala shrugged.

"I'll tell you Quail's real name. It's Sylvia. She came out here as an escort, if you can believe it."

Nala believed anything and everything these days. A woman in The Aviary being an escort? Super easy to believe. Nala was practically one for a few weeks. *And my sugar daddy boyfriend is still paying me.* Would Vincent keep gifting her a thousand dollars a week until they died? Maybe. Hopefully. Nala would not say no.

"Her and Sebastian are still a pretty new couple. I don't know much about Quail's past, but I know that she and Sebastian aren't as serious as they look. They live together, but I'm not sure how *serious* it is. I think it's a business deal, if you ask me."

Nala hadn't, but that was okay. "But you and Lucian are totally a real thing, right?"

"Oh, yes! He comes here every day. He's cried so much… I never saw him cry hardly in my life until I ended up in here. You know how those types of men are. They don't want to cry, either because they think it's unmanly or… I dunno. It's not healthy, if you ask me. People are supposed to cry to keep the stress out of their bodies. Does Vincent cry?"

So rarely did she ever call him by his first name. "I've never seen him cry, no."

"Oh. Sounds like Lucian. Well, as I said, I've been seeing him cry a lot lately. Made me realize how much I mean to him. I mean… I always knew he *loved* me, but I could see how scared he was to lose me! It scared me a little too. I've never meant that much to somebody before. I'm not even sure my mother would cry that much to lose me. I think it might really be forever with Lucian, if I ever get out of here."

"When will that be?"

Robin sucked her face inward, as if she tasted something unbearably sour. "I don't know,' she said carefully. "The doctors say that, despite my injuries, I'm doing well. I could probably go home in a few days if I wanted."

"If you wanted?"

"I don't know if I actually will."

"I see." Nala didn't press that issue. Clearly, Robin was scared. Lucian was probably even more afraid, especially if he knew the source of his girlfriend's pain. *What did he do to piss Crow off?* Vincent was right. They picked Robin not only because she was Nala's friend, but because they wanted to get to Lucian as well. A double-whammy. "Do you remember what happened?"

She treaded dangerous waters here, and Nala knew it. If Robin wasn't being forthcoming with what she knew about her own attack, then she probably didn't want to share. If she even knew…

Robin set her face into a grim look. "I'll tell you the same thing I told the police every time they were in here. I don't remember anything. One minute I was walking in my neighborhood, and the next thing I knew, I was in here with Lucian crying beside me. What happened in between? I couldn't tell you. I don't remember any event, and I definitely don't remember any people."

The way she said it betrayed her lies. The police probably thought the same thing, if they came in multiple times trying to get something out of her. *She knows who it was. She's too scared to mention it.* Nala didn't blame her, but having Hawk's involvement confirmed would mean so, so much in the world of getting to the bottom of this.

"Well, I hope that you can get out of here sooner rather than later," Nala said. "It's awful seeing you like this. I really mean that."

Robin smiled. "Thanks so much, Nala. I mean…"

Nala sat up straight in her seat. "So you know who I am…"

"Yes. Lucian told me a while ago. He said that you had a pretty name and that Vincent was lucky to have you."

"Did he, now?"

"I hope you're not angry, Nala. I assumed that you knew my name anyway. It's hard to keep a person's identity a secret in this day and age."

"Do you know my last name?"

Robin squinted. "I remember something Russian. I'm sorry, I'm terrible with foreign words and names."

"I'm sorry you found out too much," Nala said, standing up and zipping up her jacket. "I'm sorry that he decided to make an example out of you."

"Nala…"

"No, don't say anything. It's best that way." Nala nodded to one bandage on Robin's hand. "It's best that you don't find out more about me. Or Vincent. Make sure you tell Lucian that the next time you see him."

"I don't understand."

"Then understand this. Vincent and I are involved with something very, *very* dangerous. If you knew anything about our histories, then you would know that… well, I won't get too much into it. I'm sorry you got caught up in this, but it's important that you try to avoid The Aviary as much as possible until things blow over. You're not safe there. None of us really are."

Robin still made that sour face. "I know. We haven't been safe since the day it began."

Nala didn't know what that meant, but she would leave Robin to it. After a curt but polite farewell, she stepped out of the hospital room and took a meandering path down to the sidewalk, where she hailed a cab to take her back to Vincent's loft. *I should have brought the bodyguard, I guess.* Vincent was adamant that Nala never leave by herself. Yet how was she to trust a hired hand? For all she knew, they were really in Crow's pocket. Right now, Nala assumed that everyone was in Crow's pocket. Except for her and Vincent. She kept reminding herself that as the cab went down the road into downtown.

Vincent was home, although he was not locked at this work station like he had been when Nala left a few hours ago. Instead, she walked into the loft to find her boyfriend in a far, empty corner, shirtless and beating the shit out of his punching bag. Every *wumpf!* echoed in the loft, sounding like the largest scuffle of the century going down in one abandoned warehouse. *This isn't abandoned, though. This is our home.* Nala dropped her things by the living room couch before wandering over to Vincent, still punching his bag as if he never noticed Nala walking through the door.

He was gorgeous, with copious amounts of sweat streaming down his skin and even getting on the bruised and battered red punching bag. Enough sunlight came through the upper windows that Nala could see every streak of pink flushing Vincent's skin as he worked out until he couldn't anymore. *A man should not be this good looking.* The idea that he was hers for the taking whenever she wanted… that seemed ludicrous. Was it even possible for him to think the same way about her? That she was so crazy beautiful that he often stopped to stare at her in wonder? *Because that's what I am doing to him right now.* Nala felt better for the first time in days. Not just because Vincent was there – and the sexiest man on the earth – but because looking at him, at his strength and his ability to do such things, made her feel safe. Right now, especially after seeing Robin in the hospital like that? Nala valued safety above all else.

"You gonna keep punching that thing and ignoring me?"

Vincent gave the bag one more hard smack before stilling his equipment and looking at her, hard of breath. "How was your visit?" It was almost cute how easily he spoke after that much exertion.

"Interesting. Robin claims to not know anything about her attack, which is of course bullshit. Also, she knows my name."

Vincent stripped his hands of their protective gear and tossed them to the side. *Finished, are we?* Was there enough testosterone in his system to take her for a spin in the shower? They had yet to have any fun in there… and they had yet to have any *real fun* at all in a good while. *Get some of this before my period arrives.* Nala coyly stripped her sweatshirt off, but Vincent appeared too engrossed in his routine to pay her any mind.

"That's not surprising," he said. "Both of those things." Sweat trickled down his back when he bent down away from Nala and fiddled with his shoes. "She must know that it was not a random attack, and the person who attacked her has a lot over her head. Even if the police came for her, she wouldn't give it up if it meant keeping her and Lucian alive. She must know what happened to those two old members."

"Speaking of, did you find out anything?"

Vincent grunted in neither affirmation nor denial. "I thought I made headway earlier. Managed to break through some bit of security finally. Then I hit another dead end. Didn't lead to where I thought it would, in other words. The security I broke through led me to personnel files, but not the fun kind. His butlers and landscapers and shit." Vincent sighed as he switched feet. "You'll be impressed to know that I now know who has requested two weeks' worth of vacation later this year so they can go on a honeymoon in Thailand. Also, someone named Albert hasn't taken a sick day in fifteen years. They gave him a raise for it."

Nala sighed right alongside him. "So now what?"

"So now I find something else to break into."

"Are you going to keep doing this until you get what I want?"

Vincent snatched her arm and brought her near him. *Hello there, body odor.* Nala reveled in it, running her hands along his sticky skin, feeling the sheer power of his muscles and the overall spoils of his intense workouts. For all the easy breathing he did in front of her, the man puffed a little beneath her hands. *Good to know he's still human.*

"I always get what I want. Eventually."

Nala purred against his chest. "Just don't get us in even more trouble."

Vincent put both arms around her, practically inhaling her throat as he kissed her there. "Trouble is my middle name, madam. Shall I show you?"

She liked post-workout Vincent. He was virile as hell and fresh from having his mind cleared of all the toxic shit. "Is trouble in your cock?

'Cause I think he's already trying to make a point to me." Nala slid her hand between them, feeling what hardness he already had.

Before they could kiss, however, his phone buzzed a few feet away.

"Some mail came, Mr. Lane," said the man in charge of the patrolling security. "We checked it. It's clean."

Groaning, Vincent pulled away from Nala and went to the door. There was a man standing on the other side, handing over a stack of envelopes. "Thanks," Vincent muttered, shutting the door in the man's face.

Nala was on the couch by the time he rejoined her. She heard him further mutter about bills, junk mail, and…

"Great," he said with a bite to his voice. "The fucking Aviary is calling again."

Nala curled up on the couch as if it could shield her from Xavier Crow. "Tell him we're still not buying what he's peddling. Even if you're making shit up again."

Paper rustled behind her. She could practically feel Vincent reading over whatever invitation Crow had sent this week.

"This isn't a regular invitation. He says that in lieu of a regular meeting this week, they will be promoting swinging meetings."

"Joy. Please tell me we've been paired with Lucian and Robin so we don't actually have to do anything." She knew that wouldn't be the case. Swinging only worked if there were an even number of couples.

"Sorry, darling. We've been requested by a different couple." The invitation landed in her lap. "Your new best friend wants to ride my dick."

"My new best…" Nala held up the invitation in front of her. Maggie and Jay's names loomed before her eyes. "Fucking hell."

"I know I'm not turning them down." When Nala shot him a dangerous look, Vincent explained, "*Not* because I want to sleep with Maggie, okay?"

"Uh huh."

"Because there's a lot we can ask them. There's a reason they chose us, Nala. I'm guessing they want to finally talk about what's going on. Maybe we'll find out who they are."

"I'm not holding my breath. They're more likely to kill us, I think."

"You're cynical."

"You're not?"

Vincent pointed to something else on the invitation. "Two days from now. You ready to go pretend to be hot for Jay's dick?"

"Shut up." Nala snatched his chin and held him place. *No way you're getting away from me right now, buster.* "I am not going to have sex with him. And *you* are not going to have sex with her. Got it?"

"Let's see how the night unfolds."

The way he backed away from the couch implied that he was giving his girlfriend a hard time. Nevertheless, Nala leaped up from the couch and nearly chased Vincent down to the bathroom, where he was halfway to locking the door in her face. "Don't you dare!" she cried. "You're all mine, Vincent Lane! Do you hear? Your dick only goes in me!"

"Why, Miss Nazarov," he said, peering at her through a crack in the bathroom door. "You're feisty when you're jealous."

He latched the door in her face. In another minute, the shower turned on, and Nala had a whole slew of crap to whine about.

Entry #20

Tomorrow I hope to find out a truth in The Aviary. But what amuses me more is how jealous Nightingale is at the thought of me sleeping with another woman.

It shouldn't amuse me so.

But it does.

Chapter 40

No matter what Nala did, she found herself in an infinite loop of toxic thoughts. *Xavier Crow will want me dead. I have to meet Maggie and Jay, whom I barely know but are somehow involved in this. Xavier Crow will want me dead…* Nala took multiple deep breaths. Not even when Vincent crawled into bed the first night and made love to her did Nala feel better about the situation.

See, there are two problems here. The first was Xavier Crow. That was obvious. The other was this supposed swinging with Jay and Maggie.

Nala was a jealous creature after all.

She didn't think she was until now. With her previous boyfriend, everything was relaxed and… detached. So what if he quickly moved on after her? They had never been serious. Nala had never been in love with him. Not like she was in love with Vincent. Between the girl at the bookstore and the idea of him on top of Maggie… with her toned figure… and clearly knowing what she wanted at any moment… no matter how much Vincent told her that nothing would actually happen that night, Nala couldn't help but imagine *her* boyfriend fucking another woman, and the thought made her livid.

So wound up in these thoughts was she that she never stopped to think about what would happen on *her* end. Supposedly, she would have sex with Jay. A man she hardly acknowledged because his wife overshadowed him so fantastically. Jay was good looking and kindly enough. Alpha? Not really, and as Nala was quickly discovering, she was into those alpha males when they did the right things for her.

"Would you calm down?" Vincent said in his car the night of their meeting. They were both dressed as if they were going to The Aviary, with Vincent in his cut suit and Nala in a slinky black dress that accentuated what curves she had. Vincent had declared her "stunning" before they left his loft. "Nothing's going to happen. I promise you."

"What if they have other ideas?"

"I highly doubt that."

"Do you know something that I don't know?"

"No. I have a gut feeling."

"Oh, well, if you have a *feeling.*"

"Stop it." Vincent happened to stop at a red light at that moment. "You're being irrational, which is the last thing you want to be tonight."

"Shut up."

He did, but not because she told him to. If anything, he was probably ready to give her a few more testy words.

They were meeting Maggie and Jay at a downtown hotel. One that Nala and Vincent happened to stay at when they were playing hotel roulette right after Robin's attack. *When Maggie gave me that picture…* Vincent claimed to have no further information about that. All Nala could do was try not to think about it. With any luck, he would be able to press her for information. Did Jay know anything? Would Nala be able to get anything out of him… and not *that?*

They checked in using their Aviary names of Vincent and Nightingale. They were informed that the rest of their "party" awaited them in their rooms, and were given copies of the key. As they entered the elegant elevator with a number in their hands, Nala gave Vincent one final admonishment.

"If you stick any of your body parts in any of her orifices, you will never know the end of my fury."

"Duly noted."

She turned to him. "Why are you so nonchalant about this? Do you want me to sleep with Jay? Doesn't the thought of him slamming me against the wall, against the bed, or even against the fucking floor make you rage with jealousy?"

Vincent raised a single eyebrow at her. "Not really. Because I know that's not going to happen."

"You're driving me nuts right now."

"I do what I can."

They watched the floor numbers tick by in silence. Or at least they did until Vincent broke said silence again.

"Slamming you against the floor…" he chuckled.

"What's so funny?"

The elevator doors opened. Vincent stepped out, glancing over his shoulder and extending his hand to take Nala's. "That man won't go anywhere near you, and not out of fear for me. Trust me, Nala, Jay has no interest in you."

Well, that was almost insulting!

Before Nala could dwell on any of it, however, they were at their assigned room, Vincent inserting the key after giving a hearty knock announcing their arrival.

Sure enough, Jay and Maggie sat side by side on a couch, looking cozy.

They were not the only ones there.

"Why hello," Hawk said, standing and coming dangerously close to where Vincent and Nala stood in the tiny foyer. *Oh my God.* Shivers as sharp as daggers stabbed Nala in the spine. "So glad that you could join the fun tonight. Hope you don't mind that I'm here… to supervise."

Everyone exchanged glances, including Jay and Maggie, who almost looked apologetic. *What is going on here?* Nala never had any idea anymore.

"Certainly was not expecting you, that's for sure." Vincent helped Nala with her coat before leading her into the main room. Hawk stared after them, a devilish grin crossing her hawkish face. "I was under the impression that these were discreet affairs… no pun intended."

Hawk rejoined them in the main area of the hotel room. "Things have changed recently. I'm sure you've heard about what's happened to our poor Robin."

All eyes were on Vincent and Nala. *Of course we've heard! It happened at our place, and* you *did it!* Nala had to use every practiced lie in her body to not give herself away. "We have. Are you guarding us tonight?" Vincent didn't mention he had his own security team circling the perimeter of the hotel, on permanent call for the night.

"You don't think one of our own attacked her, do you?" Maggie asked Hawk. *Balls. She's got them.*

Hawk was not perturbed. Her feathery mask spread across her face as she forced a polite smile. "It's highly possible. After finding out where she was found…" She glanced at Vincent. "Well, let's say that Master Crow doesn't want to take any chances."

"I'm sure he doesn't." Nala squeezed Vincent's arm before going to sit on the couch next to Maggie and Jay. "I can't blame him, either. I think it's great that he sent you here to watch out for us." Nightingale was too good at lying – because that's who was pulling these antics. Nightingale knew how important it was to deflect off herself and flatter the assassin in the room. *Has she been sent to kill us all?* Maggie stiffened next to Nala. *Is she afraid too?* Because deep inside… Nala was a tad petrified.

"You're too kind. I'm sure tonight will be fine." Hawk perched on the edge of a chair as Vincent slowly joined his girlfriend on the couch. "Pretend I'm not even here. I want you four to enjoy yourselves as you usually would. In fact…" She stood again, heading toward the door. "I'll be right outside should you need anything. Have fun!"

She left them alone in due time. All four of The Aviary members sat in the knowledge that she could come back in whenever she wanted. Nevertheless, Nala released a pent up breath.

"Well," Maggie said, pulling her skirt down toward her knees. Nobody touched anyone, much to Nala's relief. "That was most unexpected. Anyone want a glass of wine? Because I am dying for one…" she caught herself. "I mean…"

"Great idea." Vincent stood, going to an ice bucket and rummaging for some glasses. "Wine is a terrific idea. In fact, let's have a toast. To all that happens tonight."

He poured four glasses and passed them out. Nobody was in a hurry to drink it. *Is this poisoned?* Nala sniffed it. Smelled like regular wine, but who knew? She had no idea what to look out for. Maybe it was spiked with the shit that killed her sister. Wouldn't that be something? *Slightly ironic.* She hated irony.

In a brazen move, Maggie took the first sip, her eyes locked on everyone around her. "Mm. Delicious." She lowered her glass. Nala couldn't help but continue to stare. *Well… is she going to die?* When a minute passed and she appeared unfazed, the others drank as well. At least they were on the same page. A page of fear.

"Should we get started?" Vincent finally asked. "I have a feeling we're not people who talk much. Perhaps we should get straight to it."

Nala took another swig of wine and shot him a look. *Don't be too eager.* She needed more wine already. Especially if she was going to watch her boyfriend go into a bedroom with another woman. Especially if she was going into a bedroom with another man.

"Yes," Maggie finally said, uncrossing her legs and standing. "Let's get to it. I think we've all been looking forward to tonight."

Speak for yourself. Nala pinched Vincent's arm to make sure he got the right idea. She could practically hear him groaning.

Here Nala was, watching Vincent hook his arm with Maggie's as if that were the most natural thing to do. They walked like this into one of two bedrooms, shutting the door quietly behind them. Jay followed suit, getting up, putting down his half-consumed glass of wine, and extending his hand to Nala.

"I know we haven't spoken much to each other since meeting those few weeks ago," he said with a smooth, almost melodic voice. *How have I never noticed the way he speaks before?* "I hope that you would join me in the other room, though. I'd like to get to know you." Jay's wink would send trembles of anticipation through a normal woman, but Nala was too uptight to enjoy such a flirtation from a good-looking man who wasn't her boyfriend. "If you know what I mean."

Nala tentatively took his hand and stood, pulling down the skirt of her dress as Maggie had. *Was she trying to be modest as well? In this sort of situation?* Nala glanced at the bedroom door. What were they doing in there? Maggie better not be half naked and going for Vincent's trousers…

"Don't mind them, Gale," Jay said, putting a strong hand on her shoulder. *Oh my God. Please don't kill me. Please don't make me get Hawk and put my life in her hands. Please don't.* "Let them have their fun, and we'll have ours. We can compare notes later."

He said this so loudly that his voice bounced around like a confused echo in the main chamber of the room. Jay opened the other bedroom door and helped Nala in, quick to shut and lock the door behind them. *Here we go…* Nala didn't know what to expect. Should she be worried that Jay wanted to have sex? Even if she were interested, Nala had made such a big deal about Vincent and Maggie that it would be the most hypocritical thing in the world for her to go ahead and find out about Jay's cock. Or anything else about him, for that matter.

Nala sat on the edge of the bed for a lack of anywhere else to sit. Jay stood between her and the door, hands in his pockets and looking like he was in control of everything. *Well, he is supposedly an alpha male.* Nala let out her pent up breath. That got Jay's attention.

"You can calm down, Gale. We're not going to do anything."

She looked up again. "We're not?" While that was a relief, and proved Vincent right, it also confused her even more. "Then what are we doing?"

Jay put his ear to the door. "Well, right now I'm suspecting that my partner and yours are having a very deep discussion about what's been going on lately."

"That so?"

"Yes, Gale…" When Jay didn't hear anything, he turned around and crossed his arms as if he could singlehandedly protect them both. Maybe… The more Nala looked at him, the more she realized he was bigger than she ever took him for. Then again, the only times Nala looked really close at the male members of The Aviary was when they were practically naked, which Jay had yet to be. Now she saw the outlines of muscles beneath that gray suit. She would daresay the man was fitter than Vincent. *Do he and Maggie date at the gym or something?* They were both muscular. Between Jay's biceps and Maggie's calves of steel, they could probably win a competition or two. Well, for all Nala knew, they did that in their spare time. Or professional time. *What do they do for a living?* Nala figured this was the wrong time to ask.

Nala drew her legs up on the bed, making sure her thighs were covered once more. "You know my real name, right? Cut the Gale crap. Show me that much respect."

Any hint of a smile disappeared from Jay's face. "I see. If that's how it is, then I'll honor your request… Nala."

"I'd ask how you know my name, but you being some rich asshole, I'm guessing it's easy enough to figure out."

"Yes. Now, if you knew who I really was, then I would be in a lot of trouble."

"I'm sure. And, of course, you're not going to tell me who you are."

"Not anytime soon. Hopefully you can find out eventually."

Nala dangled her legs over the side of the bed. She wanted to flop down and stare at the ceiling, but was afraid her skirt would ride up her ass. *Why did I wear this tonight?* Blech.

"Do you know why Maggie gave me that awful photo?" Nala finally asked. "Since we're having heart-to-hearts around here. I'm assuming you know what your wife is up to in her spare time."

Jay nodded. "I know about that. I'm sorry you had to see it. She wanted you to know."

"How did she get that photo?"

"Now, let's not ask too many questions. You don't need to know the answer to that."

"Yet."

He smiled again.

"I don't like being kept in the dark. Vincent keeps me in the dark too much. I know I'm not computer savvy and able to hack into shit, and I can barely Google what I need to find, but I'm not stupid. I deserve to know what Vincent knows."

"I'm sure Vincent will…"

A thump interrupted them. A loud thump, followed by a louder, angry grunt.

"Jay!" Maggie's voice burst through the door. Not frightened. Not panicked. Definitely anxious. "The chicken has hatched an egg!"

Before Nala could ask what the fuck was going on, another thump - a bunch of thumps, really - flickered in and out of her ear. Jay held up a hand and pressed his ear to the door. "Nala," he whispered. "Get in the bathroom and lock the door. Do not come out until we tell you it's clear. Do you understand?"

She was off the bed before he finished his sentence. "What if they get in the bathroom?"

"I hope you know self-defense."

She didn't. That was a gross oversight.

Still, she sprinted to the bathroom, latching the door behind her the moment Jay flung the bedroom door open. As much as she wished she could see what was going on, Nala knew it was nothing good.

Perhaps only a minute passed by, but it was a long, infuriating minute. Where was Vincent? Shit! Nala didn't have her phone. This was only compounded when the bumps entered the bedroom, followed by…

"I said get back here!" Hawk. A very angry Hawk. She swooped into the bedroom, whooshing through the air before something heavy hit the floor. "Why won't you fucking die?"

Oh my God!

Nala wished she could say she was the bravest woman in the world. She wished she could say she burst through the bathroom door and took her sister's killer head-on. Maybe snatch something sharp in the bathroom and drive it deep into that tall Amazonian's jugular. But, oh no. She was far from the bravest woman in the world, as proven when Nala hopped in the shower and drew the curtain closed - as if that would protect her.

Oh my God, oh my God…

She was about as religious as an agnostic, but Nala said a prayer anyway. Where was Vincent in all of this? Holy shit! Was he dead?

"You two are really pissing me off!"

"Fuck off, you runway reject." Nala had never been so relieved to hear Maggie's deep voice. "This is your last warning. Get down on the ground!"

"For fuck's sake, shoot the bitch!"

"You think you're getting out of here alive?" Hawk's maniacal laughter pierced every space around Nala. She rocked back and forth in the tub, trying to block out what happened. Because if Hawk made it into the bathroom? Nala was as good as dead. "As soon as I'm done with you two, I'm going to shoot that smug fucker in the head and skin the little bitch alive!"

"You do that, hon."

Nala's blood left her face with the rest of her breath when a loud, earth-shattering gunshot went off.

Silence. Then, a scream. Someone hit. She couldn't tell who, aside from a woman. More thumps. More grunts. Radio static crackled. Nala squealed into the back of her hand and wished beyond wish that Vincent was there to hold her and tell her everything would be all right.

The ensuing quiet nearly gave Nala a heart attack. What had happened? Were people dead? Should she brave going out there? Fuck, she wished she had a gun. A machete. Anything that could take down an assassin. Ahaha. Who was she kidding? She would be killed first!

Someone pounded on the bathroom door.

"Nala!" Vincent! "Nala, we gotta get out of here! The security detail is on their way but I don't want to wait!"

She scurried out of the bathtub and hurried to the door, flinging it open to reveal Vincent's arms coming through and scooping her up. *Thank heaven!* She clung to him, being whisked away from that evil room and whatever had transpired there. While Vincent deftly carried her out of the hotel room, she braved opening one eye and seeing upturned furniture and the comforter on the bed nearly torn to shreds. There was no blood, and definitely no bodies.

"What happened?" she cried, nearly vomiting in relief when their security backup showed up in the elevator. Vincent put her down and joined their small team of men in black jumpers, all of whom remained stoic and quiet while they got on radios and phoned police. *It won't do any good. Don't you get it?* "I heard a gunshot… Maggie and Jay…"

"Are nowhere to be found." Vincent put a heavy hand on Nala's shoulder and turned her toward him, his voice lowering as he tried to speak out of security's hearing range. "Something is going on, Nala. Something neither you nor I can comprehend. I don't know who those people are, but…" He motioned to a small envelope tucked in his inside pocket. "We are definitely not safe. Hawk was going to kill us all tonight."

I knew it. Nala sucked up her fear and tried to put on the bravest face she had. "Are you hurt?" she asked meekly. Her fingers clutched his jacket. "I'm scared, Vincent…"

"I know, darling." He pulled her into his embrace, letting her tears hit his clothes. "We'll get through this. You have to believe me. You are never leaving my side until this is over."

What he didn't tell her was that "until this is over" could very well mean their deaths.

Chapter 41

Nala was still shaking when they returned to Vincent's loft. The security team did their customary sweep and didn't find anything. Vincent told them to bring in more people and double their vigilance. When the captain suggested they officially go to the police with everyone's testimony - and the captain swore up and down he had a very good relationship with local law enforcement - Vincent convinced him that when it came to Xavier Crow, nobody else could be trusted. Not even the police.

Vincent consented to two bodyguards staying inside the loft that night, taking shifts with another pair. He and Nala went upstairs with drinks while the security detail sat on the couches downstairs, doing more sweeps, looking out windows, and communicating via their phones. With so much activity going on, Nala and Vincent were forced to keep their voices at lowered whispers.

"Who are they, Vincent?" Nala huddled in her sweats as she continued to lightly shake on the bed. "I've always known there's something off about them. Please tell me you've looked up their real identities."

"I did a long while ago. Jay and Marguerite Jones. He's in hedge funds and she… well, there was nothing about her besides basic profile shit. They were both squeaky clean. Nothing stood out."

Nala furrowed her brows. "You mean it was eerie how nothing stood out."

"I don't think they're who they say they are, but if they have real information out there, I can't find it. I can barely break into Crow's security."

"Maggie gave you something, right?"

Vincent pulled the small envelope form the end table. "She told me to open it with you. It was the first thing she gave me. There was no time to discuss further, because Hawk wasted no time. She wanted to take us out first. I think she was actually targeting Maggie before me. I was lucky that she was already so alert."

"So was Jay. They knew that was going to happen."

Vincent nodded, opening the envelope. Inside was a single piece of paper containing a typed letter. He spread it out on the bed and focused the nearest lamp, so the soft yellow light illuminated Maggie's words.

I cannot tell you my real name. I risk even telling you this much. Whatever you do, do not dig into my identity. You could possibly greatly compromise what I have already achieved, and I will have to kill you.

They were off to a fantastic start already.

I am on your side. I am like you in that I have been touched by Crow's evil hand.

Two years ago, I lived in a community not too unlike this one. Xavier Crow was buying up land all over Washington, which included my town. On one of his parcels he built a daycare. I enrolled my son, who was four at the time.

It turned out that Crow over-purchased the town. Soon his allotted funds dried up with little return. Whispers of him going after phony insurance claims arose, but nobody could prove anything. I should have acted, but I didn't expect the worst case scenario. See, I had my son in daycare because I was a single mother with a full time job that often went into overtime. On the night I will never forget, I had to work late. I phoned the daycare and one lovely lady there agreed to stay late with my son until I could pick him up. By the time I got there the whole daycare had burned down. Both my son and the woman died inside.

I do not doubt that Xavier Crow burned down the place to get insurance money. Whoever did it for him must have thought nobody would be there so late. There hasn't been a day that goes by that I wish I had gotten there even half an hour earlier. Maybe I could have done something. Maybe I could have saved my son and that woman. But mostly my son, who was the most precious thing in the world to me.

My son is not the only victim. I know others have died by command. I will not rest until there is justice. You are meddling. I infiltrated long before you, and I must ask that you back off. For your own good, and for the best chance at justice that we have.

I am sorry about Tasha Nazarov. I am sorry about Desirée Whitmore. Their deaths did not have to happen. I sent Nala that photo that I stole from Crow's personal office because she needed to know the truth. I recognized Nala the moment she entered The Aviary for the first time. I know that Xavier Crow did too. You were made the moment you started lying.

Tasha was known as Raven when I first infiltrated The Aviary. Of course I did not know her relationship to Crow until I did some digging. When I found out she was one of his top researchers, a lot of things started to make sense. For one, the girl was never happy in our group. I could tell that her relationship with Crow was not her choice. If you told Tasha Nazarov that she would never have to come to another club meeting again, she would be the happiest I ever saw her. I won't upset you with the things they did there, but as far as I can tell, there was some other reason Raven was in the group, and it was not because she was Crow's real girlfriend. Since her death, Crow has not had a partner aside from Hawk. I'm sure he wanted us to think that he was grieving. Nobody asked any questions. We all long learn to not ask about group members who disappear. I knew Othello and Sparrow as well. Othello cost Crow a lot of money with a bad shipment, and he moved to Germany to get away from his wrath. If you've seen the news lately, you'll notice that it didn't work out that great.

Vincent, I do not have any information on Desirée's death. I'm sorry. I've done my own digging and my guess is probably as good as yours.

Please do not interfere with me. I am on your side in that we both want justice. But I will not stop until it's done. If you get in my way? I apologize in advance for what I have to do.

Maggie.

Nala could not face the piece of paper after she was done reading. "I don't believe it," she muttered. "How could Tasha have been that man's partner in any way? She would have never been into that sort of thing. She was as vanilla as basic ice cream." Nala knew that a woman who appeared vanilla on the outside may very well be kinky on the inside, but she knew her sister. Tasha liked flirting, she probably liked sex, and she was always going on about guys when her time allowed, but the idea of her being into BDSM was about as likely as Nala becoming a housewife. Nobody would have been surprised with Nala being kinky. Submissive, maybe, but overall kinky? Yeah, right. Nala should have seen it for herself before meeting Vincent. "There must have been something in it for her. Why would Crow risk her quitting? She was one of his top researchers."

"Do you still think that he had her killed because of her research?" Vincent folded up the letter. "I've been questioning that myself lately. Then again, I don't know what the alternative could have been."

Nala shook her head. "A part of me doesn't want to know. I think it would hurt me even more than I already am." Nala thought back to that photo, of her sister trapped next to Xavier Crow, looking like the most miserable woman in the world. *This was happening to her and she never told me. Why? Because she thought I was too young? Because she didn't want to scare me?* What else was going on in her sister's life that Nala never found out about?

"I'm sorry you had to know any of this." Vincent put the letter away. "I'm going to go downstairs and start my research again. Maggie can tell us to stay away from her investigation, but I have my own to continue. I have to know why Desirée was killed. I have to find some piece of evidence we can use against him."

"Please be careful." Tears were spilling from Nala's eyes again. *I cry so much lately. I didn't cry this much before.* She had been holding too much in, apparently. "I love you, Vincent. I don't want to lose you too."

He kissed her forehead and caressed her cheek. Even so, his legs crawled off the bed and took him away from her. "You won't lose me, and I won't lose you. Starting today, you're not leaving my side. I can't risk it."

Nala waited until he was downstairs before burying her face in her pillow. *I'm sorry, Tasha. I'm sorry I could have died tonight.* How many times had she almost died now? This was her first official encounter, but what about the things that were caught before she ever knew about them? How many plans that were never carried out? Where was Hawk right now? Maggie? Who was Jay to Maggie? He was never once mentioned in her letter.

She felt like she had more questions than answers now. When sleep did not come easy, Nala focused on the sounds around her. She settled on the sounds of Vincent typing downstairs. The man was going to give himself blood clots and carpal tunnel working on those computers all day, but Nala knew it would be worth it. Everything they did had to be worth it now.

***

Vincent wasn't kidding when he said Nala had to constantly be by his side. When she attempted to go to work the next day, he told her to call in sick. "Quit, honestly," he told her. "You don't need that job. If you want a job when this is over, I'll help you find something much better." Instead, he had to swing by his office to contend with some neglected business, and Nala went with him - at his insistence. Because nothing was better than being tailed by bodyguards and looking Andrew in the smug face while she sat on Vincent's office couch and played escapist games on her phone.

She wished that there was something she could do to help, but she didn't know coding. She didn't know how to hack. Those things were so beyond her that she couldn't tinker with the fans on Vincent's machines even if she wanted to. The fact he put them together was too much to fathom in the first place.

My boyfriend is a computer genius, and I'm useless. Nala's anger had abated recently. Now she was more sad than angry. Sadness did not fuel the need for revenge.

When they were home, their lives revolved around what the security brought them to eat and otherwise live. They didn't dare go out. When Nala asked why they were not hotel hopping again, Vincent told her that it was pointless. Hawk would always know where they were. That didn't make much sense to her, but she decided to trust his judgment. Every day the security team - that she had no choice but to trust as well - swept the loft and Vincent's car for anything nefarious. They had yet to find anything, but Nala knew it was only a matter of time. She was starting to become more paranoid than Tasha was in the end. *Because I know what's going on. Did my sister have any idea?* Just how scared was Tasha in the end?

She often counted in her head. Maggie and Jay were an outlaw couple. Robin and Lucian were not much better off. That only left Sebastian and Quail, as well as Joseph and Starling. Would Crow try to off them too? Was he going to nuke the whole Aviary before the tell-alls began? If Crow was ever arrested, surely every Aviary member would be brought in for questioning.

Nala lost herself whenever she could. Video games. Phone games. Books. Anything was better than watching Vincent haunch over his dining table, surrounded by large machines as he tried to hack into Xavier Crow's private databases. The man needed a team, but he was only one man - one very, very smart man who knew what he was doing, but one man nonetheless. The frustration on his face was enough to make Nala throw up sometimes. All she could do was cook him dinner and try to entice him with video games as a break. That lasted about half an hour at a time. Then Vincent was back at the computers, grumbling, cursing, and threatening to throw machines across the room. The security personnel ignored them both unless otherwise summoned.

Nala got used to their presence to the point she stopped recognizing them. Oh, there were some men and occasionally a woman wandering around the loft while she watched TV or cut onions in the kitchen. They walked around the building outside at all hours of the day. They were armed. They were dangerous. Yet as long as Vincent kept paying them, they stood around his house utterly silent, and always observant. They were like the shadows in the corner.

Two days later, Nala heard something she never thought she would.

"Holy shit!" Vincent leaped up from his seat, staring wide-eyed at a white screen on his main monitor. "I fucking did it."

Nala turned on the couch, wondering what that meant. "You did what?" Hey, if he was excited, then so was she! "You found some evidence?"

"I hacked into his personal email. Nala!" He pivoted toward her, eyes wide and wild. "Do you understand? I broke through to his email! Not his business emails, although I can use this to access those too. But his personal emails."

Nala stood, letting the TV remote she held fall to the floor. "Have you found anything yet?"

"I don't know… but I have little time. I'm sure he has it set that he'll be notified of another IP address accessing his email. I probably have a few hours at the very most!" He sat back down, focusing on the screen as if it were a giant Christmas present. "Don't bother me, okay? I'm going to be printing like a mad man for the next few hours."

He did.

The printer never shut up. Nala did what she could to help, such as replacing ink, refilling the paper, and then going up to one of the security guards to ask for a paper run down at the local office supply store. By the time a man returned with a stack of computer paper, Vincent had queued a hundred emails to start going through.

Nala organized them for him. Emails about private holdings. Emails sent to Aviary members, sometimes about business deals and others chastising them for not participating enough. One sinister email to Lucian last week said, "Now, Mr. Clark, let's be reasonable… your darling girlfriend is in the hospital. Perhaps it's time to pay up what you owe."

The emails Nala let herself read were truly a sociopath's diary. Veiled threats. Direct threats. Musings between him and other close confidants about what it would be like to do this and that, none of "this or that" being anything cheery. Did red-heads really feel more pain? Or was it less pain? Would Melanie feel a lot of pain in the hospital? When he more or less told Hawk to cut the break-lines to Othello's car when she "went on a sojourn to Germany," he implied that he wanted Melanie to live - and feel pain.

"The beautiful birds of The Aviary need to have their wings clipped eventually. Otherwise they will stray too far from their nests and learn too much of the world. Women should be submissive, demure, but always available. To me and other men. That is true joy."

Vomit!

"This is so much fucking evidence," Nala muttered in awe. "Vincent, we've got…"

A loud clatter erupted as Vincent dropped his cup. Nala's head shot up. What she saw was the death of her boyfriend's ability to keep his cool.

"GET OUT."

The nearest bodyguard slowly lifted his head with only mild interest. "Excuse me, sir?"

"I said get out!"

Vincent shouted at every man in the room, until all three bodyguards shuffled out, mumbling about a crazy client. Nala stayed in her seat in the living room, holding a stack of emails she was in the middle of organizing. When Vincent returned from his frantic, frothing pacing, it was with total darkness in his eyes.

Was he going to tell her to get out too?

"What is it?" Nala squeaked, holding the papers in front of her mouth. "What did you find? Vincent…"

He sat back down in his seat, head in his hands.

Nala got up. This was the first time they were alone in days, and there was hardly any intimacy between them. She wanted to touch him. She wanted to pull his head to her chest and run her fingers through his dark hair. "I don't know what you found," she would say, "but know that I'm here and that I love you." Yeah, right.

She glanced at the computer screen. An email, like all the others. An old email, based on the date stamp. Three years ago. Apparently Vincent decided there was enough damning shit already and started honing in on the crap he really cared about - Desirée and her death.

In fact, the email that was open on the screen came from Desirée.

"Mr. Crow, let me say that I do not intend to press any charges. Please do not think that! I want this to blow over as smoothly as possible. I do intend to leave the project, however. I'm sorry that I have to do this, but I hope you understand the conflict of interest we now face.

On the subject of the child, I have not had the paternity test completed yet. However, since my fiancé and I have been mostly apart these past three months due to our schedules, I hope you understand when I say that… without a doubt, this child is yours. I will not be pressing charges for the event that brought this child's creation, but I do hope we can work out some kind of support. My fiancé and I have considerable debt and raising a child is not cheap in this day and age. I feel that for a man of your standing this is not too much to ask. My lawyer is willing to work with yours over whether to do a monthly stipend or an upfront amount to cover the child's life. It can be put into a trust, if you'd like. I also do not expect you to be a part of the child's life, and, as I'm sure you will agree, it may be best that you are not. I am not going to tell my fiancé about these events. Of course, this will all be settled for sure once I get the paternity results back, but please know that I am a confident woman."

Nala didn't read any further.

She stood, confused, her brain knowing what it read but rejecting every word. She looked to Vincent, who had the appearance of a man who was about to go mindlessly into war.

"What in the world is this?" Nala asked.

His head slowly turned toward her. The man looking at her wasn't her boyfriend Vincent. It was a different Vincent. One from a long, long time ago. This was the Vincent who found out something awful about his fiancée. His dead fiancée.

"You don't get it?" Vincent's voice was laced in poison. "Desirée was pregnant when she died. It wasn't mine."

Chapter 42

Nala sank against the table. She felt the whrrs of the nearest computer fan blow hot air against her back.

"You're not saying…"

"I didn't believe it at first when I saw his other emails regarding the subject." Vincent curled a hand into a fist and smacked it against the table. His fist turned red, but he did not react to any pain. "Then I did more digging. I found emails from Desirée briefly mentioning a pregnancy. I thought she was talking about the first one that…" He choked. "Then I dug more. Do you know what I found, Nala?" He didn't wait for her to respond. "I found references to a night she worked late with Crow. A night she says she doesn't remember but somehow woke up naked from."

"Vincent, don't do this yourself…"

Too late. "She would have never cheated on me!" Both fists hit the table now, sending Nala up and a good step away. Vincent's rampage was only getting started. "Do you know what that monster did to her? Do you?"

Nala swallowed. "I have a good idea." Neither of them would say the word.

Vincent jabbed a finger against the monitor. "This is dated one week before she died. There are references to her going to meet her lawyer to talk about child support. Do you know what was going to happen two days later?"

Nala shook her head. Of course she had no idea, but she was sure Vincent would tell her.

"She was going to come home. I remember getting a call from her, saying she had to get away from work for a while. That she couldn't wait to see me. That she wanted me to give her a lot of hugs and kisses."

A shiver tore down Nala's spine.

"She was scared and in pain. And pregnant. I don't doubt she was going to tell me about the pregnancy, at least…" Vincent turned away from the computer. "For fuck's sake!"

"Is that why she was…"

Vincent glared at Nala. "I found an email to Hawk along those lines, yeah. Desirée was killed because Crow didn't want a crowling out there in the world."

A car accident is an effective way of making sure that at least a miscarriage happens. Desirée dying was probably a cherry on the man's sundae.

"Desirée would have never cheated on me. Nor would she have ever done anything to make a baby go away. She wanted kids so badly one day. She was…too much of a liability."

His voice finally softened. Nala looked at him, seeing a man battered and broken. Again. He had already lost his fiancée. *Now he finds out that she had been assaulted by the man he already hates the most… and that she was pregnant.* If Vincent was heartbroken before, he was probably decimated now. Nala did not deny her heart's desire to go to him.

There was nothing she could possibly say. Whatever darkness Vincent now found himself in was nothing compared to what Nala felt regarding Tasha. When his arms wrapped tightly around her, bringing her in while breathing heavily into her sweatshirt, Nala thought back to all the other things Vincent had told her. Not just losing Desirée. Losing a baby. Losing parts of his youth, his life to grief and the constant, toxic black cloud it brought. Nothing - and she knew this as well as she knew her own heart - that happened between them over the past several weeks could possibly overshadow that. *I'm not enough to make that pain go away. Even if he loves me now, it's not enough to soothe this shock.*

"You can cry, you know," she said, smoothing down his hair. "I won't think any less of you. Go ahead. Cry. When you're done, we'll take the next natural course of action." Nala desperately hoped it involved lawyers and the police. "I'm here."

Whether or not he cried… well, Nala would not divulge that to anyone. That was between him and her.

***

"It feels like a stab right to my fucking heart. Multiple stabs. Like I really have been murdered, and here I am, suffering from my wounds."

Vincent rubbed the fatigue from his eyes, lying back in bed and attempting to stare at his bedroom ceiling. Nala also lay beside him, holding his hand and fighting back the urge to put her soothing touch all over his body. Kiss his face. Smother him with affection he probably didn't want right now. "I'm so sorry," she said for the hundredth time that night. They were still alone, with a bodyguard outside their door, but otherwise alone. "I can't even imagine how you feel right now."

"Do you know how happy I would have been if she got to tell me she was pregnant again? I probably would have thought the one night we had in those three months was enough to make it happen. I would have never thought it wasn't mine, even if the timing was off. I was going to be a father, Nala. A husband and a father."

"I know."

"Even though it was three years ago, I'm feeling it all right now. So many what-ifs in my head. What if I drove up there and got her myself? What if I fetched her before he laid a single hand on her? What if she had a miscarriage again? Would Crow have still…"

"You can't think like that. The man is pure evil. I read those emails, Vincent. He plays with fire and gets off on it. Everything is a thrill to him. Taking over the world. Taking over people. Taking whatever he wants, both legal and illegal. We know what he did to Desirée. Don't you think I know he was doing the same things to my sister?"

"I forgot all about that. Sorry. I've been making this all about myself."

Nala shook her head against her pillow. "Yours is the much bigger shock right now. I recognize that. I'm so sorry you had to find that out, Vincent. I'm sure Desirée never wanted you to know those details. She sounds like a woman who would want you to be happy about the baby, regardless of how it came to be."

"How can I feel anything else now? I was given something and had it taken away in the same instance. It's like whiplash. It's like we were cursed. Every time she became pregnant…"

"Stop going down those paths. They won't do you any good." Nala touched her head to his. "We need to regroup right now. You've got a mountain of evidence from his emails. We need to figure out what to do with it. Should we go to the police tomorrow?"

"I'm hesitant. I found a ton of emails between him and some big names in law enforcement. All over the west coast, not just around here. This is really big."

"Call your lawyer, at least."

"I will. Tomorrow. I'm too fucking tired right now."

"Naturally." Nala sank into the bed, hoping Vincent would cuddle her like he sometimes did. Well, he used to do it all the time. Only recently had he started sleeping far on his side of the bed, waking up to turn over and then over again. Sighing, Nala buried herself in his chest, letting her finger touch the soft fabric of his shirt. "I love you, Vincent. I may be young and dumb, but I know what it's like to feel pain. I'm here."

He stroked her hair, drifting off to sleep. "I know. Thank you."

Nala didn't expect him to say he loved her too. Especially not on today of all days. *A girl can still hope.* If the man hadn't been closed off before? He was impossible to penetrate now. Whatever he felt for her… it did not compare to the current horrors tearing through his mind and body. No, Nala wouldn't hear a declaration of love tonight, and probably not anytime soon. She could live with that. She would have to.

Entry #21

Everything is worse than I imagined.

I finally managed to break into Crow's email. His personal email. I found about what anyone would expect. Including emails between him and Desirée.

I can't believe it.

I can't fucking believe it.

Dare I even write it? That my Desirée was pregnant with THAT MAN'S child? Her own words to him and the fact I refuse to believe she ever cheated on me… they all lead me to one terrible conclusion.

I'm so sorry, Desirée. I had no idea you were in so much pain. I didn't know that you were that scared when you died. If I had known what that man did to you, I would have killed him myself! Right now I'm full of so much blinding rage that it's taking every bit of self-control I have to write these words.

Xavier Crow assaulted my fiancée. I don't want him to fucking die because he hurt the woman I loved. I want him to die because he transgressed something so deep and personal that I have no choice but to imagine him dying the most painful death possible.

I scare myself when I am like this, but how I can feel anything else? Desirée… if you're out there, please forgive me. I had no idea. You hid it so well. Please believe me when I say that I would have loved that child as my own. Even if I knew it wasn't mine. Even if I knew whose it was. Even now, I imagine you here, with our son or daughter, trying to move on from the pain you were made to feel. I would be there for you. I would share my strength with you, with our family.

If he had let you live, we would be married by now. Our child would be two. I would be the happiest man in the world.

I sit here in my bed, shaking, replaying your words over and over in my head. "I'm coming home, Vincent. Please be waiting for me." I'm here. I'm waiting. I'll always be waiting.

Don't tell Nightingale.

Chapter 43

"All right, we'll be there soon." Vincent turned off his phone and tucked it in his front pocket. "The lawyer is waiting for us on the east side. He's got his office there."

Nala nodded. East of the river wasn't as nice as downtown, but a lot of the neighborhoods were definitely up and coming. Not a bad place for a lawyer to set up a private practice and get a good piece of real estate.

"I have no idea how long this is going to take." Vincent nodded to the bodyguard on duty and backed his car out of its parking space. Rain splashed on the windshield long before Vincent was able to turn on the wipers. *Good thing no one else lives on this street.* Nala could hardly see the road in front of them. "You got the printouts?"

Nala motioned to the folder she carried in her arms. "Why would I be without it?"

"Making sure." Vincent changed gears before easing down the empty street. "We can't be too careful at the moment."

Speak for yourself. Ever since Nala realized how much danger her life was in, all she did was be careful. To the point of mayhem. Well, it was better than being dead anyway. "I can't wait to rub Crow's face in this shit." Nala grinned as they waited at the nearest light. "I mean, this was obtained illegally, but the lawyer will know where to go from here… right?"

Vincent shrugged. "That is certainly the hope." He readjusted his mirrors before putting his foot on the gas pedal. "I'm going to this lawyer specifically because he's taken down corporate giants before. Just recently set up shop in Portland. From what I can gather, he can't be bribed. That gives me a lot of hope."

Nala glanced in her mirror. Through the waves of rain crashing down upon them, she saw the glimmer of a black car pull out and follow them down the road. *Must be security.* Wouldn't be the first time they tailed them through downtown. Nala didn't want to know how much Vincent was paying these guys to be badass. They made her feel like a member of the First Family. *Too bad my parents weren't born in America.* So much for that presidential dream.

"What are we going to do when this is over?" she asked, watching dreary buildings go by as Vincent took the long way to the river. At this time of day it was probably faster than taking the main thoroughfares, especially when it came to the bridges. "I mean… I'm assuming we'll still be together… right?"

The idea that this could possibly be over soon already felt absurd, but Nala had to hold on to some sort of hope. Yet when she envisioned a future without Xavier Crow, she had a hard time imagining it without Vincent either. *I don't want to think about that.* A month ago, before she realized how much she was falling for him, it would have been a lot easier to go her separate way from him. Take his money. Maybe ask for some severance so she could move away from Portland and go somewhere cheaper, where her money would last longer. Now? Vincent was a man she admired, respected, and… adored. *Gag!* Nevertheless, Nala's heart was beholden to his. And even if he had been forthcoming with his affections, it still didn't make her assume they would have a happily ever after when all this was said and done.

Vincent glanced at her. "If you wouldn't mind. I'm not going to kick you out of my house, Nala."

He said it so softly that she almost couldn't hear him. *Does that mean he loves me?* She bit back her words. Now was not the time to ask. Vincent was the calmest he had been in a day, and Nala did not want to upset that. The last thing she wanted was to give her boyfriend a heart attack… especially since he was driving.

"Hey, Nala…" Vincent's eyes were locked on his rearview mirror. "If something happens to either one of us, I want you to know that I…"

He never had the chance to finish his thought. A bullet burst through the back window and right through the windshield.

Nala's heart leaped in her throat; Vincent swerved the car onto another street. Cracks exploded against the windshield, barring any ability to see the road ahead. Yet Vincent craned his head enough to keep his eye on the ever-busying streets of downtown Portland.

The car behind them gunned the gas and came dangerously close to rear-ending them.

"Holy…!"

Vincent whipped the wheel to the left, throwing Nala against the window - even with her seatbelt on. Another bullet whizzed by the window, but thanks to Vincent's quick reflexes, this one merely grazed the mirror on Nala's side.

When she got a close look at the reflection, she saw beyond herself. She saw Hawk in the nondescript car behind them.

"It's her!" she shouted, the car whipping onto yet another street. Vincent kept his head low as he stared at the road before him, the windshield wipers moving so quickly that it almost looked like they would fly off at any moment. "It's that crazy-ass bitch!"

"I know!" Vincent jammed his hand against the stick-shift and slammed his other hand on the horn. Some poor homeless woman with a cart full of clothes and tarps screamed before jumping out of the way, upturning her cart and spilling cloth and denim all over Everett Street. "Fuck!"

The mishap caused Hawk to swerve to avoid crashing into the woman now running around in paranoid circles. More rain came down, obscuring the scene as Vincent hurried to switch streets yet again.

They were lucky that these streets were relatively empty at this time of day. They were not lucky that a homicidal maniac was right on their tails - because here came Hawk again, a fucking fly that they couldn't swat with a rolled up newspaper no matter how much they tried.

"Vincent!"

"I know!"

Adrenaline pumped in Nala's veins. Her instincts told her to leap out of the car, to roll on the wet sidewalk and take her chances with a homeless camp set up in a nearby park. Yet the logical side of her brain said that was insane. Yeah, sure, maybe Nala wouldn't be trapped in this car, putting her life in Vincent's busy hands, but she would also be an easier target. How could she outrun Hawk? In her car? She was probably fitter, faster than Nala. She also had a gun. That was sort of a big issue.

But if I jump out, she'll probably come after me and leave Vincent alone. Nala only thought that because she would be the easier target. Perhaps Vincent was the bigger target, but Hawk probably didn't care who she killed as long as she got one of them finally. Not that there was much time to analyze this situation. Nala was fucked, no matter how she approached it.

"Ah!" Nala's bile lifted from her stomach and into her throat as a third bullet shot through the back window. She didn't know where this one went. She didn't have time to assess her body. Vincent was gunning the gas and swerving around any traffic getting in his way.

The whole situation was surreal. Nala had seen plenty of car chases on TV, but to actually be in one? To hear the inevitable sirens in the background? To feel the rush of adrenaline in the most terrible way possible? Tears of fear and anxiety wanted to burst from Nala, but she was in too much shock to process them. Trapped in a car with no control over what happened, all she could do was bend over in her seat and cover her head with her hands, making her a much smaller target for any wayward bullets.

"Hold on!" Nala didn't know what gear Vincent shifted the car into, but shit was fast, woozy, and pumping blood as much as it pumped horsepower. Tires crept onto narrow sidewalks. People out shopping or parking their cars screamed as they jumped out of the way. Nala saw a horrible end no matter what happened. Either they were shot or they crashed, like Desirée had. Like Othello had. *I think I would rather be shot in the head!*

She had to trust Vincent. She had to trust his ability to remember city geography as he sped across a bridge and entered another part of town. A flatter part of town.

Easier for Hawk to catch up.

But also easier for them to get away.

Sirens echoed in the distance. Who was chasing whom? Were they both being pursued by police? Was it Hawk being tailed? Or… the worst scenario possible… did she have them in Crow's pocket, and they were both chasing Nala and Vincent? *Make my death swift, God.* Nala didn't pray much, but she did now, with her hands folded in her lap and her lips muttering a hasty prayer.

"I can lose her!" Vincent barely touched his breaks as he swerved around a corner, honking his horn every second as people jumped out of the way. He ran a red light, causing a spattering of people and cars to compensate.

Nala saw the horror before it arrived. A large intersection. A red light. No time to stop. And no time to wait for Hawk to catch up and smack them into oncoming traffic anyway.

Vincent would do that on his own.

Screams erupted from every direction. Vincent cursed at the top of his lungs, whipping the steering wheel this way, holding himself back, and pointing in the other direction. Nala remained curled up in her seat, belt far away from her throat in case it got any ideas about decapitating her.

Horns that did not belong to Vincent's car blew up. Through every window - whether broken or not - Nala saw a riot of colors through the rain. Cars. Trucks. People. Bags. Signs. Buildings. This part of Portland was about to get a face lift. Luckily it did not come from Vincent, who managed to maneuver his way through the red light without a scratch.

The same couldn't be said for the cars behind them.

Nala would never forget that moment. When she looked in the side mirror, she saw three cars smack into one another, a flurry of pedestrians run away screaming, and enough smoke to be mistaken for another cloudy day. Before she could find out if a fire erupted from the pileup, Vincent turned down another road and swerved around cars until they were on the nearest bridge taking them into Washington.

It wasn't until they were halfway across the Columbia when Vincent finally slowed down, his eyes almost never leaving the rearview mirror. "I think we lost her in that crash," he mumbled. "If it didn't get her, it at least slowed her down."

Even so, Nala found it very fucking difficult to calm down. Her heart continued to beat incessantly in her chest; her breath was caught in her throat like a whirlwind. Nala had come this close to death yet again, and she was the one about to explode in tears and vomit.

"We'll have to dump the car," Vincent muttered. "Otherwise they'll know where we're going. Plus, cops."

Nala looked around. They were in Vancouver now, surrounded by cars with Washington plates and road signs shaped like a dead president's head. "Where are we going?"

Vincent puffed out his cheeks as his brain continued to tick off a list of things he had to do. "We'll head toward Seattle. I'll grab some cash at an ATM when we dump the car."

"Dump the car?"

"You heard me."

Oh, she did. The moment they were in the countryside, Vincent prompted her to get out before he had the chance to pull off the side of the road. He parked his car behind a small grove of trees. It wouldn't be enough to cover it forever, but it should be enough to give them a head start… wherever they were going.

They got out, taking whatever valuables they could carry… which wasn't much. Nala had her small backpack and Vincent had his wallet. He brought his keys with him, not that he would need them.

He grabbed a large wad of cash from the nearest ATM and peered around a quiet town in search of something. Hawk? Cops? No. It was a used car available for a few hundred bucks. Vincent paid extra cash in exchange for the seller's silence. The way the gruff looking man nodded... *He probably thinks we're drug dealers.* Nala had never felt dirty like this before. She kinda liked it, if only because it took her mind off the terrors they had been through.

This car was far from being as nice as Vincent's old one. It grumbled. It shook. The seatbelt barely worked, but Nala made it work, because the last thing they needed was to be pulled over by police. Vincent kept to the back roads as they headed north to Seattle, where they, in his words, could lay low for a while. Nala had no idea what to expect in the next few hours, let alone days.

They didn't say a damn thing the whole drive to Seattle. Nala fought back a wave of shivers that could have either been illness or more fear. *When will I be safe again?* She looked to Vincent, whose grim face was set and sticking to the road before them. Signs announcing turn offs to the outskirts to Seattle eventually appeared. Nala wondered what they would do once they got there. Did he have friends? A safe-house? Were they wanted now? Nala tried to sink into her uncomfortable seat and take a nap, but sleep did not come easy with her adrenaline still on high.

It wasn't until they were checked into a hotel outside Seattle when Nala finally allowed herself to breathe, and it wasn't an easy breath. Even with Vincent sitting on the bed with her, their eyes staring emptily at a picture of a vase of daisies on the wall, Nala still waited for another bullet to whisk by or for the car she was no longer in to swerve in either direction.

Finally, she threw herself into Vincent's arms and held on for dear life.

"It's okay," he said, patting her back. "We're safe for now. We've got a car nobody is looking out for. I've got cash so I don't have to use my card. I can easily hack the GPS in our phones. I've got a fake ID so I can get us rooms..."

"You've got a fake ID?"

"Sure do. They're easy to get, especially with my connections."

He's probably seen fake IDs being made since college. Those tech geeks… "Is there anyone we can trust here? I don't know anyone in Seattle. Crow owns half this city too…"

"That may be so, but there was nowhere else to go in the moment. If we have to, I can sneak us down the coast toward California. I've got some friends there who may be able to help us." Vincent pulled away from her and gave her shoulders a firm, reassuring squeeze. "Don't worry, darling. Rest. I've got some calls to make."

Except Nala couldn't rest. She lay on the bed, afraid to take off any of her clothes even though they were the only ones she had in her possession. This reminded her of staying in hotels around Portland. Except things were even worse now… it actually wasn't like their previous situation at all!

"…I'm serious. I have all the evidence we need to get an arrest and a conviction. Yeah, I hacked it. Do you think I would admit otherwise?" Vincent must have been on the phone with the lawyer they were supposed to meet. "I need your help. No, stop, listen. I know you don't want to get involved, but you were involved the moment you met that man. He'll keep making your life hell until this is over, so you really want to help us right now. Okay? Good." Vincent sat at a table in the corner of the room and jotted something down on a complimentary notepad. "Make sure you hire some security. I can give you a number. If they'll let you, have a guy at the hospital. I'm serious, Lucian…"

Lucian? Nala turned over.

"I know you're freaked out, man. How do you think I feel? It's what I've been telling you since the beginning. You think you know the guy, but he's a fucking killer. That Hawk has tried to kill us twice now, and I have all the evidence I need to prove that she killed my fiancée and my girlfriend's sister. You think he won't come after you and Clara too? He already has!"

Silence. Vincent glared at his phone as Lucian spoke.

"No. Don't leave Portland unless you have to. I need someone there, especially since I don't have access to my computers. I need you to do me favor. I need you to look up the address of Jay and Marguerite Jones. Yes,

I'm serious. They are somehow involved with this. Crow killed their kid. At this point, anyone in The Aviary who hasn't been touched in some way by Crow's disgusting deeds is probably working with him. Look into that as well. Look for any tragic or mysterious deaths in the other members' families. Yeah, you remember Crow's girlfriend Raven? That was Nala's sister. I'm not fucking with you. Start digging. You're already in hot water, you might as well enjoy the bath."

When Vincent hung up, he sat on the edge of the bed next to Nala and put a hand on her side. "So what now?" she asked. "What are we gonna do? I doubt the police here are any help either. If anything, they want our asses as much as the ones in Portland do. Or anywhere. Oh my God, Vincent, how fucked are we?"

"Pretty fucked," he admitted. "That doesn't mean we can't get through this, though. Our main goal right now is to not get killed or arrested."

"Oh, well, that's easy."

He ignored her sarcasm. "We need to get the evidence into the hands of someone who can do something with it. The news? He probably owns all of it around here. Still, it won't hurt to look into it." Vincent tightened his grip on Nala. "I'm so sorry it has come to this. I knew going into The Aviary that I was putting myself at risk. I should have thought more about you as well, but…"

"Back then, I was your means to an end. Things have changed."

He nodded. "I'm sorry. I was short-sighted."

"You did what you thought was right. Do you think I was planning things any better? I don't blame you for any of this, Vincent."

"I'm glad."

Nala sat up, resting her head on the brunt of his shoulder. "Could you do me a favor? Could you hug me and say that we're going to be okay? Even if you're lying, I want to hear it."

Vincent drew her into his arms and kissed the side of her head. Nala had to fight back the urge to cry into the crook of his neck. *Be strong. Now is not the time to show too much weakness. Anything could happen at any moment.* Fuck.

"We're going to be all right, Nala." She knew that voice was fake. There was no way Vincent could say that so reassuringly. "At the very least, I'll make sure that you'll be all right. I'll do everything in my power to protect you. Because I…"

Nala's breath caught in her throat for the tenth time that day… and this time it had nothing to do with adrenaline. *Is he going to say it?* This would be a helluva time to admit that he loved her!

"Because I wouldn't make it if I lost you too."

That was as close to a love declaration as Vincent Lane would ever make. Nala rolled into his arms, letting her cheek feel the softness of his clothes. *I'm here. He's here. We're safe for now. I couldn't be safer with anyone else in this world. I fucking love him. I know he loves me. That's all that matters.*

Whatever happened now didn't matter. Nala was scared, but she was still willing to go down if Vincent was by her side. She hoped he felt the same exact way. He had to. For his sake - and hers.

Entry #22

We are on the run again, this time in Seattle. Every time I think I can't come closer to death, I'm proven wrong again.

This time it's indisputably personal.

Not just my hatred for him.

But his hatred for me.

One of us will destroy the other before it's too late.

Chapter 44

History repeated itself. They went from hotel to hotel, Vincent using a series of fake IDs he kept in the back of his wallet. Nala's identity changed as well depending on who asked. Sometimes her name was Natalie. Other times it was Natasha. Once, she introduced herself to a hotel clerk using the name Natalya. They were easy to remember and yet so different. Not like Vincent, who was Lewis one minute and Gabriel the next.

He used his reserves of cash to rent these rooms, buy them food, and buy them small necessities. It was not a glamorous life, not even when compared to hotel hopping in Portland. That had been a warning. This was real. Nala lived under a constant threat of death. Her hotel could catch on fire. She could be shot or hit by a car crossing the street with Vincent right in front of her. What a way to go.

And Vincent? Well, all Nala could say was that she was happy he had plenty to distract himself with. Otherwise, when he suffered from downtimes, he was a bundle of negative energy.

The man was still processing the horrors. The horrors of what Xavier Crow did to his fiancée, and the horrors of almost dying in his own car. Sometimes he opened up to Nala about these terrors, but more often than not he drowned himself in phone calls and researching things on either his or Nala's phone. She tried to help where she could, but without knowing what ticked in her boyfriend's mile-a-minute brain, it was nearly impossible.

"Is there anything I can do?" she asked the second day. Vincent kicked up his heels on the hotel room couch, searching a million things on his phone. *If he had a real computer, I would be really shut-out.* The only thing keeping Mr. Billionaire from walking into a store and buying one was the fact he didn't have enough cash and didn't want to use his card anywhere. "I hate standing around feeling useless."

"You're not useless," he said. "But if it makes you feel better, you could go through those emails and highlight the really important things."

It was a task best left to some law enforcement grunt, but Vincent was right in that it made her feel better. *At least I have something to do.* As painful as some of the emails were to read, Nala re-read as many as she could, creating a color-coded system from a pack of highlighters Vincent bought at the nearby convenience store. Pink for names. Green for ordered hits. Blue for veiled threats. Etc., etc.

She nearly lost her light lunch of a sandwich when she reached the correspondence between Crow and Desirée. He did unspeakable things to her. She carried her child, and was probably never going to tell Vincent either thing. What would Nala have done in that situation? Well, she wasn't Desirée, that was for sure. She would have made very different decisions from Vincent's fiancée. One of those things would have been telling him about the acts. Then again, Nala knew a very different Vincent from the one Desirée was destined to marry.

Was she scared? Desirée must have been scared. Although her words to Crow were calm and collected, there was an underlying panic to them. She didn't want Crow to be a part of her life - not after what he had done. Yet she needed the money. She had decided to raise the baby - with Vincent, no less - and back then there was no way to know how rich Lane Technological Solutions would make everyone. *I wouldn't take that poisoned money.* Easy for Nala to say. She was used to poverty and making things work on the tightest budget around, whether or not she had to take care of people beyond herself. Desirée probably wasn't used to that. She probably grew up middle class like Vincent. She wanted a certain life for her baby, regardless of who the biological father was. Because Vincent would be the *real* father.

Nala swallowed the last of her bile for the day as she put those emails to the side. Instead, she went through some more recent ones, particularly about Othello and Sparrow. Last Nala had heard, Melanie / Sparrow was still in a coma in some German hospital. Just like how Robin was still in a hospital, probably the safest place for her to be right now.

"Lucian sent me the Jones' address," Vincent interrupted her. "They live all the way out in Hillsboro."

"What's weird about that?" It was the westernmost suburb, practically in farm country if someone strayed too far from the main streets, but not a strange place for someone to live. If the Jones' wanted extra land, that was the place. "Don't Starling and Joseph live in Beaverton?"

"That's all well and good, but the address isn't exactly high flying. They live in pure suburbia. Two bedroom house. Small yard. The house is worth about $500,000, and that's only because of the bubble. A few years ago when it was bought, it was only about $300,000."

Only, the billionaire says. "So what are you saying? That they're not exactly swimming in dough?"

"Hardly. Either that or they love living the simple life by a millionaire's standards."

Nala thought back to their dinner. It felt like months ago. "I thought they were investing in huge properties, though?"

"That's what I thought too. They're getting money from somewhere, but it's definitely not reflected in their home. The nicest thing they own is their car, and it's five years old."

"Do you know how ridiculous you sound?"

"Point being, Nala... well, I don't know what the point is. Find anything new in those emails?"

Just an exchange where Desirée condemns Crow to hell. "Not yet. I'm organizing them again. Hey, at least we have them. Who knows what they've gone through at your house."

Vincent pursed his lips. "I'm sure the police have been through a time or two by now. They probably know more about you than you do."

"Maybe they think I'm a Russian spy by now. Or a mail-order bride. Even though I was born here."

She exchanged a smile with Vincent. He found it in him to waggle his eyebrows at her. "I have very discerning tastes for a man who…"

"Who yanks girls off staircases and turns them into his subs?"

"I was under the impression you liked it."

"Oh, I do, Mr. Lane."

It was the first real flirtation - let alone one laced with promises of kink - between them in days. Maybe a week. Ever since the bodyguards started hanging around the loft, there weren't many opportunities to even make out, let alone have sex. *I'm dying.* Now that the adrenaline rush had faded for the time being, Nala's hormones took over again. Her period came and went over the past few days, both relieving her that she wasn't pregnant and annoying her that it existed during such a time of high stress, so now all she could think about was getting off and then getting off some more.

There hadn't been time for that, though. There definitely wasn't time in Vincent's world. If he longed for her like she did for him, none of that was happening until…

Nala stopped flipping through the stack of printouts. With a highlighter in hand, she grimaced, her face paling as she read her sister's name in a "FROM" field.

"Mr. Crow, I cannot thank you enough for the plethora of opportunities you have given me these past few months. Working as a researcher for your company has been an absolute pleasure. I'm sorry the latest trial did not work out like we hoped, but my resignation from your company has nothing to do with the work itself. I just can't do the personal anymore."

Nala knew that she should not keep reading. Yet she did, because she was a glutton for punishment.

"I've learned a lot from The Aviary. I've learned things I didn't even know about myself. But I think you and I both know I didn't go into it with you because it was a calling, or because I thought it would be an exciting adventure. I went because I wanted to please you. When you asked me to dinner all those months ago, I was the happiest girl in the world. I'm sure I don't have to tell you that you're one of the most eligible bachelors in the country, and you're a bachelor your whole life for a reason. It's because you're not meant to have one woman for the rest of your life, let alone at a moment. I know about you and Ms. Hawk. I also know about the woman in New Delhi and the twins in Paris.

"None of that ever bothered me. I never had any delusions that I would one day be Mrs. Tasha Crow. But I still wasn't happy. You pushed me to do things I wasn't comfortable with, but I did them because I wanted to hold onto the idea of us being more serious. Now I realize I was a pretty girl who worked in your chain of command. I caught your fancy. You had visions of me bent over and spanked, and with your power and money knew you could make all of that a reality with a snap of your fingers. Don't worry. I feel plenty stupid. I may be intelligent, but I am very stupid in other realms of the world.

"So not only am I resigning from Black Raven Pharmaceuticals, but I am also parting ways with you - personally. I hope that you can find someone to make you truly happy, Xavier. If that's multiple people… well, that's okay too. I don't regret my time with you, but I do wish I had caught on to my real needs sooner."

Nala didn't bother to read the response from Crow. She was too busy staring at the paper, digesting her sister's words. Probably some of the final words she ever wrote, judging from the timestamp. *Tasha looked that miserable and she still considers it unregrettable?* That didn't seem right. Just like it didn't seem right that Tasha would willingly go out with a man like Xavier Crow!

Oh, who was Nala kidding? Tasha was a romantic like most women. She dreamed of meeting the perfect guy and having him sweep her off her feet. Apparently she didn't care if that man was over fifty - as long as he had the charm and the funds. Love could be blind, and so was Tasha's ability to see the danger in front of her.

Why did it have to be Tasha? How was it possible that her own smarts brought about her demise? If she had never been that smart, then she would have never advanced that quickly up the ranks at Black Raven, let alone get a job there. Sure, some other danger may have come from somewhere else… but what did it matter? Nala needed to stop thinking about this crap.

Especially since it had the power to make her cry.

While she managed to hold in most of the tears, she still sniffed a little, causing Vincent to look up from his phone and in her direction. When he asked what was wrong, Nala put the emails aside and stood. "I'm going to take a shower," she announced. "I need to clear my mind."

The bathroom was one of the only places she could be alone. Not that she didn't want to be around Vincent, but sometimes a girl needed privacy, even if they were in mortal danger. Taking her phone into the bathroom and pretending to have stomach problems or taking showers that lasted a lifetime helped her regroup upstairs.

Until that day, Vincent respected her requests for privacy. He would occasionally ask if she was okay, but beyond that, he let her do her thing until she was ready to rejoin him wherever they stayed. Until that day. That day, Vincent came into the unlocked bathroom five minutes after Nala started her shower, when she stood naked against the wall and let the hot water drip down her breasts and speckle her legs.

She said nothing as he undressed and pulled back the shower door. *Haven't seen him this naked in a while.* Her eyes went straight to his chest, then his groin. *Good to know I'm still alive even after all the shit.* Thinking that meant one of the first things Vincent saw was a smile cracking on her face.

"Hope you don't mind if I crash your naked party," he said, stepping in and only flinching a little when the hot water hit his unsuspecting skin. "As it so happens, I need to take a shower too. Why waste the extra water when we could take one together?"

"Why, Mr. Lane, we don't shower together often."

"We should change that. You look great naked. And wet. I'd love to see you naked more often. And wet."

Nala laughed, the water droplets covering his shoulders, his arms, and his chest. She wouldn't mention where it was dripping from. "I don't mind seeing you naked either."

He came closer, which was a feat in a standard-sized shower. Nala pressed against the wall, not going to him, but also not declining his advances. *Make love to me, jerk. Make me forget everything again.* "Look at that. We're both naked in the shower. Who would have ever thought?"

Nala tilted her head back. "Cut the crap, Vincent. Make love to me."

"Yes ma'am."

His kisses started as tender caresses to her face, and then he pushed against her, his strong, naked body taking over her existence and blocking her in a world where everything was peachy and fine. Nobody got hurt. Nobody was in danger. It was only Nala and her boyfriend, the man she loved more than anyone else she wanted to think about.

It felt oddly safe in their hideaway. Their shower was warm, but their bodies were warmer. All Nala wanted was to feel him around her, above her, beneath her, and inside her. She was rewarded with that latter request when Vincent lifted her off the ground and pulled her legs around his waist. With the wall propping her up from behind, it was easy enough to let him fuck her without a care in the world.

That's not true. I care. She cared a lot. About him. About her. About their possible future together.

What would they do when it came to it? When Crow was gone? When justice was served and their vengeance quenched? Would they really keep being a couple? Or would the real world come crashing down on them?

Nala only thought of these things briefly while they made love, if it could be called that. Making love in the shower wasn't easy no matter who a person was. It didn't matter that Vincent could easily lift her off the ground and make her his. There was the water, a blessing and a curse. There was her, nearly fighting him every step of the way even though she desperately wanted him inside of her. Then there was his need to kiss her while he thrust into her, which brought her up closer to his mouth while he pulled her down below. *Holy shit, man, I'm still human!*

Nevertheless, being taken to a place of ecstasy was most welcomed, even in that hotel shower. When Nala began to climax, holding on to him tight with both arms and hips, she fantasized about a world where she didn't have to fantasize at all. Because everything would be as it should be. She could live in the moment. She could bask in the love emanating from both of their bodies.

Suffice to say, neither of them got very clean that night.

"That was worth every sore muscle I'm going to have tomorrow," Vincent said with a satisfied sigh as he climbed into bed later. He brought Nala into his hold, planting a kiss on her forehead. "I've missed you like that. I've missed you in a lot of ways."

"Unfortunately there aren't a lot of opportunities for a lot of kinky sex when we're on the run."

"No, but… this is nice too."

Nala sat up, rubbing her hand against his bare chest. *Good skies above, have I ever missed this.* It was a wonder she was able to speak instead of placing her lips all over his body. If stuff like this kept up, she would be forgetting all about the shit going on outside of the hotel room. That could be as equally dangerous, however.

"Don't tell me, Mr. Lane," Nala said, looming over him. "You're getting antsy for something a bit more in line with your predilections."

"Don't get me wrong. I like vanilla sex as much as the next man."

"Of course you do, but you're Vincent Lane. You also like spanking my ass and tying me up in elaborate designs."

"Would I ever deny it?"

"I hope not."

He gripped her tightly, his strong hands leaving their marks all over her skin. *Thank you, sir. I haven't felt properly owned and used by you in a good while.* If there was one nice thing she could say about that week of hotel hopping in Portland, it was that it got such needs out of her system for a while, but they were back now, demanding Vincent to flip her over and show her what she really was. Turned out that kinky role-play scenarios were her favorite form of escapism. Some women read books. Others played fantastical video games. Nala Nazarov? She pretended to be a sex demon in need of capture and taming.

Or maybe it was Nightingale who was those things.

"Let's be real. We're always going to be on edge unless we can purge those negative thoughts and feelings from our bodies. We both know how we do that." She didn't wait for his reaction. "We're going through some heavy shit right now. Things are going to come to a head. We're going to need to be as clear-headed as possible for what lies ahead of us."

"What are you trying to get at, exactly?"

"I'm saying that I think we should take a little time - maybe one night - to be as wild as fucking possible. You know it would be good for the both of us. This vanilla stuff is good for the day, maybe two days, but regardless of what we're up against, we need to take ourselves as far as we can go and fucking own it."

"My darling." Vincent grinned, his fingers combing through her hair as they loved to do. "I dare say that you and I make a great pair."

"It's because I can sense all this tension in your body." Nala rubbed his stomach. It was warm, yes, but it was also fraught with the terrible things he always thought about, tucked deep inside his gut and threatening to come forth at the most inopportune moment. "It's not good for you. Not right now, not ever. It's not good for me either. I want to spoil you, Vincent. I also want you to spoil me. We need that spoiling before we leave this city and do whatever needs to be done next."

"You don't have to keep making a case to me. I'm fully on board."

"We'll start by getting this shit out of sight." Nala climbed out of his embrace and off the bed. Naked, she crossed the room, picking up the emails strewn across a table and tucking them back into their folder. She made sure to put her sister's emails on the bottom. "Unless it's absolutely necessary, we are not to look at any of these things. Agree?"

Vincent rolled onto his side and propped himself up on his arm. "Agree. I won't look at them if you won't look at them. We should try to forget about them… until the time is right."

"Yes. Until the time is right to use them to fuel our rage."

Vincent took a deep breath. "Yes."

"All right." Nala tucked the folder deep into the back of her backpack, padded with spare changes of clothes. "That's done. You keep doing your research, Mr. Lane. After all, we need to finish our mission eventually. In the meantime, I will do some research of my own."

He raised his eyebrows.

"I'm going to come up with the perfect role-play scenario." Nala ambled back to the bed, sure to sway her hips and let her hair flow free all around her nubile body - a body Vincent never once stopped staring at. Nala didn't doubt that beneath those covers Mr. Lane was starting to stir again. Maybe it was time for a preview. Was there anything he could use to tie her up with in here? "You and me, sir. We're going to use all this crazy energy to fuel the wildest sex either of us has ever had. Cosmos willing, it will clear our heads enough to let us focus on the bigger picture. Right now, we need to focus on us."

Vincent grinned, extending a hand to draw Nala back into bed. "Living fast. Living loose. You're a terrible influence on me, darling."

She was more than happy to crawl into bed next to him, feeling his arms wrap tight around her as she sank deep into his embrace again. *His skin feels perfect against mine.* Even if they didn't make love again that night, it would still be the best day they had in a long while. "Believe it or not, I'm doing what I think is best for you, sir."

"I love it when you talk dirty."

"If you think that's dirty, then you have no idea what's already stirring in my mind."

"Oh, I have a good idea."

"No, you really don't."

"I'm looking forward to finding out, then. Just know that we don't have much time. I'm planning on driving down to California soon. I've contacted a few lawyers I know there who may be able to actually help us. Not to mention… I have a few buddies from college down in Silicon Valley who owe me a few favors."

Yeah, yeah. Nala wasn't thinking about that. Her mind was far, far beyond, already planning the best way for her to be useful. She may not be able to hack into servers, or have connections all over the west coast, or a billion dollars at her disposal, but she understood Vincent and his… needs. Nala was going to concoct the perfect scenario for them to enact. It would let her purge her brash mind. It would let him purge his mounting anger. Because Nala could feel it in every flexing muscle. Vincent might smile, he might crack jokes right now, and he may bask in the afterglow of sex, but inside he was a ticking time bomb with a very low counter. It was only a matter of time before he exploded and ruined every chance of seeing the justice he so desperately needed.

Nala knew how to curb that. She also knew how to save herself in the process. *It's kinda scary.* If her plan worked, they would both come out the other side very different people - and even closer to one another. How did one embrace such a possibility?

With an open heart and an even more open mind. Not only would Nala need both, but Vincent would as well. *This will either kill us or make us stronger.* She didn't know if she referred to the role-play or finally taking down Xavier Crow any way possible.

***

Nala went back to the convenience store and purchased a notebook. She stole pens from the hotel rooms they used. In this notebook, she copied down pertinent information she researched on her phone and wrote out drafts of a script for her and Vincent to follow. Meanwhile, her boyfriend kept to his phone, whether to do his own research or make a slew of phone calls to people all over the country. Perhaps the world.

She listened closely to him while writing her script. Particularly, she listened to his intonations and the words he used depending on who he was talking to. He called Lucian every day, either reassuring the frayed man or instilling a fear of God into him. Apparently, he was their #1 ally in Portland, for as much as that meant. That didn't mean a damn fucking thing to Nala. Lucian would do whatever he thought was safest for him and Robin. Or were they calling her Clara now?

Why was she listening so closely? Nala didn't care about the contents of his conversations. She cared about how they made her feel, on the most carnal level. Which words did her in? Which ones could be twisted in delightfully dirty ways? *Ooh, I like it when he sounds a little sinister.* That came out when he spoke to lawyers, none of whom would commit to helping Vincent and Nala take down a multi-billionaire with a shitton of connections.

Of course, doing this sent her deeper into her research. Thank goodness, because she was tired of obsessing over the terrible shit going on in the background of her life. Nala didn't need constant reminders that a powerful man out there wanted her dead. Nor did she want reminders that people she loved were dead or in danger in the hospital. Nor did she want to feel that creeping paranoia whenever she thought of other members of The Aviary. At that rate, she would be bothering Vincent to fire Andrew before he turned out to be an agent of Crow too!

No, she was perfectly happy to escape into her world of… what? Erotic fantasies? On one hand, Nala researched and wrote some of the darkest shit she ever braved. On the other, it was a welcomed reprieve from the realities around her. There would be plenty of time to take stock of what was happening in the world beyond her mind. This week did not have to be one of them.

Every once in a while Vincent asked her how it was coming along and if she would be done anytime soon. Nala would brush him off, and he would go back to doing what he did best - getting them into more trouble he would consequently have to get them out of again. *This time it's me getting us into trouble.* She wanted to laugh, but the reality was they very well could get into some trouble with what she had planned. The more her script came together? The more she started looking at Vincent through new eyes.

Would he do it? Or would he take a look at her dark words, dark dialogue, and darker actions and run far away from her? *Men think we're such delicate creatures.* Whether or not they built that world for themselves was not part of Nala's internal debate. Plus, even though Vincent often saw her tough side, he probably still saw her as a fragile waif in need of his protection. The moment he read this script once she was done? Who knew if that would change… if he would see her in a new, albeit dark, light.

I *wouldn't be writing it this way if I didn't know he had it in him too.* Nala had felt the possessive power of the way he made love to her. She knew how he could make her hate the simple act of walking for a day. He often said it himself: he could turn into more beast than man. The more Nala thought about that, the easier it became to slip into her day-long fantasies and fill her cheap notebook with the twisted shit she cooked in her brain.

One otherwise quiet day - after they had switched hotels for the sixth time since coming to Seattle - Vincent received a check from Lucian made out to one of the fake names. Nala only saw a glimpse of the amount, but it made her eyebrows go up. What a world it was when a billionaire couldn't risk withdrawing money from his own account and had to have a rich friend forward him some cash to be paid back later. Nala waited for some downtime in both of their work to go up to her boyfriend and ask for a hundred dollars. Two, if he could spare it.

"What do you need that much money for?" Vincent asked. "We don't need anything."

She still put her hand out expectantly. "I need supplies for this thing I'm working on. Trust me. You'll love it."

"Are you sure you're focusing on the right thing?"

"What should I be focusing on otherwise? You haven't given me anything to do."

Reluctantly, Vincent gave her some cash and told her to not stray too far from their block. At least he wasn't insisting on going with her. *Maybe he's getting too complacent.* Vincent had looked up the crash they were almost involved in a few days ago. One of the victims who ended up in the hospital with a concussion and pulled everything was none other than Hawk. She had also been arrested for reckless driving and possessing an unlicensed firearm. Out on bail and under house arrest in Crow's mansion in the West Hills… which meant she probably wasn't coming up for them anytime soon, assuming she knew where they were. But Nala wasn't going to give herself much room to breathe. Maybe today, but definitely not tomorrow.

She was careful, as always, making sure her hood was up wherever she went. In the Pacific Northwest, that was normal and didn't bring her any unwanted attention - it also meant people had a hard time identifying her, especially with fake IDs in tow. So when she went out to do her fantasy role-play shopping, she allowed herself to breathe for a whole four hours before going back to her and Vincent's hideout.

He was sitting solemnly on the bed, his eyes going straight to Nala - and not to her shopping bags.

"What is it?" she asked. The bags went in her corner stash of meager belongings. "Bad news? Has something happened?"

"In a matter of speaking." Vincent turned his phone around and showed her the screen. "I got an email from Xavier Crow. You will want to take a look at this."

Nala could barely swallow what fear bubbled up her esophagus before approaching her boyfriend. Her eyes went from his stoic ones to the words on the screen.

The email was set up in an elaborate, formal template. It looked like an Aviary invitation. Because it was.

She wanted to vomit when she saw what their old friend had written.

"Mr. Lane, you are a hard man to get a hold of these days! Your presence has also been sorely missed recently. That said, The Aviary will be taking a small turn in the upcoming days and weeks. Instead of the usual meetings, we will be having one-on-one interactions. It has come to my attention that some of our members are not as loyal as we would like to believe. As an act of good faith and a token of your loyalty to our beautiful enterprise, I am asking you to please let me meet with your sweet Nightingale for one night. It is my sincerest promise to return her to you as you left her."

Vincent mumbled a string of obscenities as he imagined whatever it was he did. Nala almost choked on laughter. When her boyfriend looked askance at her, she said, "He wants to fuck me. Oh my God, he wants you to sacrifice me to his cock." She had to laugh. It kept her from throwing up over the images in her head. *Don't think about it! Argh!*

"Nala," Vincent said, evenly. "It's a trap. He'll make sure you never leave his house in anything but a body bag, and that's being generous. He might have you buried or dumped somewhere."

"*After* he fucks me. Come on, the man must have some priorities."

"Nala!"

"What?" she sat back on her legs, Vincent's demeanor too delicious to pass up. "Oh, you're funny, Vince." Nala knew damn well he didn't like that name by now. So she said it, getting the rise she wanted. "You think I'll die before he does?"

"Don't joke like that." Vincent did his best to soften his voice, but Nala could still hear the disdain deep inside. Not disdain for her… but for what Xavier Crow could possibly do *to* her. "You know you would never have the opportunity to kill him, even if you had it in you."

"What do you mean by that?"

Vincent looked her right in the eye. Ripples of "this is the truth and you know it," exuded from those frosty blues. Nala shivered beneath the weight of it. "You are not a killer, Nala. You could never be like him or his merry band of assassins he probably has hiding around the world. You and I both know that the moment you confront him, you will freeze up in your fear and anger." He held up a hand to silence her before she could protest. "I don't say this to insult you. I say this because you are a *good* person. You wouldn't be able to kill him unless you had to protect yourself, and even then, no matter how good the lawyer I hire is, you will still go to jail. It's not worth it, Nala. I want revenge too, but there's no point seeking out justice that puts you behind bars as well. Your sister wouldn't want that."

What the fuck do you know about Tasha? Then again, what the fuck did Nala know about her either? *I would have never guessed that she was dating Crow…* Nala couldn't think about it. She also couldn't think about any glee Xavier felt over the prospect of taking Tasha's little sister too. Maybe their mother for all she knew.

"It's moot, anyway," Vincent said. "You're not going. We're not members of The Aviary anymore. Even if we wanted to go back…"

He didn't have to finish his thought. Nala knew what he was thinking. *We could have enjoyed that sort of arrangement after all.* Not to mention the potential friends they had made through the group. *I wish I could see Robin again.* Nala didn't know if she meant immediately or ever again. Clara Montgomery might continue her life pretending Nala never existed. It was doubtful she would return to The Aviary either. Yet all those people… almost everyone was there against their will in some fashion. They were all acting and pretending to keep Xavier Crow from ruining their businesses, buying out their properties or… killing them. Killing the ones they loved to make a point.

Nala put her hand on Vincent's shoulder. "You better come up with a plan, then. Because right now I can only think of two things: sex and murder."

Vincent shook his head. "What in the world have I done to you?"

"You?" Nala laughed, louder. "What makes you think it's you who did anything to me? I've had this in me my whole life, loverboy."

That was the last thing she said to him in a long time. *I see I'm still as brash as ever.* Nala went back to her couch and flipped open her notebook, the third draft of her script staring her in the face. *I'm going to need this. I need this to screw my head back on straight and stop being so stupid.* Vincent hadn't done a damn thing to make her the way she was, but he had the power to help this phase of her life end, and let another, more positive one begin.

It all came down to whether or not his research panned out. And whether or not he could play his part in Nala's fucked up fantasy.

Entry #23

The time has come. Nightingale and I must part, for her own good.

I'm not looking forward to telling her.

Chapter 45

Two important things happened the next day. First, Nala finished her script. Second, Vincent made some important decisions of his own.

When they sat down to go over their side of things, he was the first to speak. Probably not in his best interest. Because what came out of his mouth? Was liable to make Nala kill *him* next!

"You've gotta go away." That was the first thing he said to her. "I hate having to tell you that, Nala, but it's the truth. You're in too much danger. If you go away into hiding… maybe he'll spare you out of disinterest. It's me he's mainly after. I can set you up financially somewhere."

Nala crossed her arms and regarded him with every bit of disdain she could muster. "You're putting me in Vincent Protection."

"If you want to put it that way. You can't stay around me, though. Not for a long time."

"So you're getting rid of me?"

"Don't think of it that way." Vincent put his hand on her knee, but it wasn't enough to make her feel better. *Don't think that's possible right now.* "It doesn't mean I care about you any less. For fuck's sake, Nala, it's because I care about you so much that I feel this has to be done."

It wasn't that Nala didn't believe him. He was also kinda right. Xavier Crow would probably lose interest in her if she disappeared quietly and kept her head down, far away from him. She was inconsequential. An upstart. A way to get to Vincent. They would kill her, kidnap her, use her as disgusting fodder to make Mr. Lane fall apart at his already frayed seams.

"Where am I going, hm?" Nala laughed. "Back to Nevada? How about New Mexico, or the vacant wastes of Texas? At least your money would go far there."

"I found a place in Indiana that may suit you well. As well as it can, anyway."

"Oh, joy, Indiana."

"I'm serious, Nala. I want to protect you. This is the only way I know how right now. I have some connections that can get you a job with one of your fake names."

"What about my mom in all of this? Am I supposed to disappear? That would officially kill her." She didn't talk to her mom much anymore, but Nala wasn't keen on the idea of abandoning her to the whims of the world. All alone. Her family gone, disappeared. What would she do? Go back to Russia and try to scrounge up the last of her extended family?

Die?

Nala couldn't think about it. "You can't keep me away from her."

The way Vincent wrapped his arms around her and drew her into a strong embrace almost placated her. *It shouldn't be this easy. Now he wants to send me away? When would I eee him again?* Nala tentatively hugged him back.

"I don't want to keep you away from anyone, but until this all blows over, I'm afraid… well, I've already bought it." He pulled a train ticket from his sweatshirt pocket and placed it in Nala's hand. "Three days from now… I'll take you to the Amtrak station. You'll be riding to Indianapolis. I should be getting more money from Lucian tomorrow. I'm giving most of the cash to you to get you started. If I can see you anytime, I will."

Nala almost shoved the ticket back in his hand. "Are you fucking nuts?" Indianapolis, really? *As if that's my biggest problem…* "I'm not leaving you, Vincent!"

She didn't know what she felt. It was kinda like rage… but also a numbing sadness she hadn't felt since finding out her sister was dead.

Murdered. Yet it was also unlike anything she had ever felt before. Was this betrayal? Was this what it felt like to have the man she loved discard her on the side of Seattle roads? *I can't believe it. I might kill him first!*

"Do you think I want you to?" He grabbed her shoulders, as if he had to shake some sense into her. *I'd like to see him try!* He would probably die. By her hands. "Fucking hell, Nala, don't you get it? I love you!"

The red eased from her eyes as she looked at him through a film of milky white. She was going blind, but she was blinded by his words… the most recent words, not the ones that nearly killed her a moment ago.

It was the first time he told her such words. Even though Nala had felt his love more than once over the past several weeks, he had never vocalized it like this before. So clear. So determined. So *scared.*

He hasn't loved a woman since Desirée. She could see the pain in his eyes now. Pain and fear of losing her. Losing another woman he loved so much.

"Do you? Do you really?" Nala hated how desperate she sounded. *I want to hear him say it again.* "Do you love me?"

"Yes." Vincent pulled her into a hard, determined embrace, as if Nala was about to get on that train at any moment. "I love you, Nala. That's why I can't let you die. This time I have the power to save the woman I love. Why would I pass up that opportunity? I have to do it. Even if it hurts us both, knowing you're out there, alive, is all that matters to me. Please, Nala. Please understand."

She clung to him with as much desperation as he had. "I love you too, Vincent. That's why I can't stand the thought of being away from you, especially right now." She sniffed, even though tears did not come. Not yet. "Don't you get it? I can't be out there, in a brand new place all by myself. Not again. Not when I'm so attached to you now. I need you by my side, Vincent. I need to know that I'm not alone."

"You're not alone, darling. I'll always find a way to be near you."

They held each other as if the end of the world knocked on their door. *It does. The end of my world.* Nala couldn't stand thinking like that, and yet here she was, desperately clinging to Vincent in a vain attempt to keep him by her side. *I don't want to leave him. I need him. I can't lose yet another person like*

I lost my father and sister. Vincent said he would do everything to be near her, but what if Crow got to him? What if Hawk defied her house arrest to come get the bastard who put her there to begin with? Vincent didn't stand a chance unless he went into serious hiding as well!

"Please understand, Nala." Vincent kissed the top of her head. "This has to be done. Please understand, and please follow through."

"Let's talk about this later."

"Okay."

Nala wiped her face, sitting back as far as she dared without losing Vincent's touch. *This seems like an inappropriate time to bring this up.* Nevertheless, she pulled her notebook out, careful to not obscure the train ticket her boyfriend had given her. "I'm gonna give this to you to read through. I marked where the final draft starts." She flicked the lime green tab sticking out of the notebook. "Take your time going through it. I'm gonna take a shower. Alone." She had to reiterate that point, since Vincent had taken to showering with her as if they had done it their whole lives. It didn't always produce sex, but foreplay certainly started in there more often than not. "We can talk about it when I get out of there."

Vincent kept the notebook closed as Nala disrobed and grabbed her towel to take into the bathroom. It wasn't until she shut the door, turned on the lights, and went to latch the lock that she ever saw her boyfriend open one of her biggest fantasies. *Scary thing? It's probably one of his too.* Nala wasn't going to hang around and watch his reaction, that was for sure.

He's going to think I'm a total freak. To be fair, she wasn't too into him right now either. Mostly because of what he just did. *I still can't believe it. He thinks he can send me away?* Nala welcomed the hot water touching her skin the moment she turned on the shower. *What am I supposed to do? Just start all over again?* The thought petrified her. At least when she moved to Portland, she had a goal. Her spirit. Her name. She was Nala Nazarov, the sister of Tasha, and the harbinger of justice. If she didn't have any of that after moving to Indianapolis? Then what was the point? Of *anything?*

The off-chance of Vincent seeing her once, twice a year wasn't worth it. She couldn't live life like that. Who was to say that Vincent would live at all? What if she was killed anyway? Their distance would have been for naught.

Nala knew she didn't have a lot of experience in this realm of the world, but she was pretty sure it was bullshit. Almost as bullshit as realizing that the man sitting out in the hotel room, the man who currently wore a hoodie but could cut a suit like nobody's business, was the absolute love of her life. She knew it like she knew she loved her sister.

Nala sank to the bottom of the shower, letting the hot water hit her hair and watching it dribble off her split ends. *I need a haircut.* What was the point? Who would she be dressing and looking nice for in the next few days? Certainly not Vincent, the man half a world away.

Don't think about that. Think about what we can do together, right now. Never before had Nala thought so much about "in the moment." But then she thought of his potential reactions to her script, and she froze up again, wondering if it had been a mistake. The fantasy seemed perfectly fine in her head. Then she wrote it down and handed it to her boyfriend. A fucking Dom deep inside.

When Nala turned off the shower, toweled off, and dressed in the clothes she brought in, she assumed Vincent would be disgusted with her. But when she walked out, a towel resting across her shoulders so she could let her long hair air dry, she found Vincent sitting somberly on the couch with the notebook opened. Nala stood in front of him and waited.

"Well?" she finally asked.

Vincent looked between her and the handwritten words in the notebook. "This is totally insane, you know that, right?"

At least he went straight to his judgments. Even so, Nala thought she saw a flash of mischief behind those cold blues he harbored. "You know I'm right, though. If we played that out, we would be… pretty set for a long time."

"Because it's *insane.*"

"You keep saying that."

"You know I'm right."

Nala shook her head, suppressing a grin. The first grin she felt like showing all day. "So what if it's insane? It's a fantasy. One I'm sure I'm not alone in having."

"I can safely say I've never fantasized about some of this…" Vincent cut himself off. "Quite frankly, a lot of it made me uncomfortable, even when I read it with a Dom's eyes."

"Good. You should be uncomfortable. That means I can trust you."

"I'm not sure that's what you want to go for, Nala."

"Of course it is. If I handed that to a guy who gleefully read it and then asked, 'So when do we get started?' I would be out of here so fast. You should feel all sorts of uncomfortable reading that. But I won't blame you if your dick stirs while thinking about it."

"This is like that one night we had together times a hundred."

"What do you think I was going for? Romantic candlelit dinner?"

Nala was defensive, and they both knew it, but what woman wanted to have her fantasies thrown back in her face, let alone by her boyfriend?

Vincent flipped the notebook shut. "You really want to do that? We only have a couple of days to make something like that happen."

"Taken care of. I bought all the supplies we need." Nala pointed to her small untouched bag in the corner of the hotel room.

"Supplies? Sheesh."

"Like you're going to tie me up with your sweatshirt?"

Finally, Vincent smirked. "It would be a good challenge, anyway. Show me what you bought."

Nala did. She brought the bag over and went through every piece. Sometimes Vincent nodded, and other times he put something back and declared that it wouldn't do. When Nala thought he wouldn't tell her what *would* do, he opened the notebook back up and jotted down a possible replacement and told her where she could get one and for how much.

"There's only one thing," Nala admitted toward the end of their discussion. "I don't have my collar."

Vincent sat back in his seat before getting up and going to his bag. When he pulled the small silver choker from a pocket, Nala gasped.

"Why did you have that?" she asked. "We went to the lawyer's…"

"I always carry it with me." Vincent pushed her hair behind her ears, his touch lingering on her cheek. "Because it makes me think of you and what you mean to me."

Nala clutched his wrist, holding him to her. "What do I mean to you?"

"You're not just my girlfriend, Nala." His lips begged to kiss hers, but he refrained, content to convey his words to her. "You're the woman I love. Which means we share something much deeper than other people. You're my foil. I hesitate to call you my sub. To me, you're much more than that. You are the greatest complement I could ever ask for. You understand me in ways I didn't think a woman could. Most of all…"

Nala's eyes widened. "Yeah?"

"You've shown me that I can move on too."

She nearly melted into his arms. "I love you, Vincent."

"I love you too."

Nala eyed the spiral spine of the notebook. "Will you do it with me?"

He squeezed her tighter. "Of course I will. Even if it's the last thing we do together."

"Don't talk like that. Of course it won't be."

"That's what I want to believe, yeah."

Nala held him so closely that she was afraid he would break. Or she would break. It didn't matter which one of them broke first. All that mattered was that they still had each other for at least a few days. After that? Nala couldn't think about it yet. Her mind was already running through a list of terrible possibilities. However their role-play worked out would determine Nala's next course of action.

I love this man. I would do anything for him. I know he would do anything for me. Sometimes that was the only power Nala needed. She couldn't speak for all women in the world, but if asked, she would confidently say that being able to depend on a man like she could depend on Vincent was one of the most powerful feelings of all… and that was discounting her own inner power.

And she was about to let that loose.

Entry #24

Nightingale has come up with a plan that is just for the two of us. At first I was extremely put off by what she had written, but the more I think about it, the more I realize that it's meant to help the both of us. It's easy to see it as purely her fantasy… a fantasy that is so out there that, if I didn't know her as well as I do now, I would think she's fairly nuts.

Yet now I see how she has incorporated my needs into it as well. If we go through with this, I think that we will both be freed in ways we haven't felt in a long time.

It's amazing how quickly you forget what it feels like to breathe.

Chapter 46

They decided to implement Nala's script two days before she was to set off to Indianapolis – something she did not agree to. *I'll be damned if he gets to ship me off… but I digress.* Nala didn't want to focus on that. She wanted to focus on what would be one of the most exhilarating nights of her life.

Although she had pre-planned most of it, Vincent brought some of his own ideas to their shared hotel room table. For one, he would get them a room at one of the nicest places in town – he was willing to take that risk for her. Second, the man had a few of his own kinky fantasies he wouldn't mind incorporating whenever possible. Nala brought her script back out and went over these additions with him. They also finalized what props to use and other core locations. *Because it can't all take place in our hotel room.* That's where it would end… but it wasn't where it would begin. Nala already had that arranged by the time Vincent brought it up.

There was also the matter of safety.

"We can't get too carried away in public," Vincent said what felt like a hundred times. "If someone actually thinks I'm… well, we could get in really big trouble."

"That won't happen," Nala assured him an equally hundred times. "If anyone thinks I'm actually distressed, then they're not plastered enough where we're going."

"If you say so. All I'm saying is that now is a really, really bad time to get taken into custody, even if it turns out to be baseless."

"Yes, I get it."

Nala sure hoped so. The last thing she wanted once they started their role-play was to have Vincent completely lose it because he was afraid of what others would think. As he said before, it may be one of the last things they did together for a very, very long time. *I don't want to think about that.*

Once this was all decided, Nala established celibacy between them. She insisted that it was to make them appreciate each other more when the time came. In truth, she wanted to see Vincent squirm in desire for her. Which was readily noticeable whenever he smothered her in bed and she felt his hardness press against her. This always ended with her telling him to go take care of it in the shower – which he sometimes did.

Not that it didn't bother Nala. The heavens knew she wanted him as much, but this anticipation made the upcoming night even better.

On the day of, Nala took out her script and read it over a final time. After lunch, she would depart their hotel room dressed as the wildest Nightingale Vincent had ever encountered. A bird flying free in the wind. A demonic entity without a slick of morality. She hoped her mighty hunter was prepared to catch his siren before she enchanted half the men in Seattle.

***

From the moment Nala walked into the underground club, she became someone she barely knew, yet someone she was intimately familiar with, as Nightingale had always existed deep inside of her.

Electronic songs with low bass lines thumped through the walls, through the floor, and through her body. The bouncer looked at her fake ID and jerked his thumb inside – but not without checking out her ensemble from head to toe. Nala wore a tight, off the shoulder black dress that tapered above the knee and accentuated every curve she carried… and some curves that were complete illusions. She left her hair down. Dark.

Tragic. Sweeping across her shoulders and caressing her bare skin. The fringe of her bangs barely touched her eyebrows that she meticulously groomed before leaving the hotel room. Otherwise, her makeup was left to a minimal amount of black eyeliner and dark red lipstick gracing her mouth. Considering how dark things would be that night, she didn't need anything more.

She didn't wear the classic heels or flats the Nightingale of The Aviary traipsed around in. She had bought a pair of heeled boots with intimidating laces that wound all the way up her calf. Wherever she walked, people turned their heads. They were entranced with her simple, yet effective look. She looked like the wild, sexual creature she intended to be.

The only thing missing from her ensemble was a pair of wings. Impractical. Instead, she made sure to pick a dress that dipped in the back, exposing her shoulder blades. Nala used the last of her eyeliner to paint lines on her back to indicate where her wings would sprout should she truly be a creature of fantasy.

This was the easy part. The hard part was entering the appropriate headspace the moment she entered the club.

Look at this den of sin. I came to the right place. Nala moved effortlessly through small throngs of people out having a good time. "Good time" meant a multitude of things. A ton of pot. A bigger ton of alcohol. Men making out with women, and women making out with women while men made out with men. Nala barely reacted when she saw a man sitting with a drink and a woman kneeling between his legs. This was the kind of action she came to see.

Plus a plethora of other immoral things. Drugs. Solicitation. This place was so seedy she might as well have been an agent of hell come to take notes. *Maybe I am.*

She bought one drink, not wanting to get too inebriated. It was a strong drink, though. The moment she put her lips to the fluid, it burned her lips, then her tongue, and then the back of her throat. It reminded her of the many times she drank from Vincent's glass over the past several weeks. Thinking of him brought her back into reality. While imagining what Vincent would think of this scenario was certainly hot, the Nightingale on the prowl would not have thought of him at all.

Because they had yet to meet.

Nala ran her fingers through her hair as she kept her drink close to her chest. Her eyes scanned the room, searching for the perfect target. Her character had come to this club to let loose and take a sample from the bottoms of humanity. Surely there was a specimen worthy of her time.

She didn't have to find anyone after all.

"Hey." A young man with frat boy hair and clothes sidled up next to her as she clutched her shadowy wall. "You alone tonight?"

Nala pursed her lips and took another drink. "Sure am." Her voice was black silk. "How about you?"

The young man didn't answer that. "You're a darkish woman, aren't you? Yeah, I like the Goth thing you've got going on. Real subtle, as it should be. Nothing garish. Not like the other girls I know."

"That so?"

Aftershave filled her nostrils as the man pushed up against her from behind. Nala hugged her drink to her chest and tried not to look startled. This wasn't like being with Vincent at all. This guy had no finesse, no desire to be actually seductive. *That's my job tonight, anyway.*

"Yeah. You're really classy. You from around here? Go to the school a few blocks away?"

Nala smiled coquettishly. "No, afraid not. I'm new in town. Don't know anybody. Just out for a good time and to, ah, meet some people."

"Cool, cool."

The guy couldn't hide his true intentions if Vincent himself came through the door and offered the entirety of his fortune. The way Mr. Suave bounced between his feet, salivating over Nala, made her think he was about to burst in his pants at any time. *How lovely.* Well, Nightingale didn't care about that. It would mean an easier job for her. She was here to ruin as many lives as possible. That's what a succubus did.

She saw the guy make eyes with another woman across the room. He tilted his head up, and immediately she knew what was going on. "So you, uh, up for anything? Because my girlfriend has had her eye on you ever since you walked through that door."

No shit. Some girl dressed in a plaid skirt, punk boots, and a shirt so baggy she practically swam in it smiled in their direction. Nala had to suppress an epic eye roll to keep her propriety. "I like girls." Nightingale liked everyone. "What you got in mind?" Two birds with one stone. It was her favorite thing in the world.

"I think you know what I got in mind."

Once again, this guy had absolutely no finesse. Nala pushed herself off the wall and sauntered across the room, approaching the oddly dressed co-ed who probably either had a fake ID at twenty or a freshly minted real ID at twenty-one. Either way, Nala felt ages older than her, and biologically they probably could have been in the same graduating class.

"Hey," Nala said, smiling. "I hear you like me. Is that true?"

The guy came up behind her, but Nala paid him no mind. She only had eyes for the girl in front of her. "Yeah," she admitted, sheepish but doing her best to put on a brave face. "You've got a nice style. Haven't seen a girl like you around here before."

"Thanks. You're not so bad yourself."

In her usual life, Nala would let the conversation drop there. A little harmless flirtation with another woman. Except she was Nightingale now, and the real Nightingale was a woman who really, *really* loved toying with the hearts and loins of anyone and everyone around her – including women.

"Hell yeah!" the fratty guy cheered as Nala went for the kill right away. The girl didn't stand a chance. She folded like a sweet thing in Nala's arms, immediately sinking to her knees as the demonic succubus took her life force through her lips.

"Wow," the girl muttered. She stumbled against the wall as Nala took a large step away, content with what she had accomplished. "Hey, where are you going?"

Nala glanced over her shoulder but did not commit to anything more than that. "You're not the first person I'm going to kiss tonight."

No one stood a chance against Nala. She was a rogue on the prowl, out to break some hearts and jot down the names of every victim breathing her kisses. When she was done with this city, there wouldn't be a person left alive who could think of anyone but *her* for the next ten years. From the way that girl clasped her hand over her mouth and looked longingly in Nala's direction? She had accomplished the first part of her mission.

Nala finished her drink and slammed the glass back on the bar. The bartender gave her a wary eye before snatching the glass and nodding in understanding. Good. He was one of *her* people. A man who ran a house of ill-repute so she could have a grand hunting ground. She had been doing this for a thousand years. The more the humans of the mortal world sinned, the easier it would be for her to get her sustenance and continue on her merry way.

Nobody could stop her.

Well, except for perhaps one of *them.*

Nala – no, Nightingale – hadn't encountered a hunter in a long time. Such men had systematically fallen to the wayside over the years. Used to be she couldn't go into civilization without a hunter tracking her down and trying to do away with her. Now she was "lucky" to see one every hundred years. They were getting dumber, too. People didn't raise sons to be good hunters anymore. Humanity had given itself over to sin and other delights. Nala reveled in it as she leaned against a dark wall and watched a man light something that was definitely not a cigarette. All she could do was laugh and try to avoid the smoke wafting in her direction.

She sauntered into the next room and nearly had her heart ripped from her chest.

A devilishly handsome man stood on the other side of the room. Tall, toned, and the right amount of carefully groomed facial hair. Of course, any man could do that and try to pull it off. Except this wasn't any man. This was a man who instantly looked up and made eye contact with Nala.

It wasn't often a man made her feel like this. Not just interested… but *aroused.* Let alone with only one look! What kind of magic was he using to rope Nala in so quickly?

That's when she knew. In those precious few seconds in which she spotted this man for the first time, she realized that he was more like her than she could have ever anticipated.

Legend said that a creature like her could change sex and gender at will. Whenever she heard this, Nala laughed. How was that possible? The people who started that rumor wanted an excuse for their homoerotic activities. As far as she knew, she had been a woman her entire existence, as long as it had been. She loved indiscriminately – if it could be called love – but she had always been *her*. The idea that she could change her sex with a snap of her fingers was ludicrous.

Nevertheless, she rarely met the foil to her womanhood. She heard about them all the time – more often in the past than in the present – but encountering a male of her kind was about as likely as her being caught by a hunter. *I've often wondered if they had gone extinct.* As far as Nala was concerned, she may be one of the last of a dying species. She had no intention to be like her mother and take the seed of a worthy man and use it to beget a child. In this day and age? Nala loved her existence as a seductive succubus, but it was pointless to bring another of her kind into a world where they didn't matter anymore.

While she had both these pleasant and unpleasant thoughts, Nala maintained eye contact with this desirable man. *Look at him. In his nice clothes. With his nice grooming. I bet he smells good too.* She might have to go up and find out for herself. The man smirked, flashing a smile he probably flashed at a thousand women before Nala.

She walked the perimeter. While music played and people drank and made merry, she intermittently glanced at the man near her. Likewise, he continued to glance at her. Was he marking her as a target, like she was him? *This is pointless. Why would I waste my energies on someone of my own kind?* Then again, Nala had never been with a male of her kind before. Perhaps it was time to have some new experiences while she had the chance.

Mating with an incubus didn't further her innate goal of bringing the moral downfall of mankind. They couldn't even have children, although

Nala often thought they should be able to. *Some powerful children right there…* She blushed. Nala never blushed around a man.

Then again, this was no ordinary man.

How did she know that he was one of her own? Perhaps the same way he could tell that she was too. A powerful aura extended from him. Sexual. Dominant. *Masculine.* Mortal men could exude that sort of aura too, but not like this. This male creature was masculinity incarnate, like Nala was born to broadcast her feminine, sexual wiles. No wonder the people in the room were looking curiously between them. They could sense their power. They could sense what would happen if these two came together and created a cosmic harmony to end the world.

Her mother never warned her about this. Some flippant words about their existence and their role in lore was all Nala heard. *She didn't tell me what would happen if…* If they made love.

Nala wanted to find out. The other men – the mortal men – could wait for her to have her strength again. She had a feeling this creature staring her down with nary a foul bone would tear her up and leave her to nurse her wounds when this was said and done. Good. That's how a demon like her liked it.

She wasn't going to wait for him to meet her halfway. Nala approached, closing the enigmatic distance between them. If there was one thing she could say about her seduction style, it was that she never waited for a man to make the first move. Not even an incubus. She wouldn't let him have the satisfaction.

"Wait," Vincent said, holding his hand halfway up. Nala stopped, although she wasn't sure why she listened to him. *I'm already giving in.* Fancy that. "Sorry. I wanted to make sure I got to drink all of you in before you said anything."

Nala cocked her head. "Why is that?" His voice almost melted against her skin. If this was how he sounded now… with a deep, almost sonorous quality that could lure a girl to sleep… *well.* "Do you recognize me?"

She wanted him to say yes. How could he not recognize her? She was one of his kind, a woman always on the prowl and ready to pounce on any unsuspecting prey. Surely, he could sense her aura like she could sense his.

Vincent still smiled. "I suppose you could say that. Come here often?"

What coded language they used. Once the people around them gave up interest and went back to their hedonistic lives, however, Nala appreciated being left alone with her handsome stranger. "It's my first time. You?" Perhaps this was his usual hunting ground. Nala had already discovered the amount of prey readily available in such a den of sin.

Yet Vincent did not answer. Instead, he sipped from his glass of dark alcohol, eyes never leaving Nala. "It wouldn't matter, because I can safely say I've never seen a woman as beautiful as you before now."

A mortal woman would roll her eyes to hear that. Nala? She wanted to shrug, because every man told her that. She was sure they often thought that, since it was in her biology to make them think so. *Of course I'm the most beautiful woman around. Why wouldn't I be?* She wouldn't be very good at her destiny if she couldn't seduce a man – or woman – with a single look. *Nevertheless, I like the flattery.* Of course she did! It made her more powerful to be recognized!

Nala laughed. "You are good, that's for sure."

"I must be, if you came right over here."

Nala batted her eyelashes, but kept her hands to herself. *Not that I want to.* No, she definitely wanted to put her hands all over this man and turn him into an extension of herself. It wouldn't be too hard. Wiggle her hips. Wrap her arms around his shoulders. They had to be careful. Their combined power might be too much for the others to handle. *Do I care?* Not really. That was the best part.

"There are a lot of reasons to come over here. Do you know me?"

Vincent's smile faltered. "You keep asking me that. Why? Should I know you from somewhere?"

"I mean… do you know what I am?"

He shook his head, but his look was knowing. "I know a lot of things in this world. What I know about you is that you're a gorgeous creature."

"A creature, you say."

"Should I call you something else? Do you prefer to be called a woman?"

"Don't most?"

"Actual women, yeah."

"That's where you're making terrible assumptions." Nala leaned against the wall beside him, crossing her arms and forcing a sweet pout. "Regardless of what I really am, I'll always be a woman. It doesn't matter what you call me or how you dress me up. You think I can't be as womanly as the others in this room?"

Vincent gave the space a cursory glance. "Just as and more."

"Damn straight." She let her fingertip touch the soft fabric of his sleeve. "You're quite manly yourself. Don't you think of yourself as a man?"

"I am certainly a man."

"Then I'm a woman. Do you know what men and women do together?"

"I've heard a few things."

"Done a few things?"

Nala almost couldn't stand this verbal foreplay. It was foreplay, right? *Please let it be so.* She didn't often beg to be with a man.

"I may have done a few things, yes. Why are you asking?"

"You are coy. I kinda like that." Nala ran her tongue over her teeth. "Usually men fall over backward for me."

"I'm sure they do. I think you'll find, however, that I'm not as easily swayed. Or seduced for that matter."

That so? "You're the kind of guy who gets to have his pick and then goes for it."

"I suppose you could say that."

"I am saying that." Nala touched him, letting herself feel the strength within his arm. *Wow.* This guy was strong. Too strong, almost. "You're used to entering a place, picking out a woman for a night, and having no issue getting her into bed. Or keeping her out of bed, if you're more into that. Let me guess…" she continued, interrupting him before he had the chance to speak. "You leave them completely worn out but still insatiable. I know that feeling well." Men could run out of stamina, and even if they wanted to keep going, their little friends – and many of them were sorely little – would put a stop to it. But they always wanted more. They begged Nala to finish them off for good. She used to do that. Then it got harder to cover her tracks and keep the hunters off them. Now she usually left men in a stupor. Better that way. Easier. Cleaner. *I don't get as much benefit, though.* That meant she had to go through more men. She wondered if she could get her fill with a man like this.

Vincent leaned his head in toward hers. "You know an awful lot about me for a woman who has just met me."

"Naturally. I'm observant." Nala pushed out her chest. Surely, that would get his undying attention. "So, what do you think? Am I the kind of woman you decide on and then leave completely insatiable in bed?"

"You're bold. You don't even know who I am."

I know that you are like me. "I don't need to know you. You don't even have to tell me your name. In fact, I could go this whole night without knowing your name and be quite satisfied. Do you want to know my name?"

"I suppose there's no harm in that."

Strange thing to say. Nala cleared her throat and gestured to herself. "My name is Nightingale."

"Ah, the beautiful nightingale. A bird that sings a gorgeous song of mourning. Who knew that death could be so sweet?"

"Are you a learned man?"

"I've been around."

Nala wrapped her hand around his arm, indulging in how powerful his muscles felt beneath her touch. "What can I call you?"

"Vincent is fine."

Vincent, huh? Men of their kind had names given to them at birth, but most chose their own names to go by after a while. Nala liked the name Nightingale and the atmosphere it conjured wherever she went. Vincent, on the other hand, was a strange name for an incubus to take. "I like that name. Sounds… scintillating."

"I suppose."

"You haven't answered my question, though." Nala wrapped both arms around his now, looking up into his shining blue eyes that managed a luminescence even in that dark pit. "Do I seem like the type of woman you wouldn't mind taking out your energy on?"

"Like I said, you're the most beautiful woman I have seen in here all night. That doesn't mean, however, that it would be a good idea for us to go together."

Hmph. Fine. Nala could play this game. She always seduced her target in the end. Granted, this was her first time going after an entity like her… well, it would be a good challenge, at least. "I don't see why not. Unless you have a woman I don't know about around here." Nala smiled. "Fine. I don't mind adding her to the mix. Or if you've got another man?" There were definitely incubi who targeted men, but they usually didn't bother unless it was a person in desperate need of corruption, and those did not come easy in a place like this. Too bad. Nala wouldn't mind seeing action like that erupt before her. "I really don't care. I like everything."

"I don't have another woman, no," Vincent admitted. "Nor a man. Let's say that you're usually not the type of woman I go for."

"You mean because I'm… like you?"

"Something like that."

It could be dangerous to openly admit what they were. Even if Nala was 100% certain she was dealing with a fellow creature and that Vincent recognized her as well, stating what they were could create a rift in the universe. Nala was already shaking the dirty water by flirting with the man and trying to get him inside her. Maybe he knew something that she didn't. Incubi could be so incredibly sexual that it wouldn't be beyond them to track down their sisters-in-crime and have their way with them for a quick, powerful fix. Perhaps this Vincent had a bad experience before. Nala could see the results going both ways. Unfortunately, she was bored enough to find out for herself. In real time. Like right now.

"Well, that's a real shame, and I am disappointed to hear it." Nala pushed away from him, but only a little bit. She didn't want to make him think she was off the table, after all. *Unless you want me off the table and in bed or something. That is definitely more comfortable.* "Still, I would implore you to think it over. We could have a lot of fun, you and I."

"I'm sure we could, Nightingale. I'm sure you have experience doing what you do."

"Yes." She could be coy like him. "Many years. You could say it's felt like millennia."

"Yes, Nightingale," Vincent said, more evenly. "I know what you are. No need to dance around it. I know you won't openly say it, but know that I know you. I knew you the moment you came into this place and I felt your energy attempt to take it over."

"Attempt?"

"Why, yes. Because I already had taken it over."

"Is that how it is?" Nala grinned. "How many have you had tonight?"

"In truth?" He shrugged. "None. I'm still biding my time, waiting for the right person."

He's discerning, then. Perhaps she was dealing with someone older than herself. Nala was still "young" for what she was. Not so discerning. Taking whatever came her way and reveling in it. "And who is the right person? Maybe I can help you find them."

"That would be the feat. I don't even know who I am looking for."

Nala looped her finger through one of his belt loops. Getting dangerously close to his zipper probably wasn't a good idea. Even so, she would wait for him to stop her. "Perhaps she has been right in front of you all along."

She didn't think it would be so difficult to seduce a fellow creature. Yet Vincent remained unmoved as she came close to touching what many claimed to be cold as stone. So far, she didn't feel so cold around this man. Then again, many said that she was made of cold and ice as well. No one had complained thus far.

"You are eager, that is for sure."

"Well, if you know me, then you know that my existence sort of counts on shit like this."

"Why me, though? Do you know what happens when a pair like us comes together?"

"No, what?"

He bent down and whispered in her ear. Breath that was sheer delight tickled her skin, peaking her nipples and making her mouth slightly open. "Terrible, terrible things, Nightingale. I'm afraid that not even a man like me can succumb to you. As nice as it would be to give in to the way your body moves and how your voice taunts my ear, I'm afraid it's impossible. At some point, we would regret it."

"I don't see how." Nala refused to move away until he did too. Instead, she was happiest leading his hand to her midsection, letting him feel the intense heat emanating from her core. "This could all be yours. Don't you want it?'

Vincent snorted. "Of course I want it. What do you think I'm hunting tonight?"

His eyes bore into hers. Nala felt the weight of his judgment, and it almost made her quiver in her boots. "You're hunting the same thing I am: the depraved sexual energy of humanity."

"I suppose you could say that."

"I am saying that."

"Actually," Vincent said, lowering his voice and turning his head to hers. "I'm looking for a more specific kind of energy. Do you feel it? It's bouncing off these walls. It's echoing in the hearts and loins of every man and woman in this room. It's what drew me here in the first place. I could have gone anywhere in this city and had my fill for the night, but I came here. Do you know why?"

Nala let her fingers travel up his arm. "Because you felt a powerful energy heading in this direction. It must have been mine."

"Yes." Vincent pulled his lip inward, licked it, and pushed it out toward her. *The things he could do to me.* "My instincts said that I should come here because a divine creature was ready to meet me. Perhaps she didn't know it yet. Perhaps she was merely on the prowl. Either way, I knew I had to intercept her here. My existence may have depended on it."

"Have you found her?"

"I sure did. Now I don't know what to do. She may test my limits."

Nala shuddered. "I've been known to do that. Unless you mean some other creature walking these halls. I haven't sensed her." In this era, they were so uncommon that they tended to have their separate hunting grounds that they rarely transgressed. Nala's was in this city. If another she-demon appeared, it would be grounds for a territorial brawl. Nobody wanted to deal with that, especially in the modern era. It would draw way too much attention.

So the idea that there could be any other siren song being sung in that club was ridiculous. Nala would have sensed the bitch, anyway. Vincent must have meant her. She was certainly haughty enough to believe it.

"I mean you, Nightingale. You are the one I came here for."

She tried to not show her satisfaction. "Then what is stopping you? If you knew me and followed my energy here, then you must be interested in what we can offer one another. Surely, you're not scared of me."

"If I were scared of you, I wouldn't be doing my job very well."

Nala tilted her head. "What do you mean by that? Your job is to follow your instincts. If they led you to me, then it's only natural we explore what two beings like us can accomplish."

"This is what you tell me, and yet I feel pressured to tell you otherwise."

"Why is that?" Nala wished she weren't so much shorter than this man. She would love to plant a kiss on his cheek and show him how right she was. "Don't tell me you're thinking about taking your life on a different path. How would you survive?"

"It's not that, believe me." Vincent inched away from her. "I told you, Nightingale. I was drawn to your energy. I came here with a purpose that included you."

"So what's the problem? Everything works down there, right?"

He snorted again. "Oh, yeah, it works."

Nala wrapped both arms around him. Slowly, but surely, she was enticing him into her world. "Then what are you waiting for? Kiss me, and let's see where this story takes us."

She didn't think he would do it. Nala wasn't deluding herself yet into thinking that she had him wrapped around her finger. Yet… when Vincent knelt down and kissed her forehead, she felt warmth cover her skin and try to take her to another universe. *So this is what it feels like to be kissed by an incubus?* If this is what Nala felt, then how did those mortal women contend? She was already swaying back and forth on her heels.

His lips moved from her forehead to her mouth, and what a blessed state of affairs, because the moment he properly kissed her she nearly fell over and died. For a demon like her, that sort of death was something she could eventually come back from.

Nala had kissed many men in her long existence. Usually she kissed them as a precursor to taking their vitality and using it to sustain her own life. Sirens didn't need to eat, or drink really. They only did those things for pure pleasure. Mortal women quelled to see Nala drink all the beer she wanted and then chase it down with cake, never to be bothered by a thing. No, the only sustenance she really needed was the sexual energy of mortals, particularly men. Vincent wasn't like that, but he certainly had as much, if not more, sexual energy than the woman he was drawn to.

She melted in his embrace, letting her body fuse with his the longer this tantalizing kiss lasted. Vincent tipped her head back and plundered her mouth with his tongue, eating her up, devouring her like such a wretch like he did to other women who were not as strong as her. *This is almost too much.* Nala almost never said that, in all her years. Yet the power emanating from this man was too much to resist. She could barely stand it! *Is this what my prey feels before I do them in?* If Nala could harness even a bit of his power for her own, she could be sustained for years. *Years.*

Her thoughts disappeared the moment Vincent pinned her against the wall and proved to the whole room that she belonged to him.

Had two entities ever appeared so famished in this place? Probably, but none of them could have possibly made Nala feel as she did now, with her body opening to take this man in. Everything inside her readied for him. Her heart quickened. Her breasts begged to be touched, squeezed. Her legs opened and her hand pulled on the hem of her dress when she had the chance. All it would take was one drop of this man's pants and they could have all the fun they wanted. It didn't matter if it was in front of others. Why would it matter at all? Let them bask in their fucking glory.

It should have been simple. She seduced him. Or maybe he seduced *her*. Either way, Nala was at his mercy, or so she let him think. Many men pinned her to things. Vincent may have been like her, but he was no different in that regard. A man was a man, whether mortal or not.

It should have been simple.

It should have been simple.

Her revelry came to an abrupt, terrifying end when Vincent snatched his hand around her neck and held her still against the wall, his other hand rooting for something in his front pocket. Nala squirmed, fighting for air and looking at him as if he had lost his mind.

When the cold metal of a collar replaced his hand around her neck, she knew she was doomed. When a leash tugged on her throat, ending in Vincent's hand, Nala knew that the one thing she had been taught to fear the most had finally come for her. Like a fucking idiot, she walked right into his trap.

Betrayed… The weight of the collar would have drowned her in water. Even if she were a *rusalka* of Slavic lore deep inside, she could still drown, again and again, but the only one who could make that happen was a hunter. The hunter who now pinned her back against the wall, tightening the collar and pulling the leash taut.

"I've been tracking you for too long, Nightingale," Vincent hissed in her ear, his hips pushing her against the wall. His cock stirred in his pants, and yet he didn't stop threatening her like this. "Tonight it ends. Tonight I wipe your menace from this city and the earth as a whole."

The siren felt something she hadn't felt in at least millennia: fear. Terrible, arousing fear.

Chapter 47

"Release me," Nala growled, struggling beneath Vincent's weight. "What right do you have to do this to me?"

In truth, she was petrified. Her life could end tonight. Or, even worse, if the hunter didn't eradicate her correctly, she could end up trapped between this world and hell, forever sliced in half. While that sounded like a just punishment to those afflicted by her blight, half a demon on a rampage on Earth was worse than a whole one minding its own business. If Vincent had been this cautious going in, then he was probably going to do the job correctly.

She hoped.

I'm hoping for a good demise? Curse me!

"I have every right in the world. It's you who doesn't have the right to inflict your horrors."

He said it so banally, even after he released her from the wall and presented her to the room, collared and leashed. *I'm trapped.* Every siren like her knew that a hunter wrapping sweet metal around her throat was certain death. She was powerless to fight against this enchantment. Nala only had two options to ensure her continued existence. She either had to get him to let her go…

Or she would *really* have to seduce him.

Easier said than done. Hunters were trained to no longer feel the magic behind a siren or succubus. They were immune. No matter their own sexual desires, seducing a hunter was like killing one outright. Only few creatures had ever done such a thing, and every time it happened, the hunters got smarter.

By this day and age, they were probably invincible once their target was trapped.

"Please don't," she begged, forced to follow him out of the room while others looked on. *This is the part where we have to be super careful.* They didn't exactly want someone calling the cops on Vincent. So when he tugged on her leash, he did so gently, urging her forward as she grasped his free hand and whimpered in his unsympathetic ear. "I'm not really hurting anyone these days! I haven't killed anyone! It's not my fault if people who shouldn't be out looking for trouble succumb to me!"

It was tough being a creature like her. People never understood. They didn't get that she couldn't help who or what she was. Nala was born like anyone else – just because she was born deviant didn't mean she had to give up her life. People were always hurting and killing themselves in the dumbest ways. Sure, some of her brethren took things too far and killed some dumbass by draining him of every bit of energy… but she had never done that.

"You know I can't do that." Vincent yanked, harder, forcing Nala to stay right by his side as they traversed the next room of the club.

"Where are you taking me?" Did she sound scared? She didn't mean to sound scared. The last thing she wanted was for anyone around them to think she was *scared.* "If you kill me, they will come for you."

Vincent stopped between rooms, pulling Nala as close to him as he dared. When he spoke, his breath hit her face with the force of a blasting furnace. "Nobody will come for me. Because they're all gone. You're the last one."

Nala couldn't believe it. *Me? The last of my kind?* Was that why she was so unbothered for so long? Tears gathered at the corners of her eyes as she was led out of the club and down the dark streets of Seattle. They weren't too far away from the downtown district. They couldn't be, considering the seedy club they emerged from. And, lo' and behold, nobody looked at or said a damn thing about what Vincent was doing with this unassuming young woman. Nala stumbled through dirty alleys, wondering if this was where she would cease to exist, or maybe in that dumpster… or next to that homeless person…

"I'm not the last," she insisted, as the cold started to get to her. "I would know. I would know if my sisters were all gone from this world."

"They are."

"How do you know?"

Vincent stopped, staring at her in the sinister shadows. "Because I exorcised them all, like I will with you."

It seemed so helpless. A seasoned hunter. A man who could kiss her and not succumb to her energy. This man was real. Experienced. Perhaps a demi-god in his own right…

Nala had a sudden thought, as he yanked on her leash and brought her close to the street again. *Didn't I sense my own energy around him?* It wasn't him in search of her. There was something else at play.

Hunters could certainly deafen their ears to the song of a siren. They didn't all have to be eunuchs, although many of them in the old times were. But Nala knew, as she knew that she was a helpless creature in the thick of it all, that the only entity capable of spurning a siren's kiss was a member of their kind, male or female.

The best hunter would be one of her brothers.

Nala tuned out her fear so she could concentrate. It was in time, too, for they entered the lobby of a grand, gorgeous hotel with crystal chandeliers and valets that spoke better English than a Shakespearean actor. Vincent hid the end of Nala's leash beneath his sleeve and led her to the nearest elevator. She scanned the room, searching for any other possible source of the foreign energy she picked up on since the moment she first saw Vincent.

Just as she thought, there was no possible source. It was Vincent. It *had* to be him.

Did he even know? Was this why he was chosen to be a hunter? Because whoever brought him up knew that he was the only one who could spurn a fellow demon's advances?

They were alone in the elevator. Well, not completely alone. A camera taped them in the corner. They would still have to be careful.

"You're quiet, for a woman who is about to be exorcised. I'm sure you know it won't be pleasant, and you'll never be allowed to come back to this realm – forced to suffer wherever you're sent."

"Is that what you think it is? Repentance?"

"Why else would you have been born as you are?"

Nala cocked her head. Although she couldn't see it on his face, she saw it in the mirror before them. *Guilt. Shame.* Perhaps he did know who he was after all.

Was it possible? Would one of her kind betray them all out of guilt for who he was? For how he was born?

"So you're one of those who was taught that anyone like me must be a *demon.* Excuse you, nobody gets to call me a demon except me and my close friends. Wherever they were." Whoever they were… it had been a while since Nala could have real friends. Not since everyone scattered to their own private hunting grounds. *To be killed by this asshole.* Oh, excuse her. "Exorcised."

"You do nothing for society except harm people. How many men have you tainted with your poisoned kiss?"

"Don't forget my poisoned pussy."

"Whatever."

"Look, I'm not crazy about the idea of us having some philosophical discussion about my existence while you get ready to kill me. So let's cut the crap. You want me to go away because you're under the impression that I was sent to this earth to be punished by my overlord or whatever. I've heard all the theories. The truth, *sir,* is that I didn't ask for this kind of life. It was foisted upon me at birth. What choice did I have when I became conscious to having a mother who tried to prepare me the best that she could? If I want to keep living – and I do, thanks – I have to drain a man's vitality. I don't *kill* the poor bastards who have the time of their lives. Okay, so there was that one guy who passed out for three days because he didn't know how to give up. But he lived! And was infertile after I was done with him, but… he already had five kids."

"Five kids and a wife."

"You want to talk about guilt and shame? How about a guy who can't keep it in his pants. I didn't *make* that guy stray. He did it on his own. He made the conscious decision to follow me and stick it in me. It was *consensual.* Don't give me your fucking guilt trip about how…"

"How he had no choice? How his mere human brain melted at the sound of your song? There's no man on this earth who can resist a siren's temptation."

"You did. Back in that club. You kissed me, and I felt your dick start getting hard, and yet you had the wherewithal to collar and leash me like you've been trained to do."

"Indeed I did."

The elevator opened. Vincent led her down the hall, to a room he had a key to. *His den of deceit and lies.* That's all Nala could think as the door opened and she was dragged into a five-star hotel room.

How could she appreciate the expense when her uncertain future lay before her? Vincent dragged her to the large bed and unceremoniously pushed her on it.

This was it. Nala had to fight.

Yet how could she when she was enchanted with her collar? Every thrash of her body was met with more resistance. Vincent was much stronger than her. He could pin her down, easily, which he did as he pulled out bind after silk bind, each of which were probably also enchanted to keep her from moving. As she feared, she could not move as both wrists were tied to the headboard.

She looked in Vincent's cold blue eyes, appealing to him with the only tool she still had. *He will never release me. I must seduce him.*

"Hey, no, no *listen*…" Her legs kicked as he pulled her boots off and tied her ankles together. "You're not seeing the whole picture here."

Although Nala struggled, she couldn't stop the ceremonial bindings happening above her head. Vincent weaved designs that were as old as her kind. They looped in and out of the headboard, falling around her head, connecting to her wrists and arms, draping across her breasts as they threatened to spill from the top of her dress. "You're not any different from me!"

Her shout echoed in the large bedroom. Vincent stopped. "What do you mean by that?"

She had to laugh. Was he really that dumb? Hot, but dumb. "You're one of my kind. I know it as much as I know myself. From the moment I saw you, I knew that you were one of my brothers in creation. I see the guilt in your eyes. You say that we are born to repent for sins we once did long ago. Sins we don't even remember. Maybe performed in some world far away from here. Were we really, though? Is that why you hate yourself so much? Is that why you have this tremendous power, and you use it to become the perfect hunter? Are you going to eliminate all of our kind from this world until you're the only one left? Then what? Will you die too? What a fucking martyr you are."

"I am no martyr. I am doing the right thing."

Nala withheld a hiss as he continued his weaving. When she craned her head back, however, she noticed something very, very *wrong.*

This wasn't the ceremonial design of eradicating a siren from the realm of men.

This was something else entirely. Nala had never seen it in her life, but she had heard about it, and she had seen the legends played out in books and told from the lips of her old brethren.

"What are you…?"

"You're right, Nightingale." Vincent finished his knots and loomed over her, a sinister grin spreading across his face. "I am exactly what you think I am. A monster. A beast. I know what it's like to thirst for a person's energy and then harness it for myself. What do you think I've been doing all this time? I've never touched a mortal woman, though. Every siren I've taken to a bed like this has only known pleasure before she left this world.

It was fitting, I thought, but you're different. You're the last one. After you, I'm supposed to be banished as well? It doesn't work like that. I don't care what they say. That's why I saved you, the most beautiful and vivacious siren of them all, for last. You're too perfect to send to some other realm. Think of all the good you could do here. With me."

"You're not…!"

He grasped the bust of her dress and tore it down, exposing one of her most prominent tools of seduction.

"Oh, yes, Nightingale. I'm going to make you my bride."

Chapter 48

Nala strained against the binds holding her to the bed. *Our marital bed my ass!* Hell no. Hell, *no!* She didn't think such a thing was possible. She had heard about this, but it was so far removed from her reality that she couldn't imagine it being a plausible part of her existence.

"Why are you resisting?" Vincent leaned one knee against the bed while crossing his arms. "This is a great opportunity for you, Nightingale. You've been *chosen.* By the last incubus in this realm – to be his bride. Don't you know what that means? Do you know how many of your sisters would have begged to have your spot right now?"

Nala grunted as she futilely pulled against the silk binds. "What makes you think I'm excited about this? Why would I want to become any creature's thing?"

"One hour ago you were in that club rubbing up against me. How was that any different?"

I had freedom! There was a huge difference between two of their kind mating and becoming a beast's *bride.* That meant every bit of power shifted to Vincent. It took all of Nala, except for her body, out of the equation. She would be no better than a mortal woman being torn apart by an incubus.

He had bound her. Enchanted her. Was he really a hunter? He sure knew how to work like one. Perhaps he was. That's why he was so good. But deep down, he was still a plotting beast who would turn on his masters when the moment was right. For if the last of their kind were to marry, the power could very well take down swaths of reality. *What better way to get back at his enslavers?* By enslaving Nala!

She knew how this went. He would own her. She would be *his*. There was no escape. When two minutes ago Nala wanted to seduce him to secure her own future, now she wanted nothing more than to be released. *Don't say the safe word….* She had to remind herself that, taking herself out of the role-play *she* scripted. *This is a part of the fantasy, okay?* Sometimes she got so into her own world that she forgot she was supposed to be Nightingale, the last of her seductive kind. The creature who managed to seduce Vincent Lane.

She only hoped that he didn't forget *his* part of the play.

From the way he tightened her binds a final time before grabbing one of her breasts and squeezing until she whimpered, he hadn't. "*Be rough. Be demanding. Be everything you've fantasized about being with me.*" That's what she wrote in the notebook in the corner of their hotel room. Now she looked her boyfriend in the eye, hoping he would come through. Unlike Nightingale, the real Nala wanted desperately to be *his*. "Go ahead," she whispered. "Make me your fucking bride."

Whether or not he heard her affirmation while he straddled her and fixed a kink in the silk binds, she had no idea. Vincent did not let on as he stood back up and started unbuttoning his shirt.

"Give up, she-demon. You've been trapped and caught." Vincent lined his phone up so his screen was full of the intricate design he created in the headboard. *Yeah, add that to your artwork. Go ahead.* A flash nearly blinded Nala before he put his phone away. "You belong to me now. When I'm done with you, you will know what it means to be my bride. You will want no one in the world but me."

He lowered his head, hot breath cracking in Nala's ear.

"I'll do to you what my brothers have done for millennia. You'll be the first siren to know what it feels like to be seduced and claimed by the entities you call your brothers."

Nala shivered. Nightingale recoiled.

In time, Nightingale will submit. This is our origin story. The Nightingale of The Aviary was a trained succubus. Her Master? The greatest – and the last – man of her kind to ever live.

She was his possession.

She was his bride.

Together they would conquer the sinful.

First, however, they had to fully complete and acknowledge the erotic ceremony that made them as strong as they would be.

"I've been dreaming of this for so long." Vincent carefully splayed out Nala's hair, creating a halo effect across her pillow. She no longer had the energy to fight him – she would rather save her energy for what he would do to her. "The day I would have Nightingale in my bed and make her my bride." He lightly kissed her cheek. "I don't expect you to go down without a fight. It's not your nature to be controlled. As you've named yourself, you're a bird constantly in flight. Constantly flying away, singing your sad song of seduction. I'm going to put an end to that today. I'll clip your wings and make you mine. After tonight? You will do my bidding. You will *want* to do my bidding. Together we will rid this realm of those who truly deserve to be exorcised from humanity. I chose you not because your body calls to mine more than anyone else's…" He pinched her nipple, as he always loved to do. Nala squirmed, whining in both pleasure and denial. "But because you have the right personality for the job I have in mind. I need a bride who will fulfill all the right duties. Not only please me physically… but be the feisty bird with a set of fearsome talons I desire."

He flicked the nightingale charm on her collar. Nala whimpered. A whimper of anticipation… and possibly love.

"I'll know if I made the right choice when I make my claim on you. I've already caught and trapped you, Nightingale. You can't escape… but you can prove yourself worthy."

Shivers shook her whole body. Was it because her exposed skin was cold? Because she couldn't wait for what Vincent would do to her? Or because she knew she needed this as much as he did? *When this is over, we will be stronger than ever.* She knew it like she knew there were stars in the sky. A chasm of stars awaiting her arrival.

"When this is over," it was like he read her mind, "I'll be your Master."

His hand gently landed on top of the collar, fingering the pendant before stroking the underside of her chin. *Deep inside, I am already in love with this man. But right now I need to fall in love with him all over again.* He would have to claim her. And she would have to put up a rough fight.

It was all part of the script. Something Nala had fantasized about time and again. Yet now that they were at this pivotal moment? A bit of fear gripped Nala's heart, as if she had something to fear. *I trust you, Vincent. I trust you to give me exactly what I want, and to liberate yourself in the process as well.* This wasn't just for her. This elaborate role-play, the culmination of their relationship so far, was as much for him as it was for her.

"I don't need a Master," Nala insisted, speaking on Nightingale's behalf. "I cannot be tamed, and I cannot be made to submit!" In truth, Nightingale probably would have spat on this brute – but Nala figured that was taking things a bit too far.

"You say that now, but eventually you will give in to the desires lurking within you. I will have you, Nightingale. You will be my bride from this night until the end of our lives. You think I give you nothing in return? You're beyond wrong. I will give you protection beyond your wildest imagination. You will never live in fear of being hunted or exposed. You will never have to worry about having a place to live or sustenance to consume. By becoming my bride, you can feed off my energy – as I will take from yours. We will spare the innocent and only go after the guilty. You're being given a gift, Nightingale. Fight me all you want, but in the end, you will see what I mean."

She felt like a bird now, desperately flapping her wings in a bid to get the fuck out of there. She needed to escape this beast before he consumed her – before he turned her into his thrall. Every story Nala heard of an incubus taking a fellow creature as a bride ended with the death of her free will. To a siren? Free will was everything. It was better to die, to be exorcised to the other plains, than to lose free will to any man, mortal or not. At least if she were a torn demon between realms, she would still be free, and still be herself.

"You will make a stunning bride," Vincent said, casting his shirt aside. He untied her ankles and caught them both in his hands before she could flail about. He wrapped them tightly around his waist, her thighs brushing against the erection growing in his trousers. "When I'm done placating and taming you, you'll see. Our shared power will change our fates."

Nala did not let him have her easily. She strained against her binds, moving her hips erratically in an effort to outsmart him. If nothing else, she would go down knowing she did everything in her power, exerting the last of her free-will.

"Hold still!" Vincent lay upon her, and Nala knew she was in trouble now. Everyone, even the most common layperson, knew that an incubus had you when he lay upon your body and began his feast. "For God's sake, Nala, don't overdo it. I don't want to actually hurt you."

His break from character stalled her. Nala sucked in her breath, feeling his lips press heavily upon hers as Vincent claimed the bounty of his long and arduous hunt.

For Nightingale, the long-lived entity who knew a thing or two about seducing men, this was the worst part. Because the moment Vincent kissed her, she felt her energy suck from her. No, not her energy. Her essence. Her free-will. He took it from her, one penetrating kiss at a time as his hands roamed the length of her body, stopping to massage her breasts before yanking up her skirt. Perhaps it was his real strength. Perhaps it was something else, but Vincent managed to tear away her lingerie in one move, and promised to tear more of her clothing if she continued to misbehave.

This was what it meant to be seduced by an incubus. Except Nala was probably the first living being in history to not readily succumb. *I won't go down without a fight. I will prove him worthy of me.* Nevertheless, she moaned against his mouth, feeling her legs willingly open around his waist and her body release what was the first of many waves of arousal flooding her loins.

No, no, no! Don't fall for it! Euphoria. A distanced detachment. Floating on air that was not really there. If mortal women suffered like this, then how did a siren like Nala fare? Was it worse? Better? Did she moan louder or make the meekest sounds known to man? How quickly did she make Vincent hard compared to the other women? *I better make him the hardest the quickest.* She already knew that he was making her the wettest she had ever been. With so little effort, too!

She was succumbing. She was losing herself to the thrills of sex. Only there was so much to lose in this situation. It wasn't about swapping energies and sustaining herself for another hundred years. It was about losing herself in the process.

Or so she thought when she went into this. Now that Nala accepted her fate as a beast's bride, she had to work it to her advantage. How could she prove to herself and to the universe that this was truly a good thing? How could she make Vincent prove that he was worthy of having her body, her soul, and her heart? How could she show herself that it was worth all those parts of herself to submit to this man? For him to become her *Master?*

"I bet you can't do it," she snarled against his lips. "I bet you can't get it in me."

"Is that a challenge? Because I will do it." Vincent sat up, his hands still on her breasts as he thrust his hips forward. He still wore his pants, yet the fabric rubbed against her inner thighs, his cock hard against her slit. *Fuck that zipper.* That was both an exclamation and a demand. She hated it. She hated that her body craved sex, let alone with this handsome beast who was going to take a piece of her spirit for himself. All so he could make her his bride. *What a night.*

"You're gonna be shocked, *sir,*" Nala spat. "It's not as easy as you're hoping."

"I like a good challenge. It would be boring if this were over in ten minutes."

He could be fucking me in two minutes. Maybe fewer. Nala trembled at the thought. When she realized it was a tremble of desire, she nearly fainted. "Tell you what." Her thighs were wet by the time Vincent finished tearing away the last of the fabric covering her slit and center. "If you can get it in my cunt and actually fuck me, I'll give in. I won't have a choice at that point, will I? I'll be so in lust with you that all common sense will fly out the window."

"You promise, huh? What good is a siren's promise, anyway?"

"As good as I can make it… but I promise. You've gotta get it in me, though."

Her grin would be menacing to most men, but not to Vincent, who probably anticipated this streak within her. That's part of the reason he chose her, right? "I don't think that will be a problem."

"You might be surprised."

He kissed her, wiping the grin off her face as she pulled and pulled against the elaborate ceremonial binds keeping her tied to the headboard. *I'm his for the taking.* Would he be able to do it? Or would Nala prove herself to be the most worthy opponent in love and lust?

She didn't mean to moan so loudly when his tip met her spread opening. *Am I falling this quickly?* According to the script, she would fall eventually, but even Nala didn't anticipate feeling so damn good when Vincent tried to enter her the first time.

Tried being the operative word.

"Damnit," he cursed, ignoring Nala's knowing chuckles. "Would you sit still? You've got to give a man a fighting chance."

"Who said you got any breaks? You either do it or you don't." Nala narrowed her eyes the moment he looked at her visage. "If you want me that badly, if you want me to submit, you'll have to *make me*." Wink, wink.

Thank goodness Vincent wasn't stupid. He knew what she meant right away. And, fueled by crazed lust as he was, he was quick to pull her hips into his hands and bring *her* upon his cock instead of trying to impale her.

"I made you, now didn't I?"

Oh, he sure did.

Nala wailed in the sudden bliss overtaking her, like Vincent overtook her body. He was halfway inside her, fighting to know her, own her. Nala wanted so badly to succumb like any mortal woman would. Why wouldn't she? This man was gorgeous. He was the king of the alphas in any realm they spoke of. He would ensure she felt this good for the rest of her life.

So what if her brain turned to mush in the process? Perhaps it was an existence worth experiencing. Nala had done things for herself for far too long. It was time to *let go.*

"Holy shit!" Whether or not Nightingale would say that, those words came from Nala's mouth and echoed with Vincent's determined grunts. He was not gentle. He was not forgiving. The challenge was set before him, and unless Nala uttered her safe word, he would continue to pursue what he really wanted.

All of her.

Nala cried out, every part of her giving in to the lust and carnal pleasures surging through her. This man wasn't just a beast. He was a professional. Nala wasn't the first siren he tamed, but she would be the last. The one he chose to be his bride, the shadow lurking in every corner wherever he went. There was a lot of honor in that. What had she been so concerned about?

"Fuck me!" Her hips thrust against his, desperately trying to take him into her depths. "*Fuck* me!"

Once he found his hold on her, Vincent did not hold back in doing so.

Nala's eyes slammed shut, fending back the exuberant sensations filling her every crevice. It was a ton to take in at once. How had the mortals done it? Or was it in Nala's nature to feel everything more intently? Especially with a beast like Vincent?

"I'm fucking you, Nightingale." Vincent pulled on her leash, forcing her torso up with her arms still splayed behind her, hips digging into the bed as he thrust into her below. *It hurts. It's amazing. I don't care how it feels.*

It's what I want. "You're mine, now. You must give yourself to me in every way I demand."

"Yes!" Whatever energy he injected into her, it was working. No wonder he was the best. Even Nala had fallen easier than a tower of cards. Now she was at this man's whims. No, her *Master's* whims. "I'll do whatever you want! Please!"

"Please what?" He stilled within her, taunting her with how he filled her. *He's going to kill me, I swear.* Nala's legs remained spread in the air, any shame she felt about this situation completely obliterated. What shame? Ha! Who had time for *shame?*

Vincent, that was whom.

In all her fun, Nala had almost forgotten what Vincent got out of this. *I made sure to write it in.* In fact, she was more focused on his growth than her own. Easy to say when she was begging him to fuck her harder than he ever had before. "*Don't show any mercy on me tonight.*" Those were her parting words to him earlier. "*And I love you.*"

Yet now she could see in Vincent's terrible eyes that plenty of shame still lurked within. Sure, they could make up fanciful stories about how he was raised to be ashamed of his birthright as a taker of essence, a lover of women. But even after all their weeks together, Nala still knew that deep inside Vincent Lane felt guilty about loving her.

With any luck, he wouldn't after tonight.

"Please use me however you want, Master," Nala finally said. "Use me freely. You've already hunted me down and speared me where it counts. Now reap your reward and show me what it's like to see nothing but the beautiful darkness you offer."

Vincent kissed her throat, bruising her flesh as his hand mauled her breast. "You already demand so much of me," he growled. "If I didn't know any better, I would say you're trying to take over me instead, succubus."

"No way. I'm yours now. Now make me really feel like I am."

He pulled out, leaving behind an emptiness that only he could fill now. Vincent released Nala from her binds – she did not struggle or try to escape. Like she said, why would she? Every part of her body, her being belonged to this entity flipping her over and retying her to the headboard. It was so wonderfully familiar. Nala's heart alit in anticipation as she remembered the first night her hunter came and tamed the demon inside of her.

Yet she knew that this would be incredibly different.

"Use me," she whispered, her face pushed into the pillow and her ass pulled up. Vincent practically bit her there, his red blood running hot in his veins – Nala was certain he had never felt so feral in bed before. "Use me until your whole being is purged."

He nipped her ear, his tongue snaking deep within and tantalizing the last of Nala's sanity. "You too, darling."

After that, Nala was at his complete mercy.

She screamed, as loudly as she could, into her pillow, knowing that it would muffle her voice. But not too much. She wanted Vincent to hear her scream in surprise, in pleasure, in sheer jubilation the moment he thrust into her, taking her body as coarsely as he dared. Pain mixed with pleasure. Need burned with desire. There were no walls between them. Nala loved him, and she knew that Vincent loved her in turn. This was it. This was everything they wanted and more from a partnership.

Pain.

Pleasure.

There was no difference.

Just like there was no difference between Vincent making gentle love to her or treating her like an exquisite princess in need of the greatest pounding of her life. Nala's throat conveyed a mixture of delighted moans and anguished groans. Vincent, in turn, continued to growl as he clawed her back, bit her shoulder, and pried her thighs apart so he could fuck her harder and deeper. When his hand grabbed the scruff of her neck and held her down, his hips thrusting so hard that she cried out in amazing agony, Nala finally saw the empty darkness she begged to experience.

If Vincent needed to let go of his grief, his guilt, and even the pieces of shame still plaguing his soul, then Nala needed to expel the rage holding her back. That black cancer eating away at her spirit. That toxic disease clouding her mind, her judgment. She needed to remember that she had reasons to live, to experience a full life long before her. *It's right here. My first reason is right here.* Vincent might be the only man in the world who could fuck the rage and complete disregard for reason out of her.

Nala had never known what it was like to have a clear head. To see nothing. To experience everything at once. She didn't know what people meant when they said they "didn't think about anything." She was always thinking about something. Her father. Her sister. Her deplorable economic situation and her even more deplorable future if things kept going the way they were. The fact she had lived in someone's filthy closet and couldn't make a living sorting through the equivalent of dirty laundry.

Most of that was over now, but even if Vincent could eliminate the financial burdens, he could not sew her heart back together after the world had broken it so many times. Only she could do that.

Seeing that blessed darkness was the first step.

In all her research, she discovered a blissful state known as subspace. Scores of people told of forgetting who they were, where they were from, and even their biggest ailments. All they recognized was the vast love and care of their Doms. Men – and women – who took their partners' lives into their hands and promised more than the moon. Nala didn't want the moon. She wanted the expanse of space to open before her. She wanted her brain to start over. An elusive reset button was in her grasp. All she had to do was reach out and touch it.

"Who do you belong to?" Vincent grabbed her hair, pulling it with the leash. Nala came up for air, then disappeared back into her pillow. The pressure from Vincent's hand was even more damning as he surged into her, expanding her body, making her crave that delectable release. "Whose bride are you?"

Nala had to find the words buried deep within her throat before she could answer. "Yours!"

"Who do you love?"

Her heart beamed. "You!"

He said other things. Asked her other questions. Each was dirtier than the last, stirring up more carnal yearnings that would take her to another dimension if he kept this up. Maybe he was banishing her to another realm. Maybe all that stuff about becoming his bride was hogwash, meant to make her feel more comfortable about her fate. Nala didn't believe it. This man loved her. This man would be with her for the rest of her life. It didn't matter what he called her body parts. It didn't matter what he called *her* or the acts performed upon her. All she knew, felt, and heard were promises of release.

Nala was already detaching from the world by the time Vincent stilled himself within her, his groans turning into a loud, deafening roar.

By then, she was long gone.

Chapter 49

Splendor was the word of choice as Nala lay in bed, exhausted, her eyes glued – albeit hazily – to the ceiling as Vincent gently kissed her skin and rubbed her aching muscles.

No pain mattered. Not even the words entering one ear and leaving the other. Sometimes Vincent would wrap his body around hers, fondle hips and breasts, and ease her legs open so he could lazily take her from behind. She didn't care. She barely registered anything happening, even though she was there, she felt it, and every time she connected to his heart again.

"You're beautiful," he said more than once. "I love you. Do you love me? Everything will be okay, I promise. You were amazing. That was better than I thought it could be. Maybe next time I'll write the script and you'll see the depths of my own fantasies."

The man would not shut up. Eventually, Nala pushed him off her, out of her, and rolled over until her mouth met his reemerging hardness. She could taste herself on him, and yet she still could barely register what she did or what was going on. The haze she traversed was laced in self-administering opiates.

Was this it? Was this the darkness she craved, manifested in untold ways? Her thighs were sore. Her core ached for more of what Vincent offered, but knew she should hold off. Her breasts tingled for him. Her mouth called to his, wanting a million kisses that lingered on her lips and plunged deep into her throat. When she finished rubbing herself against his hardness, Vincent rolled on top of her and made slow love while his tongue claimed the depths of her demeanor.

There was no one in this world she trusted more than him. Surely, there were others she could eventually trust, but why would she seek them out? Even when their role-play came to an end because Vincent told her he needed to embrace reality, Nala continued to stare at the ceiling and feel so, *so* fucking relieved that she no longer held onto the negativity plaguing her form for untold time.

"I love you." No matter how often she heard it, Nala remained unfazed. She managed a nod when Vincent asked if he could make love to her once more, his body all around her as he filled her with his strength, youth, and virility.

Who knew how much time passed when she felt his fingers grazing her forehead, detangling her hair and touching her as lightly as his kisses did? Nala didn't care. She was so *gone* that she felt like she was drunk on the power it eventually gave her. The power that could change her fucking life.

Eventually, she closed her eyes and dozed off, feeling Vincent's hands still all over her. She went to sleep feeling like more than his supernatural bride. She was his very real partner. She was his Nightingale, a shadowy agent of change – and, most of all, rebirth.

***

Nala awoke sore, but refreshed. She rolled over in the big hotel bed, opening her eyes to find Vincent sitting half naked on the floor in front of the French doors leading out to a balcony that was too cold to visit tonight.

She gazed at him for a long time, mesmerized by the lines and ripples of his body. He looked like he was meditating, although he did nothing more than sit cross-legged with his hands on his knees. Or maybe he was enjoying the clear night sky. It was hard to tell from Nala's vantage point.

"How are you doing?" *Wow, my voice is hoarse.*

Vincent slightly turned his head at the sound of her voice. "I'm better than ever. You? I thought I lost you for a while there."

Nala inhaled deeply, filling her body with the air it desperately needed, apparently. "Not doing too bad at all. I got what I wanted."

"Good." Vincent stood, his softened countenance turning toward Nala. "So did I."

She pushed herself up, tangled hair falling across her face and twisting on the pillow. "Do we have a new plan? Or am I still going to Indianapolis in a couple of days?"

Vincent came to her, his hand instantly reaching for her cheek. "More than ever I want you to be safe. Tonight was fantastic, but once we leave this hotel tomorrow, we're back to being on the run. There are people who want us dead. I won't let them lay a hand on you, so help me."

"Hm." Nala didn't say anything beyond that. She invited Vincent into bed with her, where they made love once more, her body calling to his in ways it honestly did not need to bear any more. Nala ignored the aching muscles and soreness elsewhere. She knew that, come two days, it may be a long time before she made love to her soul mate again. If ever.

Nala didn't want to start the next phase of their renewed relationship with a lie. Yet she lied when he asked her if she would go to Indianapolis. "Of course I will," she said. Of course she wouldn't. Nala and Nightingale were truly one now. Nala wanted to run away to safety and think of only her boyfriend, but Nightingale knew that her battle was not yet over. The mourning bird did not stop singing when justice was so within reach.

Entry #25

Even if I never see Nightingale again, I can say that I regret not a single thing.

I love her. I will do everything to protect her. The most damning thing, however, is that I have so much more money now than when Desirée… and yet it doesn't seem like enough. I feel like I'll never have enough money or power to protect the ones I love.

But I can do this for her. I can send her where she will be safe. Where I can keep an eye on her, even if she can't see me.

It won't be much of a way to live… but it is better than the alternative. I will do it because I love her more than I have any right to love anyone these days.

If that man lays one hand on her…

No, I can't think about that. Only her. And how much I love her.

This will probably be my final entry. I want to end it here, because whatever happens next? Doesn't matter. All that matters is right now. This moment.

I've never felt so free.

Chapter 50

Nala had never been to King Street Station before, and she never intended to come back again.

"You're gonna smother me," she mumbled, while Vincent held onto her as if she really were a bird about to fly away. "I'm serious!"

Finally, he pulled away, his hands resting on her shoulders. *Don't look so glum, bud.* Vincent looked like he was about to lose yet another lover. *Don't put that thought in my head.* From Vincent's point of view, his girlfriend was about to go into hiding half a country away. Who knew when he would have the chance to come see her? The fact he was returning to Portland that same day to rendezvous with Lucian and figure out their next plan was probably bad enough for him.

"You got everything you need? You got enough money?"

Nala had to smile. "No way. Five thousand in cash ain't enough. You better make it ten."

"Well… that's a lot to carry in cash…"

"I'm joking." She kissed his cheek and gave him one last hug. "We should probably pull off this Band-Aid right now. My train leaves in forty-five minutes. You know how security is…"

Nala wasn't in a hurry to leave Vincent's side. Quite the contrary. She was a big fan of staying curled up in his arms and never thinking about anything ever again. Too bad she didn't live in that kind of reality right now. She would be lucky to see Vincent again in…

"Nala." Vincent's hands squeezed her shoulders, nearly shaking her where she stood. "I'm gonna put a stop to this madness. I swear. You won't be gone for long. We'll find a way to bring this guy down. I swear."

She wrapped her arms around his torso and pressed her face against his chest, inhaling his familiar scent. "I know you will. I love you, Vincent."

"I love you too, Nala. Don't ever forget that."

She stepped back, giving him a coy look. "How could I? I doubt you say that often."

"Hmph." He smiled. "Still cheeky."

"It's how I want you to remember me."

Vincent kissed her, his strength powering into her as he rocked them both back and forth. Nala almost forgot what she was doing. *Why can't I stay here and be with him?* She had no job to go back to. No family. No friends, really. She had come to the Pacific Northwest with one objective only. Falling in love had not been on the docket, and yet here she was.

"I've gotta go." Nala pulled out of his embrace and turned toward the waiting area. "I'll see you later!"

It was the hardest thing she ever had to do, and when she spared Vincent a glance… that look on his face nearly killed her. It was the look of a man who wanted to believe her, but had enough life experience to tell him that she was probably full of shit. *After what happened to Desirée, he probably doesn't trust a single "see you later."*

Nala would prove him wrong.

She was lucky that her boyfriend couldn't see her in the waiting area. To be on the safe side, she pulled on a brand new sweatshirt that he wouldn't readily recognize, tucking her long hair into the hood and hunching down so he would never guess it was her. Why would she do something like this? Because Nala had no intention of getting on the Empire Builder and heading toward Chicago, where she was due, in about two days, to switch to a train to Indianapolis. Instead, she was taking a much shorter train. To Portland.

***

The sun was already threatening to go down by the time she arrived in Portland and switched to the MAX light rail. She was heading out to the burbs, with nothing but some texts from Lucian she had forwarded from Vincent's phone to guide her.

She had no idea what she would find out in Hillsboro. She had never been out this far west in the metro area before, and seeing the suburban sprawl almost sent chills down her spine. *God, I could never live out here.* As she swapped to a bus and then started a long walk down a longer street… she was glad she did not live out in the middle of this nowhere.

The house was small. Smaller than any multi-millionaire couple had the right to live in. *Do they really live here?* Nala caught sight of a black van rounding the block. She almost ignored it, until it slowed down next to her, the driver hurrying to step on the gas when she noticed him.

Well, this place was weird.

Nala straightened out her hair and clothes before knocking on the door. Then she rang the doorbell. Then she knocked again. When a minute went by, she saw a curtain slightly open and a familiar face peer through. Within the next ten seconds, Maggie answered the door.

"What do you want?"

She was the most no-funny-business Nala had ever seen. Under the weight of that heavy glare, she almost felt like she was about to be crushed.

"I need to talk to you."

"About *what?*"

Nala did not miss the black van circling the block again. Nor did she miss Maggie glancing at it.

"About what happened that night at the hotel."

Maggie finally lowered her guard. "Is Vincent with you?"

"He doesn't even know I'm here. He thinks I'm on a train to Chicago."

Maggie opened the door. "Okay. You get ten minutes. You'll be lucky if I tell you anything."

Nala had long suspected something about Jay and Maggie. Until she walked in and saw the sparse furniture, a complete lack of photos, and a pair of paranoia-inducing binoculars on the windowsill... yeah, her suspicions were not that crazy.

Nala told Maggie her plan. Every so often the other woman asked her a pertinent question, poking holes in her plan and then buffing them up with her own ideas. There were times when Maggie insisted that Nala was completely crazy, but did not discourage her from her plan.

"You might die."

"I don't care, honestly."

"Wouldn't Vincent care?"

Nala sighed. "Of course he would, but I can't think about that. What's going on here is more important than my own life."

"If you can pull this off…" Maggie shook her head. "Well, you've got serious balls, kid."

"Bigger balls than Jay?"

Maggie's eyebrows crawled up her face. "I honestly wouldn't know."

"I figured as much."

"You're not going dressed like that, though, are you?" Maggie quickly changed subjects by bringing up the jeans and sweatshirt on Nala's person. "Even I want to laugh."

"Nope." Nala swung her backpack around and opened the top zipper, revealing the black dress she wore the night she role-played with Vincent. *It's clean… enough.* "Can I change in your bathroom?"

Maggie gestured to the room in question. "Make it quick."

Oh, Nala did. She had places she needed to be at after sundown.

"Well, don't you look like the pretty birdie?" Maggie grinned at her when she emerged from the bathroom. Hair down. Dress tight. Boots clanking against the floorboards. All Nala was missing was her fake pair of wings. "Good for you. That's exactly what he'll want to see."

Nala handed the other woman the manila envelope full of printed emails. "Just in case."

Contrary to what Nala ever expected from someone of Maggie's disposition, the tall, unbothered woman pulled Nala into an embrace and held her tight. *Whoa.* Maggie patted her back a few times before finally releasing her, the sweet scent of a floral perfume lingering between them.

"Good luck," Maggie said. "It's gonna be a long night for you."

Nala pulled on her jacket to fend off the Portland chill. "Thanks. And…" she braved saying what was on her mind all this time. "I'm sorry about your son."

Maggie didn't say anything, not that Nala gave her anytime to do so. She was out the door and down the street long before the other woman had the chance to react.

Nala shuffled down the sidewalk in her boots, boosting herself up in the hopes that she could feel more empowered before she got on the bus. The one thing not helping, however, was that damned van making another lap around the neighborhood. This time the driver did not dawdle and give Nala the chance to see who it was.

Considering the time, Nala decided to forego the bus and instead hailed the first taxi she saw. *I'll have to get one eventually anyway.* When she showed the driver the address she wanted to go to, he looked at her as if she were crazy. "Don't worry," she sweetly told the man. "I've got an invitation to an event there."

"You better, 'cause I don't feel like getting booted off the property for your mistake. I get in trouble for that, you know."

"Don't worry! I'm expected."

The taxi pulled away from the Portland suburbs. The next stop: the West Hills.

***

There was a kerfuffle outside the gate to Xavier Crow's property. The security guard was ready to raise hell to the taxi driver before Nala brought up her "invitation" on her cell phone and showed it to the man. He looked her over, taking in her outfit and the smile on her face. "All right, but he's not expecting anybody. Don't be surprised if you have to wait."

"Oh, of course."

The taxi was waved through. Nala was not surprised when a security patrol car followed them down the driveway, but the driver sure was.

"What kind of mischief are you into?" The driver waved his hand. "No, wait, I don't wanna know. I don't wanna be an accomplice."

Nala started counting out some of the bills Vincent gave her. "I'll make sure you're tipped well for your trouble."

"Honestly, I better be!"

The taxi pulled up to the main entrance. The driver was not wont to get out, but he didn't have to – the surly old butler was there to meet Nala, offering to open her door for her.

"He's expecting you, Miss."

Nala batted her eyelashes at him. *Come on, tell me your blood flows through your veins.* Were this a thousand years ago, she would think this guy was a eunuch. Now she thought he was out of touch and too blinded by the shit Xavier Crow made him look at on a constant basis.

"Miss Nightingale!" the butler bellowed in the foyer. Nala stepped in behind him, hearing the doors close and the chill instantly leave her skin. Although still a little cold, she did not resist when a maid offered to take her coat. She wanted to make sure that Xavier saw exactly what he expected when he turned the corner of the stairs.

She only had to wait a few seconds.

Years later, Nala would wonder where she found the courage she had in that moment. Here Crow was, leering at her, the piece of prey who marched willingly into his cage. Nala knew that the moment those doors latched shut, she had signed herself up for God knew what. *I know what he's done to Desirée. He could do the same thing to me.* Nevertheless, she had to keep her smile on her face and look as demure as a falling snowflake. *I cannot be as fragile, though.* That was the worst possible idea.

"Ah, Nightingale…" Xavier Crow began his descent down the stairs, removing his hat in mock formality. "So nice of you to finally swing by.

You've been expected for a long time. Come, come… there are drinks upstairs."

Nala wasn't going to drink a damn thing he wasn't already. Unfortunately, she still had to follow him upstairs and hope she wasn't surprise attacked by an assassin under house arrest.

"I'm glad that Vincent finally came around." Nala wanted to tune him out as she went up the stairs, but the only thing worth focusing on was Crow's smooth voice. *It's a lie. It's all a lie.* There was no such thing as a Xavier Crow who was genuinely kind and philanthropic. Every action of his had a reason. An ulterior motive. Something dark and sinister. Something that was likely to get Nala killed at any moment, especially if she lost her cool.

Never before had she been so pressured to be the Nightingale that Xavier expected. As she followed him down a hall and entered a different salon from the last time, Nala remained mindful of her posture and the look on her face. She did not want Xavier to think that she was here for any reason other than to make amends and have the multiple hits called out on her and Vincent to cease.

"It's an honor to be in your company like this, Master Crow." Nala sat on a plush couch and accepted a glass of wine. She didn't take a sip until she saw Xavier sip it first. "When I was invited to see you, I had to admit… what made me so special as to receive such an honor?"

"Ahh…" Xavier sat on the other end of the couch. Nala was relieved that he wasn't sitting any closer. "As it turns out, you're a very special lady, Miss Nightingale. Or should I call you Miss Nazarova?"

The corner of Nala's mouth twitched. "I hate to be so rude, Master Crow, but it's Nazarov. Nazarova is my mother."

"Of course, of course." He crossed his legs and finished half his glass of wine. *Yes, yes, get drunk. This will make everything easier.* "Did you know that I knew your sister? I knew her very well."

Nala had to check the anger burning in her body. *Don't you even mention my sister, you piece of shit.* The irony? This was the perfect segue into what

Nala wanted to bring up first. "She mentioned you a time or two, for sure… before she…" Nala looked away.

"Ah, I'm sorry. Yes, it was a terrible tragedy what happened. So young! So gifted…"

"I hear she was awfully close to a cure for cancer…"

"Hmm, is that so? Well, Tasha was very confident in her research skills, but I'm afraid she was mistaken. She came close to a couple of very promising leads, but the trials didn't pan out. She was no closer than anyone else on my research team."

Nala was not expecting this. "I've never known my sister to inflate her own ego like that."

"Like I said, she was very determined and self-assured. It's one of the reasons I hired her, even though she was so young."

Is that why you seduced her too? Nala couldn't believe it. Just looking at this man made her want to vomit. Then again, she was never into older men. Maybe Tasha was. *Older men with a lot of money, anyway…* "She mentioned you a lot, actually. Said that she was quite… close to you."

Crow's face twitched. "Is that so? Well, I don't wish to speak ill of the dead… and I certainly don't like to kiss and tell, especially with family members, but…" he chuckled. "Let's say it was highly ironic that you walked through the doors to my Aviary that day, Miss Nightingale."

"When Master Vincent told me about it, I told him we had to go. I had to see the man my sister fell in love with for myself."

She had to rely on her lying skills more than ever right now.

"Fell in love with? Why, I didn't know Tasha felt that way." Xavier continued to stare at her while he drank, looking for her tells. "As for you and Master Vincent… we didn't expect him to have a partner so soon, let alone you. I was under the impression that he was single."

Nala blushed, turning her head away so she could act like a treasured kitten. "We were not serious before The Aviary. We decided to become exclusive afterward." Were these lies believable? They had to be.

"I see. I'm glad you made that decision, Miss Nightingale. The Aviary wouldn't be the same without you."

"It's the strangest thing, though…" As if Nala would let him change subjects. "The way she died… who has a heart attack so young?"

"I hear it does happen."

"You know, I've done some research… and apparently one can make someone of any age have a heart attack if they poison them with potassium chloride. Completely untraceable. Did you know this?"

Xavier was not looking so amused now. "I may have heard of it. Why do you want to talk about such unpleasant things? There are so many… better things for us to talk about."

Now he scooted closer, and the barrier Nala mentally erected between them did nothing to stop him.

"That may be true, Master Crow," Nala said. "But forgive me if I get hung up on my sister. I didn't always know her so well growing up." More lies. She hoped they worked.

"I suppose it's normal for a young girl to want to know more about her big sister." *I dare him to call me "young girl" one more fucking time.* Nala was young, all right, but a girl? She knew how this man thought of women… pretty soon he would be calling her a female to spite her. "Do you want to know about your sister? I can tell you all about her."

Xavier stood from the couch, carrying his empty glass and not offering to refill Nala's. Fine with her. She looked to the side, retaining her cool while also suppressing her anger. The Nala of a few months ago would have lunged at this guy already. "You spoil me, sir," the Nala of today said.

"Tasha was an exemplary woman," Crow began, pouring his new drink. He kept his back to Nala. He was either more foolish than Nala took him for, or he truly didn't think she had it in her to stab him in the back. "So bright at such a young age. Beautiful, too. I may have made a fool of myself around her a time or two."

Nala kept her eyes down.

"I wish I could tell you that she and I had a whirlwind romance, but that simply wasn't the case. There was a lot of trust to build up. She didn't say yes the first time I asked her out… and, ah…"

"No need for those details, sir. Some things are best not known about family members." *Like how you… I don't know…* Had Tasha consented to all of it? Or did she feel pressured because she didn't want to be cast aside by her boss and lover? Did even Tasha know the truth? Nala knew as well as anyone by now that sometimes the lines blurred between knowing one wanted to do something and being pleasantly surprised.

"We broke up shortly before her death, you know. Don't suppose she told you that."

She didn't tell me anything. "She did, sir. She was shaken up about it. Said that she was the one who wanted to move on?"

Finally, Crow stiffened, his glass shaking in his hand. "That she did. Was a real shame losing her from the company too. You Nazarov women seem to have a lot of will."

Nala got up, hair swaying across her chest as she walked straight and tall toward Xavier Crow's form. Every step was a knowing one into a pit of vipers, a den of dogs, a cave of bears. Nala could not relent. She could not let this man see the fear gripping her bones and shaking her from the inside. Even her face, carefully made up in Maggie's bathroom, remained unflinching as she reached out and put a hand on Xavier Crow's shoulder.

"It's hard to believe my sister would let go of such a… well, do I have to say it? Such a fascinating man. I wish I knew what she thought was so much better than a life like this." Nala gestured to the lavish room around them.

Xavier looked as if he didn't know quite what to make of her. "You like a lavish lifestyle, do you Nightingale?"

She nodded, slowly. "I am a creature who appreciates the finer things. Good wine. Better food. *Fine* delights, sir." The purr in her voice was something she should have reserved for Vincent. *Now is not the time to feel guilty.* "I don't ask for much. As you can see from my style, I'm pretty low-maintenance. I speak my mind a lot, but I also know when to stay quiet." Nala shrugged, reclaiming her hand. *I need to douse it in lye.* "In return, there is a lot that I can offer the right man. I thought Tasha was much the same way. Which is why it's *so* curious she would leave you and quit her job. Marrying well and having a prestigious job were her two main obsessions."

"Marriage… well, perhaps that was it, eh? I am not the marrying kind of man. I'm also not very committed. She knew that getting involved with me, though."

I bet she loved that. Tasha was a poster child for monogamy.

"Now I want you to tell me something, Nightingale." Xavier turned, backing her against the wet bar. Nala's hand bumped against an ice bucket as her ass remained the only thing between her and a bunch of shot glasses. "Why did you come here tonight? Does Vincent even know you're here?"

Nala tilted her head and grinned. "No."

She didn't know how he would react to that. Would he find it intriguing? Would he call her a liar? Tell her she was a bad sub who needed to return to her Master and accept punishment? Or would he be pleased as punch, knowing he had her right where he wanted?

Oh, the latter, of course.

"That's right. I'm sure he would never let you come here on your own like this. Why do you think I sent for you?"

Nala snorted. Now she had to play her final card. "To kill me and send Vincent my body."

This time, she got an appropriate reaction. Xavier blanched as if she had accused him of directly murdering anyone. "Excuse you…"

She shrugged. "Someone's been trying to kill us. Someone killed that couple in Germany. Someone killed my sister." Nala glanced away before looking him in the eye again, fervor renewed. "And someone killed Desirée. You know. Vincent's pregnant fiancée."

Crow walked away from her. At first, Nala thought she had pushed too hard. Maybe they had even been wrong about a few details and she sounded stupid now, but when Crow looked at her again, this time with anything but grandfatherly flirtation in his eyes, Nala knew she had struck a nerve.

She also knew she would probably pay for it. She didn't imagine him calling for a guard.

***

Being tied to a chair in a madman's office was a helluva lot different from being tied up in Vincent's bedroom.

"Don't bother struggling, dear," Crow said, leaning against his desk and lighting a cigar. Two armed guards stood on either side of Nala, who was tied tight to a Robert chair. The only reason she now knew this basic kind of chair was called a "Robert" was because Crow called it that about fifty times, in case his guards hadn't known him for long. "As much as I would love to see you struggle, my dear, it won't do either of us any good. It will exhaust me to watch. And, well, you won't make any headway. All of my top guards are well versed in knotting."

Nala made a sour face. Did this brute know what that meant to someone in her generation? *I've read too much fanfiction.* Terrible prose about dudes and… well, never mind. Those weren't what she wanted to be her last thoughts in life, anyway!

"Why look so upset?" Xavier moved his cigar before approaching her, placing both hands on her face. "Any death should be perfectly beautiful. Second only to the body they place in the casket… and don't worry. Since you're Tasha's little sister, I'll make sure you have a peaceful death, body fully intact. It was the least I could do for her."

Nala shirked away, trying her damndest to get away from this monster's cold touch. "But not Desirée. Fuck that pregnant bitch, right? How dare she get knocked up after you *raped* her!"

"Shut your foul mouth. I would never do such a dire thing."

"Not according to those emails."

"Ah, yes, such an astounding hack job. I admit, I was impressed your boyfriend could hack through my firewalls. Then again, I was impressed with how good his app was for my company… I shouldn't have been impressed that second time." Crow smirked, finally drawing his hands away. "What happened between me and that sweet, curly-haired vixen is neither here nor there anymore. All I'll admit is that we had relations. She was a magnificent sub, by the way. Your boyfriend had trained her well."

Nala knew she shouldn't, but she couldn't help it – she surged against her bindings, growling in rage at the kempt man before her. Xavier remained unfazed while two strong hands pulled Nala against the back of her chair. The guards gave her stern looks that would make a woman *not* overdosing on adrenaline squirm in her seat.

"Possessive, are we? Don't like the thought of him being with another woman?"

"Fuck that! I don't like the idea of *you* having innocent people killed!"

"It's a rough world out there, Miss Nightingale. The more successful you become, the rougher it becomes protecting your holdings… not to mention your ideals. As for Desirée…" he looked away. "How unfortunate. I believed she would keep quiet about our affair. Then that thing happened."

"A baby, you sick, twisted fuck. A *baby* happened." Nala was one of the least maternal women in the world, and even she was beyond horrified by what he had done. "Not any baby, right? Your baby. It had to be yours, because you were the only man she was 'with' while she was separated from her *fiancé*. She wouldn't get rid of it, would she?"

"Now would be an excellent time to shut your mouth."

Didn't he know Nala didn't take orders well? "Did you know that Desirée had a miscarriage before? She would have given anything to have a baby. Even if it was *yours*. No. That took things too far. That took power out of your hands, and you are not the type of man who has power taken away, are you?"

Xavier Crow mindlessly buffed his nails with his thumb as he regarded Nala with a toxic look. "You are very different from your sister. You're lucky I liked her so much. She's the only reason I'm not having someone slice that mouth off your face right now."

"I'll be sure to thank her for it when I see her."

"You do that."Crow motioned something to his guards. Something like, "*Time to get out of here.*"

"Wait," Nala said, before the man before her could suddenly disappear. "Just tell me one thing. Something I haven't gotten a straight answer for."

Crow gave her a numbing look. "What?"

"Why did you kill Tasha?" When he was not immediately forthcoming, she continued, "Was it because she was too close to a cure, and that would have ruined your business?"

A snort shot through his puffy nostrils. "I've already told you that Tasha was no closer to a cure than anyone else. I never lied about that. Besides! Why would I kill her for *that?* A cure would only increase my brand and fortune! The Nobel Prize, for God's sake!" He shook his head. "Do you want to know why your poor sister had to be taken care of?"

Nala steeled herself. "Yes."

Xavier Crow picked up his hat and put it on his head before gesturing to the guard again. "Because, my dear, if I couldn't have her, then nobody could. I don't like it when my toys take themselves home."

The guards left. Nala sat alone, with Crow, almost in complete disbelief. *She died because of a creepy, possessive boyfriend?* It seemed too unreal. Too… anticlimactic, almost. Nala had built a narrative about cancer and pharmaceutical conspiracies in her head for so long that this was a fucking disappointment. Tasha was nothing more than a statistic for college campaigns and public TV PSAs.

"So," Nala chuckled, grinning at Crow, "you loved her back, huh?"

He turned. "What?"

"In your own twisted way. You loved my sister back, after all. That's all she fucking wanted." Nala didn't touch the other shit that would've doomed her sister anyway. She wanted to get a final jab in before dying.

So did Crow.

"You know what the most satisfying thing about seducing Desirée was?" He loomed over Nala, a man who wasn't so big when she was standing, but now seemed like a shadowy giant. Nala shivered to smell that strong cologne and realize that his face was coming closer to hers. Cologne turned into aftershave. Smelling his breath meant he was way, way, *way* too close. "Knowing that she belonged to another man. Those are always the most fun. And… oh, you both belong to the same man, don't you? I wonder… how would Vincent feel knowing that two of his precious women knew me last?"

All the blood froze in Nala's veins.

No matter how much she struggled in her bindings, no matter how far she twisted her head, and no matter how she bore her teeth once he had her mouth open, Nala could not stop Xavier Crow's version of a kiss.

Fucking. Kill me. Now.

To think that her sister had kissed this mouth *willingly*… to think that Desirée hadn't.

That was his point, wasn't it?

"We're done here." Xavier adjusted his suit jacket before heading toward the office door. "I'll give you a few minutes to think about your life. Treasure them. I won't be more generous than that, Nala Nazarov."

He left, locking the door behind him. Nala stared at the office before her, tasting that sludge of a kiss still on her lips. *Am I really going to die? With that on my mind?* Until now, Nala foolishly hadn't considered that an immediate possibility. She was prepared for anything, but to be left here, alone, wondering about her fate? It seemed almost too simple for a man like him.

Vincent… What would happen to him? Nala was prepared for something bad to happen, but… for him to lose two lovers like this… *At least I'm not pregnant.* Nala had to find some bright side.

She slumped against the chair. *I wish he were here.* She wished he would come crashing through the window, untie her, and make off with her in his arms. She knew that was stupid. Not only did he not know she was here, but what could he do? Throw himself into danger as well? Ha.

Just as Nala wondered how she was going to die, she realized she had been staring at the same paper weight on the desk for five straight minutes. That the world was becoming blurry. That sleep sounded like a very, very awesome idea.

Her eyelids became unbearably heavy. Slowly, they fluttered shut, and the last thing Nala remembered were two memories coming together: her tenth birthday party, wherein her sister and mother pooled their money to buy her a handheld video game she had always wanted… and those walks on the beach with Vincent.

I'm sorry, Mama. You've lost everyone. I'm sorry Vincent, you've lost another one.

She fell asleep.

Chapter 51

"Nala…" The voice was far away, threatening to break at any moment.

"Nala!"

The haze was too hard to navigate. Nala wanted to respond, but she was so sleepy, so tired that it made more sense to sleep forever. *No, Mom, I don't want to go to school… dumb chemistry test today… I know Tasha said she would help me study… but she was busy….*

"NALA!"

She was on the floor, untied, but unable to move. Whoever untied her picked her up and hoisted her over their shoulder. Nala recognized the soft fabric of a Stanford sweatshirt and the scent of expensive cologne.

"Vincent?"

"Don't," he whispered, carrying her. "Don't inhale. Don't make *me* inhale…"

He jumbled the door handle. When it wouldn't work, he stepped back, raised his foot, and took it down with one heavy kick. Nala felt it all vibrate through her floppy body.

Fresh air hit her. She didn't realize she needed it, yet she awoke from her dreamworld and sat up with a start. Before she could tumble to Xavier Crow's hallway floor, however, Vincent put a firm hand on the small of her back and took in the biggest gulp of air Nala ever heard a man take.

"What happened?" she asked. Her brain was still fuzzy, but with Vincent with her, everything was okay, right? Wait…

Vincent?

"Oh my God, what are you doing here?"

Finally, Vincent pulled her off his shoulder and tentatively put her feet on the floor. His hands remained firm on her shoulders. "Don't make any sudden moves. You were poisoned."

"Huh?"

"He pumped a shitton of carbon monoxide into that room. I got in through the window. Climbed in from outside… was *not* easy."

"What? How did you know I was here?"

"GPS on your phone, Nala."

If she had the energy, she would be more enraged. "What!"

"Let's not argue right now." Vincent hoisted her back over his shoulder again. Nala's stomach did a few somersaults as she watched the carpet rush by beneath her eyes. "We're gonna get caught within about…"

"Halt!"

Vincent stopped, clutching Nala as if she were his precious possession.

Footsteps thumped against the carpet. When Vincent quickly turned around, Nala caught sight of the armed guards – four of them. From the sounds of the footsteps behind her again, she guessed more were coming down from the other end of the hall.

"You're surrounded!"

Nala waited. For gunshots. For a bomb. For *something.* Yet all that happened for a few seconds was the feeling of Vincent's heavy breathing and the sounds of footsteps thumping against the ground.

"Take them into the salon."

Vincent was forced to drop Nala, who was still woozy, but what choice did he have, when at least ten of Xavier Crow's security personnel surrounded them?

"I said the salon."

She heard that man's voice far away, but had no time to think about it as she and Vincent were herded into another nearby room. Larger than the office, but still not quite big enough for the amount of people forcing themselves inside. Wherever they were on the premises, they were in a rounded room, with windows on all sides. Nala stared into the bleak, black darkness and held her breath.

"Both of you better fucking kneel right now."

Nala knew that voice. It made her bristle, all the way down to her knees, while her hands went tight behind her head. Vincent followed suit, his face grim. He looked at Nala. Apologetic. No regrets. Loving. *Yeah, I know. We're gonna die, but I love you too. Romantic.* Nala smiled at him. It was the least she could do for running away on him.

Hawk thumped into the room, her clunky tracking bracelet on her ankle making her walk with a strange gait. Great. Lot easier to kill when the victims came to her instead of her having to go to them. "These are the fuckers who got me arrested. For *driving recklessly.*" She cackled, taking a gun from one of the armed guards. "This is going to be so satisfying! My only debate is figuring out which one I want to kill first!"

The barrel of the gun pointed at Nala.

"Do I kill the obnoxious child and make our hero *cry* because this is the second time I took away the only thing he loooooved?" The gun switched to Vincent. "Or do I put you out of your misery first so the girl can find out that there are no happy endings? Either way, one of you has to die first."

Both of them remained silent, although their eyes never left the other's. "I love you," Nala mouthed, as she heard the gun click. "I'm not scared."

That was a lie. Her body trembled. Her throat was dry. Her knees were sore against this carpet. Her body was prepared to fight for its life, but with so many people in the room, it was impossible. Plus, they all had guns.

Vincent nodded. "I love you too," he said.

"Fucking piss off with this smarmy shit."

Nala knew that the gun was pointed at her. Hawk wanted to torture Vincent with his new girlfriend's death. It was her style.

She waited.

And waited.

Finally, a gun went off.

Chapter 52

Hawk hit the floor, dropping the gun and bleeding.

The rest of the room went into chaos. Guards yelled at one another. A bright light blew up outside the semicircle of windows. When one guard pointed to a bullet hole in the window, the hole suddenly got a lot bigger.

Every window crashed as shadows came flying through. Glass rained, sending half the guards scrambling out the door and the other half to stand, dumbfounded. Voices raised. Nala fell to the ground, covering her head with her hands as Vincent threw himself over her. Words like "FBI!" and "Stay where you are! Drop your weapons!" echoed around them. It wasn't until someone grabbed Vincent and then Nala that she finally opened her eyes and looked at a big fat "FBI" printed on a bulletproof vest in front of her.

Her hands were tied behind her back. Vincent was shoved back to the ground next to her. More FBI agents came swinging through the windows, raiding the whole damned place as they crunched broken glass beneath their boots and chased after more of Xavier Crow's personnel.

The commotion they heard throughout the rest of the house was like the entirety of the military raining upon Crow's palace. The raid lasted only a few minutes, at most, but the whole time Nala gaped in awe at the scene opening up around her. *Holy fucking shit!* This was the kind of stuff people only saw on TV! So many people, dressed all in black and wearing helmets, their visors pulled down, throwing smoke bombs into rooms to drive people out… putting the butts of their large guns in people's backs to make them march to the grand foyer downstairs, where Vincent and Nala were eventually taken as well. *Do they think we're anything but victims in this? Are we being arrested too?* They did have fake IDs, and who knew what else they had done that was technically illegal.

Nala and Vincent stood among the usual suspects, like corrupt security personnel, a beautifully injured Hawk who was cursing and punching anyone in her way before one big and burly FBI guy smacked her in the back and sent her to her knees, and generally sketchy looking people. But there were also scared witless maids, concerned chefs, and a couple landscapers who swore they didn't speak English.

They were rounding up *everyone.*

Including the man of the hour, Xavier Crow, who was marched down his stairs with his head still high. His hands were cuffed behind his back, but one would have never guessed this was anything but his own plan based on how he surveyed the land around him.

Once he hit the bottom of the stairs with his black-suited entourage, a familiar face walked through the main entrance.

Maggie pushed her rain jacket behind her as she sauntered up in the same dark denim jeans and beige peasant top she wore when Nala saw her earlier that evening. Her demeanor was both determined and satisfied, as if this were the greatest moment of her life – it probably was.

"Xavier Crow!" she called, pulling something from her pocket. Nala half expected a gun, but it was a leather wallet instead. "Margaret Jameson, FBI."

His eyebrows went up. Nala's practically leaped off her face. *I will never be that cool.*

"You're under arrest for extortion, insider trading, kidnapping, unlawful imprisonment, and multiple counts of conspiracy to commit murder." When Hawk squawked in pain a few feet away, Maggie continued, "That one's arrested for *just* murder. What a pair you make."

Jay approached, also wearing a FBI jacket. "Great job, babe. We got everyone."

She did not smile. "I know. Don't call me babe."

Maggie pushed past Nala and Vincent without regard. She only had eyes for Crow.

"A pest in my own Aviary," Crow said, before she had the chance to speak. "I always knew there was something off with you."

"Kinda like how everyone with half a lick of sense always knew there was something or fifty off with *you*."

"Nothing you have against me will hold up in court. These scandalous lies you tell will do nothing but hurt your institution instead."

Maggie smirked before landing a punch right between his legs.

Nala almost laughed as the man slowly sank to his knees, containing a painful expression that she recognized as *balls breaking*. Maggie told her FBI partners that her hands slipped.

"You have confessed so much already, Xavier." Maggie gestured to Nala. The nearest agent pushed her down and ripped something off her back. When she looked up, she saw that she had been bugged the whole time. *When she patted me on the back… she bugged me?* "We've got your full confession on there."

"Nobody will believe it," Crow wheezed.

"Shut the fuck up, baby killer."

"You better do as she says!" The only man dressed in a dark suit came through the front door. Even this one surprised Vincent, who stared wide-eyed at Joshua making a lackadaisical entrance. "You've had two official investigations going on for a while, Crow. If it weren't the FBI, it would've been the police. You've been making negative waves in this city for a while."

"You stupid little…"

"Let me guess? Mama's boy? Wouldn't be the first time I heard that." Joshua didn't have a gun or cuffs to show off, but he did pull out his credentials. "Cromwell is my real name. You might know my mother, Madeline Cromwell, the woman who does all those pesky business corruption investigations in the PNW. She asked me *personally* to work with the FBI on this one."

"Because you're a pervert," Maggie muttered.

"No kidding," Jay echoed.

"Why do you think I didn't say no?"

"So good to know that my judgment in character over the past year has been totally shot," Crow said, attempting to have the last word. "Now I'm going to shut up and wait for my lawyer."

"Wise idea. Take him away."

Before the FBI agents could parade him through the foyer and out the front door, however, Vincent leaped to his feet and cried, "Wait! Please!" He was let go, his hands still tied behind his back, but his feet swift as they took him to Crow. "I want to ask him one last thing."

Crow sighed. "What is it?"

"How?" Vincent looked like he wanted to throttle Crow, and Nala wouldn't blame him. "How could you kill a *pregnant* woman?"

Crow's demeanor remained unchanged. "Why do you care?" he asked evenly. "What would you have done when it inevitably came out that *your* precious little Matthew or Magda was actually *mine?*"

Vincent bit back a growl. "Kept loving it like my own."

"Hmph. How fucking noble."

"All right, that's enough," Jay said. "Get him out of here."

Vincent was pulled back and Crow marched out of his own home. Some of the FBI agents started cuffing Crow's security and taking them to vans to load up and haul downtown, while others started questioning the staff. Nobody touched Nala and Vincent. Except for Maggie, who came back down the stairs with her hands in her back pockets and a gun poking from a holster. *Wow. I want to believe she shot Hawk.* Nala would believe it until she died.

"Sorry you two kept getting wrapped up in this," she said, taking out a pocket knife and cutting apart their binds. Vincent shook out his wrists while Nala braced herself against the ground. "Because of your fucking stupidity, though, we got the last of the evidence we needed to finally raid this place. Jay and I have been undercover for over a year now."

"I helped!" Joseph called.

Nobody heeded him.

"Glad I could help," Nala muttered.

"Hey, don't be too hard on yourself. We're all young and dumb once."

"...Thanks."

"Don't mind her," Jay said. "She's tough on the love. Makes her pretty endearing, right? She's great at Thanksgiving dinners." He smiled. "My husband *adores* her."

"Your husband would think Paula Deen is great company."

"For all the wrong reasons."

When they both caught Nala looking askance at them, Maggie explained, "We're not a real couple. Jay and Marguerite Jones were our undercover names. That house is a FBI house."

"I would have never guessed," Nala sighed.

"You should get some medical attention. You may have only got shot with CO2 for a couple of seconds, but that's enough to do some damage. I'll get you a medic as soon as one's available. Hold tight." Maggie patted her shoulder. "Need you nice and healthy so we can take your statement. Might need you to testify."

Vincent turned to Jay. "Are we being arrested for anything?"

"No. Although we know about the fake IDs."

Vincent groaned.

"We'll look the other way regarding any of the... questionably legal things... you've done since entering The Aviary as long as you give us official statements about everything's that happened. Your records stay clean and your reputations strong. We all go home happy."

Vincent exuded a sigh of relief. Nala leaned against his shoulder and almost wept to feel his arm wrap around her.

"By the way," Jay said to Nala. "I'm sorry about what happened at the hotel. I couldn't blow our cover to anyone. Hawk had made us as some sort of spies, which caused the shootout. Obviously we were all right, but I know it scared you two shitless."

"It's all right," Nala said, starting to shiver in the drafty foyer. "I'm used to that by now."

"Found this one in the master bedroom."

Maggie, standing on the landing of the grand staircase, looked up and saw one of her colleagues bring down a woman in a gold dress. *Oh, no.* "Well, you were around after all."

Quail looked her in the eye before grunting in disapproval. "And you were a cop after all. Should've sniffed it out."

Maggie finally got to pull out her handcuffs. "I hate to do this, but…"

"Do it already. I got a lawyer on speed dial by this point."

Rolling her eyes, Maggie took Quail from the agent's grip, turned her around, pulled her hands behind her back, and cuffed her. "Sylvia Rogers, you're under arrest for multiple counts of solicitation and prostitution."

"No shit. I'm a fucking escort and a girl's gotta eat."

"Anything you say can and *will* be used against you… so you might wanna shut up."

They started marching down the stairs, Quail's head held high and her face so stubborn that she looked like she was about to turn around and smash her heel on Maggie's toes. Instead, she said, "I can give you Sebastian! He's a dirty bastard with…"

"Yeah, we know all about your client's workings with Crow. Save it."

"I used to be a real respected girl, you know! One of the most sought after on the east coast!"

"Yes, and you had protection over there, didn't you?" Their voices echoed in the foyer until they were at the front door. "Don't have a powerful madam to protect your ass this time. You're a fat little quail sitting dead in the road after all."

Jay turned away from the scene as soon as they were out the door. "Poor thing. We had our eye on her for a while. Had quite the fall from grace since she used to work for a high class BDSM dungeon back east. Was engaged to some bigshot before she caught him cheating." He shook his head. "Next thing we know about her, she's out here turning tricks in the big leagues."

"Apparently," Nala muttered.

"Well, I'll leave you two to it. We won't detain you or anything, but don't stray too far away. We'll need your statements before you can go home."

Once they were finally left alone, Nala fell into Vincent's arms and let out a repressed sob. He rocked her back and forth slowly enough to make her feel at ease with so much pumped up energy around them.

"I almost died…"

"I know, darling."

"But you came for me…"

"I did."

"You stalked me… but you came for me…"

"I had to make sure you were safe. I normally wouldn't do something like that."

"I know." Nala began to shake as a powerful realization claimed her. "It's over, Vincent. It's all over. He's not going to hurt anyone anymore."

"I sure hope not."

"Don't say that. Tell me he's not going to hurt anyone." Tears started to fall from her eyes, dampening his sweatshirt. "Tell me it's all over and we got the justice we set out for."

His lips buried in the crook of her neck. "It's all over, Nala. It's all fucking over."

"I love you so much."

"I love you too."

They kissed, not for a lack of anything else to do, but because they were so overcome by emotion that nothing else needed to be done. Nala fell back, feeling Vincent hold her with one arm and overpower her with his kiss as if that were the most natural thing in the world. *It is now.* Heavy boots stepped this way and that. The occasional words of derision were exchanged outside. Sirens sounded. Medics came. People wanted their statements. Soon there would be reporters. Until then, Nala was content to spend the first few moments of her new-found freedom sharing her joy with her boyfriend.

Are you okay, Tasha? Are you happy that I got you justice? Or are you angry that I hurt the man you loved?

Nala opened one eye as lighter steps walked by. It was two women, wearing FBI gear and reporting back from their superior. One woman had big, bushy hair, and the other long, black hair that looked too Slavic to ignore.

"I'm gonna need a cigarette after this," the curly-haired agent said. "I've never smoked."

"Buy me a coffee first. As soon as we get back to HQ I've gotta go back to those criminal pathology classes. Thinking about it is wearing me out. Fuck it, we're wanted upstairs to process the office."

Both women turned in the couple's direction, briefly exchanging glances with Nala and smiling. She smiled back, watching them walk by, self-assured – tired, but self-assured.

"What is it?" Vincent asked, nuzzling her. They still sat in the middle of the damned floor in the foyer, but Nala didn't care. She was wrapped in his arms, and as far as she was concerned, that was the safest place to be.

"Nothing. Kinda funny how many doppelgangers there are."

"What do you mean?"

"Nothing."

"You keep saying that."

"Shut up and kiss me."

He did, going so far as to slip some tongue in the middle of a crime scene. That's how he was, and Nala easily accepted it – because that's how she was. The world could be collapsing all around them, and she would be content if it meant kissing a man like Vincent Lane.

I'm glad you're not mad at me, Tasha.

She kissed Vincent harder, finally garnering the jabs of a few agents around them. Somewhere in the distance, a man was asking them to stop long enough to answer a few questions. Except nobody was able to stop such a formidable pair once things started to heat up. Especially when someone like Nala was *happy*. Right now she was mostly relieved, but she knew she would wake up the next day feeling pure happiness for the first time in…

Well, she didn't know in how long.

Far away, a little bird perched in its cage, singing a song of mourning. Nala used to be like that. A nightingale, crying desperately over a broken heart. The most beautiful song in the world. Beautiful because it spoke to the darkest, most pitiful parts of the human condition.

Nala used to be like that. Then someone opened her cage door and finally let her fly away, right into the arms of the only man who could change her life in such a wonderful – and unexpected – way.

Epilogue

Waves crashed lazily against the beach. The cloudy sky almost seemed cheerful in its disposition. Seagulls squawked and crabs scuttled sideways.

Nala Nazarov perched on the hood of a luxury sedan, taking in the fresh, salty air.

It was the most at peace she had felt in so long that she almost felt like she was dead. A blissful, heavenly death. As she lay back and let her hair be whipped around by the sea breeze, she imagined rose petals cast around her body and candles burning on the ground. A fitting farewell to someone only a few people knew.

"They said if we keep going south, we'll hit the caves soon enough."

Nala turned her head and opened her eyes, finding Vincent leaning against his car. "Come sit with me," she said. "It's a beautiful day."

Vincent stared at the white, somewhat gray sky before looking back at her. "You have a funny meaning of beautiful."

"It's beautiful to me."

The car sank as he sat next to her, his jeans stiff but his cotton T-shirt flexible. The suit jacket he wore over the shirt had a habit of turning Nala on every time she looked at him. The stubble he had yet to shave off made him look dark and dangerous. She knew he was anything but.

"I think you're beautiful."

Nala smiled. *Thanks for proving my point.* "Bring me a maple bar?"

Vincent leaned his head back. "Forgot. Was too distracted by the waitress's, erm, assets. She had a lot, and they were pushed into my face."

"Uh huh. Checking out another woman's tits. I see how you are."

"To be fair, unless I closed my eyes or put my hand over my face, I didn't have a choice."

"You saying mine are too small to have the same effect?"

"What? No way!"

Nala shoved his shoulder. "I'm joking."

"You better be."

"I am!"

It was one of many pranks she had pulled on him since life settled down again. In the several weeks since the raid at Xavier Crow's house in the West Hills, Vincent and Nala had made strides to work more like a real couple and less like partners in crime. That meant more dates. And less espionage. *And a whole lotta sex.* She was afraid happy Vincent wouldn't be as into the kind of sex she liked, but Nala had been pleasantly surprised at how often she needed to recuperate her ability to use her legs again.

Other, sometimes more personal things had transpired as well. Nala officially changed her address to Vincent's. She also didn't get a new job. Instead, she decided to live off her sugar daddy boyfriend's money without any guilt and do something else with her life. Namely enroll in the local community college with the goal of eventually transferring to a four-year university. Her first classes started in two weeks. Until then, she was enjoying the time she had to go shopping, play video games, and go on driving excursions with her busy billionaire boyfriend.

Vincent was in a lull between projects again. Whenever this happened, he got the traveling bug, insisting on a weekend in San Francisco, a night out on the town that consisted of a ton of alcohol and a bunch of people nerdily arguing over different editions of D&D, or driving to the other side of the state to take in the natural sights. Nala was always invited. In fact, it was mandatory that she go.

Vincent didn't have any new projects lined up for a good while. He said he was taking extra time off until Nala started her classes, knowing that she would be spending a lot of time studying since she was such a serious person. Yet when he asked what she wanted to focus on and she said, "Coding, so I can be better than you one day," he had to punish her for insubordination. *Found out that night how much this girl likes a sore ass.*

Yet the craziest thing wasn't that they kept up the Dom/sub shenanigans when the mood struck them, or that they were asked to submit official testimony against Xavier Crow and his henchmen, or that Nala felt comfortable dropping thousands of dollars on a shopping spree – to buy more video game equipment she knew Vincent needed for his nights off. No, what she was shocked to find out was that she and Vincent would keep up some of the more public qualities of a kinky sex life.

They found another club – a real one – for people like them and tested the waters by doing a trial membership. There was no pressure for them to do anything in front of anyone. They could enjoy the other members and their shows without fear of committing to anything they were uncomfortable with. There were leaders who kept things running smoothly, but they weren't, well, *sociopathic freaks.* Nala was also able to cultivate her own personality that was more true to her, even when Vincent latched her Nightingale collar around her neck and told her to grind against him in a private room. She was more than happy to oblige.

They also stayed close with Lucian and Robin, the latter of whom continued to blow up Nala's phone whenever the mood struck her. In a way, they were best friends now.

"What do you think?" Vincent asked, showing her a picture on his phone. "That's the one I did at work yesterday. Think I should post it?"

Nala glanced at the weaving Vincent pulled off with a few ropes and silks he kept in a drawer in his desk. Since dating Nala, he had immersed himself in the world of artistic bondage, and often practiced during his brief downtimes. Sometimes he depicted scenes. Other times they looked like dark spider webs. This one was a large flower, like a daisy, spiraling out of control. Sometimes Nala modeled for him. In bed or in a chair, of course. She liked being his muse.

"Post it. Build that portfolio. You're gonna do that demonstration at the club… next thing you know? You're Vincent Lane, billionaire tech guru *and* that guy who makes art with women and ropes!"

"Let's not get ahead of ourselves. It's an Instagram account."

"I keep forgetting you can do that with phones."

"Sometimes I think you have to be kidding."

Nala leaned her head against his shoulder with a pleasant visage. "I love you. You're my favorite thirty-year-old."

He snorted. "I love you too. I could love worse twenty-one-year-olds."

"I'm twenty-two now. Ex*cuse* you." What a great birthday. Cake, orgasms, and video games. In that order.

"Ah, yes, huge difference."

"Like our ages!"

"Would you stop bringing that up? It's clearly not like that."

"I'm practicing for what my mother says when she finds out."

"Your mother?"

"Uh huh. Now get in the car. It's a long drive to Nevada from here."

"We are going to Nevada, huh?"

"Yup. You're going to meet my mother. Then we're going to Fresno so I can meet your mother."

"Whoa, whoa…"

"Yup! And you're going to introduce me as your fiancée so she knows how serious it is."

"*Whoa.*"

"Relax. I'm not telling you to marry me." Nala slid off the hood of his car and opened the passenger side door. "Yet. Let me finish school first, cradle robber."

Sighing, Vincent joined her in the car and started the ignition. "The things I do for love."

"I've thought that a lot over the past few months."

He looked at her, fondly. "Me too."

Nala met him halfway over the front seat of the car for a light kiss. She sat back, pulling on his seatbelt and giving him a wry smile. "Look at you. My hardworking, super hot boyfriend who likes cramming it in like he's never gonna get the chance to again. However will I compete in the coding world with you?"

Vincent put the car in reverse and eased into a turnout. "I know. You'll be spending most of your time in bed, so you won't be able to."

"That's the *only* advantage you have over me."

"The only one?"

"Why, yes. I come from a proud line of Nazarov women who kick ass at science and fuck Doms. It's just my sister was smarter at the former and I was smarter at the latter."

Vincent pulled his sunglasses on and turned onto the nearest roadway. "This is going to be a very interesting relationship."

"Would you have it any other way?"

"Nope."

He hit the gas and took them south. To California? Toward Nevada? Who knew. Furthermore, who cared?

The day was young and Nala was in love without a care in the world. This was what she was meant to do with her life – and it was only getting started.

Cynthia Dane spends most of her time writing in the great Pacific Northwest. And when she's not writing, she's dreaming up her next big plot and meeting all sorts of new characters in her head.

She loves stories that are sexy, fun, and cut right to the chase. You can always count on explosive romances - both in and out of the bedroom - when you read a Cynthia Dane story.

Falling in love. Making love. Love in all shades and shapes and sizes. Cynthia loves it all!

Connect with Cynthia on any of the following:

Website: http://www.cynthiadane.com
Twitter: http://twitter.com/cynthia_dane
Facebook: http://facebook.com/authorcynthiadane

www.ingramcontent.com/pod-product-compliance
Lightning Source LLC
Chambersburg PA
CBHW030740030726
47497CB00001B/72

* 9 7 8 0 6 9 2 6 9 5 5 3 1 *